The Fool's Tale

NICOLE GALLAND

A hardcover edition of this book was published in 2005 by William Morrow, an imprint of HarperCollins Publishers.

HarperCollins books may be purchased for educational, business, or sales promotional use. For information please write: Special Markets Department, HarperCollins Publishers, 10 East 53rd Street, New York, NY 10022.

FIRST HARPER PAPERBACK PUBLISHED 2006.

Designed by Judith Stagnitto Abbate/Abbate Design
Map by Steve Lewis, the famous fourth-grade teacher

Library of Congress Cataloging-in-Publication Data has been applied for.

ISBN 0-06-072150-2

ISBN-10: 0-06-072151-0 (pbk.)
ISBN-13: 978-0-06-072151-0 (pbk.)

08 09 10 ❖/RRD 10 9 8 7

Sarah Mayhew

About the Author

Award-winning screenwriter NICOLE GALLAND was raised on Martha's Vineyard and divides her time between the San Francisco Bay Area and New York. Her second novel will be published this spring by William Morrow and she is working on her third book.

Harper

An Imprint of HarperCollins*Publishers*

FOR LOTHLÓRIEN HOMET

CONTENTS

Acknowledgments

he completion of this story in itself makes quite a story, and perhaps someday I'll write it. Until then, it must suffice that I acknowledge and thank the featured characters.

Above all, I salaam my personal holy trinity: Marc Glick, who gives attorneys a good name, and thank God knows how to spot a diamond in the rough; Jess Taylor for brilliant editorial assistance and hilariously helpful sarcasm along the way; and Liz Darhansoff, agent extraordinaire and superwoman. Steve Breimer and Jon Karas round out an exceptional teulu that I feel blessed to have on my side.

Jennifer Brehl, my editor at Morrow, has the amazing ability to help me actually *enjoy* performing surgery on my firstborn child.

Alan and Maureen Crumpler were so generous that folks assume I'm exaggerating when I describe them. They had barely met me when they invited me into their home to finish the manuscript, providing the best writer's retreat I could ever ask for—as well as fonts of knowledge on nearly every topic, and delightful dinner conversations to boot.

Ray Thomas—innkeeper of The Lion, raconteur, and native son—brought Radnorshire (Maelienydd) to life for me far beyond mere bookish scholarship. He also afforded me the chance to see the land from horseback (and J.S. the horse helped me to examine the bracken at very, very close proximity). The next time you're in Wales, stay at The Lion in Llanbister.

On the home front, Steve Lewis offered extraordinary support, belief, patience, love, food, and computer help throughout the first draft. The second draft would have been so much harder to complete without the assistance of my father, Leo Galland, in getting to Wales; the third draft likewise was abetted by my grandparents Rachel and Hans William Galland.

Brian Caspe and Eowyn Mader were my first readers and critics; their enthusiasm gave me the enthusiasm to go on to a second draft.

Beryl and David Vaughan, like the song says, made me a pallet on their floor when I had no place to go; Robert (Jippity) Sicular has done likewise through the years, as have my parents Mike and Karen Colaneri. Laurence Bouvard was and is a font of linguistic insight, hospitality, and camaraderie in London. Alene Sibley and Bonnie Corso offered spiritual sanity, and Paul Hyman all the other sanities. Julian Lopez-Morillas provided some eleventh-hour reality checks, and Bonnie Akimoto offered end-of-the-haul enthusiasm. And Lorien, praise be, both listened and *insisted*.

Sion Davies set me straight on history and tried valiantly to keep me honest. I am responsible for any failings, deliberate or otherwise, therein.

Paul Remfry's writings on the castles of Radorshire grounded my imagination in reality. I'm also indebted to the work of John Davies (*A History of Wales*), Thomas Peter Ellis (*Welsh Tribal Law and Customs in the Middle Ages*), H. W. Howse (*Radnorshire*), and editor Thomas Charles-Edwards (*The Welsh King and His Court*). The full list of source material is far too long to include here, but for those interested in primary sources, Gerald of Wales (see chapter 4) is very readable and can be unintentionally hilarious. There is also the *Law of Hywel Dda* and *The Chronicle of the Princes*.

I also want to thank the many people who contributed in smaller but still deeply appreciated ways. This includes Carys-Hedd of the Mid-Wales Film Commission, and other helpful souls, who know more than I ever will, at the British Library, the National Library of Wales, and St. Fagins; it includes also Mary Remnant, the patron saint of early music, and Gail Tipton, my intrepid fellow wanderer on my first two trips to Wales. I often relied on the kindness of strangers, especially in Cymru. Sundry passing navigators at each crossroad that I came to helped me in all sorts of ways. There are too many to keep track of, but they include: the entire village of Llanbister, Rhian Davies Wooldridge and Glynn Davies, my grandmother's ghost (for telling me to take the tart), Kalimata, David Hatcher, Cadw, and all the folks who played traditional music for me. *Diolch yn fawr*.

Finally, a special thanks to each genuine, rare Fool it has been my pleasure, pain, and privilege to know—and you know who you are.

PRONUNCIATION GUIDE AND GLOSSARY

PLACES

CYMARON: Cum-AAR-on (sounds like "Aaron"), the castle
MAELIENYDD: Mile-ee-EN-ith, the kingdom
GWYNEDD: GWIN-eth, a kingdom to the far north
POWYS: POW-iss, a kingdom to the immediate north and west
DEHEUBARTH: De-HI-barth, a kingdom to the south and west

PEOPLE

MAELGWYN: MILE-gwin, ruler of Maelienydd
CADWALLON: Cad-WA-thlon, ruler of Maelienydd
GWIRION: Gwir-EE-on
TEULU: TIE-lee, a lord's bodyguard and personal warband
PENTEULU: Pen-TIE-lee, the title for the captain of the teulu forces
GWILYM: GWI-lim, the castle steward
MARGED: MARE-ged, the castle cook
DAFYDD: DA-vith (Welsh David), Marged's grandson
EFAN: pronounced "Evan," the king's penteulu
HAFAIDD: HAV-eye-th, the castle usher
GORONWY: Gor-ON-wee, the royal judge
GWALLTER: GWATHL-ter, the king's chamberlain
HYWEL: pronounced "Howell," the king's bard
CADWGAN: Cad-OO-gan, the castle marshal

EDNYFED: Ed-NUV-ed, the marshal's son

ANGHARAD: Ang-HAIR-ad, the queen's woman

GENERYS: Gen-ER-is (hard *g*), the queen's woman

MADRUN: MAD-rin, the queen's woman

LLWYD: pronounced similarly to "Floyd," the queen's doorkeeper

HUW: pronounced "Hugh," a baron of Maelienydd

OWAIN: OW-in, a baron of Maelienydd

HUMFFRI: HIM-free, a baron of Maelienydd

LLEWELYN: Thlew-EL-in, prince of Gwynedd

CYNAN: CUN-an, a baron of Gwynedd

RHYS: Rh-ees, the deceased ruler of Deheubarth

NOTES

1. A "dd" is pronounced as "th" (as in *leather*); "th" written as "th" is pronounced as in *smith*.

2. The Welsh double "l": an aspirated "l"; the nearest description for someone unfamiliar with Welsh is "thl."

WALES AT THE CLOSE OF
THE TWELFTH CENTURY
Maelienydd under
Maelgwyn ap Cadwallon

GWYNEDD

POWYS

England

River Severn

Newtown

Owain's Manor

Wigmore

Rhaeadr

Cymaron

MAELIENYDD

MORTIMER'S

Lands

River Wye

to Gloucester

deBraose's

Lands

DEHEUBARTH

St. David's

Cardiff

Scale in English Miles

5 10   20   30   40   50   60

Prologue

Late September, 1179

he prince was fully a head higher than his friend, but Gwirion was cleverer; Maelgwyn won all their fistfights and Gwirion all their arguments. They were a contrast in temperament as well: Maelgwyn already had unnerving poise for one so young while Gwirion was an unruly imp. Some council members had fretted to Cadwallon that the dark-haired foundling needed reining in, that he was old enough now to realize his constant playmate was also his future sovereign and needed to be treated with some deference. The king doubted Gwirion was capable of grasping that sentiment—and anyway, he almost envied his son for having such an unself-conscious friendship. He had a soft spot for Gwirion, in part for the youngster's musical gifts (he had leave to practice on the king's own harp), and in part for the unfettered playfulness that made him disregard the tense sobriety of court. He was at the moment, for example, trying to practice equestrian acrobatics: He perched behind the prince's saddle,

clutching Maelgwyn's blond hair for balance as they rode. Maelgwyn as always calmly ignored the mild indignity.

The riding party was returning home from King Henry's court in Gloucester, and this foggy afternoon found them on a road rising over a valley of harvested farmland. They were ten in all: King Cadwallon, Prince Maelgwyn, Gwirion, and some of the king's personal warband, the teulu. It was both boys' first time in England and they were delighted by it, especially Gwirion, who loved exploring and had announced that he would chart the length and breadth of all Britain as soon as he was old enough to travel without a chaperone.

"If these are Mortimer's lands, won't he try to kill us?" Maelgwyn asked his father hopefully, a cocky nine-year-old's reaction to romanticized danger. He knew all about the Mortimer clan, powerful English barons whose properties served as a buffer between Wales and England. He knew, for example, that they had murdered most of his family, that they had tried for a century to conquer his small Welsh kingdom of Maelienydd. He knew that they had on occasion been successful, that the very castle he lived in had been built years ago by Hugh Mortimer during an Occupation. But he also knew that his father, with the help of their cousin Lord Rhys, had always driven Mortimer away again.

Gwirion looked alarmed by Maelgwyn's question, and Cadwallon smiled reassuringly. "It is Mortimer's land, but there's no danger to us. We're traveling under Henry's writ of safe passage. Hugh Mortimer is Henry's subject and that means he must let us pass through without harm." As if that were the cue for a macabre joke, an arrow flew past his arm and struck one of his teulu in the shoulder. Both boys screamed.

The second arrow hit the king in the chest. He slumped in the saddle with a grunt, groped toward the shrieking children on the palfrey beside him; ignoring his son, he grabbed Gwirion from his precarious perch to haul him closer. They slid to the ground between the two mounts and landed in a heap on the hard dirt road as shouts and horses' screams broke out around them. For one moment in the midst of panic and confusion, Gwirion thought he was being singled out to help the wounded monarch. Then he realized he was a decoy.

The furious stamping of hooves around their heads made him wince even as he shrieked, but Cadwallon's unridered stallion galloped off and they were left exposed to their attackers, which was worse. An arrow passed so close before Gwirion's face he could nearly have bitten it. Terrified, he looked back up toward the palfrey but Maelgwyn was already gone, spirited away by one of the teulu. Four more of the soldiers leapt from their horses and ringed their fallen sovereign, shields facing out, from the boy's perspective towering yards over them; the attackers, who seemed to come from all directions at once, shot at the soldiers' shins, barely above the level of Gwirion's head, and when the men tried to avoid the arrows, a second spate was already on the fly toward the breaks in their defense. All four were pierced through their leather armor and staggered out of Gwirion's view. The horses were fleeing; the indifferent grey sky above seemed full of arrows and the air was shredded by the sound of their flight. Out of the corner of his eye Gwirion saw two more of Cadwallon's men fall near the bracken. Then he heard the triumphant attackers riding toward them, whooping.

"Sire," Gwirion begged, near hysteria, turning to the large man beside him. His mantle was trapped beneath Cadwallon's heavy arm. "Sire, what shall I do?"

Cadwallon's face was ashen. He just managed to turn his head toward Gwirion and breathed, "Protect your king."

Gwirion desperately tugged the cloak out from under Cadwallon's arm, and tried to climb onto his body to cover it with his own. He gagged when he realized that the warm dampness his fingers sank into was the king's bloody tunic. "Not me," Cadwallon coughed, lacking the strength to push him away. "Protect Maelgwyn, or we fall to Mortimer."

"Hugh Mortimer?" Gwirion cried. "But you—"

He stopped as Cadwallon's glance moved past him. Safely beyond the skirmish and watching it with satisfaction, a young man dressed in blue and gold was reining in a large grey destrier. Gwirion recognized him: It was not Hugh Mortimer, but Roger his son, whom they had met at Henry's court just two days before, a youth already known for his rash ambition. The king whispered something weakly but his words were inaudible under a chilling new sound: The attackers were plunging their swords into the wounded riders' guts. Cadwallon took a final breath. "I go to God," he murmured with angry resignation, then closed his eyes and did not move again.

Gwirion tensed and waited for him to go to God, but nothing happened. The soul was not material, but he was sure there must be some evidence of its departure or else how would Father Idnerth know to speak of it? Hywel the bard said even an oat stalk had a soul, although he never spoke of it going to God. Gwirion waited without moving for a long time, fearfully breathing in the odor of sweat, blood, and earth, his focus desperately and entirely on the corpse beside him. Nothing changed. The king's body was unnaturally still.

Shouts had dulled to weak moans, and even these were fading. He raised his head carefully and looked around, suddenly shivering with cold. The dirt road was trampled nearly to mud all around him, and every one of the soldiers who had been riding with them was dead or dying. The horses had all fled, he hoped back home to Castell Cymaron where their presence would summon an alarm. The six attackers had dismounted and were gathering less than a dozen paces away from where he lay, giving each other congratulatory slaps on the shoulder in greeting. He couldn't believe there were only six, for all the arrows and all the damage done. He didn't dare look at their faces, but their strange foreign gibberish sounded rougher, harsher, than the foreign gibberish in the English king's court. Two of them stopped at a fallen guard close to Gwirion and he held his breath as they leaned over the inert body, frisking it. They found nothing of worth, and spat on the corpse in annoyance. Then one of them saw a sealed parchment rolled up in the dead man's belt, and pulled it out. He unrolled it, glanced at it, and held it out to his companion, who laughed.

Gwirion recognized it: King Henry's writ of safe passage. The man tore off the seal as a keepsake, crumpled the rest of the writ, and ground it under his heel.

They noticed Gwirion at the same moment and he didn't know if he had shut his eyes fast enough to fool them. One of his legs was twisted uncomfortably under him; he was afraid it would begin to shake and they would notice. But they gave him only a cursory look, assuming from the blood and the awkward posture of his body that his soul was wherever Cadwallon's might be.

Roger Mortimer had dismounted and joined the huddle. Gwirion lacked the French to understand what they were saying, but Mortimer was displeased about something and kept repeating a word Gwirion thought he recognized, from eavesdropping on the prince's language lessons, as "boy." He rested his head against Cadwallon's stiffened arm and watched Roger through lowered lashes.

They were obviously looking for the prince. The bracken on these hills was high enough to hide a child, but three of the marauders had tracked some broken fronds and were heading into the dying, waist-high greenery with purpose. There was nowhere else Maelgwyn could have been; if he'd fled, they would have seen him on the unsheltered hillside. Panicking, Gwirion glanced at the dead man beside him. Protect the king. He tried to think clearly: If he leapt up they would know it was a deliberate distraction and they might ignore him, so he would have to get their attention but make it seem accidental. That was as far as his foresight went. He never considered what would happen if he succeeded.

He rolled his head back onto the ground and moaned slightly, moved one arm limply, then was still again. It worked: The men all turned at once away from the bracken and ran toward him, shouting with excitement. Looking dazed, he pulled his twisted leg from under him and struggled shakily to rise. From the corner of his practiced eye, he saw a few fronds rustle slightly and knew Maelgwyn was moving out of danger. Gwirion was not yet to his knees when a violently strong hand grabbed the front of his tunic and hoisted him roughly. He found himself staring at the blue-and-gold tunic, and as he was released and felt his feet touch the ground, he looked up into the enemy's face.

Roger Mortimer was giving him an eerie, almost dreamy smile. With a monotone accent like King Henry's, he announced in Welsh, "You are not the prince." Gwirion said nothing. "But I remember you—you're his bosom friend. Almost as valuable."

The king was valuable and the king was dead. He didn't want to be valuable. "I'm just a peasant, sir."

"A peasant? Dressed like that?" He poked the shoulder of Gwirion's worn but finely woven tunic—like all his clothes, a castoff of Maelgwyn's.

"We dress our peasants well in Maelienydd," he said in a voice of utter innocence. The situation now lacked all sense of reality, and therefore danger. "Especially our royal servants."

"A real servant would not have phrased it like that. I saw you at the court, boy, you never left the prince's side. You're much more than a servant."

Gwirion's nimble imagination failed him. "The prince is blind, sir," he said, trying to sound earnest. "I'm his guide, I can't stray more than a few inches away or he might hurt himself. I'm not his friend, he never even says my name right."

Mortimer laughed briefly. "The lie is feeble, but I commend your excellent delivery."

"It's not a lie," Gwirion insisted. "Didn't you see me standing on the horse when you attacked? I had to steer, but Cadwallon doesn't want—"

"Cadwallon *didn't* want. Cadwallon is past tense." He grabbed Gwirion's collar and pivoted him around to face the corpse. "He's dead. *Your king is dead.*" He was annoyed that this failed to break the boy, although he felt him shudder. "They are all dead except you and the prince, and you'll be dead too if you don't cooperate. Are you truly nothing but a Welsh peasant?"

"I'd sooner be a Welsh peasant than a filthy English lord."

Mortimer ignored the comment, bored by the finer points of ethnicity. He calmly pulled a large knife from his belt and pressed the tip into Gwirion's throat near his ear. The boy blanched and almost pissed himself. "Where is your prince?" Gwirion pursed his lips closed and Mortimer pressed harder. "You know where he's hiding," he said in a soft, almost hypnotic voice. "And this blade is hurting you. All you have to do is tell me where he is and I'll stop hurting you. It's a very simple game."

"I don't know where he is. You were the one interested in him, not I."

"You're not being very helpful," Roger Mortimer observed quietly, and whisked the blade up to Gwirion's head, nicking the skin at the temple. The boy cried out in startled pain and clamped his hand over the cut. "There'll be more of that if you don't tell me where your prince is. I don't want to kill him, I want to speak with him."

"Attend his coronation, then," Gwirion suggested through clenched teeth, both hands now pressed to the wound. "He's sure to give you a seat of honor, since you've helped get him there so early."

Mortimer looked grudgingly impressed by the boy's pluck. He lowered the knife but did not return it to his belt, and spoke in French to his men, who exchanged looks that made the bottom of Gwirion's stomach drop out. Mortimer addressed him again in Welsh. "As entertaining as you are to chat with, I have better things to do with my time," he explained in the same false dulcet tone. "I'd kill you for your cheek, but you're the prince's friend. So you will be our bait."

The first blow, across his face, sent him spinning into the damp roadway spitting blood. He heard loud, hooting laughter that seemed to come from all sides at once as Mortimer reached down and hoisted him to his feet again. "That won't work," Gwirion managed to protest thickly, trying to feel his tongue. "Told you . . . just a servant . . . I'm nothing to him."

"I'm a betting man, and I bet that's a lie," Mortimer replied and added, pleasantly, "But if we kill you and he does nothing, you've won the bet."

H E knew his father was dead and he knew he would soon be distraught, but he wasn't now. Now he thought of nothing but survival, horribly aware of how immensely more important his existence had just become, furious that such awareness required him to stay hidden in the damp bracken. He had a dagger, a recent gift from his father, and he had fantasized about having cause to use it; it was grotesquely ironic that the best way to preserve himself now was to refrain from action.

He'd seen Gwirion distract the men and could tell it was deliberate. He wanted both to throw his arms around his friend in gratitude and to scream at him for his idiotic and misplaced selflessness: *I could have taken care of myself*, he thought. Usually it was he who looked out for Gwirion, whose size and heedlessness made him the victim of harassment from the teulu and other castle youths. The prince had often needed to go to his defense.

Mortimer did not actually think Maelgwyn would come leaping out of the bushes like an avenging devil, but he was certain he could get the prince to give himself away. He assigned three of the men to study the bracken for movement, especially where the likeliest trail began. There was no wind. Maelgwyn did not allow himself to move, tried not even to breathe too hard. Hard eyes scoured the bracken fronds near him—and one pair locked onto his and stayed there. He tensed, and tightened his hand around the dagger hilt, ready to spring. But the eyes did not actually see him, they moved on and after a moment he made himself relax his grip. He would have given anything for a bow and arrow—he knew he could hit Mortimer and was sure the others would flee if he did. He was ashamed to realize he was trembling.

Maelgwyn saw Mortimer strike Gwirion once, then he closed his eyes and cupped his hands over his ears, his heartbeat amplified and filling his head, his throat a knot of tears. He could hear the Norman's hollered offer that they would release Gwirion if the prince revealed himself—not to surrender, simply to talk. He knew it was a trap and prayed Gwirion knew that too, so he would understand why Maelgwyn couldn't act on it. He dimly heard his friend's voice crying out in fear and pain and outrage, and the offers gradually turned more sinister: The boy would be taken hostage and subjected to continual torture if the prince did not come out; he would be killed; he would be skinned alive; he would be skinned alive right now, in front of the prince's eyes. Gwirion's cries grew louder and Maelgwyn wondered, with the dispassion that comes from shock, if either of them would survive the afternoon. Three times, unbidden, his eyes flickered open and then shut again—and then he kept them shut to keep from shrieking.

After a very long time, there was quiet and the prince hesitantly lowered his hands from his ears, fearing the worst. He heard voices and opened his eyes to look.

They had released Gwirion, literally dropped him onto the road, three of the disheveled thugs breathing hard and grinning at their handiwork. Mortimer, who had stepped back to watch the scene with dispassion, was leaning over Gwirion and speaking to him loudly. He was asking Gwirion to help them find the prince, in exchange for a reprieve. Gwirion stubbornly said nothing.

After a long beat of silence, Mortimer stepped back and gestured for one of the men to resume, when Gwirion stammered, in a thin voice of defeat that Maelgwyn could hardly make out, "All right, then, I'll tell you where the prince is." Maelgwyn tightened his hand on the hilt of the dagger, his pulse racing.

Mortimer signaled his man to retreat and leaned over Gwirion again. "Yes?" he said.

For a moment, Gwirion stared at him, glassy-eyed, his face pressed against the road and his mouth half full of dirt. He spat the dirt out weakly. "I shoved him up my arse," he muttered. "I dare you to look for him—he's waiting for you with a naked blade."

After an astonished pause, Mortimer burst out laughing. "I don't know if I should kill you or *adopt* you," he declared admiringly, and drew his sword. "I've never been so sorry to reduce the Welsh population." Before Gwirion could answer, a distant cacophony of hunting horns sounded over the valley floor, a celebratory stutter of notes, and church bells began chiming far down the valley. Mortimer looked delighted by the interruption. "*Alors*, good news of some sort," he announced to his men. "Anna's time was upon her when I rode out this morning—I want to get back to Wigmore to hear if I'm become an uncle." He sheathed the sword and made a dismissive gesture toward the battered child lying at their feet. "That's enough. The little whoreson's gone. You accomplished a fair amount today; I'll call it a good day's work." In Welsh he said very clearly to the boy, "Your friend left you here for us to torture you. The friend you risked your life for doesn't care a whit for you. You Welsh are all alike." Gwirion did not rouse himself for a response. He lay limp on the cold earth; his fevered mind wondered randomly if Cadwallon's soul had finally gone to God. Mortimer crossed to him and stood directly over him, his feet in front of Gwirion's bruised and muddied face. With a final smile of satisfaction at the royal corpse, and a passing glance at the other dead surrounding it, he mounted, gestured to his men to mount as well, and led them away down the valley.

When he knew for certain they were gone, Maelgwyn crept out of the bracken and ran on stiffened legs to his friend, sobbing angrily. Gwirion lay like a doll tossed aside by a truculent child. Maelgwyn ripped off his cloak and wrapped it around Gwirion's trembling body. The two boys looked at each other. Each almost began to speak and then each stopped abruptly.

"I'll carry you, I'll take you back to Gloucester," the prince finally ventured hoarsely.

Gwirion's eyes widened in fear. "No!" he whispered. "Take me out of here! I'm going straight home to the castle."

"We're much closer to Henry's court than we are to Cymaron—"

"I don't care," Gwirion interrupted. "Take me out of England." Wincing, he picked up a corner of the cloak and brought it to his lips, then pressed it ceremoniously to his friend's chest and added, with pained reverence, "Please, Your Majesty."

HONORING tradition, Cadwallon's murder was at once added to every Welsh bard's repertoire of lamentation. Gwirion's ordeal was not. They both knew they were forever marked by this, and for nearly twenty years they never spoke about the horrors of that day.

ENEMIES

May Day, 1198

SABEL WAS OLD for a bride, nearly twenty, and orphaned with little dowry beyond her bloodline. She was considered a great beauty in her own country—small and boyish in build, with an intelligent, squarish face and a high, graceful forehead—and supremely desirable for her education, skills, and absolute lack of feminine triviality. But she had always known she'd be married for politics. It never bothered her; until she'd heard Chrétien de Troyes's romances of Lancelot and the Round Table, at the age of thirteen, it had never even occurred to her that there could be other reasons to bind herself to a man. She remembered Adèle chasing away the minstrel reciting them, then chastising Isabel for corrupting her own wits and sense. So she had never dwelt on the possibility of romantic love. But she'd assumed a match would at least be within her own race, and she had been taken aback when her uncle Roger had revealed her suitor's identity: not only a Welsh prince, but the only prince still referred to by the English chroniclers as "Rex"—*King*. A small kingdom, and a poor one, but

she would be a queen. And the king, when she'd met him, was so disarming and handsome and his accent so melodious that it had made her knees weak, although she was hardly the sort to get weak knees. When the date was set and the terms agreed upon, she had spent a fortnight smiling to herself.

But that smile waned on the journey to a land that was far too alien, considering it began almost at her childhood doorstep.

They had left the homey fields of England for windy Welsh hillsides, hillsides carpeted by dead bracken that looked like russet snow, and nothing else for miles at a stretch but grass and prickly gorse—not a tree, not a house, not even a rocky outcrop to vary the landscape. Nothing but herds of white sheep and black cattle being driven upland for what passed as summer. The songbirds had been cacophonous, magpies and curlews, red kites and buzzards perched on the skeletons of sheep that had not survived the winter. In England there had been farmers, already sowing, bowing respectfully as they passed; here they'd found undernourished peasants digging up peat under the damp grey sky and pointedly ignoring them. Isabel tried not to be disheartened by this; she hoped she could eventually make these people understand that not all Normans were butchers. Below them, the valleys and lower hillsides were impassable bogs shadowed by dense groves of scrub oak (considered by the natives sacred and haunted), so the ancient Roman roads had kept them high on the slopes, windblown, chilly and exposed. She had known it would be highland, and she'd thought that meant mountains, which would have at least been *interesting*. The first few hills had been promising, with lovely sweeping views of river valleys, but by the time they were well into the kingdom, the entire country was high, with decidedly undramatic undulations from valley to hilltop—there were no peaks to speak of anywhere. It looked, her brother Thomas had muttered, like the English moors flung over a gigantic bowl of lumpy porridge. Wigmore Castle was only a day's ride off but in that day she had been transported farther away than her pilgrimage to Santiago de Compostela had taken her.

G WIRION had been incensed when he'd learned the wedding was set for May Day, and the Spring Rites canceled because of it. ("Usurped," he'd protested, "by a *Mortimer*, by a bitch of an English virgin.") When the king warned him not to use this public gathering as a chance to make sport of anybody, Gwirion had rebutted that he would never condescend to dignify the occasion by immortalizing it with a prank of any sort. And so the entire castle population knew there would be trouble.

It was May Day at last. Boughs of birch twigs hung over windows and everyone wore brilliant colors—even the usually bedraggled dwarf Corr wore green hose under his linen tunic. The one exception was Gwirion, who had donned sackcloth to mourn the end of the king's finest years as a bachelor. He insisted the day was too splendid to waste on a wedding, particularly one involving Mortimers, and would have avoided it altogether if Corr had not begged him otherwise.

"You know how ladies react when they see me for the first time," he lamented, his colorless lashes blinking almost spastically in the sunlight. "If you're beside me I can pretend to myself it's partly your hideous mug."

Gwirion grinned at this and then a thoughtful gleam warmed his eyes. It was a look Corr was all too familiar with.

"Whatever you are thinking of thinking," he said, "don't think it."

"It seems to me," Gwirion mused, ignoring the request, "that we've never fully exploited that particular aspect of your appearance."

"I doubt she'll give us much satisfaction that way. I've heard she has a sensible head on her shoulders."

Gwirion considered this. "But what has she got on the *rest* of her?" he asked. Rhetorically.

Corr sighed in capitulation. "And how severe a whipping will this be bringing us?"

Gwirion lowered his voice even though they were yards above the crowd. "This wedding is an invasion. She'll try to coerce us to join her Norman civilization." A loaded pause, and then he grinned. "If we're expected to become like her, why don't we just become her?"

The two of them stood atop the king's tower, watching people mill about in anticipatory disarray around the ashes of the Beltane bonfires in the courtyard below. They descended the wooden stairs that hugged the stone curtain wall, bickering over the details of their plot, and began to scout for the bride's brother. He was a younger brother, named Thomas, and he was hardly in whiskers. Gwirion discovered him by the stables. He was standing near a cluster of dangerous-looking youths not much his senior—the infamously rowdy teulu, the king's resident warband. Their massive leader, Efan the penteulu, was showing off his horse's battle scars. Thomas, a doughy-faced boy with light brown hair, was looking very short and very young, and embarrassed about it. The teulu glanced toward Gwirion, realized who his target was, and returned to their boasting.

"Thomas Mortimer, isn't it? Your presence is required above," Gwirion whispered in his ear. The boy didn't recognize the oddly dressed man, but he was so grateful to be taken seriously by somebody that he went along, unquestioning. He failed to notice the looks of the young men he walked away from.

Gwirion led him past the pipers trying quietly to tune, past the large stone well, and up the wooden stairway to the top of the curtain wall. The garderobe up here, intended for the king's use, was not as foul as the one below—Gwirion was willing to incur only so much wrath for his prank. Thomas was too bewildered to understand what was happening; even after Gwirion had chained his makeshift gate fast across the open doorway, and the boy was penned into the toilet, he continued to ask innocently where his sister was.

"I'll just get her for you," Gwirion said cheerfully, and departed with no intention of returning for hours.

At least three hundred people were crowded around the large courtyard. Most were landowners of Maelienydd, handsome, sturdy Welshmen, many claiming distant kinship to the king. There were a few visiting dignitaries from England, but Roger Mortimer, Lord of Wigmore, baron of the March, was not among them. To pass the time until Corr was in place, Gwirion thought to seek the presence of Hywel, the old court bard who would bless the ceremony for real after the queen's priest performed his doddering church ritual. But he was arrested by better entertainment: His Majesty the bridegroom was forcing himself to chat with a cousin they both detested. Anarawd, the man next in line to the throne, obviously did not like this match. Besides the fact that he would soon be supplanted as heir, his father, like the king's, had been ambushed and killed by Roger Mortimer. He was a violent man himself—he'd blinded his own brothers and taken their inheritance—and he'd raged against this latest treaty with the Marcher baron, but today he was trying very hard to appear respectful and resigned because he knew the teulu would have been all too pleased to disembowel him. King Maelgwyn smiled politely as they spoke, visualizing just such sport.

He had no personal interest in his wedding or his bride. This union was only to seal an uneasy truce. Over the course of two decades he'd thrice thwarted Mortimer's attempts to conquer Maelienydd, but earlier this year, when the king's powerful comrade-in-arms Lord Rhys had died, Mortimer had redoubled the effort in a raid that had severely taxed both sides. With this wedding that would all be—theoretically—behind them now. There were several benefits to such a match: Although he could have made any son his heir, even a bastard, a child of this marriage would be half English—*Norman* English, the ruling class—and would be safe no matter which side ultimately prevailed.

The king was dressed magnificently in green and gold and he truly looked heroic, if not especially Welsh. Fair-haired and tall with fierce blue eyes revealing a sliver of Viking ancestry, he was as ever poised and effortlessly charismatic, and Gwirion conceded silently that the king deserved in earnest the title he had once given him in affectionate mockery: Maelgwyn Urddol, Maelgwyn the Noble. In their adolescence, this private joke—inspired by a summer of sexual exploits of questionable virtue—had spread throughout the castle and out to the surrounding countryside, the irony replaced immediately by earnest images of an able and handsome young ruler, and for years now he'd been referred to admiringly among his people, and by Gwirion, mostly by this sobriquet.

Noble excused himself from Anarawd, only to be immediately overtaken by Lord Ralf, one of the queen's maternal uncles, who was no improvement. "Your Majesty!" he trumpeted, a sharp-featured bearded man with hawkish eyes. He loudly began an inventory of his niece's many qualities as if Noble and the populace at large still had to be convinced of the match. "I'm sure you know that she was her brother's regent until this year—very unusual situation," he announced, with a smugness that suggested it reflected well on him somehow. "Excellent administrator. Did you know she's multilingual?"

"French, Latin, Welsh, and a little of the Saxon tongue," Noble recited sardonically. He'd been told this near a dozen times.

"Yes! And an able horsewoman."

"I intend to speak to her only in Welsh and I do not expect her to ride into battle with me," Noble said, smiling dryly. "But I do appreciate the match's value. And I assure you all my subjects do as well." *With one exception*, he thought, watching Gwirion slip through the crowded courtyard.

Gwirion had finally spotted Corr, his white hair gleaming as he whispered to the quartet of young women huddled near the dovecote. These creatures had been brought in from around the kingdom to become the new queen's officers and attendants, and Gwirion had already established that they were the silliest women he had ever met. They were bending over Corr now. Two of them looked confused, but the little redhead managed a smile and the tallest one even giggled. A grim, sharp-eyed old woman dressed incongruously in silk, who must have been Adèle, the queen's English attendant, had been inside the chapel with the as-yet-unseen bride, and stuck her head out to examine the crowd at a most inopportune moment: She caught Corr whispering to the girls and marched toward him with a frown.

Gwirion was afraid Corr would falter and tell her everything. He had to prevent them from speaking. He had to create a distraction.

"Friends!" he yelled with a piercing bray into the droning hubbub. He scrambled up onto a stack of upright mead barrels for nuptial celebrations, which made him high enough to command instant attention. The sight of the slight, wild-haired man who looked like Pan in sackcloth startled everyone and the yard fell quiet. He saw the king, just outside the chapel door, turn toward him and purse his lips. He had been listening to one of the bearded foreigners, but now he absently motioned the man to shush. "Friends!" Gwirion repeated. "Before we begin today's solemnities, we must introduce the new faces you see here today. I trust you shall receive them graciously." Adèle ignored him, continuing toward Corr. Gauging the distance to the ground, Gwirion leapt high off the cask, somersaulting in the air as people scrambled to get out of his way. He landed hard on his feet on the stone paving, as the crowd scattered from him, then he shook his head once to clear it and ran toward where Adèle was just about to accost Corr. Before the old woman could entirely register Gwirion's presence, he had crawled between her legs and stood again, hoisting her brittle frame up on his shoulders and gathering her skirt behind his head. She let out a short, undignified squawk, which delighted the crowd.

"Behold Adèle," he intoned, grabbing her ankles to keep her secured. "Lifelong companion to our new queen. This is the closest she's ever come to having a man between her thighs, and we owe her a debt of gratitude for raising her ladyship to be the chaste and lovely creature that she is. Salute her!"

Most of the assembly burst into good-natured applause and cheers. Adèle looked livid. But she restrained herself to a dull scowl and once he had set her on her feet, she glared at him then slunk away, forgetting about the dwarf, just as Gwirion had intended. Corr nodded to him and slipped quietly behind the king, toward the chapel door.

Noble could barely maintain his composure when Gwirion

hoisted the old woman. He wanted to let him go on, to test his shamelessness, but the bride's uncle was standing gaping right beside him and he couldn't risk it. "Gwirion!" he snapped. "Stop that nonsense at once or I'll have your head."

"But I have two heads, sire. Shall I give one to you and one to your fair bride? The inferior one would probably be of more interest to her, don't you think?" He pointed broadly with both hands at his groin, an exquisitely grotesque grin on his face. "I'm quite sure it's superior to anything you can offer her!"

The Norman uncles exchanged looks of shocked disgust across the yard, and the crowd in general hesitated, especially those who saw the ladies in the retinue blush purple. A disappointing response, Gwirion thought—the locals would have laughed. The king gestured sharply to Efan the penteulu to remove Gwirion from the yard. Tiring of the prank, he ignored the fact that Corr was in place and relying on him; he went with uncharacteristic cooperation, and waited patiently in the kitchen for people to get drunk enough to appreciate him.

THE queen apparent, hidden behind the chapel door until the moment the ceremony began just outside it, missed the entire episode. She'd been in here since dawn, when she had celebrated mass for the first time with her future husband, and despite the high-arched windows the room was starting to feel very claustrophobic. She was trying gamely to keep in good humor, but she hated the gown Adèle had insisted on lacing her into, an excessively tight kirtle with an equally suffocating surcoat over it, and under the elaborate gold circlet on her head, cascades of silk that distracted her like a swarm of flies. For the years Isabel had stewarded her brother's estate, she'd worn only the loosest-fitting kirtles she could convince her seamstress to fashion for her. "I'll be tied up tight enough when I'm married," she had reasoned to Adèle. "Let me breathe a little until then." Adèle's rebuttal—which she now saw the truth of—was that when she was finally tied up tight it would be far more uncomfortable than if her body had developed into womanhood already constrained. This outfit, which any other female her age and build might have been comfortable in, took her to the point of fainting. This was the first time she was wearing a wimple, which made her feel like an aging abbess, and the thought that her glossy, rosewater-scented coil, the sole thing she was prideful of, the source of so many admiring stares, would now be forever hidden from the world depressed her. Her heart was beating faster than she wanted to admit; for the thousandth time she repeated to herself she would someday be at home here—more than that, she would enhance the well-being of those who now probably considered her kin to the devil himself.

She was aware of the crowd noises, but hardly noticed what they were. At one point she did hear the king's raised baritone, and assumed he was gathering people to congregate just outside the door. That meant Thomas would be stepping into the chapel for a final embrace, then escorting her to the priest, who would give her to the king.

But the person who entered wasn't Thomas.

It was an albino dwarf. Being startled by a stranger—and particularly this stranger—made her take a sharp breath in, and the dress was so tight that she nearly swooned before he even began his patter.

"Your brother is detained, milady," he said by way of greeting, polite and expressionless.

"Detained?" On reflex she reached for her belt, for the rosary and precious crucifix holding the saint's relic.

"A bad flux of the bowels. He can't leave the garderobe just now. The priest asked me to escort you outside in his place."

She stared at him, dumbfounded, the ringing in her ears getting worse. He held out his cocked arm for her to take. She tried to back away, straining to keep her composure. "Why are you doing this to me?" She spoke so softly that Corr felt ashamed. But Gwirion was relying on him; he had to see it through.

"Doing what, milady?" he said innocently, and reached for the furred hem of her sleeve. Instinctively she released her rosary to grab her eating knife, then remembered that the wedding outfit had none. Corr took her slender hand in his knubbly, callused one and—as Gwirion had instructed—sloppily licked her palm with an expression of deadpan reverence on his face. She made a strange, unpleasant sound, and fainted.

"YOU'RE the one who fouled it up," Corr snapped. "Where *were* you? You were supposed to come in through the side door!"

"I told you, he sent me to the kitchen. Apparently I overstepped my bounds."

"And what did *I* do, then?" demanded the dwarf. "I only nearly gave the bride a concussion!"

Gwirion said nothing.

They sat glumly in the castle prison, a dank, clammy cage dug into the basement floor of the barbican. Despite Noble's frequent threats, neither of them had actually been locked in here before and they were both unnerved. They were hungry and sober, which neither of them had expected to be by this hour of the king's wedding day, and it did not help their mood.

"He's coming," Gwirion suddenly said into the tense blackness, and grabbed the bars. The cell was half a level lower than the rest of the basement. Gwirion could look out—or could have looked out, if there had been any light—but Corr was too short.

Moments later, a torch glimmered above them, and Corr heard feet on the stone floor. The king appeared in his long green-and-gold wedding tunic and his heaviest ceremonial crown, dazzlingly overdressed for his surroundings. He had brought the unsociable-looking porter Einion and a guard, both holding torches, and three other men. No . . . two other men and Thomas. They all crowded into the tiny antechamber outside the cell and the visitors' extremely annoyed faces peered down to inspect them. The strangers wore Norman beards, and clothes similar to Thomas's in cut and color. Gwirion and Corr knew what this meant: They were not about to be released, they were about to be humiliated.

"Let me handle this," Gwirion whispered.

The dwarf made a derisive sound.

Noble crossed his arms and glared down at Gwirion. Gwirion mimicked him. For a long moment they stood there glowering at each other, until finally the king let out a sigh of disgust. "I hope," he said, "that you're both ashamed of yourselves."

"I certainly am," Gwirion said. "I've never botched anything so thoroughly. I say I should be whipped for incompetence."

"Yes, you should," Corr muttered, as one of the strangers demanded, with an atrocious accent, "Are you saying you did not intend for that to happen?"

"Of course not," said Gwirion. "I never should have got myself thrown out of the yard, that was thoughtless on my part, I lost interest in the whole affair, and that was irresponsible, because it left Corr to fend for himself, and it was a two-man affair. There's really no way he could have managed it on his own."

"What are you saying?" the stranger pressed him, not looking pleased.

"Well, when she fainted—we were nearly certain she would faint—I was planning to—"

"You *intended* for my niece to faint?" The man's sharp face looked menacing, and Corr wished he could hide.

"Of course we did, that was the whole *point* to it. I was right, you see," he added in a conversational aside to Corr. "About the kirtle."

"What about the kirtle?" the uncle demanded.

"Wedding gowns are always tight—it's the bride's last chance to show off her wares, isn't it? And she was probably nervous, probably not breathing right. They swoon very easily when they're not breathing right. But we didn't want her to hit the floor that way. I was supposed to be there to catch her. To keep the gown from getting dirty.

Because the laundress has been ill and I couldn't bear to give her any more work than she already has. But then——"

"Hang him," said the stranger, straightening, and left with one of the torches.

After a startled pause, Gwirion asked, "And who was that?"

"He's my uncle Ralf and he's important," said Thomas, trying in vain not to sound like a whining child. "His approval is worth more than a parasitic——"

"That's enough," Noble said brusquely. "When you're wise enough to not follow strangers into strange dark rooms, you may insult him all you wish."

Demoralized, Thomas shut his mouth.

"But don't you want to hear how it was *supposed* to happen?" Gwirion said to Noble with a cherubic smile.

"No, I don't. Idiot." He turned to the other Norman, the tallest and gravest of the three, and said something in French beginning with "Walter." Walter said nothing, merely stared in disgust at them. After a moment, he signaled to Thomas and the guard. They lit a wall sconce for the king and the porter, and exited.

For a long time, Noble stared at Gwirion, until the prankster, who had nearly convinced himself he had done nothing wrong, had to look away.

"Have you any idea how stupid that was?" Noble demanded in a quiet, dangerous voice. "This marriage is to secure their loyalty. The ceremony today was to show them how civilized and respectable we can be. The English mock us and belittle us. We finally had a chance to show them we're to be taken seriously, and you ruined it."

"I didn't want to, sire, it was his idea," Corr said miserably.

"Spineless," Gwirion spat at him. "I didn't have to hold a knife to your throat for it." Beaming boyishly, he insisted, "It truly was clever, sire, subtle and sophisticated—we even worked the 'Norman usurpation' theme into it."

"Stop it, Gwirion," Noble said shortly. "Do you understand me?"

"You're telling me I must behave myself until they leave,"

Gwirion said, sighing. "And if I don't, half of England will attack us." He smiled with satisfaction. "I had no idea I was so dangerous."

"I'm not of a mind to jest now, Gwirion," the king continued evenly. "There's only one way to make certain you're not either. You're staying down here until they're gone."

Gwirion was shocked. *"Sire?"*

"You heard me. Both of you. Until they're gone."

"Oh, sire, for the love of God—" Corr began.

"That's final," Noble said. "When I let you out, you'll pretend you've been whipped within an inch of your lives. And you'll be decent to my wife."

Gwirion, as if stung, jerked away from the door. He curled up against the cell wall, and tried to sweep the meager straw into a pillow. Noble peered down at him for a moment, then turned to Einion. "Bring them blankets. And food. See if anything's left from the feast, but don't say it's for them. And send your boy down here to watch the door—Gwirion can pick locks."

The porter nodded gruffly, separated some burning rushes out of the wall sconce, and departed, leaving the king completely alone with the prisoners.

Noble turned back to the cell. "Well?" he said after a pause.

Gwirion said nothing. Finally Corr very hesitantly asked, "Well what, sire?"

"How was this subtle and sophisticated prank supposed to work?"

Corr glanced at his cell mate. There was a moment of stillness. Then Gwirion, without quite uncurling himself, looked over his shoulder at the king. "If she was completely out, I would take her veil and Corr would walk me out of the chapel and hand me to you in front of the priest. If she came to, I would carry her in my arms out the door, and then run past you and through the gate as if I were abducting her."

Noble's face betrayed the faintest tic of amusement. "Christ in heaven, I'm grateful you botched it, then."

"You have a strange way of showing it," Gwirion said, and turned his head away.

THE bridegroom was gentle with the bride that night, even gentler than he had assumed he would need to be, because of the afternoon's misadventure. He disappointed the revelers by cancel-ing the traditional bedding ritual, refusing to allow the carousing guests to come with them into the wedding chamber. When they were finally alone together for the first time he was surprised, but not displeased, by her absolute stubbornness: She would not let him touch her until he swore to send at least one of the offenders away. He relented, refusing to provide details, then caught both of her hands in one of his and reached for her wimple, and she looked down, blushing, and became at once obedient.

She was far from his ideal. He liked trollops, he liked wild dark hair and curvy flesh and the fluid peasant accents of his mother tongue. She offered nothing coy or feverish. Her hair was the color of hay, and hung heavily, with startling flatness, nearly to her knees. Her eyes were such pale brown they looked feline, entirely too calm for him. And naturally there was some part of him that saw her flesh only as a piece of Mortimer's. Here it was, literally in his grasp, un-der his weight, crushable and trusting—a limb of the animal that had murdered his father and damaged his friend. It was his. The flesh that had wronged him was finally in his hands, spiritually obliged now to bend to his will, and he found this so thrilling that it almost made him dizzy.

But he did nothing untoward. His better side won no internal moral victory, nor did he remember that he had entered into this marriage in service to his people's need for stability, not his own need for vengeance. Her safety was secured by something far more ele-mental: He loved the female form too much. He could not have forced his hands to touch her for any purpose but pleasure.

IT was neither as tremendous nor as terrible as she'd thought it would be, their first night together. From almost the moment he touched her, Isabel felt safe. But the part of her that knew it wouldn't be terrible had expected it would actually be marvelous. That there was a mystical secret she was to be let in on. That they would be joined soul to soul afterward, and that did not happen.

Still there was great pleasure in it. Vague urges that her body had felt for years overwhelmed her, and he knew just where to touch and what to do. She assumed some older woman must have instructed him in these arts, and she was grateful for his education. He was patient with her bumbling shyness, and promised her that the physical union itself was all he required for satisfaction, a polite fiction he would rectify when she was ready for it. It did not hurt the second time, and without the pain, she shivered with the pleasure that he brought her. Adèle had never even hinted that the burden of womanhood could be so agreeable.

GWIRION picked the lock their first night of confinement when the porter's boy fell asleep. Corr wouldn't go with him, terrified that they should further anger anybody. So Gwirion went alone, slipping silently through the dark of the porthouse, out of the barbican and into the bailey.

The daily life at Cymaron took place around this bailey, a large walled courtyard with corner towers and several freestanding buildings within. Across a steep trench to the south was a smaller but much higher earthen motte, which housed the looming keep tower used for protection during sieges. The moon was only a few nights past full and shining defiantly through a cloud cover that had slunk in from the north, and Gwirion knew there was a watch on the roof of the keep, so he didn't dare walk straight through the courtyard to his destination. To circle the yard to the left would take him past the great hall and then the kitchen, both full of lightly sleeping servants trained to wake at the slightest sound. Instead, he took the long way around, skirting silently along the curtain wall to the right, past the chapel, the dovecote, and the steward's corner tower with its snoring court officials; along the western wall where the kitchen garden and council chamber stood; past another corner tower and then along the southern wall—past the kiln house where the unkempt chief hunts-man slept, the kennels where an early litter whined for its absent mother, the stables housing Cadwgan the marshal and his grooms. The large D-shaped tower in that southeast corner held the king's bedchamber; Gwirion had learned long ago to scale the wall, despite the sleek external whitewash that made the castle look carved from a single piece of stone.

He climbed up past the room of the sleeping judge and cham-berlain—the fattest and thinnest men in the council, respectively—to the top floor, where he peeked into the room through a window whose shutter had been left open in the cool spring night. What he saw nearly made him laugh aloud.

The new queen's most impressive addition to the castle, a source of fascinated and suspicious gossip, had been a wedding bed—a large canopied, curtained feather mattress far softer than any self-respecting Welshman should ever sleep on, Gwirion had scoffed. The bed curtain facing the open window was pulled aside. He had never laid eyes on the queen until now, when she was splayed naked under her husband. Not really interested in her, Gwirion noticed only that she was very slender and small, and therefore would be of no lasting interest to the king. What was of interest, and amusement, was how she moved beneath him: She looked excessively virginal. Over the course of years, Gwirion had seen the king with women of all sorts, and this was sending him back to the nursery. He must have been so bored, Gwirion thought sympathetically. And of course he wouldn't tell her that, so he was in the unusual position of having to be bored and polite about it. That was what had made Gwirion want to laugh. When looked at from such a perspective, he decided, this marriage could be exactly what Maelienydd needed after all: The king might develop a working sense of diplomacy.

GWIRION and Corr were ecstatic to be out in the air again, especially after Noble made them sit through a sermon by the chaplain on their moral perdition. They danced about the fog-dampened courtyard drunk with rowdy laughter, and no one could quiet them for half an hour.

"So did you even meet her?" Enid asked when Gwirion finally stopped for breath by the herb garden to steal a sprig of mint. Enid was a pretty, dark-haired kitchen girl brought to the castle for the Spring Rites four years earlier, and had been the king's favorite ever since.

He shook his head and grinned. "Caught a glimpse of her, though—certainly no threat to you."

"What about a threat to you?" she teased.

HIS glee was shattered an hour later when the king announced he would—eventually—be sending Corr away. "It's my fault—I even admitted it!" Gwirion protested angrily in Noble's private receiving chamber, pounding his fist against the mantel stone. "And I think the valor required of me to admit that should cancel out all blame against both of us." Noble, slouching in his leather chair, responded with a droll expression that showed he disagreed. "Then at least send *me* away!" Gwirion shouted.

Noble gave him one of those slow stares of his, the hypnotic gaze that Gwirion thought must explain his sway over the entire court. "You know you're not going anywhere."

"The mischief was my brainchild, I bullied him into it," Gwirion insisted. Corr stood quietly by the door, cleaning his fingernails, fretting as he always did when he was made the center of attention.

"He was the one caught in the act," Noble said, shrugging.

"I locked the boy in the garderobe!" Gwirion stamped his booted foot in exasperation. "Half the teulu saw me take him there!"

"The teulu will never testify against you, Gwirion, you know that. You're the only entertainment they've had since I made them stop vandalizing the abbey."

"Noble," Gwirion said sharply, shedding the feigned adolescent tantrum. "You know I'm the one to be punished."

Noble folded his arms and pretended to consider this. "You're right," he said at last. "You should be punished. Your punishment is to remain at Cymaron and learn to tolerate the Mortimer-born queen consort. Corr will be spared this dreadful fate by retiring to someplace far away, once I have found him a suitable guardian."

"That's not amusing!" Gwirion said through clenched jaws.

"I find it hilarious," Noble said in a humorless voice that ended the discussion. "Let's have a song. What key is your harp in?"

Gwirion scowled and with annoyance ran his hand through his unkempt black hair. "I invented a new tuning in honor of your wife," he answered, with a mocking bow. "Every string is tuned to the same pitch. I call it 'the Anglo-Norman Drone.' "

· 2 ·

DECORUM

Approaching Midsummer, 1198

 OBODY AT CASTELL Cymaron knew what to make of the new queen, of her brocade Norman kirtles, bewimpled head and foreign manners. They'd all heard that English women were trodden on by their men, and had vaguely expected her to be submissive, but Isabel never was. Awkward or socially shy occasionally, high strung not infrequently, but submissive never.

She was out of place, however, and she knew it. Her accent alone set her apart: The murmuring monotone of Norman French lacked all the punchy singsong of the Welsh. Assuming he would in time control the whole of what he coveted, Roger Mortimer had insisted that his extended household learn to speak Welsh; even Adèle was fluent. But Isabel, although technically proficient, had found little occasion to practice, and it dazed her to face a castle full of talkative characters who spoke nothing else. She felt lost in this new home, further lost in this new culture, a world that seemed at first simply a primitive version of her native England but was at second glance alien in a hundred subtle ways.

She had been master and mistress of a large estate—unheard of for a young woman in her circumstances—and had anticipated certain sovereign privileges as the consort of a Welsh king. But she found herself instead an outsider in a tight household that already had a master and had functioned smoothly without a mistress since the queen mother died years earlier. She would have no political power, and because she was socially superior to the court, court officers claimed even the domestic duties she had assumed would be hers. The tall understated man named Gwilym, the steward, ran the household and oversaw the use of the great hall, the nexus of castle life; Marged, the cook's rotund, aging widow who had ascended to her husband's station, was not only the overseer of all provisions, but the spiritual mother of Cymaron. Everyone was unfailingly respectful to their queen, but she could tell that they considered her superfluous; they certainly would not interrupt their comfortable routines merely to accommodate her. She suspected that if she had been a military strategist, a horse breaker, or a smith, there would be much to occupy her here on the harried fringe of civilization, but she was not. The hardest thing for her was to feel useless; beyond her political worth as queen consort and mother of the heir, she would be almost useless here.

She had say only over her attendants. She did not know them, and their collective intellect was not quite equal to a rabbit's (which Isabel doubted was common of Welsh women), but she took them in hand to make the best of it, since they were a privilege she had petitioned for. The royal court was rigidly structured and the officers she was entitled to were of tradition male. She'd accepted many of these: her doorkeeper, her groom, and others. But for the offices more intimate to daily life, positions nearer an English noblewoman's retinue, she had requested female attendants—and she was beginning to wish she hadn't. The only things they knew how to do were the distaff chores she had always loathed: spinning, weaving, and sewing. It became clear, too clear, that these were also the only things that would be expected of her. And in this backward land, even the local technology of weaving seemed primitive to her.

After mass on the morning that she and Noble came out of their connubial seclusion, she had first entered her new solar—a painfully ironic term considering how little sun there was to warm it. As well as the second curtained bed she'd brought, this chamber had been outfitted with spindles, two upright looms, and Adèle's sole valuable and exotic possession: the spindle wheel. Isabel's spirit sank at the sight of it all. Her sovereignty, the steward Gwilym explained with a kindly voice and an awkward bow, would be limited to this room.

It was a room, he added tactfully, that she was fortunate to be housed in. The great hall had been built snug into the courtyard corner by this tower; her solar opened directly onto a balcony with stairs leading down to the hall floor. The apartments in the other towers, even His Majesty's, required their occupants to cross either through the courtyard or up along the wall walk to reach the hall. This one bedchamber had the luxury of internal hall access, which would make all the difference when winter came. With a forced smile, she told Gwilym she appreciated it.

This was to be her world, then: a round, whitewashed stone room some ten paces across hung with bright tapestries, with one large fireplace and windows looking out over the undulating, grass-crowned hills of Maelienydd. Even now, at the height of spring, it was a watery grey light that filled the room; here it was even cloudier than England, and there was a constant subtle clamminess that she could only hope to grow inured to. During the day, she and her women would be joined by any female servant with a passing free moment. They were all entertained on occasion by Hywel, the old bard, with his muted hair-strung harp on his lap. He knew a stream of stories, poems, elegies, and sagas, but for all his vast impressive repertoire, his was a humorless sentiment and his voice was not what it had been, so everything sounded like a dirge. The entire arrangement depressed her, although she knew that most women would be honored, even ecstatic, to begin married life with all of these amenities. Her husband, or Gwilym, or whoever furnished the solar, no doubt meant to please her. And she was never one to brood, so she pushed her despair into that corner of her heart reserved for such indulgent emotions, and concerned herself solely with mastering each day.

There were four girls, differentiated almost exclusively by looks: Angharad (blond and delicate), Generys (brunette and sturdy), Madrun (a petite redhead, the youngest), and Gwen (tall and curving, with a wild dark mane). Like all Welsh women, they had cut their hair fetchingly short across their brows, and covered their braids with a simple white veil. Isabel wanted to imitate the style—it must certainly be more comfortable than the wimpled headdress Adèle wrapped her into every morning—but Adèle insisted she maintain her native grooming as a silent reminder of her intrinsic superiority. They were poised, could all read and write, but to her mind they were disturbingly unlearned and superstitious, although Noble had chosen them out of highborn families from the four most far-flung corners of his realm. Two of the girls excelled at general sewing, and the other two were very fast weavers. Adèle jealously guarded the spindle wheel, which dazzled them all with its newfangled efficiency, and the spindles and teasels for carding the wool were usually shunted between servants over the course of the day. This left Isabel at a loss. She took up some embroidery, but she realized within a week that she would go mad if she spent her life like that, and begged Adèle to let her take on the spinning.

"It will callus your fingers," said the old woman without pausing from her work.

"My fingers were callused before. My hands need useful work."

"The king won't want you if you have callused fingers."

"That is absurd," she answered. "Let me at the wheel."

When Isabel had the wheel up to speed, she was surprised by how relaxing it was. The monotony was soothing. She remembered the feeling of Noble inside her, and a pleasing chill ran down her spine. If only they could have spent a few more days doing nothing but that—the pleasure of his closeness, his skin rich with a warm

smell that made her want to leap up from the wheel and run through
the castle to find him. It was the only thing in this new life that
helped her feel alive.

THE recent death of old Lord Rhys, ruler of Deheubarth, Noble's powerful cousin and long a companion-at-arms (when
they weren't fighting each other) had made all of Wales uneasy. Rhys
had been both stabilizer and protector, always ready to assist his fellow princes with the Marcher lords. For decades he'd been
Maelienydd's staunch supporter in her defensive campaigns against
Mortimer, without once suggesting that Maelienydd's king was in
any way his vassal, even when that king was a boy of ten. Upon
Rhys's death his own kingdom had been thrown into near anarchy,
torn apart by his inept, ambitious offspring; Powys, directly to the
north, had suffered similar internal intrigues and been splintered in
two, with terrible bloodshed.

And yet even knowing how fruitless warfare had been for all the
kingdoms, the council was (respectfully) leery of Noble's declaration
that sustained diplomacy might be a true alternative. "This is an experiment," he repeated calmly, "to see how far Mortimer can be
trusted. Now that we have the English border stabilized by this marriage, we don't need so many troops on the Marches there. If Roger
gives us any reason to mistrust him, we can call them back there
within days, and remind him that we have his niece. Otherwise I want
to redeploy those men; we need them near the deBraose lands. In fact
we might even be able to coax our new English allies into sending
some of their men to strengthen our southeast border. Somebody find
out who's in charge of the troops that are potentially accountable to
my wife—surely not that idiot boy Gwirion locked in the garderobe?"

"Do you mean your brother-in-law, sire?" Gwilym ventured
dryly.

Noble responded with a dismissive wave. "Don't refer to him

that way in my hearing. But it's not him, is it? We need to find out if it's Mortimer or those two boors who were at the wedding." He smiled bitterly. "That would be ironic, Mortimer securing our borders at his own expense."

The burly red-haired marshal Cadwgan offered to make inquiries, and a courier was sent ahead to inform the idiot boy that he would be receiving an emissary from the King of Maelienydd. They reviewed the status of the northern and western borders, and agreed that, for a change, nobody in Powys was behaving in any way alarmingly.

When council was adjourned, Noble told Gwirion he wished to have a nap. This was flatly unimaginative code for an afternoon assignation in his private receiving room, usually with Enid. Gwirion looked for her in the kitchen, but was told she had gone up to help in the queen's solar. He made a face and mounted the steps.

ONLY Enid could have charmed Adèle into letting her try the precious wheel; only Enid was that thoroughly disarming. She looked so delighted by the privilege that Isabel was almost ashamed of her own grudging attitude toward the work. The coordination of it was beyond the girl, so Adèle turned the wheel for her and Enid's brown eyes danced when the wool was nearly torn through her fingers as she drew it away from the spindle. "We should have one of these for each of us!" she announced.

"And where would they fit?" asked Generys as she finished weighting the warp of the larger loom. "There's hardly room to sleep all of us now."

"Especially when His Majesty visits," whispered Madrun, the petite one, mischievously. The four attendants exchanged looks and guilty grins. Isabel turned crimson and lowered her face, sticking the iron needle so hard into the linen she was embroidering that she stuck herself.

Enid alone laughed. "He takes the five of you at once?" When Adèle scowled at her she grinned in response. "Oh, pardon me,

Adèle, I didn't mean to slight you—it's all six of you, then, is it?"
Even the queen smiled at the absurdity of that and felt slightly less
embarrassed. But Adèle stopped the wheel abruptly. "That's
enough," she grumbled, and gestured for Enid to yield the stool.

There was a single rap on the door, which swung slowly open as
the girl stood, and everyone in the room stiffened when Gwirion
stepped halfway through the crack. Ignoring the eyes upon him, he
gave Enid a look that she read at once. "Where are you going?"
Adèle demanded as Enid, looking down, headed for the door.

"She's wanted," Gwirion said coolly, and ducked back out of the
room and onto the shadowed balcony. Isabel swallowed her indignation: He had not even acknowledged the queen's presence, had ignored her just as thoroughly as he did on every rare occasion they
were near each other.

Enid met him outside on the balcony looking over the hall. She
whispered, "Couldn't you tell him it's my—"

"I tried that last time," Gwirion said, anticipating her. "It excited him."

She saw that he was struggling not to turn back to the queen's
door, and she knew him well enough to almost read his thoughts: He
wanted the newcomers to know where Enid was going; he wanted
them to understand that the king preferred a Welsh peasant girl to a
Norman gentlewoman. Her hand moved nearly in unison with his as
he reached again for the door latch, and she slapped his knuckles.
"Don't do anything stupid," she said.

"Or you neither," Gwirion retorted, but stepped away from the
door. "He's a married man now, remember."

She chuckled. "Oh, that makes a difference, does it?"

Gwirion followed her down the steps. After seeing her to the
door of the king's receiving chamber, he wandered into the kitchen
and eyed the supper preparations. Marged was severing rabbit meat
from its skeleton while her grandson helped the baker, a smiling,
silent man, prepare barley quick bread for supper.

"Where is Enid?" demanded Adèle, from behind him in the
doorway.

Marged and the others suddenly found their work vastly more preoccupying. Gwirion smirked but did not turn around. "I told you, she was wanted."

"She works here."

"She works here, but she was wanted elsewhere." Adèle sighed and exited again, ignored by all of them. "Here, lad, let me do that," Gwirion said grandly, nudging the boy out of the way. "You help your grandma with the rabbit."

"He's too young for that knife, now," Marged objected, but Gwirion smiled at her.

"I'll keep an eye on him. I want to make the loaf for the high table tonight." He winked at her. "A special little treat for Their Majesties."

A T supper that night, the loaf laid before the center of the high table was shaped like a pair of buttocks, and decorated: On each cheek, outlined by sprigs of herbs, was a decorated shield. It was somewhat warped and blurred from baking but it took little imagination to delineate the geometric pattern that was the Mortimer coat of arms. Noble found it hilarious; Isabel was outraged. Gwirion's name was never mentioned. It went without saying.

"Please," she begged as they undressed for bed later in Noble's chamber. "Muzzle him somehow."

"He can't be muzzled," he replied in an indulgent tone. She wasn't sure if the indulgence was for Gwirion or for herself, but that seemed to end it for Noble. He kissed the top of her head as she sat undressing, and smiled down at her. His face, Isabel had decided in an uncharacteristic flight of romantic fancy, was the human equivalent of a lion's: handsome, calmly arrogant, cool and yet unflappably paternal. "I'm growing fonder of you," he said. As her face warmed to return the smile he added, "How can you possibly be a Mortimer?"

She stiffened. "Is it absolutely necessary to insult my family?"

"Absolutely? I suppose not," he admitted. "But it's certainly a pleasure."

"Not for me."

He grinned and slid his hand down to the small of her back. "Well, now that I've had my pleasure, let's attend to yours."

SOMETHING about that evening affected her in a way Isabel had not expected. If asked, she might have said she had fallen in love—a common mistake, to confuse love with the more advanced mechanics of fornication—and the next morning, she awoke with a new delight in her married life. She reached for Noble in the bed, and was disappointed to find him gone. Then she remembered that he'd suggested riding out beyond the village gates in the morning and dining together on the hillside across the Aron. She smiled and got out of bed.

It was not sunny—she hadn't seen the sun since her wedding—but the diffused early-morning light felt more silver than grey today, and seemed to promise better weather later. Dressed and freshened, she made her way out of the king's chamber, down the wooden stairs and through the already bustling courtyard. In the great hall, Enid was placing cups of ale at the high table as other servants set up trestles for breakfast. She was the only one who bothered to smile at Isabel, so the queen headed toward her.

"Good morning," she said as the girl dropped into a curtsy. "Where is my husband?"

"Gwirion begged him to ride out alone together this morning, Your Majesty," Enid replied.

"Gwirion?"

"That's what I was told, Your Majesty."

"They're already gone? Before mass even?" Enid nodded. "When will they be back?"

"I'm not sure, milady, but they took their dinner with them." Seeing some squelched emotion on the queen's face, she asked gingerly, "I trust this news is not disturbing to you, milady?"

Isabel cleared her throat, hating how stuffy this made her sound, and said with a feeble pretense of offhandedness, "My husband had asked me to join him for a ride this morning."

Enid silently cursed both men for putting her in this position. "That's an unfortunate complication," she said vaguely. "I'm afraid Gwirion's infamous for those. Is there something I might do for you?"

"No. Thank you. I . . . would like some breakfast." She had paled almost imperceptibly.

"Shall I bring it up to your solar, then, milady?" Enid asked. "You look like you may be wanting to rest for a bit."

"No," she said shortly, then reconsidered. This girl was the only person other than Adèle who had expressed the slightest solicitousness toward her. That was not something to shrug off. "Actually, yes, in my solar. Thank you." She walked stiffly toward the stairs to her room.

WHEN Enid entered, with wimberries and oat bread, Isabel was standing with her arms folded tightly before her, vainly willing herself to calm, determined not to let a servant perceive how furious she was. Enid seemed to consider something briefly. She placed the platter on the bed, curtsied, and quietly announced, "You should understand, milady, that no one comes before Gwirion."

"I beg your pardon?" the queen said, playing with the tassel on her belt to feign indifference.

"Gwirion, milady. He'll always come first."

Isabel stared at her. "Gwirion is just an entertainment."

Enid hesitated, but she knew it would be said eventually and at least she, perhaps, could soften it. "No, milady. *You're* just an entertainment."

Before Isabel knew what she was doing she had smacked the girl, hard. Enid recoiled and Isabel, shocked, stared at her own hand as though it were possessed. "*Mon dieu*, did I do that?" she gasped, and gave Enid a troubled look. "Did I really do that?" Stammering, she switched to Welsh. "Forgive me, please forgive me. Are you hurt?"

"No, milady," Enid said, but stayed several paces away. "I'm sorry, I didn't mean to be impertinent. It's just that you're still a stranger here and perhaps you don't know our ways."

After a pause, Isabel sat down again and asked, warily, "What do I need to know, then?"

"I wouldn't presume to have all the answers to that," Enid began carefully. "I only know that you're here for the king, but Gwirion is also here for the king, and he's been here longer."

"But I'm the king's *wife*," Isabel snapped back. "I'm his political ally and his social consort and his bedfellow, and I'll be the mother of his children. Gwirion is merely *diverting*, he's not *significant*, he isn't *useful*—"

"Your Majesty," Enid interrupted gently, "Gwirion is necessary." She said this with such simple conviction that Isabel, without understanding the words, suddenly knew better than to contradict them.

But she wanted to make sense of them. "Why?" she demanded. "What does he *do*?"

Enid looked at once surprised and awkward, both rarities for her. "It's what he *did*," she said delicately. "Your Majesty doesn't know? He saved the king's life when they were children."

Isabel frowned. "Really? When?"

Enid blinked. She did not want this responsibility. "I wasn't quite born yet," she replied evasively. "But everybody knows about it." Although she'd never heard him even mention it, she cautiously suggested, "Perhaps if you asked Gwirion for the story, it might afford you a chance of civil conversation from him."

The queen laughed humorlessly. "Yes, I'm sure he'd love the opportunity to gloat about his preciousness to Noble."

Enid pursed her lips a moment then said, almost furtively, "Don't envy that attachment, milady." The queen gave her a bemused look, but hurriedly she added, "I hope you'll eat now, Your Majesty," and withdrew.

"WHY did you ask me to ride with you this morning, sire?"

"You suggested it," Noble informed him.

"No I didn't. When do I ever ask to leave the castle?"

This was a rarity for the king: a pleasure ride near the royal hunting area across the River Aron, a hillside almost overgrown with bracken. He was riding the large grey-spotted Spanish charger he'd claimed as booty from an English raid three years earlier; Gwirion rode an aging, native Welsh hill pony, a mare that the king had jokingly gifted him long ago. The mare was strong and fast, but her legs were very short; she always had to trot to keep pace, and the charger, used to her, allowed itself to be reined in more readily than otherwise. Two of the teulu, carrying spears and the royal dinner, had followed at a respectful distance; otherwise, the men were alone. They'd turned off the road, which was barely visible on the wide, bare hilltop, and settled in a shallow dip on the slope to dine.

The youths had laid brychan and board for them, then retreated a hundred paces. Now Noble and Gwirion were stretched out comfortably on the brychan, sharing the wine flagon and eating by hand from the same hardened trencher loaf. Gwirion swallowed a final mouthful of lamb, and rolled over onto his back to contemplate the sky. It was still grey, but the clouds seemed farther away now. He watched two red kites circle lazily on a rising column of warm air. He was edgy: Open hillsides always felt exposing. "I never ask to leave the castle," he repeated, a distracted murmur.

Noble gave him a significant look. "You suggested it. It was just a whim you had. I indulged it."

"So you won't tell me the reason."

"I don't need a reason."

Gwirion laughed. "Now I *know* you're up to something."

Noble gave him the sardonic stare that Gwirion knew so well. "Was there something better you had intended for your morning?"

"Endless fornication," Gwirion replied cheerfully, shifting his back on the blanket to avoid a pebble. "Not with you, if you'll excuse the insult, but perhaps with those charmingly articulate attendants of your wife."

Noble pursed his lips thoughtfully. "I don't know how successful you'd have been. You can't offer position or wealth—the usual aphrodisiacs."

"What are you saying?" Gwirion protested. "I can be any lord that a lady wishes me to be—I've studied the rutting vocalizations of every man in court, I can imitate them all."

Noble was delighted with this news. "Really? Show me one."

Gwirion laughed briefly. "I was lying."

"It's a splendid idea, though. Improvise." Gwirion made a face. "Go on, show me someone. Einion the porter."

Gwirion sighed. "When he's with a woman or a sheep?"

Noble grinned. "Can you do the sheep as well?"

"With pleasure." Gwirion pulled himself up, then balanced on his haunches and mimed bending over a stout body. A hundred yards away, one of the teulu nudged the other and they turned to watch: Like any males old enough to shave but not to marry, the teulu adored Gwirion's libidinous humor.

Thrusting his pelvis back and forth, he rolled his eyes up and stared slack jawed into the recesses of his skull. The king snorted with amusement, and after a few moments, Gwirion went on to the moans. "Oh, lovely. Lovely," he droned earnestly with each thrust. "Yes, lovely, *bah*—lovely—ugh—lovely—ugh—ugh—*bah*—lovely, *lovely!*" His whole body began moving with the thrusts, and the slack look on his face tightened into anguish. The soldiers inched toward them as Noble bellowed with laughter. "Yes—yes—oh, lovely, *baaaah,* lovely!" Gwirion cried, and finally, after several moments of increasing hysteria, screeched out, *"Lambikins!"* and collapsed.

Noble applauded. "That was marvelous," he announced. Gwirion sat up and rubbed his neck. "We'll do it at the next feast."

"Sire?" Gwirion looked at him, ignoring their guards' whooping approval.

"You'll work your way right through the court." Seeing Gwirion's alarm, he placated, "Or just a few of them. We'll use a lottery to select the victims."

Hoping to avoid this assignment, Gwirion insisted, "It's not a bachelor household any longer. The queen and her women wouldn't care for it."

"Pff," the king said, dismissively. "You have no sense of Isabel at all, Gwirion. She's quite a little tomboy, really."

"Ah. I see. Being a tomboy allows her to appreciate grotesqueries."

"It wasn't grotesque, there was something charming about it. Wasn't there, lads?" he called out to the teulu. They cheered.

Gwirion looked at them in disbelief. "You have the sensibilities of rodents in heat!" he shouted at them.

The king smiled broadly. "That explains their passion on the field," he said.

THEY returned in the early afternoon, and Noble stayed at the stables to summon the rest of the teulu for a mock skirmish in the tangled woods of the lower hills, despite the light rain that had begun. Gwirion at once made his way through the dampening yard to the kitchen in search of Corr, who was still waiting anxiously for further word of his banishment—Noble refused to send the little fellow away until he knew there was a good home waiting for him.

Nobody was in the kitchen but Enid, minding some leek-and-cabbage stew in a huge cauldron hung over the fire.

"Oh, you're finally back," she said, sullen.

"And what's up your nose?"

"Nothing." He waited, refusing to play along. Finally she explained, airily, "It's just that His Majesty had told Her Majesty they'd be spending the morning out riding together, and she wasn't pleased to learn he'd gone with you instead."

Gwirion stared at her. "You're not serious."

"I am."

"Who told you?"

"*She* told me. We had a right good talk. And afterward she invited me to serve her at dinner." She smiled coyly. "I think there's a promotion coming."

"Oh, good, you can sit in that cage of a room and listen to cackling dullwits all day."

"I might *replace* those cackling dullwits." Enid beamed. "She seems to prefer me to them, even the grouchy one she brought with her."

"Why? Gave her some hints for tickling the king, did you?"

"Certainly not! I wouldn't tell her that, it'd break her heart."

Gwirion was genuinely surprised. "She doesn't know?"

"She doesn't know about any of his women—and don't you even *think* of telling her. You've disturbed her enough as it is."

He was astonished. "This is a pretty change of tune. When did you defect to the French side?"

"Gwirion, Christ," she sighed, and returned her attention to the stew. "It isn't a matter of sides. We all have to live here." She glanced over her shoulder at him. "It's a small place, suddenly. It's different. It can never go back to what it was."

"It's just a few more girls shoved into one of the towers."

"It's not that simple—"

"Yes it is!" he snapped, with such anger that she stopped fussing with the pot and turned fully around. He was self-conscious for a moment, but then continued. "It's not as if we've been invaded or there's some sort of plague. He's got another belly to jump on, and a consort for feasts. That's all it is. For the love of God, Enid, she's a *Mortimer*, it's not as if he'll ever *like* her."

Enid looked at him for a moment. When she finally spoke, she was almost as cross as he was. "Do you know how stupid it is for you to be scared of that poor lady? She's not here to replace you."

"I know that!" Gwirion snapped back scornfully. "That's what

I'm trying to say! D'you—d'y'think I'd have been invited to ride along with him today if *she* had any say over it? So there!"

"Christ, you're such an ass!" Enid threw the wooden ladle at him. He leapt at it and caught it between his teeth—one of her favorite tricks, but she ignored it now. "Don't you understand *anything*? He set up the whole thing."

"Whuh?" Gwirion asked, the ladle in his mouth.

"He told her he would be riding with *her* today, and then he went out with you instead."

Gwirion took the ladle out of his mouth. "So?" He shrugged. "He's entitled to change his mind."

"He *didn't* change his mind. He made plans with her with the *intention* of breaking them. He told everyone the ride was your idea. He said he was—"

"—indulging a whim," Gwirion said in unison with her, startled.

"You see? But it wasn't even your whim. He set up the entire thing just to show her—"

Gwirion nodded, understanding her point. "He wants her to see that he'll throw her over if I want his attention. He wants her to know I matter more."

They stood silently for a moment in the empty kitchen, looking at each other across the chopping table. Enid could almost see the thoughts crowding his brain as he considered the responsibility this placed upon his shoulders. The king had raised his status without telling him, but now that he realized his position, Enid doubted it was enviable. How could one face a friendless woman, armed with the power to make her loneliness even more absolute?

Gwirion moved closer to her, and Enid realized he was handing back the ladle. "Well," he said. "Thank you for telling me. Do you know what this means?"

"Of course I do. What matters is do *you* know what it means?"

"Of course." He gave her a most solemn gaze, and then suddenly threw his arms around her and burst into delighted laughter. "It means I've won!"

Knowing that he spoke more from fear than malice, she could not bear to chastise him.

ADÈLE was too irascible to offer good company, and her women's chatter was, as ever, substantial as milk bubbles, but with Enid's deliberate and distracting attentions Isabel had weathered the day, and was trying hard not to brood now. To show Noble the insignificance of the slight. The effort was not lost on him when he found her in his chamber late that afternoon.

He entered in the sweaty leather corselet and red linen tunic that he always wore with the teulu, and his dusty blond hair still had tiny wet twigs clinging to it. The mock battle had been, as usual, deep in the recesses of wooded slopes: groups of young men armed with blunted spears and arrows, trying as much to outwit as to outfight each other in the confusion of scrubby overgrowth and treacherous footing, an imitation of traditional Welsh warfare. His team had won the skirmish. His team almost always won. And as so often in the aftermath of such brute exhilaration, he wanted a woman. Any woman, even his wife with her small breasts and lack of ingenuity in bed.

Isabel pretended to have been working on some embroidery that she'd actually borrowed from one of the bevy in her room. "Did you have a good ride this morning, milord?"

"Yes, and thank you," Noble said with a smile. "Gwirion wanted to visit one of our childhood haunts."

Isabel, petulant despite herself, ventured, "Forgive me for saying so, but he really is the most indulged fool I've ever seen."

"Gwirion's no fool," Noble said sharply. "You'll gain no ground with me by insulting him."

Pretending to focus on the embroidery, she said, in a tone that implied it should have been self-evident, "I didn't mean I think he's feebleminded. I meant an *allowed* fool." Noticing his blank look, she added, with tentative condescension, "As they have on the continent?" and returned to her sewing.

Noble shook his head. "What are you talking about?"

She set the embroidery frame aside on the bed. It was pleasing, under the circumstances, to feel worldlier than he was. "Fools are the latest rage in the continental courts. You haven't heard of this? The princes and barons take in eccentric ragtag confidants, as pets almost. They have license to do whatever they want—they make a lot of mischief and everybody thinks it's very witty."

Noble looked delightedly intrigued. "Are there really that many impish foundlings in the world? I must tell Gwirion he has a brotherhood."

Isabel made a dismissive gesture. "They're not foundlings. They're usually just clever vagabonds out to make an easy living by the entertaining shock of saying things other people dare not even think. They earn their keep entirely by personality, not usefulness. Roger finds them repulsive, and so do I." She returned her attention to the embroidery pattern.

Noble's face lit up. "Well, that settles it," he said congenially. "If Roger Mortimer dislikes them, there must clearly be value to them! I take back my chastisement—the term applied to Gwirion is highly complimentary."

She looked mildly exasperated. "I only even said it because I assumed you'd hired Gwirion to play that role."

Noble shook his head, looking superior. "Gwirion's no vagabond, and he's certainly not *hired* to the task. So I suppose with him it's more of a . . . spontaneous vocation." He smiled, nodded his head a little, tickled. "I rather like that. Gwirion: my Fool."

"I stand by my observation that your fool is very much indulged."

A pause, as he crossed to her and lifted her chin to face him. "He's feeling a bit threatened by your arrival."

"I don't see why. My presence has no effect on him. We've never even spoken to each other."

"I know, but I had to reassure him." He smiled at her then

turned away, shrugging out of the corselet and pulling the tunic over his head.

"I might like such occasional reassurance myself," Isabel suggested, pretending to struggle with a snarl in the embroidery thread.

"I can hardly imagine why you'd require it, milady." He looked at her meaningfully as he brushed the twigs from his hair, and she knew that if she let it, the conversation could end right here, with her complaint unheard but her dignity intact—and her subordination to Gwirion cemented. She'd known that to accept any man's hand was to subject herself to certain elemental insults, but being bested by a parasite was not among them.

He was waiting to see if she would pursue it.

"I was hurt to hear you'd forgotten about our ride this morning," she announced, almost defiantly, and tossed the embroidery frame to the ground.

"I see." He sat beside her and caught her off guard by running his tongue under the edge of her wimple, along the side of her face. He knew they had to have this conversation—he had planned it— but now he was really only interested in removing her clothes. "Surely you're not jealous of Gwirion?"

She jerked her face away from him. "I am trying not to be."

"But, madam, that's a waste of your time," he insisted, taking off her circlet and laying it near the bed. He tugged at her veil with a playful grin; she tried to maintain a dignified expression and ignored him. "You can't replace him, and he can't replace you." He ripped the wimple from her head, exposing her chin and neck and the great coiled whorls of her braids. Isabel bristled but otherwise wouldn't acknowledge the action.

"Envy isn't jealousy. I don't envy him. But I trust I will occasionally be the one whom you will choose when there's a clash of interests."

"No," he said casually, "that will quite certainly never happen."

She looked so annoyed by the declaration that he barely had the patience to go on. He was pleased she understood that this was a lesson, but he didn't want to take up time with an argument just to lay the ground rules. So he reached down to the silver belt at her hips, and began to unfasten it as he spoke. She did not move. "But don't fret about it. It's unlikely your requests for my time and attention will conflict very often. Gwirion has a habit I quite approve of and strongly recommend." He tossed the belt on the floor and picked up the hem of her long silk kirtle. "He befriends everyone. He doesn't sit on his *posterior* waiting to see if I'll pay attention to him." As he said the word, he shoved the back of her kirtle up under her buttocks while she sat stubbornly immobile on the bed. He reached up the front of the skirt, and rested one hand on each of her thighs, high up her lap, and his splayed fingers pulled at the flesh of each leg, parting them. She flushed and her body lurched toward him despite herself. "Do you have an argument with the attention I pay you? I thought you enjoyed it." His fingers crept inward. "If you don't, I'll withdraw it." And he began to pull away. Almost not knowing she did it, she clapped her hands down hard over his to keep them where they were. This was the one thing Gwirion could never threaten. She released his hands, returned his smile, and drew up the hem of her skirt.

THE next morning, Gwirion was playing harp in the hall in the rapid Celtic style Isabel still found amazing. The horsehair strings gave the harp a clearer sound than the gut-strung instruments she was used to, and every little grace note stood out clearly. It was a soft, mellifluous effect; it did not, in her opinion, fit Gwirion at all. Nor did his pleasant composure this morning as he relaxed beside the fire, chatting with Noble, with a comfortable familiarity she had yet to attain. He looked like a well-bred young musician, perhaps a bard in training; the gleefully vicious adolescent lurking within showed no signs of striking out, although he still refused to address the queen directly.

Resisting the entrancing tease of the music, she retired early to her solar from breakfast while the sewing bevy and Adèle were still eating in the lower end of the hall. Stout maternal Marged, amused by the notion that one of her kitchen girls might end up in service— legitimate service—upstairs, had released Enid from morning duties to give her time at spindles with Her Majesty. The two young women found themselves alone in the queen's chamber and Isabel was about to sit at the wheel when she noticed a small silk bag lying on her bed. Curious, she opened it and looked in.

There was a large handful of Welsh-minted coins in the bag. "What is this for?" she wondered aloud, and Enid, with permission, peered over her shoulder.

"Oh," she said offhandedly. "That's your *cowyll*, milady. Hadn't he paid it yet?" She returned to her stool and picked up a spindle.

"My what?"

"*Cowyll?*" Obviously the term meant nothing to the queen. "I don't know what they call it in Norman," Enid said. "Maiden fee? What he owes you for your virginity?"

Isabel stared at her, then at the bag, shocked. "I'm not accepting this," she said.

"Isn't it enough?" asked Enid, standing again to reexamine the kines in the bag. It was a lot—more than she or any girl she knew had received, more money than she'd ever seen together in her life. "Perhaps, no offense, milady, but perhaps it's less for your being a foreigner? I thought foreign women got nothing at all, to be honest, but then it is very bad luck to deprive a woman of—"

"It has nothing to do with the amount," the queen said impatiently. "I just can't accept it."

Enid's eyes widened and she gave the queen a conspiratorial grin. "Weren't you a maiden, then, milady?"

"Of course I was!" the queen snapped. "But I did not *sell* my body to him, I'm not a—" She couldn't recall the Welsh for prostitute, but Enid understood. She laughed without malice at the confusion and returned to spinning.

"Oh, no, milady, it's not like that. The man always pays it to the woman, doesn't matter who. You don't have a maiden fee where you come from?"

"*No,*" Isabel said shortly.

"Isn't your virginity valuable to you?"

"This is an extraordinary conversation," the queen announced, shaking her head, and moved to the window seat that looked out over the river.

But Enid's curiosity was piqued now. "Pardon, milady, but do you mean where you're from, they just give it away? They're that eager for it?" She laughed approvingly. "I certainly hadn't heard that about the Saxon women!"

"I am Norman," the queen corrected.

"It's the same thing, though, isn't it, milady?" Said without intended offense, it was more statement than question, and it wasn't the first time here that her lineage had been so casually insulted. Saxon, Norman, English, French—the terms were used almost interchangeably to describe anybody, of any background, who came from beyond the border to the east, although Saxon, which was the greatest insult to Norman aristocracy, was the commonest. Frustrated, Isabel pressed her hands against her forehead and leaned back in the felt-covered cushions of the window seat.

"I need an interpreter. Speaking the language does not begin to suffice for comprehending anything here."

Pleased by how fortune was smiling on her today, Enid put aside the spindle and stood up. "If Your Majesty wouldn't be offended by a villein's daughter from the kitchen . . ." She let it trail off as the queen looked up with obvious interest. But before she could actually speak, the door opened and Adèle's wimpled head popped into view.

"What's going on here?" she demanded, stepping fully into the room.

"Do you know what that is, Adèle?" the queen responded, pointing to the bag on the bed. She looked resignedly amused now, the first flicker Enid had ever seen of a possible sense of humor in the woman. Adèle glanced at the sack and used a finger to draw it open.

"It's that Welsh money, kines, isn't it?"

"It's a bit more complicated than that, and we would both have made fools of ourselves wandering around the bailey asking people why it was lying on my bed this morning. Enid is going to ensure that we do *not* make fools of ourselves. With that or anything else."

"Why Enid?" Adèle asked at once, leveling her eyes on the girl. Enid looked entirely untroubled by the scrutiny.

"Because I *like* her, Adèle," said the queen with patient amusement. "Enid, what is the legal procedure to have you added to my retinue?"

Adèle glanced at Isabel and said something in the dull nasally language Enid could not understand. There was a brief exchange between them without apparent emotion—neither of these women was very expressive, which Enid knew the entire castle found unattractive. She wondered if that should be on the list of things to explain to them.

"Excuse us, Enid, that was rude," the queen said in Welsh. "Adèle is concerned about the dynamics of raising a villein to court level."

"Oh, I doubt it's even allowable, I'm not freeborn," Enid said comfortably. "But the cook will let me go whenever you need me to explain something for you." She smiled and politely excused herself, knowing there were certain things that would never be explained, and glad she had control of them.

SUCH bright colors," Enid said admiringly some days later, looking at a red-and-yellow kerchief that Adèle had left on the sill after wiping off the rain. "It's rare to see a linen take the dye so well."

"It's from France, they're more advanced with textiles," the queen said offhandedly, squelching the impulse to add that they were actually more advanced with everything. She smiled as Enid's pretty eyes grew round. The sewing bevy exchanged looks: They were tired of both the queen's trumpeting her foreign identity and the servant girl's fascination with it. The woman was *here* now. She should try to be *Welsh*. They had already weathered a disagreement between the royal couple over this room's decoration: Isabel had started to wainscot it in the French style, until her husband, leaning languidly against the door frame, began reciting worthier uses for both the wood and the laborers. Everybody knew this was not the real issue, but it accomplished what he wanted: She had called off the work herself.

"May I hold it?" Enid asked, her hand hovering near the kerchief.

Isabel looked up and considered Enid for a moment. The peasant's occasional cheekiness was worth the cheer she added to the solar. "You may keep it," the queen said, smiling, and returned to her sewing.

The Welsh women at once exchanged expressions usually reserved for gossip. Enid blinked. "Your Majesty, are you sure?"

"Yes, of course," Isabel answered, a little confused by the group reaction.

The women once again swapped glances, quickly, and then deliberately busied themselves in their sewing. Enid pressed the kerchief to the good-luck amulet she wore tied around her neck, then tucked it into her belt. "Thank you, milady," she said. "May I be excused to the kitchen, then?" She lowered her voice. "I'd like to show Marged."

This seemed a dramatic reaction to receiving what was practically a rag, but the queen nodded, and Enid scampered off. Again there was a quick exchange of glances among the women and then they busied themselves in their work again.

"What is going on?" Adèle demanded.

"Nothing," Gwen said quickly.

"Somebody explain what is wrong with Her Majesty giving Enid a gift," she insisted. They stared at her blankly.

"Is it favoritism?" the queen asked, knowing that of course it was. The eyes all swiveled from Adèle to Isabel. "Is it wrong to have given her a gift without giving the four of you one? I didn't mean to insult anybody; it's just a trifle."

Again the exchange of glances. "You didn't insult *us*, milady," stout Generys hummed.

"Then whom did I insult?"

And yet again the exchange of looks, as if they were clairvoyantly discussing who should next speak for the group. "Nobody, yet, milady," Gwen finally answered, the only one who seemed amused. "But wait until Enid opens her mouth."

Frustrated, Isabel dropped the discussion. It was always like pulling teeth, trying to speak to these four; if it would not have been a diplomatic disaster, she'd happily send all of them home to their parents. She returned to her embroidery.

B Y the time Isabel went down to supper, the entire castle knew that she had given Enid a used linen kerchief. The queen was aware of cold eyes on her in hall, especially from the officers and particularly from Gwilym the steward, who was a man of great dignity and usually most civil. Enid, and only Enid, looked content, although people were eyeing her as much as they were Isabel. Enid didn't seem to care.

There was a flurry of bows around the room as the king and Gwirion entered from the courtyard, their hair and long tunics damp from the dense evening fog. Noble was laughing at a story Gwirion was telling with the aid of obscene gestures, but he stopped himself and elbowed his friend when he saw Enid standing near the kitchen screens. "It's the kerchief that brought down Cymaron! I *knew* it was a French conspiracy," the queen heard Gwirion declaim, grinning, as he went to get his harp from its chest. Noble began walking toward Enid. Concerned that she had gotten the girl into trouble, Isabel watched him. As Gwilym and Hafaidd, the wiry court usher, helped people into their seats for the meal, the queen moved toward her own chair, her eyes still on her husband. Enid curtsied deeply, and when Noble spoke to her, she proudly presented the kerchief. He swiveled so that his broad shoulders and back blocked both of them from general view, and they fell into quiet conversation. Isabel noticed Gwirion watching them too, as he set his harp on its back a few yards from the hearth. He still sported a derisive grin. What was going on?

When she turned her eyes back toward the conversing pair, Enid had vanished into the kitchen and Noble held the kerchief. He presented it to his wife with a small ironic flourish when he reached his seat.

"You can't do that," he said quietly, and gestured to the chamberlain to pour his ale.

"Why not?" she whispered.

"Not here," he muttered back. He turned to Hafaidd. "Ask Father Idnerth to begin the blessing."

WOULD you like me to explain your blunder, then?" Noble said after the chandler had left them with a blazing hearth that evening.

"*Please.*"

"We have a custom here of handing down used clothing through the ranks."

"We do that in England too, especially at Christmas." Isabel began to unfasten her wimple, readying for bed.

"I think we must do it differently here, at least when it comes to livery." He stretched out on the bed and crossed his booted feet, clasping his hands comfortably behind his head. "It's a very structured system. To step outside the bounds of it . . . discomfits our charges. It makes a bit of a statement."

Isabel sighed. "And what statement did I make?"

"Well . . ." he said, with wry amusement. "You realize that red and gold happen to be my colors. Considering the queen gives the gift of linen livery to court officers by rank, and Enid was the only one who received any from you, you effectively raised her status above everyone else's, even Gwilym and my penteulu Efan. And Father Idnerth. And Justice Goronwy. And Cadwgan the marshal. Shall I go on?" He glanced up at her as if they were sharing a private joke.

She scowled in frustration as she unplaited one of her braids. "I gave her a used piece of cloth."

"Used by you," Noble corrected. "That only makes it more valuable; it is imbued with the essence of royalty. Father Idnerth receives an entire outfit of my used clothes for Lent each year—I give him the rattiest thing in my chests, to be honest, and he responds as if it's manna from heaven. It's rather endearing. But when it comes to the queen and linen, it's very strictly regulated. If you'd given her a silk gown, there would have been less fuss."

"She wasn't interested in a silk gown—she liked the kerchief! This is absurd."

"Structure is proof of an advanced society," Noble said complacently.

"*Success* is proof of an advanced society," Isabel shot back, too aggravated to be prudent.

His humor vanished; he sat up snapping, "And what is that supposed to mean?"

"Nothing." She hesitated. "I just mean there's no sense in having all these rituals and beliefs and traditions if they don't help you to thrive. And, Noble"—she paused again, but decided she had to say it—"Maelienydd is not thriving."

He looked at once disappointed and relieved, and threw himself back down into a comfortable slouch. "Yes, and it's entirely because I won't let you give Enid a rag. Regicide and genocide and treachery have absolutely nothing to do with the state of my kingdom." He gave her a withering glance. "I didn't ask to spend all of my resources fighting off Norman persecution, you know."

Isabel let the loose hair fall so that it blocked her face from him. Very quietly she said, "It doesn't have to be persecution."

He froze, and then looked genuinely alarmed. "What does that mean?"

She hesitated again, but decided to press on. This was her belief and it would out eventually. She could not conceive of speaking to a man of her own race this way, but surely as a Welsh queen of Norman blood she was entitled. She pushed her hair away from her face and looked at him directly. "If you let the Norman influence in. It would take so much burden from your shoulders and your people could embrace modern civilization—trade and scholarship and statecraft—that they have no access to now because your minds are all as guarded as your borders."

He gaped at her, furious and horrified, and stood up. "Is that why your uncle sent you here, to lull me into this most singular reasoning?" he whispered, then grabbed her roughly by the wrist, jerking her toward him. *"Answer me!"*

"Of course not," she stammered. "I'm sorry, that's not what I—" She silenced herself as he released her arm and shoved her roughly down onto the bed. She had misjudged, she had gone too far even as queen consort, and she steeled herself for punishment.

But Noble, his quicksilver temper instantly reined in, only looked at her curiously. "Why are you cowering?" he demanded. "You look like you expect me to strike you." She said nothing, and he took a step away to view the whole of her posture. He had never seen her like this. "You do expect me to strike you, don't you?" he concluded, the harsh amusement she was already too familiar with creeping into his voice. "Why?" She said nothing. He nodded, the derision growing. "Is that what an Englishman would do in my position? Strike you for no good reason? Strike you for having an articulate opinion that happens to oppose his?" She glanced at him awkwardly and then away again, and slowly straightened up. Her behavior only offered him greater entertainment. "One of your own would have struck you for that, is that it?" He laughed. "And *we're* the barbarians, are we? Is this a part of the enlightened Norman influence you think I should introduce to my primitive people—telling the men they can slap their women around just for challenging their authority? How extraordinary."

"Then I may safely challenge your authority?" Isabel ventured, collecting herself.

"If you ever speak again of 'letting in the Norman influence,' your king will deal with you very harshly," he assured her. "But you may challenge your husband. That doesn't mean he'll acquiesce, but he certainly won't *beat* you for it." He seemed almost tickled by the image.

"Then I'm challenging your authority," she
giving the kerchief back to Enid."

"No you're not," he said firmly, serious again.
allow it."

"Then your wife shall withhold her affection from yo.

"If you insist on punishing yourself," he said agreeabi,
opened his door. Gethin the doorkeeper took a step toward him.

"Sire?"

"The queen is feeling poorly this evening and would like to retire to her own chamber early. See she gets there safely." He handed
her off to Gethin, her hair uncovered and half unbraided, and then,
without another glance in her direction, he began to undress for bed.

SOCDE called it Midsummer and some St. John's Day. Mostly,
for them, it was the day to celebrate the end of sheep shearing,
and weather permitting it called for a great supper to be taken in the
courtyard under the latest twilight of the year.

Noble knew, as had his forefathers, that a land of shepherds and
poets would not happily yield up their traditional solstice celebrations, so the emphasis around Castell Cymaron was not especially
Christian. The evening before, lintels and sills had been festooned
with St. John's wort, dangerously large bonfires lit in the courtyard
and village, and birch poles raised to dance around. The chaplain and
the village priest grudgingly acknowledged the nature of the day in
mass, but few rose in time to attend mass this morning anyhow.
Egged on by Gwirion from the castle walls, some of the local peasant youths rolled blazing wooden wheels down the steep castle
mound and into the Aron, crowing that they were Llew the sun god
incarnate.

The war began that evening after supper.

Despite damp from the intermittent morning rain, the evening
feast was held outside. The courtyard easily had room for the

dred-odd souls who, in addition to Noble's teulu, made up the
population of the village, as well as dozens of families within two
hours' walk of the castle, and a few of the nobility within an hour's
ride. The high table was on a small dais beside the steps to the hall,
and trestle tables ran lengthwise from it to the kitchen garden at the
far end. Servants circled the tables with fronds of bracken to keep
the evening midges at bay. Castell Cymaron was brilliantly sited for
domestic comfort—Isabel's own ancestors, not Noble's, could take
credit for that. It was on an elevated spot within the valley, warmer
than the surrounding hillsides: high enough to be out of the river
mist and valley bogs, but low enough also to be sheltered from the
wind. Although the stone was far inferior to anything in England, the
bailey afforded one of the most pleasant courtyards Isabel could
think of, somehow both spacious and cozy. Her grandfather had
built this place—she chose not to think about why—as a literal
home away from home, not simply a military outpost.

With Enid's assistance, the queen was finally adjusting to Welsh
dining habits. These people were as clean and fastidious as the Norman English, perhaps more so, but the stilted patterns of etiquette
she had been raised with were almost unknown here ("here in the
wilderness," Adèle muttered in French). And it was supper rather
than dinner that constituted the largest meal of the day. From what
Isabel could tell, the wild-eyed young teulu, who lived in the village
but ate at the castle, did not even stop for a midday meal, and entertainment was nearly always reserved for the cooler evening hours. It
had taken her a while to develop any taste for the food at all. Even in
the castle, they seemed to live on meat, oats, and vast quantities of
cheese; wheat bread was entirely missing and barley was a sour substitute. There were no vegetables but leeks and cabbage, and there was
such a narrow range of culinary herbs that Isabel sometimes wondered what the kitchen garden was really used for.

But there was a stranger thing about the Welsh at board. At any
well-mannered English table, people sat in pairs, with a cup, platter,
and trencher loaf between them. Here, they shared these things
among three people, which led to a louder, messier, but more con-

vivial mealtime. She and Noble were exempt from this, partaking only with each other; Gwirion and the yet-to-be-exiled Corr, who sat not at board but behind the king's left shoulder, had nothing except their laps with which to share their portion. Their meals were the most convivial of all.

Isabel was happy, especially to be in an official capacity at her husband's side tonight. After weathering their first real argument, she actually felt closer to him. And there was, for the populace, still a vague aura of romance to her presence—it was pleasant to feel admired for a change, even if they still considered her an outsider. It was almost a relief to have the villagers and farmholders present. For all the aromas they brought with them there was also a freshness and vigor compared to the stilted atmosphere of her solar, which she was beginning to hate. Only Enid's sunny company, a presence she had called upon often these past few weeks, made that room bearable to her. At her insistence, and to the usher's perturbation, Enid had been temporarily promoted to queen's cupbearer, and rather than joining the other servants at the lower tables, she was attending to the queen's mead, displacing Generys of the sewing bevy. This had caused some friction in the solar—although not as much as the kerchief had. Isabel didn't care; by her reasoning, honors ought to be bestowed by merit, not exclusively by birth. She had given the kerchief back to Enid in secret and the girl kept it tucked into her belt, underneath her apron. She understood it did not signify the outrageous honor she had thought at first, but it was still a favor and she cherished it.

The evening wore on while the sun lingered, as if suspended in hazy indecision, just enough silver cloud cloaking it to spare their eyes as they sat facing into it. The old bard Hywel lugubriously recited the adventures of the hero Pryderi and of Arthur, the gigantic, terrifying warrior-ruler of the ancient Britons. Council members and freemen made speeches to the queen, the king, and the two of them together. Bawdy toasts regarding the number of their offspring were offered throughout the meal; she had blushed at first, but by the time the tables were being cleared and villagers were unwrapping musical instruments, she'd grown immune to it, and understood that they were meant to be flattering. The Welsh of Maelienydd were surely an earthier lot than her own people, but there was something welcoming about them that warmed her.

The only dark spot of the evening was upon them now. She'd known that Gwirion would perform beyond his traditional opening song, but what he was doing—at Noble's insistence, which made it worse—was disgusting. And the commons' delight with it dampened her joy of their presence.

It was entertainment that would never have been allowed at Wigmore. Gwirion stood on each of the five long tables in turn. At each table he would roll a small ball from one end toward the other, and people would grab for it. Whoever caught it was invited to name any one of the landlords or appointed officials who lived in or near the castle, and Gwirion would do a crude imitation of that man in sexual congress. Noble justified this rancid debauchery as "entertainment befitting the heat of the day," but she was certain Gwirion was itching for any excuse to do it. He was very specific and very lewd, and the crowd adored him. The sewing bevy had faces so red their eyes were nearly bloodshot; Adèle, appalled, had retreated to the far end of the courtyard. Each subject of imitation turned even more crimson than the queen's ladies, but Cadwgan the marshal was good-humored enough to laugh at his caricature, and the subsequent victims felt it only manly to follow suit. Noble had announced that if Gwirion failed to perform to the ball catcher's satisfaction, the ball catcher could whip him, which put a certain forced enthusiasm into his act.

Finally, as the air was turning periwinkle under a cloudy, moonless sky and the silent chandler had begun to light the torches, Gwirion stood on the final table. By now everyone was exceptionally drunk and anything resembling manners or decorum was forgotten. Mothers from the village had gathered up their younger children and departed, but the crowd was still large. As the ball bounded down the length of the table, a very tall man reached out with an enormous paw and almost caught it—but a wizened arm elbowed past him and someone else had claimed it. The tall man sat back, drunk beyond caring. Noble, Isabel, and Gwirion were all surprised to see Adèle's bony hand clenching the ball.

"Show us the king," she challenged.

The crowd lost itself for a moment in a collective, drunken mumble, trying to decide whether this was riotously funny or offensive to the point of corporal punishment. *What are you doing?* Isabel thought. Adèle's behavior lately had bordered on eccentric.

"I don't believe the king is on the list," Gwirion called back to her.

"You said any lord or official. His Majesty is both. Of course, you could do the proper thing and refuse." She smiled up at him with rheumy eyes. "I won't whip you too hard."

Their audience exploded with laughter and began to pound on the table boards. Hating his life, Gwirion in the dusk turned to look at Noble. Noble stared back at him, his face unreadable. Gwirion looked then at the queen, who was giving Adèle an expression of alarm. He saw Enid scowling at him from the foot of the dais; remembering her lecture in the kitchen, he grudgingly squashed his first instinct, which was to portray the king nodding off from boredom while mounting his wife.

He looked once more at Noble. The courtyard grew silent with tense expectation. The king, who enjoyed this sort of spectacle, sat back in his chair savoring the crowd's collective bated breath. He offered an innocent shrug in his friend's direction, leaving it to Gwirion.

But then he smiled slightly, to encourage him.

"His Majesty will certainly excuse me from a whipping if I fail to comply?"

"Of course not," Noble replied pleasantly. "I can't break my own rules—what sort of ruler would that make me?" The crowd cheered him, then settled back into their edgy anticipation.

Finally Gwirion looked back down at Adèle. "Well then, madam," he said, sounding more nervous than he'd realized he was. "I always try to think of the ladies' best interests, and I don't want you to jeopardize your health by beating me just for the king's amusement."

"It would be for my own amusement," Adèle assured him, and everyone laughed.

"I'm sorry to disappoint you, then," he said, shifting his attention to the yard at large. "Ladies and gentlemen—and all the rest of you as well—with tremendous reverence and respect, I give you His Royal Majesty in the heat of rutting."

Everyone wanted to clap and no one did; instead they all looked up at the dais. "Oh, God," Isabel whispered, and reached out instinctively for her husband's arm. "Make him stop. Nobody should be allowed to be so disrespectful."

Seeing her distress he promised, "I'll stop him in a moment, I just want to see him squirm a bit." He gave her hand a reassuring kiss, which the audience responded to loudly, taking it to mean the royal couple was amused to see themselves caricatured. He gestured to the chandler, and a torch was held up near where Gwirion stood.

On the near end of the table, Gwirion had already begun his performance. "Good evening, love," he purred, with an overdone affectation of the king's velvet baritone. "Don't you like my beautiful blue eyes? I'm delighted to meet you—now come over here at once and take your clothes off." The crowd guffawed.

"Get to the good part!" an anonymous drunk called out from the back.

"Watch yourself, you're next," Gwirion hissed, and willed his attention back to his lamentable situation. Adèle, apparently, had vanished. He hoped the queen would give her a good beating for setting up this unfortunate scenario.

He couldn't be humorous without getting into trouble. The previous caricatures had been easy: His marshal was more interested in cleaning tack than the fellatio he was receiving; his horny young penteulu got stuck in a series of contorted positions trying to prove his ruggedness; his deadpan steward suffered satyriasis; and his chaplain was a marvelously subversive study of equating guilt and pleasure. But the king would not take kindly to an unflattering portrait, so Gwirion opted for a routine of generic mimed humping, punctuated with occasional interjections of lust. There was nothing clever to it, but the simple fact that he was depicting *the king* made it electric to his audience, king included. Every now and then he would pause in his acrobatics to announce with withering suavity, "Don't worry, then, you marvelous creature, I've barely started here." The crowd loved this, and so did Noble, so Gwirion decided to keep the routine going for as long as he could. He was pleased with himself for saving the situation and hoped that old bat Adèle was watching, wherever she was.

Isabel was surprised. She was certain Gwirion would have tried to humiliate her, but this was almost flattering. She and Noble exchanged looks and grinned, although her cheeks felt hot in the torchlight. He kissed the palm of her hand, which made her shudder pleasantly and added fuel to the crowd's rising heat. Gwirion's imitation of Noble's voice in the midst of abandon was almost unnerving. As a performer—even of such a perverse entertainment—he had surprising charisma. She could see his satisfaction at owning the crowd's collective mood: He knew exactly how far he could take this before they became bored, and although she found the idea unsettling, he must indeed have seen his master in the act once. She blushed more deeply, hoping it wasn't with her.

"Oh, Lord, yes, oh, God—" Gwirion groaned. "Oh ... oh ... oh ... oh yes ..." He swiveled suddenly so that his upturned face was turned straight to the king and queen, and as loudly as he could he finished off with an ecstatic cry of "I'm coming, Enid!" Then he leapt nimbly off the table to sprint past them, up the steps and into the hall.

Pandemonium broke out instantly. The crowd bellowed, some with hilarity, others with indignation that the queen had been so publicly embarrassed. She snapped her head toward her husband and saw Enid, between them, pale to the color of cold ashes and run from the dais out of sight. Isabel leapt up, half determined to quiet the yard with her own wrath, but the pained amusement on her husband's face humiliated her beyond words, and she stalked off the dais and toward the stairs without a word. Adèle, seething with an enraged thrill from the back of the crowd, went after her.

Meanwhile, across the tables, those who found Gwirion clever (mostly the teulu) were scolded by those who found him rude (everybody else), and inevitably drunken brawls broke out. It took the castle garrison the better part of an hour to clear the yard.

S HE won't see you, sire," Adèle said coldly. They were standing on the balcony outside the queen's solar. Irritated, he grabbed her by the shoulder and pushed her aside, snatching the torch from the chandler's grasp.

Isabel was alone in the darkened room, fuming. She turned her head slightly when the door opened, but recognizing his step turned away again. "I'm not going to look you in the face, I don't want to be bewitched by those beautiful eyes you use on kitchen sluts."

He drew his breath in sharply, but stopped himself from speaking on impulse. "Isabel," he ventured after a calming pause, and placed the torch in a wall brace. "It was a performance. It was not meant to be taken seriously."

"Are you saying you've never been with Enid?"

"No, I'm not," he answered. "I had a life before you arrived, you know."

"So did I," she replied. "I did not bring mine with me into this marriage."

"Of course you did," he corrected. "I'd have gained nothing by marrying you otherwise."

"Are you in love with her?" she blurted out, and instantly regretted it.

But he only laughed, relieved by the absurdity of the question. "I had no idea you were such a child! I barely know the girl, I never bother about friendships with women. If I falter as a partner, it's because I lack experience that way. In fact, that's part of what upsets Gwirion about you. He prefers knowing my women are only—"

"Your *women?*" she repeated, and despite herself turned to glare at him. "Would you please explain that phrase?"

"Don't do this," he said in a tired voice. "I was warned that this is what wives do. You're an intelligent woman, I thought you were exempt. Please don't prove me wrong now."

"What are you talking about?" she demanded.

"The oration on fidelity." He closed his eyes and rubbed his temple. "I'm sorry Gwirion did that, but if his intention was to hurt you and humiliate you, remember that you're just letting him win if you get upset. Come to bed now. Or would you rather sleep in here?" He opened his bleary eyes again.

Isabel was standing directly in front of him, shaking with anger. For a moment he was simply amused by her exaggerated expression, but then he realized the anger was directed at him, and he'd have to deal with it before being allowed to retire. He looked at her ruefully. "Give me the speech, then, if that will offer you relief. But be quick, I'm likely to fall asleep standing up."

"*Get out!*" she hissed, and slapped him hard across the face.

Like a serpent springing, he grabbed both her hands and pinned them fast in one of his. "That is not allowed," he said as if speaking to a willful child, and held her chin. "You will not strike your sovereign lord. Ever. Do you understand?"

"Bastard!"

He slapped her. Unlike hers, it was controlled and deliberate, intended not to hurt but to startle. "Don't become hysterical or I won't talk to you. Do you understand?" After a sullen moment of resistance, she glanced down and nodded. He released her hands. "Then you're free to speak."

She looked up at him with angry eyes. "I want to know what you meant by your 'women.'"

He considered this. She probably did not really want the truth, she simply wanted something that would mend her pride.

"What do you want to know?"

"I want to know what you meant," she insisted.

"I meant women I have nonconjugal fornication with." It was an effort not to laugh at himself for sounding so formal.

"In the present tense?"

He wished Gwirion were here, there was probably a pun in there crying out to be discovered, but he couldn't get his mind around it. His delay upset her.

"In the present tense?" she demanded.

"Of course in the present tense," he said impatiently. "Go on with the pontificating, just be quick about it."

She looked up at him for a moment. "No," she said sadly. "If this marriage is a sham, no pontificating is going to change that."

Again he laughed at her naiveté. "It's not a sham, what an absurd thing to say. It's a political contract. I have no personal obligations to you." This was, in fact, a lie, but she with her stubborn adherence to foreign custom wouldn't know that, and he was content to keep it that way for as long as he could. "You think like all the other wives, don't you? That's a disappointment, but I'll get over it." He surprised her by kissing her affectionately on the forehead. "I hope you'll come to me tonight. But if you don't, I'll see you at morning mass."

He left, taking the torch with him.

HE stepped into his own chamber to find a candelabra blazing on the floor by the unlit hearth. Sitting beside it was a familiar dark-haired figure, his sharp features strangely shadowed in the candlelight.

"And what are *you* doing in here?" Noble asked.

Gwirion looked over his shoulder at him. "It's the one place I was certain she wouldn't come tonight."

Noble sat on a chest near him and leaned back against a wool tapestry. "There was no need to be so cruel, you know."

"There would have been no *chance* to be cruel if you hadn't *insisted* upon that absurd game."

Noble shook his head. "That's a specious defense. I never suggested that the game include humiliating my wife."

"I was trying to get back at the old lady."

"You didn't upset the old lady nearly so much as the young lady."

"It's ridiculous for her to be upset about your romps," Gwirion
protested, fidgeting with the tuning key he kept tied by a string to his
belt. "I can't believe she didn't know about them until tonight."

"I was a little surprised by that myself," Noble admitted. "But
even if she had known, Gwirion, it was a nasty thing to do. It's one
thing to face it—it's another to face it in front of half the kingdom."

The smaller man sat up very straight and looked at him with
hard dark eyes. "I'm not saying it was kind of me," he admitted. "But
honestly, what's really upsetting her now? That I embarrassed her? Or
that you have a healthy appetite?"

"That's not the issue—"

"No, that *is* the issue. She'd be upset no matter how she heard the
news. She's upset with you, Noble, not with me."

"She's upset with both of us."

"She'll recover," Gwirion said with a deliberate yawn. "I'm glad
we had this little chat, but I'll be off to sleep now."

He rose with angular, feline grace and took a step toward the
door, which suddenly opened as the queen stepped into the room.
Seeing Gwirion, she stopped. Seeing her, Gwirion stopped. The king
rose. There was an awkward moment of silence.

"I don't believe the two of you have been formally introduced,"
Noble finally said. This seemed extraordinary given that she'd been
there over a month, but Gwirion had managed to avoid it. "Gwirion,
this is your queen. Pay your respects to her." Gwirion looked at him,
incredulous. *"Now."*

With the enthusiasm of a punished boy apologizing under
duress to some smaller child he has tormented, Gwirion approached
her and presented himself with a deep but grudging bow. "Milady,"
he muttered, not looking at her. Still bent over, he glanced at Noble.
"Shall I kiss the hem of her train?" he asked sarcastically.

"No," she said firmly. "I don't want it soiled." She heard Noble chuckle at this, which pleased her. Gwirion stood up abruptly, black eyes sparking, but her satisfaction waned when she saw that he was not the least insulted.

"Perhaps she has promise after all," he said to the king, and walked out of the room without further acknowledging her.

"I'm glad you came," Noble said quietly after a moment.

"I couldn't bear the thought that you would bring another woman in here tonight."

Noble laughed harshly. "What do you think I am? Under the circumstances, that would be cretinous."

"Oh? Then how does it work? Do *you* go to *them*?" she asked, angry with herself for caring.

"Isabel—"

"Or perhaps you do it in the stables with the other beasts."

"For the love of Christ," he muttered, irritated. "I won't discuss this." He gestured. "Undress now, and come to bed."

She pulled away from him and left.

Once he knew she was safely gone, he opened his door a crack to speak to his doorkeeper. "Enid," he said.

But he was relieved when Gethin returned with the message that Enid had refused to come.

3

USES OF ADULTERY

High Summer, 1198

HAT SUMMER, Noble's greatest headaches were domestic, but he could not ignore the forces at his borders. The late Lord Rhys's kingdom of Deheubarth was close to anarchy as his sons squabbled over it; north of Maelienydd lay the divided and increasingly unstable Powys, half its forces slaughtered in a recent misguided uprising against the English.

A bigger concern for Noble, however, lay farther to the north, in Gwynedd. Llewelyn ap Iorwerth, an upstart would-be prince just a few years his junior, was fighting and strategizing his way toward a united crown of Gwynedd on a wave of public adoration. An able warrior and charismatic leader, he promised to be unreliable as an ally—he did want stability, and wanted all of Wales to throw off the Norman yoke, but to Noble's mind, he wanted the ultimate glory in this achievement to be reserved only for himself. Even if he proved to be, in power, the next Lord Rhys, Llewelyn did not seem the sort to encourage a true confederacy of fellow rulers. He made no aggressive gestures; he was still working on uniting Gwynedd, and anyway, a thick slab of Powys served as a buffer between them. But Noble didn't trust him, and was determined to glean what his intentions were toward the English—and particularly toward King Richard's brother John, who watched Wales in his brother's absence, and who might succeed the bellicose monarch once he killed himself on a continental battlefield. Richard's reign had not been good for Wales; the Marcher barons had run wild with frontier ambition during his perennial absence from England. But John might strike his own bargain with the Marcher lords. He had been one of them, and he was not averse to guile. This thought, in turn, reminded Noble of the worst of his worries.

"Damn Roger Mortimer," he grumbled, his head on Enid's lap, reclining nude beneath a sheet in his receiving room. Their afternoon dalliance had been intended to get his mind off politics. It hadn't worked. Nothing worked.

Gwirion had been called in to play for them and he was helping Enid, wearing only her shift, to tie her veil back on. It was the first time since the Midsummer feast that she was civil to him; she'd refused to even speak to him until he had admitted, in front of Noble, that he'd been a malicious ass to the queen. "*Now* what has our beloved Roger done?" Gwirion asked.

"Nothing yet," Noble muttered. "Literally nothing—my scouts have all vanished into the ether. I send new scouts to find the old ones and they vanish as well."

"And which one is Mortimer, again, sire?" Enid asked playfully.

"Trade lives with me, won't you?" Noble pleaded, reaching up to tweak her nose. "I want your ignorance."

"I am not ignorant, Your Majesty!" Enid replied with cheerful indignation, and swatted his hand away. "But which is Mortimer? All those Norman names sound the same to me."

"I believe," Gwirion said, reading a small gesture from Noble and moving toward the door, "that I'll depart and let the king"—he waggled his eyebrows—"fill you in."

Enid laughed. "Your subtlety is deafening, Gwirion."

Noble sat up, stretching densely muscled arms as the sheet rolled off him. "Where's my wife?" he asked, and for a fleeting moment Enid shifted uncomfortably. Gwirion looked bored and pointed at the ceiling to the queen's solar above them. Noble rolled his blue eyes slowly toward Enid and gave her a seductive smile. "Just the very thought of Mortimer's exhausted me. I need another nap."

She grinned as he reached for her again. Gwirion, grateful not to be held in attendance for a second round, opened the door—and found himself face-to-face with the queen, who carried a heavy book under her arm. "Your Majesty!" he said with genuine alarm, and behind him heard the king curse under his breath. Gwirion reflexively raised the harp to his chest and wrapped his other arm protectively around it, as if she might injure it. "I was just looking for you, milady. I was wondering if you could give me lessons in that beguiling language of yours." He loosened the grip on the instrument and took her arm, trying to back her out of the doorway. "If you could—"

With a glare, she pulled her arm free and pressed past him, holding out the book. "I need to speak to my husband about a matter of Welsh law that—" She stopped.

It was impossible to hide what was happening. Enid had the sheet wrapped around her and was huddled facing away from the door. Noble sat in profile to his wife, splendid and naked, not looking at her but not deliberately avoiding her either. For a long moment she stood staring silently at one, then the other, her face unreadable. Finally, Noble, as much out of boredom as charity, took a breath to say something, and as if that were her cue, she turned sharply away and walked out of the room. After an awkward beat, Gwirion closed the door.

"Pardon me," he said, "but was I the only one who found that amusing?"

"Gwirion!" Enid snapped.

"At least she had some warning!" Gwirion insisted. "Imagine if I hadn't given her a hint."

"Shut up," Noble muttered, getting to his feet and reaching for his drawers. With a long-suffering sigh he started to pull them on.

"Mortimer had better behave himself for all this," he said under his breath.

NOBLE, like most Welsh rulers, kept his barons committed to him by personal loyalty. Several times a year, he made a circuit of the kingdom, spending weeks in transit visiting his lords, giving gifts, hearing local cases with Goronwy his judge, checking the training progress of the barons' own youthful teulu forces, taking time to speak even with the villeins along the route. It reassured him politically, but he also loved the fuss people made. Even the humblest servants and villagers around Castell Cymaron grew used to him eventually; on the road, amidst the far-flung collections of his subjects, he was a permanent celebrity. Tournaments were held for him by the local teulu, feasts were thrown, and he and Goronwy dispensed their royal justice to plaintiffs. The plaintiffs were often charmingly sycophantic.

His absence allowed his servants to have something like a holiday. Nearly all the court officers went with him, and those of the teulu who didn't serve as bodyguards went off on a circuit of their own to keep them out of trouble, so there were few officials in the castle to cater to. This year it was to be a short tour; he was too concerned about the general political climate to be away from Cymaron for very long.

He avoided the east and his English border, where his scouts were still mysteriously silent and invisible. It was a feint: If Mortimer was up to something, Noble wanted him to proceed as carelessly as possible and thus give himself away, which was less likely if he knew the king was traveling nearby. So he sent Efan, his own penteulu, east to keep a subtle eye on Roger, but he himself moved much more ostentatiously along the southwest border, an area that he and Lord Rhys had tussled over more than once. Custom decreed that at this time the queen go on a circuit of her own, but she had not yet estab-

lished diplomatic ties with any of his people, so he had brought her
with him hoping she'd develop some. This meant dragging her
through the wind-beaten, heather-crowned hills of one of the bleakest parts of his kingdom, but it also meant that they would have
hours a day on horseback with little to distract them from coming to
a personal understanding.

Isabel had been stone-cold to him at first and turned away from
his touch in bed. Against his native inclination, he persisted with patience and indulgence, allowed Adèle to travel beside them instead of
at the back of the train with the rest of the queen's officers, indulged
his wife's peculiar newfound fascination with Welsh justice and per-
mitted her to bring the codex of the *Law of Wales* with her. He gave her
not one moment to suspect he was straying. She gradually softened,
and one afternoon on their trek between manors, their bodyguards
began unsentimentally to place bets on the king's chances of riding
his wife that night.

They were in the far west, heading north from the village of
Rhaeadr on a hillside blazing yellow with gorse, in that awesome
quadrant of the kingdom boasting dramatic cliffs and precipices. Isabel conceded a growing fondness for the landscape: As with the castle courtyard, there was somehow both a coziness and spaciousness
about it. The royal couple had spent a genuinely pleasant morning
together under clouds that looked, as usual, almost close enough to
touch. They raised their voices over the slow, damp gusts that cooled
the hilltop roads, discussing safely neutral topics like Roman ruins
and folk beliefs about the spirits of the local flora. The casual ease
between them, as companions, seemed secure enough that even
Adèle stopped hovering obsessively, and warily slid back into her assigned place in the procession.

Isabel noticed a small stone pillar high atop a hill on the far side
of the valley to the north. She asked her husband if it might not be
the remnants of one of the Roman hill forts he'd described. He
glanced to where she pointed, and stiffened. "No," he said. "That's a
monument." After a pause, he added, "To mark where your uncle
killed my uncle." Caught short, she drew a sharp breath. "*One* of my

uncles," he went on, gratuitously. "I believe the final tally was approx-
imately three uncles and one father, limited of course to the one generation. Would you like to go across for a better look?"

She closed her eyes against his icy sarcasm. "Your grievances are
starting to resemble boasting, sire. Have you never killed a man?
Have the men you killed had no families?"

"I've never killed a man in ambush days after celebrating Christmas with him," said Noble caustically.

She snapped her head around to glare at him. "Roger would
never have done such a thing," she declared.

"I'm glad to hear it," he said. "While you're rewriting history,
please expunge my father's murder too."

"There must have been some provocation, then."

"Oh, great provocation. Cousin Rhys hosted a Christmas festival
at Aberteifi, to celebrate the unprecedented state of nobody being at
war with anybody else for more than a week, and my uncle Einion
Clud's team bested your uncle Mortimer's in a tournament there.
Clearly murder was the only possible response to such an insult, so
Roger ambushed him on the ride home. Or perhaps that was just a
convenient excuse to take up his father's hobby—the obliteration of
my line. Two years later he killed my father and tried to kill me too."

She'd known about Cadwallon, but never having heard the bardic
laments, details were unknown to her. "You were *there?*" she gasped,
louder than she meant to.

He snorted with contempt that this was news to her. "Don't
your minstrels crow triumphantly about it?"

Suddenly she felt very tired. "I'm appalled that he did that, but
it's not my duty to atone for him."

He swung around in the saddle to glare at her. "Yes it is," he
growled. "That and more. Doesn't it strike you how few men in the
prime of life there are about Cymaron? That most of my officers are
approaching old age except for Efan, who's barely a grown man?" He
spoke rapidly, a recitation too familiar to dwell on: "Gwilym and
Hafaidd lost their sons, each about to have ascended to his father's
post, less than a year ago in Roger's last attack. Efan's father, who to be

honest had not quite prepared his son to take over my personal teulu, let alone my entire army, was killed the same day. Marged, in the kitchen, has lost a husband, half a dozen sons, and four grandsons over the past ten years. Cadwgan the marshal lost a son, Einion the porter a brother, Father Idnerth and Hywel several nephews each. And many women were lost as well but I'll spare you the particular details. The only native soul in Cymaron who has not lost close family to your uncle within the last decade is Gwirion, because he has no family to lose. Even your women, your doorkeeper, your groom. These people see your Norman face at the king's table every meal eating the food they worked to put there. Don't expect them to stomach that if you offer no atonement." He began to urge his horse ahead of hers.

She grabbed his arm and when he looked back at her, she tried not to sound imploring. "You resent me for my heritage but you don't help me at all to embrace yours. I'm no use to you unless I belong to both and you know that, that's why you chose me."

His laughter was harsh. "Oh, it's my fault, is it? I must convince my people to embrace you although I know you won't embrace them back—what you want is to soften them to the man who killed—"

Fed up, she almost spat at him: "Have you atoned for the sins of *your* people, Noble? I'm not entirely ignorant of your family." She felt her throat tighten; if they'd been in private, she would have shouted at him. She had been taught a recitation too, less personally bitter but still damning, and keeping her voice low and her face neutral in case anyone was watching them, she hissed it all at him in French. "One of your cousins killed his own brother, another *blinded* both of his brothers, and your own sainted father sold his brother as a hostage. That's what your family does *to its own*, not to its rivals. You are *dazzlingly* sanctimonious." She let go of his sleeve, took a deep, satisfied breath and looked away. That had felt wonderful.

He stared at her so hard she felt it as a physical force, and reluctantly found herself looking back at him again. "Yes, my family did all that. After your family had distressed them beyond reason," Noble said quietly, all trace of humor, even sarcasm, vanished. "We must both of us atone for the sins of our families. Anarawd, who blinded his brothers, is my legal heir, and the only way to save the kingdom from his hubris is for me to have a son. Do you think I've spent the last two weeks coddling you because I'm sorry you were upset about Enid? Listen to me!" he snapped. She had looked away, and he grabbed her palfrey's rein to force her toward him, which brought the palfrey to a jerking halt. The train behind them awkwardly pulled up. Noble was angry now, and the entire entourage could see it, but he lowered his voice for her hearing alone. "Caring what we think of each other is not a luxury allowed to us. I'd prefer not to force myself on you, but you're bordering on treason if you would put your own petty pride ahead of giving me a child, when you know that if I die without issue, this kingdom will fall into such hands. Would you do that to your own people?" She looked stung, and he tried to speak in gentler tones. "When you've reconsidered the consequences of your selfishness, I will be ready for you." He released her horse's rein and spurred his own mount on ahead.

THE king never brought Gwirion with him on circuit. Gwirion hated leaving Cymaron, and anyway, His Majesty claimed, he was far too unpredictable. When Noble was away, Gwirion tended to slip into lackadaisical ennui. This had not always been true; in earlier years, he had made it a habit to steal the great seal, which was kept in the royal coffers, and use it on a variety of interesting proclamations. One year he demanded the arrest of all fleas, another time he issued a warrant outlawing the issuing of warrants, and once he officially declared that on the first of June all goods in the village could be paid for by the sound of money in lieu of actual currency. When following a bad harvest he managed to send out, to the entire kingdom, an edict that all land-use fees for the year could be paid in human excrement, Gwilym the steward—never losing his calm demeanor—seized the seal and kept it with him at all times until the king returned. He had ever since maintained a vigil over it whenever Noble left Cymaron. On only one occasion in over a decade had Gwirion managed to spirit the seal away from him, and used it to stamp an order that made dying a capital offense. The steward's vigil had tightened after that, and Gwirion resigned himself to boredom in Noble's absence. It was still better than being out on the open road.

When the watch on the keep roof called down that the royal party was in sight of home, the announcement set village and castle into a frenzy of activity. The mayor oversaw the village and Gwilym the castle, organizing the populace as they raised the images of Noble's gold lion, *rampant regardant,* on a field of crimson. The porter's deputy ran down to the village and offered the children a halfpenny an armload for flowers to strew along the hamlet's single thoroughfare. In the castle, everyone assembled outside on the steps leading up to the hall, in formation according to their status—this meant Gwilym, followed by the smith in his black conical hat, followed by officials' wives, followed by everybody else. Except Gwirion. True to the ambiguity of his rank, the man who was not even given a place at table stood in front of everyone else to welcome his monarch home.

Enid hesitated to join the welcome party. The queen had stumbled upon them a second time before the circuit started, under even more compromising circumstances, and had forbade Enid entering her solar or even straying unnecessarily into her view; the girl was debating whether anybody could really hold a grudge for weeks. "Look at you," Gwirion said, shaking his head at her uncertainty. "Further evidence of the damage that Saxoness is doing all of us. It takes a potent dose of poison to dull your pretty smile." She scowled at him, which to him only proved his point. "You'll be out there to greet *him,* not her," he insisted. "What has he done to you for you to disrespect him?" Ten minutes later, she was standing with the kitchen crew watching the gates draw open.

There was a small vanguard of teulu and then the king himself entered on his Castilian charger, in his red-and-gold traveling uniform, looking as ever casually bedazzling. The queen was behind him in similar colors, small and demure, looking and feeling almost invisible. Grooms stepped forward to take the horses' heads and the couple dismounted while behind them the rest of the retinue continued to ride into the bailey. Following Gwirion's lead, the assembly on the hall steps bowed in unison to their sovereign, and Noble, followed by his wife, formally bowed in response. "Now get you back to work, you lazy scoundrels!" Gwirion cried out playfully, turning around. "Haven't you anything better to do than stand here and gape at the king's consort? It's the same woman he had when he left . . . well, *that's* novel, anyhow," he admitted, intending no real malice. To his mind it was even a compliment. He turned back around toward the king, and saw the queen walking past him briskly, her expression unreadable behind the linen veil that had shielded her face from the road dust. She made such a show of ignoring him as she passed that for a minute he actually pitied her ineptness, and very nearly offered to show her how to snub somebody more effectively. Instead, he took a step down to join the king, who was watching her go with a look of exasperation on his face. Gwirion was about to offer him sympathy when he realized the exasperation was aimed at himself.

"It took some hard words, but I had her feathers smoothed before you started in," Noble said. "Thank you."

"My pleasure," Gwirion said brightly, not sure how else to respond. "Are you in need of a nap?"

"No, Gwirion," Noble said with tired patience. "I am in need of domestic serenity."

"Ah." Gwirion considered, briefly. "I don't think I can help you much with that."

Noble looked at him. "That is more than abundantly clear. Make yourself useful somewhere, would you please?" He passed by him and up the steps.

THE queen took supper in her room that night, citing travel exhaustion. Adèle was in the village arguing with the tanner about a belt for her mistress, so taking the platter up to the queen was left to Marged's discretion.

Ever since Noble's rebuke above Rhaeadr, Isabel had been troubled and meditative. There was a large chasm in her mind between her initial awed thrill at the title "queen," the notion of all the useful Christian work that such a role might offer her . . . and the sole obligation to bear a son who would exist only to rule bogs, hillsides and shepherds. She was seeking solutions to her internal dissonance when there was a knock on the door and her doorkeeper Llwyd stuck his head in. "Your food, Majesty," he said in his soft, somnolent tone. She put down the enormous law book she had been reading in the last stretch of daylight, and got up from the window seat. When she turned her attention back into the room, she was shocked to see Enid laying the platter on the bed. "Here you are, Majesty," she hummed, curtsying and sounding chipper. The queen did not acknowledge her. "Would you like company while you're eating?"

"Not yours," Isabel said shortly. "Thank you for bringing my supper, but please have somebody else come for the platter." She sat again and pointedly looked out the window.

Enid sighed and straightened up from arranging things nicely on the tray. Her impulse was to roundly scold Her Majesty, arms akimbo, but instead she clasped her hands sedately before her. "Milady," she said, "it will not be possible for me to hide from you for the rest of my life. If I may be presumptuous enough—"

"You've already been more than presumptuous, Enid."

She paused, and tried again. "You have forgiven him, milady, and his crime against you is worse than mine."

"Is it?" Isabel asked in an ironic voice, looking at her.

"It's his body you engage with, milady, not mine."

"Your crime is not your body," Isabel scoffed. "It's encouraging my intimacy on false pretenses. You knew the significance of what you were hiding from me and you hid it so that you could worm your way into my affections." She spoke with bitterness. "You were being duplicitous."

"I thought I was being discreet, milady," Enid answered quietly.

"How long did you expect that to last? What were you planning to say to me when I finally found out? What could you possibly have said that would preserve amity between us?"

"Preserving amity with you was not my first concern, Your Majesty," Enid said. "You seem to think we are talking about a man, milady, but we are talking about the king, and my duty to the king comes first. I'm sorry for deceiving you, but my presence here does not diminish who you are. You are the queen. Doesn't that satisfy you?"

Isabel stood up from the window seat. "You may not presume to tell me what I should be satisfied with!"

"Exactly—because you're the queen and I'm not. Good evening, milady, and as you asked I will send somebody else up for the platter." Enid was unused to the frustrated anger the conversation evoked in her; she had to get out of there before she said something she'd regret. She began to wonder if Gwirion was right about the queen's universally poisonous effect. But it saddened her too. She liked the young woman and had even fancied there was something of herself in there, some happy spirit begging for release.

WHILE the queen was preoccupied with Welsh law, Corr was preoccupied with confirmation of his banishment.

"It's not banishment. It's retirement! How many parasites ever manage to retire? With full corrodies—lodging, food, clothing, everything! What a luxury," Gwirion insisted, forcing cheer. Humffri ap Madoc, a baron to the north and the last stop on the king's circuit, had volunteered to take the dwarf into his care, offering to give him a minor position in his own kitchen. Corr, who had always yearned for the pride of actually earning his own keep, almost wept with gratitude, and began counting the hours to his departure with happiness instead of distress.

The night before he left, with filial affection, Gwirion organized a farewell party for him. Adèle bristled when she learned of it: Corr was supposed to be leaving in shame as punishment for distressing the bride on her wedding day, but this was a near heroic send-off. Isabel did not bother sharing Adèle's indignation; she had ensconced herself in her room, contemplating the various paths the *Law of Wales* might allow her. Nobody at the court paid her enough heed to wonder at her sudden interest in legal matters.

Noble composed Corr's traveling party the next morning to his own advantage. Besides two members of the teulu, one of them about to leave to take holy orders at Cwm-hir, he ordered Gwirion and Enid to go along. This was a peace offering to his wife: Now the people she least wanted to see would be out of sight for a day, and perhaps he could coax her back out of her shell. Besides, although Gwirion usually refused to leave the village walls without the king, he was anxious to see where Corr would be spending his greying years, and Enid had long desired to visit her parents, who lived a few hours north of the castle. She would ride behind Gwirion on the mare, stopping on the way, and they would pick her up on their return.

The dwarf on his own tiny hill pony looked like a swaddled infant, wrapped protectively against the white-hot sun that would damage his fair skin so easily. The trip out was uneventful, but leaving Corr was far more distressing than Gwirion was prepared for. His usual endless chatter grew still, and he was a morose traveling companion as they headed back south. He rode very slowly through the dense yellow gorse, claiming it was his mount's discomfort in the summer humidity; whatever the cause, they didn't reach Enid until nearly sundown.

Enid's parents, who were so aggressively dull that they left the source of their daughter's buoyancy and beauty a mystery, breathlessly offered to host the royal party in their shoddy hovel on the edge of a hamlet. When Gwirion realized this meant they were planning to go without supper and sleep on the ground outside, giving their food and bedsheets to their guests, he refused. To the soldiers' annoyance but Enid's profound gratitude, he declared his intention of

making it back to the castle by midnight; once they were safely out of
sight of the hut, of course, they stopped again to make camp. They
were at least off the main highway, he pointed out, far enough down
the hillside to be out of the wind, but shielded from the cold valley
mist by an oak grove below them.

The teulu mounts were always outfitted with travel gear: a small
tartan brychan, flint, a water skin, and a miserly ration of cured meat
behind each saddle. Once Gwirion volunteered to poach fallen
branches from the oak grove—Enid and the guards were too superstitious to enter any grove of sacred trees—they were able to make a
fire and a woefully thin meat broth to share, but there was an awkward moment about the sleeping arrangements. Enid had ridden behind Gwirion on the pony, so there were only two horses and
therefore two blankets. Two blankets, and four people. It would be
common enough to share a brychan, but these were cut too small for
two men, even if one of them was slender Gwirion.

Since one guard would always be awake on watch, only three
blankets would ever be needed, but that was still more than they had.
Gwirion was about to offer Enid the second brychan when
Caradoc—the stocky young soldier who was clearly *not* about to enter the brotherhood—asked Enid to share his with him. She laughed.

"I'm not for general consumption," she said.

"His Majesty need never know," Caradoc offered, and gave his
cohort a meaningful glance. The monk looked disgusted and went to
tether the horses away from the poisonous bracken. Ignoring
Gwirion's presence, the wooer turned his gaze back to Enid who, despite her youth, was probably older than he was. "Come on, then.
You're a fine girl and I'm not so bad, am I? We could have some fun,
no harm done, and none's the wiser." He licked his lower lip. "I've
fancied you for months."

"Jesu, that's enough," Gwirion interrupted. "Enid, you take the
second brychan. I'll sleep in the bracken." He began to walk toward
the monk's saddle.

"No," said Caradoc in a menacing voice, moving toward Enid
with ogling deliberation. "She's mine."

Enid stared at him, suddenly very aware of how large he was. Alarmed, she glanced at Gwirion, who changed course and immediately put himself between the two of them, glowering up at Caradoc, arms crossed. "No she's not, Caradoc, she's under my protection."

The younger man laughed derisively and patted his sword hilt. "Your protection? Is that meant to intimidate me?"

"Think on who I am, you idiot," Gwirion said in a calm voice, trembling in the darkness.

Caradoc considered him with an angry frown, then snorted with resignation and turned away, making a dismissive gesture. Gwirion barely managed to hide how relieved he was, but decided not to leave Enid's side for the rest of the evening. He announced that she would sleep on the near side of the fire in the second brychan, and he would sit guarding her. The soldiers would split the night into two shifts, one of them sleeping at the far side of the fire, the other keeping the watch from near the top of a sheltering incline.

The monk had soothed Caradoc's frustrated intentions by miraculously producing fermented liquid rye, and plied him with it until Caradoc fell asleep. Gwirion sat cross-legged at the corner of Enid's blanket. "You look so maternal," she teased, as she lay down on the tartan. He smiled, uncomfortable. He had seen Enid naked on the king's bed and other places on plenty of occasions, but there was an unsettling intimacy to her snuggling down for something as innocent as sleep right in front of him. "You know," she added, "we're both small, we could probably share the brychan."

He caught his breath. "Oh, no, that's all right, I'm fine. I've got to keep my eye on Caradoc."

"Caradoc's asleep," Enid whispered.

"Well . . . the young monk, then."

She gave him a savvy look. "Gwirion, do you really think he's going to try anything? Get some rest." She moved over on the blanket and patted the empty space.

"Mmm—no. Many thanks." He nodded almost spastically. "I'll be fine."

"Gwirion! Are you trying to insult me?"

"No," he said in a voice tenor with tension. "I just want to be honorable. And see that you sleep unmolested."

A coquettish and purposeful grin spread across her face. "Are you saying you'd molest me if you slept beside me?"

"Oh, no, I didn't mean—that's not . . ." His breathing grew shallow and quick and he looked pained. Delighted, she sat up, grabbed him by the shoulders, and pulled him back down on top of herself. "What . . . what's this about?" he asked in the same boyish treble.

"I have a present for you," she whispered into his ear. "To thank you for protecting me."

He swallowed hard and tried to sit up, but she clasped him close above herself. "I'm very flattered but—"

"The king need never know," Enid whispered, imitating Caradoc's blustering diction. "We could have some fun, no harm done, none's the wiser." She smiled invitingly at him. "Anyhow, you know he has no jealousy of me."

He stared at her, bemused and almost unhappy, for a long moment. Then he firmly removed her arms from around him and sat up. "Why are you doing this?" he asked quietly.

She sat up too, to stay near him. "Because I like you, Gwirion. I think you're sad right now about Corr, and I want to take your mind off it."

"I've known you since you were a girl," he said softly. "Since nearly before you had *breasts.*"

"Is it the breasts you don't like?"

"Lord, no, you have beautiful breasts. Fit for a king," he said sheepishly.

"If you don't object to the breasts, what is it you object to?" she pressed.

He blushed. "I just don't . . . it's been a long time since I—"

"Well, let's make sure everything's still functioning, then," she purred.

He stopped resisting. Trembling, he watched her reach up under the short skirt of his linen tunic to loosen his drawers and tug them down below his bony knees. He stared at her stupidly, hardly breathing, afraid even to touch her. His eyes jerked nervously toward Caradoc across the fire, but the guard was sleeping soundly, turned away from them. A wriggling movement beneath him snapped his gaze back to Enid. She was lifting her skirt. Her eyes flickered up to meet his, and she smiled.

"I can't," he whispered hoarsely.

"Why not?"

He couldn't answer that. To hear she was like a little sister to him would only make her laugh, and he had been present at her intimacies with Noble too often for a claim of modesty to ring true. "It's just conditioning," he said at last. "I see you with that look on your face and my fingers start itching for a harp."

"I think we can find a better way to scratch that itch. Close your eyes if you need to. I'm not going to, though." She grinned. "Half the fun in this is that it's *you.*"

"Oh," he said stupidly, not sure what she meant, and then bit his lip to keep from crying out as she reached up under his tunic and closed her hand around him. She guided him down on top of her and, with nearly maternal affection and attention, shifted her hips to give him access to her. He almost passed out before collapsing against her, trying to choke back sobs that were a confused mixture of pleasure, gratitude, and shame.

Across the fire from them, Caradoc slept soundly.

THEY returned to Cymaron by midmorning, crossing paths just outside the village gates with a departing emissary from Llewelyn, the upstart prince in Gwynedd. When they reached the stable, Enid skipped at once through the yard and into the kitchen to see if Marged needed her. Things were nearly prepared for dinner, which was always a simple meal, and after minding the stew for a short while, she headed into the hall to help the steward's workers set up the trestle tables.

Too late, she realized the queen was standing in her path, reviewing a saint's-day calendar with Father Idnerth and Gwilym. Not
wanting to draw attention to herself, Enid hesitated, and overheard
enough of the conversation to sober her. The queen, her face as inexpressive as ever framed by the dark red wimple, was being informed
of what would take place on each of the feast days. She was not dis-
pensing orders herself; the officers were not asking her opinion on
anything, or even seeking her approval. They were, as always, respectful, even kindly, but aloof. There was an easy camaraderie between
the two men that had nothing to do with rank—Enid knew even she
would have been welcomed into it but the queen was absolutely ex-
cluded. She wished she had a reason to interrupt; she wasn't fooled by
the patient resignation plastered on Her Majesty's face. She knew
what was under it.

"Excuse me, milady," she said on impulse, stepping into the triangle and nearly shrugging the frail old chaplain aside. All three of
them stared at her, astonished by her impertinence. "May I speak
with you for a moment?"

The queen's face registered polite disinterest. "Certainly. Excuse
us, gentlemen." The tone was of dismissal, not departure, and after a
pause they understood, drawing away with slight, stiff bows. She
considered Enid for a moment—confusing Enid because, far from
its usual coolness, the queen's face suddenly seemed bordering on
conspiratorial amusement. "What do you want?" she finally asked.

Enid scrambled for an excuse. "Lady Humffri sends her
warmest regards."

The queen gave her a droll look. "I was not aware you met with
Lady Humffri."

"No, that's true, she gave the message to Gwirion but I thought I
would spare you the displeasure of being approached by him."

"I've been learning about Welsh law," Isabel said abruptly. Her
voice was low, eager and confiding, and for a moment Enid almost
believed the queen had been awaiting her return to Cymaron just to
share this with her. "Do you know much about Welsh law? There is
no love lost between myself and the elements of this hill country,

and I would welcome an excuse to leave, politics be damned. If I catch the two of you a third time, I'll have that excuse—I can divorce him. But if I do, Enid, however content *I* might be with that, the 'Saxons' you all sneer at will have killed him and overrun the kingdom within a month. Apparently Welsh law *is* more progressive than Norman—where I come from, a kitchen servant fucking the king could never wreak that kind of havoc."

Enid gasped to hear such language from the queen's mouth, but before she could reply, her eye caught sight over the queen's shoulder of the king. There was something about his posture that made her look twice; for a flash she was more aware of him as a burdened human being than as a ruler or even as a bedmate. She remembered the messenger they'd passed outside the gates; whatever was distressing His Majesty must have something to do with Llewelyn. He walked slowly from the door of his receiving chamber to the hall hearth, stared into it for a moment, then lifted his head, looked around— and fixed his hypnotic gaze on Enid. Seeing her in civil conversation with his wife, his eyes widened briefly, then he shook his head and began walking toward them. Enid knew the expression: He wanted her, alone.

"Did you hear me?" the queen demanded. "I have been discussing Welsh law with Judge Goronwy. I know what my rights are."

"It's not for me to say anything, milady," she stammered.

"Yes it is," Isabel retorted sweetly. "Jealousy is not the issue, Enid—I would *like* to catch you in the act again, I could be home in England by harvesttime. One more time, let me surprise you just once more." She lowered her voice to an intimate whisper. "Give me that, Enid, as atonement for your sins against me. Wigmore is so lovely in the autumn," she sighed, then turned officious. "But you must be willing. He can't force you. Do you have any idea what it would cost him if you accused him of rape? I read that part of the law as well."

"Did you read the part that says the king is, under all circumstances, exempt from punishment?" demanded her husband behind her, quietly. She started and turned to face him, but he switched his blue gaze to Enid. "I could take this adorable harlot by force if I chose to, but happily that's never necessary with her. And while we're on that subject, Enid," he went on, in a suggestive tone, "go to my receiving room immediately."

"I'm coming too," Isabel announced. She glanced triumphantly at Enid but veiled her excitement from her husband lest he understand it.

"Very well," he said, not looking at her. "You are, as ever, utterly transparent. I'm not going to alter my plans, but you're welcome to watch."

"Sire," Enid said nervously, "Marged requires my presence—"

"I require it more," he said with calm authority, and turned to head back to the audience chamber. "Come along or I'll have to carry you, and that will make quite a scene."

When both women had stepped inside, Isabel nearly humming with perverse anticipation, Noble shut the door with a small flourish and turned to Enid. "I was just speaking with that young would-be Cistercian. He brought distressing news about something that happened last night."

"It was nothing, sire," she insisted.

"He said the other guard made an unwelcome advance on you."

"Caradoc. It was nothing. Gwirion stared him down."

"That was honorable of him."

"Yes it was. He's an honorable fellow," Enid said, and added for the queen's benefit, "in his own strange way."

"I'm also told that after Caradoc turned in, you and Gwirion were intimate with each other."

This caught her completely by surprise and she blushed for perhaps the first time in her life. Isabel involuntarily recoiled. "Well," Enid stammered. "Yes, sire. That's true."

"Who initiated it?"

She hesitated. "I did."

Noble took a breath that almost sounded like satisfaction, but his response, incongruously, was, "I'm not pleased about that, Enid." He looked at his wife. "You're welcome to stay but this topic is the

sum of my interest in her today. This particular liaison will afford
you no grounds for divorce and I'm sure there are more satisfying
ways for you to spend your time."

Isabel was so unprepared for the direction in which the encounter was going that it took her a moment to answer. "Yes, there
are," she agreed, and opened the door to leave.

But when she'd pulled it shut behind her, her curiosity kept her
there. She lingered for a few moments, tempted to go back inside,
and she had just convinced herself not to, had nearly taken a step up
the stairs toward her solar, when the door was suddenly flung open
and the two of them came out in a rush. Noble was angry and Enid
looked shocked, almost dazed. He had her by the back of the neck,
pulling her along beside him as he walked quickly toward the main
door to the hall, with his captive scrambling not to lose her footing.
"Sire, please—" she heard Enid say, sounding frightened, and she
rushed to intercept them.

"Noble, leave her alone!" she insisted, stepping directly in front
of them. He stopped short but did not release his grip on Enid's
neck. "You don't own her."

"I do, actually, but that's beside the point—and you have no idea
what the point is, so stand aside."

"Where are you taking her?"

"Away from mischief," he announced, and elbowed his wife aside
to continue the harsh promenade to the hall doorway.

AFTER seeing his mare safely to the stable, Gwirion retreated
into the tiny closet off the kitchen that had long ago been designated his sleeping quarters. He fell asleep effortlessly, grateful to
be back under his own blanket and enjoying that rare privilege of privacy. He was surprised to be awakened by Marged's grandson with
the news that the king wanted to see him at once. It was after supper.
He had slept more than eight hours.

"Can't he entertain himself for once?" he grumbled, but he went along obediently.

Noble sat alone in the audience chamber. This was Gwirion's favorite room in the castle, small but brightly whitewashed, and carpeted with pale pelt rugs. Although wall paintings and tapestries throughout the castle offered color and cheer, there was something almost celestial in the simplicity of this space. The king's elegant leather chair faced a padded settle across a low table—actually an ornate chest—and there was a cushion at his feet where Gwirion sat sometimes. Otherwise the room was empty. It had only the one door opening into the great hall, and no window but a high-up slit of an air vent, too small even to shoot an arrow from, that opened away from the yard. But the glazed white walls, broad hearth, and generous array of sconces kept it from ever seeming dark or stuffy. Gwirion performed what passed as a bow and at Noble's gesture, sank down on the cushion with his harp beside him.

"This is formal," he commented. Noble looked tired and careworn; probably from being left alone with his wife for a day and a half, Gwirion decided. Then common sense intervened: He knew the source of the king's distress. "We passed a courier by the gate this morning—was he wearing the colors of Gwynedd?"

"Yes," Noble sighed. "The upstart prince Llewelyn has requested an official diplomatic relationship—not as an upstart but as a prince. As a peer." He did not sound pleased about it, but his tone hardly explained how grim he looked. "That's not why I called you in here, Gwirion. I know about what happened last night."

"It wasn't a problem, sire," Gwirion waved it off. "Caradoc—"

"Not that. I already have a full confession from Enid. I know she pushed you into it. I don't hold you responsible." Gwirion's face reddened and he uttered a sound that wasn't quite a word. "What's the matter, didn't you enjoy it? Your monk friend seemed to think you enjoyed it quite a lot."

"I wasn't planning, I mean, I had no intention—"

"I know that."

"And I'll never let such a situation hap—"

"No, *I'll* never let such a situation happen again," Noble snapped. He sat up very straight and stared down at Gwirion with an alarming expression. "It was such a *trespass* for her to do that. I couldn't let such wanton use of power go unpunished."

Gwirion leapt unsteadily to his feet. He hoped he misunderstood. "Sire? What do you mean?"

Seeing Gwirion's face, Noble couldn't help a short, harsh laugh. "Calm down, I haven't killed her." Gwirion relaxed. "I've just had her sent away."

The alarm sprang back to Gwirion's eyes. "What?"

"I didn't hurt her. Just had them shave her head a bit before they drove her out."

"Drove her *out*?" Gwirion echoed. "Why?"

Noble gave him a long, slow stare. Then he abruptly changed his expression and said, lightly, "The queen was troubled by her presence. It's just as well she's gone."

Gwirion frowned. "You threw her out because the queen was upset that you had her, or because you were upset that I had her?"

"Neither," said the king. "I was upset that *she* had *you*." Gwirion gave him a bemused look. "It's a matter of ethics, Gwirion, so you probably wouldn't understand: you mustn't take other people's things." Gwirion started at what this implied and tried to protest, but impatiently the king added, "Actually, Isabel was waiting to catch me with her a third time to sue for divorce, so now I've removed the temptation. That's all. I just wanted to tell you what had happened." Gwirion stood openmouthed before him. "What?"

Disoriented and not knowing which explanation was the truer, or what to make of either one, Gwirion managed to stammer, lamely, "Won't you miss her?"

"Probably, but I'll find someone else. I might even give monogamy a try—my wife really is plotting to divorce me otherwise." He laughed. "In fact, I think I'll take her right to bed. The least she can do is give me a son."

HE felt no stronger affection for her but his need to make his cousin Anarawd irrelevant compelled him to take her frequently, until it became almost a chore for both of them. Although a private skeptic, he even consulted his physician and his bard to see if there were any astrological considerations, amulets, or spells that might assist; the suspicious silence from his border with Mortimer and the too eager whispered rumors of Llewelyn's rising star made him desperate for an heir.

He did at least take steps against Gwirion to keep things comfortable for the queen. Gwirion rebelled as much as he dared, and protested ferociously that after robbing him of his only two companions, Noble had no right to make his life even more miserable by muzzling him. The king stood firm. So Gwirion was called upon to play the harp in the evenings after the bard had finished his more respectable performance, but he was not allowed to speak publicly in hall. His position had always been peculiar and his status a source of perennial dissent—in a world of strictly established court positions, he conformed to nothing. Noble had despaired of passing him off as the chief of song, because the office required things that were beyond him. He should, for example, have begun each evening's entertainment with a song of religious praise, but he was already perceived as such a rascal that on the few occasions he'd tried to do it, it had sounded like a parody.

So Gwirion lived in an odd limbo. He was allowed to play the gilded willow harp with the carved lion's head, loaned to him by King Cadwallon years ago—the most valuable object in the castle outside the relics of St. Cynllo in the chapel—and he played nearly every evening, but only after the official bardic entertainment had finished. He maintained his stool just behind the king's chair at board, and they often whispered together, snickering, when there was no other conversation, but Noble was aware of his wife's eyes on him and would be careful to give her equal, if dispassionate, attention.

Robbed of his usual outlets for both anger and amusement, Gwirion turned his attention to writing letters to Corr. He did not have a pretty script, and he was nearly positive Corr could not, in fact, read. But he needed to express his indignation to somebody and no one else would listen. The consensus of the court was that this was simply how things would be from now on—less entertaining but more civil—and it was Gwirion's problem if he could not adjust.

IT'S a hopeless situation, my friend," he scribbled. "It's the most ill-starred marriage since Adam and Eve. It's just as well Noble won't let me mock her, I wouldn't even know what to say, she gives me nothing to play with. It's very frustrating.

"He is truly restraining from all entertainment outside the marriage bed, the poor bored lad. She seems to take this as her due, as if it were to be expected. She has no idea what a monumental, even heroic, effort it is on his behalf—not only to restrict himself to one woman, but for that woman to be her! She should be kissing the hem of his robe, and instead she struts around smugly as if she were entitled to the preferential treatment! She seems to think it will always be this way. I tell you, Corr, she'll be disappointed. And probably soon."

THE betrayal took place on her own bed. She had been vaguely aware that Gwen, her tallest attendant, resembled not only Enid, but nearly every woman who caught Noble's eye: wild dark hair, impossible to tame even braided under a veil, glistening dark eyes and most of all, extraordinary curves. "You could fit the queen's buttocks into that girl's cleavage and there'd still be room left over," Gwirion had made the point of saying loudly in hall one afternoon. Noble, grinning, had lined the two of them up as if measuring them for the accuracy of this assessment, and Isabel had assumed that his public playfulness meant he would go no further in private. She was wrong.

Gwirion entertained that evening after Hywel the bard retired to the village. He was very solicitous toward the queen, asking what she would like to hear and playing with extraordinary grace. Somewhere he had found a set of gut strings and restrung the harp with them; that simple, subtle change in tone, to the more resonant flavor she was familiar with, made the music even more distracting. He was an excellent harpist, which annoyed her: It seemed unfair that such a cretinous soul should have that talent.

Her suspicion of his motives began when he apologized profusely, almost self-flagellating, for being ignorant of the excellent and varied Norman repertoire. Then she realized that the king, who had excused himself to the garderobe, had been gone nearly half an hour. When Gwirion finished "Rhiannon's Tears" for the second time—his signature tune, which she was unwilling to tell him was also a favorite of hers—she thanked him for the recital and excused herself to bed.

"Bed?" Gwirion echoed with a blink. "You mean the king's bed, surely. He'll be wanting you there." This was true: Noble had given Gwirion orders to distract the queen as long as possible before sending her directly to his room, to keep her out of her own, where Gwen was finishing a weaving project.

"I assumed my husband had already retired for the evening," she said, acutely aware of the entire court, officers and servants, ogling their interaction. It was rare for these two to acknowledge each other directly.

"Oh, no, milady," Gwirion said with slightly too much insistence. "He expressly asked me to tell you to retire to *his* chamber." He had the gift of telling the truth as if it were a lie, and she thought she was catching him in a falsehood. Just as he had counted on.

"Is he in his chamber now?" she asked.

"He'll be there," Gwirion said, nodding his head earnestly.

"Where is he now?" she pressed.

"He'll be in his room soon, Your Majesty. That's where he wants you to go."

Isabel rose from her seat. She didn't know what was going on, but anything to do with Gwirion made her uncomfortable, and that, in turn, made her want to withdraw. "I am retiring to my own chamber," she informed him, unaware he'd neatly shepherded her to this decision. "When you see the king, please invite him to send for me when he's ready to retire."

"If you insist, milady," he answered, and remained expressionless until she had mounted the steps. Then he grinned hugely, tickled by the prospect of approaching chaos.

Adèle was near the kitchen screens and saw his glee. She thought she understood it, and raced across the width of the hall after her mistress, hoping she could intercept her.

She couldn't. She slipped on some wet rushes, and as she recovered and scrambled up the stairs to the queen's solar, it was clear from the sounds within what had happened: The queen had found her husband undressing dark-haired Gwen.

She glared at them in silence, but her appearance and expression so frightened Gwen that the girl shrieked in alarm, and it carried clearly down into the hall, where Gwirion fell off his stool from laughing. Noble tried to assuage his wife, who was almost too furious to speak. When she found her voice, she was barely coherent and switched between Welsh and French without realizing it. "You're finished!" she whispered furiously at the traumatized, confused Gwen in a language the girl didn't understand. "You will be out of this castle tomorrow and I never want to see you again." Gwen, trying to get back into her tunic, looked at the king in confusion. Adèle shut the door behind her to keep them from continuing to entertain Gwirion, and very brusquely started to help Gwen into her surcoat.

"She's throwing you out," Adèle explained shortly, and escorted her to the far side of the room, beyond the tapestry that closed off the attendants' sleeping area, so that she could finish adjusting her clothes.

Isabel's anger transformed into vengeful ecstasy as she turned her full attention to her husband. "That's the third time I've caught you, Noble! I can do it now. Even as a king you have no right to stop me." She pointed triumphantly to the heavy law book beside her bed. "I," she announced, looking radiant, "am suing for divorce."

Noble crossed his arms and gave her the overly patient look of a tired parent. "And what will you be going home to, madam?"

4

FALSE DISPATCHES

Around Lammas, 1198

HE DID NOT sue for divorce, but her increasing malaise began to infest Cymaron. All day the solar was a silent, humid, dreary cage; at night she regularly refused her husband's summons to his room. Determined for an heir, he began coming to her bed, and for the first time in a decade found himself lying with a wholly unreceptive woman, which only reaffirmed for him how much he liked his wantons. Had he not so despised and distrusted the cousin who was next in line to the throne, he would almost have preferred not bothering with issue. His wife understood him well enough now to know how to play against him: She acted bored by his attention, unimpressed when he tried to arouse her. That was not a game his pride would indulge, and one night he spent half an hour coaxing a physical response from her—but even then she was so doggedly still and silent that he would hardly have known she'd climaxed if he hadn't been inside her. "An interesting skill," he mused sarcastically, hovering over her. "Not es-

pecially useful, but interesting." She blinked away humiliated tears and would not look at him.

Adèle, desperate to see her mistress's spirit restored, begged a private audience with the king to offer a solution. The Cistercian abbey of Cwm-hir was less than three hours' ride to the west; Cadwallon had founded the retreat in the serenest, most beautiful valley in the kingdom and the holy brothers were in the process of building an enormous church there. Noble regularly gave them money in his father's honor, but he was their official patron and he'd been remiss in patronizing them. The queen, Adèle proposed, might go in his stead. The church would be under construction for years—as royal overseer of the project, it would keep her occupied for a very long time, doing something genuinely useful. Adèle suggested the idea because it was a religious house and therefore civilized; Noble approved it because it was Cistercian and therefore not English. He was impressed that the increasingly truculent old woman had presented a constructive idea. A lay brother was summoned from the abbey early one morning to show the queen simple hand signals should she need to communicate with the silent monks. Then the royal couple, Adèle, and a small van of bodyguards followed him back to the holy valley so that the king could officially introduce the abbey to its new patroness. He ruefully suspected she would not receive a warm reception.

But he hardly recognized the woman he rode out beside. Despite the dull white sky, Isabel's mood obviously lifted once the riding party was out of sight of the castle. She cooed over the gentle open countryside as if she had never encountered such beauty. Noble hid his surprise, watching her smile with a warmth he'd never seen, at the smallest things, bumbling lambs and mewling calves, children playing with their grandfather on the edge of a village, even a cavorting couple they surprised in the sea of green bracken. He shot a glance at Adèle and read from her giddy expression that she had anticipated this—which meant, amazingly, that there must be some precedent for it.

They arrived at Cwm-hir in time for dinner, and the queen disarmed the wary, white-robed congregation of the complex—none of whom had ever seen a woman so elegantly dressed—by insisting upon leaving her husband's party to join them in their simple, silent meal. They were all flummoxed but cautiously accepted, afraid to insult either royalty or Normans. Noble felt Adèle scrutinizing him, and granted her the satisfaction of looking pleasantly impressed. He took no meal at all: Intrigued by the alteration in his wife, he watched her from behind as she broke bread with the monks. She refused a better portion or preferential treatment, communicating entirely with the sign language she'd practiced with the lay brother as they rode.

After dinner the royal couple met with the abbot, who showed them plans for the church. Isabel examined them quickly then made several astute suggestions; Noble's wonderment increased and he was afraid Adèle might explode from too much gloating when a tour of the construction revealed that the queen knew more about church architecture than the abbot did himself.

They stayed for nones at Isabel's insistence, and she left a gift from her own coffers in honor of Maelienydd's patron, St. Cynllo, whose feast day it was—something the native-born King of Maelienydd himself had not thought to do. By the time they headed home in the late afternoon, Noble was almost speechless with admiration and determined to keep Isabel in this spirit indefinitely. Adèle was all pleasure and relief to see her mistress once again behaving like herself. This was the girl she knew; this was the pluck with which to win over Cymaron. This was a strength that neither Gwirion nor the king could sap.

THE king returned from the abbey in an unusually genial mood, and Gwirion found himself entertaining informally in the hall for hours after supper had been cleared away. Nearly everyone played an instrument, but nobody played as well as Gwirion and he was always in demand. There had been many nights like this before the queen arrived and he was happy for a return to normal—and even *she*, returned from Cwm-hir, was behaving like a pleasant human being tonight. Noble stretched out with her on what would later be bedding for the unmarried servants, drinking wine; farther away from the fire, Gwilym, Hafaidd, Efan, Marged, and (remoter yet) a few of the kitchen workers were settled on the floor with beer. The servants whose bedding Noble had commandeered were gathered in the lower end of the hall, quietly gossiping or playing dice, while couples and families sought slumber behind curtains in the side sections of the great room. Gwirion performed the simple, often bawdy songs that were forbidden at board or when court was even marginally in session, those that no bard had in his repertoire. Those, in other words, that most people privately preferred to hear.

As he was loosening a string to go into his favorite key—"the drunkard's tuning"—he unexpectedly addressed the queen; it was a civil gesture to acknowledge (grudgingly) her civil mood, although he was suspicious of the royal couple's sudden easy amity together. "And so, Your Majesty, what do you think of our little Abbey Cwm-hir?"

"Little?" she said, almost stammering in her surprise that he'd addressed her without sarcasm. "That church is going to be the size of a cathedral. You have excellent stonemasons." Feeling generous, she added the highest compliment she could think of: "It will be quite as grand as any church on the continent."

"With all respect to Your Majesty's weakness for Frenchiness," Gwirion commented, keeping his attention focused on the harp peg, "nobody here has been to the continent, so we can't appreciate how profoundly you must be flattering us."

"My husband has been there," she corrected him complacently.

"I have?" her husband said, taken aback.

She frowned up at him. "You went on Crusade."

He was even more astonished. "I *what?*"

She faltered. "Years ago. I thought—"

"Where did you hear that?" He looked amused, as if it were a preposterous suggestion. She felt foolish and wished she hadn't started the conversation in front of others. But surely Noble wouldn't brush her off or bruise her dignity, not now that he had seen how desirable a companion she could be for him when she was treated fairly.

"In a book," she muttered, trying to sound offhand.

"In a *book*?" Gwirion echoed, and looked at Noble. The king straightened, staring down at his wife. "What book?" Gwirion asked. "What else did it say about him?"

"It was just the one reference," she replied quickly in the same quiet voice, feeling the heat rising to her cheeks.

"And . . . ?" Noble prompted when she said nothing else.

"It was only a private manuscript one of the Benedictine brothers wrote. Uncle Roger loaned it to me before I came here. It mentioned all the Welsh princes, and naturally I read about the man I was about to—"

Gwirion could not contain himself. "This is brilliant!" He affected grave fascination. "Tell me, then, Your Majesty, is this typical of French scholarship in general?"

"Who wrote it?" Noble demanded. "What did they say about me?" He did not share Gwirion's amusement.

She should never have mentioned it. She glanced at Adèle, a ubiquitous shadow near the kitchen screens, and knew the old woman was thinking the same thing. Her recent stiff self-consciousness came crashing down upon her, erasing the ease of the day. "Archbishop Baldwin made a tour through Wales," she began awkwardly. "To enlist men for the Crusade, and he brought a Welsh brother named de Barri who—"

Noble almost choked on his relieved, dismissive laughter, and relaxed back onto the blanket. *"Gerald?* It's my cousin's cousin, for the love of God. Gerald de Barri—a spy for Canterbury, eh? Who would have thought it?"

"I remember that visit!" Gwirion announced, his face lighting up. "We all drank like fish! Don't you remember it, Noble?" he asked the king, forgetting to use an honorific in front of members of the court. "Gerald kissing Baldwin's buttocks all night? That man is a predicant phenomenon," he told the queen. "His head is bigger than Noble's and his mouth is bigger than mine."

"Good God," she said without thinking, sounding horrified, but Gwirion only laughed and asked, now with genuine interest, "What did he write, then?"

"He kept a journal of the trip, and published it. Noble met them at some fort—"

"It was Eryr, Crug Eryr," Gwirion said, grinning at the recollection. "Noble nearly had to drug me to get me to go with him. What did our little Gerald write?"

She hesitated. "He wrote that Noble took the cross. That he swore to go on Crusade—"

"Yes!" Gwirion crowed, remembering the detail, and erupted again into laughter, turning to the king. "Your mother was *furious*. Cadwallon left you with an abbey full of Welsh Cistercians to support and there you were offering your soul to the Archbishop of Canterbury. She didn't want to let us back in when we came home. Now *that* queen," he said with a nostalgic chuckle, "was a queen to *worship*."

Noble finally recalled it too. "Oh, yes," he said dismissively, amused. "That was just political farce—nobody intended to go to Jerusalem."

"That's shameful," Isabel chastised.

"No, it's not," her husband said, sobering a little. "The Crusade was a front. Baldwin wanted to remind us that Canterbury controlled the Welsh church."

"I'm surprised you agreed with him," she said, trying not to sound sarcastic, trying to reclaim some sense of their earlier rapport.

He shook his head. "Like everything else, love, it's tit for tat. Once you take the cross, you're a soldier of God and woe to any man who wrongs you. We sold our souls to Canterbury so that Canterbury would forbid the English barons to attack our lands. The barons attacked anyway, and more than once. And your esteemed archbishop did nothing. When the shepherd stands idly by as the wolf wounds his flock, the flock does not feel much indebted to the shepherd."

"But the wolf does," Gwirion said dryly, plucking out a dissonant chord.

"Anyhow, they were boors," Noble went on, lightening the mood again. "Even without the politics, we'd have agreed just to shut them up and make them go away. And we're all clever fellows, we'd have each found plausible reasons not to follow through."

"Rhys said his wife wouldn't let him go," Gwirion chortled. "The Lord Prince Justice of all South Wales, henpecked out of going on Crusade! And Gerald, that sanctimonious woman hater—Gerald fell for it!" He and Noble starting laughing convulsively, remembering.

As they quieted, Noble affected nostalgia. "Ah, Cousin Gerald."

"Ah, good Queen Efa," Gwirion said in exactly the same tone. With all apparent friendliness he told the queen, "I do wish you could have met her, Majesty. She might have helped you find your feet more easily."

She was completely taken aback by the tone—and so was everyone else. There was riveted silence as she asked, tentatively, "How?"

Never losing the guileless, helpful look, Gwirion explained, "She didn't want Noble learning about women from the teulu, so when he was thirteen she sent her attendant to his room for a nocturnal education. A very practical lady, that one. She could have set you straight about the monogamy problem right away and it would have saved us all a hell of a lot of grief—we might have had so many lovely evenings like this one."

"Gwirion," Noble chastised wearily, his smile vanishing. "That was uncalled for."

"It was also accurate," Gwirion said pleasantly, and began to play "Rhiannon's Tears." Isabel was already standing, and without addressing any of them she began walking toward the stairs to her room. Gwirion watched her go, looking disappointed. "She might have stayed and fought a little," he sighed. "The Saxoness has no play in her at all." He heard a rustle in the shadows and looked over to see Adèle glaring at him as she headed after her mistress.

THERE was another courtyard feast in early August. It marked the start of harvest, and caused Adèle apoplexy because it did not even try to hide its heathen roots: It was proclaimed even by the chaplain as a day of homage to the pagan god Llew, and the populace

celebrated it like all the other feast days. Isabel ignored Gwirion's jubilant afternoon rhetoric in the sweltering courtyard, claiming that
Llew, as god of both the sun and harvest, offered manifest proof that
even an oat stalk was animated by a divine spark. Except for the sac-
rilegiousness of it, it seemed utterly out of character for Gwirion to
turn his attention to anything divine, but he was as casual about it as
if he were explaining why the rain falls. His audience—villagers, castle workers, and some landed gentry arrived early for the feast—listened to him with the same placid interest with which they had
earlier listened to his tales of the last dragon in Wales, asleep in Rad-
nor Forest. It was off-putting to Isabel, but fascinating, how matter-
of-fact these people were about even their most fanciful and
superstitious beliefs. Sorcery was not a sin to them, but simply a
power that could be used for good or ill; dead kings seemed closer to
a second coming than even Christ himself. Especially when the bards
got hold of them.

For the feast itself that evening, Gwirion was not asked to entertain, but by the end of the evening Isabel almost wished he had been,
for she found it excruciating to sit through the alternative. The aging
bard Hywel donned his long blue ceremonial robe and spent the entire evening reciting elegies to fallen heroes. They were exceptionally
wordy and filled with linguistic tricks; this in itself she would have
found merely tiresome, although she enjoyed watching how intensely
emotional everyone—landowners, villeins, teulu, castle servants, and
even her own husband—became over the stories. But the finale,
which took up almost half the evening, was an epic poem about the
valor of the kings of Maelienydd through the years, and the theme
became tedious. For years the princes and their retainers lived out of
saddlebags, battling to win control of Maelienydd back from the evil
Mortimers. Finally, after more than a decade of battle and intrigues
that followed the assassination (by the evil Mortimers) of good King
Madoc, his surviving son Cadwallon reclaimed Castell Cymaron
(from the evil Mortimers). For more than three decades, there was
glorious stability, and every attempted invasion (led, usually, by some
evil Mortimer) was valiantly rebuffed. The fair-haired Prince Mael-

gwyn was born to the incomparably beautiful and righteous Queen Efa and all was well in the kingdom of Cadwallon, who was referred to as "the holiest flame of all humanity" and a few other things Isabel considered just a bit excessive . . . and then, moaned the bard, came the day that changed everything. In late September of '79, Cadwallon was summoned to Gloucester to meet with Henry of England. It was a large party that rode to the high king and a large party that began the return . . . but only the young prince and his companion made it back alive. At this point the evil assassin's name was so obvious it did not have to be mentioned, but of course it was anyhow, at least five times. Gwirion was absent for the recitation and she wished she had been too.

"I assume you are aware of how humiliating that was," she said later in the king's solar, in a cadence intended to be calm but instead sounding standoffish.

"It could only be humiliating if you think yourself a Mortimer," Noble retorted. "Call yourself the Lady of Maelienydd and I think you'll feel quite different."

IT was very warm the next day, despite the silver barricade of clouds that blocked the sun from view, and at Noble's request, he and Goronwy held court outside. The queen was not welcome to participate, but he did not begrudge her watching, although the cases were almost always very dull. They were not, however, as dull as sewing. Her presence at the abbey, although welcomed, was not useful more than once a week, and she was desperate for distractions from the distaff life. She knew Noble was finding other women again, and she resented it, but not enough to estrange herself from the entire castle by being peevish—that was Adèle's pastime. So she made it a habit to insert herself, however silently, into court life as often as she could. This was not the manner of Welsh queens, not even the incomparably beautiful and righteous Queen Efa, but the king's benign neglect of her behavior afforded nobody the chance to challenge it.

When Hafaidd brought her chair out for her to sit behind Noble, the first case of the morning had already begun, and this one showed signs of intrigue. A young woman, hardly more than a girl and dressed very demurely in a worn-looking long tunic with a high collar, was standing before Goronwy's chair tearfully murmuring her version of whatever the argument was. Behind her, looking agitated and resentful, was a rough-looking man dressed all in leather, nearly old enough to be her father. They were not from the castle village; they must have come from several valleys away. The chubby, pink-faced judge, sitting on a lower level to Noble's right, listened attentively and occasionally murmured asthmatically to his assistant, who took notes. When the girl was finished, she curtsied and backed away from the low dais.

The man glared at her and moved closer to Noble and Goronwy. "She's lying if she says I touched her. She's claiming she was virgin when I took her—well then, she's virgin yet. I swear that on the holy book, and it's all I have to say."

King and judge exchanged meaningful glances, sharing some unspoken knowledge that seemed to burden the justice but tickled Noble's sense of humor. "Where's your heir?" Goronwy asked, which struck Isabel as a remarkable non sequitor.

Noble shook his head. "My beloved cousin is a day's ride away and I don't care to have him near me anyhow. I'll appoint a worthy substitute." Then he grinned, and Goronwy sighed with resignation.

"Sire, it's a delicate matter, by the rule of law it ought to be your heir—"

"I can appoint someone else my heir for the next hour," Noble said reasonably.

Without waiting for the king to say the name, the judge phlegmatically dispatched Hafaidd to find Gwirion, and Noble relaxed against the back of his tall wooden chair looking pleased with himself.

Gwirion was in the kitchen with his harp, in a silk brocade tunic that had once belonged to Noble, too old now for its color to be clearly discernable. He was entertaining Marged's workers with improvised, outrageous divinations. Absolutely straight-faced, his right hand fluttering dramatically over the lower strings of the harp, he claimed that the bard Taliesin's prophecies (which had never been wrong in over six hundred years) predicted that the world would end the following Thursday unless they all rose in revolt against the king and replaced him with whoever in the castle could drink the most cheap ale without passing out—so they should all start imbibing immediately, for the good of humanity. Hafaidd caught him in the midst of this exhortation, ignored the treasonous commentary that would have hanged anybody else, and briskly escorted him out to the yard.

Arms crossed, blinking his dark eyes in the harshly hazy daylight, Gwirion considered the two suppliants warily and then looked at the king. "Why am I here, then?" he asked.

Noble folded his hands together, made a steeple of his forefingers and tapped it against his lips, a lifelong habit Gwirion knew meant he was trying not to laugh. "This young woman," he said matter-of-factly, "claims this man forced her to yield him her virginity, and he denies it. To begin examining the case, therefore, according to the rule of law, we must first examine her to see if she's intact." He allowed himself the slightest indulgent smile. "That's going to be your job."

"*What?*" It came in stereo, from both the queen and Gwirion at once. "Noble, are you *mad?* Have a woman do it! Or at least the physician," the queen insisted. Gwirion was too shocked to say anything else. Even the two suppliants were astonished; the girl looked outright alarmed.

"It's not my place to change the law," Noble said with mock humility. "I confess it sounds peculiar, but who am I to challenge Hywel the Good?" He smiled beatifically. "It has been the law in rape trials for centuries. The notary of maidenhead is supposed to be my heir, but he's too far away, so I'm appointing Gwirion as substitute. Go on, Gwirion."

"Not in public," Isabel announced firmly, standing. "That's *barbarous.*"

He shrugged agreeably. "Very well, in private, then, but you'd best go along as my representative to keep an eye on him."

For one disorienting moment, the queen and Gwirion were united against him, as Gwirion made generic sounds of protest and the queen declared, "*I'll* examine her, don't subject her to a man."

"You?" Noble crossed his arms and looked at her, his sarcastic smile twitching the corners of his mouth. "I didn't realize you were experienced with women's private parts."

There was squelched laughter from onlookers and the queen shot back, "I didn't realize Gwirion was either." This earned a bigger reaction and for a moment she was pleased, until she realized that she had just cemented the situation, for now Gwirion would be goaded by them into proving her wrong.

Gwirion stood in the middle of a circle of teasing spectators who were all ignoring the usher's stern requests for silence. For a moment he stared at Noble, his face unreadable. Then he turned to the nervous girl and said in a tone of resignation, "Let's go in here," gesturing to the ground-floor room of the nearest corner tower. He turned toward the queen without quite looking at her. "Are you coming, milady?"

Childishly, she wished that Adèle would miraculously appear from the solar and deal with the situation. With a heavy breath, which she hoped made her appear disdainful, she nodded and followed. "Remember, she's there to keep you honest," Noble reminded him cheerfully as they entered. "There's a very hefty fine at stake here."

This room, below the steward's well-appointed chamber, housed several of the lower officers. Their beds were mats of brychan-shrouded heather and the room, ill ventilated, had a heavy, sweet aroma to it. The wiry Hafaidd escorted them in and crossed at once to swing open the shutter of the only window, letting in some light and air.

When the door was closed behind them, Gwirion turned at once to the girl, who looked traumatized. "Are you devout?" he asked. She glanced down shyly and nodded, and Gwirion held his hand out to the queen. "Your rosary, milady, if I may."

Isabel hesitated. She didn't trust him and the piece was precious to her—Adèle had fashioned the beads by hand from the pulp of crushed roses, and the crucifix held a lock of hair from the head of St. Milburga, at whose abbey she'd been baptized.

"I'll be careful with it," he promised impatiently, understanding her expression. She gave it to him, frowning, and he pressed it into the girl's cold hand, bending over her. "Will you swear on Her Majesty's cross to be truthful?" Her eyes flickered up to his, then down again. She pursed her lips together and nodded. "Are you still a maiden?" he asked quietly. Her face crumpled and she nodded again, close to sobbing, but his calm reaction reassured her and she kept herself in check. "Why are you doing this, then? Who put you up to it?" She shook her head, pursing her lips again, and he sighed. "You'd better tell me or you're in a lot of trouble." The girl shifted her eyes pleadingly to the queen, hoping for feminine sympathy.

She found none. The queen was waiting for her to speak; her expression was far less lenient than Gwirion's, and framed by her wine-red wimple it looked especially severe. "My brother," the girl finally said, whispering miserably, then blurted it all out at once. "That man killed our sister when she refused him years ago and he made it look like an accident, like a drowning; I saw it but I was only six then and they wouldn't take my testimony in court, so he was acquitted but I saw him do it and he never paid the blood fine for it and we need money terribly so Iorweth thought to get it by accusing him of something else we could fine him for."

Isabel wanted to be sympathetic but she couldn't let this pass. Anticipating Gwirion's thoughts, she warned, "Even if you play along with her and say she's been deflowered, he can claim it was by someone else's hand."

"We don't use *hands* for that here. You English are a weird lot,

aren't you?" Gwirion retorted, and was relieved to see the shadow of
a grin on the girl's face. He patted her shoulder. "What's your reputation where you come from?"

She sobered instantly, looked guilty. "It never occurred to anybody in the village to question me when I said it, and anyway he's
known for taking anyone he pleases."

Gwirion looked up at the queen with an expression of satisfaction. "I think it's very obvious what to do here."

"I can't let you," she said with sympathetic firmness.

"Oh, for the love of God, milady!"

"First of all, you don't even know that a thing she says is true,
and anyway, I won't let you lie to the court, it makes a mockery of
justice."

"Letting a murderer go free *isn't* making a mockery of justice?"
he demanded and then, before she could reply, he gave her an ironic
look of comprehension. "Ah! How could I forget, milady, you're a
Mortimer, your sort does that all the time."

She wanted to hit him. "I believe in the rule of law," she said
through clenched jaws. "Perhaps you haven't heard of that here." She
turned to the girl. "We can try to exonerate you from this scheme,
but you're taking justice into your own hands and I can't condone
that." Seeing the look on Gwirion's face she added, "I'm representing
the king, Gwirion, you know I have to do this."

He stared at her for a moment. "Allow me to treat you precisely
as I would the king on this occasion, then," he said, and walked to the
exit, grabbed the latch, and threw the door open.

Twenty paces away sat Noble and Goronwy, on the far edge of a
ring of waiting onlookers, most of them starting to perspire in the
summer-morning haze. All eyes were immediately on Gwirion.

"And how was the anatomy lesson?" Noble called out.

Gwirion ignored him and crossed to the accused man, standing
alone in the middle of the circle, idly picking at a scab on his elbow.
Barely moving his lips, in a voice too low to carry beyond the two of
them, Gwirion muttered ominously, "I know about the sister and I
have the proof to hang you if you don't confess to this instead." The

man's alarmed reaction, although quickly buried, was cognizant enough to satisfy him. He turned to Noble and the judge. "This man is guilty," he said loudly, with finality, and marched back to the tower.

The queen was at the threshold, on her way out, as Gwirion returned. To a collective gasp from the onlookers, he grabbed her arm and pushed her back inside, hesitating for a moment in the doorway until he heard the man start to confess the rape. Then he slammed the door closed.

"Let go of me!" Isabel ordered.

He released her but kept his hand leaning on the door. "Milady, if you call this girl's bluff now, that whoreson will go free, unpunished—"

"For something he didn't do!" she snapped.

"And also for something he *did* do!" he insisted. "And the family, who has been wronged, and by that man, never gets any reparation. I would never let Noble do that and I won't let you do it either."

"You think you're above the law?"

"Oh, no, milady, very much below it," he said comfortably.

"I'd say so," she muttered. "Even your charity is underhanded."

If it was meant to insult him, it failed. Looking pleased with himself, he collected the rosary from the shaken girl and held it out to the queen. She snatched it up from his open palm and headed at once toward the door.

"He just confessed to the lesser charge, milady. If you tell them all the truth now you'll be doing nobody a favor, except perhaps God, but in that case I must say that God is a twisted bastard."

She winced at his impiety. "The law is not for doing people favors, Gwirion, it's for *justice*. Nobody's being punished or rewarded according to their just desserts and that's an affront to the rule of law itself—*and* to the king who executes it."

He considered this briefly, then shrugged. "Well then, tell the king to sue me for it." He walked past her to the door, exited the tower, and walked through the court, straight back to the kitchen, his harp, and his audience.

A mockery of justice?" Noble echoed her in disbelief that night. He was in bed, waiting—very patiently, he thought—for her to calm down and join him for her wifely duties.

Isabel was pacing his chamber in her shift and his bedrobe, which was far too big for her. With her long braids swaying and the robe dragging behind her she looked like a child playing at being an angry adult. "Gwirion mocked the law today—because you decided to *entertain* yourself by giving him authority you shouldn't have given him."

"I don't exist to serve the rule of law, Isabel—the rule of law exists to serve me."

"It exists to serve the *kingdom!*" she insisted hotly.

"I am the kingdom," he said, quite cool.

She began pacing more excitedly. "That is the most hubristic, self-centered definition of kingship I have ever—"

"No, it's not, Isabel," he said with an exaggeratedly tired sigh. "In fact, it's absolutely self-*less*, but it's too late for political philosophy, as charming as it is to find that you are so inflamed by the subject. Come to bed now."

"How does appointing Gwirion in that way serve the kingdom?" she demanded, her pacing bringing her no closer to the bed.

"You would rather I'd called Anarawd over from Elfael to molest her? Just because that would be the legal thing to do, you'd subject that poor child to him? Come to bed."

"No, I wouldn't want Anarawd either," she said impatiently. "But if you were reassigning the job, you should not have given it to a rascal like Gwirion. If you're going to manipulate the law, do it *responsibly*, do it with *sense*," she insisted, slapping the back of one hand upon the other palm for emphasis. "Just because you're the king doesn't mean you can reorder the universe to suit your whim."

He raised his head off the cushion and gave her a look of amazement, almost choking as he laughed at her. "My *whim*? I've never done anything in court to suit my whim! Short of picking the women I bed for pleasure I don't think I've ever done *anything* to suit my whim."

"Assigning Gwirion to that position was a whim."

He shook his head. "I knew the girl was virgin, I could tell by the way she *walked*, let alone that she was a truly incompetent liar. Gwirion was the best choice to resolve the situation, never mind why. Come to bed, Isabel, that's an order."

"You treated it as if it were a whim," she insisted.

"Of course I did," he said in exasperation, relaxing his head on the cushion again. "Half Gwirion's value is that nobody, including Gwirion, takes him seriously except for me. It's part of that fool mystique I'm so charmed you introduced me to. If you don't come here at once, I shall summon someone else to take your place, and I'll be glad of the replacement."

Her anger suddenly refocused, she spun around to glare at him. "It *is* possible for you to philander without insulting my station that blatantly," she informed him.

"Yes, it is. But it is not possible for me to procreate without a willing partner. I have a genocidal Norman baron, an upstart Welsh prince, and a criminally-minded cousin to ward off with the fruit of my loins. Where would you prefer that fruit to ripen?"

Looking sickened, she forced herself to join him.

HA! I knew the monogamy experiment would never last," Gwirion wrote gleefully to Corr, some two weeks later. "He's returned to his natural ways with a vengeance. It's refreshing. I myself think he should try to seduce that addle-pated Adèle, just on principle.

"Our Saxoness queen consort is showing a little more mettle now, which I actually admire although it's not nearly as entertaining. But her entire life revolves around where he shoves his cock, and she's being incredibly backward about it. After raising such a fuss about Enid, she could have divorced him over Gwen, but she didn't—apparently in England that would make her 'damaged wares,' and I understand that's even worse than having a virile husband. And now that she's put up with him for more than three episodes, of course, she's even lost her right to ask for reparations, so we are all doomed to listen to her rant and rave when any reasonable woman would have dealt with the thing by now." This was a fiction of Gwirion's; the queen's reactions were as always icy, not volcanic. "At least I finally have something to make fun of. But he won't let me *use* it.

"And Adèle is becoming a nuisance. Is it *my* fault that the queen is always within earshot when I'm practicing a new verse about the king's latest conquests?"

An hour after handing this last letter to the increasingly fidgety messenger, Gwirion was in the kitchen showing Marged's grandson Dafydd some sleight-of-hand tricks with a kerchief. The kitchen workers were taking a short break outside, soaking in a rare moment of genuinely bright, dry sunshine and blue sky. Marged, relaxing on a sack of oats that was only marginally wider than she was, nursed a mug of ale before starting in on supper, watching these two with a contented grin. She remembered when Gwirion was that age. She even remembered when Corr was that age.

The peace was shattered by Adèle storming into the kitchen from the hall, her face nearly purple, murder in her eyes. She rushed up to Gwirion and without warning or explanation slapped him across the face as hard as she could. Astonished, he stood up and glared down at her. "What in hell was that for?" he demanded, as the boy leapt away and Marged scrambled to her feet.

Adèle, almost too outraged to speak, shook a handful of documents in his face. It took him a moment to recognize that they were the letters, *every* letter, he had written to Corr. They had never left the castle. "That's private correspondence," he cried. "You had no right—"

"I have the right to do anything in defense of my mistress," she shrieked. "You heartless bastard!"

"That's just me sounding off to a friend who can't even read!" Gwirion shot back. "I'm not planning anything against her, there's no malfeasance—"

"You sent her to find the king with that whore in her room," the woman shouted, shaking the packet under his nose.

"No I didn't!" Gwirion shouted back. "She found them on her own! You silly, ranting—"

She slapped him again. "Get out of this castle," she ordered. "Get out of my lady's life. You're good for nothing here, you're nothing but a parasite."

Gwirion laughed bitterly. "Do you think I don't know that? You convince the king to get rid of me, and I will readily go wherever he sends me. But he'll never do it."

"Then go on your own," Adèle said. "You're obviously miserable here. Go someplace where they'll let you unleash your vicious humor. Just walk out of here and go somewhere they'll appreciate you. If there is such a place."

Gwirion shrugged. "I can't," he said. As if that settled it, he resumed his seat and gestured for the boy to join him again with the kerchief. Adèle pushed between them and chucked the letters under the cauldron, into the flames of the gaping fireplace.

"What are you doing?" Gwirion yelled, trying to grab them back. He salvaged only half of one burned page, puckering his nose against the smell of burning parchment. "Those are mine! You have no right!"

"Sully her name one more time," Adèle threatened, "and even if nobody reads it, I swear on all I hold sacred, I will make you suffer. And I'll make the king suffer for keeping you."

She looked alarmingly serious, but Gwirion calmed at once and gave her an appraising, almost approving look. "Very well, I'll take that dare," he said. "You're *far* more satisfying to bait than she is—I wish you'd've let me know that sooner! As soon as I've taught my little friend this trick, I'll get a fresh quill."

ADÈLE decided she would have to get rid of him. It became her monomania; she made it her business to learn everything she could about his background, certain there would be grounds for an accusation of unchristian ways, but she was disappointed. Father Idnerth was helpful with the start of the story, which was disappointingly mundane. Gwirion had been a foundling; the holy man had wanted him christened and when nobody else expressed an interest in naming him, the priest himself had chosen Gwion, the birth name of the legendary bard Taliesin, who had also been a foundling of sorts. When Prince Maelgwyn as a toddler, stumbling over his expanding vocabulary, called him "gwirion"—not a name, just a word meaning both innocent and foolish—the entire court had humorously taken up the misnomer until the orphan thought it was his real name. Maelgwyn and Gwion, the chaplain pointed out with parental and slightly senile affection, had rechristened each other.

Marged—not yet the cook then, but the cook's wife—was Gwirion's wet-nurse, and he slept with Corr in the little closet off the kitchen, which was unorthodox since private sleeping quarters, even modest ones, were unheard of for anyone but royalty. Because he was of an age with the prince they were sometimes left together, and Marged noticed almost at once that Gwirion was the only one whose presence calmed the infant prince's tantrums. This elevated his potential from domestic drudge to royal companion, and when the prince began his studies Gwirion was not officially tutored, but he was invited to learn on the periphery. So he learned to ride, but not to lance; to fight, but not with sword or arrow or spear, only with fists. He never studied politics, but he learned to read and write faster than the prince, and when he took an interest in and had an aptitude for Hywel's harp, Cadwallon invested in training him to music.

There was one detail that challenged credulity: Older castle residents insisted that Gwirion, although never respectful of authority, had been the sweetest-tempered child until the murder of Cadwallon. Again and again she heard the chorus that Gwirion had saved young Maelgwyn's life that day, although nobody seemed to know or care about the details. In fact, nobody seemed to care about much of anything about Gwirion's past, including Gwirion himself. Adèle realized she would have to look to the present or worse, the future, to find a way to deal with him.

And then the queen presented her with an unexpected opportunity.

NOBLE was surprised that the tentative knock at the door that wet September evening was his wife's. He had asked for one of the steward's girls, but she must have seen her mistress on the way and wisely dropped back. Thanks to Gwirion, the queen's tantrums were legendary, despite the fact that she had never thrown one.

"Milady," he said, and stood up, straightening the tunic and drawers that he slept in, glad he hadn't yet removed them. "I wasn't expecting you tonight."

"Do you want me to leave?" she asked quickly, hesitating to take off her cape, already soaked from the short walk across the bailey. She was in a strange mood, tense and yet distracted. Usually when she was upset about something she had the focus of a hawk. Now her attention was turned inward.

"No," he said, placating her. "I . . . perhaps I just misread the moon, but I assumed—"

"You did misread," Isabel said. "My flux should have been upon me nearly two weeks ago. Nothing has come." She didn't know where to look. This was why they had married, after all, it should have been an announcement of extraordinary joy, but she had sobbed in Adèle's arms for most of the afternoon.

Noble took a breath and found his hand at his chest. He pushed the cape off her and had his arms tight around her, his lips pressing her brow. "This is wonderful!" he announced, almost trembling.

She managed to give him a weak smile. Her hands were cold.

SINCE he now understood exactly who his audience was, Gwirion obligingly tailored his wit. "To my revered correspondent," he scribbled onto a pilfered piece of the king's best paper, sitting by Marged's hearth, and paused. He wanted to provide material worthy of Adèle's awesome wrath. "The queen is suddenly no longer allowed to ride out to the abbey. No one is saying why, but I'm sure she's with child. Why must they all be so *precious* about it? Why can't someone just say, 'Ah, he finally ploughed her deep enough,' or words to that effect, and be done with it?

"My personal theory is that his other women enjoy him so much that they don't want to lose his favor by becoming fat with pregnancy, and they take precautions, so he's never sired a bastard. I'm glad they know to do that; she'll be so swollen and crabby soon that he won't want to touch her, but you know as well as I do that he can't go more than a few days without activity. I suspect he'll be riding the entire female population of the castle by Advent. Perhaps he'll even make her watch, so that she might finally learn a little of what really pleases him.

"Or perhaps, once there's an heir, he'll dispose of his marriage altogether. I don't think Mortimer is behaving himself anyhow, so she's essentially useless. The gaggle of girls who do nothing all day but play with balls of yarn and giggle at each other's stupid jokes have been displaced from her solar and are spending their time in a corner of the great hall, where they get in the way of the people who have real business to attend to. Only Adèle spends any time with the queen now. How could anyone possibly have a healthy pregnancy with such a humorless, mad old shrew hovering about? Half the time she won't even let the king in to speak to his own wife! Well, she's such a frail little thing, she'll probably die in childbirth, and then we won't have her to deal with anymore. Then he can find himself a nice Welsh wife and restore Cymaron's dignity. We all pray for such a time—and if he has any sense, he prays so too."

HE found Adèle by the hall fire. "Here you are," he said angelically, handing her the letter. "Do let me know when you're ready to begin the persecution." He bowed extravagantly and went back into the kitchen. She pursued him with her eyes.

"I'm ready now," she gloated.

5

So Shall Ye Reap

Harvest Festival, 1198

INALLY, AFTER FAR too many hours, the audience-chamber door was opened to let in the cool air of the September afternoon. The king, beginning to recover from being shut up with Gwilym the steward and Gwallter the chamberlain settling the state accounts of the past year, had been interrupted by a runner from the English border with disturbing news of Mortimer—after all these months, at last, concrete news of Mortimer, and astonishingly damning too. After receiving it in brooding silence and dictating several sharp responses to send back east at once, Noble could do nothing further for the moment, and he was trying to push it from his mind. Now he just wanted to be down on the tourney field with his men but there were other domestic duties to attend to first.

He did, however, indulge himself in a few moments of Gwirion's prattling.

The prattling had sunk to this level: "Think of all the furrows you've ploughed, and never a seedling or even a weed reported yet.

You haven't the power to spawn. It's God's punishment upon you for seducing that darling bride of Christ when we were young."

"She hadn't yet taken the veil," Noble insisted mildly, nostalgia pulling at the corner of his mouth.

Gwirion was already back to the present. "Face the truth, sire," he said with a mischievous grin, knowing there was no danger he would be taken seriously. "Your wife is obviously having an affair. It's another man's son."

Noble laughed a little, stretching across the leather chair back with leonine indolence. "Even for a fool, that's dangerous territory."

Gwirion rose to his knees on the cushion and leaned against the king's shin. "She's so distraught when she learns of your indiscretions. A little upset would be one thing, that would be her being a woman. But she becomes hysterical," he insisted, although he knew she didn't. Working within the inconvenient confines of reality was Noble's burden, not his. He lowered his voice conspiratorially. "The one who cries 'Foul' the loudest is usually guilty of the very sin he denounces. That's an ageless truth. I warn you, she's been carrying on with another man."

Noble, grateful for any trivial distraction, played it out. "And whom do you suspect?" he asked with all apparent seriousness.

"Well, sire," Gwirion answered, equally straight-faced, "she's very religious. Do you think it might be Father Idnerth? I think it might be Idnerth, sire."

"He's old enough to be her grandfather."

Gwirion gave him a knowing look. "Some women prefer older men for their experience."

"Of which Idnerth must have untold thimblefuls." Noble laughed and stood up. "Thank you for bringing it to my attention. Go make mischief elsewhere. I must visit with my wife, assuming her living chastity belt will let me through the gates."

"There's no one left for me to make mischief with." Gwirion frowned, also rising. "You've disposed of everyone who made good company."

"*I'm* still here," the king said expansively, affronted.

"I said everyone who made *good* company," Gwirion corrected, and Noble, grinning, made an obscene gesture at him.

"Then go harass someone," he said, picking up the Mortimer scroll from the arm of his chair. Turning toward the door, he was surprised to see Adèle standing at the threshold, in a dusty shaft of sunlight from a hall window. "There you are, Gwirion, practice on that." He walked past the old woman without a greeting, and disappeared into the hum of the great hall.

Gwirion and Adèle stood for a moment staring at each other, two wiry bright-eyed creatures in their masters' castoffs, aflame with mutual defiance. Suddenly Gwirion smiled and said heartily, without sarcasm, "I appreciate that you hate me as much as I hate you. It takes a certain courage for anyone, especially a mad old woman whom nobody likes, to be that genuine. But weren't you going to persecute me? After that delicious fodder I provided? I almost offended my own sensibilities," he said, confidingly.

"What has my poor girl ever done to you," Adèle demanded, "that you would try to convince the king she's been unfaithful to him?"

"He didn't believe me."

"Of course he didn't, but you were in earnest."

"I was not!" Gwirion said, laughing.

"That's blood lust," she insisted with intensity, as if she hadn't heard him. "You're a sick creature, and a demeaning influence on His Majesty." She turned to walk away.

"Wait a moment, then!" Gwirion cried. "Why don't you ever fret about His Majesty being a demeaning influence on *me*? Do you think I was *born* to be this way?"

She paused, looked back into the room, and for a flicker of a moment seemed on the verge of lowering her armor. "Do you think *I* was born to be this way?" she asked, quite earnestly.

"Of course," he answered at once. "That face was never beautiful. You're not going to be her midwife, are you? You'll scare the wee one half to death, one look and he'll try to climb back into the womb. Then he'll rupture her spleen in the effort and she'll die and it will all be your fault. There truly are such things as killing looks!"

THERE was a slightly awkward formality between them, and he would have to be the one to overcome it: He knew her pride was wounded that he now no longer sent for her, that both he and Gwirion were so casually blatant in setting up his trysts. It did not inflame her righteous indignation as it did Adèle's, thank God, but it took a toll on her already rattled spirits.

"You are well?" he asked at last.

Isabel was having a difficult time of it, but she only nodded and adjusted her wimple in the mirror. The silver threads caught the fading daylight from the window and glittered prettily about her wide face, but they were stiff and confining and she would happily have traded the whole thing for a simple Welsh veil. Adèle still insisted on the wimple. "There is only the nausea, and Adèle has concoctions for that. I've invited Thomas for a visit."

"You've what?"

"When I wrote my family, I invited Thomas for a visit."

A cold hand closed over his heart when he heard this and he gripped the scroll harder. With effort, he kept himself calm and asked, "Are you sure it was wise to tell them?"

She frowned. "Why wouldn't it be?"

"Your status has changed," he said. "You'd make a far more attractive hostage now, carrying my child."

Her eyes widened and she turned from the mirror to face him. "Noble, don't be ridiculous. They're my family, not my enemies."

"No, I'm your family and they're *my* enemies," he said.

"You married me because you aren't enemies anymore," she said with some exasperation.

"Then why is your uncle acting like one?" Noble snapped.

She hesitated. "What do you mean?"

He threw the scroll down onto her bed, almost as if he were expecting a confession. "Mortimer tried to buy the loyalty of our eastern and southeastern guard," he announced. "He's been working on them for months. My men have been playing along with him to see what he's up to—"

"Southeast?" she said, confused. "Your southeast border touches the deBraose lands, not Roger's."

"Yes," he said, annoyed. "*Our* southeast border does. Either Roger is trying to hire my men as mercenaries to attack deBraose, which I would consider ungentlemanly but forgivable, or he's trying to use deBraose as a shield to plan something against us. Which do you think is more likely?" She was too shocked to speak. "I'm sending more men to the area and I've already written deBraose and Prince John. This will be resolved quickly now. But nothing is what it seems at the moment, Isabel. I won't stand any hostile elements having access to you."

"You consider my own brother a hostile element?"

"Not Thomas," Noble said impatiently, "Roger. Roger will see this child only as a prince of Maelienydd—a new target to dispatch."

"All of that is over now," she said firmly, with a frustrated sigh. "And justice was served, after all, he paid for his crime *years* ago."

"No he didn't," Noble snorted.

"Yes he did," she corrected. "Henry imprisoned him for two entire years. Do you know how extraordinary that is? For the English king to imprison an English lord for killing a *Welshman?*"

"For two years!" Noble flared. "Two years! What kind of punishment is that for regicide? Anyway, it *wasn't* for regicide, it was for disregarding the writ of safe passage—it's a debt Mortimer paid Henry Plantagenet of England. It has nothing to do with the debt he owes Maelgwyn ap Cadwallon of Maelienydd."

She shook her head. "What are you talking about?"

"He owes me a blood fine."

"What, an eye for an eye?"

"No," he scoffed. "How pathetically English of you. It's to *prevent* an eye for an eye. It's the law of Wales—I thought you studied that this summer with my pudgy little judge; didn't you bother with anything that wasn't to do with my cock? The killer pays a fine—a galanas—to the victim's family. And *then* it's over."

She tried, and failed, to imagine her uncle acquiescing to this. "And if it's never paid?"

"Then we devolve to the barbaric customs of your own beloved nation," he said dryly, "and it does become an eye for an eye. But it need not be Roger's. Any Mortimer suffices."

"Is that a threat?" she demanded sharply.

He had meant it merely as a barb, but her response made him think. "Only if you consider yourself a Mortimer."

"Don't play games about this, Noble—of course I'm a Mortimer. If I'm *not* a Mortimer, why did you marry me?"

"If you *are* a Mortimer, why did *you* marry *me*?" She blinked at him, and he nodded. "You understand, I hope, that I require an answer before I can allow you to see your kin again." He left, pulling the door closed behind him, as the severity of this sentence sunk in.

She rushed after him and threw the door open again. "Noble!" He paused on the first step, his back to her, his broad shoulders silhouetted against the light from the hall below. "What exactly did you mean by that?" she demanded.

Without turning to look at her he said firmly, "I mean that I will not allow fraternizing between a Mortimer who is in physical possession of my heir and Mortimers who would like to dispossess my heir."

"But I'm not a Mortimer, I'm the Lady of Maelienydd," she said, trying not to sound desperate.

After a pause, he turned and with a cocked eyebrow appraised her. "Is that so?" She nodded. "I'm glad to hear it. The Lady of Maelienydd has no earthly reason for wanting to spend time with those wretched Mortimers, so obviously the issue of doing so, or even writing them, will simply never arise. Until the child is safely delivered and can stay in my custody should you make the questionable choice of discoursing with Mortimers, you shall not be discoursing with any Mortimers at all." He gave her a politely triumphant smile and descended the staircase, not noticing Adèle in the shadows of the balcony. The old woman gave him a murderous look as he passed by her.

THE harvest feast that night, the feast of Michelmas, would include the official announcement of the queen's condition, as well as a celebration of her birthday, but it was mostly a festival of thanksgiving for a successful harvest and an acknowledgment of the leaner months to come. It was the time of year when masses of Noble's subjects migrated with their herds and flocks from summer farms in the hills to the winter dwellings closer in to the villages. The valley of Cymaron saw its population increase by nearly a third this month.

The hall had been swept, the floor covered with dried rushes and aromatic meadowsweet, and the heavier winter tapestries hung upon the walls. Some of these were new, brought by the queen from England and mostly religious in theme. Gwirion had stood in front of each of them in turn, caricaturing Christ and paraphrasing scripture—obscenely—with an exaggerated French accent, until the chaplain arthritically swatted him away. The other hangings, although not as colorful as the English ones, were old favorites of heroes, battles, and hunting scenes. Above the main door hung an elaborately braided ribbon of what looked like hay: the very last tuft of grain harvested that day in the king's fields, brought into the court earlier amidst laughter and ceremony that Isabel could not begin to comprehend. Adèle assured her, bristling, that it was not Christian.

For the feast, hundreds of oaten threshing cakes with thyme and savory had been prepared; rook cakes with thyme and savory were baking; gallons of rabbit stew with thyme and savory had been seasoning for days. This year there would be an additional and exotic treat, wholly novel to the Welsh palette: a ginger dish, with neither thyme nor savory, that the queen's woman had brought from beyond the border. Adèle was given a corner of the kitchen and enough eggs and milk to make jance sauce for several hundred—a chore even for her industrious hands. Marged the cook, proprietary and motivated as much by suspicion as curiosity, loomed over Adèle as she worked and insisted on sampling it before allowing it to be served to the king. With an unpleasantly surprised expression she spat it out, but having recovered, she demanded to sample it again and then, after another involuntary grimace, a third time. Gwirion, chuckling, pronounced it a success, reminded Adèle with a hopeful grin that he was waiting to be persecuted, and returned to the bustling hall to wrestle with his harp. Noble had bought him wire strings from Ireland, which he was having a calamitous time experimenting with. The bright, almost harsh sounds they made as he tried to tune the instrument reverberated off the rafters, and half his notes, it seemed, were swallowed up by the echo. "Crazy Irish!" he spat at last, and changed back to gentler horsehair.

I T was unthinkable to Noble to apologize for anything, but when he saw his wife approach the high table as the feast began, her face so grim within the pale wimple, he regretted what he'd said to her and drew her to him to whisper that she was free to welcome Thomas for a visit. She relaxed into his embrace, grateful and appeased; there was something more vital than mere affection binding them together now and her respect for that was visceral. But she couldn't bring herself to reciprocate any show of affection, feeling Adèle's eyes on the two of them: In Adèle's very black-and-white world, the king was very black, and tonight Isabel lacked the energy to fend off her chastisements for weakening to him. Even she was getting weary of Adèle's venom, although the old woman only ever deployed it in service to her mistress.

Hafaidd called out sharply for silence so that Father Idnerth might deliver his blessing. It was in Latin, which meant nothing to most of them, and almost at once he was competing with a dozen whispered conversations round the hall about more important things, such as who was joining in the peat-stacking party this year, or whose ailments had been healed magically by the old wise woman in the hazel grove. When Idnerth had said amen, the smith was given, as he always was at feasts, the first drink of the evening. "That's because," Gwirion called out approvingly, "a sod like you needs an early start to get at all inebriated!"

When the meal was over (Adèle's jance sauce having been admiringly discussed but not much eaten), servants cleared away the board and trestles, and the guests gathered around an open space in front of the dais to dance and play games. Gwirion was in his element here, and despite her general resentment, Isabel finally saw a side of him that was not entirely repugnant to her. He was by instinct a common entertainer, and harvest was a time for common revels. Almost everyone had brought instruments of some sort—crwth, pipes, and harps of a dozen strings at most—and when Gwirion began a tune they all joined in, those without instruments singing. It was a raucous but innocent and truly joyful din and Gwirion, Isabel realized with grudging appreciation, was its natural conductor.

But when the third or fourth tune was in full swing, just as she was willing to concede that he might even have a winsome touch, the common entertainer in him once again appalled her. Carefully he laid his harp down on its back, then leapt up from his stool and in rapid succession grabbed a young woman and some half-dozen men out of the torchlit crowd. He steered them nimbly through a short, bizarre ritual in which the girl and one man were tossed into the air together by the other men, her skirts flying and their legs tangling together while everybody roared with approving laughter. Isabel had no idea what they were doing, but it seemed obscene, the leavings of some pagan fertility ritual of which Gwirion was a perverted form of minister, and at the end of it she was dismayed that the entire hall, even children, burst into deafening applause and cheering. She caught Adèle's eye; the older woman shook her head. "Godless heathens all,"

she mouthed in French, and exited calmly to the kitchen to prepare
for Gwirion's death.

AFTER about an hour the general hilarity of the crowd was
softened by the ready flow of ale, and the guests' instruments,
at Hafaidd's urging, were finally put away. Now there would be gentler entertainment in honor of the queen.

Gwirion (under orders he resented) began this too, leading a
pack of village men through a Christian hymn in stunning close har-
mony, with more parts to it than a full English choir. Hywel the
bard, his voice growing ragged from years of overuse, told a story of
King Arthur's heroic exploits that startled Isabel with its violence.
Poets and musicians attached to the households of visiting lords contributed songs and stories, including one praising Noble's maternal
family line, which went back to Rhodri the Great and the legendary
Elystan Glodrydd. There was a rash of obsequious toasts, and then
the messengered greetings were read aloud; even Anarawd, the cousin
who would no longer be the heir, sent warm regards that sounded
plausible. The only moment that displeased the king all evening was
a last-minute delivery on horseback: the proclamation of congratula-
tions sent from Llewelyn of Gwynedd—a patently political move,
nothing more than an excuse to have his status as Noble's supposed
peer trumpeted in front of Noble's subjects.

Adèle hovered in the kitchen by the screens to the hall, watching
the bustle of servants going in and out, waiting for one of the sewing
bevy to pass through. Fortune favored her and Madrun, the most
trusting and naive of the trio, entered through the screens, carrying
an empty pitcher. She deposited it on the central table and was
headed back toward the hall when Adèle called out to her and she
turned back.

"Run an errand for me, the cook's instructions," she ordered the
girl with brusque offhandedness. She held out a wooden cup.

A S Isabel sat envying a silken-voiced songstress with a harp, she felt a tug on her sleeve and glanced back. Madrun stood in the shadow behind the throne, her wild red hair a demure auburn in the low light. With an innocent smile, she presented a wooden chalice. "Your Majesty's medicine?" she offered.

The queen looked at it in confusion, then rose and slipped back with Madrun to the shadows behind her throne. She reached for the cup and glanced at the contents, no more than a mouthful. "What is this?" she asked.

"From the kitchen," Madrun said, as she had been instructed to. "To settle your stomach."

Isabel sniffed it. Adèle had exhausted her own knowledge of the herbs but Marged was still gamely experimenting, and sometimes something helped a little. The oily liquid smelled like ginger and nutmeg, but there was a hint of other things she could not recognize. Ginger sometimes helped the nausea, so, desperate for relief and suspecting it would taste foul, she brought it to her lips and downed it in a single swallow.

It choked her. Juice of raw ginger made her eyes and nose smart fiercely and her throat constricted in pain—but it was only masking some other taste, something oily, alien and bitter. It burned her all the way down to the lining of her stomach. She grabbed the girl's arm in alarm, gasping for breath. "What was that?" she demanded, not quite in a whisper. *"What did I just drink?"*

"It's fine, milady, please don't distress yourself," Madrun said assuagingly. "The cook said it would go down very harshly, but it does marvels when it starts to work." Noble was glancing back over his shoulder at them, frowning and looking concerned. Isabel raised a hand dismissively to tell him not to worry himself. Madrun, her task not quite completed, returned to the kitchen.

Noble gave his wife a passing smile as she rejoined him, then returned his attention to the female musician who was performing. She was not a pretty woman to his eyes—too small in build, too placid in demeanor—but she sang like an angel, and played a better harp even than Gwirion. Her master was staying overnight as a guest, so a proposition would be easy. He glanced at his wife, glad for both their sakes she couldn't read his mind.

Something about her complexion made him look again. She was very pale and a fine sweat had broken out over her face. "Isabel," he whispered, frowning, "are you unwell? Should you be lying down?"

"No, no, I'm fine," she said hoarsely, and reached out to touch his hand. He was surprised and pleased by the gesture, and held her hand in his, stroking it. She smiled gratefully, which was the best moment of the night for him. He smiled back.

"Do you need anything?" he pressed. The song had ended; the herald introduced another singer into the performing space.

"No, I'm all right, really. It's only that the mead tastes off to me."

"Gwilym tested it. That's the best in the kingdom, it's been waiting some eight years for a celebration like tonight. And so have I." He lowered his head toward her, pressed his lips against her fingers, and then, more intimately, against her palm. The throng, watching them, cheered. King and queen smiled tentatively at each other.

"When they do that, it almost feels as if they're our children," she whispered.

He nodded, and then winked at her. "If this one goes well enough, we might start work on a brood that size."

She blushed despite herself. "Noble," she murmured, confused by her own pleasure at these words, "that's hubris."

"A king should be allowed a little hubris," he said, and then shifted his attention to the crowd. "We thank you for your spirit, people. The singer may begin now."

Half an hour later they were nearing the end of the night's entertainment, and Isabel felt far worse than she had before she had drunk Madrun's offering. It was not nausea now; it was something more acute, as if a hole had been drilled through her stomach and her

muscles were clenching around it. Concerned, she was about to excuse herself to the kitchen to ask Marged about the concoction, when
she found Madrun standing demurely at her elbow again, trying to
stay hidden behind the thrones. "Excuse me, milady," she whispered
in the queen's ear. She spoke hesitantly, bemused by the instructions
that this message required delivery at just this moment and no
sooner. "But now I am to tell you it was not Marged who made up
the potion you drank earlier. It was Adèle."

A DÈLE in her grey wimple, ignoring and ignored by the harried workers cleaning in the kitchen, had moved nearer the
doorway leading out into the courtyard, fidgeting with a piece of paper and awaiting the familiar footsteps. She looked up calmly when
she heard them.

Isabel stopped beside her, pale, frightened—and furious. In a
slow, threatening whisper she demanded, *"What have you done?"*

"Come with me," Adèle said quietly, and went outside. She
closed the door behind the queen and stayed on the steps overlook-
ing the yard, their privacy assured and the torch offering the fire she
needed.

"Adèle, you *must* tell me what you've done."

"You know what I've done," Adèle said. "And you know why."
She hoped she had timed this to accommodate her mistress's wrath.

Isabel slammed the back of her hand to her mouth to stifle a
horrified cry. "I'll vomit it out," she announced, furious.

"It's already in your blood," said Adèle complacently. "But go
on, feel free to try if it will ease your conscience." She gestured to
the far side of the stairs, where it was dark enough that nobody in
the yard could see anything. Immediately Isabel crouched in the
shadows and frantically took herself to a state of pained gagging
that brought nothing up. After a long, shuddering dry heave, she

gave up and collapsed, gripping the cold stone steps for balance. Adèle waited.

At last the queen rose and returned to her, lashes wet, contained but more enraged than Adèle had ever seen her. "I won't do this, Adèle!" she whispered, fuming. "Give me an antidote."

"There is none."

Isabel spun away and slammed her foot hard on the stone step in a childish, impotent explosion of rage. She took a few ragged breaths and then turned back to Adèle, demanding, "Was it oil of pennyroyal?"

"And other things. If you're thinking of asking Marged for help, don't bother. There's a lot of ginger in it and Marged never saw ginger before this week, she knows nothing about its properties and won't dare interfere with a mix she doesn't know, for fear of complications. And it's too late now anyhow."

"Dammit!" Isabel hissed, her throat constricting again, barely controlling the urge to throttle Adèle. *I should have seen such madness coming,* she thought with a wave of panic. "I'm telling Noble this minute—" She began to push past her for the door. Adèle stopped her by holding out the paper.

"Read this first."

"Later—"

"*Now,*" Adèle said in a voice from Isabel's childhood, and Isabel stopped at once.

But she didn't take the scroll. "This is *treason,*" she whispered, glaring at the old woman and starting to tremble. "And anyhow, how could you do this? It's *my child,* Adèle, you had no right—"

"It's not your child, it's his heir," Adèle said harshly.

"That makes it worse!" she insisted. "I'll tell Noble, perhaps I can convince him it was a mistake and—"

"You can always make another one. I'm doing this for you, don't muck it up."

She shook her head, incredulous, and stared at Adèle as if she'd never seen her before. "I don't want this! Have you lost your senses?"

"Don't become hysterical," Adèle said without quite meeting her eyes. "You're a practical girl and you'll see in time the value of this action. There's nothing you can do to prevent it now, so your choices are to tell the king at once and gain nothing by it but my execution, or to help me use this to the best advantage." She waved the scroll. Isabel shook her head, hugging herself and shaking from the cold and the drug, her face starting to crumple into tears. She released one arm and began to cross herself repeatedly. "Be despondent later," Adèle ordered fiercely. "Pay attention now or this really will be for nothing."

The queen blinked back the tears and stopped crossing herself. Feeling ill, she slowly took the scroll and hesitantly unrolled it. " 'To my revered correspondent'—Who is this intended for?"

"Does it matter?" Adèle replied serenely. "I intercepted it. Read what it says and then tell me if you'll work with me."

Isabel looked down and squinted to read it in the torchlight. She was trembling so badly now that Adèle had to hold the paper for her. "The queen is suddenly no longer allowed to ride out to the abbey. No one is saying why, but I'm sure she's with child." She looked up. "Who wrote this?" Adèle gestured for her to keep reading. "Why must they all be so precious about it? Why can't someone just say, 'Ah, he finally ploughed her deep enough,' or words to that effect, and be done with it?" She closed her eyes a moment, knowing who the author had to be, then resumed reading in silence. She grew paler as she read and chewed her lip ferociously to keep her bitterness in check.

" 'She's such a frail little thing,' " Adèle recited with righteous disgust when she saw Isabel reach the words, " 'she'll probably die in childbirth, and then we won't have her to deal with anymore. Then he can find himself a nice Welsh wife and restore Cymaron's dignity. We all pray for such a time—and if he has any sense, he prays so too.' "

Isabel closed her eyes again when she had finished, light-headed now, and Adèle reached up and fed the scroll into the torch fire. "An unborn child is easily replaced. That villain, thank God, is not. Will you work with me?" she asked.

WHEN the final guest performer had graciously dipped his head to acknowledge the applause, Gwirion stepped out away from the shadow of the dais and moved into the empty space. Noble, after playfully grilling Isabel on the finer points of continental foolery, had ordered him to change his outfit to a deliberately clownish one for the evening, with ass's ears attached to a cap on his head, and the audience hooted at him now. He tried to ignore them and begin his dancing prattle, but he couldn't. "So you think this is ridiculous?" he demanded.

"Hell, yes!" several drunken voices chorused in reply, accompanied by muted chuckles. He glanced down at himself.

"Well," he said. "You're right. I look absurd. Of course, many say I *am* absurd, so that's all well and good. But I worry about those who look absurd when they're not supposed to. The king, for instance," he offered, and headed up the steps of the dais. Noble theatrically rolled his eyes, and people in the front laughed.

The queen shrank back as Gwirion approached them. The moment she'd seen him as she was returning to her seat, sanity returned and she'd determined to sabotage Adèle's ludicrous, murderous scheme, but by now she was having a hard time thinking clearly. Still she managed to keep a small smile plastered to her lips.

"Stand up, sire," Gwirion was saying loudly. "I want to show the crowd that your attire is also absurd."

Misreading his wife's discomfort, Noble reluctantly shook his head. "No, Gwirion, none of that tonight."

"It's fortunate you never say that to the queen or we might not be celebrating this happy occasion," Gwirion chortled. He turned his face but not his attention toward her, not noticing her jaundiced flush. "Now here's another absurdity," he announced to the crowd, gesturing to her silk kirtle and pelisse. "Here we have the expectant mother dressed in silver and the palest of flowery hues. She looks veritably *virginal*. But we're here tonight in testimony that she's certainly no virgin!"

The room was spinning; she was about to lose consciousness. This was the moment Adèle had told her to act but she was sickened with guilt for even considering it. Confused, fighting an encroaching fog, she could remember only that his proximity was what endangered him, that she was to get as near to him as possible, so that Adèle, stationed in the crowd, could convince the drunken revelers that they had seen him lay hands upon the queen. She cowered away from him, and disoriented by the drug that was making her belly clench, shouted what she meant to whisper, desperate and unhinged: "Move away, for God's sake, Gwirion, move *away* from me!" She flailed her arms at him and he worriedly shot a look at Noble. Noble made a gesture to carry on as he leaned in toward his wife and put a reassuring arm around her, gently hushing her and checking her forehead for a fever. As if it were a delirious litany, she continued pleading for Gwirion to keep away from her.

Unnerved, Gwirion jumped down to the open space on the floor and tried to continue his patter. "Is this some peculiar Norman custom? If anyone can explain to me why we should celebrate proof of her fecundity by dressing her as if she were a little girl—"

He was interrupted by a scream of pain. He spun around to look, and fell victim to the general panic that swept the hall.

There was a growing streak of blood across the skirt he'd just mocked, and the queen, vomiting blood onto the dais, had turned a disturbing yellow. For one shocked moment, nobody was capable of movement but the queen herself, as she stood then convulsed violently and doubled over, clutching her abdomen. The last word from her mouth, still pleading and barely audible, was "Gwirion." She began to tumble down the dais steps, but Noble leapt from his seat and caught her. He lifted her in his arms as she fainted, her body still convulsing, blood seeping from her nostrils and the corners of her mouth. Women screamed as the blood continued to splatter the steps, some people pressing forward, others frantic to back away.

Gwirion tried to run back up to the dais, but the guards had stepped in to push the mob back, and within seconds many people—starting with a woman's voice that was distinctly accented—began to cry out his name accusingly and claw at him, murder in their eyes. Suddenly terrified, he changed direction and began struggling to get away from the guards and out of the hall, but his costume made him easy to identify. He felt a tug on his leg, and as he pulled away his cap was torn off. People grabbed at him from all sides as he ducked, pushed, scrambled, and climbed out of the crowd, his heart rippling in his throat.

NOBLE refused to leave her side. Too distracted to heed Adèle's hints that she needed to be alone with Isabel, he sat by her bed and would not release her hand. Finally Adèle gave him a damp rag and told him to make himself useful by keeping his wife's brow cool. Her priest hovered near her other shoulder muttering something ominous in Latin, the sewing bevy rushed to fetch rags and poultices to stem the flow of blood; Angharad asked to drape a cord of sheep gut on her as a talisman but the priest shrilly denounced the idea. With his approval, though, Adèle placed the handmade rosary housing the relic of St. Milburga around her neck. There was much more blood than Adèle had expected, and she was frightened for a while. Isabel was pale and sickly yellow and unconscious for over an hour. By that time, the women had cut her out of her bloodied silks, sponged her clean, wrapped her in a warm mantle, and placed her under the blankets.

Noble, hovering anxiously by her head, was the first to hear her speak. He couldn't make out what she was saying over the priest's endless intonations and the women's talking, and he held up his hand. At once there was silence and all attention in the room was on the bed.

"Adèle," she moaned softly, her eyes still closed. "Adèle, what's happening?" She spoke in French.

Adèle sat across from the king, on the bed. She placed her cool, weathered hand on Isabel's damp cheek, kissed her forehead, and answered in their mother tongue.

"You're safe now, child, you're safe and back with us. You're beyond harm."

She opened her eyes, and blinked in the muted candlelight. Her eyes glanced at Adèle, at Noble, and quickly back at Adèle.

"You lost the child," Adèle whispered in Welsh. No one had actually said the words aloud and when he heard it, Noble grunted and gripped his wife's hand harder. Isabel erupted into furious, impotent tears. "The parasite had just come up uninvited onto the dais and was very close to you, in fact I think he was touching you—"

"That's enough," Noble interrupted in a low, threatening voice.

"Sire, you can't deny—"

"I can and I do," he said, keeping his voice quiet for his wife's sake. "She was feeling ill well before that. If you try to turn this against Gwirion, Adèle, I warn you, you'll regret it."

"Where is he, then, Your Majesty?" Adèle asked, defiantly. "If he were innocent, you'd think he'd make some gesture of sympathy toward his sovereign lady."

Noble let go of Isabel's hand and turned his full attention on Adèle, his blue eyes blazing angrily but his voice controlled. "Gwirion is hiding somewhere right now because you convinced four hundred superstitious people that Isabel was accusing him."

"I?" the old woman said, defiant and incredulous.

He gave her a knowing look. "However backward you think my people are, none of them would have made that inane association on their own. I heard your voice, Adèle."

"You're mistaken, sire, but he's certainly an evil influence in this court, and this was a sign from God that he should no longer blight these walls."

"That's nonsense."

"With all respect, sire—" the priest began from the across the room.

"This is beginning to sound like a conspiracy," the king said, in a warning tone that silenced them. Now the only sound was Isabel's bitter weeping. Noble stood up. "Look to my wife; I'm going to find Gwirion."

GWIRION was not to be found. Anywhere. The castle denizens had gone through the bailey and keep several times throughout the night, finding nothing even with the help of sunrise. A hue and cry was raised, and by early morning scouting parties formed and were sweeping the countryside, beating through heather, gorse, and bracken, hacking through the dense undergrowth of the valley floors. Noble had immediately sent messengers conveying his proclamation that he, the king, personally guaranteed Gwirion's innocence, but it had little effect. Seeing the royal scouts work their way across the hills only incited rural imagination, and soon illicit well-armed posses were also beating through the bracken. It made the people feel important to think they were on a holy crusade against the demon who had robbed them of their baby prince.

Noble was finishing a belated hasty breakfast before returning to his wife when Gwilym approached him hesitantly, his calm demeanor shaken. "Sire." It took him a moment to continue. "There's a rumor of a reward for bringing Gwirion's head into court."

Noble sighed heavily. "As if there weren't enough nonsense to deal with. Do what you can to dampen it. Cadwgan, Goronwy, get their help." He began walking toward the stairs to the queen's solar.

Gwilym looked pained. "Someone is here to *claim* the reward, sire."

Noble froze. He jerked around and stared at the steward, wide-eyed. "No," he said quietly, and for a flash Gwilym remembered the child Maelgwyn after his father's murder. The two men turned together to march quickly in long, matching strides to the door toward the barbican.

From the hall steps, the barbican was within spitting distance, and Noble, blinking fast in the sudden brightness, saw a man with a peculiar package, standing at the open gate arguing with Einion the porter. A step closer and the thing became identifiable: It was a dark-haired human head stained with fresh blood, and the man grasped it by a set of ass's ears sewn into a cap tied under the chin. The king stopped in midstride and blanched. He closed his eyes briefly to collect himself, then nodded curtly to Gwilym and they continued to the gate.

"This man is a criminal," the porter growled to the steward. Then he saw who Gwilym's companion was and quickly bowed. "Sire. He's committed butchery—"

"Let me see it," Noble commanded sternly, pushing past him. He braced himself and examined the monstrosity.

Blood had seeped everywhere from the ass's ears; they were from a donkey that must have been alive an hour earlier. The head itself was from a half-rotting corpse, unearthed for the occasion. Noble let out a breath, almost laughed. He turned to the perpetrator, who did not realize the game was over and grinned at the king expectantly as he bowed.

Noble replied to the grin with a look of contemptuous disgust and tersely ordered Gwilym to have the man publicly flogged. "And make sure people hear about it," he growled before walking away.

MIDMORNING, despite the priest's insistence that the queen was still too weak for conversation, Noble pushed his way past the sewing bevy and into her chamber. She was sitting up in bed; her women had bathed her, clothed her, braided and coiled her hair. Adèle had nursed her with nettle juice to cleanse her blood, and some color had returned to her face, but she was still exhausted and unnaturally yellow. The look she gave him—grief and apology and tentative affection all mixed together—wrenched his heart. "Isabel," he said gently, sitting beside her pillow. "Tell me how you are."

She leaned her head against his arm. "I'm alive and grateful for it."

"The physician saw you?"

"Your physician said he knows nothing of women's ailments, Noble. There were only my ladies and my priest to attend to me."

"They don't know the cause?"

She hesitated and lowered her eyes, suddenly transfixed by the embroidered stitching on the border of her blanket. "You heard what Adèle—"

"Don't," he said in an iron voice. He looked around the room. Adèle was asleep on a cushion by the hearth. She awoke at once when he called her name, and didn't want to leave the room, but the king gave her one of his stares and she finally obeyed.

When he was alone with his wife, he took her hands in his and kissed them. "I don't mean to scare you," he said. "But Gwirion's life hangs on this issue now. Wherever he is, he won't be safe until his name is cleared."

"I almost died last night. You lost your child. But what matters to you most is clearing a parasite's good name?" Her tone was tired but not peevish.

Reflexively furious, he pulled away from her for a moment, but then with a resigned sigh moved back and took her hand again. "Of course I'm grieved for our loss. And concerned for your health too. But there will be more loss to mourn if I don't get this situation under control."

"I don't feel well, Noble, I need to sleep."

"I'll let you sleep in a moment, as soon as you tell me what happened."

She pretended again to be absorbed in the bedding's embroidered edge. "I've already told Adèle everything, why don't you ask her."

"I want to hear it from you, I don't trust her," he replied. "Please." He waited for her to make brief eye contact, then pushed on. "You were unwell while the woman was singing, weren't you? I noticed you were in a sweat while she was still singing. When did you first feel ill?"

She couldn't look at him. "It's hard to say, I have morning sickness so often—"

"This was different. You turned a strange color and seemed to have trouble breathing. When did that start?"

"I don't remember, Noble, I'm sorry."

He pressed her. "Your redhead gave you something to drink. Could that have done it? What's her family background—might her people be in with Anarawd?"

Horrified that she had put the girl in danger, she looked up and said with absolute sincerity, "It wasn't Madrun's fault, Noble, don't suspect her." Then she looked harder at his eyes and realized she'd given too much away.

"I didn't suspect her, actually," he said, his tone triumphantly flinty. "But if *that* is your reaction to mistaken accusations, I am intrigued by some of your other responses." He kept staring at her and she looked down, fidgeting with the blanket. "Adèle prepared that draught for you, didn't she?"

"Noble, please, I'm dizzy, I need to rest—"

"This is *important*," he insisted, taking her little chin in his broad hand and forcing her to look into his face. "Did Adèle mix that potion?"

She nodded reluctantly. "But I was already feeling ill when Madrun gave it to me."

"It clearly didn't help. It might have made it worse. What was it?"

She couldn't move her head from his grip, but she lowered her eyes again. "I don't know. You might ask Adèle."

"She said it was ginger water, but I don't know what that is. Why did she have Madrun give you the drink? I don't remember you asking for anything."

She knew she should look up at him to seem sufficiently defiant, but she couldn't. "Are you suggesting Adèle would try to harm me?" she asked, willing her lips not to quiver.

He let go of her head, his attitude softening. "Look at me, Isabel," he whispered, very gently, his baritone voice fatherly and soft as velvet. "Please look at me."

It was Adèle's undoing: Isabel met his gaze and started sobbing. "I didn't know what it was," she blurted out. "I didn't know, and then there was nothing I could do."

He swallowed a wave of nausea, stunned by the revelation although he had suspected it, and clutched her tightly, rocking her against his chest. He would have held her that way for hours, even days, but she forced herself to almost instant recovery, angry at her own lapse as her mind raced in fruitless panic trying to concoct anything to save Adèle.

He helped her lie back against the mound of felt cushions and they looked at each other for a moment in pained silence. "This makes her a criminal," Noble finally said.

"I don't think she meant for it to happen—"

"Of course she did. She planned it exactly." Suddenly it was so obvious, he was angry for not realizing right away. "Is she mad to think such a thing would work? She drugged you. She timed it to affect you at the end of the evening, when Gwirion would be performing and you—" He cut himself off and sharply pulled away from her, eyeing her as if she were something poisonous. She chose to become fascinated once again with the embroidered border of the sheet, picking at the stitches. After a moment, forcing himself to calm, he continued. "Was she the one who told you to wear light colors? It wouldn't have been nearly so dramatic if you'd been wearing your usual colors, your reds and maroons. You trust her like a mother—she knew you would drink whatever she gave you." He stood, agitated. "That's what happened. She killed my child for the sake of trying to kill him." He ran to the door, hurled it wide, grabbed Adèle by the arm from out of the small waiting huddle on the balcony, and pulled her roughly into the room, slamming the door closed again. He pushed her down to the wooden floor hard enough to knock the wind out of her.

"Noble!" Isabel begged.

"Be quiet," he snapped, and turned all his fury on Adèle. He hauled her up, smashed her hard across the face, punched her furiously in the ribs. Something cracked and she gasped, clutching her torso and convulsing in pain. He shoved her to the floor again and slammed his boot into her over and over, forcing her slowly across the floor with the impact of each blow.

"Stop, sire, please, sire, I'll explain," she begged between kicks, grabbing her ribs and shuddering.

"Noble, stop!" the queen screamed, sitting up in bed, but he didn't stop. She cried out wildly for help, and two of the teulu came through the door at once, bearing knives. When they saw that the king was the attacker, they hesitated.

"Stop him!" she yelled at them. "He's killing her! Stop him, *stop him!*"

The two of them, barely more than boys, looked at each other in confusion. No one had told them what to do in such a situation, and they were too stunned to try anything on their own. "Stop it, Noble!" Isabel screamed again, and pulled herself out of bed. She could barely stand, but she stumbled toward her husband, collapsed against him, and tried to pound against his back. He shoved her away with a wave of his arm and continued his attack on Adèle.

She landed on the floor with a cry, and the cry won his attention. He left Adèle in a trembling heap, and turned at once, breathing hard, to pick up his wife and place her back on the bed. He handled her gently—but he glowered at her.

In the sudden quiet, the door opened again and the priest stumbled in, followed cautiously by the others. Noble followed their gaze to the old woman's softly moaning form. "She did it," he said, sounding disgusted and exhausted. "Adèle did it. Someone fetch the physician."

"He's in the village," one of the teulu said, heading back out the door. "I'll go."

"Who else can heal?" Noble asked.

"Adèle," said the priest. "Marged."

"You"—this was to the other of the teulu—"take her down to the kitchens and see what Marged can do for her. But stay with her—she's a condemned woman, I don't want her trying to escape."

Isabel made a wordless sound of protest from the bed. The priest begged for an explanation but Noble impatiently sent everyone back out of the room, Adèle voicing agony with each forced, assisted movement. Alone with his wife, the king crossed his arms; unspeaking, he pierced her with a scrutinizing stare that made her skin crawl. He leaned back against the wall as if waiting for something.

"Noble, she's very old," she said nervously, to fill the icy silence. "I think she's senile. I can't believe she set out to endanger me or the child."

"Then what was she up to?"

"I don't know. Perhaps she just wanted me to faint."

"Why?"

She had no answer.

"She has to hang."

"*What?*"

"Public hanging. She brought it on herself."

"Noble—"

"It's treason. I have to obey the rule of law."

"But you can't prove it!" she said desperately. "Even I couldn't swear that she did it—I really don't know what was in the drink."

"That can be traced. Goronwy will have no choice in the matter."

"You can pardon her—you're the king, for the love of God, you can pardon anyone for anything," she implored.

"I will not exercise the privilege of pardon unless you can explain to me how that benefits Maelienydd. And even if I were to pardon her killing my child and nearly killing my wife—which I'm not inclined to do—there is still the other matter to consider." His voice was suddenly harder, flatter.

She shuddered without knowing why. "What other matter?"

"The matter of your singling out Gwirion before you fainted," he said coldly. "I'll pose the question that I hope to God you have an answer for, but to be honest I can't imagine what it is. Can you explain your behavior in a way that does not implicate you in this catastrophe?"

She took a breath, silently exhorting herself to face the moment calmly.

But another voice preempted her reply. "*I* certainly can't!" It was anxious, muffled. The king jumped and put his hand to his belt, forgetting he had no sword. They both looked around in alarm, but there was no one else there. Then Noble's eyes widened. He dropped to his knees and reached deep under the bed. With no resistance, he pulled out a very dirty creature wearing the tattered remains of a jester's costume. He hoisted him to his feet and looked him over: Only once before could he remember Gwirion ever looking so pathetic. "I commend your choice of hideout," he finally said with a small smile, feeling far more than he was willing to show either of them. Isabel sighed hugely with relief.

Gwirion backed away against the wall farthest from the door, looking leery of the queen. His face and arms were stained from the dust under the bed that had caked itself to his sweat. He had soiled himself and one cheek had three small parallel scabs across it, the scratches of a sharp-nailed hand reaching out to grab at him.

"Have you been here the whole time?" asked Noble.

"I'd just slipped under the bed when you brought her in last night," he stammered. "I didn't think anyone would look for me here, and here I'd know when it was safe to come out."

"You look dreadful."

"I feel dreadful." He jutted his sharp chin toward the queen. "She didn't answer you."

Noble sighed. "No, she didn't." He turned back to her. "I believe we were on the threshold of confession."

She grimaced nervously. "By then, yes, by then I knew. I was actually trying to *protect* him, though, not accuse him. I was trying to put distance between us, I wasn't thinking clearly—and I swear I didn't know what was in that cup when I drank it."

"But you drank it knowing what it would do?" He sat by her again with a dangerous heat in his eyes.

"No!" she insisted.

"Prove it," he demanded, grabbing her wrist hard. "Now."

"Ask Madrun," she gasped. "Madrun will tell you I was unaware, I thought Marged had mixed it up for my nausea."

"Why did you do nothing when you realized?"

"I did! I tried to vomit it up, but it had already started working. Adèle claimed there was no antidote and that if I asked Marged to help she must refuse for not knowing the properties of an ingredient."

"This was certainly staged to assure you could exonerate yourself," Noble said sarcastically. He released her wrist and stood again, looking agitated.

"I'm not pretending I deserve an unconditional pardon," she admitted, rubbing the freed wrist nervously. "I was drugged, I was confused, and I changed my mind at once, but I had one moment of intending to act against him, and that robs me of true innocence, I confess that." She took another breath to calm herself. "But, Noble, guilt rests in the *act*, not in the impulse, and my actions on the dais were a confused attempt to *protect* him."

"If in the span of half an hour your impulse and then your actions both endangered him, it's mere semantics to suggest the two have no connection." He looked at her with disgust. "I should charge you with conspiracy to murder."

"Sire," Gwirion interjected quietly. "I believe her."

"Thank you," Isabel whispered.

"It doesn't matter what you believe, Gwirion, only what I know," the king announced flatly. He took a step toward the bed and looked down at her threateningly. "I hold her accountable for a long chain of events, and justice will be served accordingly—as it just was to Adèle."

Isabel stifled a squeal of fear and curled up defensively under the blankets. But his expression changed, and he flashed a peculiar, brittle smile. "Indeed," he said tightly. "And considering the net effect you've had on Gwirion's well-being, I have no choice but to exonerate you."

They both stared at him. The queen cautiously half uncurled.

"Sire?" Gwirion questioned. "I am not asking you to punish the queen, but what inspires you to say that?"

Noble looked between them for a moment, weighing something. Abruptly, he turned his gaze to the window and the hills beyond, and after a silence said, "She saved your life." There was pained amusement in his voice.

They exchanged bewildered looks. "How?" Gwirion finally demanded.

"By being born."

Gwirion at once felt as if he was both airborne and under water. He staggered to his knees near the fire, holding out his hand to grasp at a tapestry for balance. "The hunting horns?" he asked faintly. "The horns and the bells?"

"Announced her birth, yes. I sat in the bushes with a naked blade, and I could do nothing—*because* I was the king, I could do nothing," he emphasized bitterly. "Mortimer wanted to go back to Wigmore to see if the child had come. You don't understand French, so you couldn't have known that. But that was the reason he let you go. Bask a moment," he suggested, finally looking back into the room, "in the poignant irony of that thought."

"What are you talking about?" Isabel asked.

Noble turned to his wife. "You haven't heard the famous tale of Gwirion saving my life? He was with us when your uncle ambushed us, and Roger was about to kill him. These past two decades would have been unbearable without..." He looked at Gwirion, who appeared the least likely of worthies in his torn and dirtied clothes. Noble made a sound that was both mocking and affectionate, and gestured grandly toward his friend. "Without *that*," he said, laughing. Gwirion was dazed, still in the past. "He manages both to distract me from reality and to make me face it clearly without the warping camouflage of court etiquette. He is the only luxury I am allowed in life, and he would be dead nineteen years by now if you had not been born. The bargaining chit that saves you today is that you were the agent by which he was restored to me. I thank you for that."

He gave her a small smile and the tension in the room relaxed. For a moment there was peaceful silence.

Then his smile devolved into a severe look of warning. "But Isabel, that chit is spent now. If you ever again become the agent by which I might lose him, I will make an example of you as I just did of Adèle."

Gwirion, recovering, saw alarm on the queen's face and protested with a nervous, forced laugh, "You've already beaten one defenseless Saxoness to death this lifetime, isn't that enough?"

"Don't speak that way," Isabel said crossly. "She didn't die, she didn't even swoon."

He shook his head. "I'm sorry, Your Majesty. I saw the light go out of her eyes."

"She was still breathing when they carried her out of here," the queen corrected him.

Gwirion shook his head. "She was letting go. She's gone by now. I'm sorry."

"Noble," she said firmly. "He's wrong. Tell him he's wrong."

The king held up his hand for quiet and went to the door to ask after Adèle.

The priest was already waiting on the balcony with a leaden face, and stepped into the room at once. "We did not even get her to the kitchen, sire." Isabel gave a cry of shock and buried her face in the embroidered sheet. "I just gave her last rites, and called some men up from the yard, but I don't know where you want us to place her."

Noble sank heavily on the bed. "Oh, Christ," he said slowly. "Father, I don't know where she should be. Leave her where she is—"

"She's lying at the foot of the stairs."

"Take her to the chapel," the queen said in a broken voice, without looking up.

"I'm sorry, Your Majesty, I can't allow that," said her priest awkwardly. "She's accused of a mortal sin."

"No she's not," Gwirion piped up. The priest saw him and did a double take. Gwirion coughed, trying to look dignified in his torn, befouled clothes. "She did nothing wrong. The miscarriage was an act of God. But . . ." He scrambled mentally. There was no plausible way around this, so with typical Gwirion instinct he simply let each phrase tumble from his mouth without knowing what would follow it. "The queen thought I was responsible—that was a mistake—and God was displeased with the queen for putting my innocent life in danger, and Adèle, Adèle is such a God-fearing woman that when she realized her mistress had erred she asked God if she could take the queen's sin on herself and God afflicted her for the queen's failing by sending her into an epileptic fit, and she beat herself to death against the walls in here." He laughed nervously, patting the curved wall, which was plastered over and padded almost everywhere with tapestries. "So she's exonerated her mistress's mistake and proved her own worth, and she should be taken to the, uh, to—" He looked at the queen. "The chapel?"

"Yes," Isabel said quietly, teary and astonished.

"The chapel. God has forgiven them both—especially our revered queen—and Adèle deserves an honorable burial."

No one spoke for a long moment.

"I think we can all live with that chronicle of events," Noble finally said.

"Thank God the *rule of law* is not for doing people favors—it's only for *justice, n'est-ce pas,* Your Majesty?" Gwirion, recovered, muttered quietly—but not very quietly—to the queen. She pressed the fingertips of one hand against her closed eyes, too overwhelmed to manage a response.

"Father, you heard him," Noble said heavily. "Adèle should rest in the chapel until burial arrangements can be made. I'm going there with you. I need to go to shrift."

Alone, Isabel and Gwirion looked at each other in self-conscious silence.

"Thank you," he said tentatively, almost as a question.

"Please," she said with a teary sigh. "Please, Gwirion, I haven't the energy for sarcasm."

"I'm not being sarcastic," he assured her, awkward. He looked like a wreck, but the dark eyes considered her with a deference she'd never seen before. "I'm forced to contemplate the fact that as well as being the source of all my woes, you're also the reason I'm alive."

She shrugged, not knowing how to answer. "I owe you thanks as well," she said, barely above a whisper. "However absurd that explanation was, she'll rest in hallowed ground for what you said."

"I had as much to gain as you did," he replied.

"No," she said. "You could have saved yourself without saving her."

"I didn't save her, Majesty. She's dead. I'm alive. For that, you are not actually grateful." His gaze, cold again, turned away from her, and bowing, he left the room.

THE funeral was modest but respectable, and Isabel went into seclusion for a week, spending her waking hours in chapel. Her rosary was almost always in her hands, her fingers touching the home-made beads as affectionately as if they were Adèle herself. Gwirion, still wary of the general public, was afraid to leave the castle, and spent much of his time in the receiving room failing to distract the abruptly brooding king.

Adèle's violent dispatch in front of his wife had been unavoidable when he considered it strategically, but he hated having the need for it. Although it had made Isabel understand at once the power and position of the king, it had made her demonize the nature of the man, and Noble couldn't blame her.

It rained unceasingly for days, the first severe rain of autumn; it added a pallor to the world. Even the sconces that the small audience chamber depended on seemed to shed a watery light. Gwirion played for hours at a stretch without speaking, the harp in its sad tuning, the music melancholy.

"How is she recovering?" he asked after three days.

"She's a little stronger, and trying to forgive me. We've reached certain . . . understandings."

"Such as? You're not being yoked into monogamy again, are you?"

Noble shook his head. "That romantic bubble has burst, thank God, but we have an agreement now that I'll be more discreet."

"And which testicle did you have to cut off in exchange for this?"

Noble gently cuffed Gwirion's head. "Neither. All she wants is dignity, and Lord knows Adèle's the only one who ever really gave her that. She'll have a little more say over the household, but you know how Gwilym is, he won't yield pride of place. And she doesn't have to sew anymore. Apparently she doesn't like it."

"That's it? And what's the catch?"

"No catch. No, that's not quite true." He gave Gwirion a pained, wry smile. "Anglo-Saxon law has finally insinuated its way into our court. Do you remember we pressed King Henry for the blood fine from Mortimer when he killed my father?"

"Of course."

"She considers it paid."

Gwirion frowned. "How? You've never received anything from Mortimer."

"We believe in restitution—the English believe in revenge. As far as she's concerned, it's an eye for an eye. Adèle's life for my father's, and now the score is settled."

Gwirion laughed in scorn. "A serving woman's death avenges a *king's*?"

"Adèle was like a mother to her. A mother's death avenges a father's."

Gwirion shook his head. "You can't expect someone who's never had parents to begin to understand that." They sat in silence for another moment and then Gwirion ventured, tentatively, "Of course, there's a true poetic irony—"

"I know that, Gwirion," Noble said in a voice that forbade further comment. Adèle had died on her mistress's birthday, the anniversary of Cadwallon's murder.

6

DAY OF THE DOGS

All Hallows' Eve, 1198

S THE DAYS shortened and the wind grew sharp, Isabel tried to turn away from her losses to help to prepare the castle household for the winter. Between the queen and Gwirion there was a kind of truce. They had nothing to talk about, but with Adèle as agitator replaced by a shared remembrance of her death, they were finally at least tolerant of each other.

The rising star, that upstart Prince Llewelyn of Gwynedd, continued to make his presence known at Cymaron, sending first a flowery message of condolence and later an offer to fill Adèle's office with the spinster sister of a minor official in Llewelyn's court. Noble, after spending weeks convincing his wife he was not really a monster, allowed her to respond to this herself. She graciously declined the offer. With equal graciousness, Noble himself declined Llewelyn's suggestion that they consult toward forming a confederacy of Welsh princes—which Llewelyn, as prince of the once and future greatest kingdom in all of Wales, would naturally lead.

Something had derailed Mortimer's ambitions to the southeast with the deBraose family. There was much dissension about it in the council—Gwilym and Efan, who differed in philosophy even more than in temperament or age—were clearly annoyed with each other for some reason, but the issue was never discussed openly outside the council room and Isabel sensed that nothing good would come of her prying for more information. As long as Roger's mischief didn't reflect poorly on her own character, she decided she could not waste the time in thinking much about him anymore. Her brother's struggle to run his estate as well as she once had, a challenge frequently bewailed in his letters, was the only piece of her family's fortune she indulged herself to care about.

It was the last day of October now, the beginning of winter and the end of red-deer season, and the king was preparing to ride on the annual first hunt. On this daylong outing, the youngest hounds were taken into the hills without their elders, to gauge their general competence and maturity for hunting winter game. This year, it was particularly significant, since fate and illness had conspired to kill many of the older dogs. The first hunt would let the huntsman know what sort of pack he had to see him through the winter. This in turn affected much of the rest of the castle: November was the month to slaughter livestock and today would give the butcher a sense of how much stock would have to be killed, which would in turn alert Marged and Gwilym to how much brining salt would be needed to cure the meat, which would in turn determine how Cadwgan would go about securing it.

Gwirion, generally reluctant to leave the castle in any event, had been wary of even an unescorted walk down to the village since the night of Adèle's death, and he had never been one to enjoy a hunting day. But he made it very clear that he wanted to go this time, and the chief huntsman warily welcomed him. He wrapped an extra mantle around himself and went on his pony beside Noble and the other riders, out the main gate and down over the River Aron, through grey fog as thick as fleece at an hour he would not normally consider decent.

IN the dark of the morning, an early mass had been held to bless the dogs and the hunters. They were gone, lost in the heather of the higher hills, by the time the castle as a whole had risen, and they weren't expected back until well after dinner. They were not missed; that evening would be the sober festival of All Hallows' Eve and those in charge of preparing for it were glad to have fewer extra people underfoot all day. There were the common feast foods to ready—geese, pork, lamb, vegetable stews, white barley bread, and mounds of cheeses—as well as whatever the hunt would bring in. But today people also had to prepare food for the dead, tiny loaves made of barley, water, and so much salt they were inedible to any sentient tongue. The village children would collect these soul cakes later—and, of course, demand payment for seeing to it that the dead received their nourishment. There were similar customs in England although they were confined to the lower Saxon classes. But the queen, still grieving for Adèle, went to the kitchen early on in her somber surcoat, gown, and wimple to make a dozen soul cakes with her own hands. Her presence caused a wordless stir and she was awkwardly avoided by everyone but Marged, who enjoyed watching the foreign woman trying to conform to their ways.

Outside, once the mist burned off, all of the men who were not on the first hunt were helping the fueler collect enough wood for the evening's bonfire. In a land devoted to celebratory flames, this would be the biggest blaze of the year. The entire castle would spend most of the night around the fire playing games, feasting on apples and nuts, and indulging in divination—something Gwirion was particularly called upon to do because he could improvise nonsense and deliver it with such convincing, deadpan earnestness. As with every other feast day she had spent in Maelienydd, when Isabel heard of these festivities she shook her head at how much more cheerful, loud, and outright pagan the formal observations were here compared to her native Wigmore Castle.

There was a feeling of morning levity around the bailey. For the first time in months, the sky was completely cloudless, and brilliant blue above the crisp autumn air. Most court functions had been suspended for the hunt, and the officers who remained behind, led by grinning Maredudd the brewer, collected together in the wide courtyard. As they helped assemble the bonfire on the middle of the courtyard paving stones, the men sang rowdy tunes accompanied by teulu members on the bowed crwth and the pipes. Some of the older teulu (all of one and twenty years) dragged a few of the hall maids out into the yard for an impromptu dance. The kitchen servants began preparations for curing the meat that the hunt would bring in, doing as much of it as possible outside the kitchen scullery to enjoy the weather and the music. Even when Marged sat down with Gwilym to finesse details for the supper feast, they sat on the hall steps watching the dancing and marveling at the warmth in the air. It was an afterthought, but Gwilym politely invited the queen to join them, and so only the sewing bevy remained inside, within the queen's solar, working on a couple of twill weaving projects and staring out over the river at the gentle swell of hillside, watching for the hunting party.

When the meeting was over and the spontaneous carousing in the yard had quieted, the queen helped Marged in the kitchen until there was no room for her unskilled hands in the growing crowd of workers, and finally, brushing oat flour off her skirt and feeling happily involved with something other than distaff chores, she retired toward her chamber. It was barely midmorning. On the balcony outside the door, she heard the three young women murmuring together with a growing urgency. "Milady, look!" they said nearly in unison as she entered, and they gestured out the window together.

The glorious blue still dominated the sky, but huge white clouds in exotic shapes were rising over the northern hills. Standing out in sharp relief against the clouds was the hunting party, returning early, two dozen men on foot and horseback meandering their way slowly down the grassy slope, skirting gorse bushes and green-and-russet swaths of dying bracken. The marshal led a pony in full tack that had no rider in the saddle, and the huntsman, his scowl visible even from a distance, led a sumpter horse that had something thrown over it. Something like an animal but far too large for winter game.

"Who is that?" Isabel asked, squinting and moving toward the window.

"We think it's Gwirion," Angharad replied. "Isn't that his mare?"

"What's happened? They shouldn't be home for half a day yet."

"*He* must have done something," announced Madrun, wide-eyed, but Angharad shook her delicate blond head.

"He looks hurt, I think someone did something *to* him."

"And where are the dogs?" asked Generys. "The dogs aren't with them."

"They sent the runner ahead this way," said Angharad.

"Stay here," the queen instructed. "I'm going down to meet them at the gate."

She rushed back down the stairs and crossed the hall to the crowded, noisy kitchen. "Has there been a messenger from the hunt?" she demanded above the din.

A score of voices called, "No, Majesty," and she headed out of the kitchen and into the yard. A long-legged boy in Noble's livery was approaching her from the barbican gate, out of breath. In this high country, footing everywhere was treacherous, so swift travel on horseback was impossible; runners were the preferred couriers.

"Your Majesty," the boy gasped, and bowed. "I have a message from the king."

"Rise and speak."

"I am to give the message to the steward."

The steward, of course the steward, not the queen. Peeved, she gave him leave to find the man. "I'll be in the king's receiving room," she said, "should Gwilym condescend to share the news with me."

Gwilym and the runner arrived at the round white room just moments after she had. The boy was not recovered from his final sprint, but he couldn't wait to give his important news, so he blurted it out between breaths. "His Majesty is bringing a criminal home and wants the prison cell prepared to receive him. He'll hang him to-morrow at dawn in the village, and in the meantime, there is no game meat for tonight's supper and the feast of All Hallows' is canceled."

"Who's the criminal?" she asked, perversely thrilled. Based on what she'd seen, the crime was obvious: Somebody had hurt Noble's darling Gwirion.

"The criminal is Gwirion. His crime is sorcery," the boy an-nounced.

They gaped at him. "Sorcery?" stammered Gwilym, barely main-taining his unflappable demeanor.

"Yes, sir. He bewitched the dogs and made them afeared of the animals they were supposed to hunt."

Queen and steward exchanged amazed looks. "You can't mean that, boy," Gwilym insisted.

"Milord, I wouldn't believe it if I hadn't seen it with these eyes. We put them on the scent, and they yelped and whined like someone had stepped on their paws. They put their tails between their legs and tried to hide behind the horses. It was the most unnatural thing I've ever seen."

"How did the king stop them?"

"He couldn't stop them, Majesty. Nor the chief huntsman. They told Gwirion to take the spell off; he laughed and laughed and said he couldn't, it was no spell, it's how they were. His Majesty thought it was funny at first, but not when Gwirion said he couldn't fix it. They even put the whip on him to make him undo it, but he wouldn't."

"My God, he's so perverse," the queen said under her breath.

"I wouldn't know anything about that, Majesty," the boy said, looking briefly embarrassed. "He thought it was right funny, though. He laughed up until they started whipping him."

She winced. "I saw him slung over the packhorse."

"Yes, Majesty. He's not laughing anymore. I think he's scared now."

"Disaster always follows when Gwirion gets scared," the queen muttered. She turned to the steward, who looked to be in shock. "Gwilym, take the news to the kitchen, and ask them to put it around the court. I'm going to meet the hunting party at the gate." She'd never given Gwilym an order before and despite the upset of the moment, she was pleased with herself. He bowed his head with dignified coolness and she hurried out of the room, wondering what was really going on. Obviously Noble could not mean to do it.

As she reached the steps of the hall, the riders entered the bailey, and the solemnity of the procession made her stop short. Gwirion still lay facedown over the sumpter horse, strapped by his wrists and ankles. He was whimpering and he looked too miserable to be alive. His face was a shocking greyish-green, his belt was gone, his faded tunic and shirt were both shredded along the back from the whip, and angry welts were storming up where it had dug into the skin.

Noble, by contrast, was furious but elegant and collected. His broad, grandly handsome face was as stony as a statue, his brown hunting outfit was unsullied by an actual hunt, and his horse was barely exercised. He dismounted, handed the reins to his groom, and gestured toward Gwirion without actually looking at him. "Have Einion put him in the cellar," he said, between clenched teeth. "Waste no food on the wretch for dinner or supper." Head bowed, he began walking toward the tower that contained his bedchamber, his fists clenching and unclenching.

"Noble, wait!" the queen cried out after him, rushing down the steps to catch up with him near the well. He stopped and turned back to face her, and she went down on one knee, her silk skirt pressing into the sandy mud.

"Oh, for God's sake don't do that," he said impatiently, and pulled her up with unusual roughness. For a moment their faces were very close and she saw something in his eyes that frightened her— beneath the cool exterior he looked crazed. By now the entire hunting party, a number of the teulu, and many of the kitchen staff were watching, and he addressed the whole yard, looking annoyed that he was expected to speak. "There is no game today. At all. And there'll be no meat for the rest of the winter, unless we slaughter *all* the livestock, and even then some of you will probably starve. He did something to the dogs, they wouldn't hunt. That's not a prank, it's not the license of a fool, it's treason. He's put the court in danger."

"Where are the dogs?" Isabel asked.

"The dogs are dead," he said harshly, and turned the crazed glance back to her as if daring her to criticize him. "I had the archers shoot them all. He'd ruined them."

"Sire, as I tried to point out—" stammered the agitated chief huntsman, whom Noble was not fond of under the best of circumstances.

"I am not interested in anything you have to say on the matter," Noble cut him off angrily. "The dogs would not hunt, they were *afraid* of the scent."

"Ask the barons for dogs as part of their tribute for the year," the queen said. Noble stared at her.

"I intend to," he replied. "That's not the issue here." He turned and continued toward the wooden staircase outside his tower. She moved with him, lowering her voice. "Noble," she whispered, their backs to the yard, "I agree he should be punished for this, but a death sentence is absurd." He glared at her and began walking faster, balling one hand into a fist and closing the other one around it. She forced herself to continue, straining to keep her voice too low to be heard. "Noble, stop. You're angry right now, and you're right to be angry, but please don't act out of anger." They were at the bottom of the stairs now, and he took the first step up, cutting her off from following. "You regretted it with Adèle—you will never forgive yourself if you hurt Gwirion. He's your closest friend. You don't know what that loss is like. I do." She took his hand, which was still a fist, and tried to meet his eyes; he wouldn't look at her. He turned on his heel and walked slowly up the wood steps toward his room, signaling the porter before disappearing from sight.

She wrapped her arms around herself, suddenly aware of a chill. She'd slipped off her surcoat while she sat listening to Marged and Gwilym and wore only a thin kirtle now. Several people approached her offering her their mantles and cloaks, but she brushed them all aside. "I'm fine," she announced. "Someone make certain Gwirion is fed."

"Your Majesty," said Gwilym quietly. "The king said there will be no food wasted on—"

"Give him my portion," she ordered.

She stood there, unmoving, and listened to the buzz behind her slowly fade. She heard Gwirion lifted off the horse, moaning as he was carried to the barbican and down into the holding cell. She heard the horses led past her to the stables, and the hushed gossip of teulu and castle workers fade away. The playfulness of the morning was harshly extinguished.

By now the sky was definitely clouding over. She wished her husband were superstitious enough to take this as an omen that he was making a mistake. Certainly she had never liked Gwirion, but she'd never truly wished him dead. Only Adèle had made that mistake. How could Noble possibly exterminate the only person in the world he loved?

With a gasp of insight, she ran up the stairs, into the tower and Noble's chamber. "Sire," she called from the anteroom, pounding on the door, choking back relieved laughter now. "Noble, I know what you're up to, and you've won your point. You don't have to go through with it."

There was a moment of silence and then he pulled the door open so fast that she jumped. "And what do you think I'm up to?" he demanded, glowering down at her with the furious gleam still in his eyes.

She was taken aback by his intensity, but made herself smile up at him. "You want to make me beg for his life. You want me to come to his defense so I'll appreciate him. And I do, I do appreciate him, so you're very clever and devious and it worked brilliantly, but please, *please* don't continue this nonsense." She sank to her knees and looked up at him. "I am officially begging for Gwirion's life."

He was condescending and disgusted. "I wouldn't threaten Gwirion's life just to make you 'appreciate' him. But by your reaction,

I *could* be doing it—although I'm not—to test the theory that you *always* oppose me, no matter what the circumstance."

"Noble," she protested, getting to her feet. "That's nonsense."

"You defend a man you despise rather than support me," he said. "You beg clemency for a man whom you yourself *conspired to kill* little more than a month ago, just to contradict me—trust me, madam, I won't forget that." She tried to interrupt but he silenced her with a furious glare. "And for Gwirion, this will be an actual execution, and he brought it upon himself, with no assistance from you. What we saw today frightened my bravest men. It truly felt ungodly. It has nothing to do with my personal feelings." His voice caught and he looked away from her angrily. "Cutting off my own arm would be less painful—but were it gangrenous, I'd cut it off."

"I don't understand how you can do this," she protested.

He touched his slender crown of gold and garnet, and then her slighter circlet. "That is because I wear this and you wear only that," he said coldly, and slammed the door on her.

GWIRION was in the same cell he had shared with Corr less than six months earlier, but the internment was infinitely more traumatic this time. Despite the cooling unguents Marged had slathered on his wounds, he was in throbbing pain, and lay curled on his side on the damp floor. He knew the king's step and it was not the king who was approaching. It was a woman. But not Marged coming back. Not Enid, even if it could have been Enid. He had never bothered to learn the queen's step. This could have been her, but there was no reason for her to come down here. Except perhaps to gloat. In her position, Gwirion admitted to himself, he probably would have.

Einion stood straighter, and awkwardly bowed his head toward the approaching person. Without uncurling, Gwirion stretched his neck slightly up toward the bars of the door to see.

"Your Majesty," he said, still confused, when he realized it was the queen kneeling down to see him. "Pardon me but I'm not getting up."

"It wasn't really sorcery, was it?" she asked. She felt ridiculous. "Why don't you tell him what really happened?"

"I *did*." This was a piss-poor time for the woman to decide to play the good Samaritan, he thought. What feminine self-indulgence. "I told him what I did and he refused to believe me. Even the huntsman backed my claim, and he hardly knows how to open his mouth."

"What did you do?"

"I switched the dogs," he said, and laid his pounding head back down on the cool stone floor. "Last spring, Corr and I saved a litter of runts from drowning, and I hid them with a farming family near the village. The son Ithel smuggles them into the woods by the tourney field and we've been training them this whole time to go against their instincts and act frightened when they smell their prey. They were so good at it!" He sounded almost fatherly.

"And you switched the runts with the castle dogs?"

"Yes. Of course the huntsman could tell right away, but I begged him not to reveal it, and he likes me, so he kept mum. Then when we found the scent . . ." He chuckled painfully. "It was extraordinary. You've never seen so many bewildered men in your life." He sobered. "And the king killed all of them. All of my pups. Right in front of me—they were like *children* to me."

"He thought you'd bewitched the real dogs."

"But the huntsman *told* him. As soon as he saw what I was up to, as soon as he saw that I'd be in trouble for it, he told the king these weren't the castle hounds, and the king would not believe him."

"Why not?"

"I think you refused to spread your thighs for him again unless he got rid of me."

"Gwirion," she said sharply, and moved away from the bars. She had been leaning into them, hanging on his words, without realizing it.

"He was willing to *entertain* the notion that they were changelings, but I couldn't prove it," Gwirion explained, too exhausted to go into detail. "We were near the farmstead, and he sent Efan, the penteulu, there to find the boy and the real hounds, but he came back saying the farm was deserted. I don't understand that part—Ithel was supposed to be waiting there with the real pups to return them." He sighed. "Please let me sleep. I'm in a lot of pain right now."

"Of course you are, I'm sorry," she said, and stood to leave. "Is there anything I can do for you?"

There was a pause, and then a slight rustle, as if he was trying to move. She couldn't see clearly enough, and anyhow he grunted and stopped abruptly. "Tell him I'm sorry for offending him," he said. He sounded bitter. "But I'm flattered he found my prank so . . . significant." A pause. "And tell him I hope he has a long and joyful marriage, and many healthy sons."

"Thank you," she said awkwardly.

"I didn't say with *you*."

He grinned despite his pain, listening to her irritated departure.

A FTER letting the chandler in to light the fire, the king refused to speak with anybody for the rest of the day, with the brief exceptions of the court justice and the chaplain. Goronwy appeared at His Majesty's door, wheezing slightly from the effort of lifting his weight an entire flight of steps but insisting it was his duty to intercede: Only a judge might mete out punishment. The king welcomed him into his chamber long enough to point out that the judge meted out punishment according to the *Law of Wales*, which did not recognize sorcery, and the case was therefore out of his jurisdiction. The meeting lasted less than a minute. An hour later, Noble summoned knobby-knuckled, liver-spotted Father Idnerth to his chamber to write out the official condemnation, to be read the next morning on the gallows.

After Idnerth was free, Gwilym as steward called an urgent meeting in the council chamber, even remembering to invite the queen, but it came to nothing beyond frustrated, baffled conjecture. The chaplain and judge both testified from their brief encounters with him that the king was deeply distressed but absolutely inflexible about his decision. The huntsman swore they had not been his dogs, but he couldn't find his own anywhere to prove otherwise; Efan had said they hadn't been where Gwirion claimed they would be. The penteulu himself was absent, leading his charges in some solemn All Hallows' Eve tradition—which probably had something to do with scaring young women out of their skirts, Gwilym observed sardonically.

SHE did not go to her husband's chamber that night. But he, claiming lonely wretchedness, came to hers.

She refused him.

"Are you frightened of me now?" he demanded, impatiently. He looked terrifying, his expression one of the fevered intensity of a man who had strayed from reason.

"Of course not," she lied, pulling away as he tried to push her down onto the bed. "Noble, stop it!" Always uncomfortable when he came to her room, she fidgeted with the tapestry that provided the only privacy from the sewing bevy. "I don't want his death on my conscience."

"There's no reason it should be." He sat on the bed and gestured for her to come to him. She ignored the gesture.

"He thinks I won't lie with you unless you kill him."

"No he doesn't," Noble said contemptuously. "He's playing with you."

"I need to know in my own heart that that's not the reason," she insisted, suddenly grateful that her women were in the room, and the doorkeeper outside was within easy earshot. "The only way I can do that is to refuse you unless you agree to pardon him."

"And yet a new way to oppose me," he said, irked. "You will espouse *any* philosophy, grab *any* opportunity that lets you thwart me from an heir. Condemn Gwirion, defend Gwirion—whatever will forestall my fathering living issue. Who are you in league with? My cousin? Your uncle? Perhaps Llewelyn? Does Adèle manipulate you still, even from beyond the grave?"

Her eyes widened. "Noble, you don't mean any of that. That's ranting."

"No it's not, madam," he said in a low, lethal voice. "Strategy does not become you. If you're determined not to have my child, just say so, don't muddy the issue with Gwirion's fate."

She almost laughed from frustration. "Gwirion's fate is the only issue!" At a loss, she untied her robe at the throat and waist and pulled it off, tossing it to the bed. The cold air bit into her skin and she tensed, but she began to pull off her shift as well. "Bed me, then," she said. "If that's what it would take to convince you I am only after saving a man's life, bed me. I will do and be whatever you request if you will just call off this nonsense."

Noble made a face. "Put your shift back on, your Norman blood can't take this cold so early in the season. I don't want to lie with you tonight anyway, it's not a night to indulge in any form of pleasure. *That wretched fool,*" he added under his breath, miserably, and left the room too quickly for her even to try to hold him back.

She redressed quickly and went after him. Although the usual games and gatherings were canceled, the courtyard was brilliantly lit by the bonfire, but even so, she lost track of him. He wasn't in his room. She found him finally in the chapel on his knees, in a pose so mournfully and deeply meditative that he did not hear her approach. His hands were clutched together tightly, his knuckles white. After a few moments, she touched his arm. He opened his eyes and looked at her blankly, with a frightening glint as if he were quite mad. He would not speak, and when she tried to speak to him, he signaled her own priest to remove her.

IN the middle of the night, Gwirion was awakened by Einion prodding at him from above with a stick from between the bars of the cell.

"Get up, you," the porter said in a muffled tone. "Show some respect for Her Majesty, now." He thrust a rush light into a brazier by the door.

"Oh, Christ," Gwirion groaned, and didn't move. "And what is it this time?"

This was not the reception she'd hoped for. "Gwirion, I want you to know that I did everything I could to talk Noble out of this."

There was a pause.

Then his voice, reedy and weak: "I'm still in here, so I assume you failed."

"I'm sorry, but I want you to know I tried."

"That makes a hell of a difference."

"You could at least appreciate the effort," she huffed, and instantly regretted her pettiness.

With a grunt of pain, he raised his head a little to look straight up at her. His face was pale in the rush light and the large eyes were bloodshot, but without his comical grimace, she could hardly recognize her tormentor lying in the straw; indeed, in Noble's castoffs, he almost looked like an imperiled aristocrat. "I'm sorry, I hurt the lass's feelings. You're such a good lass. Doesn't matter that you've spent the last six months trying to estrange me from him, no, all that matters is that at the last hour when it was obvious you could do nothing, you decided to wake me up from my last night of earthly repose just to tell me you could do nothing. Thank you. Thank you! That makes you a good girl, so of course I'm obliged to absolve you from all those sinful months of wishing I was dead." He tired of the rant suddenly, but she was too shocked to speak. "Milady," he said in a kinder voice, "you're doing this because you feel guilty for hating me. You're not doing it because you crave my continued existence or even my gratitude. It's the guilty conscience of past days. That's all it is. Good for you for wrestling with your conscience and letting it win. But let me sleep now."

She wanted to rip out his tongue. She opened her mouth for a stinging response, but he was quicker.

"The angrier you are, the more what I've said is true. And you're a smart lass, after all, you know I'm right."

She forgot her retort, but he didn't expect a reply.

IT was raining slightly, and still dark, when the tiny village green at the foot of the castle mound filled with well-wrapped and bundled-up onlookers: The entire population had come to watch. News that Gwirion was in trouble for a prank would not have made an impression on anyone; even news of his impending execution would have been dismissed as another crazy rumor about him. But the feast of All Hallows' being canceled affected everyone directly, and gave an unpleasant, heavy credence to the gallows being erected that night. Sudden piety ran rampant. Father Idnerth had offered to hold midnight mass in the village—the king insisted on having the castle chapel to himself—and there was a bigger turnout in the cramped church than anyone could remember. The bard Hywel joined him and in an unprecedented meeting of old and new traditions, half of the evening was given over to the recitation of the bard's oldest and most sacred poems lamenting dead heroes. This was the day when the veil between the worlds was most transparent, and people were troubled enough about the dead impinging upon the realm of the living; Gwirion's execution at dawn would reverse the flow in a way that was even more disturbing.

No one in the castle had slept well—except for Gwirion, at last. The superstitious porter had drugged him to keep his powers at low ebb. He would have been grateful if he had known.

While it was still dark, he was roughly woken and hauled out of his cell. In place of regular garrison guards, a dozen armed teulu were to escort him to his hanging. He was told this was a great honor, and responded with a tired, sarcastic laugh. Gwilym silently delivered to him a special outfit of black brocaded silk, and the youngest of the teulu—a boy of fourteen, the only one who didn't look hungover— helped him to change in the darkness of the porthouse, since his muscles were too cramped and sore, and the skin on his back too raw, for him to manage on his own. The clothes felt strange, only in part because he'd never worn anything so new before. He lived in Noble's oversize castoffs, but somebody had troubled themselves enough to take in the tunic, the drawers, and even the hose, and he faced the last morning of his existence with the novel experience of wearing clothes that fit properly. With his hands manacled before him, he let the boy escort him out into the courtyard. He was sur rounded by the teulu and marched down into the village, squinting against the spattering of raindrops.

He squawked in amazement when he saw the crowd in the cold, grey light creeping over the hills. "All of these people want to watch me die?" he whispered to the little soldier who had helped him dress.

"I wouldn't take it personally, sir," the boy replied uncomfortably. "Everyone's fond of you. But a hanging is a hanging, it's an event."

Gwirion looked at him angrily. "Thank you for putting it in perspective," he said sarcastically, and wouldn't look at the abashed young man again.

It wasn't, in the end, to be a hanging. An hour earlier, as the crowd was gathering in the wet, Noble had conferred wearily with the butcher, who doubled as executioner, and decided a beheading was a better idea. It was a more honorable way to die, and Gwirion de served at least that much. So the low scaffold remained, but the gal lows were struck and an executioner's block was waiting for them. The king in sackcloth, a growing look of madness on his face and his hair as unkempt as the convict's usually was, sat with his irate wife who clutched her rosary, on a temporary covered dais that had been erected to the side of the green.

In the cold, ashy dawn, one of the teulu nudged Gwirion toward the rough wooden step to the scaffold with the butt of a spear. He raised his foot onto the first step.

Another nudge. The next step.

Another nudge. The next step. It was the slowest climb up a flight of stairs Gwirion had ever made.

His insides felt full of mud. If he could somehow wash the mud away, the insanity would stop and Noble would restore him to grace. When he reached the top step and saw the executioner's block rather than the gallows, he froze.

"It's a token of honor," the king called out.

Without taking his eyes off the block, Gwirion called back, "I don't want honor, I want life."

The crowd collectively made a strange sound, as if it had expected to hear a quip, was already prepared to laugh at it, and then realized it wasn't one. It was unnerving to see the antic fellow dressed not in his usual ragtag garments, but in a neat black silk tunic and hose. Someone had combed his hair and even tamed his cowlick—a rare event—and rubbed water across his face. He looked presentable. He almost looked handsome, his sharp, wily features suddenly seeming chiseled. Worst of all, he looked *normal*, no less and no more eccentric than anyone else in the square. There was nothing there but a frightened man who couldn't take his eyes off the executioner's block.

"Someone offer him water," the king said in a tight voice, clearing his throat, and his hands clenched briefly into fists. The executioner's young son, dressed and masked like his father, stepped forward with a bucket of water and a wooden ladle. He offered it to Gwirion, who wanted to refuse it but couldn't. Despite the rain his lips were dry and cracked, and he was hungry. He could hardly swallow, but the boy held the ladle steady for him and he awkwardly sipped some.

"Thank you, lad," he said. The boy put the ladle aside and wouldn't look at him. Gwirion studied the boy's mouth, set in a tight grimace, and his nervous, fidgety body language. He remembered when he'd taught this boy to juggle.

At an anxious nod from the king, the teulu fell into formation around and behind Gwirion holding up their spears, and moved closer to the block. He hesitated but then moved with them. A trumpet sounded. Father Idnerth's assistant, as herald, unrolled the parchment scroll that the king had dictated the night before. "Gwion called Gwirion of Maelienydd, you have been sentenced by Maelgwyn ap Cadwallon ap Madoc ap Idnerth ap Cadwgan to die," he read loudly and unsteadily. Noble shifted his weight in his chair, looking burdened by the recitation of his formal name. "Insofar as you bewitched the royal hounds to turn them off the scent, you have rendered the castle incapable of self-sufficiency and placed the lives of His Majesty and members of the royal court and all their servants in dire jeopardy. You are therefore doubly condemned, for sorcery and for treason." He lowered the scroll because it was getting rained on, but continued to recite, without looking at Gwirion. "What are your last words, sir?"

Gwirion couldn't think of anything to say. Something cutting and witty would have been best, but anything at all would have served. His mind was blank. He opened his mouth relying as he often did on intuition, and realized he had lost his voice. Finally, in a hoarse whisper that couldn't be heard beyond the scaffold, he managed to sound out the words, "Don't you want to know where the real hounds are?"

It was repeated by one of the teulu so that the king could hear it. He frowned and made a desperate, impatient sound, caught between annoyance and pain. "No, Gwirion, I'm not playing that game. This is unbearable. Get on with it," he ordered, his voice on the edge of breaking. He looked away, and at his gruff but shaky signal the penteulu shoved Gwirion down onto his knees before the block.

"Noble!" Gwirion suddenly screamed across the green. "Don't do this! These people know our friendship—if you cast me off like this, they'll know you for an irrational tyrant and they'll rise up in arms!"

"Noble, please—" Isabel said at once, turning in desperation toward him as the crowd began a distraught mutter.

"Enough!" Noble thundered, his eyes flashing. He pointed to the executioner and demanded in a quavering voice, "*Do it.*"

Efan tied a rag around Gwirion's eyes and then with a jerk lowered his forehead onto the damp block. The crowd froze. Gwirion trembled violently but made no sound. Isabel turned her head away. "Watch," Noble commanded, grabbing her shoulder in his trembling grasp. There was a bitter intensity on his face, almost a brutality, that terrified her.

The executioner cleared his throat, and lifted the axe to his shoulder. Behind him, Idnerth began chanting quietly in Latin, although he had not formally given Gwirion last rites or even offered a final shrift. He knew the fellow would not have accepted.

The executioner lifted the axe over his head, and looked at the king.

The king nodded, looking wretched.

The executioner glanced at his son.

The son dumped the bucket of water over Gwirion's head. Gwirion yelled in shock and fell over.

A mass of confused faces turned toward Noble, who opened his mouth wide and roared with laughter. A nervous chuckle of relief circled around the green, but the hundreds of onlookers combined did not drown out his hilarity.

The executioner had put down his axe at once, and had already unshackled Gwirion's hands and removed his blindfold. "Here you go, then," he said gently, and tried to help Gwirion to his feet. But Gwirion could barely sit up. He glared at the king like a frenzied bantam cock. The expression, familiar in its ferociousness, reassured the crowd and they laughed.

Isabel did not laugh. She rose and marched down from the covered dais, and on foot made her way through the rain, back up toward the castle, appalled and unescorted. Noble didn't notice her leave.

"I convinced you, didn't I?" he howled. Gwirion glared at him. "I convinced the lot of you!" He slapped his hands on his knees. "A round for the executioner and his son!" He began applauding them and the crowd obediently followed. The two masked figures nodded sheepishly and looked as if they wanted to hide.

Aᖴᴛᴇʀ inviting the assembled crowd to join him in the great hall for ale, which rendered them even more appreciative of his handiwork, Noble went in search of Gwirion.

He made straight for the kitchen, knowing that Marged would be mothering him after the shock. His Majesty seldom came in here and the kitchen workers were flustered, but he waved them aside.

"Where is he?" he asked, grinning, and they parted for him nervously.

Marged had settled Gwirion on her only comfortable stool, by the fire, and wrapped him in a brychan snatched from his bed. He was holding a cup of something steaming hot, but he was trembling so much he spilled a bit every time he brought it to his lips. The king slapped him chummily on the arm, and the cup crashed to the floor.

"Oh, dear." Noble laughed. "Someone get him another." Nobody moved, but the king didn't notice. "That was brilliant, wasn't it?" he chuckled. "I bet you can't top it."

"You should be whipped," Gwirion said. Noble laughed and the assembly tittered nervously. "I'm serious. You really should be whipped."

"Can't you swallow your own medicine?" Noble teased.

"What medicine? I've never pretended I was going to kill anyone!" Gwirion squealed. "That wasn't amusing. Embarrassment is amusing. Comeuppance is amusing. *Terror* is not amusing."

"You don't think that was inspired? I gave a consummate performance—nobody understood me, but *nobody* thought I was faking." He was too pleased with himself to stop smiling.

With a deliberate grunt of righteous annoyance, Marged picked up the spilled cup and signaled Dafydd to get a fresh one.

Gwirion continued to stare at the king. His relief at being alive was almost entirely negated by his fury. "Dignity can be trifled with. Not mortality."

Noble was abruptly sober. "You're absolutely right," he said pedantically. "Which is why I had to punish you for making thirty men believe they'd starve this winter."

"If you hadn't meddled, they'd only have thought that for a moment!" Gwirion snapped. "I stared my mortality in the face for the whole of a day and a night!"

"I was visiting upon you the collected fear those thirty felt both for themselves and for their families." He smiled, softening. "With a little interest, perhaps, just to raise the stakes and prove that I can beat you at your own game."

Gwirion grabbed hold of a hearthstone and pulled himself up. His green pallor deepened into a very unattractive purple and he hurled himself at the king, screaming. There were no teulu here, no guards, no one but the kitchen servants, and they were all far too flustered to do anything besides gasp and yelp and wring their hands. But Noble was stronger than Gwirion and managed to fend off his friend's enraged attack. He held Gwirion almost like a poppet at arm's length, and shook him hard to get his attention—but the king was more startled than angered. "You're a terribly sore loser," he complained.

Gwirion sprang to life again, trying in vain to scratch at the king's face. *"Ogre!"* he screeched. "You bastard son of a whore devil, I'll rip your liver out with my teeth, you mud-sucking leprous swine!"

The crowd drew back with eyes widening and mouths closing into nervous little Os. Noble was hard-pressed to keep Gwirion under control; he finally shoved him back down on the stool, pulled a dagger from his belt, and pressed it against Gwirion's throat. Gwirion grunted and then sat back, panting, staring murderously up. "Go ahead, do it," he snapped. "Or better yet, pierce me enough to do some serious harm and then tell us all it was just a prank."

"There's been no serious harm, you fool," Noble said with condescending affection. "You're fine."

"I am not fine! You scourged me yesterday for no good reason, you whoreson!"

The dagger remained where it was to keep Gwirion seated; otherwise, Noble acted as if this were a friendly chat, enjoying his performance and his audience. "That was to make it believable," he said reasonably. "If I didn't seem absolutely incensed, someone—you, even—might have known it was all in play. My God, do you know how difficult it was? I didn't tell *anyone*—except Efan before I sent him out to find the farmstead, so he would know to say it was deserted, but otherwise not a *single soul*, until this morning when I met with the butcher. I had an elaborate plan for a false hanging, but he warned me something might stick and you'd get hurt, so we agreed on the bucket of water instead. It wasn't gratuitous violence against you. I did what was necessary for the trick to work, that's all. Trust me, if you really had done something to the dogs, you'd have been in for a far worse fate. The flogging was a mild one, Lord knows you've weathered worse. You'll be fine."

"I just faced my own death," Gwirion said.

"So did my entire court," Noble said sharply, but then he grinned and gave Gwirion a comradely nudge with his elbow. "You're taking this in the wrong spirit," he insisted. "Honestly, Gwirion, you disappoint me. I think of you as a master craftsman. Can't you appreciate somebody else's comic craftiness?"

"It would have been comical," Gwirion said, "only if I'd died of fright when the water hit me. That would have been comical."

"No it wouldn't!" Noble said, shocked. "That would have been horrible."

"And comical," Gwirion insisted. "Then at least there'd be irony."

"You don't think it's ironic as it stands?" demanded Noble. Gwirion ignored him.

Little Dafydd carefully handed Gwirion another cup of the

brew. There was a commanding silence as he wrapped his hands around it and shivered from the pleasure of the heat.

Noble finally put up his blade. "I am disappointed," he said. "I really did it to entertain *you*."

Gwirion gave him a weary and withering glance. "I do a grand job of entertaining myself, sire—it's not something you're properly trained to do."

"The crowd liked it."

"How lovely for the crowd. How lovely for the chroniclers. You'll be remembered as the king who pretended he was going to kill his prankster—as a prank. Don't tell me you didn't think of that." He took a slow sip of the infusion. There was brandy in it, he noticed gratefully.

"It wasn't *just* as a prank, Gwirion. Besides." Noble smiled. "There are other things I hope to be remembered for."

"I meant things they can tell children about," Gwirion retorted. People laughed nervously. Noble looked at all of them, considering something.

"Leave us," he ordered.

He watched the servants scurry from the kitchen, and when he was alone with Gwirion, turned back to him. Gwirion would not look him in the face, just continued to sip his warm, inebriating medicine. There was an awkward silence.

"I did nothing wrong," Noble finally said. "But I am sorry this did not go over with you the way I thought it would." Gwirion said nothing. Noble cleared his throat. "And I am sorry you suffered such anguish, really I didn't think it would affect you so deeply. I was seeing myself in your situation—I would have responded differently, but that's how I was trained."

"Oh I see," Gwirion said with cold sarcasm. "I was supposed to see it through the eyes of a trained soldier. My mistake entirely, Your Majesty. I was seeing it through the eyes of a young boy who decided to throw himself to his king's assassins so as to distract them from murdering—who was it now? oh, yes—you, *Your Majesty*."

Noble was silent for a moment. "I propose a truce. Assure me you understand there must be limits to your mischief, and I will offer restitution for what I put you through."

"How? Let me get away with something that really is a hanging offense?"

"I've done that many times over the years, Gwirion," the king said patiently. "Perhaps something more immediate."

"Gold?" Gwirion asked at once. It was a long-lived joke between them that the king would provide Gwirion with anything but money. Gwirion, who could break into every coffer in the castle, didn't really mind.

"If that's what it would take. But anyone with means can give you gold. Ask me for something that only I might give you."

Gwirion nodded, and briefly glanced at his master. "That's tempting," he admitted. "I'll think about it."

"There isn't something that comes to mind right away?" Noble pressed, anxious for levity.

"I would ask you to get rid of the queen but she's the only one who was decent to me yesterday, even when I was a lout to her, so I suppose that maybe she can stay."

Noble grinned. "She is my wife, you know."

Gwirion gave him a questioning frown. "Meaning . . . ?"

The king winked.

"You're disgusting!" Gwirion cried. Then calming himself he immediately added, "You could at *least* offer me one of your mistresses." He made a face. "The queen. Yech. I said she could *stay*, I didn't say she was *attractive*. Jesu, Noble, but you're full of charm today, aren't you?"

SHE avoided him all day; he hardly noticed. He was enjoying being congratulated by everyone he could find for having staged such a clever prank. That night, he went again to her chamber, and in a rare instance of genuine naiveté, expected a warm response.

She refused him.

"You said you'd refuse me unless I spared his life. I did better than that—I never even meant to take it in the first place."

She calmly sidestepped away from his reach. "You are demented."

He pretended to pout. "If Gwirion had no problem with it, I don't see why you should."

"I heard about the row in the kitchen. Don't tell me Gwirion had no problem with it." She took the stool from the wall loom and placed it by her small dressing table, then began brushing her hair, that heavy mane that always disappointed him with its simple sleekness.

"You of all people ought to understand what I was demonstrating to him. I do not enjoy tormenting my best friend, but my duty is to protect my charges, and the situation required dramatic action."

That was Adèle's reasoning, she thought, and nearly said it aloud.

He relaxed onto her bed, watching her. "And I wanted to see what it felt like," he added, with a confiding smile.

"To kill someone for a thrill?"

"To be Gwirion."

She put the brush down and stared at him. "Which part of this conversation was I asleep for?"

"I wanted to spend a whole day getting attention for making mischief instead of order. It was wonderful. I wish I could do it more often. Gwirion has the best life of any man alive."

"Gwirion dresses in rags and isn't allowed to make eyes at a woman without your permission. And I can't believe those words are from the man who boasts of never abusing his authority to indulge his whims."

"It wasn't a whim, it was valuable research," Noble said with an impish smile. "To *continue* such a delightful practice might constitute a whim, but I shall selflessly refrain from doing so."

"Thank God for that much," she muttered under her breath. "You'd do less damage making Gwirion king for a day."

Noble sat up, beaming. "That's a wonderful idea!" He leapt playfully from the bed and wrapped his arms around her. She tried to push him aside with the brush, but he spun her around to face him, kissing her forehead. "You are my little muse!"

"Be quiet, you'll wake my women," she hissed.

"That's exactly the way to make it up to him. I'll make him king for a day."

"*What?*"

He grinned at her. "Just for a day. Tit for tat. He's earned it and I can certainly undo whatever mischief he creates in one day." He hooted with laughter, ignoring her attempts to shush him, and got to his feet. He hovered over her to rifle through the random trinkets on her dressing table. "And especially with your family coming. That uncle of yours, what's his name, Ralf I think, the one who—what is it?"

She was staring up at him, astonished. "My family? My family is coming?"

"Didn't I mention it?" he said with false offhandedness and began pacing the room, peering into chests in search of something. "Your brother and your insufferable uncles. Not our beloved Mortimer, of course—just the old coots from the other side. You haven't got a quill in here by any chance, have you? I really must write this down or I'll forget it. King for a day." He chuckled softly to himself.

"When are they coming?" she demanded. She had not seen Thomas since the wedding.

"I expect them tomorrow, probably in the late afternoon. I sent a writ of safe conduct three days ago."

Her eyes rounded. "When were you planning to tell me this?"

He shrugged. "It's a working visit, it doesn't involve you. Do you really have nothing in here to take dictation with?"

"It's my *family*."

"Meaning?"

"I want to see them! I can't believe I should even have to explain that to you."

"I didn't want to interrupt your sewing," he said mischievously, and leapt toward her to grab the brush away because she truly looked as if she was about to throw it at him. He added, placating, "Family to me is so ubiquitous it's absolutely meaningless." He handed her back the brush like a peace offering. "You're the only family I have that counts," he said quietly, kissing her neck.

"I'm touched," she said. "But I don't believe you—what about Gwirion?"

He made a dismissive gesture. "That's so much more than family." He leaned toward her to peck her forehead again, but she pushed him away with a look of annoyance.

She turned back to her mirror, one of the few extravagances in her room, and continued to brush her hair. The thick, straight strands were silky and glistened in the rush light. This was a ritual she relied on whenever there was tension between them in private. She loved her hair, and she knew that he didn't. It was a perfect way for her to soothe herself without providing him any satisfaction.

"Why is Thomas coming?" she asked.

Noble abandoned his search for a stylus and threw himself sprawling back onto the bed, affecting ennui. He was glad there was an English-style bed in both their chambers; it was a luxury easy to grow used to. "It's nothing of import to you. Just a few new problems with the border."

She put down the brush and swiveled on her stool to look at him warily. He was never so casual about these issues. "How can that not be important to me? That's my land, those are my people."

The king raised his head slightly and craned his neck to meet her gaze. "You're a little slow about this, aren't you?" he said. He gestured around the room. "This is your land now. I am your people."

"You can't expect me to stop caring about them just because I'm no longer there. I tended to those people for years. I'd like to know what the problems are."

"I don't want you worrying about it." He grinned. "Women who worry lose their looks."

"I'm going to worry more if you don't tell me. Or I'll ask Thomas tomorrow and believe his version of it."

Amused, he relaxed his head back against the bed pillows. "Such a stubborn little thing. I forget that sometimes." He rolled onto his side and propped up his head on a bent arm. "All right, then. Your dear innocent devoted brother has been plotting with Roger Mortimer to invade our kingdom."

She leapt to her feet, panicked. "That's a lie!" She rushed to the bed and grabbed his arm, trying to propel him up and off. "Get out! I won't speak to you if you say such rubbish."

He laughed and went limp, sprawling on his back again, ignoring her anger. "Be quiet, you'll wake your women," he teased. She was bending over him seeking the leverage to pry him into a sitting position, and their faces were close. He smiled at her, an expression that frustrated and perplexed her because it looked so genuine, so utterly without malice, even as he made this inflammatory accusation. "I just need to have a little chat with the boy about some rumors I've heard." He reached out and stroked her cheek. "Just rumors. I don't want to trouble you with it."

"Don't insult me by infantilizing me."

Impatience flickered in his blue eyes and he spoke more genuinely. "Actually, Isabel, I'm trying to protect you, not insult you."

"Protect me from what, the real world? You don't think that's insulting?"

He scrutinized her for a moment, then chuckled with affectionate sarcasm. "You really are enthrallingly artless. I'm trying to protect you from slander, dearest. Suspicion of all foreigners is high right now and you have not exactly distanced yourself from your Norman identity. Reminding any Welshman of your ties of love or blood to any Norman is not in your best interest." He looked at her more seriously. "My councilors aren't idiots, Isabel, they all have suspicions about what really happened when you lost the child. You're on very thin ice and it grows thinner every time you so much as glance out your solar window to the east. I'm manufacturing your indifference. Then if there is something nefarious going on with Thomas, you might be shielded from being associated with it."

One panic subsided in favor of another. "I'm sure there's a reasonable explanation for whatever you think is happening," she insisted.

"There is no reasonable explanation for my brother-in-law signing a sworn oath promising to fight beside Mortimer in all circumstances."

"His allegiance is with you. You're holding his sister hostage."

Noble, still slouching, laughed. "Is that what I'm doing? Let's agree not to share that perception with our devoted subjects. And for the record, I seem to recall some sort of marriage ceremony last May that we both entered into of our own free will."

She pulled away from him with frustrated disgust. "What kind of free will? What would have happened to me if I'd refused?"

He propped himself up on his elbow, amused again. "Are you telling me you didn't want to be a queen?"

Some string inside her pulled so tight it broke. "Queen of what?" she spat, forcing herself to whisper. "I might as well be some minor baron's wife in England—at least then I'd be a member of civilization and run my own household. I have no sovereignty here at all. You won't let me oversee anything but an unfinished abbey in the middle of the wilderness! I have no political power or even domestic power, and really, what else is there?"

"Pardon me if I'm putting this too bluntly but there are supposed to be children." He had sat up on the edge of the bed, his humor replaced with a harsh matter-of-factness. "And I can't beget children if you won't let me have you, so if you really want something important to do, take off your clothes and lie down."

She instinctively clasped her hands over her chest in a protective gesture. "You are a brute."

Standing and taking a step toward her, he gestured to the bed. "I'm serious, I won't be refused." He pulled her to him and uncrossed her arms, cupping a hand over one of her breasts. He felt the familiar flicker of disappointment that she wasn't more buxom. He would have to find a replacement for Enid soon, someone he could reliably turn to without any of these exhausting complications. He would ask Gwirion to start looking in the morning.

He saw her jaw was twitching, and softened despite himself. Releasing her breast, he put his arms around her gently, a platonic gesture of comfort, kissing the top of her head, rubbing his cheek against her satiny hair. "Never mind, then, I won't trouble you tonight. I only hope your brother doesn't trouble us tomorrow."

7

COLLABORATORS

All Souls' Day, 1198

GWIRION DIDN'T KNOW the purpose of their visit, some diplomatic thing about the borders, no doubt. It was always the borders. He wished there were a huge wall built around the kingdom, like the walls around the castle and the village. He thought about suggesting this to Noble, but the king was in a foul mood, as he usually was on All Souls' Day because the land-use fees came in and it created havoc that took half the court half the day to control. Each village and farm in the kingdom owed the crown a portion of its worth, and most of it came due today—and never in anything as simple as coin. While the usher efficiently directed traffic and the chaplain noted down what came from where, it took the marshal, the steward, the falconer, the huntsman, the butler, the cook, the baker, and the brewer most of the day to send the sheep, cattle, pigs, vessels of butter and honey, vats of mead and ale and wine, and cartloads of oats and barley flour in the right directions for care and storage. Gwirion's assistance, it was universally agreed, was the last thing anyone needed.

Which suited him. He was still recovering from both the trauma and the pain of his mock execution, and anyway he remembered the glaring, speechless Lord Walter and the other uncle, the one who had demanded his death. He wasn't eager to cross their paths, nor did he particularly want to see Thomas, the poor boy he had so humiliated the day of the wedding. Gwirion grudgingly conceded a growing respect for the queen's character and found it hard to believe that Thomas had sprung from the same loins.

After sleeping for most of the day, he was in the kitchen having his welts dressed by an exhausted Marged and evaluating, in the weak rays coming in from the setting sun, a half-dozen oblivious kitchen girls as potential royal playthings. Noble flattered himself by not possessing any woman who wasn't eager: He never took one by force and was even known to decline, without penalty, those who were simply lackluster. One of Marged's helpers, a new girl Gwirion didn't know, had promise. She was hardly Enid, but there were curves and curly hair, and no indication of prudery. Gwirion wondered if he should try her out himself so that he could deliver a more thorough report, but dismissed the idea with irritation, knowing he would never actually take such initiative no matter how extravagantly he fantasized about it.

He glanced through the window into the courtyard, and saw the group from the Marches heading toward the council chamber, their vague shadows stretching long and misshapen behind them in the sunset. He was surprised to see the queen accompanying them. Perhaps they were planning a family dinner.

THE king glared across the table at them. "I consider it an act of war."

Thomas and his uncles were white-faced. The queen stood behind her husband, out of the circle at the table. He had told her she might attend but not speak, so she gave her uncles pointed looks, silently begging them to make the obvious arguments that would protect her brother. Noble had posted as guards his most intimidating teulu—four of them in one small room—and armed them rather extravagantly with spears, swords, and daggers. Their presence alone made the visitors almost too cowed to speak.

"It's not an act of war," the queen said, quietly but firmly, feeling her pulse beating in her throat, and all the men in the room turned to stare at her.

"Madam," the king growled low, almost a whisper.

"You have no idea how complicated relationships are between the Marcher barons and the crown," she protested, speaking slowly because they were using French, and she wanted to make sure that Gwilym—the only senior councilor the king listened to—understood each word. "Uncle Roger needs reassurance about who his English allies would be against other Englishmen, not against you! Six weeks ago, when you suspected him of colluding with deBraose against you on the southeastern border, he was probably plotting somehow *against* deBraose in his own defense." The councilors all exchanged quick, impressed glances and she realized, with relief, that she had guessed right about that. She pressed on. "Everyone's afraid of him, but that means everyone wants to see him fall—"

"I'm not asking to see him fall," Noble said. "But I refuse to fall *to* him. That's the only issue here."

"No, it's not," she insisted. "Please try to see this in context—"

Noble leapt to his feet, turning on her, and she sank down onto a chest against the back wall. After a final harsh look, he turned again to Thomas. "If you swear allegiance to Mortimer, you must also swear it to me."

"You're married to my sister," Thomas said cautiously. "Isn't that enough?"

"You're a *blood relative* to Roger Mortimer. But *that* wasn't enough?"

Thomas fumbled for an argument as Father Idnerth quietly summarized a translation to Efan and the other officers who had no French. The penteulu looked expectantly at Thomas, as if waiting for him to say the wrong thing so he'd have an excuse to pounce upon him. "It has nothing to do with the Welsh borders," the boy finally stammered. "It's an internal English issue."

"Good," Noble said briskly. "Then swearing amity toward me should not cause any conflict of interest for you. You'll be doing that before you leave here."

Thomas blanched and glanced at his uncles, who suddenly seemed to be sitting on something extremely uncomfortable. Clearing his throat and trying to sound like an adult, which he wasn't quite, he answered, "I'd like to hear your terms and discuss them with Roger first."

"Very well," Noble agreed. "My terms are that I'm holding you hostage until you swear amity to me." He switched to Welsh. "Escort the little Saxon to the cellar."

Everyone reacted at once. Isabel clamped her hands over her mouth to keep from shrieking; her uncles stood up spluttering in unison; Thomas fell back in his chair and nearly swooned as Hywel, Efan, and Gwilym leapt out of the way, anticipating the two larger guards who made straight for the boy and had raised him up and bound his arms behind him before he registered what was happening. The two remaining guards shadowed the uncles, discouraging any physical protest.

HIS cry of distress was not loud, but it carried. Gwirion heard it even in his little closet, where he was dressing gingerly after Marged's ministrations, and its plaintiveness brought him back to the kitchen window. He saw, across the dusky yard, two of the biggest teulu lugging a teenage boy out of the wood-frame council room.

"Oh my!" he chortled. "Marged, look at this! You too," he said specifically to the new girl. This turn of events suggested she would almost certainly be invited to Noble's room later that night. "Her

Royal Majesty's esteemed brother is being trundled around like a sack of barley!"

The two women came to the window, everyone else crowding in behind them craning to see. They watched in dumbfounded silence as Thomas, hands bound, was led roughly through the courtyard toward the porthouse by the barbican. His two uncles came chasing after him, but they were coaxed toward the guest quarters by their guards with the wordless efficiency of sheep dogs.

"Where are they taking him?" asked the girl.

Gwirion kept staring out into the yard. "The barbican. I'd say they're either throwing him out entirely or putting him in the dungeon."

"The dungeon!" she gasped.

Marged made a face. "It's not a dungeon, it's just a little holding pen. Don't frighten the lass."

Gwirion kept his gaze focused out the window, then finally turned away and moved through the kitchen, heading for the side entrance by the well. "This is simply too intriguing," he announced loudly.

"Hey, boyo!" Marged snapped, more maternal than chastising. "Stay out of it. You're not to be seen today, remember?"

"I won't be," he promised, and was gone.

T HIS is a classic example of what we refer to as *irony*," Gwirion said to the youth, who was too distressed to register a word.

"What," he answered stupidly, as Gwirion settled down on a moldy pile of straw outside the cell.

"Irony," Gwirion repeated. He adjusted the rush light to give Thomas's new quarters better illumination. "The last time we saw each other was at this very spot, but we were on opposite sides of the bars."

Thomas registered at last his visitor's identity. He took in a dis-

gusted breath and made a face almost identical to one the queen often made—an expression which, for reasons he pretended not to
fathom, Gwirion frequently inspired. "You were supposed to be
hanged."

"You were supposed to stop getting yourself locked into dark
rooms. What happened?"

"I will not discuss it with you."

"And what's wrong with me?"

Thomas gave him the look of an emperor disdaining the suppli-
cations of a beggar. "You are beneath contempt," he said slowly.
"You're a nonentity."

"I'm the king's favorite nonentity," Gwirion warned him. "I
don't know what you did to get in here, but unless Noble's attempting another stupid prank, you're in serious trouble right now, and it's
only myself who can make him reconsider whatever he plans to do
to you."

Thomas shook his head at him. "My sister's interceding for me.
She'll take care of it."

Gwirion laughed. "You poor idiot, do you really believe that?
Your sister has no power over the king at all, except perhaps at the ex-
act moment of sexual climax, but even that's debatable—especially
tonight when I know for a fact he's riding a pretty kitchen girl. No, no,
lad, if you want help, you'd best tell Uncle Gwirion all about it."
Thomas's flustered expression was irresistible and Gwirion felt compelled to make it worse. "What's the matter, laddie, does it embarrass
you to think of your sister copulating? That's the only reason we
brought her here, you know that, don't you? So that our king could
plunge his great Welsh spear into her moist, submissive little Norman
crevice."

Thomas was instantly crimson. "How dare you talk that way!"
he shouted, smashing the heel of his hand against the iron door.
"About my sister *or* your queen!"

Gwirion gestured calmly to their surroundings. "Do you see
where you are? Do you see where I am? If I want to help you, I'll talk
however I please."

Thomas glowered at him. "Why do you want to help me? You hate me and you hate my sister."

"Aha! And therefore, nobody would expect me to help you. Anything involving irony—there's that word again—that's my specialty." He winced as he shifted to lessen the pull of his tunic across his tender back, and added more seriously, "Plus the king is in need of severe comeuppance right now. I'm not wont to place a Mortimer's well-being above my monarch's but I'm perfectly willing to use you as a tool for my own retribution. Tell me what the problem is and perhaps we can assist each other."

"You'll want gold, I suppose," the boy sniffed, trying to maintain a disdainful and contemptuous facade as his insides wobbled.

"No, I don't want gold," Gwirion said impatiently, lying. "I just want gossip. Tell me what happened."

LONG after night had fallen outside, bringing sudden clouds and rain, Thomas finally finished explaining the situation to Gwirion. He had been surprised by the Welshman's quick understanding of subtle details, but frustrated by his obsession with going off on tangents, punning, or caricaturing the different people mentioned, most of whom he'd probably never met. He went on about Roger Mortimer for nearly twenty minutes with more gleeful venom than Thomas thought was deserved. What should have taken a few minutes of simple description took more than an hour, and half the time Thomas had no idea what Gwirion was talking about. Although Gwirion was clearly entertaining himself, the boy could see that he was also trying in some odd way to entertain him, and he grudgingly appreciated it. That was probably the fellow's only stock-in-trade, which explained his nearly frantic need to turn everything into the butt of a joke, usually sexual or worse. He wondered how his sister could bear the fellow's presence, and remembered with sorrow her letters lamenting that she couldn't.

"Well, knowing the king and knowing the history, I understand why he reacted as he did," Gwirion said. "I don't think what you did was intelligent, but I wouldn't call it an act of war."

"Will you help me?"

Gwirion gave this question much more thought than Thomas felt it required. He was finally about to speak when he was distracted by approaching footsteps, and Einion came toward them, someone in a damp cape following.

"The inmate has a visitor," he informed them tersely.

"We're busy," Gwirion informed him just as tersely in response and began to turn back toward the boy, when the figure cloaked in purple surprised him by stepping forward and revealing itself as the queen. "Milady," he said, sheepish at being found here. He chuckled awkwardly. "We're spending far too much time down here together. People will be saying things."

She spoke without shrillness or pleading. "If you have any human decency, Gwirion, you will not taunt my brother now."

He was annoyed for a moment, but realized there was no reason for her to think he was here for any reason but ill. "I'm actually here to perform an All Souls' mass for him," he said. "I know what pious Christians you Mortimers are and I didn't want to deprive him of an opportunity for monotony. You're welcome to join us, though." He pressed his palms together before his face and chanted in Gregorian tones: *"O nominae patrie. Nobilitae es jackassium. Gwirionius assistium Thomassium."* She gave him a strange look and he lowered his hands. "Milady, he's told me of the situation and I'm trying to find a way to help him."

She blinked. "You are?" she asked, and when he nodded, demanded suspiciously, *"Why?"*

"Repaying the king's abuse of me by aiding a Mortimer—isn't that a *perfect* irony?" he asked blithely, and returned his attention to the boy. "Answer a few questions so I have the whole of it. Why can't you do as Noble wants? Why don't you simply swear an oath of amity?"

"Uncle Roger would react to that the way Maelgwyn is reacting to this—he'd see it as double-dealing. I just want to explain the sit-uation here to Roger before I make such a commitment to Mael-gwyn."

"So then, why couldn't you have explained Mortimer's situation to Noble—Maelgwyn—before you made such a commitment to Mortimer?"

Thomas shrugged uncomfortably. "He's a long day's ride away in another country. Uncle Roger is breathing down the back of my neck. And he is my overlord after all. Your king isn't."

Gwirion took a new tack. "Well then, on the topic of kings, what does *your* king think of his barons plotting to attack each other?"

"*Our* king," Thomas corrected, then hesitated before conceding "... is not in England."

Gwirion gave him a sardonic look. "Is Richard off fighting infi-dels again? Never you mind, he'll get himself killed off any day now and then we'll all have brother John to play with, and—"

"And until that happens," the queen cut in, to preempt Gwirion's tangent, "the Marcher lords consider themselves accountable to no one. They're all but sovereigns unto themselves, and Roger sees him-self as Noble's peer, perhaps even his superior."

Gwirion shook his head. "Noble will never concede that," he said.

"That's not *my* problem," Thomas said desperately.

"Gwirion is saying that it has *become* your problem," the queen said. "And I agree." Gwirion did a double take and then pretended to gape at her. She saw the look out of the corner of her eye and smiled wryly. "That's right, Gwirion, we're in complete accord on some-thing. And the lion shall lie down with the lamb."

"What, the Second Coming? You're rushing things a bit, aren't you? We haven't even come once yet." He leaned toward her with a lecherous expression in his impish dark eyes. "Would you like to be the lion or the lamb?"

She made a disgusted face but then, despite herself, shook her head with grudging amusement.

THE next morning the castle was thrown into chaos with the news that the prisoner had escaped. It had been raining on and off for hours, and the lack of footprints in the mud around the barbican defeated even the marshal. Mass was canceled, a hue and cry was raised, and search parties were sent out through the downpour to comb the towers, the village, and the hillsides, with their dying bracken groves so thick a person could easily disappear in them. Messengers staggered through the mud to the nearest landowners to warn them against harboring the fugitive, and a search party in oiled cloaks was sent to the eastern border. The king, his council, the queen, and her uncles convened in the chilly wood-frame council chamber for what quickly devolved into a rabid, bilingual frenzy. Noble accused the uncles of spiriting Thomas away; the uncles accused Noble of murdering him. Efan threatened Ralf theatrically for making such an accusation; Gwilym threatened Efan subtly for being so theatrical. Einion the porter was called in to give his brief, unhelpful report for the seventh time in twenty minutes: He believed he had been drugged, had fallen into a deep sleep, and when he'd awakened, not only the prisoner but the prison key was missing. Outside help was presumed. Noble and Ralf growled at each other for nearly an hour, arguing loudly and angrily over who would have custody of the boy when he was found. The council was endlessly breaking down into side arguments, tangential conversations, brainstorming sessions, and name-callings, when the only person who could make things worse entered the room.

"Excuse me," Gwirion stammered, thrown by the disorder. He gave his soggy tartan mantle to the guard, shaking the rain from his hair. The only one who noticed him was Ralf. It took him a moment to place Gwirion's face, but it was clear the moment he did.

"You!" he snapped, turning all his attention to the smaller man. Gwirion recognized his rodent-bright eyes and reflexively took a step backward. Enraged, Ralf spun back around toward the king and managed to cry out above the din: "You were supposed to hang this thing!"

"I never said that," Noble called back.

"Never mind that now!" Lord Walter snapped at his brother in French.

"Excuse me——" Gwirion tried again, but got no further because Ralf was brandishing a knife. "Christ!" Gwirion scrambled frantically to the other side of the room, Ralf behind him knocking into things and people in his rush to catch him.

"Sit down!" Noble shouted at Ralf. "Put that away! Nobody draws steel in this room, ever, under any circumstances!"

Half the men around the table gasped as Noble reached out with his unprotected hand and grabbed the bare knife blade, staring Ralf down with his mesmerizing glare. Ralf froze and the room quieted at once. "Put the knife away," Noble said slowly to the older man through gritted teeth, and released his grip. Fuming, Ralf obeyed, sending killing glances at Gwirion.

"Excuse me——" Gwirion started again.

"Not now, Gwirion, this is a crisis," Noble said impatiently, and pickup conversations returned the room to auditory chaos. "I'll send for you later. Your presence will not help right now."

Looking uncharacteristically crestfallen, Gwirion began a slow cross through the room, back toward the door, absently fingering his cowlick. Without looking at anyone, he collected the gazes of the officers as he passed by them, his very docility making them suspicious. He saw the queen from across the room and she gave him a troubled, questioning look. She knew no details of his plan to help Thomas, and had no idea if this was a part of it or an unexpected complication. Gwirion did not try to communicate with her, just continued trudging past the bank of bolted windows toward the door. He retrieved his sodden wrap from the young teulu guard and began to thank him. And then he did not stop, even to draw breath. "I do so appreciate you holding this for me," he said, speaking not loudly but very rapidly. "Especially as it's wet and malodorously aromatic, and I hope you don't think that I equate you with a cloak peg, because I don't. To tell you the truth, I think your job is very difficult and I hope these gentlemen are treating you well, or at least better than they're treating me—well, you saw how the English gentleman was treating me—and forgive me for asking, but I can't help wondering, is it hard for you to just stand here like this and keep a straight face while they're all rattling on to each other?" The guard's mouth twitched as more of the men turned toward them and the room gradually stilled. "Or is it harder for you to keep a straight face while *I'm* rattling on to *you*? Do you ever have a chance to rattle on to somebody? I suppose it must be very difficult to hear the rot that goes on in council all day and not be able to—" When he sensed that he had everyone's attention, Gwirion cut himself off abruptly and looked at the staring faces as if just noticing them. "Pardon, did I interrupt something important?"

"I told you to leave," the king warned him in a baritone growl.

In the jot of time between the end of the royal dismissal and the recommencement of the debates, Gwirion tossed something directly onto the middle of the table. It landed with a soft clack on the layers of maps and castle diagrams.

It was the prison key.

After a startled moment, an entire room of heads—bearded, mustached, clean shaven, bald, wimpled—snapped toward Gwirion, who shrugged and turned to leave. But the cacophony of shouts to the guard, although none clear enough to understand, made him slam the door closed. Noble stood up and glowered over the table at Gwirion.

"What have you done with him?"

"I'm not prepared to share that information quite yet," Gwirion said placidly.

"Fiend!" Ralf hissed. "Whip him!" He signaled to one of his own attendants and the man took a step toward Gwirion, who ducked away from him.

"No," the king said, holding up a hand. "No whipping. Gwirion, tell me where he is."

"Whip the bastard! He's not going to cooperate!" the Norman insisted. "His impertinence alone is grounds for the block!"

"They tried that just the other day," Gwirion informed him confidentially. "It didn't take."

"Gwirion, I'm serious," the king said in a threatening voice. "Where is he? I'm sure you've rigged up some very clever gag out of this whole scenario, but you can't go through with it. Do you understand? This is bigger than you. It's bigger than *me*." He gave Gwirion a look that made it clear he was absolutely serious, with no hidden wink or grin or wagging eyebrow. Gwirion was surprised by how furious he looked—but also how frightened. It was satisfying, and he toyed with the idea of keeping His Majesty in this state for as long as possible in revenge for the mock execution, but decided there were better things to do with his morning. And in the end, this was about Roger Mortimer, who would always be their shared enemy. So he met Noble's gaze and walked toward him around the conference table. When he reached the king, he continued to look at him steadily, then nimbly leapt onto the table and took a large step into the center of it, scuffing the maps and diagrams with mud.

Noble killed the growing murmurs around them with a look, and gestured up at Gwirion. "All right, go ahead," he said in annoyance. "Give us your performance."

"The performance is for after supper. This is *serious*, Noble— have you no sense of propriety?"

"Get on with it!" Noble snarled as Ralf muttered in audible French to his brother, "I can't believe he allows himself to be subjected to such humiliation."

Taking his time, Gwirion swept the maps together into a neat pile and handed them politely to Father Idnerth. Then he sat cross-legged, facing the king, suddenly all business. Those at the table he had his back to shifted slowly toward the king's chair, unable to resist seeing the encounter unencumbered—except for the uncles, who remained tense in their seats. The queen hovered behind her husband, watching anxiously.

"I'll produce Thomas on one condition."

"You do not presume to give the king conditions!" Ralf said from behind him, but Noble waved him to be quiet and said, listening, "Go on." The Normans exchanged disbelieving glances.

"The boy realizes he was in error, and he's sorry for it. He has a new proposal for resolving the situation fairly, which I shall now share with you. You will accept it without reservation and take the first step toward putting it into action. And then I will tell you where Thomas is."

"Aren't you still in welts from the lashing the other day?" Noble demanded with quiet fury. "Do you really want another one already?"

"As you said, this is bigger than me," Gwirion answered coyly, and batted his eyelashes at the king. "My pain isn't a deciding factor."

"Maybe your life will be," Noble said dangerously. He gestured Efan toward Gwirion.

"You've already tried that threat, I'm not falling for it again," Gwirion said, laughing, unfazed by the large gloved hand closing on his shoulder.

"Gentlemen, if you will just step across the yard with me," the king announced in an annoyed voice, ignoring Gwirion's laughter. "We'll need a water tub. This should not take long."

Reassembled grumpily outside the kitchen with their mantles wrapped to protect their heads from pelting rain, they clustered around a wooden tub filled with well water that Marged's grandson had been summoned to fill. Noble pointed to the tub.

"Gwirion, your head is going in there unless you tell me where Thomas is at once."

Gwirion, the only one with no wrap, frowned at the water tub. "I could use a hair wash, is there any soap?"

Glaring at him, Noble signaled Efan. Gwirion made a pained face as the huge young man shoved him down onto his knees in the mud, then grabbed a hank of his dark hair and pushed his head completely underwater.

For a long moment, Gwirion neither breathed nor struggled,

holding his breath as they all watched. Then bubbles disturbed the surface, slowly. Finally, when it felt as if minutes had passed, the bubbles stopped and Gwirion's body jerked. The penteulu looked at Noble, who nodded, and Gwirion's head was hauled out of the tub. He was gasping for breath, painfully, but his black eyes sparkled.

"There're some trout in there that are simply enormous!" he announced.

"Where's the boy?" Noble demanded.

"I can't tell you until you've heard his new terms," Gwirion said, and took a deep breath, anticipating another submersion.

Three more times they dunked him, each time for longer. On the fourth round he began to convulse in earnest, in true distress for the first time, his hands grabbing at Efan's forearms in desperation until Gwilym grimaced and Isabel couldn't watch any longer. "Don't kill him!" she begged reflexively in French. "We'll never find Thomas!"

"Please, sire," Walter seconded. Noble immediately gestured to Efan, who was grinning; he hauled Gwirion's head out of the tub and this time pushed him to the ground. Gwirion lay purple-faced in the mud on his side, retching, gasping for breath and getting rained on. Nobody moved to help him. He appealed for no sympathy. They stood around him, their breaths congealing in little puffs, awkwardly waiting for him to get his own breath back, and when he could finally croak out a sound, he pulled himself gingerly to his feet. "Cold," he managed, hoarse and shivering. "Inside."

Noble, avoiding his eye, nodded. The group squelched back across the yard to the council room, except for Gwirion, who was temporarily dismissed to the kitchen to recover. He staggered to the door by the well, stumbling, shaking his head and trying uselessly to wipe his face dry and wring the water from his sodden, muddy clothes. Marged had watched the whole episode from the kitchen in extreme indignation, and already had a blanket and hot brew waiting for him by the stool near the fire.

He sipped slowly and mused that he was back where he'd been two days ago, only now in addition to everything else, he was freezing wet. *I seem to be on a downward spiral,* he thought, and opened his mouth to share this insight with Marged, but it hurt too much to talk. Then he noticed that Marged had risen to her feet with a nervous huff and was staring over his shoulder.

His cold nose caught the hinted scent of rosewater. "What's the rest of your scheme?" said the queen's voice in his ear.

"I thought *merci* was the word for gratitude," he croaked without looking back at her, and rubbed his throat.

She blushed. "Forgive me—and thank you. Thank you a thousand times. But what happens now?"

"Now I tell them Thomas's conditions."

"Which are what?"

He made a pained face, not wanting to speak. "I'm not much good at political strategy, Your Majesty, I rely on impulse and intuition. I'll just say whatever comes into my head at the moment."

"You can't do that now," she countered. "Not with such a delicate matter."

He looked up crossly at her. "Do you have a better idea?" he whispered mockingly.

"I do, actually," she said, imitating his tone. "Would you like to hear it?"

"Not really," muttered Gwirion, and turned back to the fire.

A few minutes later, he was back in the council room, sitting on a chest against the wall. The queen had managed to slip in separately, unnoticed.

"Thomas proposes a neutrality statement," Gwirion said in a voice so husky it was hardly a voice. "He'll swear allegiance to Mortimer in matters of English politics, and to you in matters of Welsh ones." He winced and rubbed his throat, struggling with a deep breath that was as loud as speech. "But he'll also swear an oath to both of you saying that he will not raise a hand against *any* family, neither uncle nor brother-in-law. And most important, he will not allow his land to be used as a staging point for either of you to attack the other. Since his estate is really just a long strip by Llanandras, that creates a safety buffer for you—it gives Mortimer almost no place to launch an easy attack."

Noble considered the proposal as Ralf translated for his brother. "That will never work," the king said at last.

"Why not?" Gwirion challenged, trying to suppress a painful cough.

"Mortimer will never accept it."

"Sorry, if you want the boy back, you have to agree to at least trying it. Draft a proposal to Mortimer and send it off immediately."

Ralf stood up to protest but his brother pulled him back down. "It's this or Thomas as Maelgwyn's hostage," Walter murmured in French. "If he is so deranged he'll let his parasite dictate policy, close your mouth and be grateful."

Noble crossed his arms, then leaned back in his chair and crossed his legs at the ankles, scrutinizing his friend. "It's rather ironic this is happening now, you know," he said, suddenly conversational. "Just two nights ago I was playing with the idea of making you king for a day, but I postponed it because I couldn't have you at the helm while we were navigating the hazardous waters of Marcher politics."

"Yes, another lovely example of irony," Gwirion said, smiling, but his voice and his breathing were still husky and strained. "I was explaining irony to Thomas only last night. I'm not sure he quite understood."

His eyes still on Gwirion, the king called for paper from the chapel stores, which brought protestations from some of his own men. The two uncles were caught between appalled incredulity that he was obeying Gwirion's orders and relief that Thomas would be out of harm.

Gwirion dictated the proposal to Father Idnerth, in the form of a letter from Thomas to both Noble and Roger Mortimer. The queen penned her brother's name, and Noble signed to indicate he endorsed it. While the ink was drying, Noble sat back and asked, "Just out of curiosity, who devised that proposal?"

"Thomas," Gwirion replied promptly.

"Not Thomas," the king said. "I don't know him well but a boy sitting traumatized in a prison cell is not coming up with a new model for border politics."

"He may have had a little help," Gwirion said noncommittally, with another painful swallow. The king grinned.

He turned to the rest of the council and announced, "We've just implemented policy invented by a fool." He seemed tickled by this, almost more so because nobody else in the room found it amusing.

Gwirion leaned forward, gathering the woolen blanket about his shoulders. "Actually, sire, it's more subversive even than that," he said hoarsely, in a tone that sounded confidential but was loud enough to be heard by all. Because it sounded confidential, it caught everybody's attention immediately. "You've just implemented policy that was invented by a woman."

"A woman?"

"Your wife, sire," Gwirion answered, nodding toward the queen. "It's a *French* woman, no less." Before she could catch his gaze, he looked away and stood up. "We'll give your runner a three-hour start, then I'll bring you the boy." He met Noble's eye one final time and Isabel saw an entire unspoken conversation flash between them; she half believed Noble approved of what Gwirion had done. Gwirion headed out of the room, drawing the brychan over his head against the rain. Noble saw the Normans' attendants make to follow him, but he called out to them sharply and they did not persist. Then he stood and turned to stare at his wife.

"When did the two of you begin collaborating?" he asked, looking amused despite himself.

She laughed dismissively. "I'd hardly call it a collaboration," she assured him.

*T*HIS is why women don't make policy," Noble spat. It was two weeks later and an exhausted, filthy messenger, shadowed by the hulking young Efan, had burst into the hall, interrupting the breakfast meal to hand a rolled and sealed parchment to the king.

"What is it?" Isabel asked, laying down her oatcake and leaning toward him for a better look. Gwirion had finished eating and was already huddled near the fire, where he was restringing the gilded harp. The king tossed down the parchment with an annoyed gesture. Concerned, the queen grabbed it up from the table before Goronwy could get his stubby hands on it, and looked at the broken seal. She recognized it: her uncle Walter's. Her eyes glanced over the words and she paled.

"What's happened?" demanded the judge.

"Roger Mortimer responded to the neutrality proposal by taking Thomas hostage," Noble announced, grim. "His own nephew."

"We have to raise a ransom," the queen said in a faint voice, struggling to keep her composure. Noble stood up and turned on her, his grimness fast evolving into anger.

"Did you read what Walter wrote?" he snapped. "Mortimer doesn't want a ransom. He wants Thomas's lands around Lingen. So that he can launch an attack on my eastern border. That's all he ever wanted—it's what he was after when he asked Thomas for a loyalty pledge. It had nothing to do with deBraose or any other English baron. In fact for all I know, Thomas is not even hostage, this is all an involved pretense to make him appear innocent so they can use him as a pawn against me in the future."

"He's too guileless for that, Noble, you would have seen right through it when he was here," she countered impatiently.

"I'll have to back that," Gwirion said from the fireside. He lay the harp aside, realizing the situation was serious enough to require even his fickle attention. "The boy is hardly the model of fearless integrity but he's too simple to pull off a double cross."

Noble grimaced but made a dismissive gesture that they both knew meant Thomas was, for now, not under suspicion.

"What is going on, sire?" Gwilym asked calmly, striding in toward the high table from the kitchen.

"Our darling Mortimer is raising a hostile force near your queen's birthplace," Noble said with irritation.

"That doesn't make any sense," she insisted. "He endorsed our marriage to stabilize the border."

"No, madam, he endorsed it to give me a false sense of security!" Noble thundered, slamming his hand on the table so hard the platters rattled. Isabel started. Even Gwirion sat up straighter; he had never seen the king so publicly explosive. "Without this marriage I'd have no responsibility to that idiot brother of yours locked up in Wigmore and I'd have an entire company of defensive troops on the other side of Offa's Dyke *right now*. Clearly all Mortimer ever had in mind for this fruitless union was taking over Maelienydd." He turned on her in wrath. "And so help you, if ever I have reason to suspect you knew——"

"Noble!" she gasped, horrified.

Ignoring her, he swung around to face the steward. "Summon the council." Goronwy and the other officers still at breakfast rose at once; Gwilym did a head count, nodded, and walked out quickly, taking a cloak from a servant by the door. The other councilors followed him into the courtyard, scurrying to the council chamber.

"I'm sitting in," the queen announced, standing and gesturing to Generys for her mantle. Noble shot her a derisive look.

"You most certainly are not," he informed her.

"It's my brother!"

"It's my *kingdom*," he hissed through clenched teeth.

"It's my kingdom too," she protested.

He stared at her. "Is it?" he demanded in a menacing voice.

"Noble, don't be ridiculous," Gwirion said, his focus back on his harp, perfectly aware he was being inexcusably rude. "If she were that duplicitous, don't you think she and I would have taken to each other at once? She's never fit in because she's too artless to

be capable of anything as charmingly twisted as what you're suggesting."

Within minutes the council room was filled with the high officers of the court: bard, steward, penteulu, judge, marshal, chaplain,
physician, usher, chamberlain, falconer, and huntsman. They met for
less than half an hour, in a rare show of complete accord about what
had to happen. Troops would go at once to the eastern border. Runners would be sent around the kingdom to convene a war council beginning in two weeks, on the first of December. A missive of official
rebuke was drafted and sent to Roger Mortimer, demanding that he
release Thomas, remove his men from Thomas's land, and cease any
further preparation for hostile acts. Prince John would be petitioned
too, although he hardly had the power to do much more than chastise, and Mortimer was already known to hold the royal family in
contempt. Finally—and this was the sole source of brief debate—a
message was sent to Llewelyn ap Iorwerth in Gwynedd, alerting him
to Mortimer's preparations and apparent intentions. Llewelyn would
have no more patience with an Anglo-Norman occupation force
than Noble would. He was invited to attend the war council or send
a representative, although they doubted that he would condescend to
participate in something he was not leading.

Gwilym immediately settled into urgent efficiency, organizing
their limited resources to host such a congress. The king, regretting
his outburst against his wife, invited her to help him summon and
greet the barons. Marged was informed with minor apology by
Hafaidd of the meeting's outcome, and almost threw a fit at the
prospect of feeding the hordes who would come just as winter and its
privations descended on the castle.

8

A Suitor at Council

Early December, 1198

 HERE WERE THOSE at Cymaron who thought things might actually be better with Norman overlordship. Nobody was stupid enough to say it, but the king knew who they were; he knew as well that they would not go against the collective will of his barons, which he could usually manipulate. Some of the barons would also be inclined toward capitulation, but he knew how to handle them. He was almost looking forward to it now that they were all here.

Gwirion's work would be simple that night, just a few tunes after Hywel's raspy recitation of "The Sovereignty of Britain." But he was fascinated by all the faces, both the familiar—Anarawd, the king's cousin, for example—and the unknown. He scrutinized the guests as they laid their weapons in a pile by the door and made their way to the dais to receive a formal welcome from their king and queen. Of the forty or so men who attended the war council, more than a dozen had brought their mates, and of them, seven or eight had young children underfoot, offspring not yet old enough to have gone to wardens and foster parents for their upbringing. These men were mostly from the eastern border near Mortimer, and they had chosen the inconvenience of traveling with children over the anxiety of leaving them behind. Gwirion adored the children, and even had a sentimental flash that first chilly afternoon of wanting the queen to produce offspring so he could play with them. Ashamed of himself for falling prey to such sentimentality, he banished the image from his mind. She would probably never let him near her children anyway.

MORE than one man who was meeting his queen for the first time looked into her bewimpled face with surprise, and commented that he hadn't heard her beauty praised as it deserved. At first she dismissed this as flattery, knowing the Celtic aesthetic differed from the continental, but when enough of them had said it, always after a brief, surprised stare, she beamed, beginning to believe the compliment. Noble enjoyed the glow in her tawny eyes. He still did not consider her beautiful—handsome, yes, perhaps pretty with her petite, efficient features and high forehead, but not beautiful—and he found it as surprising and flattering as she did that so many men were struck by her appearance. It made him want to gloat. They were an elegant couple tonight, matching in their heavier ceremonial crowns and long tunics of brocaded crimson silk edged with gold, she with a surcoat of velvet from England that all the women eyed covetously.

A dark-haired young man, her age or likely younger, knelt at their feet now, and kissed first the king's hand, then the queen's, before even lifting his eyes. He wore a green woolen tunic onto which had been sewn a yellow eagle *displayed*, and he was handsome, his features sharp and aristocratic. He too did an appreciative double take when he first saw her, but unlike the ones who had come before him, he seemed struck dumb. He took in a breath and finally turned to the king with a dazzled, guileless smile. "Your wife her ladyship is the most beautiful woman I've ever seen."

"I thank you," Noble said. "You may tell her so directly."

He looked at the queen and then quickly back at the king. "I don't think I can," he said with complete sincerity.

Noble chuckled. "Conquer your shyness, lad." He kept an eye on his wife, seeking her agreement as he added, "Sit by us tonight and share our cup if you like. See if you can bring yourself to talk to her."

The young man's face lit up. He nodded his thanks, and began to descend from the dais. "What is your name, sir?" the queen asked, holding him back with her words.

For a moment, he looked as though he really didn't know the answer. Then he beamed reassuringly and announced, "Owain ap Ithel, milady."

"Owain is a good name. We say John in England."

"You may call me John if you like, milady. I would turn Norman for your sake."

Noble almost snapped at this—but seeing that the young man was obviously too flustered to realize what he'd said, he smiled broadly instead and clapped him on the arm. "Good lad, not only talking to her but flirting! We'll make a man of you yet."

Owain nodded and excused himself. While waiting for the next man to cross up to them, Noble glanced at the queen and quietly baahed like a sheep.

"That's not nice," she scolded, laughing, both of them grateful for the moment of levity between them.

AFTER the official greetings, people dispersed to dress for supper. It was crowded, and most of them would be sleeping in the hall for the duration, pushing the servants to the lower end near the door. There were curtains hung for nighttime privacy along the outer edges of the room, and these were pulled closed now to change behind, while every pitcher and basin in the castle was collected for people to wash the road mud off their hands and boots. The custom of washing guests' feet was suspended with the understanding that there were far too many feet and not enough washers.

The king had chosen two parties to honor with the only separate apartments the castle offered visitors. One was Anarawd his cousin, the man who was still for now his heir. Although Noble found him hateful he felt obliged to honor the kinship, so Anarawd's entourage would stay in the king's snug, unadorned audience room directly off the hall. Huw ap Maredudd was being coddled for quite another reason: His large manors high on the hills near Llanidloes, although poor in soil like much of northwestern Maelienydd and therefore nearly worthless in themselves, were full of mountain passes and put him closest to Llewelyn's siren call, which he was openly intrigued by. He was one of the very few wealthy landowners with no traceable lineage to the king, and Noble needed to keep him pleased with his current sovereign; he would be staying with his wife above the steward and usher, in the quietest, most private room in the castle.

But Gwirion noticed the portly, middle-aged Huw standing now in the upper half of the hall near the fire, in personal audience with Noble as people unpacked and settled in around them in the din. The unobtrusive chandler had already lit the hall—it was dark hours before supper now, and a room with more people in it seemed to require more light. As Huw and Noble spoke, there spread across the king's face an understated slyness that Gwirion historically associated with secret assignations. It surprised him: Noble nearly always used Gwirion as his interlocutor for intimate arrangements. He supposed Noble was requesting to detain some attendant lady in Huw's retinue, but he idly wondered why the king was doing it himself instead of sending him.

Before he had a chance to glean the answer, he was conscripted into duty. The children, ten in all, were scampering through the hall, darting around the screens wreaking havoc and spreading mud, glee-

ful the journey and then the tiresome formalities were over, and a harried Hafaidd gave Gwirion the job of keeping them from mischief.

He decided to settle them by the hearth and explain to them
what their parents were too busy or nervous to explain: why they were
making this visit, and what the fuss was all about. He had finished
his main narrative and was answering their questions when he noticed the young dark-haired baron who had been so inarticulate with
the queen on the dais, his face washed and his travel outfit exchanged
for a long black ceremonial tunic. He approached Gwirion and the
children, and stood watching him with quiet interest.

Not noticing Owain, Isabel caught Gwirion and the children in
her peripheral vision, and immediately handed the brychans she was
carrying to a passing hall servant. "Take these to the men in that corner," she ordered, and headed briskly back toward the hearth. She
didn't trust Gwirion with youngsters, so she was surprised and impressed to hear him engaging the children in an apparently sensible
conversation, and paused out of sight to listen.

"But why do they want our land?" asked a six-year-old boy.

"I don't really know, to be honest." His face brightened. "Let's
ask the queen the next time we see her—she understands all about
the English, she's very fond of them. Those English seem to delight in
taking other people's things." She bristled in her hiding place, but decided not to intervene. She almost hoped he'd say something worse
and get himself thrown out of hall for the week.

"But why so much?" another child demanded.

Gwirion looked at their trusting, upturned faces and wondered
if he should give in to a terrible impulse. Probably not, he thought.

Oh, what the hell, he thought.

"It has to do with genitals," he said gravely. "Do you know that
word?" They didn't. Around the corner, listening, she assumed she
had heard wrong, and tried to figure out what he'd actually said.

"When boys piss—you know how that's different from girls
pissing, of course."

They all did, from the family livestock if nothing else. "You
mean a penis," said a little girl, gravely.

"Exactly." Gwirion smiled. "Some men have very small penises. Roger Mortimer, for example, has a *very*—"

"That's enough," two voices announced in unison, as Isabel and Owain descended upon him from opposite sides at the same moment. They startled each other more than they startled Gwirion or the children, but both recovered at once, with a formality that was almost as risible as their embarrassment. Owain bowed—gracefully, to Gwirion's surprise—and the queen nodded her head in acknowledgment.

"It's Your Majesty's prerogative," he insisted, gesturing toward Gwirion as if he were a piece of furniture.

She smiled and shook her head. "I have such ample opportunity for this particular chastisement, I've grown weary of it. Please continue, I applaud your initiative."

"They're discussing who's going to bawl me out over pissing," Gwirion explained loudly, annoyed. He glanced up at them. "May I finish?"

"No, Gwirion," Isabel said firmly, "it's—"

"But why does having a small genital make someone want to take our land?" an older girl, about seven, asked. She was pleased with herself for incorporating the new vocabulary word. "Girls have smaller ones than boys and girls don't do such things."

They all looked expectantly at Gwirion. He held up his hands. "Alas, my friends, I've just been banned from speaking to you about this very timely topic. Query the grown-ups." He lifted himself up from the hearth and walked off toward the side door with a huff of exaggerated indignation—then immediately ducked to hide behind the corner of the fireplace, where the queen herself had just been eavesdropping. Owain and his hostess were left looking at each other and the children in silence.

"So then?" one of the boys finally ventured. "Do you know the answer or not?"

The queen looked down at them. Other than Thomas she had no experience with children, and he had never demanded this kind of explanation. "Of course we do," she said gamely. But her mind was a blank.

"Here's what it is," Owain announced, and gave her a reassuring smile before turning his attention to the children. "Men think the bigger they are there, the better they are. So men with smaller ones act the way they think men with big ones act, so everyone will think theirs are bigger too." The children exchanged perplexed looks: This was so stupid, he had to be making it up.

"So why do men with *big* genitals take over land?" the seven-year-old pressed on behalf of the group.

"Oh, but they don't," Owain assured them, with doe-eyed sincerity, and without thinking it through he added, earnestly, "I've never stolen so much as a handful of dirt." Her Majesty's surprised laughter made him blink, and then blush. He glanced quickly at the children, but they hadn't followed the logic and were already bored with him. He turned his attention nervously back to Isabel, who couldn't check her amusement. After a hesitant moment, Owain chuckled sheepishly with her and when their glances met again, they both began laughing in earnest, although the blush stayed on his cheeks.

The exchange was delightful to Gwirion until the moment he realized they were enjoying themselves. That robbed him of his pleasure, and he skulked off toward the kitchen looking for something to eat. If he had to listen to them *giggling* all evening he would lose his appetite.

NOBLE was astounded by the change in Owain's composure by the time the trestles were set up and supper served. Isabel must have taken the effort to put him at ease, and he was so guileless about his admiration of her that it was hard to begrudge him his oddly unassuming familiarity. There was nothing predatory in his attentions; he had no thought of his worship being given weight either by a married queen or by her lord. The dais had been disassembled and replaced by the high table before the fireplace, hosting only the royal couple and certain members of the court. But none of the dignitaries sat as close tonight as Owain did, right at the queen's side and serving her from the platter they both shared with the king. She was unused to portioning food among three, and it was occasionally awkward keeping track of who wanted the mead and who the milk, but it was an awkwardness she found herself enjoying, and she laughed throughout the meal.

Owain and Isabel shared an interest in the stars, and each knew many constellations, although they ascribed different names and legends to them and it took some puzzling to figure out who was discussing what. Noble, amused by Owain's uncomplicated amiability, suggested the three of them repair to the wall walk before the end of the council week to stargaze, and they both nodded, forgetting there was a full moon that would wash out the heavens. Gwirion rolled his eyes, but nobody saw him.

The king was enjoying his wife's hilarity. Earlier in the evening she had been merely cheerful. Now she was effervescent. He had never seen her so lighthearted and he liked it. If this was the effect of her being unabashedly adored, he would have to round up lots of adorers to keep her in good humor. It could do remarkable things for his domestic life. As the tables were being cleared away he even suggested this to Gwirion, but Gwirion scowled at the idea. "And what if she falls in love with one of them?"

"Gwirion, look at him," Noble scoffed. "His voice has barely changed—he only came into his inheritance last month. I'm not sure he's even realized he's flirting."

The queen settled in her chair near the fire for the evening's entertainment, and invited the young man to sit beside her until the king joined them. Owain pointed to Noble and Gwirion's huddled conversation nearby. "And what's that about, milady?" he asked.

She shook her head. "They have the strangest friendship. I don't think I'll ever understand it, and I am not sure I care to." That was a lie. She wanted very much to understand it.

"Is he a bit off, then, that fellow?" Owain ventured thoughtfully, watching them. "May I ask Your Majesty what he does here?"

She laughed ironically. "What doesn't he do would be easier to answer. He certainly doesn't do anything useful." She softened. "That's not true. He saved my brother's life a month ago."

"Really?" he asked. "I'm glad to hear it. What was it, then, an accident?"

She gave him an awkward smile. "Not quite. Mostly he pulls elaborate pranks that take weeks or months of planning, and he doesn't care about the victims as long as the prank comes off. He's insulting, rude, bawdy . . . and very good at what he does. We despised each other the first six months I was here." She was surprised, and glad, that she could put that in the past tense.

"Why?"

She didn't discuss this with anyone, even her ladies, and she knew it was impolitic to broach it with one of the men Noble needed for his mission. But she liked the easy innocence in his eyes. And she was lonely; Noble was the only one she could talk to without enduring officiousness or boredom, and his attentions had been entirely on this conference for a fortnight. "We were both mad with jealousy for the king's attention," she explained and then, oversimplifying, "It took a while to accept the pecking order."

Owain made a face of expansive sympathy. "I can see how it would be hard for him to yield up pride of place."

"He didn't."

He was incredulous. "The funny fellow comes before you? How could the king make such—forgive me, Your Majesty, but how could he make such a choice?"

She smiled tightly and shook her head; Noble was making his way toward them and they dropped the matter. When he reached them he gave Owain a warm smile of greeting, then settled between them into his cushioned chair and took his wife's hand. "That's enough gallivanting for you tonight, young lady," he teased, kissing her cheek. Her unprecedented levity made him sincerely grateful for the first time since last spring to have her as a companion. There was something almost Enid-like about it. With Lord Huw's cooperation, he had already negotiated an early evening rendezvous, but if she was still glowing like this later on . . . He kissed her quickly on the lips and then turned to listen to Gwirion play, not noticing her smile waver for a moment.

It was the condescension that annoyed her, the assumption that his wife would docilely obey the marriage vows he so blithely broke. *If my receiving such attention is amusing, I'll amuse you with it until it's not amusement anymore.* What a simple plan. She should have tried it months ago.

A FTER Gwirion's performance that evening, Owain asked a dozen harried servants where to find the harpist, and finally somebody suggested that he try the king's private receiving chamber just off the hall. Owain was shown to the room and knocked. When nobody answered, he tried the latch, and the big oak door swung inward.

The room was crowded with sleeping blankets, but none of their inhabitants had claimed them yet. The usual furniture—Noble's leather chair, the cushioned settle, and the chest that doubled as a table—had been pushed to the side, and across the room was a blazing hearth. The room, with walls almost twice as thick as the solar above it, was cozy and wonderfully warm. It was a relief to be out of the crowd.

Gwirion sat curled up like a cat in front of the fire, gazing into the flames. He did not turn when Owain entered.

"Excuse me," Owain said pleasantly. Moving only his eyes, Gwirion briefly glanced toward him, then back to the fire.

"It's you," Gwirion said, as if that implied something.

"Yes," Owain said, smiling, as if he was content with whatever it might imply. "Me."

A silence. Gwirion wondered whether his ease came from stupid-ity or cockiness. Or perhaps—although it was hard to imagine it—genuine innocence.

"Do you want something, then?" Gwirion asked, still not turning toward him.

"You play exquisitely."

"Thank you."

"Do you compose as well?"

"Ah." Gwirion uncurled and finally turned toward the younger man. "You want me to compose a song on your behalf extolling the beauty of the queen."

Owain was surprised. "Yes!" he said, pleased. "How did you know that?"

Gwirion was about to give a mocking answer but reconsidered and simply smiled. "Call it a hunch," he said. "But I can't help you."

"Why not?"

"I don't find her attractive, myself. I think she's sexless."

"How can you say that?" Owain scolded gently. "Those eyes? That smile?"

Before Gwirion could pretend to vomit, the door opened and the subject of their conversation stood in the doorway, looking slightly less elated than she had before. Because he had taken a few steps away, Owain was hidden behind the door as it swung inward, and Gwirion was backlit by the fire, his face in shadow. "I wondered if you would care to join me on the wall walk to look at the constellations," she said to Gwirion. "I have been displaced from my quarters for a little while and I thought to enjoy your company until my bed is ready."

"Oh, Christ," the harpist groaned, standing up and moving toward her so she could see his face in the light from the hall. "You're even worse than he is."

She started when she realized who it was. "I thought you were—"

"Yes, I know. He's right behind the door. Take him and good riddance. I assume you don't want a threesome."

He left. She took a step farther into the room so that she could see Owain. "That was embarrassing," she said, not sounding embarrassed. "Did you hear my invitation?"

"Thank you, milady, I'd like that very much. But don't you think the king might like to join us?"

"The king is otherwise engaged," she said with tight finality. "He is entertaining one of our female guests." Seeing the startled look on his face, she laughed in the dim light. "I'm telling you all our little secrets. You must forgive me. I'm so desperate for somebody to talk to. And I've had more wine than usual. Would you like to come up and look at the stars?"

Owain said he'd be delighted to.

GUIRION wasn't sure what to do now. It was one thing when their guest was innocently drooling over the queen, but for the queen to encourage or return the attention drastically altered the picture, and suggesting they stargaze when there were no stars was a declaration of mischief. She must have learned that the king had gone for a "nap" and was motivated by a reckless sense of revenge. Surely she wasn't actually interested in Owain? Impossible, he decided, and dropped it. Noble had enough on his mind already. He didn't want to be a snitch.

SO it was without malice of intent—quite the contrary—that he worked his way through the crowded hall, across the chilly yard, and up the stairs to the king's chamber. As he expected, the king's massive doorkeeper Gethin was standing in the anteroom looking bored, ignoring the sounds of sexual rapture from within. Any vicarious thrill to be had from the job had worn off years ago.

"Some servant of Lord Huw's, is it?" Gwirion asked, remembering the conversation he'd overseen earlier.

"Actually it's his lordship's wife."

Gwirion looked impressed, then confused. "His lordship condoned it?"

Gethin grinned confidentially. "For a price. The king offered him a stable boy he had his eye on."

Gwirion was stunned. He forced himself to leer. "Ah. So everyone wins."

"Except the stable boy," said Gethin, and chortled. Gwirion pretended to join him, but turned his face away to hide a flash of anger. That explained why Noble had not used Gwirion as a go-between; he knew Gwirion would never broker such an arrangement, would probably even sabotage it. He sat on the floor, resting his back against the wall. It was cold down there, but the cold was numbing and he needed to calm himself.

After half an hour, the noises from the inner chamber stopped for good, and a few minutes later the door opened. A tall, graceful woman noticeably older than the king came out of the room in a very elegant russet gown that was in slight disarray. Her hair was uncovered and loose, tumbling long, dark, and unruly down the curves of her body, and she looked both sleepy and giddy at the same time. She was strikingly beautiful and exuded that rare smoky sensuality that deepens with maturity. Not noticing Gwirion, she gave the ogling doorkeeper an engaging smile as she passed him to descend the steps. Gwirion had never seen her here before today, but she must have had some arrangement with her husband to be so casual about cuckolding him. He tried to imagine the queen agreeing to such an arrangement and shook his head.

"Scrumptious," he said when she was out of earshot. "I want one." But he was still angry about the boy.

The king's voice called out. Gethin stuck his head into the room, received an order, and shut the door again, heading for the stairs down to the yard. Gwirion leapt to his feet. "The queen?" he asked.

The man nodded. Because of the horde of guests, the queen's chamber had been turned into a dormitory for the children, with her three women and several visiting nursemaids jammed in as well, so she and her husband were sharing his bed for the week no matter what his recreational intentions.

"She's not in hall, I'll get her," said Gwirion. "She's outside, it's cold, you stay snug in here." Before Gethin could respond Gwirion dashed out onto the open wall walk.

The temperature had dropped while he'd been waiting by Noble's door, and the cold hit him like a slap. He wrapped his arms around his body wishing he had brought at least a cloak. The winter night was biting but mesmerizing, cloudless, the moon so brilliant its light washed out the constellations. A hundred feet away from him, near the opening to her own antechamber, stood the queen and her admirer, each wrapped in purple cloaks, absurdly pretending to stargaze and clearly distracted by their proximity. Gwirion observed them for a moment, fascinated.

It had never occurred to him that the queen could feel desire, attraction, any independent emotion at all besides peevishness. He felt no protective loyalty toward her, but he knew he had to nip the infatuation in the bud. Their backs were to him and he could hear an unfamiliar cooing quality in the queen's voice that made him ill. Soundlessly, he drew up behind, easily visible but entirely unnoticed in their mutual absorption. As a silence settled on them and the queen smiled at her escort with an inexcusably stupid level of invitation, Gwirion lunged forward and clapped his hands together between them.

Isabel gasped and they both spun around. His teeth flashed in the moonlight.

"And how is heaven this evening?" he asked.

"What are you doing here?" demanded Isabel.

"Saving you from yourself," Gwirion replied loftily.

"You can't be serious," the queen said. "We're not even alone." She gestured to the guards standing watch over on the tower keep, a hundred yards away across the trench and twenty feet above them.

"You might have had an orgy and those men wouldn't have known of it. It would behoove Her Majesty to keep a guard with her at all times now," Gwirion retorted testily. "The castle's full of strange men. Even their allegiance to the king can't guarantee their behavior toward you. They can be very dangerous—one of them even wanted to compose a song about you."

"All right, now," Owain interjected awkwardly.

Ignoring him, Gwirion jerked his head up the walk. "He's ready for you."

Isabel looked down at her feet for a moment, stalling, pushing a stray pebble about with her shoe. "Is he in his chamber?" she asked at last.

"Better than that, in his bed. Probably asleep. Be grateful—he really worked over your proxy, she could hardly walk when she left."

"Don't speak to your queen that way!" Owain gasped, shocked, and raised a gloved hand to smack Gwirion, but she grabbed his arm and stopped him.

"Don't hurt him, it's the only hanging offense in the castle," she said resentfully.

"I'm doing you a favor coming here," Gwirion snapped. "He sent his doorkeeper for her. Do you know what would have happened if he'd had to look all over the castle for her and then bring her back with the report that she'd been alone up here with you? *Stargazing?*" he added sarcastically, waving at the moon.

"How is it any better if *you* tell him?" she demanded.

"I'm not going to tell him."

In the diffused light he could clearly see her surprise. He didn't know if she was relieved or annoyed—it must have been the latter, if she was doing this just to get back at the king for his tryst.

"Thank you," she said stiffly. She turned to Owain, bid him a polite but impersonal good night, and headed along the walk until she disappeared into Noble's tower.

Alone, the two men looked at each other in the moonlight.

"I'm sorry," Owain said, sincere and slightly sheepish. "I didn't realize how serious it was."

"Were you raised by wolves? A married woman, any married woman, knows better than to be alone with—"

"She invited me!" he insisted.

"Of course she did, she wanted to enrage her husband. You should have respectfully declined." Gwirion began to head back toward the stairs. "Excuse me, there's a boy in the stables who needs tending."

"Ah, did old Huw get his hands on him, then?" Owain asked casually.

Gwirion stopped and turned back to him. "You know about that?"

"Everyone in the western baronies knows Huw," Owain said with an awkward smile. "Not that anyone cares about Huw, but his wife . . ." He laughed nervously, then explained in a confiding tone: "She gave him three boys, but late in life, and something happened with the third and she couldn't conceive anymore. So he decided he didn't care what she did as long as she didn't care what he did. Their marriage is, mmm, well-known near the border. I doubt there's a local gentleman who hasn't . . . been affected by it."

"Are you one of them?" Gwirion demanded.

"It would be ungentlemanly of me to reveal that," Owain stammered.

Gwirion felt a wave of alarm. This cherub might be capable of things the king assumed he wasn't. "Owain, the king and queen don't have such a relationship. Her attentions toward you are not foreplay, they're to punish the king for his philandering. You're just a pawn. Don't think you're anything special."

By the following evening, Gwirion was painfully eating his words.

9

Uses of Loyalty

Early December, 1198

WAIN WAS BUSY all day in council, which was convened at the upper end of the hall since the council chamber wouldn't hold everyone. Mass had been said here as well, and when it was over Gwirion was entrusted with the children again, with admonitions not to discuss genitals. The usually unflappable duo of steward and usher were so overwhelmed with the details of feeding and housing the guests while also maintaining a presence in the war council that Gwilym, conquering his pride, asked Her Majesty for the honor of her assistance overseeing the daily operations of the household. She was delighted by both the distraction and the chance to be useful; other than the official greeting ceremony, which the king had offered her to be conciliatory, her presence was unwelcome at the war council. The sewing bevy was put out by the new assignment, although it gave them greater opportunity to cross through the hall, hurling demure glances at certain younger members of the court. They dutifully followed

their mistress into the kitchen and even kneaded bread, but they had an impressive range of excuses to refuse anything that might splatter sauce or oil on their tunics.

By suppertime Isabel was tired, but revived when they sat at board, returned to the radiance born of Owain's wide-eyed reverence. She behaved as if the awkward moment on the wall walk had never happened, and before the end of the meal, she was not merely basking in the youth's attention but actively encouraging it. She made little darting glances with her cat's eyes at him, often with a smile that bordered on coquettish. She used every excuse to brush against his sleeve or shoulder as they ate, and—apparently—a thrill ran through her with each contact. Gwirion watched with disgust, wondering when the king would correct her, but Noble seemed oblivious.

When supper was over and the trestles struck, the queen allowed Owain to follow her around the hall like a pup, trying to be helpful as she organized the servants to prepare the room for bedding down. There wasn't a thing he could do, being a guest, a lord, and especially a bumbling, smitten boy, but she encouraged his shadowing because it further publicized the infatuation and that would make it hard for Noble to ignore it. She sent a hall boy to get fresh bedding for one of the spaces that was sectioned off for privacy, and she managed very casually to herd Owain into the area that would be hidden when the curtain was pulled closed. She was reaching out for the curtain when a hand appeared from the other side of it, grabbed it, and whipped it aside. She started as she found herself looking directly into Gwirion's hard dark eyes. "People are talking," he muttered under his breath.

She shrugged, a triumphant twist in the corner of her mouth. "Let them talk," she said, and began to pull the curtain out again. He grabbed it just below her hand and stopped her. "They're not talking about you. They're talking about him. You're going to cause him trouble. To feed your pride." He gave her a knowing look.

She flushed with anger. "You're meddling," she said.

"No, milady." He smiled. "You are." He flashed the curtain closed again between them and was gone.

She turned around to look at Owain, who was standing near her politely waiting to be useful, or at least noticed. For a long moment she gazed at him, troubled by Gwirion's words. Owain, who hadn't heard the exchange, returned her gaze worshipfully. "Your Majesty?" he whispered at last.

"Owain." Expectant, even nervous, he took a step toward her. His closeness in the intimate space made her heart beat faster and she suddenly wanted to touch him. Instead she withdrew a step, nearly backing into the curtain, and cleared her throat. "Owain, there are certain circumstances in which men and women may be playful with each other without it ... meaning anything." He blushed. "Apparently that's not the case here. I'm sorry if I misled you. You are a darling man and I enjoy your attention. But—" The curtain whisked open again behind her and Owain winced. She growled, "Leave me *alone,* Gwiri—" but was interrupted by her husband's voice.

"Gwirion?" he asked in an ironic tone. She spun around, inches from his chest, and he looked down at her without expression. "Gwirion is on his way to my chamber. In lieu of public entertainment, the two of you will join us there."

G UIRION didn't want to perform privately for this trio, but he grumpily made an excuse to the steward, wrapped his harp in its felt sheath, and downed a mug of ale before trudging as slowly as he could across the bailey, slushy from a wet afternoon snowfall, to the king's tower. He was the last to arrive. The king stood facing the other two in the middle of the well-lit room, a handsome, patient father hovering over his wayward offspring. He held a slender walking cane that Gwirion thought he remembered seeing earlier with one of the older visitors.

"Sit down, Gwirion, make yourself comfortable. Put the harp anywhere, you won't be playing it."

"Am I not performing?"

Noble shook his head. "No. You're here as witness. As audience. Isn't that a welcome change?"

Gwirion didn't respond. As he sat by the fire and laid his harp near him, he saw worry on the queen's face and troubled confusion on Owain's.

"Now then," Noble began, calmly and without a trace of anger. "There's no need to make a scene over this, but I want to clarify a few things. I am your king. This is my wife. Do you understand?"

Owain blushed and looked astonished. "Sire, I hope you don't think I had any intention of—"

Ignoring him, Noble turned to her. "It's not just a matter of your honor, or even my honor, it's a matter of the realm's stability. The mere appearance of impropriety from you right now is as dangerous as any reality, especially with Anarawd skulking about with his eyes glued to you. Until there is a son that is absolutely, inarguably mine, your dallying with another man will bring chaos. Even then, you are still *mine*. Do you understand that? If I see fit to dole you out to some young stud, then I will, but you don't make those decisions on your own."

She was aghast. "You may not dole me out to some young stud!" she hissed. "If I'm yours, then I'm only for you."

"That's true for my wife, but you're also my subject," Noble said evenly. "Are you not? Am I your sovereign?"

"Yes," she said impatiently.

He turned at last to face Owain directly. "Am I your sovereign?"

"Yes, sire," Owain stammered.

"Good," Noble said, smiling. "And here's a little trial to make sure we all understand what that means." He backed a step away from them. "Kiss her."

Owain blinked. "Sire?"

"I told you to kiss my wife. I know you want to and now I've ordered you to, so there should be nothing holding you back. Take a step closer to her, place your hand at her waist, and kiss her on the lips."

"Noble, don't do this," she said in a strained voice. "We understand your point, I understand it, I'll be obedient."

"If you want to show me you're obedient, kiss him back when he kisses you. Owain, begin please. Can you see, Gwirion?"

Gwirion said nothing. Owain turned to the queen and bent toward her with an apologetic expression, pecked her on the lips, and pulled away. The king laughed scornfully.

"Not like that!" he said. "A real kiss. Long. Slow. Taste each other's tongues. *Now!*" he demanded, banging the cane on the floor.

Again Owain moved toward her. She looked down, her jaw twitching.

"Chin up, madam," Noble said harshly.

Slowly she lifted her head. Any ambivalence Gwirion had had about this gathering was smashed by the heartbreaking humiliation on her face. Her skin was splotched and her expression was unbearable to Gwirion. He ducked his head away embarrassed, but he heard everything. There was a kiss, a long one, barely maintained through the queen's ragged breaths. Finally Noble gave them permission to pull apart and Gwirion heard her gasp for air.

"We're not through," her husband informed them. "Owain my lad, give me your hand."

Holding Owain's right hand in his left one, the king abruptly ripped open the front of her crimson kirtle and slapped Owain's hand onto her exposed breast. She cried out and tried to pull away but Noble's free hand held her fast. The fingers of his other hand pressed directly over Owain's and he squeezed Owain's fist open and shut around the giving flesh.

"Keep touching her," Noble ordered, releasing his own hand. "Squeeze her very small breast." Owain did, again with a profoundly apologetic expression. She looked over his head into the darkness, refusing to satisfy her husband with any reaction. "Slide your hand to the other breast," Noble ordered, and Owain hesitantly did it. "Does that feel good? Now put your mouth on her breast and suck on it like a mewling baby."

"Sire, please——" Owain began.

"*Do it!*" Noble shouted, furious. Owain, grimacing, kissed the queen's breastbone. "No, not there!" Noble chastised angrily. "Do what I tell you."

As if her flesh seared his lips, Owain gingerly moved his mouth over first one breast, then the other. She teetered, barely breathing.

Finally Noble announced, "You may stand up," and Owain pulled away from her, avoiding her eyes, his cheeks crimson. For a long moment there was complete silence in the room except for Isabel's unsteady breathing. Then Noble smiled at them with tremendous indulgence. "I know it's hard to believe right now, but I've done this as a favor to both of you. Oh, yes," he said in response to the glare his wife gave him. "Now that your attraction is irreversibly intertwined with humiliation and guilt, it will be much easier to resist it. I'm assisting you in averting adultery. Admittedly I have something to gain from that, as does the entire kingdom of Maelienydd except perhaps my cousin, but the real onus is on the two of you. Do we all understand why this had to happen? Do we?" he pressed when they didn't reply.

"Yes, milord," they both murmured.

"Good." He smiled. "But I want to be certain. So, my good friend Owain, you are going to do one more thing to demonstrate that you understand both your own status and my wife's." Cordially, he held out the cane to him. "You are going to beat her."

Owain stared at the stick as if it were poisonous. "I will not harm the queen," he said in a shaky voice. "She is my sovereign lady——"

"Nonsense. I'm your sovereign lord and she's my consort, the rest is all polite trimmings for minstrels to sing about. If I hadn't married her, the kingdom wouldn't even be in this predicament with Mortimer. We may be out on a battlefield together soon, my friend, and I must believe that I can trust my men to follow my orders without question. If you can't do that here, you can't do it out there, and I'll have to treat you as a deserter. You know what I do to deserters. So take the cane and hit her. Hard."

Owain looked ill as he reached out for the cane. Noble turned his shaking wife around and swept the long train of her headdress forward over her shoulder, then calmly ripped open the back of the kirtle so that she was exposed from neck to waist. Too disturbed to resist, she crossed her arms over her breasts and tensed against the blow.

Owain raised the cane to the level of his elbow. "Higher," Noble demanded. Owain raised it an inch. "Higher," Noble said, and repeated the demand until Owain held the cane far above his head. He drew a breath and steeled himself to strike.

In the hesitation before Owain's blow, Gwirion darted from his place by the fire and leapt up high enough to grab the cane from Owain's uncertain grasp. As soon as he landed he broke the cane over his knee with a muttered curse. He threw the pieces to the floor at the king's feet and glared at him, rubbing his shin.

The king glared back.

Then he burst out laughing.

"Anyone but you would already be halfway to the gallows, fool," Noble said companionably.

"If you'd kill someone over that, you're not even fit to rule sheep," Gwirion snarled.

Still the king smiled. "And you're the only one who can get away with that as well. You owe Twdor a cane, by the way." Gwirion glowered at him. "But you realize, of course, that you must balance rights with responsibility. You're allowed such behavior only because you're also obedient. Be obedient now, and kiss the queen."

"Go to hell!"

"Or I'll have you publicly whipped."

"And what reason are you going to give out? You're punishing me because I refused to molest your wife? Me, Noble?" Gwirion demanded in disgust, and throwing the door open he walked out of the room, limping a little from the cane's resistance.

They stood there a moment looking after him. Then Noble cleared his throat and turned back to his two pupils. "Well, that ruined the mood, now, didn't it?" He smiled. "All right, then, lesson learned." Turning to Owain he said in a very deliberate tone, "I am sure we can all agree that this never happened." The young man nodded, silent and distressed, and Noble sent him away with an almost smarmy wave.

Alone, the royal couple studied each other. He picked up a blanket lying near the hearth, and wrapped it loosely around her shoulders. The gentleness of the gesture startled her, and she almost collapsed against him. He put his arms around her and helped her to the edge of the bed, then sat her down and lifted her legs onto the feather mattress so that she was reclining. He kissed the top of her head. "I'll have the kitchen send you up metheglin to soothe your nerves," he said softly.

"Where are you going?" she asked as he went for the door.

"To find Gwirion."

"Please—" She sat up, with a desperate look on her face. "Please don't punish him, Noble."

He stared at her. "You still are such a foreigner here," he said quietly, and left.

NOBLE went personally to the kitchen to order medicinal mead for the queen, and then to ask for Gwirion. "I need to speak with Huw ap Maredudd and his wife," he told another servant. "If they're not in hall listening to Hywel, they're in the visitors' tower. Tell them to meet me in the audience room."

It took longer to find Gwirion; by the time he was ushered into the whitewashed chamber, Noble had completed his business with the famously unorthodox couple, and Huw had already departed. His wife reclined quietly on one of the guests' bedrolls. She wore a dark long tunic, blending into the low-lit room. Gwirion was too busy being sullen to notice her. He cleared his throat to announce his arrival and crossed his arms, radiating sulky defiance.

"The queen asked me not to punish you," Noble said, standing in front of the fire.

"You weren't planning to punish me," Gwirion snapped back. "What do you want?"

"I have a peace offering, actually."

"Gold?" Gwirion said sarcastically.

"No, better than that. A woman."

"Your wife?" he asked with disgusted sarcasm.

"No, a willing woman. A wanting woman, even." A throaty female chuckle from near the floor made Gwirion turn to look just as Noble introduced her. "This is Branwyn, wife of Huw ap Maredudd. You intrigue her. That makes you a lucky fellow, trust me."

Gwirion recognized the siren who had exited Noble's room the night before. She was lounging in a position intended to encourage him to simply fall on top of her, and for a moment he gawked, astonished and willing to forgive the king anything. Then, unexpected and unwelcome, a wave of anger smashed against him. "Where's your husband?" he demanded.

"Gwirion, that's rude. Introduce yourself properly."

"My name is Gwirion and I want to know where your husband is."

Branwyn, amused by his brashness, purred, "He's occupied."

"Is he occupying the same boy as last night?"

"I don't know, it might be a girl tonight," she said mildly, and rearranged her limbs a little, invitingly.

"It's no concern of yours, Gwirion," Noble said, shifting with almost imperceptible discomfort.

"I saw the boy this morning. He was in bad shape."

Unconcerned, the woman shrugged. "They bounce back quickly at that age."

"That's an appalling attitude."

She had a low, throaty laugh. "It's just a servant boy, I'm sure he's used to it. You surprise me, Gwirion. You struck me as someone who'd approve of entertainment no matter what the form."

"Is Huw with the boy right now?" Gwirion demanded.

"I believe he was headed that way, but I don't spy on him."

Gwirion spun around and ran out the door. There was a pause.

"Did I scare him?" Branwyn asked.

"No," Noble said in an aggrieved voice. "He's going to the stables."

"Does he know that boy?"

Noble hesitated. "He's been that boy," he finally said, a rare note of pain in his voice.

THE stables and smithy were across the courtyard from the hall. Gwirion approached at a run, skidding on slush, and came to a slithering halt outside the tack room. The noises coming from within needed no explanation. He shoved open the door and rushed in.

Huw had set a torch in the wall brace and what Gwirion saw made him shriek with rage. He flew at the baron and tore him off the boy, pushed the boy out of the room, and then shoved Huw to the floor and threw himself on him. Huw fell hard under his own bulk, but he was a trained fighter and collected himself immediately, and once Gwirion lost the element of surprise he was in trouble. When the king ran into the room moments later, Gwirion's face was cut and bleeding and one of his eyes was swelling shut. Huw was threatening him with a dagger, indignantly tugging up his drawers with his free hand.

"*Stop!*" the king demanded in panic. Huw checked himself with disgruntlement.

"This mongrel attacked me unarmed, without provocation! I—"

"He's not right in the head," Noble said quickly. "He's out of his wits, you can't hold him accountable for his actions."

"I was assaulted! Who's responsible, then?" Huw demanded.

"I am. Petition to me for redress."

Huw was angrily taken aback, and Noble didn't wait for a reply.

He knelt down beside his cowering friend, lifted him in his arms, and carried him out of the room, past the dumbstruck baron.

S HE had almost drifted off to sleep when a commotion outside startled her to alertness. Gethin threw the door open and Noble entered hurriedly with something in his arms that looked like a huge rag poppet. She gasped when she realized it was Gwirion and saw the state that he was in.

"What happened?" she cried as he laid Gwirion before the hearth.

"He was playing Defender of the Subjugated again but he took on a little more than he could manage," Noble said, annoyed, and stuck his head out the door, asking the doorkeeper to bring Marged up with her healing tinctures. "He'll have to stay up here tonight."

"On the floor?"

"What choice is there?" Noble said sharply, pushing the harp out of the way.

He moved briskly around the room, opening the carved wooden chests lining the walls in search of brychans and cushions. As he set about making a nest for Gwirion to curl up in, she swept the blankets off her legs and got up. "Let him have the bed," she said. "That chest is nothing but blankets, there's more than enough for the two of us."

He stopped what he was doing to look at her. "Are you sure?"

"I owe him at least that. He saved me from a beating."

"And I saved you from something worse."

"Fine. You take the bed and Gwirion and I will sleep on the floor together."

Noble glanced down. She thought it was a gesture of shame at first, then realized he was actually trying to hide a smile. "You don't have to believe this," he said, "but I wouldn't have let him strike you."

"How gracious of His Majesty not to oblige me to believe it," she said indifferently, going to the chest and flipping up the lid. She began to pull the blankets out, tossing them into a pile. Noble lifted Gwirion up from the hearth and laid him on the bed.

"I intended to stop his hand. The purpose of that exercise was to make sure of his obedience, it wasn't to inflict pain on you. You were pained quite enough by then. I wouldn't have let anything happen."

"I wouldn't have let anything happen either."

"It was already happening," he corrected. "In front of the collected powers of my kingdom, you of all people were not treating me as king. In front of Anarawd, of all men, who would leap at any excuse to invalidate my offspring."

She paused in her activity and looked at him for a long moment. Then she turned her attention back to the chest.

THE next morning at breakfast, an uncomfortable silence filled the great hall. Everybody knew that strange things had happened the night before but almost nobody knew what, although it obviously involved the king's odd little confidant, who walked with a limp and sported an immense black eye. Huw and Branwyn avoided mass and demanded their breakfast brought up to them, and Noble followed it to their private tower room. He spent an hour placating and threatening by turn until Huw let the matter drop, and agreed to come down when the council resumed.

In the hall itself, over breakfast, Owain stayed as far from the queen's table as he could. Gwirion did likewise, unwilling to decide how nice he ought to be to her without the king around. This made it easy for Owain to approach him—or rather, to corner him, since Gwirion had no desire to speak with him, anticipating how the conversation would go. But Owain trapped him just outside the kitchen as he was peeling a hazel twig to clean his teeth.

"I want to thank you for last night," Owain began in a chagrined voice.

"You're welcome," Gwirion said awkwardly, squelching the impulse to find sexual humor in the line.

He looked shamed. "I'll always have to wonder what I would have done if you hadn't—"

"Oh, spare me, please. Spare yourself," Gwirion pleaded, chewing on the twig. "Forget it happened."

"I also know what you did later." Owain pressed on. "My man heard the servants discussing it at mass. They're all astonished. They're calling you the patron saint of stable boys."

"That's ridiculous, look at me, he ground me to a pulp," he muttered.

"I just want you to know, for whatever it might be worth, that I think you're a good Christian," Owain said, with such unselfconscious sincerity it made Gwirion himself self-conscious.

"Well, that makes everything all right, then," he answered sarcastically, clapping Owain on the back harder than necessary. He began to walk off but Owain detained him with a gentle hand on his arm.

"And I want to tell you that I envy you." His eyes had a childlike surety that unnerved Gwirion.

"You want to be the patron saint of stable boys? It's really not as glamorous as they say, and the wages are dreadful—"

"Not that. Everything else. The liberty."

Gwirion dropped the twig into the floor rushes, gleefully relishing the absurdity of this assertion. "The *liberty*? I can't take a wife or a mistress without permission of the king. I can't go anywhere without permission of the king. I can't *possess* anything, including money, and even when bighearted guests give me a gift on the side, for trifling favors such as saving them from having to flog defenseless women, say—no, Owain, it was a joke," he said, interrupting himself, as Owain immediately reached down to his belt for his purse.

Owain dropped the purse and looked back up at Gwirion. "Isn't that freeing? It simplifies everything. You don't have to worry about practical matters at all."

"Because I'm a parasite!" Gwirion snapped. "He keeps me completely dependent on him for *everything*. I live in a state of permanent humiliation. Liberty? You have no idea what you're talking about."

"You have the liberty to do what you did last night," Owain pointed out.

Gwirion frowned at him and then declared, "I'd trade that in for a chance to earn my own keep."

"Why don't you leave, then?" Owain asked.

"And do what?" Gwirion demanded. "He doesn't want me to go. The only skill I have is the harp and he'd have no trouble finding me if I were out in the world doing that. I have no other skills, I have no way to survive."

"What if somebody hired you into their household? Anonymously. You can read and write, can't you? You could be almost any official's assistant. Those are freemen positions—they pay well. If you moved up to an officer's status you might even get land."

"Who would hire me?" Gwirion asked in exasperation, more than ready to end this.

"I would," Owain said.

A day earlier, Gwirion would have laughed right in his face. But now he couldn't. He couldn't respond at all. He just stared.

"I'm new to my patrimony, I'm still establishing my household. Anytime you choose to free yourself of this place, my manor stands ready to welcome you. Not as a parasite, as a man. There is no reason for the king to ever know you're there. I'm the least of lords in the outlands of Gwerthrynion; there never was much traffic past my father's door and I don't think that will change."

Gwirion's knees almost gave out. It frightened him how seductive the offer sounded. Scowling, he asked, "That means no privileges, though, right? I can't attack pederast lords or serve arse-shaped bread loaves or insult stupid visitors, can I?"

Owain considered this. "Well, that sort of thing would likely get back to the king."

"So I'd have to give up what you call my liberty here."

Owain nodded. "Yes. In your own interest, yes."

It seemed a small price to pay for dignity.

"Thank you. I'll consider it." He leaned in to Owain. "You're a good man too," he allowed, grudgingly.

He worked his way through the hall to see if any children had finished their breakfast yet. That had been an aggravating conversation and as soon as he was free of Owain he knew the idea was preposterous—Gwirion could flee to Jerusalem and Noble would still find him. Anyhow, he would hardly know how to comport himself in the world away from Noble's side. It was the boy's ignorant earnestness that had made it seem possible for even a moment.

The queen caught his eye and gestured him over to where she sat alone at the high table. *Oh Christ,* Gwirion thought, *and now there's this one too.* Still, he flushed when her face registered anguish at his bruises.

"I heard how that happened. It was charitable of you."

"It was just stupid," he said dismissively. "Now I'll have to watch my back until Huw leaves. What do you want?"

"What was Owain talking to you about?" she asked, dropping both her voice and her gaze.

"He was singing my praises." That was all he'd intended to say, but something made him go on. "And he invited me to join his household if I want to escape this insanity."

She clapped her hands over her mouth and stared at him.

"What?" he asked, impatiently. It wasn't an outrageous proposal, and this morning she of all people should appreciate the temptation.

For a moment, she stayed looking at him, hiding most of her face behind her hands. She lowered them at last and gave him a sheepish smile. "For the longest time nothing in the world would have pleased me more than your going away," she said. "Now that there's actually a chance of it, I realize . . ." This was hard to say. "I realize you're probably the best friend I have here, and I'd miss you."

"Friend? When did we become friends?" Gwirion demanded, alarmed. Isabel straightened, looked embarrassed.

"Allies, at least. If not friends, allies. You've shown me I can rely on you and I'm grateful."

"No, no, we're not allies," Gwirion said, holding his outstretched palms toward her and sounding almost panicked. "I don't do things for your sake. I do things for my sake. Period."

"You helped my brother—"

"That was to punish Noble for whipping me."

"Last night—"

"When something sickens me, I do what I can to stop it so I don't feel sick anymore. That's all," Gwirion said firmly. "Don't take it personally. I'm not anybody's ally—and *certainly* not a Mortimer's."

FOR days Noble spent sixteen-hour stretches huddled in the council room with smaller groups, interspersed with assemblies in the drafty hall that often became shouting matches. The queen, barred from politics and increasingly burdened with running the household, could not participate; in the evening her intention of querying Noble was checked when she realized how exhausted he was.

She puzzled about the understanding with Huw, but Gwirion's behavior confused her more. He was cold and snippish toward Noble, refusing to engage in their usual private banter at the supper table and one evening making a very public fuss about performing after the meal. Noble was gently solicitous toward him but the whispered, ferocious private conversations they had, at least once a day, appeared always to consist of Gwirion demanding something and the king, in a variety of sympathetic but condescending moods, refusing him. She was vaguely aware of Huw's continued evening activities, which she found distasteful but hardly outrageous, and supposed this was the source of contention, although why Gwirion would care about it so much was beyond her. Huw and Gwirion never spoke but glowered at each other across the hall. The entire dynamic confused Isabel, but she had no time to spare for asking subtle questions or even eavesdropping.

And when she did, it was to try to follow what was happening in the war council. Gwilym in their morning meetings would speak of nothing but domestic matters, so her only knowledge of what was going on was what she could pick up on the periphery. The collected barons of Maelienydd were split into at least five different camps at the start of the council and Noble was by turns bullying and reasoning to bring them all into accord. A small majority followed his way of thinking: establishing a larger, permanent guard and possibly earthworks along vulnerable sections of the border, without actively seeking hostilities. The section of Maelienydd nearest to Mortimer's troops had been briefly taken by the Saxons long ago, and its reconquest by Noble's ancestors made it hard to defend because it was on the far side of Offa's Dyke, the enormous ditch that ran the entire eastern length of the country, built many centuries earlier by a Saxon ruler to keep the Welsh in Wales. The dyke had largely accomplished its task—but not in this small section of the middle March, where Maelienydd now spilled east beyond it by some two hours' ride. The area's few inhabitants just wanted to be left alone to raid black Welsh cattle or their English counterparts as fancy struck them. This was rich farmland valley, a rarity in Maelienydd, and yet privately Noble would almost have relinquished it—to anyone other than Mortimer. But whoever held it would then be perfectly positioned to launch a campaign of absolute destruction throughout eastern Maelienydd. With Mortimer's troops gathering on Thomas's land, the area had to be secured immediately. Noble acknowledged that winter was an ill-conceived time to set out on a campaign, but, he argued, it was a mild winter and Mortimer, in his slightly more temperate homeland, was in any event not going to accommodate their seasonal vagaries. He pressed that he was not advocating a military campaign for midwinter, only a preventive one. Thomas's release, he argued, should be obtained through diplomacy or not at all.

Others, led by Anarawd the Default Heir, were more traditionally Welsh and bellicose, and saw this crisis as an opportunity to push Mortimer farther east, take more farmland, and raid his thriving villages with impunity. It was, they agreed, a green winter, so supply sources would not be dire; in fact, there would be better winter fodder for the horses lower down, closer to the border. Some went so far as to demand they besiege Wigmore Castle to free her brother, although everybody knew by now that Thomas's fate really only mattered to the queen. She silently applauded their sentiment but considered the plan a death wish. Another group, she gleaned, even thought that this was the perfect opportunity for Noble to reclaim true self-sovereignty and stop paying yearly homage to the English king, which made her want to laugh. That was *definitely* a death wish. Others just wanted to fight, with neither rhyme nor reason. Unsurprisingly, Efan, as captain of the teulu forces, was the ringleader of that group.

Still others, whose philosophy the queen was able to overhear in hall one morning after breakfast, gingerly brought up the idea of capitulation. Like Noble, they were tired of bloodshed; unlike him, they thought the best way to end it was to let the Normans claim themselves overlords and then go about their own lives, which would not really change a whit beyond higher taxes. They all detested Mortimer, but he was an excellent administrator over his own properties.

Noble smiled contemptuously at this argument. "The Mortimers have not been systematically killing off my family for the last five generations because they want to help you run your estates more efficiently," he informed them, in a mockingly gentle cadence, as if their feelings might be wounded by the revelation. He went on, slowly, speaking to them as if they were dull-witted; this same argument came up anew each day without its supporters ever acknowledging his rebuttal. "Mortimer has many relatives and retainers. He wants to keep them loyal, so he has to keep them in his debt, and what they want is land. Not just to live on, but to *own*, to collect taxes on, to work villeins on. This isn't the same as when Rhys and I would argue over Rhaeadr—that was about who would receive the land-use fee. This is about who receives the land itself and if we capitulate, it won't be you. The villeins are the only ones who wouldn't be massacred or at least left homeless, and frankly I don't think they care who's in charge as long as they get a hen and a week off from duties at Christmas."

The queen took a step into the hall from the kitchen with a deliberate cough, and the entire company of men turned around to stare at her. Noble shot her a furious look that ordered her to go away, but she stayed there, taking in everybody's gaze, from Owain's bemused but supportive smile to the many looks of suspicion and resentment. They saw her only as a Mortimer, she knew, and she had done nothing much to make them think otherwise. Of course he could not let her sit in on council; to them it was arguably like having the enemy eavesdropping. She would not have been surprised if they had asked him to divorce her now. "His Majesty my husband is telling you the truth," she said in a clear, loud voice, putting more than her usual effort into combating her accent. "Trusting Roger for anything will be your doom. He'll kill every landowner without compunction. You must do everything possible to keep him out of Maelienydd. Even—" Her voice nearly quavered, but she controlled it. "Even if it means removing Thomas from the issue entirely. I would be grateful for his release but he . . ." She almost couldn't say the words. "His fate is nothing compared to the fate of our kingdom. In fact," she pushed on, "although I realize much of what you need cannot be obtained with gold, half the sum of the queen's coffers will go to whatever effort His Majesty my husband deems most advisable. I challenge all the faithful among you to meet me in that endowment. There is nobody in this room who better knows the mind of Roger Mortimer than I do, not even Maelgwyn ap Cadwallon. I am telling you to trust our king." She turned abruptly and walked outside, taking deep, calming breaths in the relative quiet of the courtyard's damp grey morning.

She had not seen Noble's face change as she spoke. For the rest of the morning he was in better spirits, glancing now and then at the hall door to see if she would return. When dinner was called, he spirited her away to his chamber and made love to her with an affectionate exuberance she could barely remember ever existing between them.

There was another, final faction at council, perhaps the most troublesome, and the queen's conversion did nothing for it. This group was made up of all the men from the northwest, including Owain and Huw ap Maredudd, who was their spokesman. Llewelyn

of Gwynedd did not appear, but these border barons were intrigued
by him. He had a great swath of Gwynedd under him now; he would
reunite that ancient kingdom soon, and there was no reason to think
he would stop there. He was phenomenally popular, his successes
public mandate. His undeclared philosophy was that to defy the English invaders, the whole of Wales had to be united—under him. He
had recently been wooing barons near his eastern and southern borders to align themselves with him. He had been delicate, almost discreet, with the hope that he could work his way outward through
wobbling Powys and convince Noble and the scattered princes near
him to acknowledge Llewelyn their overlord. Noble was faced with a
bloc of fighters and landowners who wanted to throw their lot in
with Llewelyn and let him decide how to use their collective resources. Noble was urged at least to marry one of his near kin to one
of Llewelyn's as soon as possible. The arguments he made against ca-
pitulating to Mortimer were no good with this crowd. Unlike Mortimer, Llewelyn would not slaughter the landowners or even (it was
posited) depose Noble—he would, at worst, merely demote the king
to a petty prince. They said Llewelyn had an army of ten thousand
men, mostly peasants but like all native fighters vicious and compe-
tent. They wanted that size host fighting with them; more important,
they did not want it turned against them. Eventually, this faction argued, some form of central power would be needed to keep Wales
out of English hands, some brilliant overseer to replace the remarkable, but lamentably dead, Lord Rhys of Deheubarth. It would almost inevitably be Llewelyn, so for Noble to align Maelienydd with
him now, when he was offering and not ordering, was not weakness—it was savvy. Gwilym suggested asking Llewelyn to help them
with this struggle, whose outcome would affect his own future, without discussing the fate of Wales as a whole (or any potential nup-
tials) until the border had been stabilized.

The king couldn't afford to alienate a single baron in his process
of forcing consensus. His resources were too limited and his border,
suddenly vulnerable on two fronts, could not afford a weak point.

The brief moment of levity from his wife's declaration had evaporated entirely by noon of the following day.

GWIRION was also busy, but his business was a mystery. More and more often, he turned the care of the children over to Angharad or Generys and disappeared. He would be spotted during the day, usually outside, in brief but intense discourse with one or another of the grooms or squires attached to the visitors. If the king had heard of this he would have interpreted it instinctively, and canceled the informal tourney that was planned to celebrate the end of council. Isabel noticed enough to wonder if she should mention it to him, but her curiosity was piqued. She couldn't believe Gwirion, for all of his recent anger, would try to undo the king's coalition efforts. Noble enjoyed any prank Gwirion came up with, and took it as a sign of affection for himself, so surely after this troubling week he would welcome a little harmless mischief.

BY the end of the fifth full day of arguing, a grudging consensus had been reached, and the forty guests swore an oath to stand behind their king and his decision. Noble would send more men east immediately, both to secure the area from Mortimer's potential raid and to scout out the weakest natural defenses in the border. He would approach Llewelyn, asking him to join him on the endeavor, but he would not consider yielding sovereignty to him as part of any strategy—nor would he offer up a relative for marriage. He would also call reserve troops to go into training should there be urgent need for an expanded army: Every healthy male of fourteen and older would be given the privilege of serving the king in arms.

After a supper that used up most of the remaining fresh meat, when the tables had been struck and the large and now familiar crowd had collected in a huge cluster as close to the hearth as possible, Hywel—and only Hywel—performed. The king had decided the tenor of the day called for serious, heroic, and patriotic recitations, and Gwirion had never bothered to learn any of these. The selection was familiar and inarguably appropriate: It was the epic elegy of the kings of Maelienydd in defense of their realm. The long climax, describing Cadwallon's murder by her uncle, did not humiliate Isabel as it had last summer. Now it upset her, deeply, and she felt a hopeless despair for the future of her two lands. "The hero has been slaughtered," droned the bard, "he who was so brilliant to behold." She had thought Roger sent her to Maelienydd so that a Mortimer heir might lawfully ascend to the throne within a generation, but she realized now that that was a diversion on his part, and romantic folly for her to have believed it. Roger Mortimer wanted Maelienydd for himself and he wanted it immediately.

She listened more carefully to the words this time, curious for a reference to Gwirion's supposed heroism. But there was nothing, only a passing comment that the brave and valiant prince had had a boon companion with him when he miraculously escaped Mortimer's assault. For a moment she was tempted to discount what Enid had said last spring, what the king himself had told her in September. But she realized that the duty of all bards was to elevate the king alone. It would not read well in the chronicles of history to know the kingdom owed its survival to a parasite.

To her side, Noble's face was wet with tears. More surprisingly, Gwirion—who had not spoken to the king for days—was on the floor beside the throne, away from her, sobbing into the skirt of Noble's long red tunic. Noble's hand brushed against Gwirion's dark hair in a vague, unconscious gesture of comfort. She suddenly understood that they were listening to a narrative whose details—or lack thereof—they themselves must have provided. She looked away, feeling intrusive.

But later in the evening, as the king was about to exit the hall, the queen saw the two men in confusing, bitter argument again. It ended with the king ordering Efan to keep Gwirion in custody until the castle had retired for the night. She tried questioning the pen-teulu, but the burly young man clearly knew nothing and lacked all curiosity.

THE next morning was sunny, and despite the cold the entire castle and much of the village turned out to watch the tourna-ment. The tourney field lay within the village walls, between the steep base of the castle mound and the lazy River Aron. It was small, the only level field for miles around and absolutely flat. There was a wooden terrace built out from the rampart below Noble's tower and Isabel had taken her accustomed place there; the wives and children of the fighters joined her bundled in mantles, cloaks, and blankets. The king, having finished an attractive but gratuitous romp around the field on his spotted Spanish charger (just to remind his people how magnificent a leader they had), arrived on the terrace, kissed his wife's hand, then stood up to declare the start of the tournament.

Most of the landowners and fighters were taking part in the mock battle, which would be fought with dulled lances and blunt wooden swords. The Welsh did not usually fight the way these men were about to. Welshmen were expert archers and spearmen and they eschewed their many chances for open battle to move, frequently on foot and without armor, through the wooded hills to surprise ene-mies who were playing by more conventional battle rules—and who, after more than a century, never seemed to learn better. That was how their fathers and grandfathers had defeated Henry of England more than a generation earlier. But it was part of any gentleman soldier's training to learn the Norman style of warfare, which was far more en-tertaining to watch than a spearing match.

At Noble's gesture, grooms held the horses' heads and the participants prepared to mount. He raised his hand so that he could signal the commencement as soon as their weight hit their saddles—but for many of them their weight never did.

It was a bizarre scene, three dozen well-bred, well-trained chargers bucking and rearing as they tried to unseat their own masters. More than half of the riders went down hard before the other half realized it was a universal problem and backed away from their mounts.

Twenty dizzy warriors stumbled about wondering what had happened to them while their grooms scrambled to reclaim the horses, most of whom shuddered indignantly, snorted, and trotted briskly away to the edges of the field. Nobody offered a solution and finally Cadwgan the marshal angrily ordered the saddle be removed from his own mare. He tore off the saddle pad, removed his gloves, and began to work his fingers around it. A moment later, he stopped, examined something he had found, and ripped it out of the blanket. He held it up for everyone to see.

A small iron spur had been embedded deeply in the blanket. The press of the saddle itself, even when firmly cinched, had caused the mare no discomfort, but the moment her rider's full weight bore down on the stirrup, the metal barbs on the spur had bitten into her back. All of the horses were reclaimed and unsaddled, and within moments every one was found to have at least one such burr in their saddle blankets. Anarawd's and Huw's had seven each. The villagers on the ground, and the castle staff high above on the wall walk, began to laugh, knowing at once who was behind it. The riders themselves were furious and began shouting at each other.

On the terrace, the amused children demanded of their nurses what had happened, as Noble shook his head and groaned softly to himself. "Good morning, Your Majesties," said a voice behind them. Everyone turned to see Gwirion, his eye still discolored and puffy from Huw's attack, wandering through the small crowd, tousling the heads of the children within reach as they called out to him affectionately. He had a grey mantle wrapped around his slender shoulders, and he settled kneeling on the floor between king and queen

without bothering to look down at the tourney. He was still annoyed at Noble and ignored him. "I overslept. Have I missed anything?" he asked the queen.

Noble clasped his hands, the two index fingers steeplelike pressed against each other, and hid his mouth behind them. The gesture usually implied suppressed amusement, but there was no amusement now. "You whoreson," he said quietly, staring down at the field. "How did you manage that?"

Gwirion peered over the edge of the railing to see what was happening. Several fistfights were about to break out among the fighters. "Oh, that was easy. The blacksmith's an obsessively devoted Christian."

"And?" Noble prompted crossly when that seemed to be the end of Gwirion's explanation.

"And you'll be needing a new silver cross in the chapel."

"You didn't!" the queen gasped, as Noble made a disgusted sound. "Gwirion, you must return that, you can't steal from the house of God."

"Oh, that's all right, I gave myself license to do it as long as I put it to good use, which I think this was."

"It's good use to infuriate the men I rely on to keep the kingdom whole?" Noble demanded, watching the collective reaction of the fighters grow uglier. "This is going to alienate—"

"I have it in hand," Gwirion said. He rose gracefully and waved his arms wide in a greeting to the crowd. There was a roar of approval from the commoners and a dawning bellow of indignation from the lords. The squires and grooms were conspicuously silent. "You seem to be having some difficulties down there," he chirped.

Among the angry cries, Lord Huw's voice boomed, "What's the excuse now, you little ass? This isn't the work of somebody who's out of his head, it's the work of somebody with too much idle time on his hands!"

Anarawd's voice, distinct and slightly nasal, added more loudly and threateningly, "What's the *king's* excuse? He binds us to an oath and then makes fools of us! Is this a man who deserves our obedi-

ence?" The rest of his accusation was drowned out in furious, loud agreement from the others.

Noble, his face like Gwirion's looking out over the crowd, leaned in close to him and whispered threateningly, "If he foments rebellion from this, I'm hanging you for treason."

Gwirion ignored the comment and held his hands up for silence, which took a moment to achieve. "Do you believe this to have been a prank? This wasn't a prank! This was a lesson! How do you think I did it—all by myself? Of course not. I had the help of everybody's grooms and squires. Everybody's. *Wait!*" he called sharply as the men, now furious at their own underlings, looked for those it was within their power to punish. "Wait! Hear me out! I asked no one to plot against his own master. I asked them all who their masters had any minor grudge with, and then convinced them they would be acting in their lord's interest to perform a small act of mischief against that person—one single, apparently harmless action. Your lads all acted in service *to you.* That's their duty, don't punish them for it. The lesson here, however, is that they were acting in service *only* to you. The spirit of this past week, all your striving for cohesiveness and unity—you haven't bothered to share that need with them. To communicate it to *your people.* Have you? And this is the result. Consider it. And now, if you don't mind, I have other tykes to enlighten—"

The children cheered behind him, thrilled that their favorite nurse had turned out to be the perpetrator of the entertainment, but the men were not going to let him go.

"You're not getting away with this!" Huw called out. "You shamed us, now you come down here and be shamed yourself!" This got everybody frantically excited. Gwirion tried to quiet them but they were too exercised.

Suddenly Noble leapt up and shoved him aside, so roughly that he stumbled into the queen. Isabel, wincing at the enormity of trouble Gwirion had just brought upon himself, reflexively held out a hand to steady him. The king held up his hands and the lords silenced themselves at once. There was a pause. "Tell me what he's done wrong, and I will punish him accordingly," His Majesty offered.

"He's made fools of us!" Huw declared in outrage from below.

"Has he?" Noble seemed to muse. "I would say rather that he's demonstrated something we should have understood ourselves. This will *prevent* us from making fools of ourselves again, when the stakes are higher. If anything, we owe him a debt of gratitude."

"*Gratitude?*" half the lords cried in a shared, incredulous voice.

But the king's glare was enough to silence them again. "I am your king," he reminded them, slowly. "And I'm telling you we are grateful for the lesson we've just learned. Who defies me?" There were unhappy looks and noises exchanged, but nobody spoke another word. Noble smiled down at them with all apparent calm. "Then we are all in accord, and Gwirion shall have the best cut of lamb tonight at supper for his thoughtful demonstration."

Without another word, he turned his back to the field and began to walk off the terrace, gesturing for his startled wife to follow him. He grabbed Gwirion's wrist on the way and pulled him brusquely along beside him. They stopped at the back edge of the platform and he pivoted Gwirion to look straight at him. Knowing there were many eyes upon them, he seemed to smile at his friend as he informed him between clenched jaws, "I should have killed you right in front of all of them." Then he released Gwirion's wrist and began to climb the steep wooden steps up to the base of his tower.

"That was very dangerous, Gwirion," Isabel whispered, more amazed than chastening.

"Of course it was *dangerous*," Gwirion retorted, watching Noble ascend. Despite his cocky tone, he fidgeted a little. "There'd have been no purpose to it otherwise."

"You would really risk your life just to show the barons up?"

Gwirion made a face and shook his head, his eyes still raised, following the king. "I didn't risk my life. He *should* have killed me, but he never *would* have."

"How can you be so confident of that?"

Gwirion gave her an arch look. "Apparently, Your Majesty, it seems that I'm a fool." He mounted the stairs, following the king.

10

ENGAGING ENEMIES

Winter, 1198–99

N THE DEPTHS of the midwinter holidays, Noble made the decision he'd grimly anticipated for a month.

Immediately after the war council, Llewelyn had agreed—in theory—to go with him to confront Mortimer. Unsurprisingly, the other Welsh princes all demurred, with the promise that if it turned into a military engagement they might reconsider.

The mild weather had brought no snow, but they went three weeks without an hour of clear sunshine and Isabel thought she would soon go mad. Throughout December Noble was rarely at Cymaron and hardly ever off his horse, riding hard from one section of his kingdom to another, checking the state of the reserve host being trained, conferring with the border troops, meeting with Llewelyn to get a measure of the man, and vainly seeking council with Roger Mortimer himself. The single time Mortimer agreed to meet, exactly on the legal border at the windy crest of what the English called Stone Wall Hill, he sent an envoy in his place. Noble recognized the man and was convinced he had been part of the ambush twenty years ago; that struck him as something Mortimer might do, but he held his tongue and his temper for the sake of diplomacy. The envoy claimed that there was nothing to discuss. There were no hostilities planned; the troops massing on Thomas's estates were simply training for a possible Crusade—Noble was even chastised for reneging on his own pledge to take the cross years earlier. Thomas, it was finally claimed, was his uncle's honored guest at Wigmore Castle, remaining entirely at his own pleasure.

Llewelyn offered more satisfying audience. Noble was impressed with him at once, finding himself for the first time in his life in the company of a true peer. He was a great strategist and had a zeal, a focused ferocity for a united Wales that made it necessary to take him seriously. As adversary or comrade-in-arms, he was clearly a force to be reckoned with. It was almost enough to make Noble reconsider the idea of marrying their families somehow. But the price of his assistance would not be cheap: Noble would not only back him in his claims to the throne of Gwynedd, he would lend material aid for Llewelyn to achieve it. Noble demanded a written oath that the younger prince's sovereign ambition would find saturation at Gwynedd's borders, then clasped hands with him on the agreement and hurried home to Cymaron to arrive on Christmas Eve.

Christmas, beginning with the solemn predawn caroling in chapel, was understated and grim. Rituals both familiar and exotic to the queen's sensibilities were observed with lackluster obedience. Even the much heralded passing on of linen, which she had wondered about since her blunder with Enid and the kerchief, was anticlimactic. It was exactly as in her own home: She gave the court officials linen underclothes and the king gave them woolen dress livery, red emblazoned with his golden lion *rampant regardant*. The upset over the kerchief remained inscrutably stupid to her. The teulu were given their yearly gift of a pound each in coin, and every family in the village was sent a Christmas hen. All other Yuletide rituals were ignored; there was no impetus for cheer.

IT was Thomas's letter to the queen that tipped the scales toward action. Noble had been willing to keep a minimal force at the border, to train reserve troops without conscripting them to duty—until a letter arrived in Thomas's hand, addressed with sensational rudeness to Isabel Mortimer of Cymaron Castle, affectionately begging her to "join the family" at Wigmore Castle for a New Year's visit. It was neutrally worded, too neutrally worded, and obviously dictated. Her husband was not included in the invitation.

"That's not even *subtle,*" Noble complained with a harsh laugh when she brought it to him. He had not seen her so upset since Adèle's death.

Once it was clear that hostilities were imminent, most of the penteulus in the kingdom begged permission to pillage Mortimer's villages on day raids and snipe his armies as they camped. The king appreciated the impulse, but refused it. His people had reacted that way for centuries and had little to show for it now. The Welsh had never been partial to diplomacy, and with Richard on the English throne the Marcher lords weren't either. Noble was determined to change that: For the first time since King Henry's reign, a territorial issue would be resolved by parley.

But parley only worked when one did not seem desperate for it, so he summoned the largest host the kingdom had ever seen, intending to bring them to the border, ideally to do nothing but sit there for weeks and look fierce. There were desperate outcries against this unorthodoxy, of course: A winter campaign was a death wish. Yes, said the envoys from the lords who protested, it had been a mild winter so far and yes, all signs suggested it would continue to be so until Lent, but winter was winter—they would all be hard-pressed for food and fodder. Noble listened and nodded and continued to prepare. Mortimer was collecting a massive army on Thomas's land and he had to be blocked from using it. Nothing else mattered.

When Llewelyn of Gwynedd agreed to join the Maelienydd host

at the border, with his own men, the protestations instantly and reverently subsided.

THE collected host, all under the charge of the king's ecstatic penteulu, was organized into five small armies. Those from the center of the country would convene outside the castle the night before setting off to the border, bivouacking on the tourney field while their commanders slept in the castle hall. The western, southern, and northern forces would join them at the eastern border, where troops had been since right after the war council. For a week before they set off, the castle was a maelstrom of preparation as rations for both the men and those who stayed behind were assigned, measured, packed, and stored or carted eastward. The baker took over the village oven to make sure there would be enough bread the first few days at camp, and brought huge stores of oats plus dozens of hens for the eggs. He left his son behind to bake for the castle household, which would have to survive on barley and rye. The butler took his wife, and three kitchen girls in training under Marged went as well. The blacksmith closed his forge and fit what he could into half a large cart; the other half was piled with tents for Noble and the other commanders. The beds the queen had brought from England were not collapsible, but the king did not even seek one that was, choosing instead to sleep like his men, on a brychan stretched over straw. Most of the castle officers went along, leaving only Marged the cook, Gwilym the steward, Hafaidd the usher, and Goronwy the judge to command a sea of pages, chambermaids, aging attendants, and villagers under temporary hire. Ordinarily in war, the queen would go on circuit for safety, but there was no precedence for a winter campaign and anyway, Noble had insisted again, it was not yet a war and hopefully never would be.

The night before the host left for the Marches, a supper of roast geese was prepared for the commanders and the teulu in the hall, and double rations of ale were given to the men bivouacked outside. This could hardly make up for the near scandalous disruption of calling people to arms during the Christmas holidays and squelching riotous evenings of songs and caroling, but it would have to suffice. At evening mass the chapel was lit brilliantly with hundreds of candles; after the ceremony, Noble offered a week's leisure for all when they returned.

"Unless you lose," Gwirion commented later, during a quick moment alone with the king before the audience-chamber hearth.

"I've never lost to Roger Mortimer," Noble said.

"You've never faced Mortimer without Lord Rhys beside you," Gwirion said, speaking the thought Noble had been trying to will out of his mind. "But he is dead this time, you know."

"Well, now I have Llewelyn beside me, and judging by popular gossip that's even better," the king said with minor irritation. "And I truly hope it never comes to fighting."

"That's blasphemy! Aren't we supposed to be bloodthirsty?"

Noble closed his eyes, looking exhausted. "Even I have sickened of the battle."

Later in the evening, Hywel, almost doddering now, attempted to fill the hall with his shaking voice while Gwirion was called down to the field to entertain. A cozy, dull cloud cover masked the waning moonlight and made the evening mild. It was Twelfth Night, and a farmer-soldier from Llanbister had brought to camp a decorated horse's skull, a Mari Lwyd, so Gwirion traded in his harp for a pipe to lead a cheery, drunken procession around the camp. But out here there were no women to tease and no feast to sit down to—the main reasons to ramble about with a skeletal horse, after all—and when the paraders were drunk enough to fall over, he returned to the castle. It was an early night. There had been a short round of carols inside, but the usual merrymaking was canceled.

Before Gwilym the steward retired for the evening, he went into Noble's audience room to receive the great seal for safekeeping from Gwirion's mischief in the king's absence. Before he left, he made an offer—looking slightly self-conscious but, as ever, dignified—that would once have been unimaginable.

"My duties will be doubled in your absence, sire."

"You always handle it with grace." Noble managed to smile, although he looked very stressed and tired. "As you did for my father before me."

Gwilym grimaced. "Thank you. It has always been my honor to be your deputy." He paused. "Considering the circumstances, Her Majesty will have a hard time of it here. There's little to occupy her attention—I understand construction has stopped at the abbey for the winter."

Noble gave him a disbelieving, conspiratorial look. "Are you saying what I think you're saying?"

"If it would assist to . . . maintain her current desirable demeanor, I will yield some of my castellan privileges to her. I must admit she has more than proven her potential."

It took Noble less than a second to decide what he wanted to do with this opportunity. "That's very generous of you, Gwilym. She may well take you up on that."

S HE was already pacing around his torchlit chamber when he arrived, even tenser than she had been for weeks now. He understood, more than he could afford to let her know, how difficult all this was for her. When he returned, when it was over, he would tell her how genuinely he admired her reserve, but the comment given now would likely, under pressure, somehow lead to argument. She was wearing only her silk shift and Noble's large woolen chamber robe, her braids hanging down to her waist, and as always in this outfit she looked like a child playing dress up. When Isabel heard him entering, she stopped her pacing and took a deep, nervous breath. "I want to go with you," she blurted out.

He stared at her and then laughed gently. "That's not even open for discussion, madam."

"If I stay here with so little to do, I'll go mad."

He couldn't help smiling at how neatly she'd walked into the game. "I seem to recall your poring over law books last summer with Goronwy. Would it help distract you if you stood in for me at court?"

She frowned. "But that's the steward's privilege."

"It could be yours," he said. "And so could many other things."

"Gwilym would be outraged. Goronwy would throw a fit!"

"I don't make offers I can't honor, Isabel." He raised one brow at her. "Let's play a little tit for tat. One castellan duty for every novelty you agree to try tonight."

She almost laughed, but duly made a disgusted face instead. "That's perverse."

"I need some perverse distraction and so do you, I think. Take off your things and lie down on the bed." She realized he was serious and stared at him in silence, unmoving. "Excuse me," he said in a sterner voice. "I am leaving here in ten hours to put my life at risk for your idiot brother—because of a marriage contract that has yielded me nothing that it should have. Take off your things and lie down now."

With a loud sigh of annoyance she obeyed him, pulling off her shift as he unlaced his boots and stripped off his own tunic, hose, and drawers. He sat over her on the bed, unceremoniously pushed her legs apart, wet his fingers with his tongue, and lubricated her. She made a constricted sound in her throat and growled at him, but he only gave her a mischievous smile and shook his head.

"I'm seeing you beg me to bind your wrists to the bedposts."

"I'm seeing you being mistaken," she retorted. She crossed her arms across her bare chest and glowered up at the bed canopy.

"If you'd like to be my deputy in court," he said, grinning, "you will beg me to bind your wrists to the bedposts. To start with. I promise you'll enjoy this game more if you play it with enthusiasm."

He ran his tongue across her lower belly and she gasped, then broke into frustrated, angry laughter from the sheer tension of the night.

H IS final farewell was to Gwirion, whom he scared by awakening, personally, two hours before dawn.

"Sire?" Gwirion whispered when he sensed rather than saw the familiar presence kneeling in the entrance to his closet. "What are you doing here?"

"If these are my last two hours alive at Cymaron," Noble whispered in response, "I shouldn't be sleeping through them."

"Molest your wife, then," Gwirion said, flattered by the visit.

"I already did that. She surprised me tonight, but she hasn't Enid's staying power."

"Neither have I," muttered Gwirion, but trundled the covers away. "Well then, are you coming in or am I going out? It's warm in here at least, and I don't think there's much privacy anywhere else."

The king ducked his head down and crawled into the space. Gwirion lit a candle and the two of them glanced briefly at each other in the dim light. "This is homey but it's rather tight. How did you and Corr both fit?"

"We were *very* close," Gwirion lisped precociously.

Noble cleared his throat. "I have something to say to you," he whispered, suddenly serious. Gwirion considered him for a moment, guessed what it was, and made a face of mock amazement.

"Don't tell me His Royal Highness is about to apologize," he said. "Not now! We have no witnesses, no artists to immortalize the moment, no bard to compose flowery monotony about your spiritual transformation."

"Be quiet or I'll cut your tongue out," Noble said impatiently. "I don't have much experience with this and I don't want you misunderstanding."

"My ears are yours."

Noble grimaced. "I don't care that Huw prefers partners that are half the size of his wife. And I don't care if he prefers it when they're not very eager about it."

"*You* don't even do that," Gwirion protested.

"Gwirion," the king said bluntly, "there is absolutely no difference between Huw and myself."

Gwirion gave him a disbelieving look. "There's a huge difference. Huw is bad to his partners, you're good to yours."

Noble gave his friend a didactic smile. "Only because I enjoy it. That's not a difference in morality, Gwirion, it's only a difference in taste."

"You give them a *choice*, he forces them."

Noble laughed comfortably. "And what sort of choice does a woman have when she's invited to go to the king, when she knows the king can take her anyhow?"

"Noble, you don't touch them if they're even just a little bashful. I've *been* there, I've *seen* you."

"That's a choice I'm entitled to make because I am the one with all the power."

"It's a choice you make because you're a good man," Gwirion declared firmly. "I wouldn't pander for you otherwise."

"You're confusing goodness with preference," Noble corrected him. "I take no pleasure in a woman's indifference, and certainly not in her resistance. I wrestle with enough recalcitrance in council—and with you, for that matter, although at least with you it's occasionally entertaining. I like the flattery of ready enthusiasm in *some* facet of existence. That's the premise of my gallantry—I'm simply taking what I want in the manner that I want it." He gave his friend a droll look. "That's sensual gratification, Gwirion, not goodness. In that way I'm no different from Huw." Gwirion looked stricken, almost nauseated, and said nothing. After a moment Noble, his expression softening, pressed on. "You were right, though, there's an apology in here." He paused, took a breath to collect his words. "It was not wrong of me to offer Huw those children. It was a kind of quid pro quo—and not for Branwyn, by the way, she was just a rather marvelous perquisite."

Gwirion looked at him uncomprehendingly. "What did you get out of it but Branwyn?"

"The security of Huw's allegiance."

Gwirion blinked. "You're not telling me he swore loyalty to you because you let him sodomize your stable boy."

"He swore loyalty because we have an understanding now, that we will look out for each other's interests. That there are checks and balances, but I am the dispenser of favors, and he must be deserving of such favors if he wishes to receive them. He's seen that I will dispense with my subjects as I see fit, but he knows that applies to him as well as to a stable boy. What happened that week was a necessary transaction, and in itself it was entirely unobjectionable. My failing was in my obligation to you. You were distressed about the children and I know why."

Gwirion looked away awkwardly. "My distress has nothing to do with . . . *that*." He tugged at a fraying thread on the cuffs of his breeches.

"I thought they were killing you too," Noble said. "I thought I'd lost both—"

"We agreed not to talk about it," Gwirion insisted sharply, looking up.

Noble retreated. "Fine. That is the apology. I am genuinely grieved that what happened disturbed you. You must understand something, however, Gwirion: I'm grieved but I will not modify my behavior for it. Not because I'm a monster, but because I'm a king. I may *wish* to spare a child from trauma, I may *wish* to spare your being distressed about it, but I *need* to protect my kingdom's northwest border."

"But you do wish you could have spared him, don't you?" Gwirion demanded, sounding almost plaintive.

"My wishing something that I can't act on contributes nothing to the well-being of the kingdom, so it doesn't matter whether I wish it or not."

"Drop the king-talk," Gwirion said irritably.

"For important matters, I have no other language," said Noble quietly. "That's why your nonsense is always such welcome relief."

Gwirion said nothing for a long time. Although their faces were only inches apart, the king could not read his eyes in the dimly lit space. Finally, Gwirion looked up and met his gaze. "I accept the apology," he said aloud. To himself he kept the thought, unspoken, *You are becoming a horrible man and I must escape you.* But the native affection he had for that face, more familiar than his own, and the eyes more attentive than any mother's gaze he had ever known, made such a choice, however necessary, ultimately impossible, and he knew it.

L ISTLESSNESS settled over the castle when the king and his men had gone. The exception was the queen, who (indifferent to the indignant mutterings around her) reveled in the castellan duties she had earned. There were many: Each morning after attending chapel and breaking her fast, she met with Gwilym and Marged to go over the day's schedule. Every few days she met with the almoner, the laundress, the seamstress, the interim captain of the shriveled castle garrison, the mayor of the village, and the marshal's son Ednyfed, standing in for his father, who was with the king. After the morning meeting, once a week she would sit with Goronwy the judge to listen to civil matters from villagers and other subjects who had traveled sometimes days on foot. When there were no complications, the judge would simply rule on cases; when his judgment was challenged, the matter was normally turned over on appeal to the king or his deputy to consider with the council. But it was wartime and most of the council was at the front, so the queen found herself in the extraordinary position of being a one-woman, foreign-born appellate court. Goronwy was furious at first, but Gwilym calmly backed her claim that she was replacing him as the king's deputy—and further pointed out that there was no actual law forbidding such a thing; it had simply never been the custom. Once the judge accepted that they were not breaking any law, he rescinded his objection with almost comical speed, although most castle workers continued to cast a disapproving eye on the queen's mysterious and shocking assumption of authority. The first day of court trials, suppliants did not hide their unwillingness to receive judgment from a woman and a foreigner. She was gracious with them, offering them the opportunity to return when the king was back from the border. Most took her up on this but a few, in the end, did not, and by chance or fancy those appealing liked her judgment—the peasant who cut down a sacred oak grove; the penniless young freeman who'd just inherited his father's lands but not his title and his brother who'd inherited the title but no land; a woman accused of killing her husband's concubine. With no bias, conditioning, or instinct to control the population, she was truer to the letter of the law than Noble ever could have been and word quickly spread that the queen was a prudent, fair adjudicator. Already by the second week, people had begun to argue with the judge's sentences simply for the novelty of her attention. Native law was meticulous and complicated, and she found her eyes glazing over trying to understand all the taxation schemes for the various uses of land. For a people more pastoral than agricultural, they had rules about land use and distribution that outgarbled Norman feudalism.

She also assumed the financial burden of the housekeeping, setting the budget and keeping track of who spent how much for what. There were no fees to the crown for months to come now, which spared her from the awkward situation of accepting capital from people she knew lacked enough to spare. She had never been comfortable doing this for her brother's manors, and was glad to avoid it here. On a couple of occasions she found herself awkwardly accepting minor fees for things she could not believe Noble ought to benefit from: the loss of every maiden's virginity, for example, enriched the king's coffers even more handsomely than it did each ex-maiden's. She wondered sardonically how the math worked out when Noble himself was the responsible party.

But more than the mental gymnastics of a day in court, what left her most uncertain was what to do with Gwirion. Normally he was forever busy at errands, performing, rehearsing, or pursuing other vague activities she had never bothered to look in to. But with the king gone, he sank into almost immediate lethargy. He would do anything that was asked of him, quickly and efficiently, from performing acrobatics for the village children to helping prepare grain for the mill, but left to himself he was like a puppet without a puppeteer.

COURIERS, running in relay along preestablished routes, came to and from the eastern border regularly. The temperature held mild, but with the mountainous terrain and unpredictable weather, it took at least a day for the fastest of them to reach the front, and much longer when there was mud or driving rain.

The only thing that put Isabel on edge were Noble's reports. They had arrived without incident, he wrote, stopping only at Pilleth's holy well for a blessing from the statue of the Virgin there. But once they were encamped near Llanandras, Mortimer had mocked them and told them to go home. They had demanded Thomas's free presence in person, and Mortimer stalled for days. The next report told her that Mortimer had ambushed and imprisoned her old coot uncles, Walter and Ralf, while they were on their way to petition Prince John for Thomas's release. Finally, Noble wrote, Mortimer had come to parley at the River Lugg, but he was cagey and indirect and at the end of the discussion, nothing at all had been justified or promised. There was no further parley.

But after five tense days, a band of teulu, going stir-crazy camped out through endless winter nights, stupidly crossed the border to raid the English village of Lingen, which belonged to Mortimer— and every day since then had seen a retaliatory counterstrike from each side in turn, skirmish after skirmish that were almost as difficult to quell as a full-out battle would have been to prosecute. The messengers came less frequently, and the queen's brow was permanently creased. When news finally arrived again from the east, it came in a coffin. Hywel the bard had fallen early on, sword in hand, during the largest engagement so far: a brief battle in which Mortimer had almost effortlessly annexed the Maelienydd valley that had been the no-man's-land between the armies. He moved the whole of his force onto the richest soil in Noble's kingdom and settled them there: squatters, invaders, victors. He did not press his advantage, he did not attack the native host. He simply stayed.

When this news reached Cymaron, Hafaidd and Gwilym spent a fretful day calculating what smallest possible company could defend the castle in a siege. With the queen's sanction, they chose from among the guards those least likely to contribute much in battle. They kept these men at Cymaron to form a skeleton garrison; all the rest, they sent to the front. Years later, two old men in an altered world, they would trace the events of that winter and spring backward through time and agree that the folly of their decision was to blame for all that followed, although they could not possibly have foreseen the worst of it.

THE morning after the bard's burial, on the first day it was truly winter cold, Castell Cymaron was alerted to a sound no one had heard in years: five urgent staccato notes sounded on a trumpet, repeated many times. People looked up from their work—plucking geese, laying down new strewing herbs, fixing ploughs, balancing books, feeding horses, tending fires, hearing confession, letting blood—wondering what it meant. Then, almost as a single unit, the castle population realized they were under attack.

Panic swept the bailey and everybody instinctively scuttled into the hall, where the queen and the judge had been holding court. Gwilym, with the prescience Isabel had grown to admire, was already standing at her side. She turned to him, grim but unshaken. "The keep?" she asked.

The keep tower was intended for protection in an attack, but the castle's design required crossing over a trench to reach it from the courtyard. Since marauders were usually sighted from a distance on these high broad hills, there would normally be time to get up into the keep, but the trumpeter's signal was the code for an imminent siege; she was concerned that there would be no time to get people safely across. "I'll learn more," the steward offered, and went out to the courtyard.

Gwirion wandered in as Isabel was trying to soothe the visiting women petitioners. He had heard the alarm and imagined the queen would be hysterical, so he chose to appear with an insouciant attitude to accentuate her fear. He entered eating a heel of barley bread Marged had told him he couldn't have, chewing slowly and loudly to demonstrate how unconcerned he was about the chaos.

"Gwirion," said the queen's voice beside him, with a calm authority he had never heard and could hardly believe. "We may be moving to the keep and we'll need your assistance." She pointed to an elderly couple from another valley, at court on petition. "Help those two." Without waiting for an answer, she efficiently shifted her attention to a large man, a villager, and told him to carry a woman who was blind. Gwirion was floored by her levelheadedness; he wasn't sure whether he was disappointed or impressed.

Gwilym returned looking confused. "There's been some mistake, milady," he said. "It's nothing but a small company outside the barbican. The guards at the village gate let them in and they made their way up to the castle without incident. They're not even on horseback. I would recommend you come speak to them, Your Majesty."

"Why did our man sound the alarm?"

"We're so lightly garrisoned right now, all of the guards have been on edge." He did not add his personal opinion: Feeling insulted for being kept behind, these men were hoping for a crisis so they could prove themselves, and they were only too eager to read drama into any unexpected circumstance.

She called for a mantle and tied it closed, then stepped out of the side door with him into the cold, grey morning air, descending the steps to the main gate. She nodded to the deputy porter, a gaunt tanner from the village who bowed nervously, flustered by her proximity. He opened the small eye-level panel in the gate to reveal an enormous jowl and moustache. "Identify yourself to Her Majesty," he ordered the moustache.

Its owner descended enough to show his face in the opening. He was about Noble's age and coloring but much rougher looking, and reddened from the cold. "Good morning!" he said to the porter as if they were old friends. "Let us in, would you? We're freezing."

"Identify yourself," the porter repeated.

The man proclaimed himself Cynan ap Dafydd, baron from Gwynedd and kinsman to Prince Llewelyn.

"Why aren't you fighting with him if you're kin?" Gwilym asked, moving closer to the gate.

"I've been keeping an eye on things at home. We're on our way to the Marches now to join my prince and his men, but we needed to warm ourselves and possibly restore provisions. We'd pay for that, of course."

"And why did my man sound an alarm?" the steward persisted quietly.

"Well, there's a lot of us," Cynan said. "The whole of my company stands outside the gates. He might have been a bit overwhelmed. It's a misunderstanding. I'm not asking you to shelter all of them, just my teulu, and there's not many of them. We need a day to regroup, then we'll be on our way again. I've got Llewelyn's seal with me if you're seeking proof."

Satisfied, Gwilym looked to the queen for instructions. "We need a moment to discuss this," she said politely, and to the porter added, "Close the panel."

"Wait, wait!" the baron called. "There's nothing to discuss. I'm kinsman to your lord's closest ally, on my way to help fight for *your* border, and we need some shelter because it's colder than ice balls out here. Open the gate."

She stared at him through narrowed eyes. "You've arrived in the morning. Why does that seem strange to me?"

"We got lost in the hills, lost our bearings. All the valleys look exactly alike around here, don't they? We didn't know we were so close until we broke camp at dawn. Please, lady, we have lads out here with frostbite. We're guests! There's a code of decency! Haven't you got that in England?"

"Why didn't you send a messenger ahead to let us know you were coming?" she pressed, ignoring the insult.

The man cursed. "We did! I guess he's lost too, then. I hope he didn't freeze to death, poor lad. As castles go, this one is damn hard to find, you know that, don't you?"

She couldn't argue that point; her wedding party had almost gotten lost coming here and she hadn't had nearly so far to travel. Beginning to shiver a little in the cold, she turned to the steward. "What are your thoughts on this?"

"Saxons," she heard Cynan mutter in exasperation to someone in his party. She forced herself to ignore it.

Gwilym had a ready answer. "Your Majesty is the king's deputy in this, but I would admit them. It's a terrible insult to Llewelyn not to. They'll leave their weapons with the porter."

"Of course we will," Cynan said, impatient at having to even discuss something so obvious.

At last, displeased, she gestured for the gate to be opened. Although a man on the barbican had already vouched that the visitor spoke the truth, she didn't relax until she saw Cynan's company for herself: a small teulu of about a dozen men, and their squires who carried satchels. "There's soldiers out that way," he said, nodding down the road out of the village. "Watching our mounts. But they'll stay there unless you have the room and inclination to house them in your bailey. They're hardy enough."

She smiled stiffly without responding, and exchanged formal greetings with him as he and his men laid their quivers, bows, and swords in a pile near the gate. To reassure the queen, Gwilym signaled most of the garrison to shadow the visitors into the hall. As they

mounted the broad stone stairs, Cynan asked if breakfast was a possibility—again, he said cheerfully, just for these men, not his entire
company. Marged grudgingly agreed to scrounge something up.

People began to drift out of the hall and back to their tasks or
(after wrapping themselves snugly) down into the village, and even
Goronwy excused himself to waddle back to his room, since court
was clearly adjourned for the morning. Some folk stayed around, fascinated by the unexpected guests; the guards tried casually to blend in
with them. The queen's focus was so intently on her visitors that she
didn't realize, until the familiar strains of "Rhiannon's Tears" caught
her attention, that Gwirion was in the room, squatting on his stool by
the hearth. She had to admit to herself she was glad of his presence.

She had deliberately neglected offering to wash her guests' feet,
and denied Cynan's request to let his men enjoy free rein of the bailey, but he simply shrugged agreeably. Still there was something
about this man she didn't trust. He was enjoying himself too much
for somebody fighting off frostbite. She excused the steward and
usher to their chamber, but she did it in a tone of voice that encouraged them to tarry in the courtyard to keep an eye on things.

There was a table by the hearth for the morning audience that
had been interrupted, and the baron and his men settled themselves
there. She sat near them, partly to be courteous but mostly to keep an
eye on them. Marged managed to feed them all cheese, barley cakes,
and ale, and everyone who saw it wondered if that would be a meal
out of their own mouths before the end of winter. The men ate with
gusto, and quickly. Cynan pushed his ale away and rubbed his sleeve
across his moustache and lips, which approximated cleaning them.
He smiled broadly at the queen.

"You have a good harp there, milady."

"Thank you," she and Gwirion said at the same moment. She
glanced at the harpist quickly; he did not return the look, just ran his
hand with deferential affection over the slightly curved forepillar and
the lion head atop it, and began a new piece.

"Excuse me, milady, but did I really hear the steward call you
your husband's deputy?"

"That's correct," she answered stiffly, wondering what to say if questioned about how that had come to pass.

"Then if you don't mind, milady, there is in fact just one quick thing I'd like to speak of with you."

"It depends upon the substance of it."

"Is your ladyship aware of my prince's interest in . . . unifying Wales under a single banner?"

"A single banner of Gwynedd, do you mean?" she said coldly. "My husband has mentioned it. He's opposed, of course. I thought the issue had been dropped."

He shook his head, grimacing. "It hasn't. My master Llewelyn would like him to reconsider an arrangement."

"That should be negotiated by the two of them personally after the current crisis is settled. This is hardly the time to resolve it."

"Well, yes, that's what I told His Highness myself, but the way he saw it, the current crisis offers an opportunity to demonstrate to your husband the wisdom of cooperating."

"How?"

"Llewelyn believes it might encourage your husband to cooper-ate if I brought Your Majesty to Gwynedd for a while."

She was on her feet instantly and backing away from him, but eight of the pages, hidden knives drawn from their knee boots, were already in pairs at the exits and the foot of the stairs. They'd moved with arrow-straight choreography: Someone who knew this space had drawn it out for them. Marged shrieked from the kitchen and Gwirion, leaping to his feet, banged his knee on the harp as the few green or aging guards, taken by surprise, took a moment to collect themselves, which cost them. Cynan's teulu were far better fighters and outmanned them, and had them disarmed in less than a minute as Gwirion and the queen gaped at what was happening. The four re-maining pages, with almost mechanical synchronicity, pulled ropes from their satchels and had the men bound before another minute had passed, as Isabel stared helplessly around the hall. It had hap-pened so quickly and with so little struggle that it was hard to believe there was any real menace involved. The baron's companionable expression did not change. "It's no use running away, milady, and you won't be sending anyone for help." As if on cue, the trumpeter outside began to sound the five-note alarm again, and the church bell joined the noise urgently. The baron smiled. "So your man has finally puzzled it out. My host has the entire village surrounded now. No one will get away but by my permission."

"If you hold me hostage—"

"Oh, no, milady, it's nothing like that." Cynan chuckled reassuringly. "You'll be a treasured guest of my prince, that's all, and he'll be very jealous of your safety. You'll notice we haven't hurt your men. This isn't a siege, we're simply here to escort you northward. I'll be bringing you back with me today, and my soldiers will stay outside the village walls a few days more to make sure word doesn't travel to your king too quickly. He needs to keep his mind on the enemy, you know—wouldn't want him distracted by domestic troubles." As she calculated her chances of getting past the boys by the kitchen entrance, the baron's teulu and the remaining pages dashed through the exits in groups of four to secure the entire bailey. She knew, with a sinking feeling, that they would meet almost no resistance. Even Gwilym, despite his height and general build, was too old now to be strong in arms. "So, milady, thank you for the breakfast, that was a treat, and we'll be departing at once. If one of you lads would bind Her Majesty's hands—gently, she's a delicate thing—and where is that pretty cape you were wearing?" He looked casually around the hall, as if expecting a servant to show up holding it out.

"You're wasting your time, he won't give up a thing for that one," Gwirion said from the hearth. She closed her eyes and breathed a silent prayer of gratitude. He set the harp against the wall and walked up to Cynan. "I'm the one you want."

The baron looked at him as if he were insane. "And who in hell are you?" he asked.

"I'm a person of importance to the king—isn't that all that matters? If you're taking somebody hostage to manipulate His Majesty, you'll have a lot more leverage if you take me."

Cynan turned to the queen. "Is the fellow daft?"

"No," she said, barely able to bring her voice above a whisper. "He's not. He's telling you the truth." It was a truth she never thought she'd be grateful to hear touted.

"What sort of prat is this, then?" the baron demanded. "I don't believe either of you."

"The queen's no use to him. She hasn't brought him a son, she couldn't even carry to term. And it was a political marriage designed to help stabilize the area where—in case you hadn't heard—there is now a battle going on, so obviously that part of the union didn't work either. You'd be doing him a favor, frankly, taking the thing off his hands. The rest of us wouldn't mind either, to be honest, she's an uppity woman who will *not* keep to her place. He'll let her wither away in your dungeon or wherever you keep her. She's not even a native subject! It'll be a wasted effort."

"And you? What's to be gained by you?"

"Noble would raise the heavens to get me back under his roof. Take me, don't waste your time with the queen."

Cynan curled his lip at Gwirion. "I hadn't heard about that particular predilection."

Gwirion laughed. "It's not like that, but make of it what you will."

The baron snorted again. "This is an obvious ploy, I'd have to be an idiot to fall for it."

Gwirion shrugged. "If you don't believe me, help yourself to her, but you're wasting your time and she'll be another mouth to feed for no benefit at all. She's small, but trust me, she eats like a starving pig." He walked back toward his harp. Isabel's heart thrilled with gratitude at his convincing nonchalance.

"Why are you being so helpful?" Cynan demanded.

Looking down demurely as he settled at the harp, Gwirion said in a conspiratorial tone, "Some people here think Llewelyn would not be such a bad overlord, but nobody's been able to persuade the king of that. I am happy to offer myself up for the sake of a better future."

"Is that so?" Cynan asked, with wary sarcasm. "I'm glad there are those here with a little common sense." He studied the harpist. "If you're telling me the truth, prove it."

"You can ask anybody in this room. In the castle. In the village. In the valley," Gwirion said calmly.

"That's nothing," the baron scoffed. "That could be a stratagem you set up weeks ago."

"Naive as we are, it never occurred to us we'd need a stratagem for protection against our major ally. But if you need proof, just ask the king," Gwirion said, already sounding bored with the discussion, and picked up his tuning key to fiddle with the harp pegs.

The baron laughed. "Yes, I'll just trot over to the front lines and say, 'Excuse me, Your Highness, but I need to take a hostage and I was wondering whose absence you'd be most disturbed by.'"

"Send a messenger," Gwirion suggested casually, apparently more interested in tuning his harp than he was in the conversation. But Isabel saw a look on his face that she suddenly recognized and something inside her relaxed, trusting his instincts and knowing that things might be under control now, as preposterous as that seemed. "Send one of your messengers dressed in our livery, and have him ask the question very neutrally—tell him it's a bet we're making here among ourselves, and they need a written answer to who matters more, the queen or Gwirion."

The baron's eyes got very wide. "You're Gwirion!" he said, as if that made everything clear. Gwirion looked up from tuning, then down again in mock consternation at his own hands and arms.

"Good God, man, you're right! How did *that* happen?"

"I thought Huw had invented you!"

Gwirion and the queen exchanged looks: Huw ap Maredudd, seducer of stable boys and longtime advocate of Prince Llewelyn. Of course. He turned back to his harp, refusing to grace Cynan with a direct glance. "Will you do that, then? Send one of your boys to the king? If you've a good horse and a strong boy, he can be there and back in two days."

The baron eyed him thoughtfully. Now that he knew who the fellow was, there was actually a remote possibility he was telling the truth. Based on stories of what the king let this man get away with, there was surely some unique bond between them. But still . . .

"Don't be daft. The lady is his queen consort and you don't even exist as a political entity."

"Noble doesn't negotiate," Gwirion lied, apparently speaking to his B-flat string. "He won't make decisions from political manipulation. He's completely self-centered, a creature of whims and fancy, and you'll get far more out of him if you appeal to his emotions than to his political loyalties. He simply has no sense of loyalty." He finally looked up at Cynan. "Not unlike your own prince."

The baron ignored the remark. Gwirion's suggestion sounded appealing. This was a warm castle, and a few days' rations at somebody else's expense was always a good idea in wintertime. On the other hand, there was the garrison to deal with. Although it was only a skeleton crew, his men could not hold all of them at bay for more than a few hours. Unless—

"Madoc," he called out, as one of his men reentered from the yard. "Look at their keep. Could we lock the castle guard into it for a few days?" That might work. It would be easy to control them, they'd be removed from the unarmed civilians, and there would be ample provisions for them there. "Is there a dungeon?" he suddenly asked. He saw Gwirion and Isabel both blanch. "I'm not interested in torturing you, I just need to hole you up somewhere until the messenger returns— What?" he demanded when Gwirion laughed.

"Together? I'd rather have the rack!" the harpist answered, and ran his fingers over the strings to check the tuning. "In any event, the only cell's not big enough to hold us both, unless you want to breed us—but from an aesthetic perspective, I really wouldn't advise it. My magnificent profile would be lost to history."

Cynan ignored the flip comment. "Is there a room we can secure entirely? No windows, one door? Her Majesty is now a guest of ours, I don't want her put out."

Nobody offered information.

"Then she shall have to join you in the cellar," Cynan said with a shrug.

"There's the king's private audience chamber," Gwirion conceded, seeing the look on Isabel's face. He tightened the third peg slightly and plucked the string, his ear pressed close to it. "That would be acceptable to Her Majesty, I think. It's snugger than a nun's loins."

"Where is it?"

Gwirion gestured toward the door in the corner of the hall before returning to his tuning, and the baron sent one of his men to check the room. A moment later, Madoc returned with the report that the keep would work. The top floor was intentionally empty, to provide refuge in a siege, and the basement held months' worth of food. The baron agreed to Gwirion's suggestion, and a courier outfit in the royal livery of red tunic and yellow hose was found to fit one of the baron's pages. The baron coached him on what to say, and Gwirion put the harp down at last, to point out where the boy's accent was too obviously of Gwynedd. "If anybody asks, say you're from the northern border—say Newtown—and you've just arrived here as a page. If you use my name, or the queen's, you should get immediate access to the king, and he'll probably laugh and write you a response right away."

"Won't he think it strange that in the middle of battle he's getting such a trivial request?" The baron frowned.

"On the contrary," Gwirion assured him, picking up his harp again. "He'll assume it's part of some bigger prank of mine. It will seem so reassuringly normal he'll forget about it within an hour." He closed his eyes and began a series of melodious descending arpeggios, smiling contentedly.

"You're an odd lot in Maelienydd, aren't you?" Cynan snorted. "Anyway, now, into the chamber with you, boyo." Isabel started slightly and the arpeggio ended in midnote as Gwirion clapped his hands over the strings, his eyes springing open: Neither of them had realized they were actually going to end up shut in together.

"I thought I was going to the cellar," Gwirion said.

Cynan gestured vaguely toward the door. "In this cold? If you're the prize we want, I can't risk your taking a chill and dying off."

Gwirion, thrown, affected insouciance and made a great show of laying the harp on its back, bowing, and fluttering an imaginary cloak as he crossed to the door and finally marched in, waving gaily to everybody as he vanished into the shadows of the chamber. Cynan turned to the queen, who had watched his parade with obvious discomfort. Silently, she allowed herself to be escorted in behind her fellow inmate. The door was pulled shut, and she heard the butler's key turn in the lock.

11

UNVEILED

Late January, 1199

HE ONLY LIGHT was from the fireplace and it took her a moment to adjust to the darkness. Gwirion was trembling, actually shaking with fear, and his face was almost as pale as the whitewashed walls.

"Gwirion?" she said in disbelief.

"I was so frightened," he whispered, ashamed, and collapsed hard into Noble's chair.

"I would never have known it." She sat on the chest beside him but didn't touch him for fear of making him more self-conscious. "Why did you do that?"

"To buy time. And because what I said is true." He was trying to calm his breathing.

She pushed away the immature impulse to argue with him. "So what? What do you gain from it?" He didn't answer. "You told me you aren't my ally, you only do what benefits you. How on earth do you benefit from being taken to Gwynedd as a hostage?"

The truth was, he did not know why he'd done it, and he scrambled mentally for any excuse that wouldn't sound chivalrous. "I can escape. I could free myself from anything they would put me in within minutes. You can't."

"But how do you benefit from that?"

"Then I'm free!" he said nervously, still jangled. "It's the perfect way to desert without having Noble's hounds on me."

"I didn't think you wanted to desert anymore. You didn't go with Owain."

He'd forgotten he had confided that to her. No, he hadn't gone with Owain. And Noble had done nothing objectionable since the end of the war council . . . except for that twisted apology the morning he left, a moment of unmasking that left Gwirion with a terrible opinion of what his friend was made of—something he could never tell her about. "That was before there was *war*," he said instead. "I don't want to be confined to a castle with this sort of nonsense happening all the time."

She shook her head. "You're safer here than anywhere else. People come *to* Cymaron for safety. You're not making any sense."

He threw her a challenging look, trying to stare her down with his onyx-hard eyes. "Why do *you* think I did it, then?"

"Because you're my ally," she said, risking a shy, pleased smile.

"Why do women sentimentalize everything?" he groaned. He leapt up and knocked hard on the door. One of Cynan's teulu opened it a crack and stuck a knife through it to discourage Gwirion's coming too near. "Excuse me," he petitioned the soldier, "would you be willing perhaps to construct a rack and keep me on it in another room for the duration?"

"You are such an ass!" Isabel said crossly, standing up. Unexpectedly, Gwirion laughed and the guard slammed the door closed again.

"Thank you," he said, his humor restored. "I don't think you've ever let yourself go with me before. This might actually be entertaining! Quick, what's the worst insult you can think of? I'll win that duel, but I'd be happy to mentor you."

She made a gesture of annoyance and crossed away from him to the dark side of the room. "This is even worse than being cooped up with the sewing bevy," she muttered to herself. Gwirion, hearing her, gave her a gaping look of delight.

"The *sewing bevy*? Is that what you call your attendants?"

"Not to their faces," she said shortly, turning away from him.

"And you don't like the sewing bevy?" This, in a hopefully tentative voice as if he feared her answer might disappoint him.

She spoke clearly but without malice, still facing into the darkness. "They are a bunch of ninnies."

He clapped his hands together, nearly prancing. "Your Majesty, I wish I'd known you felt that way, I'd've persecuted them!" She looked over her veiled shoulder to stare at him. "If I knew someone might derive satisfaction from it, I would have paid them some attention, but I assumed you were all birds of a feather so I never bothered about them."

"You bothered about *me*."

"Of course I did, you're the top hen."

"And I threatened you," she said firmly, returning to the fireplace.

He stopped prancing, but grinned at her boyishly. "For about a day. I threatened you much longer than that, and much worse. I *still* threaten you. That's why we're in here right now, isn't it?"

She looked at him with wounded dignity. "If he answers that I'm the more important, won't that threaten you?"

"He won't say that," Gwirion assured her, impatiently, then grinned again. "Tell me what you dislike about the sewing bevy."

"Just because I think they're dullwits doesn't mean they deserve your persecution."

"I'll only do it behind their backs," he promised. "They'll never even know."

"And what purpose would that serve?"

"I'd be doing it for *you*, of course," he explained. "As a favor. You've never said a cross thing about them that I know of. You've been an angel, and you need a devil to let the bile out on your behalf."

"Oh, is *that* what you're for?" she asked ironically. He nodded, pleased that she finally understood. "Then I must assume you insult me because Noble hates me but can't let himself say so. You're being the devil he can't let himself be?"

He looked startled at this thought, and then shook his head. "No, that's different," he said in a rare moment of utter guilelessness. "You're an outsider who's invaded my kingdom. When I insult you, I'm doing it for myself."

She crossed her arms and took a step toward him. "Why?" She wanted to finally have it out with him.

Gwirion looked blank. He stared wide-eyed at her, at the wall, at the floor, at his own shoulder, but nothing inspired an answer. Finally, with an awkward laugh, he declared, "Because it's *fun*, of course."

She made a disgusted sound and leaned back against the mantel seeking warmth, wrapping her arms around herself. "That's the most puerile thing I've ever heard."

He moved in toward the other end of the hearth. "I insult the king too! He enjoys it! Why can't you enjoy it? What's wrong with you?" he asked, overplaying the mockery to hide his discomfort.

She gave him a killing look. "You insult him as a perverse way of showing him affection. You aren't showing me affection when you ask somebody to stretch you on the rack in order to avoid my company!"

"Perhaps I am," Gwirion shot back without thinking.

There was a pause. He considered what he had just said and fidgeted in the firelight.

"Is that true?" she demanded. Her impulse had been to berate him, but if there was any way at all, ever, for the two of them to reach a genuine détente . . .

There was another pause, this one more awkward. Gwirion wanted to rescind the statement, but didn't have the energy to get into another round. And somehow, insulting her for its own sake had lost its vicious appeal; he was simply getting bored with it.

"It didn't used to be true," he said at last.

"Is it true now?" she pressed.

"Who else do you dislike in the castle?" he asked, regaining the boyish grin. In a hopeful, conspiratorial tone, he whispered loudly, "I bet you have a terrifically twisted secret side. We might come out of this the best of friends!"

"Stop avoiding the question."

The grin faded and he turned away from her. She watched him absently brush away the hair of his cowlick as he mused, expressionless, and she decided with a certain smug condescension that he was really almost good looking when he wasn't making those ridiculous faces. Finally he turned back to her to explain in a dismissive tone: "It's just pity. I was so appalled by his treatment of you, that night with Owain, and you couldn't have gotten away with the sort of thing I did. You're still fundamentally insultable, but I had never really understood before how powerless you were."

"We're exactly the same, then, aren't we?"

He looked at her, bemused. "You mean besides the fact that you sleep in the king's bed?"

"Our only real value here is our relative worth to him. We have no independent function, either of us. That's a distinction nobody else shares." He blinked, unprepared for an insight he couldn't mock or dismiss. Finally, he nodded slowly in concession, and she added with a soft laugh, "I'm glad I did not have that thought before now. A few months ago it might have made me ill."

He leered at her theatrically. "You mean you're starting to like me?"

She mirrored the leer back at him across the mantelpiece, a mildly malicious gesture he approved of although it was startlingly alien to her blunt features. "No," she said, and dropped the expression. "But I understand you a little more. I'm on shakier ground than you are, you know. What you said about my giving him a child is right. If I'm permanently damaged, he might be pressured to . . . free himself, so he may take a wife who can produce an heir." She tried to say this in a tone that wouldn't reveal how many nightmares the thought had caused her. Divorce under canon law was practically impossible, and she'd heard more than once of a man simply killing his wife to expedite getting a new one.

But Gwirion waved the idea off. "No, you're thinking like those silly English," he said. "In Wales, any son he has with anyone, any son he acknowledges, can inherit. As long as he sires at least one bastard, you don't have to give him anything."

This did not reassure her the way he'd intended it to. "So I'm not even needed as a brood mare, I can't rely on the need for an heir as a way to make sure he keeps me. That means I'm completely dependent on his whim!"

Gwirion, for whom this had always been true, didn't understand the crisis, but he felt vaguely responsible for her agitation and in any case wanted her to calm down. "He doesn't kill people when he gets tired of them," he reassured her. "He would just get an annulment."

This didn't help either. "And that would reduce me to *nothing*," she fretted. "I would be a spinster, without power, prestige, money—"

"That's what I am now," Gwirion offered as a clumsy attempt to both empathize and distract. "Except the spinster part—but my carnal carousing is as frequent as a spinster's. If it weren't for the Spring Rites, I might still be a virgin." He pursed his lips shut abruptly.

"The what?"

"Oh, nothing," he said, too quickly and avoiding her gaze. "A . . . poem. A poem I recite that makes women weak in the knees. Shall I recite it to you now? It goes like this," he said, getting down on his knees before the fire and assuming, in his oversize clothes and featherweight stature, a mock-heroic pose. " 'In the spring, it is only right to honor my right to spring on you—' "

"Oh, for God's sake!" She strode across to the door and smacked it hard with the heel of her hand. Again, the door opened a sliver and the knife poked through.

"What?" the guard said, as if she had interrupted an important meeting.

"This is unacceptable!" she announced. "Let me speak to the baron. It's indecent to shut up a married woman with a man not her husband."

The baron had been standing behind the guard, and motioned

him to open the door wide enough to confront her. A weak grey shaft of daylight lit the air behind him. "Milady," he said politely, with a bow. "The only other place to put him is the little cell in the basement of the barbican. Do you demand that?"

"Yes!" she said at once. Seeing Gwirion's face in the firelight as he uncomfortably rose to his feet made her regret it. "Actually, no," she said, between nearly clenched teeth. That was no way to use someone who was risking his own safety for her. "But this arrangement is unacceptable. We need certain concessions or we'll both go mad."

"Such as?" Cynan asked with his maddeningly jovial smile. She saw that he was munching happily on some salted pork. It was a January morning. There wasn't enough food in the castle to justify anybody eating anything between breakfast and dinner, but she pushed her furious indignation aside to speak in a steady voice.

"We require air. There will have to be a few moments when you let us out of here, even if it is simply to walk around the hall. You may bind us and send everyone away if you like, but you can't expect us to stay in here without falling ill."

He shrugged noncommittally. "What else?"

"More light, of course. And we need a bucket to relieve ourselves and a basin of water for washing. And a curtain to have some privacy from each other when we sleep."

"And *things*," Gwirion added from the hearthside behind her. "We need *things*."

The man shifted his eyes to him. "What things?"

"The queen requires, I don't know, embroidery or spinning, have one of her women bring her something down."

"I don't care to sew," she said sternly, to Gwirion.

"Then bring her a cow to milk. I want my harp, it's lying by the hearth."

Promising nothing, Cynan shut the door. A quarter of an hour later, they were given the bucket, the basin, the harp, and a half-finished pattern in an embroidery frame. They were promised regular meals and firewood, but no exercise and no curtain; the baron didn't see why two people asleep should need privacy from each other. He did, however, give them torches for the wall sconces, which brightened the room to its usual warm glow.

"Brute," she said under her breath when the door was closed again. "Do you think there's a way to escape?"

Gwirion had immediately curled up around his harp on the padded settle like a snake seeking warmth from a sunbaked stone. He picked up the tuning key that hung from his leather belt. "No. The air vent is far too small. Maybe the chimney, if we let the fire die down, but you could never manage it in that kirtle and I'm not sure even I could get up through it. I don't even think it's in our interest to try. If they think we're docile, then they won't be so vigilant over whichever of us they take. Would you like to hear something in the turn-string tuning?"

"Whichever of us? You said it would be *you*."

"I know. But the more I think about it, the more I wonder if I misjudged. Noble might answer the question wrong just to be perverse—"

"Not possibly because that's how he *feels*?" she demanded.

"Of course not" Gwirion said offhandedly, as if oblivious to the fact that this could hurt her. "And anyway, they might decide that regardless of his response, it's still better to have a political pawn than a personal one. So I can't *promise* they won't take you, but at least we'll have delayed their plans by several days." He looked up from tuning. "You won't faint or become hysterical, will you?"

She scowled. "I am a *Mortimer*."

Gwirion gave her a droll look. "Which means . . . what? You commit regicide? Slaughter the innocent? Imprison your own family for political gain?"

"I have never been faced with a crisis I couldn't handle," she scoffed indignantly.

"You fainted when Corr scared you at the wedding."

"That wasn't a crisis, that was a *prank*," she snapped.

"Fair enough," Gwirion said, and tested the pitch of the string he'd been tuning by sounding it against its neighbor. He tightened it a fraction of a turn. "But please, if they do take you, don't be a Mortimer, just be docile. Do what they want. I'll say something to scare them out of trying to molest you, but I suspect they know better anyway. I'm not worried about the watch they've set up, I can slip out of here without being caught, so I'll go straight to the front to warn him." He smiled at her. "You'll be safe. But I really don't think they'll be taking you."

At once comforted and insulted by the assertion, she arranged her embroidery where there was the most light, as he began to play "Rhiannon's Tears." They passed the morning without another spoken word, but each relatively content in their respective distraction. It was a comfortable silence, not a cold one.

Gwirion could carry a tune well, and invent wild harmonies when he sang with the villagers, but he had never been trusted with romantic ballads or important poetry of any sort. He was, however, a profoundly gifted harpist, and it was pleasant to work to his music. Every now and then she would glance up at him bent close to the strings, his cheek almost resting against the curved shoulder of the instrument. The finial of a lion's head, looking not forward but back along the string arm in imitation of the royal coat of arms, seemed to be watching over him. The dozens and dozens of nights she'd seen him play in hall, she'd always been galled by the focused contentment on his face as he basked in the attention and admiration of everyone present. Alone with him, she didn't mind it so much. The pleasured expression was still there even without a crowd applauding him, and she was forced to consider the possibility that the smile was not for being publicly adored, but for the joy of the music itself. She realized, a little shamed for it, that she had considered herself the only one who could truly appreciate the beauty of it: Noble liked anything Gwirion did, and he had no ear anyhow; Gwirion, she had always assumed, was an attention-hungry cretin who had randomly been blessed with the gift to create something far more beautiful than he himself could understand. She was embarrassed to see that he appreciated it at least as much as she did. There was actually something winsome about the loving absorption he was giving to the strings as he sounded them; it reminded her of the way Noble looked at her—sometimes—when they lay together. Trying to imagine Gwirion looking at a woman that way, she blushed and hurriedly returned her attention to the embroidery pattern.

Eventually the door opened and a platter was shoved into the room. The portions of barley bread, cheese, porridge, dried fish, and weak ale were generous enough to feed them both, but it was all mangled; the guard had investigated every piece of food for hidden messages or weapons being slipped in from the kitchen. Gwirion lay the harp on its back and brought the platter to the carved chest that lay between the settle and Noble's chair, where Isabel was sitting. The queen, although at first resenting the sewing, had become so mesmerized by her work that she continued as if she hadn't noticed the interruption. Gwirion stood watching for a moment, then ventured up to her and gently took the frame and needle out of her hands. He laid them on the floor beside her. "Come and eat," he coaxed. "Or I'll eat it all myself. You're scrawny enough as it is."

"*Dammit*, Gwirion, *why* is everything an insult?" she demanded, leaping up with an abrupt hurt fury.

He backed away from her, eyes wide. Vicious responses spewed through his mind but he stopped his lips against them. "I apologize," he said instead, quietly, and possibly for the first time in his life. It surprised him.

It surprised her too, even more than her own wrath had. "Oh," she said after a moment, and then added awkwardly, "Thank you."

She sat across from him at the chest and began eating. Gwirion had grown unused to sharing over a meal, and kept forgetting to return the cup to a place where she could reach it. Amused more than annoyed, she would tap his wrist gently and gesture, and he would immediately grab the cup and offer it to her. Sheepish about his manners, he insisted she eat all the porridge, but she refused.

Then there was a silence. They looked at each other, never at the same time but always with the same thought: How strange to be sitting here with this person. It occurred to each of them independently that although they had never been friends, they knew each other well.

The months of his persecuting and her hostility had woven their attention tightly together, braided it with Noble's life. This person sitting across the chest was someone they'd never had a friendly discussion with but still was not a stranger, and far more than a mere acquaintance. The realization amused both of them for different reasons, but for different reasons also it was not an amusement either wanted the other to see.

So when their eyes finally did meet, they each blushed, then were more embarrassed about blushing as they looked hurriedly away. And yet even the embarrassment had a comfortable intimacy to it, emphasized perhaps by invaders just beyond the door. There was almost something pleasurable about the self-consciousness of it, Isabel thought. Gwirion did not quite admit this to himself, but he was grudgingly aware there was something he wasn't admitting.

After ten minutes of silence, she ventured awkwardly, "I'm grateful you thought to ask him for my sewing. I don't know how I would make it through this otherwise."

He nodded to acknowledge the comment, a little uncomfortably, and continued to eat. They stared at each other's hands, hesitating to reach for something the other one might want. When they had finished, he placed the platter by the door, set the bucket as far away from the fire as possible for future use, returned to the couch, and picked up his harp. They resumed the morning's routine for some three hours, Gwirion pausing occasionally to tend the fire or the torches, until finally she pushed her handiwork aside. "I can't do any more of this now," she said. "My eyes are watering and my hands are getting stiff. It's soporific, doing nothing all day, and it's stuffy in here." She yawned. "Will it discomfit you if I stretch out and nap for a bit?"

He squelched the impulse to tell her this was the king's favorite place for naps and said instead, "You won't be able to sleep through the night."

"I always sleep well. Will you help me to find a cushion?" She moved toward the deerskin rug by the hearth. "I'll just rest here."

Gwirion knew where there were cushions—and blankets, and

even a quilt stuffed with goose down. This room was designated as a berth for visiting dignitaries, but the bedding got far more use when Noble indulged himself of an afternoon or evening without his wife.

He decided not to mention the bedding to the queen. Instead he took the lambskin throw from the king's chair, rolled it up, and offered it to her. She accepted it with a smile.

"Will you think it indecent of me if I take off my wimple?" she asked, reaching up to pull the band from her chin.

"Not nearly indecent enough," Gwirion quipped.

The headdress was a little involved, but she was adept and had occasionally done it herself since Adèle's death. Noble was the only man who had seen her hair loose since her wedding, but since she saw her own uncovered head every night and morning, there was nothing exotic or unusual about it to her, and she forgot it was an unknown to the rest of the castle. Her tomboyish youth had accustomed her years ago to wear her hair in braids curled up on either side of her head. But she'd been rushed this morning, and had cheated, twisting the long, tawny locks into a simple quick chignon and covering the wimple with a longer veil in case it slipped. It took only a moment to undo. She was surprised when, after laying the headdress and hairpins on the chest, she turned and saw Gwirion's expression. He was gaping at her. "What?" she asked.

"Is that what you really look like?" he demanded loudly before he could think, staring at the honey-toned cascade that fell smooth and heavy nearly to her knees. It was the glossiest mane he had ever seen. He didn't know women could grow hair like that.

"Haven't you ever seen hair on a woman before?"

Not like yours, Gwirion almost said, but didn't, because that wasn't what had floored him. What left him blinking stupidly at her was that she had become a different person. The queen he knew had hair made of fabric, with a bald face peering out chinless and neckless from it, stiff and formal. English. Standing before him now was a pretty young woman, with hair that seemed exotic compared to the coarse tresses of his countrywomen, hair that matched her pale eyes perfectly and—most astonishing to him—a woman with a neck.

Most of the castle women wore simple white veils, so seeing a woman's neck was not unusual . . . but seeing *the queen's neck* shocked him because it forced him to admit that the queen actually was a woman, with a woman's body. Somehow, even the time he had peeked in on Noble possessing her on their wedding night, that had never been real to him. Despite the firm, square face, she had a delicate chin and a graceful neck, which only made the revelation more disturbing. It had not really occurred to him until this moment that he was locked alone in a room with a woman, and he was distressed by it. To be shut up alone with any woman would have been difficult enough; an attractive woman made him feel even more awkward, and when that attractive woman had the gall to be *her* . . .

She had considered, and completely misjudged, his reaction. "Go ahead," she said through tight lips, the afternoon's peace lost.

"Milady?" he asked.

"Whatever insulting thing you're going to say about my hair, just say it and be done with it so I may sleep in peace."

He looked at her as if she were speaking Latin. Finally, mumbling, almost sullen, he managed to reply, "I have nothing insulting to say of your hair." In response to her surprised look, he grudgingly added, "It's actually . . . pretty." He wanted to smack himself for the admission.

Her face softened. "Really? Noble doesn't like it. It's never been complimented by a man before." She bestowed a smile on him—truly bestowed it, as a favor, beaming. "Thank you."

That only made it worse. He had to turn away from her to hide his reaction. This was terrible. How ridiculous. How riotously ridiculous. Someday he and Noble would go riding in the hills and Gwirion would confess he'd had an erection from seeing the queen's hair, and the two of them would laugh uproariously and then when they returned home to the queen and her wimple he would casually insult her. He tried to focus on that future afternoon until it was safe to turn back to her.

"Gwirion, what are you *doing?*" she asked, perplexed almost to laughter by his behavior. "What's wrong with you?"

"Nothing," he said. "Go to sleep."

Shrugging off his strangeness, she stretched out on the rug and propped the sheepskin under her head.

"Wait," he said. He couldn't stop himself from performing a gratuitous act of kindness for her, which made him angry with himself. Mostly, he decided, he just wanted her covered up so he couldn't see her anymore. Her veil usually matched the color of her kirtle, blurring the outline of her figure; her hair, such a contrast to the dark silk she was wearing, suddenly accentuated every subtle curve. He wanted to hide all of it. "We can improve on that a little." He went to the chest and lifted the top.

"What is that doing there?" she asked of the luxurious bedding he pulled out, not really wanting to hear the answer because she was sure she already knew.

"King's stash," Gwirion replied unsentimentally. "Officially for visitors, but used more often—"

"I understand," she cut in with annoyance. They spread the down-filled quilt on the floor, layered the blankets over it, and Isabel chose a cushion for her head. As she settled into the bed, Gwirion turned away hoping that once she was covered up, she would cease to be fascinating.

The opposite proved true, of course, since once she was snuggled in, she was almost nothing but hair. Hair and face—but the face, because of the hair, was a new face, not that of an adversary or a familiar nuisance. He curled up on the settle as far away from her as he could, again grasping the harp to himself for comfort.

"Sleep well, milady," he called out, trying to pretend he was far enough away from her to need to call out. He just wanted her to be asleep so he could feel alone. He ran his fingers over the harp strings without realizing it, and at once tried to silence them.

"Oh, that's lovely," she said in exactly the dreamy voice that the beautiful women of his fantasies always used when they were in bed. "Play me to sleep."

He uncurled himself and began a lullaby, determined to lose himself in the music until she was awake again. But when the rhythm of her breath suggested that she had finally lapsed into slumber, he felt his fingers still the strings, and found himself drawn to her side. He could not get over the transformation of her face surrounded by all that hair. It was like a magic trick; he had a childish impulse to wake her up and make her put the wimple back on just so she could take it off again. Instead, he bent down over her sleeping form to stare at the hair. And without even feeling himself doing it, he reached down gently to stroke it. It was as smooth as a rabbit pelt and smelled faintly of rosewater. Hair exposed to weather and seldom groomed was never like this. He wanted to grab handfuls of it and rub it against his face, but he satisfied himself with stroking it, gently, so gently it would never wake her. He stared at the smooth young face that was so familiar and yet so alien.

Somehow, after a few minutes, his hand, on its own, without his knowledge or permission, migrated to her cheek. He saw it there as if it were somebody else's hand, and horrified, willed it to go away, but it wouldn't. It kept stroking the warm flesh, sending him sensations of dizzying pleasure even as he was begging it to move. Finally, with all the theatrical deliberation he used when performing for children or a crowd in the courtyard, he reached his other hand out to snatch the offending paw from her face, and pulled it safely out of reach above his head. The exaggerated movement threw him off balance and he tumbled over toward her, his own face inches from her closed eyes.

She stirred at the sound and he froze, praying to a God he usually ignored to spare her from seeing him. *Go away,* he ordered himself. *Go to the other side of the room and stay there.*

He couldn't. He meant to, and maybe he would have, but she rolled in her sleep and a thick lock of that hair uncoiled like a rope across his arm as he tried to stand, and he almost sank from the touch. He hovered over her again, staring at the sweetly sleeping face, the face that had the same features as the queen he didn't like and yet looked nothing like her. The transformation alone was so bewitching that even if it had been unflattering, he would have been entranced. Even her skin tone seemed different, rich and rosier, when it was surrounded by the living curtain of her hair. His fingers hovered in the space just below her chin, wanting to touch her there. He could barely make out her pale, slender throat in the shadows beneath it. He could almost *smell* how soft that skin would be.

She was absolutely unlike the queen he enjoyed mocking. This was just a pretty girl, a child almost, and she trusted him enough to fall into a deep sleep in his company. It was a trust he felt unworthy of. *Don't be beautiful, you irritating creature,* he thought, pulling his hand away. He tried to be as annoyed with the sleeper as he was with her animated, wimpled counterpart. It didn't work. She was too innocent.

The key turned loudly in the latch, the door creaked open and the supper platter was pushed in. He glanced down at her but she didn't stir, and he found himself smiling at her. He didn't understand what he was feeling. He would have called it lust—in one inarguable way it was obviously lust—but lust usually made him feel like a nervous puppy, silly, forward, playful. This was calmer. He was pleased to see her sleeping safely and deeply, as if she were a child he was looking after. That's what it was, he decided, ignoring the physical reaction he was still fighting. *I feel paternal because I'm looking out for her.* Feeling virtuous, and very relieved, he gently rocked her shoulder until she was awake. She blinked sleepily and opened her catlike eyes, then looked up at him with exactly the dreamy smile that the beautiful women of his fantasies always used when they were in bed, and he backed away in distress, not feeling the least paternal anymore.

12

CAPTIVES

Late January, 1199

 HAT WAS LOVELY," she said groggily. Gwirion pulled farther away and went to fetch the platter. Her behavior felt almost seductive to him and he didn't know if he should be angry with her or with himself. "The sleep of the Mortimers," she purred. "Only the strong of heart can rest well during a crisis."

"Sleeping during a crisis is just a lethargic way of swooning," he retorted. He set the platter on the chest and held out her wimple to her. "Here, you may as well put this back on now."

She took it from him but then dropped it onto the quilt as she sat up. "It will be time for bed soon, I don't feel like bothering." He said nothing in protest as they sat down to eat, but she was confused by how distressed his silence seemed now.

Supper was the same as dinner, with a little salted pork added; under the circumstances, a luxury. Gwirion had an even more awkward time sharing the trencher and cup than he'd had at dinner. He was suddenly too aware of where her hands were, seemed terrified of brushing against them with his own.

"Oh, no, please," he said at least a dozen times, yielding up almost the entire meal.

"Gwirion," she reassured him, as if he were a toddler, "there's enough for two." His behavior was inexplicable to her. He nearly breathed a sigh of relief when they put the platter aside, as if some gruesome ordeal was over.

After supper they returned to the sewing and the music for a while, but it was hard to have a sense of time in a room without windows or conversation, and eventually they agreed to face the slightly awkward task of preparing for sleep. Gwirion dragged the padded settle over before the hearth, and moved the quilt and her blankets onto it. Taking a few of the woolen brychans that were left, he made a bed for himself on the rug between the settle and the hearth, then dowsed the torches before he nestled in.

THE king had been brooding anxiously, listening to the rain on the canvas roof, already sleepless. When Gwallter the chamberlain stuck his narrow face through the tent flap with the news that there was a rider come from Cymaron, Noble welcomed the midnight distraction. He received the boy's peculiar query with warily confused curiosity, hoping whatever mischief Gwirion was up to would not overly upset the queen. Actually, though, the question was so blunt—Who matters more, the queen or Gwirion?—that it seemed almost more her style of querying than his, but the boy was too vague to give him a clear answer about its origin. A written response had been requested. He wrote it himself, and the boy, not even waiting for refreshment or dry clothes, accepted a new mount and was riding west again within an hour. The king tried to envision what prank or jest would arise from this, but his imagination failed him. Reluctantly, painfully, he returned his attention to his enemy.

He could not let Mortimer just sit there on his best soil, stalling for time, attempting no further aggression beyond keeping what he'd taken and efficiently annihilating any Welshmen who came too close. But it was an astonishingly massive army that Mortimer had planted on the Welsh farmland, and Llewelyn warned against an all-out attack, had refused to lend his own men to such an assault. This was supposed to be a *show* of force, he'd reminded Noble, not a *use* of force. Hopefully Roger Mortimer had similar intentions for his legions. Llewelyn had already lost men enough against the English in his support of other border princes.

Mortimer seemed to be taunting them with his idleness. He had enormous reserves of food and fuel, and hundreds of workers to deliver it. Spies provided unwelcome rumors: His intentions were to keep the army camped there until the Welsh froze to death, ran out of food, or just gave up and went home, and by Easter he would have lumber and stone in place to build a fortress—like Cymaron, a sturdy Norman fortress. There would have been symbolic and even spiritual satisfaction in defeating this plan in a manner that was thoroughly Welsh. But Welsh fighting was based on violent, brief surprise raids in impossible terrain and one did not stage a sneak attack on an entire army.

GWIRION was right: After her nap, however brief it had been, she couldn't fall asleep again. And she would never have admitted this, but she was a little nervous, knowing there were hostile men outside who could overpower her before Gwirion woke up, even though she doubted they would try anything that stupid. She leaned over the edge of the settle, hovering over Gwirion's sleeping form as if it somehow gave her extra protection. Ignorant of the irony, she fell into the same game he had only a few hours earlier.

She had rarely seen him relaxed, without making some grimace or setting his mouth in concentration on a melody or acrobatic

movement. This was no longer the prankster's face, it was the face of
a man she realized she didn't know. It did not affect her physically the
way it had her cell mate earlier, but still it fascinated her. But of
course she knew him, she argued with herself, it was *Gwirion*, a force
almost more ubiquitous in her life than her own husband. He was an
intimate, even if a cool one. She had known, early on, that she would
never have any meaningful discourse with her simpering sewing bevy,
and had not even tried to be close to them. After Adèle was gone,
Noble had afforded her her only real companionship, and that was
certainly inconsistent. This day spent largely without words in
Gwirion's presence was a gift; there was an unexpected and inexplicable sense of being with a peer.

Sometimes when Noble slept she would look at his face and
marvel at the transformation sleep had wrought. Little pieces of his
character poked through the mask of slumber, things that he kept
hidden during the day. He slept with his mouth closed in a tight,
straight line, looking grim, worn down, hopeless almost. She had
never seen such an expression on his face by daylight; by day he was
sometimes moody but always energetic. But the skin around his eyes
was softer in sleep. His eyes were almost never soft when he was
awake. Hypnotic, but not soft.

She didn't know Gwirion's waking face well enough to truly appreciate all the ways it changed in slumber, but she was intrigued to
see what was before her now. He was just an ordinary man, small
framed, dark hair with a cowlick and a healthy swarthiness to his
skin. The scars from Huw's attack had not quite disappeared. He
had a mole on the left side of his face, beneath his eye. She'd never
noticed. Crinkles that seemed like part of a weathered mask when he
was awake softened to very fine lines around his eyes and the corners
of his lips; he looked both older and younger in repose. Her eyes
traced his hairline. There was a scar on his temple—very old, probably from some childhood mishap—another one on the web of flesh
between finger and thumb on his left hand. There was something else
that looked like a burn wound on his throat. She wanted to touch the
white skin there, but didn't let herself. She returned her attention to

his face and wondered what personality she would assume such a man had if she came upon him for the first time, without a history. There was something pleasingly familiar about him. His face was actually well proportioned and classically Welsh, an oval with strong, fine features and what she decided was an elegant chin. He warped the natural contours of his face behind the sarcastic sneers and exaggerated impish grins of his daily life. She thought about how pleasant it had been to work to his music, what a relief to have him treat her with something other than scorn. He had been so enraptured with her hair that it was possible, however unlikely, that he'd even considered her with appreciation. The thought made her stomach tighten in a strangely pleasing way.

"I like appreciation," she whispered to the sleeping man. After a deliberating moment, she tucked her veil and wimple out of sight under the quilt.

THEY both awoke in the morning to the sound of the key in the lock. The aroma of breakfast touched them: Marged was trying to send them comfort by feeding them what little fresh meat she could pull together, an unheard-of indulgence for a morning meal in winter. Isabel was surprised their guard hadn't eaten it. A second unsmiling youth of Cynan's teulu entered with fresh light for the wall sconces, and rekindled the fire. Isabel was up before Gwirion and set the platter on the chest, then relaxed into the leather chair.

"Good morning," she greeted him as he began to crawl out of the blankets.

"Put up your hair," he said gruffly in reply, not looking at her, and began at once to gratuitously change the tuning on the harp.

She stifled a laugh, pleased. She had never had this power before, and she liked it. "Oh," she sighed, running her hands through her locks with a smile, letting them fall smoothly through her fingers, "It's a rare thing to have my head uncovered, and it feels so lovely. I want to enjoy it a little longer." She studied him out of the corner of her eye for a re-action. If she could pain him with beauty, as he had once pained her with wit, it would be such sweet vengeance, not only on him but also on Noble, who had never once given her reassurances that she was attractive. In fact, she conceded, the real impetus was vanity more than revenge. It hardly mattered what man it was who ogled her, it was good to feel *noticed*. That it was Gwirion was simply an entertaining irony. To her tremendous satisfaction, he frowned slightly and looked away. "And," she went on, "this way we're on an even footing."

"And what does that mean?"

"We are both without our protective shields. I'm without my veil and wimple, you're without the king."

He looked up from the harp pegs and smirked at her sarcastically. "Oh, very good! But I don't need the king around to be a rude, offensive ass, I'm quite capable of that on my own."

"Yes, I know," Isabel said. "Please don't feel the need to prove it."

"It wouldn't be worth the effort," he assured her.

Smiling, she began combing her hair with her fingers. She lolled her head back for a moment, pretending to stretch, exposing her neck and the underside of her chin. It was so satisfying to know he was gawking at her; she could feel his grudging attention without looking at him. Attracting him thrilled her, even though there was no love lost between them. In fact, the absence of affection made the attraction more real, more flattering: He was ogling her despite himself. She wasn't beautiful because he cared for her, she was beautiful because she was beautiful. It was so impersonal that it was almost animal. She flushed a little. She liked that sense of power and she liked him just for giving it to her. "Are you hot?" she asked, making a move as if about to remove her surcoat.

"No!" he said crossly, and put the harp aside with an agitated gesture. "And neither are you. Just eat, would you please?"

As they ate, she looked across at him. He was diligently avoiding her face, watching only her fingers to avoid touching them, so she could stare with impunity. She was enjoying this. All the things she had seen last night on the sleeping stranger's face were now animated on the man she knew as Gwirion. Again she admitted to herself that part of her pleasure was in discomfiting him, but a larger part was in realizing how effectively she could distract a man.

Gwirion wanted to throttle her. They were shut up alone together for another day at least, and this behavior couldn't possibly make it pass more comfortably. And how *was* one supposed to act, being shut up with a woman one had an abrupt feeling of lechery for, but otherwise disliked? He wondered if he should ask to be put in the cellar.

THERE had been a morning raid on the northern extreme of the camp, quickly repelled without serious harm to either side, almost as if Mortimer's troops were bored and simply seeking an hour's exercise. Cadwgan the marshal brought word that provisions would be gone in a few days, and Efan at once insisted that a retaliatory raid onto Mortimer's lands would be both strategically and logistically advisable.

Noble wanted to refuse. But he knew it would happen anyway, and if he was overseeing it he could at least make sure it was Mortimer's immediate stores, not Thomas's or anyone else's, that were plundered. So he agreed, ruefully, and Efan swaggered off to give the news to his teulu, who whooped with appreciation so loudly they could be heard a mile off. Noble turned his troubled gaze back to the east. He needed other options. This was maddening. He had to break the stalemate.

WITH no other options, they spent much of the second day as they had the first, Gwirion bent close to his harp strings and Isabel sewing, her hair pouring over one shoulder into her lap like a pool of honey. He went through his entire repertory, adjusting the strings nine different times to create keys whose names she thought he must be making up: the drunkard's tuning, the witch's tuning, the sad Irish tuning, the strange tuning.

When they needed a change, in the late afternoon, they finally risked a conversation. It began simply: She admitted how fond she was of "Rhiannon's Tears," a tune he played obsessively, and she told him her earliest memory of hearing it, in a very different form, during an English wedding dance. Gwirion promptly described English music as "the sounds of a people entranced by their own boredom," and did a cruel and witty imitation of what he thought "Rhiannon's Tears" might sound like if mangled by English musicians. Suddenly it was five hours later and they had never paused for breath.

And they had never mentioned the king.

He was alluded to. His presence hovered all around them, every moment. But they knew each other well enough now, had enough shared references, that if they chose they could forge an independent friendship, something neither of them had much experience with. At her request for a story of King Arthur, Gwirion rattled off a parody of Culhwch's quest for the daughter of Ysbaddaden, turning the characters into real people—Roger Mortimer standing in for the malevolent giant Ysbaddaden, spherical Marged the cook for his ravishingly beautiful daughter Olwen, and little Corr for Arthur, giant king of the Britons. He delivered the entire monologue in an exaggerated imitation of old Hywel's humorless melodrama, and she found herself wiping tears of hilarity from her eyes, wondering if Adèle would have banished this sort of romance from her hearing too.

"But why do the Welsh poems about Arthur never mention Camelot?" she asked.

"Who's Camelot?"

She made a face at him. "Stop that, Gwirion—even *I* know about Camelot and Adèle hardly ever let me listen to the ballads."

"What *ballads*?" Gwirion asked, incredulous. "Why would there be ballads about Arthur in *England*? He's one of *us*. He slaughtered the lot of you," he said with some satisfaction, and ran his hand over the lower harp strings to create a brief, triumphal cacophony.

"He slaughtered the *Saxons*," she corrected patiently. She'd given up on trying to explain the difference to anyone. "Six *hundred* years ago. There are dozens of ballads in French about him and his knights and his court—haven't any of them made it to Wales?"

"In French?" Gwirion gave her a look of barely suppressed sarcasm. "Please consider that he slaughtered the Saxons. Because they invaded Britain."

"And?"

It was hard to believe such an obvious point had not even entered her mind. "*You* invaded Britain. *Recently.*"

"We've been here more than a *century!*" she protested, but Gwirion just laughed at her.

"You're as much the enemy as the Saxons are by Arthur's standards. And you're telling me your courts are full of stories about him. Where he's the hero? Where the man who would butcher all of you is the hero? Isn't that just a bit odd?"

"No," she said. "They're just entertainment, they're not political."

"*Everything* is political," Gwirion chastised her, but gently. "Arthur is *our* king. If you've appropriated him, I'll wager you've changed him too, haven't you?"

"Well, he's not as violent as your version," she began, but Gwirion cut her off with a harsh laugh.

"We don't have a *version*, milady, we have history! You have fiction!" He softened when he saw her discomfort. "Tell me about the fiction, then. Let's hear what the silly French have done to our man."

She told him then the stories she could dimly remember from years earlier, of Camelot, Lancelot, Guinevere—one of the few names familiar to Gwirion—and as many stories about the Round Table as she could recall. He lay back on the settle and listened with riveted attention, then shook his head in wonderment when she had finished.

"How extraordinary," he mused, staring at the ceiling. "We give you the greatest warrior in the history of the British Isles and you castrate him."

"Gwirion!"

"He won't be very happy about that when he comes back," he insisted, playing with her now.

"He's coming back? Is that part of your *history*?"

"Of course," Gwirion answered, straight-faced. "He's just in some netherworld somewhere getting a second wind. He'll be back to scourge the land of our invaders, meaning you, as soon as things get bad enough."

"That will be hard for him to do, considering he's *dead*," she said with cheerful smugness, understanding now that disagreement was the whole point of this conversation. "They found his body at Glastonbury about a decade ago, hadn't you heard?"

Gwirion, who had heard, theatrically rolled his eyes. "And that, of course, is not *the least* political. That couldn't *possibly* be your Norman kinfolk trying to prove to us naughty natives that we have no hero waiting to reappear to throw off your Norman yoke. Of course not. And the timing is *pure* coincidence—that his demise would *happen* to be proven just as your uncle and the others decided they wanted to step up their attacks on us."

She held up her hands in self-defense against the verbal onslaught. "All right," she conceded, slightly sheepishly. "All right. You take the honors for that round. Now what?"

"Oh, fornication I think. That's always a lark to talk about."

She narrowed her eyes at him. "I don't want to hear about any more mistresses, thank you."

"There aren't any more, milady, you scared them all away." That was a mistake, he realized too late: It resembled genuine barbs not yet far enough behind them. She looked away from him. She even picked up her sewing, which he knew she had lost all interest in. "Milady," he said in a conciliatory tone, and sat up. After an obstinate pause, she glanced at him from the corner of her eye. "I must apologize for saying such a thing." She raised her head to look at him more directly, and less sourly, but clearly expected more of an apology. He did not have the discipline. "Yes." He nodded. "I didn't mean that. You haven't scared any of them off, there's dozens of them, they're crawling all over the castle."

She threw her sewing, frame and all, right at him as he

laughed—and then she started laughing too, grudgingly, despite herself. "You are such a spiteful boor," she said with amused resignation.

"Ah, the fickle flame of flattery," he intoned. "And I am so deserving of it." He liked that they could tread dangerous ground more safely now, and decided to see what else he could get away with. "I will not say another word about that. In Enid's honor."

The amusement left her face at once, but this time she looked chastened more than angry. "I am not responsib—"

"I know," he said, and stood up to hand her sewing back to her.

There was a silence. Gwirion returned to the harp, ran his fingernail across the strings to remind himself what tuning he was in, then began to play a piece she'd never heard before. It was sweet and lilting, playful yet soft, and there were no words to it. When he finished she complimented him, and he nodded thanks.

"I learned that from Hywel. It was the first full tune he ever taught me. He was never much good for a laugh, that fellow, but he was the most learned man I ever knew and I'm sorry that he's gone."

"Who do you think will replace him as bard?"

"Oh, me, I hope," Gwirion said, brightening. "And I'll encourage much deflowering to fill my pockets with the maiden fees."

She gave him a disbelieving stare. "Not the bard as well," she said. "Don't tell me the *court bard* profits from a woman's—" Gwirion nodded cheerfully and she demanded, "What is the *excuse* for that?"

He shrugged. "He gets it for his role as chief of song, so maybe his music is credited with bringing lad and lass together, although I suspect our dear-departed sage did more for insomnia than for romance. But even so, he profits by it and that's why he and Father Idnerth clashed. They had *rather* different attitudes about the value of virginity," he explained confidingly.

Mention of the bard led them to speak of poetry and music, and they argued playfully about religion. Isabel described her pilgrimage to Compostela, the towering cities of London and Gloucester, the estate she had managed from the age of twelve; Gwirion shared decades of decadent castle gossip with her that nearly made her eyes bulge, and recited his quirky interpretations of native legends that were so often alluded to and quoted from but had befuddled her out of context. She listened with grudging fascination as he spoke of Llew, who sanctified each oat stalk, Llew the god of sun and harvest—"in other words, of life"—the same Llew whose tales she had contemptuously ignored last August in the courtyard.

Gwirion had never had such an involved conversation with anyone but the king, and Isabel doubted she'd ever talked to another person for so long in her entire life. She knew she'd earned some special status when Gwirion listened to her tell stories of St. Milburga the revered abbess of Wenlock, a lock of whose hair she carried in her crucifix, without sneering at her for it. Despite the awkwardness at breakfast, she had the urge to say to him now, "Do you know, Gwirion, I actually like you," but she couldn't bear the possibility of his reverting to his usual demeanor and mocking her for it. And yet she could tell it was reciprocated, and thought happily of future times when Noble was back and order restored, of the three of them engaging each other as friends, which she realized with regret was what Noble had wanted for them all from the start. Gwirion was her inverse, all of the things she wasn't and yet both of them reflections of the king, and there was a sense of union there that made her want to throw her arms around him and declare him her brother.

But there was also a part of her that wanted to wring from him again the agitated attention a man gives to an attractive woman. How delicious and unexpected it would be to receive both friendship and flattery from the only man Noble would ever allow near her! Adèle had banished the *chanteur des romances* before he was halfway through his ballad, and she was ignorant of what disasters could follow from such affections.

THERE was no maniacal light in his eyes this time, but the entire army was convinced their king had gone mad. Just hours after the camp had settled in for slumber, he initiated the chain of communication from his officers down to the water boys, with the news that they would be attacking Mortimer—immediately. The afternoon drizzle had cleared and now the full moon was brilliant, bright enough for a simple skirmish. But the moon was inching toward the horizon now, and even if it weren't, a surprise attack of such a scale, lit only by winter moonlight, was surely the conception of a mind that had cracked. Llewelyn had nearly suggested as much when he dismissed the idea the night before. Knowing precisely what each of his officers would say in protest, Noble did not bother telling anyone else until he woke Efan two hours before he intended the attack to begin. This way, he explained hurriedly, a leak was impossible—the news could hardly reach Mortimer any faster than Noble's army would. The penteulu's response was only the first of many times that night the king was silently cursed. Absolute incredulity spread in waves across the sleep-sodden, dark encampment. But when Efan finished his reveille rounds by going to Llewelyn's tent, the northern prince agreed this time and summoned his own officers to wake his men as well. He told Efan, grinning, that this was the most foolhardy thing he'd done since he'd challenged his uncle Dafydd in battle—the first of his many victories.

Within half an hour all commanders of both armies were in Noble's tent, few fully dressed and some still half asleep; he bid them to silence and gave them each their orders, then sent them away again with no chance to register protest. The foot soldiers would go in first, relying on the Welsh stealthiness that Englishmen did not consider a battle asset. When the enemy was awake and beginning to regroup, the archers and the horsemen would begin their work. But what mattered most was taking Roger Mortimer alive. It was a simple plan, crude in fact—that was its strength.

"It is immoral," Father Idnerth argued moments later, when the commanders had been sent off. The candle he held trembled in the cold. "It's murder. You are killing men in their beds."

This had troubled Noble when he'd first contemplated it, but he had justified it to himself. "If we don't do this, my people will have their own throats cut in their sleep before long," he said steadily, as he stood spread-eagle in the middle of the tent, Gwallter fastening his leather armor. "Mortimer has shown himself utterly devoid of morals and I have no chance unless I respond to him with equal disregard for decency."

"Mortimer is not the one whose throat you're slitting, sire."

"Those throats are all Mortimer's," said Noble.

Now he was waiting outside his tent for his groom to bring his Castilian charger. He surveyed the moonlit camp around him as it swarmed with quiet, dark activity in the frigid air. As his men ceased grumbling and began to follow orders, they were all surprised—as he'd guessed they would be—by how much easier it was to prepare than they'd anticipated. It was not sight that aided them in putting on their armor or stringing their bows; it was routine, and they realized now that they could, literally, do it in the dark, half asleep. They sensed their comrades by their general shape, their smell, the singular subtle noises each one made; they could assemble without sunlight. In total blackness it would have been a disaster, but Noble, when he saw he would have a clear sky, had timed this perfectly. Even if Mortimer's watch saw movement here, they would never be able to decipher its meaning; the most reasonable assumption would be that the Welsh were packing up for a dawn retreat.

He saw his groom approaching, carrying a lantern, Cadwgan the marshal beside him. Noble's eyes were so adjusted to the fading moonlight, the little fire in the lantern was almost blinding. He waved once so they could see him, and they hurried over.

"Sire," said Cadwgan, bowing. "This is irregular, but a boy was caught by the western watch trying to slip into camp. He says he must speak to you, he won't breathe a word of his mission to another."

"Unarmed?" asked the king.

"Unarmed, filthy, hungry, and exhausted. He's lame and he's spent the past two days on foot getting here from Cymaron. That's all he'll say. He's quite frantic, he's desperate to speak to you before you ride out."

"One of our boys?"

"I recognize him, sire, but I don't think he's from the castle." A treble voice down the line, faint but growing louder, caught their attention and Cadwgan gestured. "That's him. He'll wake the enemy if he keeps that up."

"Silence him and bring him to me," Noble said. "Quickly." He took the reins from his groom, then reconsidered and handed them back. "I'll see him inside."

"Shall I stay as bodyguard?" Cadwgan asked. Noble shook his head. "I'm not worried about a threadbare child," he said, glancing toward the setting moon. "Unless he wastes my time." He drew his sword.

The boy, a skinny fellow of about eleven years with thick brown hair, dressed like a farmer's son, was unknown to Noble, but he recognized the king and calmed at once when he realized he was to be granted an audience. Noble gestured him into his darkened tent and sat him on the floor. He stood over him with his sword tip under the boy's chin. "Be quick," he said.

The boy was surprised by, but unafraid of, Noble's action. "There's a hostile force around the entire village of Cymaron," he announced breathlessly.

"*What?*"

"I'm from a farm in the next valley, but I was near the castle the morning before last, and I heard the siege alarm sound so I went up to the eastern hill to look. I'd seen a troop of foreigners just a little earlier heading toward the castle so I thought perhaps they had something to do with it. Things seemed quiet inside for a while, but then the main company of foreigners slipped around the edge of the village walls, and the alarm sounded again, with the church bells. They weren't attacking, it looked more like they were standing watch for something."

Noble was perplexed by this description. "And then?"

"All the castle garrison was marched across the bridge by the foreign fellows who'd gone inside the castle, and they were put into the keep, and then the bridge was drawn back from the wrong side so they were stuck in there. The castle's been taken, sire."

The king was grateful it was too dark for the boy to see how

shocked he was. This had to be a bad dream, punishment for the atroci-
ties he was planning. "Who was it attacked?" he said, nudging the sword
against the boy's throat. "Saxon? Norman? What did they speak?"

"I memorized the banner to describe it to you, but there's no
need to do it—it's the flag of the other camp."

"Mortimer's?"

"No, sire, Llewelyn of Gwynedd's."

He almost slashed the boy's throat from his violent start of
amazement. "What?" he demanded in a whisper.

"Yes, sire, I memorized it. The same image. I wanted to get
closer in to see what was happening but then I had the thought that
you would need to know, so I came here instead." He stretched his
neck as Noble lowered the blade and paced to the far side of the dark
tent in agitation.

"Who knows this?" Noble demanded.

"Nobody, sire," the boy answered. "I was going to just blurt it
out as soon as I found anyone to talk to here, but I saw their camp
first, I saw their standard in the moonlight and knew something was
up, so I decided to talk to no one but you."

Noble was across the tent again at once. Instead of praising the
boy's decision, he returned the blade to his windpipe, pressing hard.
"Nobody? You have told nobody? If you've told anyone, boy, let me
know now, and I'll forgive you the blunder. If I hear later you told
someone, that will be accounted treason."

"Nobody, sire," the boy insisted, looking uneasily at the blade.

"And this is not a jest?" he demanded sternly. "Another of
Gwirion's peculiar pastimes? We had a rider last night"—he stopped
himself, realizing. Realizing everything—what the question had
meant, what his answer would mean. "Oh, *Christ*."

"I saw a rider, sire, a boy my age in your livery, he passed me
coming and going. He left the castle right after they took it. Whatever he brought you didn't come from Gwirion, sire, it was coming
from Llewelyn's men."

Noble lowered the sword. He sat down hard on his bedding, and
pressed his palm across his eyes a moment, nearly cringing.

"Dammit," he whispered, and took a breath. The hand rubbed his face, moved down to his stubbled chin. For a moment he forgot the boy, the tent, the imminent attack. "What have I done," he breathed. He grimaced, then forced his full attention back to the boy and said with a focused frown on his face, "You will not tell anyone else this. Nobody, not even my closest men, are to know this at present."

"Of course not, sire, I understand."

"I cannot stress how important that is. What I am about to do requires the fiction that Llewelyn is my inviolable ally. If this were a few hundred years ago I would cut your tongue out right now just to make sure nobody else came to know."

The boy blanched in the darkness. "No, sire, I'm excellently good at keeping secrets."

"And how am I to trust that?" Noble asked.

He squirmed a little. "Well, sire, we've worked together before, in a manner of speaking." At Noble's quizzical look he added, sheepishly, "I'm Ithel, the boy who helped Gwirion train the dogs."

Noble looked at him for a moment, weighing in his mind if this meant the boy was more or less likely to be true. Finally he granted him a tight smile of approval. "So you've been trained by an expert in keeping secrets. Very well, then. Find yourself some victuals and get a little sleep. I have a Norman army to decapitate." He rose and headed for the opening.

"Sire?" Ithel cried quietly. "Aren't you going to do anything?"

"No," Noble said brusquely, barely stopping himself from lashing out in fury at the child. "From your description, they're holding all of them hostage, and they won't harm hostages. They're inconvenienced but not in danger."

"It's your *wife*, sire, your *home*," the boy said.

"Maelienydd is my home and this is how I tend to it," Noble answered.

"But, sire—" Ithel was very fond of Gwirion and was certain he'd been in the castle when it was taken.

Noble turned away abruptly. "I have a war to prosecute. Get some sleep, lad. Sleep in here if you like."

Ithel got to his feet and would have protested, but the king was already gone. The boy rushed behind him to the tent flap and stopped short in the entrance, watching. His Majesty mounted his Castilian in a smooth, liquid movement of casual athleticism, reached down for a torch from his chandler, and urged his mount through the ranks of his men.

Few of them were devout, but now all of them were praying for deliverance. Noble seemed to be looking them over, although he could not see them with the torchlight blinding the edge of his vision. But he knew they were there, and he knew they were watching him in the flickering flames, wondering if he was mad. It hardly mattered: Now that they were up, dressed, and at least half awake, their native fighting spirit was roused and it was easy to turn their irritation to battle fuel. While the whole circle of the horizon was absolutely black, his men were following him—grudging, grumbling, disapproving almost to a man, but they were following him and they were feeling their hearts pound with anger, fear, and savage raw energy in the biting dark.

"Leave a bard behind to sing about the king's folly when we're all dead—which will be in about an hour," Noble heard a foot soldier mutter, deliberately in his hearing. He smiled and ignored it. There was another torch, a quarter of a mile away, moving toward him. He turned his horse to meet the other rider. It was Llewelyn, the treacherous ally, leading his troops who were equally stupefied but equally obedient. Eyes glittering in the torchlight, the two men grasped each other's forearms in greeting—like brothers, Noble thought, like Cain and Abel—then turned and rode abreast over the black swell to the east, their silent armies rushing on foot behind them.

CYNAN had been having a pleasant stay at Castell Cymaron. He allowed his men to turn their attention only to the downstairs servants for physical amusements, but the king had stocked his larder well in that regard, and they had been feasting. The food was also excellent, and Cymaron's hall was warmer than his own. He now considered their reason for the extended visit a sham—obviously the king, no matter how much he may have preferred Gwirion's company, could not afford to make a written declaration saying his queen mattered less than his parasite. But it didn't matter, it justified their lingering, and that was enough.

He was surprised when one of the pages came running into the hall, out of breath, from the side door near the barbican. "The courier is back, sir!" he called out, waving a rolled parchment. "He has your answer!"

The baron leapt to his feet. "In less than two days?" He frowned. "Has the fighting moved this way?"

"No, sir," the page said, dipping his head respectfully. "The roads were good. And the moon's full."

The baron took the scroll from the boy. It was closed with Noble's general seal: a lion *rampant regardant* over a red kite. He broke the seal, unrolled the rough paper, and read the six words Noble had written as his answer.

"Kings be damned," he muttered. He looked up and told the messenger to wake his men.

The boy nodded and darted off. Cynan looked at the note again to make sure he wasn't misreading it, then carried it toward the room holding his two captives.

I T was perhaps the most gratifying moment of Noble's life, finally pressing the blade of his dagger against that particular jugular vein. They were on the far outskirts of the Norman camp. Efan thrust a torch near so that the king could see his captive clearly. "Welcome to my kingdom, Roger," he whispered, smiling viciously. "But you seem to be lacking a writ of safe passage. How terribly unfortunate there is no bracken here for you to hide in."

S HE loved how the natural lessening of tension, the almost al-
chemical change in the feel of the room, soothed them into
cheerful placidity together. After Gwirion had pressured her for a
quarter of an hour, she finally relented and performed her secret im-
itations of the sewing bevy, sashaying and primping and giggling like
each in turn. He fell off the settle he was laughing so hard.

"You've been masquerading all these months as an English gentlewoman," he scolded, "when the truth is you're cut from a swath of
my own fabric!"

"Thank you," she said, grinning, warmed. It was as close as he
would ever come to voicing the sentiments of friendship and affection that she wanted to hear, she knew. It was enough.

They were startled out of their laughter by a knock on the door.
It swung open as they rose, Gwirion protectively clutching the harp
up to him with one hand and holding an arm out in front of the
queen to shield her. Cynan entered. With his unrelentingly convivial
grin, he waved a scroll in the air at them. "From your king," he said.
"We leave before dawn. That's not so far from now—you children
are up late tonight." He laughed, but when neither of them took a
step to get the letter, he dropped it to the floor. As if he really did
care about them getting sleep, he made a clucking sound and removed two of the sconce torches when he left, leaving the room in a
dim glow.

After a moment, Gwirion lay his harp on the settle and retrieved
the note. He unrolled it and scanned the message silently. It read:

She is replaceable. He is not.

How this would have made him crow with vicious victory a few
weeks ago, perhaps even a few days ago. Now he cringed for her sake.
Still, he was glad of it, and it was the answer he needed.

"What does it say?" she demanded, her heart in her throat.

He looked at her for a moment, feeling trapped, then quickly crumpled the message in one fist and threw it into the fire.

"Gwirion, what does it say?" she repeated, more shrilly.

"I'm going," he said quietly, and sat down on the floor by the hearth.

She took a moment to collect herself. Noble had not chosen her. The relief was greater than the hurt, but the hurt would last longer, she knew. She noticed Gwirion was not gloating. "Thank you," she said quietly, sitting beside him. Impatiently, she swept her hair over one shoulder to contain it; her earlier preening seemed silly now. Gwirion's attention was lost in the flames. "Are you sure you can get away from them?"

He nodded. Still staring into the fire, he added quietly, "I just hope they don't come back here and take you when they realize they've lost me."

"When you escape, go straight to Noble and tell him what's happened," she said.

"They can turn around and come back here in less time than it will take for me to get a message to the king."

"Just go to him yourself, you'll have immediate access." They were both whispering, as if the guards might somehow overhear them through the heavy oak door.

He looked at her. "Don't you remember? I'm escaping. From *everyone*. I can't go to him myself because I'm not coming back to Maelienydd."

Her look of disappointment and surprise only convinced him more. What to her had simply been a lovely evening of friendly conversation had been ecstatic agony to him. She wasn't the queen anymore, she was an attractive young woman and he wanted her. But that wasn't the worst problem—lust was at least impersonal, it could be exorcised by proxy. Despite himself, he'd got caught up in conversation with her, hanging stupidly on her thoughts, wanting so to impress her, to enthrall her with his wit—the very thing that had alienated the queen. Suddenly finding himself with a woman who shared his points of reference as the queen did, but lacked the queen's usual prickly attitude, he reveled in her company almost as much as he did the king's, and he found it alarming. Affection and attraction, commingled, dizzied him—this was a new drug, and he was desperate to fight off its seductive stupor. He wanted the night to go on forever but he did not see how he could ever survive another one like it. And Noble read him so easily; if such an evening passed with Noble present—

"I'm escaping," he repeated firmly.

"You can't," she declared. "I won't let you."

"You can't stop me, milady," he said with a soft, pained laugh, avoiding her gaze.

"But we're friends now. If you stay, everything will be good. For all of us." She hadn't recognized the drug for what it was as readily as he had.

He didn't quite manage to swallow a bitter laugh. "I don't think so, milady."

"Stop miladying me. Why do you need to leave? We're not at odds anymore, and Noble's been behaving himself for months. Relatively." When he didn't reply, she challenged him. "Anyhow, you've said you were leaving before and you didn't, why should I believe you this time?"

"Please don't ask me to explain," he said, looking back into the fire.

She curled her graceful arms around her bent knees. The fire was blazing; it was so warm that she decided to resort to her threatened coquetry from earlier in the day and seduce him—chastely, of course—into staying. She stood up, slipped off her heavy, fur-lined surcoat, and sat again, in only a long kirtle that revealed more of her gentle curves than Gwirion thought he could bear to look at. She tipped her head slightly and the curtain of her hair slid down her arm, brushing against him. He tensed.

"Please put that back on, milady," he said, sounding genuinely distressed.

"I'm hot," she said, gazing serenely into the flames.

"Then please put it back on and stand away from the hearth."

She turned to him and smiled—sweetly, not suggestively. "I want to sit here. I like sitting next to you."

He looked even more distressed. *"Don't,"* he said gruffly, and stood up, moving away into the shadows. She immediately reached for her surcoat.

"All right, I'll put it back on. Come sit beside me."

"I'm fine here," he growled.

"Gwirion, I'm your queen, I order you to sit down."

"I don't obey frivolous orders."

"It's not frivolous," she insisted, with an impish grin that reminded him of Enid. "It's your last few hours as a member of my household and I want to say farewell properly." He dreaded the possible meaning of this, even as he fought to hide his body's insane, irrational delight over what the words could have implied. But she seemed completely undistressed; had she felt one jot of what he did, she would surely have been traumatized. Her very sweetness proved she felt nothing of the kind—she was too artless and too honest to manipulate anyone that way. All she meant, all she could possibly mean, was a chaste embrace and a friendly kiss. The thought of even this sent his heart to his throat. But he let himself sit beside her, grunting in annoyance to show her how put out he was by the request.

"Thank you," she said, angelic. He didn't remember her ever sounding angelic before. Why did she have to start now? She wasn't really angelic. She was really a shrew. He remembered that, in theory, although he couldn't recall any specific examples.

"So," he said when he was sitting beside her, trying to sound nonchalant. "Here I am. Farewell." He started to get up again, but she put a hand on his arm and he froze.

"Not just farewell. Farewell and thank you," she said gently. She leaned forward to kiss his cheek and he felt dizzy again. Her lips were impossibly soft, like rose petals. He was disgusted with himself for having such a hackneyed sentiment, but that didn't keep them from feeling like rose petals. He realized with a sinking feeling that he had leaned into the kiss slightly, and that she must have felt his body shift.

She finished the kiss but kept her head close to his. Their eyelashes could almost brush against each other. She had never been so
close to any man but Noble. She was fascinated by the *difference* of
him, his scent, his shape, the planes of his face. He had a sinewy
grace, feline but not feminine, so different from Noble's muscular
solidity. She remembered blushing as she'd watched Gwirion gaze intensely at his harp strings, and a shiver raced through her as she wondered how else the two men differed.

She kissed him again, this time on the lips.

He did not kiss back. He made sure not even to lean into it this
time.

She pulled away, disappointed.

"Kiss me," she said.

"Is that an order?"

She almost said yes, then saw his expression. "It's a request."

"I can't," he said. "You're Noble's."

"So are you," she said, trying to smile. "I think that makes it all
right."

"You don't really know him, do you?" Gwirion muttered.

"Just a kiss. I'm not asking you to put your hand up my skirt!
Just a kiss to celebrate that we're friends at last."

He shook his head, looking anywhere but at her. She leaned in
and kissed him again. He pushed her away roughly, got to his feet
with an expression of panic on his face, ran to the door and began
kicking it and smacking his hands against it frantically.

"What what what?" the baron demanded, when the guard had
opened it.

"Put me in the cellar until we go," Gwirion insisted.

"I will not allow that," said the queen, in a voice of iron. Surprised, they all turned to look at her. She was standing. The glow from
the fire behind her glancing off her veil of hair silhouetted her with an
aura that made her look otherworldly. "This is his last night in his
own home for what might be quite a while. I will not have him so insulted. Besides, it's your last night here as well and I would feel much

more comfortable having one of my own people standing watch over me in case you were tempted to perform any indecent acts."

The baron burst out laughing. "Majesty, we've got all the indecent acts we can manage out here already," he assured her, smoothing his mustache with one hand as he pretended to try to hide his smirk. He turned to Gwirion. "I don't know what your argument is with your mistress but you'll have to harden yourself to it. By the time we had you settled in it would be time to go. See you soon, then," he finished cheerfully, and closed the door.

Gwirion stayed with his face to the door for a long moment. "Milady," he said at last, sounding hoarse. "I won't kiss you because if I did I don't think I could *keep* my hand from going up your skirt."

"But that's all right," she blurted out giddily, unaware she was not thinking rationally and so happy to have his attention it seemed fine to say anything to keep it.

He spun around to face her and she was shocked to see he was near tears. "I did not want this!" he shouted.

She blinked, refusing to understand his distress. "What are you frightened of? You're not trapped, you're about to escape." She smiled, feeling generous and thrilled and believing herself to be sensible. "It's any man's fantasy, Gwirion—a night alone with a woman you want, who *condones* your abandoning her afterward."

Gwirion blushed, flustered. "You don't condone it, you tried to talk me out of it."

"I would be willing to lose you if only I could really have you first."

He gawked, and she almost laughed at her own brazenness. She'd never imagined she could talk or even think this way, and it gave her a heady feeling of power. Astonishing a man with her own will and desire fueled both the will and the desire. It was dangerously rash— no, not dangerous, for he was about to vanish permanently, and she would never find herself in this extraordinary position ever again.

"I won't be able to stay away," Gwirion stammered, red faced, trying to keep his senses. "I'd come back, and we'd be tormented, and, and ... besides the fact that I'm no Lancelot, Noble is hardly Arthur, especially *your* Arthur. This isn't a romantic tale. I'm flattered you chose me for your first little juvenile crush—confused, but flattered. But you don't have the luxury of indulging in it, *Your Majesty*."

She stood up, slowly, and keeping his gaze, she again removed the surcoat, pushing it slowly off one shoulder and then the other. "Come here," she ordered calmly.

He shook his head. It was maddening how heedless she was. It made his determination to behave himself seem silly. She seemed so convinced that this wasn't wrong, it nearly eroded his belief that it was.

"Please," she said.

"I'm sorry for this," he managed to say, without moving.

She walked to him. He backed up against the door, looking cornered, but she stopped a long stride before reaching him and held out the surcoat. She looked disappointed, even exasperated, but dignified. "I didn't mean to unnerve you. If you'll help me back into this, we'll pretend it never happened." He took the coat and looked at her, distressed, but held it open for her. She gave him one last inviting smile, which he looked away from, and then she began to turn her shoulder away from him to back into the surcoat. The casual tilt of her head in the firelight was so elegant and lovely it was almost physically painful to look at her. She sensed his discomfort, and still hoping that he would relent she slid half a pace toward him and deliberately cocked her elbow so that it brushed against his body as she turned. He grabbed her arm and furiously yanked her around to face him.

She answered his angry expression with an almost giddy smile, although her heart was beating so furiously she could hardly breathe. "You're touching me," she whispered, glancing at his hand on her arm and then back up at his face. "Touch me some more."

He tossed the surcoat aside and pulled her to him, and a noise that was half gasp and half laugh escaped her as she threw her arms around him, kissing him. He kissed her too, terrified and ecstatic at the same time, trying hard to forget who she was, trying to make it an impersonal meeting of flesh.

Grinning, she led him back to the floor by the fire and they sat, but when she lay on her back, trying to pull him down with her, he resisted. She reached up and ran her hand over his worn wool tunic, and was rewarded by his nearly collapsing against her, finally lowering his body onto hers with a shaky, resigned sigh. It felt strange to her, a man other than Noble on top of her, but thrilling. She had never been this aroused before her clothes came off, and there was an emotional intensity that had never been there with Noble at all. She wondered fleetingly if it was because he was Gwirion, or because he wasn't Noble, but the answer really didn't matter. The feeling was there and she loved it. He would be safely gone forever soon, and this would be a secret memory that she could cherish always.

He felt her body underneath his, felt her legs pressing against his, tangled in her silk skirts, felt the delicate torso under her belt, the very hips he had watched Noble grasping the night he'd spied on them. He cupped his own hands around them now. These weren't the same hips. They couldn't be. He tried to pull away, but she raised her face up to his and kissed him again. The impossibly soft lips parted for an impossibly strong tongue, and he knew that Noble had probably trained that tongue well, to do things that he tried very hard to keep from thinking about now. But maybe anything that wasn't technically fornication—

He cut his own thoughts short. He remembered what Noble had done to Owain and the queen just for making eyes at each other. And then, he simply remembered Noble. He pulled away. "We can't do this," he said, with a firm desperation that made her pay attention.

Breathing hard, she grimaced and pulled herself up to a sitting position. "Now you'll think me horrible," she said, morose, knowing the entirety of the day's joy was permanently ruined.

He choked back a pained laugh. "I thought you were horrible before I'd even met you. Now I think you're human."

They didn't dare eye contact, two disheveled people with sheepish smiles and pulses racing. There was a long silence.

"Where will you go?" she asked, just to say something.

"I have no idea." He pulled away to face her. "Listen. Let Marged be the one to tell him that I'm gone. She's the only one who's immune to his rages, he'll traumatize anybody else who gives him the news, including you. He needs to know that I'm not really hostage, so he doesn't negotiate, but spare yourself the experience of breaking the whole truth to him. Especially if it's coming from you, he might think you drove me to it."

"There was a time when I would have," she said, fidgeting with her rosary.

"Pretend you still feel that way."

Again they looked at each other trying to agree without words what was acceptable. Regardless of their age, all the women he'd been with—many of them handed over by the king—had seemed older. This was the first time he felt older and in some strange way wiser than the girl beside him. It was a seductive feeling and yet he couldn't bear it. He wanted to be the silly, puerile prankster who earned women's amused but indifferent favors. That was familiar, that was easy.

Forgetting himself, he kissed her, the first kiss he'd let himself initiate, and he felt her tremble against him. No woman had ever responded that way to a kiss from him. The flattery of it alone pushed him beyond reason. He grabbed her closer to wrap himself around her—but the noise of the key in the lock made them pull apart, breathless and disoriented.

"It's time," the baron declared from the door, as if he were announcing Christmas morning.

13

A Hero's Welcome

Approaching Candlemas, 1199

RMS BOUND, Gwirion was led away well wrapped against the chill. Cynan put him on a horse, which genuinely pleased him since he was so used to his pony. Isabel had slipped him her precious rosary after taking off the relic-bearing crucifix, so that he would have something to barter for food or shelter until he got his bearings. He did not tell her what he would probably barter it for instead: He'd determined to exorcise her from his mind by finding a whore as soon as he was free.

I T was over before the sun rose, and an hour after dawn Noble was reclining on a brychan, hands clasped behind his head, his legs stretched out before him and crossed at the ankle. He grinned at his captive, who was tied standing stiffly under heavy guard. The smells of a belated breakfast wafted past. Noble had chosen to take the au-

dience this way partly to hide how bone tired he was and partly to insult Roger Mortimer with extreme informality.

"Might we interest you in a traditional Welsh breakfast?"

"Richard will raise a stink about this," Mortimer said.

"About feeding you a Welsh breakfast?" Noble answered. "I
didn't know he was so particular about his lords' diets. Very well,
then, how do you Saxons break your fast?" He punched the word,
knowing it was rude. He was jubilant.

"I meant my capture," Mortimer said disdainfully.

Noble shook his head. "Let's not waste our time with feeble posturing, Uncle Roger. Richard won't even hear about this for weeks,
maybe months, and he'll just think you were stupid for provoking
me. Which you were. Of course, if you would like to be your niece's
guest at Cymaron until Richard can be bothered to raise your ransom, you're welcome, but I suspect you'd be more comfortable in
your own home, so let's settle this now." Through all the glibness, he
had one eye on Llewelyn, studying him. The younger prince either
didn't notice the scrutiny or didn't care, and in any case he gave nothing away. He was the model of a young commander whose star was
rising: cocky but deserving it, respectful and obedient to Noble's se-
niority. "I would like to get home to your niece myself," Noble said
in a light tone, and absolutely nothing was revealed in Llewelyn's face.

THE castle was physically undamaged, but the stores were plundered and the inhabitants moved about like ghosts. The serving
women who had been forced to entertain the invaders clung together in
the kitchen, where Marged warmed milk to soothe their nerves. The
queen called the castle residents together in the hall, to warn them that
there were still armed men outside the village walls who would not let
anybody leave, for any reason, and she begged them not to try. The entire assembly spontaneously interrupted her with applause for her
aplomb and poise in the face of crisis. She blushed and patiently ac-

knowledged their admiration, then pressed on to assure them that Gwirion would alert the king once he escaped, which evoked another outburst of approval. She did not reveal that Gwirion was not coming back, although she meant to tell Marged that night.

But night fell and she did not tell Marged because she didn't want to concede that it was the truth. As a comforting gesture, she requested the most indulgent supper the kitchen could muster, trusting that Cynan would be called to account to replenish their stores before the end of winter. But there was little fresh meat and no means to get any—the butcher, huntsman, and falconer were all with Noble.

For her brush with danger, the queen was instantly granted the status of an adored young saint; everybody wanted to be near her, to assist her, to receive attention from her. She enjoyed it but she was unused to it, and it seemed ironic that after months of trying so hard to win these people's hearts, she was successful only after being locked up in a room doing nothing for two days but entertaining adulterous thoughts.

Almost everyone offered to perform during and after the meal; the honor of playing first was awarded to an awkward young wheelwright who had been left behind as part of the guard. He sang and played the pipe, and Angharad, the oldest of the sewing bevy, performed next on the harp. The two of them, and the motley assortment of musicality that followed, all did the best they could to entertain, but the collective effect on Isabel was abysmal. In tribute to Gwirion, Angharad attempted "Rhiannon's Tears." Gwirion had played it half a dozen times in their two days of confinement. Once, to show off, he had played it—he claimed—backward. Angharad butchered it compared to Gwirion's finesse, but even if it had been an excellent rendition it would have left Isabel heart heavy. She remembered that his harp was still in the audience chamber, and asked that it be wrapped in its felt sheath and returned to the chest near the kitchen screen. She wondered when it would ever be sounded again. Without her rosary to worry, she began to fidget with the crucifix until she nearly snapped it in half. She put it in her purse, out of reach, and fretted with the edge of her veil instead.

It did not seem fair to her, or even sensible, how tormented she

was now. Being in his presence yesterday had suddenly been so pleasant, had made her feel light and cheerful, giddy even—and now his
absence was a wall she could not stop walking into. Noble did not
have nearly such a grip on her imagination. His absence never preoccupied her even though her well-being was more dependent on his
safe return. And he was her husband, her bedmate. Why did
thoughts of Gwirion, who had refused to undress her, make her feel
abandoned? For the love of the saints, there was nothing to miss! She
missed the conversation, yes, but how could anyone yearn more for
one evening's conversation than for nine months of domestic and
connubial intimacy? If she felt such longing for Noble, or at least his
body, she could have excused herself. But she didn't. She longed only
for something she had never even known.

Isabel slept that night in Noble's bed, unable to bear the proximity of her women. Everyone seemed pale and dull compared to the
man she had nearly forced herself on the night before. She lay beside
the space where her husband usually slept, imagining Gwirion there
instead, and almost swooned in a hazy fantasy of making love to him.

She awoke with an empty feeling in the pit of her stomach.

I T was just after dawn when Gwirion's message reached the king.
Noble was deep in slumber, a rare thing for him in any circumstance. He'd been up most of the night with Llewelyn, trying to
break Mortimer's will without breaking his body—an act of charity
Noble did not really think the Norman was entitled to. But he had
challenged convention far enough already in this venture and he
knew that to treat Mortimer as he deserved was risking censure from
the English king, the pope, or both.

Ithel was sleeping on the floor of the tent, the king's mysterious
new mascot whom nobody in camp was allowed to approach. He
awoke first and awkwardly tugged at the king's blanket until Noble
opened his eyes—and then he was instantly awake. "What?" he

demanded, and sat erect. At the tent flap stood Gwallter with a young runner wearing livery and breathing hard, his short hair plastered to his forehead with sweat. Ithel had wordlessly taken a grubby, unsealed parchment from him and offered it to His Majesty.

Noble recognized the writing and sent Gwallter and the boy away. He unrolled the scroll and Ithel watched him as he read. Noble looked up, straight at him.

"Well, lad," he said, "You were exactly on the mark." And then to himself, softly, "Christ." He had not allowed it to be real until he saw it written in Gwirion's familiar, spidery script.

"Will you send someone back now?" Ithel asked for the dozenth time. "You don't need the soldiers anymore."

"It's over," Noble said vaguely. "There was a hostage attempt and Gwirion foiled it." He tossed the parchment to the ground.

"Good!" Ithel declared. "But you had better send some troops back to be safe." Noble lay back on the brychan, eyeing the boy. Clearly he had no idea how presumptuous and disrespectful he was being, and Noble lacked both the energy and the inclination to educate him. If he was following in Gwirion's footsteps, there was little hope for improvement anyway.

"No," he answered. "And you will continue to keep your mouth shut."

The boy looked distressed. "Sire? Why?"

"We'll finish the formalities with Mortimer this morning and then we're starting for home after dinner. I'm keeping my army intact until I have a signed and sworn concession from the enemy I just humiliated. For all we know, deBraose or one of Mortimer's other neighbors is sending twenty thousand men to take us down. We are not necessarily through here, Ithel, but the situation at Cymaron is resolved."

THAT morning castle life was almost returned to normal. Queen and judge sat in hall again, and met with the villagers and other petitioners to hear their disputes. Many of them chattered excitedly about Gwirion as if he were some heroic figure of legend, happily anticipating his triumphant return. His selfless act of bravery and cunning being undertaken for her sake only added to her new popularity, and she was dizzy with compliments and adoring glances by the end of the day. She received the subjects who had come in from the countryside and been held hostage within the gates by Cynan's outside troops, and invited those who could not find lodging within the village to come back to the hall for the night.

She had hoped there would be more talented entertainers in their ranks. There weren't. But a few well-meaning souls who were praised within their own undemanding hamlets wanted to impress Her Most Esteemed Majesty, and, of course, most of them played some painful variant of "Rhiannon's Tears." She wanted to scream.

She went to Noble's bed again the second night determined not to think about Gwirion, and failed at once. He must have escaped by now. She wondered how long it would take his message to reach Noble, worried that the baron would come back for her once Gwirion escaped him. Anxiously she lit a candle, then a wall sconce, to search for a map of the region, but of course there were no maps in the bedchamber. Defeated, fretting, she darkened the room again and crawled back under the blankets, trying hard not to imagine what it would be like to have Gwirion beside her.

She drifted to sleep and dreamt that he was lying on top of her, but he was much bigger, bigger than Noble, he had grown so huge that he was suffocating her and she couldn't breathe. In a panic, she forced herself to wake up, but the suffocation didn't lessen and she realized with a painful twist of fear that it was real.

A gloved hand was clamped hard over her mouth and nose. She tried to scream, but the hand had an airtight seal. Somebody yanked her head up roughly and held her in a viselike grip against his cold body. A knife poked into her neck right behind her jawbone.

"Don't move," a deep voice whispered in the darkness. It was a northern accent like the baron's and she knew with dread what was happening. His breath smelled of cheap ale, and the stubble on his cheek raked her ear. "If I remove my hand and you scream, I'll send this dagger right through your throat. Do you understand? Nod." She nodded against his hand. The hand released.

"What do you want?" she demanded in a harsh whisper, praying she sounded more angry than frightened.

"Just you, Your Majesty." The knife poked a little. "Are you going to cause any trouble?"

"Who are you?" she asked, wishing she hadn't doused the torch. Now she realized how foolish it was to have lit it—that's how the man must have located her.

"An ally," said the voice, suddenly sounding familiar. The knife fell away, the grip relaxed, and she barely stifled a scream of pleasure when she saw Gwirion's profile silhouetted against the window.

"You came back!"

He pulled the glove off, lit a candle, and placed it beside the bed, avoiding her glance. "I'm not staying," he said.

"Then why did you come at all?"

He couldn't tell her the crude truth of it: That hours after he had escaped he had, in fact, found himself on a prostitute's pallet, unable to summon even lust. The whore had been genial and understanding, especially since she had already been paid. She told him that if a lass had that kind of hold on him, there was only one cure: He had to possess her. Whatever feverish and idealized image he had of being with her would make the real experience pale in comparison, and then, disillusioned, he would be free. This woman was not a romantic.

"I came to let you know it went off smoothly. And . . . to see you one more time," he said awkwardly, feeling like a cretin. "If you want that. Or I can just go," he added hurriedly.

Anticipation tickled her from her throat down to her thighs and for a moment she could hardly breathe. "Is *seeing* all you're capable of?" she whispered.

"I'm not going to become your lover," he said, more aggressively than he meant to. "This is one night. And then I'm gone for good."

"Then we must do things just right, so we may feast on the memories for years." If she was going to long for him, she at least had a right to know what she would be longing for. She was pleased with this rationale, believing herself the first lover in the history of forbidden desire to think of it. She stroked the stubble on his cheek with the back of her finger. "But first tell me what happened."

He jerked her hand away from his face, shaken by how intensely the simple gesture aroused him. He took a breath, then grimaced apologetically and released her. "It was simple," he began, willing himself to focus on speech. "We got just past the Severn, and they made camp as soon as the horses recovered from the fording. I got away soon after sunset and propped up my blankets to look like I was sleeping. The nights are so long now, I had ten hours' lead at least, I think. And I'd dropped a few hints during the day about having family in northeastern Powys, so I think they'll have wasted today heading in exactly the wrong direction. I went back over the Severn to Newtown, and sent the mayor's courier to the border to warn Noble." It was this mayor, thrilled at being invited into the annals of history, who had taken him to the village's one hostel and treated him to its one whore, who was his niece. That reminded Gwirion, wryly, of Isabel's rosary, which he took from around his neck now and draped over her hands. She set it beside the bed. "The fates seem to be with us—there's a good moon and it was clear, and there's a manned relay course from Newtown to the king's camp. The message is certainly at the border by now. If Noble can send somebody, you should have protection by tomorrow night at the latest. I've been hearing conflicting things about how things are faring there, so I don't trust any of it."

Noble's fool, the man she knew as her tormentor, was not capable of what Gwirion had just done. She wondered, if she could persuade him to stay, whether he would regress to the rascally waywardness that Noble so enjoyed. Perhaps he was afraid of that too.

"Thank you" was all she said. Then she took one of his hands in hers and drew him onto the bed.

He resisted. It was the personal betrayal, not the technicality of adultery, that troubled him. The king had betrayed his trust in many ways—*pretending to kill me, for example*—but in the end Noble's actions had been, however strangely, a celebration of their friendship, not an affront to it.

She slowly peeled away the layers of blankets until she sat nude beside him. This alone could have kept him spellbound for the night. Her skin was almost translucent. "My God, you're beautiful," he managed to say aloud, remembering she could not hear the thoughts that sounded so deafening to him. For nine months now, Noble had had this in his bed and he had never once spoken of it with appreciation.

She reached for the tongue of his belt. She knew how to undress a man, it was one thing her husband had taught her early on. Gwirion was stupefied; rarely had a woman so much as lifted the hem of his tunic. Even when Enid seduced him he was almost fully clothed and she had simply pulled up her skirt.

Her hands were small and soft, wonderfully warming on his chilled skin, but he became self-conscious when she tried to remove his drawers. "What's wrong?" she asked, smiling up at him. He couldn't manage to say anything coherent. "Are you afraid I'll be disappointed?"

"*Yes,*" he said. It should have been obvious. He went on, stammering: "I'm not the lover he is. I'm not as gifted, in any sense." He pushed her hands away.

She put them back. "I'm not worried about that," she whispered, and nudged his hands aside again.

When they were both undressed there was a long, indecisive moment. They stared at each other, fascinated and desirous but also stunned that they found themselves here, when a week ago they had been grudgingly civil at best. "Please," Isabel said at last. "I've dragged you this far. You must take the next step or I'll feel as if I'm forcing you."

This was the king's bed, and Noble's blue eyes, in his mind, stared down at them unblinking from the canopy. She had given herself to a man many times here but it had always been her husband. He didn't know if Noble's image was plaguing him to terrorize him, shame him, or just intimidate him, but he tried to push it away as he laid her on the mattress and hovered over her. He was frightened of the first moment, the commencement of true sin and irredeemable betrayal. Beyond that, when it was too late to turn back, there would be a sickly kind of freedom and relief. But until then the possibility of redemption gave guilt and fear their own seductive powers—

"You're thinking too much," she whispered. "Stay here."

He gave her an apologetic smile, bent over to kiss her cheek, and then he lost himself in her.

They were tentative at first. But their lean bodies fit together beautifully, moved together with one rhythm, intertwined so naturally they could almost forget they were not one. This was the mystery she had missed on her wedding night, the sense of being let into some secret. He lacked Noble's suave assurance but his touch was a hundred times more electric. She didn't know where her Christian Lord fit into it, but she knew this was a mingling that no benevolent God could have condemned. This could not be an evil thing.

She was not indulging him, as he now realized suddenly that most other women had always done. There was some fathomless craving beyond the animal need for sex and it frightened him to feel it. It frightened him much more to sense she felt it too.

Hours later, they lay beside each other on the bed, her face buried in his shoulder, arms around each other. "I want more of that," she whispered. "More and more and more." She felt him tense.

"We can't. Only tonight. I have to get out before it's light and I can't come back." He kissed the top of her head, where her tangled hair made a zigzag part across her scalp. That silky hair that had so enchanted him for the first time just a few days ago. It seemed like another era. It was another era. "Only tonight," he repeated, kissing her. "It's better this way," he insisted quietly when she frowned. "It's not complicated. We'll have unsullied memories of each other, and the part of each of us that belongs to him will never have to—" He stopped talking abruptly, realizing that she wasn't listening, and realizing why.

She was running her fingers over a ridge of skin near his spine, an ancient wound from the day she was born. "What's that?" she asked, and lifted herself up to peer over his torso in the candlelight. She gasped. "Gwirion! Your back!"

She was staring at the faded scars from the lashing he'd received on Halloween. "That's from my little misadventure with the dogs," he said dismissively, but she shook her head.

"No, I see those, but there's something else here," she insisted, and reached toward the patch of slick, taut scar tissue. "This is much older—"

"I fell off a horse when I was nine," he said quickly. "Let me dress now."

They stood before the fireplace. She slipped into a chemise and then Noble's long wool robe for warmth, and helped him back on with his clothes so coquettishly that by the time he was ready to go, their hands were all over each other again. "Please stay," she whispered into his neck and ran her hands down his front. "Just once more. Quickly, we'll stay dressed—"

"Do you want me to get caught?" he asked backing away, his voice rising in alarm. "If there's light enough to see someone climbing over the wall, those men will shoot to kill."

She threw her arms around him one final time, hating to let go, and he held her tightly, her face nuzzling his collarbone, her knees bending slightly to press against his legs. They stayed in this final clench, lost in each other's presence, too distracted to hear the dim noises rising from the courtyard on the other side of the tower, or even, a moment later, slippered feet racing up the wooden steps outside and low voices greeting each other on the other side of the door.

The king's doorkeeper Gethin rapped hard, and—against all custom or decorum—entered immediately, torch in hand. "Milady!" he cried, heading automatically for the bed before looking toward the now-dim fire and feeble candlelight. In that moment of delay they dropped their embrace and leapt apart, but Gwirion had no chance to hide.

Gethin blinked in surprise to see him and forgot to bow to Her Majesty. "How did you get in here? I've been on guard since the queen went to bed."

"Scaled the wall," Gwirion said in a high voice, trying to sound casual. "I've just terrified Her Majesty." Her Majesty was too flustered to act terrified, so he babbled on. "Saw a light in the window and assumed the king was back somehow—"

"He is!" the doorkeeper nearly bellowed, grinning. "They saw him from the beacon tower and he'll be here in ten minutes or less, that's why Gwilym requested Her Majesty to come to hall. Oh, Gwirion lad, but he'll be glad you're home safe. You must both come down to greet him."

She felt him sway beside her and she took his arm to support him. "Gwirion is feeling poorly," she said. "He's had a rough journey out and back, and he's chilled. I am excusing him from seeing the king tonight."

"Oh, Your Majesty, I don't know about that. The king would want to see him if he were at death's door. Come on, lad, I'll take you down to the kitchen and see what Marged can do for you. We'll see you when you're ready, milady."

Before either of them could object, the burly fellow had scooped Gwirion up under one arm and was escorting him out of the room, radiating cheer. Gwirion managed to turn his head and give her a traumatized look of resignation before he disappeared down the steps. Alone, she leaned against the mantel, uncertain if she wanted to laugh or weep.

THE queen's chandler hurriedly lit rushes around the hall. Outside in the bailey, the castle population had gathered in the cold to shake off sleep and greet their sovereign. Noble reined in his sweat-drenched mount, Efan and three soldiers riding up behind him looking agitated and exhausted. Everyone had tried to talk His Majesty out of doing this. The sky was clear and the moon bright enough to travel by, he'd argued. On foot, perhaps, and in familiar territory, Cadwgan had angrily admonished him, begging him not to run a tired horse through unfamiliar hills at night. The roads from Wigmore to Cymaron, Noble had rebutted impatiently, were well worn from the days of the Mortimer occupation, and traversing nothing but treeless hills, they could be trusted in dim light. Since he had no chance of changing horses along the way he would obviously not spend his mount foolishly, but he had delayed enough already and did not want to wait until morning to be gone. He'd wanted to go alone, arguing that even a single guard would slow him down, but Efan refused to let him leave the camp without an escort.

He had been supping with Llewelyn and their officers near Knighton as the armies traveled home, preparing to split off to go to their respective kingdoms the following morning and celebrating their last night of war rations by drinking as much as possible. They were cheering the settlement they'd forced on Mortimer, crowing triumphantly over Thomas's release and the terms, which were all to Mortimer's loss. Just as King Richard's benign neglect gave the Marcher baron freedom to run wild with ambition, it gave him little to fall back upon for help in a defeat. Lord Maelgwyn ap Cadwallon, King of Maelienydd, had decided all the terms.

Throughout that final supper, he'd waited. He waited as the ceremonious toasts acknowledged him the supreme and successful commander. He waited as the camp bards and the bards from Gwynedd paid him elaborate praise. He waited, barely wetting his lips, smiling and laughing with the officers who were all guzzling foul brew on the grounds that the less there was to carry, the faster they could get home. He waited until he knew everyone's attentions were truly turned away from war and toward their own homes, until Llewelyn's value as his comrade-in-arms was of substance only to the bards.

Then he had his dagger at Llewelyn's throat too fast for even the keenest guards to stop him, and cleared the tent of everybody else, declaring that only one of them would leave the tent alive if blade met blade. However savvier a politician and tactician the Prince of Gwynedd was, Noble was a better swordsman—at least when he was cold sober and Llewelyn wasn't—and Llewelyn knew that. He chose at once to admit his mischief, and Noble, not condescending to speak further with him, called in Father Idnerth to negotiate a penalty. Ten minutes later the king was on horseback racing toward Castell Cymaron.

He wondered as he rode why he suddenly felt emotional. Gwirion had obviously escaped safely and might even be back at the castle before him. The queen was safe. Nobody was hurt. The danger was over. There was no need for him to come flying home belatedly this way; he had known something was amiss for two days and nights and he'd done nothing about it, and all had come out fine. Still his breath caught, thinking what it must have been like for them, his two dependents so completely unprepared. It warmed him that Gwirion had put himself in harm's way for his wife. It was her face that hovered in his mind's eye now, and a rare tenderness threatened to weaken his limbs. He was ashamed and furious that a fellow Welshman had betrayed her trust, and he wanted to wrap reassuring arms around her and promise her she would be safe now. And he would have a chance to do that before sunup.

His spirits were high as he flung the reins to a waiting groom and tried to dismount. But the crowd—villagers, servants, the scrawny men who'd stayed behind to guard the castle, and the petitioners who'd been locked inside the village walls—swarmed around his horse and lifted him onto their shoulders, cheering, crowing with delight at his safe return and the presumed victory it presaged. He was taken aback by the excitement but then, laughing, let them carry him. A great wobbling carpet of heads and hands, they rushed up the steps to the great hall and cheered again when they saw his wife waiting to receive him.

She was across the room, standing alone by the low embers of the fire, in a chemise and surcoat, her hair braided hurriedly and hanging limply down her back. She was startled by the joyful on-slaught, but seeing who it carried, knelt down respectfully at once. The crowd, with the awkward grace of a collective entity, brought king to queen and slid him gently to his feet to stand beside her, before retreating to where they could all gawk and listen without crowding the couple. "Milady," Noble said, taking her hands and pulling her up. "I praise every god in creation for your safety." He pecked her formally on each cheek and then, so relieved to feel her small frame in his grasp, kissed her passionately on the lips for a moment, not noticing her tremulous response. There was a hearty caw of approval from around the room. Noble glanced at the congregation as if seeing them for the first time, then turned back to his wife, stroking her face with roughened hands smelling of leather and horse sweat.

"Are you well?"

"Yes, milord," she managed to say. "Just a bit overwhelmed by all the excitement."

"Things will be in order now," he assured her, and murmured quietly, a private message for the only one who really cared, "Your brother is safely back in his home." A small sob of gratitude escaped her and she hugged him. He loved the feel of her slender arms clinging to him, and stroked her hair, resting his chin on the top of her head until she had collected herself. Then he took her hand, turned to the crowd surrounding them, and announced, "The fighting is over. We are victorious and all our terms are met." They cheered again, ecstatically; they had no idea what the terms were, but "victorious" sounded promising. "And I've had it out with the upstart prince who subjected you all to his cousin's rude visit. We'll have no more problems from that border either." This had more immediate meaning for them, so the cheering was ecstatic and prolonged.

Noble was about to dismiss them all to return to bed, when he saw a small figure near the kitchen, nearly hidden behind Gethin's bulk and drinking deeply from a cup. The king's face lit up. "Gwirion!" he cried out, and instantly the crowd turned its collective exuberance in the same direction. The doorkeeper, swept up in the spirit of the moment, jovially grabbed the startled Gwirion under the arms and lifted his limp form high in the air, presenting him to all like a sacred relic.

Noble broke through the crowd to reach him. Gethin lowered him into the king's strong embrace and he hung inert in Noble's arms. "It's a master politician we have here—I should make you my heir! Our little hero, and come home already!" The castle populace cheered with approval around him and he looked so joyful it made Gwirion want to kill himself. He was trapped now. Antidotal to the alarming novelty of the last few days, Noble's familiarity calmed something in Gwirion; the seductive aroma of charisma was already weaving its way around his rib cage. His eyes met Isabel's briefly over the crowd. She knew he wasn't leaving now. And she turned away, understanding it was for the king, not herself, that he was staying.

The king dismissed the collected huddle with a gesture and turned his full attention to his friend. "How long have you been back?" he asked quietly, still smiling, as the crowd dispersed.

"Just a few minutes, sire, I'm surprised we didn't come across each other outside the gates. I've been on foot and I'm chilled through, so—"

"Come up for a bit to my room. Play for me," he said, "and for the queen. What you did was tremendous, Gwirion, for the kingdom and for me, but also for her. This is the beginning of a great friendship for the three of us, I hope."

Gwirion decided then that the only way out of the situation was sudden death. "Noble," he said miserably, in a quiet voice although people had already wandered out of earshot. "I've been with your wife."

"Yes, I know, shut up in—"

"I mean carnally," Gwirion said with a wince.

The king chuckled. "Indeed? You always were a fellow of extremes. Come on up, just a tune or two—"

"I'm serious," Gwirion said in his most humorless voice. "Christ, Noble, send me away."

He only laughed harder. "I hope this is a quick jest, Gwirion, it's too late to get into something complicated."

"And what is the jest?" demanded Isabel in a too bright voice, appearing suddenly at Noble's elbow. The bottom of Gwirion's stomach fell out.

Noble merely smiled. "I don't think it's for a lady's ears. Finish it tomorrow, won't you, Gwirion? It's an excellent deadpan." He put a hand on each of their shoulders, looking between them with satisfaction. "I'm so pleased," he said. He turned to his wife. "Do you know how extraordinary it is for Gwirion to have done that?" And back to his friend, beaming: "Truly. You amaze me. You of all people."

"It's not as if he despised me," the queen protested, slightly unnerved by Noble's wonderment.

The king shook his head. "It has nothing to do with you. I'm amazed that Gwirion left the castle at all. Gwirion doesn't take to the open road, do you, my friend?" He saw the confused look she shot Gwirion, who ignored it. Noble slid his arm around her shoulders, pulled her to him, and kissed her cheekbone near her ear. "Come to bed, and I'll explain it."

"Please don't, sire," Gwirion said in a tense voice.

"Then come up with us, distract me from telling tales with a tune on the harp." He kissed her cheek again, more ardently, and murmured, "Would you like a serenade for our reunion?" Gwirion, who heard the question plainly, shut his eyes, wishing he could disappear.

Isabel managed to be equal to it. She leaned against her husband, smiling up at him. "I thought privacy might be in order." Lowering her voice suggestively, she added, "I earned castellan privileges from you before you left. Do you wish to earn them back?"

He nearly did a double take. "I don't need to earn them, they're mine to take—but is my own wife flirting with me?" He looked up at Gwirion, delighted. "I'll have to go to war more often. Come up and play."

Gwirion willed his exhaustion to visually manifest itself. "I've been on the road without rest for two days, sire, I would be a disappointment to you. I need to sleep."

Noble shrugged, then smiled lecherously at his wife. "I hope you don't need to sleep, milady, because I don't intend to let you. Take leave of your new friend for the night." He playfully pivoted her toward Gwirion.

They avoided any direct glance. "Good evening, Gwirion. Thank you. For everything."

"Good evening, milady," he mumbled in response. "It was my privilege."

S HE had straightened the bedchamber before coming down to greet him, but as he cheerfully pulled off his dusty clothes she stared desperately about to make sure no hint of what had just happened here remained.

"What did you mean before?" she asked, to cover her fidgeting. "About Gwirion never leaving the castle?"

Noble sat down on the bed to unstrap his boots. "Haven't you noticed that he doesn't?"

"He has no reason to."

"He invents reasons all the time. Whenever he's angry with me, he threatens to run off. He never has and he never will."

"Why not?" she pressed.

Noble paused, grimacing, fidgeting with the week-old stubble he was desperate to be rid of. "It's not my place to tell you."

She looked at him in surprise; he usually took as much glee in disregarding other people's proprieties as Gwirion himself did. "Not your place? You're the king. It's your place to say whatever you wish to."

"I don't wish to say what happened to Gwirion." He grinned broadly. "What I do wish is for you to undress and lie down. Let's not waste his gallantry in saving your little body from imprisonment." Her stomach tightened as he threw the blankets aside: She had stripped the sheeting from the bed and hidden it, but had been too flustered and hurried to find a replacement.

"What's the meaning of this?" He frowned, examining the bare mattress. "Why is my bed unmade?"

If he'd asked her a question that required yes or no for an answer, she might have been able to dissemble, but inventing a falsehood at that moment was beyond her. "The sheet was stained," she said, trying to sound casual. She wrapped her arms around herself and suddenly realized that even if she could get through this moment, her body offered as much evidence as the bedding had.

He stared at her for a moment in confusion, then a look of anger crossed his face. "That whoreson," he spat. "Using my bed to rape my servants." He didn't notice her sag heavily against the bedpost as he replaced his annoyance with a suggestive smile. "Well. If the baron has desecrated our bed, then we must resanctify it, mustn't we?" He held out his hand and beckoned for her.

"You're very dusty from the road, shall we bathe first?" she said quickly, silently thanking whatever guardian angel had put the words into her mouth.

He smiled approvingly. "Lord, yes. And let's get rid of this," he added, scratching the beard. "Before I start looking like a Norman. One of those *defeated* fellows."

GWIRION retreated to his closet behind the kitchen chimney, to the warmth and privacy he thought he'd never see again, which he'd been away from for nearly four nights in a row—one of the longest absences of his life. He crawled under his blanket, comforted by the familiar space, and tried hard to pretend he didn't know what the king was doing. He was undoubtedly doing it far better than Gwirion had, which was the best reason to try to forget it was happening.

THE next morning on Noble's orders the entire castle rose late. The king, still jubilant from victory, graciously received spontaneous applause first in chapel and then again at board. The queen missed mass and when she finally appeared, to eat, she moved very gingerly toward the high table, nodding with bashful pleasant-ness to the many servants and villagers whose adoration she had earned over the past week. She avoided Gwirion's eyes. Noble, watch-ing her with a satisfied grin, whispered to Gwirion, "I gave her the riding of her life, she's never had half so much ploughing in one night."

"Probably not a quarter as much," Gwirion said quietly, feeling ill and picking at his barley bread. If Noble thought it was a deliber-ate deadpan, at least he didn't have to fake cheeriness. "I'm surprised Your Majesty didn't choose somebody a little more exciting for your homecoming romp."

"I had romps enough at the front," Noble whispered back. "This was better than a romp. And she always smells so good." Gwirion involuntarily made a distressed expression, and Noble laughed. "Stop that, Gwirion, she's not the ogress you pretend she is. Anyhow, all she's useful for now, really, is an heir, and I need one, preferably a legitimate one. This episode with Mortimer has con-vinced me of that. I'll find another mother if I must, but legitimate offspring would be best, especially if we have to deal with the En-glish in the future."

"Ah, I see," Gwirion said. "You're suspending recreational sex in favor of procreational sex."

Noble grinned. "Exactly."

"Well where's the fun in *that*?" Gwirion said, desperately grasping for something wittier to say and finding his brain turned to mush. *Sound cynical,* he thought, *and perhaps he won't notice anything's different.* He'd already retreated from the impulsive honesty that had led to his con-fession. His determination to be truthful had evaporated; now he just wanted the event and all its evidence to permanently disappear, for everybody's sake.

Noble looked pleased with himself. "Oh, I've trained her pretty well by now and she's an admirably apt pupil. When you claim them virginal, you can convince them that almost anything is normal." He grinned. "You're perverse, you might take great advantage of that. What do you say? I owe you a huge favor and you're quite the hero now. I could find you a willing concubine without much trouble."

"No thank you," Gwirion said, but immediately reconsidered. Maybe that was the way to free himself from thoughts of her. "I'd say yes, but I'm so busy saving the kingdom and all that nonsense, I just don't know when I'd find the time to train her."

"I would train her for you." The king winked.

"Aren't you saving yourself for the queen?"

"For you, my friend, I will always make allowances."

"I'm deeply honored," Gwirion said in an exaggerated monotone, and the king clapped him on the shoulder.

"Is it some experiment of yours, this new delivery?"

"Yes, sire, it's so the next time you go away, *I* can stand in for Gwilym," he said, imitating the steward's somber diction. "And nobody will notice I'm not him."

"Gwilym is twice your size," Noble pointed out.

Gwirion leaned in close to Noble. "Not where it matters, sire," he assured him, with an exaggerated wink.

She watched them whispering together and it enraged her. Obviously Noble was bragging about his performance in bed the night before, and apparently Gwirion was making crass remarks, probably about her, because Noble was smiling and laughing, sometimes folding his hands in front of his lips with the forefingers pressed together, which was always a sign he was hiding a vicious delight. She knew Gwirion had no choice, but it hurt her. He would do whatever he had to do to make things seem normal, to protect himself, and there was no reason to think he'd spare her in the process. It was safer for both of them if he didn't, in fact, but she wasn't sure she could survive it. Maybe he would decide to run off after all. The thought brought as much depression as it did relief.

After the meal, she excused herself to her chamber and closed herself in with the sewing bevy. These were her only safe companions now, she realized with an internal groan. She took up her old task of spinning and lost herself in the mesmerizing monotony of the work, remembering last summer when she had also turned to this for comfort. At least then she'd had Adèle. At least then it had been warmer too, and there was sunlight, even if it was relentlessly grey or at best silver. To keep out the winter chill, the windows were now sealed with waxed cloth, and nearly all the light came from the wall sconces. For some reason this didn't give the room the coziness of the receiving chamber below; it only made it feel that much more a cage.

Two tedious hours later there was a knock on the door. She acknowledged it, assuming it was the chandler coming in to check the fire. Instead Gwirion entered carrying a basket of freshly laundered rags. The pit of her gut clenched when she saw him. "Excuse me, Your Majesty, Marged wants to know if the kitchen may have these, or if they should be mended to be of use elsewhere first." He avoided looking at her as he put the basket down, even taking a step away when she approached, pretending to clean his fingernails as he waited. The rags were the remains of bed curtains, hung along the outer sections of the hall to provide nominal privacy at night. They were unstained but very worn.

"We can make sheets of these," she said. "If Marged needs some rags, she may have what's left over, there should be plenty."

He nodded once, excused himself, and left. Isabel immediately put aside her spinning to follow him out.

"Gwirion," she hissed in the shadows of the balcony. He froze, and turned back to her, almost squirming, his foot on the top stair.

"Your Majesty?" he replied as neutrally as he could.

Now she had nothing to say. "Was there a reason for that?" she finally asked.

"Yes, milady," he said respectfully. "Marged wanted to know if—"

"That's not what I meant," she snapped, and it made a bad impression on him in combination with the wimple. She lowered her voice to a whisper, afraid her words would carry down to the hall. "You know that's not what I meant. Why did *you* bring it? You don't run errands for her."

"She asked me to and I couldn't say no without seeming strange," he whispered back, which was the truth. "I was not looking for an excuse to get near you—is that what you're accusing me of?"

"I didn't mean it as an accusation. God forbid you actually try to be in my presence."

"I think God does forbid it," he answered. "I'm not much of a Christian so I ignore him. But I'm not an idiot either. We have to stay away from each other until we can behave normally and pretend nothing happened."

Everything vulnerable inside her wanted to shriek at him, but she forced herself to stay calm. "You're saying that once we've lost the desire to be around each other, then we may be around each other."

He almost smiled. "Yes, I suppose that's it."

"Since avoiding each other is logistically impossible, could we perhaps discuss alternatives?"

"Could you perhaps be more officious?" he answered with nervous sarcasm. But he stepped away from the stairs, then slipped around behind her and began playing with her veil, trying not to think about all that it was shielding from his view. He spoke in a low voice, not a whisper; whispering, if anyone in the hall happened to glance up and see them here, would look suspicious. "Your headdress slipped and I'm adjusting it for you." She nodded, picked up her rosary and ran her fingers anxiously around the outline of the crucifix. "First of all," he said quietly, "it will not happen again, you understand that, don't you?"

"*Yes,*" she said with exaggerated impatience, furious that he'd said it first. Or perhaps that he'd said it at all. His touch, even in passing on the back of her veil, made her light-headed. She tugged at the shadowed side of her wimple and pulled the whole thing askew, to give him something real to do with his nervous fingers.

"And it's better for us to stay away from each other until we're each . . . calmer about it."

"We can't shun each other utterly," she insisted. "He believes us to be friends at least."

"He has no idea what a friendship between us would resemble. Considering our history, simply ignoring each other could constitute profound affection."

"Maybe six months ago, but not now. Now he would notice."

"Your Majesty," Gwirion corrected, with a grudging smile at her naiveté, "Even *I* lack the exaggerated self-importance to believe that Noble will notice *anything* in the next week but celebrating his victory and dispersing the army. He won't even open court again until Lent at the earliest. There couldn't *be* a better time for us to snub each other." Inspired—and desperate—he grabbed the opportunity to estrange her and with a harsh tug on the wimple added: "You should realize that better than I, Your Majesty—you're the one obsessed with invading the enclave of courtly power. Speaking of which, how many points do you score for ensnaring the king's top man? That must be quite a coup."

She drew a sharp, indignant breath, but caught herself and said with cutting dryness, "Kindly envision me turning around and smacking you very hard across the face." He had to duck his head away to hide how charmed he was by the retort. "I presume your silence is an acknowledgment that you were speaking rubbish," she continued. "If you said it to generate antagonism, then you're very shortsighted. Antagonism *will* catch his attention. You should know that, it's how you curry favor with him half the time."

He resented how attractive the uttering of insults made her. "Then are we agreed that an act of mutual indifference is the safest course for now?"

"No," she insisted. "It must be an affectation of friendship, if you can possibly bring yourself to be decent to me. Anything else will make him suspicious."

"A compromise, then," Gwirion said stubbornly. "Two weeks of cold shoulders followed by a month of pleasantries."

"He believes us to be friends *now*."

"Well then, he's wrong. It has been known to happen. And now I must be going, I've run out of wimple." He stepped away, not looking at her.

"Do you regret that it happened?" she asked before she could stop herself.

"Considering the consequences, of course I regret it," he whispered impatiently, moving toward the stairs, but then he softened. "If I had escaped, no, I wouldn't regret it at all." He would not look her in the face. "Am I excused, Your Majesty?"

THAT evening the king and queen, standing together, opened the hall for Candlemas and the entire village walked up to the castle carrying tapers. This holiday, in the bleakest, dullest part of the year, was a symbol of hope and renewal: The procession of candles was a collective reminder that the sun, the great god Llew, was returning to them at last. This had been manipulated by the church into the Feast of the Purification of the Virgin, a day celebrating Mary's ritual cleansing after childbirth, and her return to the church ("What church?" Gwirion interrupted incredulously when Father Idnerth attempted to give his usual brief sermon between courses at the supper feast. "Jesus hadn't yet been crucified, there was no church!")

And this year, of more import than any symbolic or religious meaning, there was a victory to celebrate: Roger Mortimer had been prevented, again, from taking Maelienydd. The queen's brother was free, his lands restored to him, and his primary allegiance sworn to Noble. Thomas would host a large, permanent garrison of Welsh fighters who would patrol the border, overseeing new standing defenses: a dyke and palisade, to be built and paid for by Roger Mortimer. Noble explained all this informally to the assembly; the people were thrilled, even with the details they did not quite understand,

and the ready flow of ale made their laughter, their applause, and their general delight ring out in peals into the night. The king also took a moment to publicly acknowledge Gwilym's selfless and unprecedented yielding of castellan rights to the queen, and to praise the queen for her able job of standing in for him while he was away. "My mother Queen Efa and all who came before her would rejoice to add this woman to the roster of worthy consorts," he declared, and she blushed, more grateful for his praise than for all the adoration of their subjects. He had never so nearly treated her like a peer—all the more remarkable now, when she knew full well that the political value of the marriage had been virtually nullified. Gwirion watched silently from the hearthside, sadly dazzled by how beautiful she was when she was happy.

Isabel feared that the hour-long elegiac poem about Cadwallon's murder would be dragged out again, but instead a young poet—sent by Llewelyn as part of his damage payment—presented a poem in progress extolling Noble's virtue in battle. Gwirion, who'd resolutely refused to speak to the queen all evening, looked trapped, almost persecuted, by a verse singing his praises for heroically defending her. He did not return to his normal humor until the applause and cheering had died away and the chaplain was halfway through the blessing in honor of the spring hunt, which would begin the next morning at dawn. In keeping with tradition, most of Idnerth's hunting prayer was drowned out by urgent whispered conferences between the villagers and castle servants concerning, for example, bets placed on chess games between the mayor and the steward.

Then Gwirion was asked to perform. He had played for them all five thousand times before, but tonight it was as if an archangel were gracing them with his artistry; this was his share of the adoring celebrity the people of Maelienydd were slathering on the three of them. Noble had offered him new clothes, but he'd refused them, saying he preferred his familiar shabby, shapeless garments. He did this entirely because he wanted desperately to look handsome to the queen and refused to let himself indulge the impulse.

She'd been able to distract her mind from the poet's incantation, but the harp went right through her. As always, his first tune was "Rhiannon's Tears," and hearing it distressed her so deeply she had to make an excuse to her husband and leave the hall. Needing privacy and knowing Angharad and Madrun were in the solar, she slipped out into the courtyard, hiding in the shadowed niche between the end of the hall and the barbican tower. She hadn't brought a mantle with her, not wanting to draw attention by asking for one, and within moments she was shaking from the cold, but she hardly noticed. She knelt down and lifted the hem of her skirt to her face, wracked by frustrated sobs. When she had finally calmed herself, she pressed the heels of her hands against the frozen building stones until they were almost numb, then held them over her eyes until, she hoped, the evidence of her weeping had subsided.

Inside, Gwirion had finished playing and was sitting next to Noble—in her chair. Whose idea was that? Nervously, she approached the two men. They sat in their usual evening poses, Noble reclining comfortably, legs stretched out before him with feet crossed at the ankles and his fingers interlaced behind his head, Gwirion sitting upright and alert, almost pitched forward, as if he were about to be catapulted somewhere. They both noticed her approach and responded at the same moment but in very different ways: Noble, with an easy smile to her, signaled Hafaidd to bring another seat, but Gwirion leapt out of her chair as if the bottom were on fire. Realizing he'd drawn Noble's attention by his abruptness, he continued the natural arc of his movement by dropping into a cartwheel that landed him on the far side of the king. Then, as if this were a perfectly common mode of perambulating, he settled nonchalantly on the floor by Noble's seat and fixed his attention on the young bard who was performing.

"You needn't spring away like that, Gwirion, I don't have the plague," Isabel said in a pleasant voice as she sat, determined to show him how easy and preferable it was to be kindly toward each other.

"I'm sorry, did Your Majesty speak?" he said impassively, not looking at her. "I missed it."

"I said I don't have the plague," she repeated, still very sweetly, and busied herself adjusting and smoothing her skirt to affect offhandedness.

"I never suggested that you did, milady," he said reasonably, and straightened up again, pointedly looking at the musician.

Not even a jibe. If anything, she thought irritably, he would raise Noble's suspicions by his very blandness. And Noble did, in fact, find it an odd exchange.

"Are you being short with the queen, Gwirion?" he asked warningly.

"Not as short as I am with you, sire, considering you're a good deal taller than she is. I'll be less short if you wish it, though." In a single smooth move, he leapt up onto the arm of Noble's chair, perched on the backrest—and then sat astride the royal shoulders, as Noble lurched to keep his balance from the suddenness of the action. "Now I'm far from short!" Gwirion crowed. "I'm taller even than you. In fact, if you would just stand up, I'll reach such heights that you need never fear my being short with anyone again."

"We'll see about that," Noble muttered. He stood slowly, lifting Gwirion on his shoulders, and the entire hall turned to stare at them. The bard silenced his instrument; nobody even noticed. Gwirion, grinning, waved grandly as the king took a few steps away from the hearth toward a clump of matted rushes strewn on the floor. He braced his hands just above his knees and with an abrupt jerking motion flung his upper body forward until he was bent over double. Gwirion, with a startled grunt, tumbled off the descending royal shoulders and landed on his back on the rushes, his complaints drowned out by laughter from their audience.

"I'd rather you be short, at least then I can keep an eye on you," Noble said with an affectionate smirk, giving him a hand up.

"As it pleases His Most Royal Majesty," Gwirion intoned a little breathlessly, recovering at once and giving him a very exaggerated bow. "But now, if you'll excuse me, I'm for bed." Ignoring the queen, he bowed his head to Noble and departed for his little room, acknowledging the affectionate farewells that the crowd called out to him.

"What a silly fellow," Noble said, smiling, sitting again beside his wife, his mind a thousand miles away from the awkward moment that had birthed the silliness. She didn't reply, afraid her voice would not be steady. This was even worse than the old antagonism. Now he was camouflaging his coldness to her, not flaunting it as he had before, so there was no way to seek even sympathy from Noble, let alone reprieve from Gwirion himself.

14

Aftermath

Lent, 1199

THE KING was distracted over the next fortnight; his focus was, as Gwirion had predicted, entirely upon security and military matters. Specific conditions for Mortimer were declared, written, signed, and delivered not only to Roger himself but to King Richard's court, and to the manors of all the other Marcher lords, to warn them off interfering with Maelienydd's borders. The army came home and dispersed, which required days of delegating paperwork so that each man's military contribution to the crown could be measured and entered into the rolls. Accounts of the victorious raid were written up and sent to every manor and castle throughout Wales, an invitation to immortalize Maelgwyn ap Cadwallon in poetry and song. Congratulatory notes and gifts poured in; these were cataloged and archived and announced at supper each night, spinning out the golden hour of victory into days, then weeks.

Of greater urgency was the settlement with Llewelyn. Noble's first demand was freedom from his obligation to support Llewelyn's claims against other Welshmen—and a sworn oath that he and his subjects would never have to pay obeisance to the Prince of Gwynedd in any way, even if Llewelyn should in time conquer the whole of Britain. For Cynan's offenses, Llewelyn replaced thrice over the appropriated food and fodder, and paid a massive fine that Noble split between the state coffers and his molested servants. Llewelyn sent his own envoy to apologize and swear profusely that from now on, the rising star of Gwynedd would work in league with Noble in all things. Noble accepted the proclamation graciously, knowing it to be a lie. In private, he mused briefly on a mitigating tie by marriage between their two courts, but dismissed the thought at once—a marriage bond had not staved off Mortimer's ambition, after all.

Finally, there was Huw to deal with. Assisting Cynan to plan the infiltration of Cymaron was an act of treason and treason called for hanging. But Huw's three sons were not yet old enough to claim their patrimony and there was a very real danger his cousin would seize his lands. The cousin was in Powys, the neighboring kingdom, already causing problems for his own prince, and he was a known champion of Llewelyn. So Noble grudgingly argued clemency for Huw on the grounds, ironically, of national security. The royal court fined him nearly enough to beggar him, and three of Noble's teulu were sent to his household as a permanent guard, to be at all times in hearing distance of him—and of Branwyn, who entertained more men than he did.

Nobody, including Isabel, was entirely certain if she was still Noble's deputy in quotidian matters of the realm, matters he neglected for a fortnight. So while he attended to weightier issues, the court hovered in near stasis, tentatively taking its lead from her. The council met only once to discuss domestic matters; Goronwy heard no cases; the coffers were kept closed for all but minor expenditures, all at Isabel's authorization.

That fortnight culminated in Shrove Tuesday's final huge indulgence before the Lenten fast. The village children were hired to ring the chapel bell unceasingly for hours, as inside the hall everyone inhaled what little fresh food was left to them, smothering everything in butter, cheese, and lard. There was an air of forceful gaiety and excess to the evening, since everybody knew what was to follow come the morning mass.

Gwirion as always sat behind the king's left shoulder at the feast, managing to smile and laugh and contribute his usual puerility. He had become exhausted by the constant vigilance required in the queen's presence. Her "friendliness" was a feeble pretext for what, to him, was dangerous behavior. But he hoped that finally he had guided her to a comfortable level of coolness, in which they never spoke directly to each other (or rather, he never spoke directly to her, nor did he acknowledge anything she said directly to him), and yet they could engage in a triptych conversation when Noble was between them. Although his humor remained excessively libidinous, he made no bawdy jokes about her to her husband; in fact, he had nearly transmuted his image of her to that of a sexless curiosity who happened to sleep in the king's bed. It was a fiction he was certain he could grow accustomed to believe in time. And so by the great feast of Shrove Tuesday, he had very nearly convinced himself that everything was back to normal.

Noble rose as the final course of veal was being cleared away, and raised his cup, gesturing to his wife in her brightest veil and kirtle to stand beside him. She looked gracious and confident—even though he'd apprised her of the speech he was about to make, and it was hard for her to feel gracious about it. He gazed out over the rows of happily tipsy villagers and castle denizens, a firm but loving father. "My people," he called out, and waited for it to quiet. He spoke with unwonted formality. "You whom by the grace of all the gods I'm charged to steward. Tonight we feast together because tomorrow we bend under the solemn yoke assigned to us as faithful Christians. In addition, tomorrow my wife and I both bend under the particular yokes assigned to us by God—I by returning my full attention to the duties of the throne, she by returning her full attention to her duties as my queen and yours. I have been remiss this fortnight, neglecting my more domestic duties in favor of settling the issues at the borders. I now turn my energies home and hearth-ward, so that my gracious bride, who has been so selflessly and valiantly burdened as my deputy, may now entirely return to the role that is preferred for her by God, by nature, and by her own sweet spirit—to be my consort and the mother of our kingdom's heir." He beamed warmly at her in front of all of them and she managed to return the expression, but her throat constricted at the import of the words. Then a suggestive little smile tickled the corners of his mouth and he winked at her, reverting to his usual, more personable demeanor. "In the evening's spirit of excess, I'll be particularly ar-dent possessing her tonight, by way of symbolically repossessing my entire court." The crowd, hardly hearing what the words were, catch-ing only the tone that assured them he was being lecherous, cheered him, especially when he added, leering, "I admonish all my soldiers to similarly repossess your own private domains. Tomorrow let us greet the Lenten season knowing we are truly back in residence." He grinned. Gwirion had managed a halfhearted expression of ap-proval and was preparing to top off Noble's speech with something appropriately prurient, when the king raised his voice and finished grandly: "My castle shall be under my jurisdiction again, as shall my court of law, my council, my people, and also, of course"—he ges-tured broadly over his shoulder—"my beloved sacrificial fool!" He laughed heartily and spun to his left, startling Gwirion with an ef-fusive embrace as the crowd cheered approval. Gwirion smiled weakly, absolutely flummoxed how to respond to this. Isabel felt her knees almost buckle, and prayed no one was looking at her. Nobel, still radiating cheer, released his friend, who sat down very abruptly on his stool. "Yes," Noble continued to the crowd, grinning, "we are very grateful that she had good use of him in my absence, but now she must relinquish her hero so that my court can have its jester back. So come, madam," he finished with a flourish, "to my bed. We have a kingdom to restore to custom—all these good people are re-lying on you to give me what is mine and therefore theirs." He led her grandly around the table and out of the hall toward the stairs up to his bedroom; she followed, looking pale.

Gwirion knew he should have made some approving, lewd comment as they departed but he did not trust himself to speak. As soon as it was safe, he forced himself to wander very slowly toward the kitchen with his empty tumbler. Then he dived into his little closet room, grateful for the privacy, trying to will Noble's comment from his head.

When the meal was cleared, the happy, sodden congregation followed Marged out to the forge, where she ceremoniously gave the smith an old cooking pot. He smashed it against his small block anvil with his heaviest hammer, crushing it.

Lent had begun. It was a time to honor discipline and deprivation.

AT breakfast the next day Gwirion felt compelled to keep up an almost constant stream of whispered witticisms to the king, about any topic under heaven except the queen. Half the time he rambled incoherently and could barely invent punch lines to justify his yammering. He resented the effort it required.

Isabel eyed them whispering over the king's shoulder in the shadows, just as they had done for at least as long as she had been alive. She felt iron splinters in her gut simply watching them. Whenever Noble smiled she winced, certain that Gwirion had somehow just sacrificed her dignity. For two weeks now he'd neatly deflected her innocent attempts at interaction, distracting the king with jokes, insults, or antics. He never once allowed himself a simple, friendly exchange with her. Clearly this was what he thought was necessary to protect them both, but to her it was unfeeling and excessive. It hurt more now than it had the first day. She had to make him stop.

J UST stop it," she begged, when she managed to make their solitary paths cross by the well that afternoon. The smith was in his shop beside them and the echoing tenor clank of his hammer offered them some privacy of speech.

"But that's what the king expects of me."

"And you always have to do what he expects of you?"

"You don't?" he snapped. "He wants your body and my wit. I'll withhold my wit if you withhold your body." He fumbled, realizing it had sounded like a wish. Before she could respond he pressed on brusquely, "But that of course is not the proper *use* of royal fools, now is it?"

"He meant nothing by that comment last night," she said, nervously but firm. "That was his Welsh oratory getting the better of him in the moment."

"Of course he *meant* something by it, he was warning me away from you. That was a threat. He doesn't even want us speaking to each other."

"Don't be ridiculous," she hissed impatiently. "I was with him the full ten hours after he said it and——"

"I *know* that," he sneered, appalled at himself for speaking jealously.

"——and there was nothing off in his behavior," she insisted, ignoring his interjection. "Nothing pointed, no hints or threats of even the subtlest kind. It was only a guilty conscience that heard more than what he said."

"It's *your* guilty conscience that needs to believe something so naive about him."

Isabel frowned. "At the very worst," she said, in partial concession, "he suspects we might have strayed, that's all. He was making it clear that *if* we did, we mustn't stray again. In fact, in a way it was forgiveness, because he publicly reclaimed us both."

"Your Majesty, please," Gwirion said quietly, worried that people passing through the courtyard were noticing him upset their new darling. "We're bickering as if we were lovers, as if we were carrying on. We're not. So there's nothing more to say."

"May we at least be friendly?" she insisted. "It wasn't just lust, it was affection. We came to have real regard for each other. Can't we try to be easy in that?"

She looked small and vulnerable and he was annoyed with her for rousing gentle impulses in him. He frowned, a hard, angry expression. "No, not after his resounding proclamation," he said. "He's so possessive of us both, it's just too dangerous." But the hardness wavered. "And too ... strange," he added, sounding regretful. He walked off, briskly, toward the main gate where he had been headed when she'd stopped him. She felt her eyes smart and took a moment to steady her breathing.

Gwirion had been called to the barbican to help greet a traveling party. Although St. David's Day, March 1, was two weeks off, some folk were beginning Lenten pilgrimages to the saint's home village, far to the southwest in Deheubarth, and the occasional gentleman pilgrim asked leave to stay the night in Cymaron on his way. The flag of the approaching party, a white Maltese cross on a red field, looked vaguely familiar, but Gwirion couldn't place it—until he recognized Corr's patrons, Humffri ap Madoc and his wife. She wore images of daffodils embroidered on her veil; the real ones weren't yet available to make offerings. Humffri handed down his spear to Einion the porter and coaxed his spotted charger farther into the bailey where a groom was waiting.

A servant who had come in on a large grey pack beast at the tail end of the entourage tossed a lumpy sack of oats practically on Gwirion's head. He sputtered with annoyance and pushed the sack off him to the ground, then looked up to castigate the offender. He saw only a skirt, descending on him very fast, and he reflexively held his arms out to catch its occupant.

"You always were a gentleman, Gwirion," a cheerful peasant accent said in his ear as he got his bearings.

He looked at his burden, and with a crow of delight he

dropped her to her feet and then almost smothered her in an embrace. *"Enid!"*

AFTER Gwirion had exhausted her by dragging her all around the bailey and hoisting her onto his shoulders so she could wave to people working in the towers, Enid sat with him outside the kitchen, both of them wrapped in brychans, and they talked, their breath coming out in mist. As Noble had said, Enid had been taken from the castle, although the bit about shaving her head was an embellishment. She'd been allowed to take her clothes and a few possessions, and had even been given—at Noble's insistence—enough salted meat to last her for a month. She'd found herself at Lord Humffri's gates within a week or two; Corr had happily endorsed her abilities, and a history in the king's kitchen gave her clout. It was assumed, without ever being said, that she had been terminated because she was a favorite of the king's and therefore not of the queen's—"So I promised to keep downstairs this visit," she concluded with a grin that made her nose wrinkle. "And Corr sends greetings, of course. But I want *you* to talk now, tell me what a hero you are. I want to hear your side of this crazy tale about your risking your life to save the queen."

Gwirion rolled his eyes. "That gives it a veneer of romance that simply isn't there."

"Suddenly everyone seems to adore her—haven't you become bosom buddies with herself, then?" Enid teased innocently.

Gwirion was suddenly fidgety. "No. Nothing's changed. Nothing to tell."

"Pranks?" she asked, dark eyes glittering. "Tell me your latest prank."

He shrugged, staring at the ground. "No good pranks lately. Actually, I think he's getting bored with me." He glanced at her sidewise and leered. "Maybe he needs your sort of entertainment."

"The queen has been through enough of late without having to endure me again." Enid laughed. "She's a sweet lady underneath it all, Gwirion; I don't want to upset her." He was looking at her strangely. "What?"

It was right here, at his feet, the perfect opportunity to embrace disaster. "She—" he stammered, "she understands him a little better now. I don't think she'd be upset if he met with you. In fact, with this new obsession he has for getting an heir of her, she'd probably like a night free from him, the poor girl." He tried hard to believe that he was only doing this to give himself a respite from the gut-twisting jealousy that convulsed him every night. He would not go to her. He would simply relax with the gratitude of knowing she too was alone.

Enid smoothed a patch of mud with the sole of her buskin, considering the proposal. She hadn't appreciated, until she'd left this place, either the flattery or the actual pleasure of the king's attentions. For all of her deliberate sunniness, her life lacked enjoyable diversions. "Are you sure?" she asked.

"I'll arrange it for late tonight. In his audience chamber. Then you're not even breaking your promise about staying downstairs."

Enid grinned. "All right." She nudged him. "Since we're on the subject, have you put any notches on your belt since our little misadventure?"

"No!" he said, too loudly and too quickly. She laughed.

"That kind of no means yes with a naughty tale behind it."

"No it doesn't," Gwirion said, looking away.

She took his head and turned it toward her, ducking down to make eye contact when he wouldn't look up. "Confess, Gwirion. Is it a girl? A boy? A horse?"

He finally looked at her, considering something. "You mustn't tell a soul." He gestured her close and whispered, very gravely, "I've decided to become a nun."

"Gwirion!" She laughed and swatted him through the blankets. "I'm serious."

"So am I. What better way to get my filthy claws into a gaggle of virgins?"

Enid gave him an affectionate smile, but shook her head. "You can't distract me from this." She looked at him appraisingly. "Something's different."

"No it isn't," he said quickly.

"Yes. Something's definitely different. I noticed it in your eyes right away."

"Feminine imagination," he scoffed, and turned his head away again.

"If you don't look at me, I'll know there's something there that you're trying to hide and I'll assume the worst," she said. "So you might as well let me have the real story."

After an obstinate and nervous pause, he turned back toward her with a false front of defiance, but wouldn't look directly in her eyes. She examined his face with the absorption of a physician, and sobered. "Forgive me, Gwirion, I shouldn't have teased you," she said softly. "What's her name?"

Gwirion gave her a panicked expression. "Can't tell you," he answered, although when he'd opened his mouth, he'd meant to deny it completely.

"Does the king know?"

"Of course not!" he said, his eyes widening. "Don't tell him!"

"Of course I'm not going to tell him, idiot. I remember what happened the last time, and that was just one night with me, as if *I* were any threat! Won't you tell me who, though? I'm not going to blab."

He shook his head, jaw set, and no amount of cajoling would change his mind.

SUPPER that night was brief and informal—and Lenten, being mostly salted fish. Humffri's bard Brychan ap Caradog, accompanying him on this pious pilgrimage, was given the honor of performing for His Majesty, which freed Gwirion. The prankster whispered a brief word to the king, promising him a special treat and more than a little mischief if he waited in his receiving chamber after supper. Then he excused himself from hall for the night, afraid that given the opportunity his mouth might operate without his permission and let the queen know the madness he was trying not to contemplate.

He joined Enid with Marged's little stable of assistants in the warm stone kitchen where they were catching up on gossip, drinking, and belching. Enid was helping Marged close down the kitchen for the evening, since most of her attendants—using Enid's visit as an excuse—were already too tipsy. Gwirion was gaily called over to join the party, but people lost interest in him almost at once when they saw he was not in a rowdy mood.

Enid tugged his sleeve and took him aside. "What's wrong?" she asked. "You look like somebody's been practicing rope tricks with your guts."

"It's nothing. I just need an easy night's sleep, which I'm finally going to get." He gave her a grim smile. "Enjoy yourself tonight." He exited into his closet, yawning.

But lying in the dark, he could not begin to relax. Knowing the queen would be alone tonight was even worse than knowing she was with the king. He wanted to touch her so badly it made his throat dry. It was impotent, humiliating desire: All week she had been with a man who knew so much better than he did what to do with her. She must be thanking God for returning her to her senses. Between adultery with a clumsy oaf and sanctified union with an experienced lover, there could not even be a choice. He was almost nauseated with embarrassment, realizing he had let himself think that her annoying behavior this past fortnight was because she still wanted him.

But he still wanted her. He would not be able to sleep knowing there was even a slip of a chance that he could touch her. It was nothing personal, it was just that he was so hungry for a woman's touch, and hers was the only one he had known for so long that of course his desire would think she was the only possible source of satisfaction. But any other woman would do. If he could find himself with another woman, obviously within a night or two this obsession would have transferred smoothly to she-who-was-not-queen. But right now it drove him toward she who was.

He decided to go to Noble's chamber. On the unlikely chance she was there, he would suffer the humiliation of being refused by her, but then at least it would be over, and official. Anyhow, she almost certainly would not appear, so he would simply curl up on velvet cushions and sleep by the fire, as he did sometimes, and tease Noble when he came back from his tryst with Enid. Just like old times.

But of course he couldn't go to Noble's room. She probably would not be there, but it would raise eyebrows—having arranged for the king to be busy, Gwirion goes to the king's room, where the queen usually retires? That would look suspicious. He couldn't go.

But he couldn't sleep. He couldn't even rest. The kitchen sounds had quieted down, and throwing a blanket around himself he stepped out of his room.

Enid was still perched on the cutting table, alert and awake, while the floor around her was covered with sleeping forms on matted reeds, wrapped in mantles and brychans, huddled together for warmth. She gave him a pleased but surprised look when he appeared.

"I thought you were asleep," she whispered.

"Couldn't," he whispered back. "Too early. Why aren't you with the king?"

"I'm just waiting for the ladies to retire. He's in his audience chamber but the queen is still talking with my mistress in hall, and I can't go to him right in front of her."

He wished she would. That was a terrible, stupid, foolish wish but he wished she would. If the queen saw Enid go in to Noble, she'd know her husband would be detained all night, and perhaps she would go not to her own room, the sewing bevy within earshot, but to the privacy of the king's chamber, and perhaps if she found him there she would not refuse him, if for no other reason than anger at the king's dalliance with Enid. He almost told her to go. No. He couldn't. He had to keep himself from doing anything idiotic. He would walk. He would cross over to the keep and walk around all night, until he saw Noble's chandler light his room for him, until any possible opportunity for meeting her was over. He had been such an ass to arrange this assignation. His mischief was supposed to torment other people, not himself.

"Gwirion, you really don't look well," Enid was saying, trying to bring him back from whatever interior world he had vanished into. "Is it your stomach? Shall I mix something up for you?"

"I'm going for a stroll," he said abruptly. He picked his way over the sleeping bodies and disappeared through the back entrance, past the well, into the night. Enid, watching him go, noticed he was barefoot. *Something is going on with that fellow,* she thought, tickled and concerned at the same time.

T HE queen finally bid good night to their visitors, who had paid her priest to perform a special late-night Ash Wednesday mass for them. Noble had earlier excused himself to finish reviewing the accounts. He told his wife he didn't know when he would be finished, and that if she preferred to go up to her own room tonight, she should do so. The temperature had dropped during supper, and she decided to accept his offer, since there was no way to cross over to his chamber without going out into the frigid night. Even the hall was chilly; the servants who slept in here had decided as a unit to attend the late mass with Humffri, simply for the collective body warmth of standing close together in the relatively airtight chapel. The great hall, for the first time in Isabel's memory, was absolutely empty.

She had taken two steps up the stairs when she saw a figure slide from the kitchen and into the hall.

It was Enid.

Astonished, her heart suddenly beating very fast, Isabel came back down the stairs and took a step toward the young woman, blocking her path.

"Excuse me, Enid," she said with remarkable steadiness, and the girl jumped. When she saw who had approached her she squirmed noticeably even as she dropped into a deep curtsy.

"Your Majesty," she said, as innocently as she could, and explained almost apologetically, "I'm here with Lord Humffri."

Isabel fought hard to not sound flustered. "And I presume you're on your way to see the king."

Enid blinked awkwardly and seemed to be looking for an answer just behind the queen's head. "Beg pardon, Your Majesty? I don't know what—"

"Don't dissemble. Are you going to see my husband?"

Enid dropped her eyes, ashamed when she realized the queen wasn't going to stop her. "Yes, ma'am," she murmured, barely audible. "But I won't if you ask it, he doesn't know to expect me."

"Excuse me?"

"It was—" She hesitated. "Please don't be sore at him, Your Majesty, but it was something that Gwirion set up for him as a surprise."

Isabel blinked. "*Gwirion* set this up?" she asked in a fierce whisper.

"Yes, ma'am, but please don't be—"

"He knows the king will be down here tonight? With you?"

"Don't hold him respons—"

"Answer my question!" Isabel demanded.

"Yes, ma'am, he knows, he arranged it," Enid mumbled, looking down, resigned to once again bring royal disfavor on her friend. When the queen said nothing, she looked up again, and was confused by a feverish look on Her Majesty's face.

"This was Gwirion's idea?" she asked again. "He wanted to send you in to keep the king busy? You didn't suggest it?"

"No, I was surprised that he did. I won't go in there if it will cause problems between yourself and—"

"No, go in. Stay. Stay all night. Keep him there. *Please.*" She spoke in a half whisper glancing nervously around the hall, which made her seem deranged. She looked briefly up the stairway that led to her solar and the sewing bevy, then rushed toward the main door—where, in the yard, she could climb the steps to the king's empty room. The light from her candle betrayed how much she was shaking. Enid knew these symptoms. Suddenly she knew the cause as well.

"Oh, *Christ!*" she cried aloud before she could check herself. The queen stopped and glanced at her sharply over her shoulder.

"What?"

Enid stared at her, troubled and amazed. She wanted to say something but there was nothing she could say without being whipped for presumptuousness, even if she was right. Finally she ventured a whispered plea: "Be careful, milady."

The queen froze. After a long moment of silence she nodded once in awkward acknowledgment, looking troubled, and continued toward the door.

NOBLE'S eyes were starting to cross from the amount of paperwork before him. Except for signing an official rebuke to Mortimer—who was already tardy in observing his obligations to the treaty—it all felt like busywork, but almost anything requiring ink felt like busywork to him. He wondered how long he had been waiting. Gwirion had told him to come in here and keep himself busy. He complied because he missed Gwirion's cavorting and anticipated one of his absurd old tricks, but if something didn't happen soon, he was going to give up on it for the night.

Finally there was a gentle rap on the door. He got up and walked to it, bracing himself for some harmless attack.

He was unprepared for the familiar pretty face attached to the familiar pretty body waiting for him. Weeks of stress lifted from his shoulders and for a moment he felt like an adolescent boy with a crush. "Good Lord," he said, laughing quietly.

Enid smiled playfully and stepped into the room, pushing the door closed behind her. Seeing him up close gave her a greater thrill than she'd expected, more than sex but less than love. His warm grin banished any fears she'd had that she would not be welcome.

"How did you—"

"I'm with Lord Humffri's household. They almost didn't bring me, they were afraid it might cause trouble."

"Trouble? Darling little Enid? And I have you all to myself for how long?"

Thinking of what else was probably happening tonight, Enid smiled a sultry smile and said, "All night. I overheard the queen before I came in, she's not expecting you."

"Gwirion won't be barging in on us, will he?"

She reached for the clasp of his leather belt. "I think Gwirion is already in bed," she answered softly.

S HE was sweating in the icy air. Her heart was pounding in her chest and she dropped the candle, heard it hiss out on the cold, damp stones. She kept walking, fidgeting relentlessly with her rosary, relying on the torchlight around the bailey under the magnificently star-strewn sky. It probably meant nothing. Gwirion was trying so hard to return things to how they had been, and pandering for the king had been one of his duties, so he was reclaiming it. That was all. But just in case, just in case . . . she made herself smile calmly at Gethin's deputy, a rheumy-looking older man posted outside Noble's door. "His Majesty will not be coming in until extremely late tonight," she said, "but I would like a moment to waken and prepare myself for his arrival. When you see his light heading for the stairs, please rap on the door."

"Yes, milady," he gurgled pleasantly. "If I'm off duty before he arrives, I'll tell my relief, shall I?" She nodded and smiled her thanks, then went inside.

Too nervous to look around the room, she leaned her forehead against the door as the man outside pulled it closed and latched it. She stayed there for a moment, willing her heart to slow down. Gwirion didn't just know about the tryst downstairs, he had arranged it. Wasn't it possible that he had done it to see her? But he was so irritable, she was afraid to assume there was any remaining affection. And he had said, adamantly, that it was not going to continue. So then there was nothing ulterior in tonight's downstairs meeting. He was playing pander, nothing more. In fact, by using Enid, he was deliberately trying to upset her, to assure alienation. It was manipulative but it was smart. She felt stupid for having rushed here, and decided to go back to her own bed, reaching for the door latch.

From out of nowhere in the darkness, a hand touched her shoulder softly. She spun around and found herself eye to eye with Gwirion.

"Do you want me to leave?" he whispered anxiously. "I'll leave if you want."

In answer, she grabbed his arm and led him to the bed. For a long time they just sat on the feather mattress, looking at each other with troubled expressions in the light of a dying fire.

"Are you frightened?" she said at last.

"I'm *terrified*."

"But we'll never get caught. Nobody else would ever believe it."

"I hope you're right," he said. "Think of what it would do to my reputation. Everyone will stop offering me their sheep."

She shoved him playfully. And again they sat in silence, basking in each other's presence.

"Would you like to undress me?" she asked suddenly, with the incongruously untroubled pleasure of their first kiss. He had a physical reaction to this, which delighted her.

"I don't understand you. All you've ever known is Noble. He's beautiful and experienced, what could I ever—"

"Undress me." She stuck out her lower lip in a mock scowl. "I command it."

"I don't obey commands," he replied, but he reached for her belt anyway.

She had to reassure him that there was no need to hurry, they had hours, although he fretted when she insisted that they also had years. "We don't know if there'll be anything beyond tonight," he insisted nervously. "This is not an affair. I'm not your lover." She forced back a laugh, for he said this as he was pulling her shift off her with shaking hands. She wanted to stop him for a moment, take the time to engage on that other level, where they used words as well as fingertips to captivate each other, but she knew he was frightened of it. And it was no painful compromise to let the night be about physical satisfaction. She reclined into the pillows, shivering with pleasure as his warm mouth grazed all over her. "Your skin," he informed her earnestly, "has two dozen different flavors." She laughed softly and wrapped her legs around him. Her curious fingers strayed on their own toward the strange wadded scar on his back. This time she said nothing about it, only touched the smooth, unfeeling skin gently for a moment and then turned her attention to more sensitive parts of his anatomy. They were still experimenting when the guard rapped on the door just before dawn.

Gwirion, to her alarm, climbed out the window into the freezing air completely naked, tossing his clothing down before him. There were pocks in the whitewashed outer walls of the tower, he assured her, that he was as comfortable using as a stairway, and there was barely any moon for him to be seen by. He reminded her as he disappeared to put the blankets back on the bed, a task she rushed at and finished just as Noble was opening the door.

Gwirion had pleased her many times during the night, but at the moment he rushed off he had been in the middle of arousing her again, and it was with great difficulty that she managed to greet her husband without looking sodden with sex. Noble seemed happily exhausted, and she felt a flash of sympathy. Now he would make some excuse for staying up all night and she would have to accept it, although she wanted to say, "I know what you've been doing and I hope you enjoyed yourself; I certainly did." She thought of Huw ap

Maredudd and his wife Branwyn. Their arrangement, which had seemed abhorrent to her before, was suddenly enviable. But Branwyn had earned that right—she had provided her husband with three boys. If she could just give Noble a son, maybe . . .

"I thought you would be in your own chamber," he said.

"I didn't know you'd be so long."

"There was more waiting for me than I'd anticipated."

She smiled and wished that she could tell him she understood. "That's all right. Balancing accounts is exhausting. You get up close to some of those figures and they mysteriously suck you in." She gave him a smile that left him wondering whether she knew what he'd been doing all night.

15

STRATEGISTS

Late Winter, 1199

NID HAD BEEN given a rare privilege when the king left her: He'd invited her to sleep through the chill remainder of the night in the audience chamber, wrapped in the feather quilt from the chest, provided she was up and out before the household stirred. Gwirion did not see her in the kitchen when he returned to his warren, and guessed where she was. Knowing the castle would soon awaken, and not wanting to miss a chance to tease her, he sneaked into the darkened receiving chamber draped in a wool blanket, hovering over her dozing form with a candle. She lay in the same place and position Isabel had that fateful afternoon, more obviously sensuous, her hair dark and loose, her lips much fuller than the queen's, her complexion more hale—but it had no effect on him. He almost wished it would; he was still trying to depersonalize the attraction, convince himself it was just about a woman's body and not about *her.*

He tapped his finger on Enid's nose until she awoke with a start.

She blinked in the candlelight, laughed languidly, and relaxed back into the sinfully comfortable bedding.

"Good morning, little slut, I'm here to collect my commission."

She shook her head. "Anyone but you and I'd get angry."

He gave her a suggestive smile. "Did you enjoy yourself?"

She mirrored the smile back at him, her nose crinkling as it always did when she was especially amused. "Did you?"

His smile faded. "What are you talking about?" he asked, an edge in his voice to hide his nervousness.

"Gwirion, I know," she whispered.

"Know what?" He frowned at her with what he hoped passed for bored impatience and stood up, heading for the door. "Let's pester Marged for some breakfast."

"Don't play coy with me," Enid said, grinning. "She would have gone to her own room if she hadn't seen me coming here. If you had a good time, you should thank me for it."

Gwirion stumbled and fell into the king's chair. He stared at her with such abject fear that she made herself relinquish the warmth of the blankets to go and steady him. "He doesn't know," she said, taking the candle from him so he wouldn't drop it. She had on only her shift, so she set down the candle and picked up the quilt to wrap around herself, and they faced each other like two swaddled infants.

"I don't—" he began to protest innocence. "But how did you find out?" he asked, sheepish but alarmed.

"Ha! After your peculiar behavior, hers was easy to interpret." He looked up at her, horrified, and she patted his arm. "For *me*, I mean. He doesn't suspect. Trust me, I just spent the night with him, he doesn't suspect." He made a face and shook his head, refusing to be reassured.

"I can't believe this is happening," he whispered bleakly, frightened.

"I'm stunned myself," she admitted. "And I'm worried about you."

"Why?" he said defensively, looking away. A witness cemented the reality. It no longer existed in their shared desire—a disinterested third party had called him to account. It was a fact now, a part of objective reality. If Enid could see it, then others could too.

"Because what's next?"

"We have to stop it," he said nervously.

She shook her head with a sympathetic smile. "I don't know that you have a choice."

"I can't do that to Noble," he insisted. The answer was instinctual, and reassured him. Less instinctual was the assertion: "I'll just find someone else."

She sighed, ignoring this final comment, which she knew was meaningless. "It's like one of those long, tortured love ballads Brychan the bard likes so much."

"Those ballads always made me sick," Gwirion said angrily.

LATER that morning, despite the snow flurries speckling the air, the pilgrims continued on their way toward St. David's, embroidered daffodils wafting on skirts and veils in defiance of the weather.

Gwirion and the queen managed to avoid each other through the morning, terrified of giving anything away in their behavior, but each fell prey to that most common weakness of new lovers: stealing furtive glances, even if the other was oblivious, just for the thrilling reassurance of the other's continued and astonishing existence. Gwirion caught himself at it finally, ogling the slight curve of her hips from across the hall and remembering what it felt like to push himself against them. He realized what a danger it was and scowled at her the next time he felt her eyes on him, but she didn't understand him. More than a risk of discovery, it seemed to him an invitation to self-torture, for however resigned they were to a mutual lust, there would be no easy way to indulge it again. That frustration at least offered him one reassurance: Since they most likely could not act again, at least they could not be caught.

Isabel herself felt almost impervious to danger now. Between the public's romantic affection for her and the secret thrill of adultery accomplished, she was no longer just the brood mare who had failed to deliver. She glowed all day, even when spasms of panic over- whelmed her each time she thought her husband was looking at her strangely. Caught between fearful guilt and the pleasant fluster of proximity, both she and Gwirion tried hard to dwell on neither their desire to grope each other nor their inability to do so.

The king held council after dinner, fretting over first Llewelyn and then Mortimer. He forced himself to listen to his men's cautious suggestion that he stabilize the situation with Llewelyn by joining their courts in a confederacy, ideally by marriage. These officers, the highest in the kingdom, humbly offered their offspring or even themselves to such a union, but the king considered it a useless proj- ect. "My marrying a Mortimer profited us nothing," he pointed out. "Who among you can offer a more profitable hand than mine?"

The shine of his victory was beginning to subside and he de- bated with his huddled officers how best to chastise Roger for his sluggishness. He invited his wife to sit in for this part of the council, and marveled silently that the entire table—most of whom had been at the front with him and had not actually seen her in her castellan duties—naturally accepted her as one of them. This was unheard of; not even his mother Efa, when widowed by Cadwallon and with a young son to prepare for kingship, had been so accepted in the court. He studied how offhand she seemed about this extraordinary status, how levelheaded about pressuring her uncle.

He also brought Gwirion to council, to play softly in the back- ground, and he kept the harp within hearing wherever he was for the rest of the day, shooting his friend occasional warm smiles for his ef- forts. Gwirion was grateful for a chance to serve his monarch and his friend; in his tormented imagination, each new tune exonerated the sin of each new indecent thought he had about the queen. He had to play a lot of tunes.

That evening after supper the royal couple sat near the fire and Gwirion again unwrapped his harp to play. Because of the chill weather, most of the castle was gathered here until bedtime. It was a welcome change from the unbroken hours of political ruminations, and there was a cozy familiarity to it—it was the first time since the king's return that there had been an informal evening party. Noble asked for many old favorites until people started nodding off. Gwirion was taking a final request from Cadwgan's daughter Gwladys when the queen abruptly brought both hands to her face to cover an enormous yawn.

"Don't become sleepy on me now," her husband said. With a private, roguish smile, he added something in a lowered voice that made her blush. The harp sounded a sour note, and the king turned to Gwirion with a droll expression. "I've never heard you miss a note before, Gwirion," he scolded. "Was it something I said? Do you still disapprove of my honoring my marriage vows?"

"It's just that you'll break my poor mare's heart, sire," Gwirion replied, picking up the melody again. "You said she was the only girl for you and she's been waiting all evening for you in your room."

"Excellent, a threesome!" He winked at his wife—who almost jumped—and then turned back to Gwirion. "Come up and serenade us."

"Only if I can mount the pretty one," Gwirion leered, his eyes on the strings.

"Gwirion!" the queen cried.

"What? She's my pony, I can do what I please with her," he shot back, and Noble laughed. With pursed lips, Isabel settled nervously back into her chair.

"Of course, if you'd rather a more conventional treatment to put you to sleep," the king suggested, "just call Gwirion up to play for you."

He nearly missed another string. "Damn harp's out of alignment again," he muttered loudly, inventing a complaint. He picked up his tuning key from the string on his belt and poured his attention into the imaginary problem.

She looked at her husband as if she couldn't quite understand his meaning. "In the middle of the night?" she said. "In my room? A man?"

"It's just Gwirion," he said breezily. "The worst he can do is pun you to death."

"But . . . he needs to sleep, surely, I can't wake—"

"Gwirion exists without sleep," Noble assured her. "Don't you?"

The harpist looked up innocently from the harp. "Pardon? I was distracted."

"I was telling my wife you wouldn't mind going to her room at night to play for her if she's restless. Provided of course that I don't need you."

Gwirion's eyes involuntarily flashed to the queen and away again, and he paled. He could not square this with what he was certain was in Noble's heart and mind. "Good God, sire, I can't do that," he said.

"Why not?"

Isabel tried to breathe calmly and look unconcerned, but her fingers were clenched around the arms of her chair. "Well, sire . . ." Gwirion glanced around the hall and lowered his voice confidingly. "It's her women. They're all desperate for me—I'm constantly beating them away and I just don't think I'm strong enough to fend off all three at once."

Noble gave him a sly look. "I'd think you'd want that, the way you carry on."

"I'm waiting for a woman with lots of livestock to keep me satisfied when she's not in the mood," Gwirion explained pleasantly. "What tune would you like next?"

The queen made a disgusted sound to cover her nervousness and rose to leave. Gwirion felt his stomach tighten. "I'm sorry, Your Majesty," he called to her quickly. "I didn't mean to insult your women. I'd be delighted if they ravished me. And I'm pleased to play for you any evening you require it." He'd managed to appear offhand.

She did not smile. "Thank you, Gwirion. I'll keep that in mind." She sounded totally disinterested.

"Of course, you won't be needing it so often," he said. "You're a Mortimer after all. You can sleep through anything."

She made a face at him that made her husband chuckle. "I'll be up as soon as you've warmed the sheets," he crooned, "my little harpy." Isabel gave him a flustered smile and walked away.

Noble and Gwirion both watched her lithe body in its burgundy silk crossing away from them. Her husband took a breath and rose suddenly. "You'll excuse me," he said to Gwirion and the few others who were still awake, "I believe we'll warm the bed together." He walked with light, quick steps after her until he was beside her. Gwirion watched as the king put his arm around her slender waist and hugged her slightly to him, gesturing to a hall servant for his mantle.

R ETURNING to her own bed hours later, she sent Llwyd her doorkeeper downstairs "to fetch the harpist." Emerging from the sticky web of sleep, Gwirion was thrown by the man's inviting him to the queen's room alone and almost refused the request, but finally allowed himself to be escorted to her chamber, harp in hand, eager and reluctant at once. He desperately wished this rendezvous wasn't born of Noble's unthinking trust in both of them.

Perhaps it wasn't unthinking trust. Perhaps it was a trap.

But once they were closed in together, the great failing of this opportunity, the evidence that it was neither really a gift nor a trap, made itself plain: Her women could hear clearly through the tapestried curtain that offered the only privacy between her sleeping area and theirs. This was no recipe for trysting; they may as well have been in public, and he couldn't stop playing or he would lose his excuse for being here. So he played.

She reached up through the cold dark air to stroke his face, and the shock of it jolted him so severely that his fingers missed the strings and he smacked his head against the harp's hollowed sound box. "*Please* don't do that," he whispered. "That's worse than not being here at all." She grinned and immediately reached up again, but he pulled his head away. "I'm serious," he hissed. "I can hardly keep the harp on my lap." He started to play again, almost desperately.

She kept beaming at him in the darkness, breathless with the dangerous pleasure of their treasonous proximity. "Then we'll meet elsewhere," she decided.

"That would be madness."

She ignored the observation. "The next time there's outside entertainment and you have the evening free, we'll spirit ourselves away from the hall and meet in the guest chamber upstairs from Gwilym's room. If it's empty, there'll be no guard on that floor. It will need to be quick but it's better than nothing."

He agreed with reluctance, still wanting not to want to be with her.

$\mathcal{A}$ FTER just two days and nights of fickle snowfall, two days of Gwirion devoting himself with doglike fidelity to the king's ebbing humor and two nights of Isabel being an obedient, ardent wife, they had an opportunity. The bard from Abbey Cwm-hir came to play for the king. He was fed before supper, accepting only bread and water, and performed throughout the meal and afterward. In honor of Lent he played nothing that was even remotely enjoyable, and in the ensuing torpor that overtook the hall it was easy for both Gwirion and Isabel to slip away.

But when they met in the empty tower, they were once again slapped by disappointment. The room was clammy and dark, and they dared not light a fire or even a candle, lest the sergeant, on the lookout for unexplained fires, notice something through the sealed parchment over the windows and decide to explore. The moon was not yet a quarter full and anyway was blotted out by clouds. Unfa-

miliar with the room and unable to see anything, they could not nav-
igate to retrieve a blanket or cushion from a storage chest. They were
both distressed about time, fearful of being missed in hall and then
of being seen returning, and the bed, when they finally found it, was
missing its blanket—there was only a dense pile of dried heather,
flattened slightly from Humffri's visit.

Her teeth chattering in the cold, Isabel still let out a sigh of im-
perial annoyance. Gwirion took it personally, thinking of the feather
mattress and warm woven blankets and billowing canopied curtains
Noble offered her each night.

"This wasn't my idea," he said unhappily, rubbing his arms for
warmth in the dark. "I had no way of—"

"I know that," she cut him off impatiently.

He was almost glad this was going afoul. As desperate as he was
to feel her against him again, he was equally desperate to be free of
that desire, and two frustrated assignations in a row was an excellent
way of souring it. Noble had offered him a mistress and there was a
new hall servant whom he found his gaze drifting to at meals; maybe
he would ask for her. To be respectful to Her Majesty, he would wait
until she herself declared their liaison over, which would certainly be
soon if these frustrations kept arising. Then he would take a lover,
she would return her full attention to her marriage and all would be
well; perhaps they could be proper friends again. He missed those
hours of conversation, locked up together in the audience room.

Defeated and unsatisfied, they left separately and took different
paths back to the hall. Gwirion braved more of the cold and slush
by descending and walking the long way around the inner curtain
wall; the queen took the icy wall walk over the barbican across to her
own room, and descended back into the hall from there. Neither of
them had been missed, and they avoided addressing each other directly for the rest of the evening, but Gwirion was immensely attentive to the king.

She tried to convince herself that his behavior was prompted by
either fear or guilt, but she could not deny the genuine affection that
he exuded, almost despite himself, toward Noble. It galled her on

two fronts. First because, despite his sexual attentiveness, Noble had never extended to her whatever it was that made Gwirion cleave to him so; second—and worse—because Gwirion gave so freely to the king that part of him, the hidden human part, which had first drawn her to him when they were locked up alone together, and she ached for it.

G WIRION, feared and hoped that the fiasco in the tower was the end of it, especially when Noble sent the queen ahead to his bed to warm it for him. So he was confused when the same sleepily whispering doorkeeper came for him in the midnight hours, requesting his presence, with his harp, in the queen's chamber.

He closed her door behind him with a soft sigh, wondering why she was subjecting both of them to this torture a second time. He would have to invent a gentle refusal if she tried it again.

The room was unexpectedly warm, the fire recently stoked and brighter than a torch. "Good evening," she greeted him with polite formality. "My ladies have asked that you play as quietly as possible, so you will continue to sit beside my bed." She gestured for him. "And you will play for as long as I require it."

He acknowledged this with a feeble smile and took his position near her head. "Why am I here?" he whispered, grateful the sewing bevy was hidden by the tapestry.

"To play the harp. For now," she whispered back. "Until they've fallen asleep."

He was astonished. "You're not thinking—"

She put her finger to his lips. "A lullaby, please."

His heart pounding, Gwirion performed every soft song he knew, every gentle song, even every drinking song slowed to a lull. He tried playing the melody with only his left hand, while droning gently on the lower strings with the right, and the effect was something stuporous. His fingers wanted to rush through all the tunes, as if the faster they were completed the faster those women would succumb to slumber. He almost couldn't keep the rhythm of anything he played, all of it moved so much more slowly than his own heartbeat in fearful anticipation. Every few minutes he looked anxiously toward the door, expecting interruption. "I can always hear him approaching," she whispered reassuringly, but he wasn't reassured.

After almost an hour, when even he was having trouble staying focused and the fire was dying down to embers, she nodded to him to stop, and drew the curtains closed all around the bed. Except for one small opening, through which she beckoned him to enter.

He mouthed the words "Are you mad?" to her, but she only smiled.

"They sleep through it when Noble comes, they'll sleep through it now."

"How can you possibly—"

"Even if they hear something, they'll think it's him come during the night. They can't see anything."

He glanced at the tapestry that hid the women, his heartbeat quickening. To help him make a well-reasoned choice, she slid her hand along his lap toward his groin. He spun around to look at her, a wild, pleading look in his eyes.

"Why do I have to start everything?" she asked in a coy whisper. "Couldn't you just once pretend I'm irresistible?"

He blushed, and after a hesitation, he laid the harp on the floor and crawled in through the curtains. "Do you prefer hanging or dismemberment?" he asked as he straddled her.

As she undressed him, they were nearly as aware of the sleeping attendants as they were of each other, but for her it only fueled the excitement. She almost wished one of the women would call out in her sleep, just to add an adrenaline rush to her own already soaring state. Gwirion would have given anything for the surety of privacy, but her enthusiasm was contagious and he managed to put the images of hanging and dismemberment out of his mind for a while.

She radiated heat from the blankets and the pleasure of sliding against an entire female body of such warmth was nearly as intoxicating as the consummation.

"We can't do this very often," he whispered afterward.

"Of course we can!" she whispered back, absently fingering the scar on his back.

He shook his head. "My nerves would be ruined by the end of a week and I'd have a stomach ulcer the size of Wigmore."

She grinned. "It's always funny to hear a Norman word said with a Welsh accent. Do it again." She whispered even more quietly, "Say my name."

He stared at her, shook his head nervously. "That's dangerous. I might get used to saying it, I'd get sloppy—"

"We've already been sloppy," she said, sobering. He guessed that she meant Enid, and nodded. He ran the side of his thumb across her lips. Already he couldn't remember how he had ever looked at that mouth without wanting to taste it. Seeing that he was getting distracted, she frowned at him in the darkness and pushed his hand away. "What do you suggest, then?" she asked.

"I suggest losing interest in each other. But I don't imagine that will happen for a while." He glanced at her for confirmation and she pressed her nose against his cheek. "All right, then. Random encounters. When it's safe. No more than once a week." By his standards, that was decadently frequent.

"No!" she begged. "More than that!"

"Twice, then," he relented as she slid her leg over his thigh. She wiggled up against him, grinning. "Oh, Christ, as often as you want. But only when it's *safe*. Not near the full moon, people don't sleep as deeply, there'll be more open eyes around. Not if Noble's in a mood—"

"If Roger doesn't start honoring the treaty, Noble will be in a permanent mood," she sighed.

"If you don't like it, then help him out of it," Gwirion said, almost chiding her.

"That's your responsibility, fool," she retorted. "Keep him pleased so that it will be safe for you to come to my bed."

He sat up and pulled away from her. "That will never be the reason I please him," he said sternly.

NOT every night throughout the next three weeks, but often, the restless queen would excuse herself from the king's bed to her own, and send for the harp. Once her women were asleep, Gwirion would slink through the curtains and warm himself against her, amazed each time that she wanted to give herself to him after being with her husband. It was almost enough to make him religious. The need for silence forced them to find other ways to express desire and satisfaction. They learned to read each other's subtle shifts of weight and movement, the scents of the other's body changing with excitement. It was reckless of her but she actually enjoyed knowing they were never safe. It added romance and intensity to their lovemaking. Because they were unable to converse freely, they focused all their energy on physical intimacies, and he would leave almost immediately afterward, as if neither of them knew what to do with each other when they weren't actually making love.

Strangely, once they had established that they could have each other almost as often as they wanted to, the dynamics of their daily routines were undisturbed by their affair, and they were able to treat each other with friendly indifference in all but the most awkward circumstances. Perhaps this was because he never stayed with her beyond the lovemaking, and so there were two parallel worlds between them whose rules of conduct never overlapped. In one they were unspeaking carnal partners; in the other they were the king's two devoted dependents, still adored, as he was, by the populace. But there was a jealous tension between the two worlds, and both lovers noticed, with more attention than either would ever have confessed to,

whom the other one spoke with and for how long. There was no opportunity to complain in daylight hours, and the night was too precious to waste in words. So she bit her lip when he ogled the new
buxom black-haired hall maid or flirted, however innocently, with
Marged's workers, and he looked away whenever the king's hand casually touched her sleeve, her cheek, her knee, and most of all when
Noble sent her to his bed each night, smiling with royal anticipation
at the thought of warming his own limbs against hers in his comfortable feather bed. That moment was always the hardest for
Gwirion. Despite the quiet drone of guilt that filled his head, sometimes he had the sense that he was being robbed.

There were of course the deprivations that late winter wrought,
the tensions at the court from Mortimer delaying reparations, from
rumors that Llewelyn's ambition was on the rise again. Gwirion dutifully applied himself to offering distraction, although his genius for
clever mischief had gone into hibernation. A routine of sexual intimacy caused unforeseen distractions and he now found himself more
aware of women's bodies at the most inopportune of times. Not
only breasts and hips and lips and eyes, but the collarbones, elbows,
jawlines, knuckles of all his female acquaintances and friends seemed
suddenly rife with potential sensuality and he blushed more often
than he had since puberty.

For relief he would escape outside, to snow forts and vicious
snowball fights organized by Efan to train (or so went his excuse) the
next generation of potential teulu. It was a matter of debate whether
Efan or Gwirion offered more rigorous training in winter sports.
Gwirion's exercises were the more unorthodox, of course: snow
sculptures of half-size troops, dubbed as either Mortimer's or
Llewelyn's, would be overwhelmed by means of bodily fluids, leaving
melting, golden lumps of snow in the corner of the courtyard for
Elen, the marshal's wife, to grouse about to Noble.

Noble had far more pressing issues to attend to, and took to
keeping Gwirion with him almost every waking moment—sometimes to listen to him play the harp, sometimes to listen to him ramble comically, sometimes to try to interest him in statecraft or war

sports on the grounds that he was, after all, the new hero of Maelienydd and could surely find a better way to manifest it than pissing on snowy effigies of his enemies.

He kept his wife near him frequently as well, for different reasons. He continued to invite her into council, but her suggestions for strong-arming her uncle hadn't been successful, and as Roger's stonewalling increased, Isabel's value in the officers' eyes threatened to diminish. Begetting an heir was still a constant goal—and generally more pleasurable than it had once been—but until he had her with child, he could not rest easy that he had a useful marriage. Then cousin Anarawd wrote, asking after Her Majesty's health and wondering when he might have the pleasure of attending a christening. Noble frowned and burned the letter without showing it to anyone.

ONE day in early March, when the snow had receded to a negligible six inches, news arrived that Humffri's party, returning at last from their early pilgrimage to St. David's, had begged the honor of stopping at Cymaron for the midday meal before the final leg of their journey home. Noble had been cooped up in the council room all morning and was glad of an excuse to take the air: He stood waiting to receive his baron, quite informally, with his wife beside him on the hall steps, both of them in winter reds and golden circlets. Humffri's retinue was small, but he was escorted to the gate by a most peculiar and unnerving entourage, consisting of the entire village of Cymaron—carvers, weavers, wrights, carpenters, tanners, smiths, bakers, and dozens of others with their wives and children and aging parents, and finally, one skinny long-legged breathless boy in Noble's livery.

The runner, not the baron, was the focus of the mob's attention when two hundred soggy brogues, buskins, and boots stopped obediently at the gates. The crowd was well behaved and courteous of convention; they made no move to enter. Einion came out of the porthouse, gaping. The king, startled but affecting indifference, sent Gwilym to the gate to glean the cause of this spontaneous congress. The steward brought back with him not only Humffri, his lady, and their riding party, but also the gasping courier and an explanation. It was mere chance that baron and boy had arrived at the village at the same moment. A pretty village gossip, flirting with the gate watch, had seen the boy arrive from the northwest—*the northwest*—and within ten minutes the whole of the village knew there was news of the feared, distrusted, and despised Llewelyn. They wanted to know what it was.

Noble climbed the steps to the top of the barbican, looked down on the silent, anxious crowd, back toward the runner who was too exhausted to reveal much emotion, and finally informed Einion and Gwilym that if the villagers truly had nothing better to do with their dinner hour than hear trifling tales of a petty prince, they were welcome to enter the bailey.

INSIDE the hall, king and queen took their seats at the high table with their aristocratic visitors to their right and Gwirion, as ever, behind the king's left shoulder. The villagers, obedient but dogged, had poured quietly through the castle gate, and with the collective focus of a school of fish had gone straight to the hall steps. Both doors had been opened, and the human mass split itself spontaneously in two, each half crowding around a broad threshold, eyes on the high table, waiting to hear what new pillaging of trust the powerful, dreaded Llewelyn had accomplished. Noble and his officers paid them no attention. The rest of the diners squirmed under their scrutiny.

The first course of dinner was already laid out but Noble ignored it, which required everyone else to ignore it as well. The king turned his attention to the boy and the boy handed him the scroll.

He looked at the seal on it and raised his eyebrows. "Your lover, madam," he said to his wife in an arch tone, and showed it to her. The seal was Owain's.

She said nothing, content now to let him say that, even think it. Gwirion feigned indifference as Noble signaled the hall to begin eating, but he himself began to read the missive, and nobody so much as picked up a knife. He read in silence, his face growing somber. The court officers had watched him break the seal, anticipating a call to council. He felt the collected eyes upon him and looked up from reading. "Hubris," he spat with sudden venom. "Llewelyn is creeping ever outward in his quest to conquer—pardon, *unify*—Wales. He's appropriated yet another county in Gwynedd." He threw the scroll down onto the table with a sharp, angry gesture.

There was an uneasy exchange of looks around the upper end of the hall and the crowd huddling at the door murmured as if they were watching a performance. Isabel's guard went up at once. This was hardly damning news to her ears, and had nothing to do with Maelienydd. Noble was genuinely angry and dismayed about it, but she wondered if he was not, in fact, performing.

"It may have been under Norman control," Father Idnerth observed.

Noble shook his head. "Welsh."

"He does have birthright over certain areas," Goronwy said. "Perhaps he was reclaiming—"

"No."

There was another awkward silence.

"Perhaps he seized it from a rival," said the queen.

"Owain seems to think he *convinced* the baron to yield to him. I find that more alarming than if he'd taken it by force." He got to his feet so abruptly he almost knocked his chair over, and Gwirion, who recognized the mood, asked, "Harp?" at once. Noble jerked his head once in response, and distractedly signaled ease to the other diners, who had all in turn nearly knocked their benches over in a rush to stand. His Majesty walked around the high table and into the central area of the hall, where he began a round of long-legged pacing, deep in thought, his jaw hanging slightly slack, brow furrowed, blue eyes pensively downcast. The whole room and the entire population of Cymaron village hung in suspension, waiting on him, privileged to see the king in a moment of such vulnerable introspection. As Gwirion moved to the hearth he unintentionally swapped glances with the queen and saw plainly on her face the wariness already in his mind. It was unlikely that Maelgwyn ap Cadwallon had ever in his life suffered a bout of vulnerable introspection, and he most certainly would never suffer it in public. Unless, that is, something was very wrong. Gwirion, trying not to feel spooked, settled with his harp and began to play, not an actual melody but a series of simple descending arpeggios.

After a moment, without pausing in his movement, Noble made a sharp gesture toward his audience chamber. "Senior council," he said tersely, and turning toward Humffri, announced, "I'm appropriating your bard for the while." He nodded in response to Gwirion's questioning expression, and harpist followed steward, penteulu, chaplain, and judge into the audience room. "No, madam, don't even ask," Noble said, anticipating his wife. "How could we be so rude as to leave our guests unattended? Pardon me, Humffri, this will be short. Continue your meal. My wife will provide company until I return."

Brychan, Humffri's recently appointed bard, could not have looked less bardlike. He was short, compact, thick-necked, and red-haired, his face constructed so that he looked permanently alarmed at the prospect of public speaking, and he was barely seasoned enough to be a bard of his own standing. But bard he was, and obedient. He followed Noble's flourishing gesture with his eyes, then belatedly rushed into the receiving room after the castle officers.

Noble looked at the bizarre collection of faces stuffing the doorways, pink and splotchy from the cold. "We are going to close the doors now. Your presence is not required at this moment," he informed them, but none of them moved. He reviewed them a moment longer and then groaned theatrically. "You may as well come in, then," he declared, ironical, long-suffering. "We've lost enough of you to war, let's not have winter claim the rest. But I'm not feeding you today." He disappeared into his receiving room as the village—voiceless, spooked, polite—flowed into the hall.

I N the receiving room, they stood. The little round chamber was always lit and heated, but there was not enough seating for the seven of them. Noble nodded respectfully to Brychan. "We lost Hywel in the Mortimer campaign, as you know. We've managed to stumble along, but what I need to know now is distinctly a bard's area of expertise." Noble looked grim. "You are, I believe, versed in all the genealogies of the royal families of Wales?"

"Yes, sire," Brychan answered, wide-eyed.

"Can you tell me if there are any marriageable women in Llewelyn's close family?" To his startled men he said, heavily, "Perhaps all of you are right, and that's the best way to control him."

"If I may, sire," Brychan stammered, bowing. "I require a meditation alone someplace to review within my mind's eye the tributaries of that family river." Gwirion almost shouted with laughter at his language but Noble, anticipating that, preempted him with a stern look.

"You may be hard put to find privacy with that silent mob outside," the king said. "The chapel is empty, but it's frigid in there now."

When Brychan was gone, swallowed at once in the eerily quiet throng of onlookers in hall, the council members exchanged solemn glances. Young Efan and old Gwilym, the two highest-ranking members of the court, shifted self-consciously. "We are all your servants, sire," Gwilym said. "But which of us do you consider weighty enough to give to such a union?"

"None of you," the king said, and turned briskly to Idnerth. "The second thing I need to know is in your jurisdiction, Father. How may a king sue for divorce under canon law?"

SHE sat down hard on the settle, holding out her hand for balance.

"Am I that disposable?" she breathed. "I thought we'd finally . . ." She had to take another breath. Gwirion continued to play the same soft chords, sitting backlit by the hearth. Noble had dismissed the council. "I thought you and I had finally come to a genuine—"

"We had," he said, gently, and sat in his chair across from her, reaching for her hand. "That's the sad irony here—you truly have become a consort worthy of Maelienydd. But your family is treacherous. Your uncle is treacherous. Our union buys me nothing that way, and the victory I just won over Roger was completely hollow. He's not going to honor the treaty, we both know that. Besides, Mortimer is not the nemesis to fear. Llewelyn is. Mortimer is just another foreign headache; Llewelyn is a native danger." That observation genuinely pained him. She wavered in her suspicion that this was just a trick. "And Llewelyn is encroaching," he went on heavily. "Roger killed off so many of my menfolk, there's nobody else to seek a marriage with but cousin Anarawd and I would never trust him to be closer knit to Llewelyn than I am." He released her hand and waited for her to speak. She still said nothing. "As I said, this will happen only if there's a match to be made that would be more useful than ours. If there is, and we divorce, I'll have no hold on you. But if your heart is truly in Maelienydd—and I believe it is now—I have a proposition that will serve us both extremely well. This is personal, would you have Gwirion leave?"

"I don't care either way," Isabel said with perfect offhandedness, her pale brown eyes artless. She was telling the truth, both grateful and resentful that Gwirion was responding so indifferently.

Noble said nothing to their musician, whose fingers moved automatically over the horsehair strings while his attention was bent entirely on keeping his own breath steady. He had no idea how plausible or possible this scheme of Noble's was; his old fears were reignited and he was half convinced Noble had rigged the entire scenario just to test them both. Why else would he subject her to hearing such a cruel plan before it was even a reality?

But now Noble was giving her a look that Gwirion recognized for its sincerity. The blue eyes beamed beneficently; the king considered whatever he was about to propose a boon bestowed, proof that he was the most indulgent of sovereigns. "I want you," he informed her, "to marry Owain."

"*What?*"

"It's a happy solution for both of us. Even if I marry into Llewelyn's line, that corner of the kingdom is not secure. Owain is alarmingly naive, Huw has far too much sway over him and Huw has ambitious kin in Powys. I require an intelligent, loyal soul minding that border and you've proven you are that; you want a partner who reveres you for more than your political worth, and our little Owain has more than proven himself in that regard."

Gwirion sneezed. "Excuse me," he said gruffly, when both of them snapped their heads to stare at him.

"Our sage Gwirion sneezes at this idea," Noble said with lofty mockery. "Perhaps he will be so good as to tell us why?"

He wasn't sure yet, Gwirion decided—he only suspected. They could disarm his suspicion if they handled it adroitly; he had probably even invented this outrageous scenario as a test to let them prove their innocence. "I think after the king's bed, she'll find herself bored to tears to lie with him," he answered in a leering tone. "You've ruined her for anyone else."

Noble laughed lightly and turned back to his wife, who dutifully made a little sound of annoyed disgust. "We may always rely on Gwirion to remind us of what matters most in life," he said. "What do you say to the proposition, madam?"

She lowered her eyes. "I'd consider it if it would help you, sire, but I think I would lose my mind with boredom to spend the rest of my years in that dull corner of the world."

Noble looked as if he was about to make a sarcastic remark in response, then controlled the urge and said instead, "Your alternative would be a nunnery. Or, I suppose, you would be free to return to your beloved Wigmore."

"I have no longing to return to Wigmore."

"Well, you can't stay *here*, that would be rather awkward for my bride," he said wryly, then sobered. "You will not contest a divorce? I'll make it clear to everyone it has nothing to do with my regard for you. I won't let you be insulted by the process."

"The process itself is an insult," she said tightly.

"But you won't contest it?" he repeated, biting back his impatience. She said nothing, just stared into the fire. He grimaced. "Madam, here we have an excellent example of abusing power, which you've accused me of doing more than once. You have the power to contest this. Exercising that power suits your whim, it does not suit your people."

"Grand words if your plan were necessary for the people," she said, still staring at the fire. "I don't think it is."

He sat back and waved his hand impatiently. "Go ahead, then, make your case."

"If there is a useful match to be made between Llewelyn's court and yours, make it with someone else. Your court is full of bachelors and widowers."

"I've already considered that. Llewelyn won't waste a marriage opportunity on a mere officer. It would have to be my near kin to be of value. Thanks to your uncle, the only near kin I have left is Anarawd and I refuse to give Anarawd that kind of power, I may as well abdicate."

She suddenly knew how to pass this test. She was certain it was not about the prince of Gwynedd. "Llewelyn knows from experience who's of real value to you. Should he have a bride to offer, marry her to Gwirion."

The two men started at the same moment, and Gwirion, picking up her lead, cried, "Oh, please do, sire! I've heard about those girls of Gwynedd, they entertain themselves with stallions when their men are away fighting. And sometimes, they say," he added, lowering his voice and speaking with a thrilled and knowing tone, "the stallions don't survive the night."

Noble laughed suddenly and hard at this, his face crinkling with genuine levity for the first time all day. The queen and Gwirion did not exchange looks this time but both of them relaxed: The test was over.

But then Noble, quieting, shook his head and the heaviness settled back upon him. "We don't even know if Gwirion is freeborn or not. He's politically unmarriageable. Otherwise, I applaud your suggestion. But I'm afraid I have only myself to sacrifice in this. And by extension, you." He stood up. "We've left our visitors too long and the stew is getting cold. Come to board with me, Gwirion. Madam, you will not contest this?"

He really meant to do it. Flummoxed, she looked down into her lap, nodding weakly, and he seemed satisfied.

"Your people thank you. Would you like a moment alone?"

She nodded again.

Gwirion followed Noble out, trying not to stagger.

Nobody was seated anymore. The meal and the day's tasks were forgotten. The news had exploded as soon as the council had adjourned and people were swarming, buzzing about it—villagers, castle workers, officers, Humffri's retinue. Again Llewelyn posed a threat to their beloved queen. That their own king's decision was to blame this time meant nothing to them—he was, after all, being forced into this sacrifice by Llewelyn's hubris. Already a crowd of those in warmer layers and slush-proof brogues had formed around the chapel door, waiting for Brychan the bard to emerge into the grey afternoon to tell them if this shocking insult to their queen was in fact to pass. A few earnest adolescents even knelt on the chapel steps praying aloud for God to smite dead every female in Llewelyn's line.

Noble took a speechless Gwirion with him through the ripple of bowing peasant heads in the hall and out to the buzzing courtyard, ignoring the murmurings—but hearing them all the same. His subjects noticed him, of course, and besides bowing hurriedly and giving

him a wide path to walk through, they were as blunt as decorum
would allow. Nobody petitioned him directly and nobody spoke
rudely in his hearing, but however demure they were in their language, it was clear that the castle and the village wanted to hold on to
their lady. Now and then the king would raise one astonished brow at
something that was said. "Can you imagine this reception last
spring?" he whispered to Gwirion. "What wretched timing that
they've come to love her only when I must be rid of her." Gwirion
smiled politely, still trying to recover from the shock that Noble was
entirely serious about divorce.

They made a beeline for the chapel. By the time they got there,
the murmurings proved that not one of these xenophobic peasants
would willingly trade Isabel Mortimer for some native princess.
When they reached the chapel steps, the curious villagers moved to
give way to them. Noble nodded a dismissal to Gwirion, and after
the slightest hesitation, pushed open the chapel door to join the bard
inside.

Perplexed and disoriented, Gwirion stood alone on the stone
steps. He wanted to run back across the yard and into the great hall,
to throw his arms around the queen to comfort her. His muscles
tensed to hold himself in check. Suddenly a pair of arms had
grabbed him from behind around the waist, a woman's arms but very
strong.

"Gwirion," said Enid's voice softly from behind his left shoulder.

He turned fast, and embraced her hard in return without speaking. People excitedly crossed below them in the slush, gathering at
the chapel steps to wait for the bard, back to the hall to see if the
queen had emerged to face the news yet, gossiping and conjecturing
self-righteously.

When they disengaged, Enid took a moment to peruse his face.
Self-conscious, he began to speak, but she quickly held up her hand.

"Don't tell me anything," she commanded quietly. "Unless you
can tell me that there is nothing to tell."

He looked down, his forehead wrinkling with distress. He'd followed the king out here without bothering to get a wrap, and he shivered now, rubbing his knuckles up and down his arms for warmth.

"I can't say that," he whispered.

Enid reflexively reached up to touch the amulet around her neck. She gave him a look of maternal worry. "Gwirion, Christ, you're such a fool."

He grimaced. "Yes, that's what Noble likes about me."

I SABEL was terrified of stepping out into the hall, terrified of how she'd be received. If any of them still housed some secret hatred of "the Saxoness," this would be the time to gloat, although she feared indifference more. How naive to think Noble's decision was anything personal toward either of them. She wondered if Gwirion had also realized how entirely political the situation really was. She doubted it.

She straightened the gold circlet crowning her wimple, smoothed her skirt, adjusted the silver brooch on her breast and the rosary hanging from her belt, pinched her pale cheeks to bring some color to them, and pulled open the door.

She strode through the hall briskly toward the side exit, the crowd parting for her like the Red Sea. She knew so many of these faces from the passing patterns of daily life. The same wash of gazes that had once been cool to her now looked sympathetic, even troubled. She had earned their attachment, and she was about to be deprived of it. She wanted that to be the thought that most upset her. It would have been a month ago. It wasn't now.

When she reached the threshold, she looked out over the courtyard, aware that eyes out there were also turning to stare at her, that the bailey was falling silent at her appearance. Angharad appeared behind her with a red wool cloak and she nodded, allowing her attendant to tie it on her as she scanned the yard. Generys appeared on the

other side and gave her a cup of warmed metheglin, which she took
with a grateful nod.

She recognized Enid by her billowing dark hair, before she
even realized whom the girl was talking to. Then she saw Gwirion's
face in the hazy light and felt her heart thud. Oh, God, she wanted
him to come to her. She watched as he slipped his arm around
Enid's shoulders to give her a gruffly affectionate squeeze, perhaps
the resolution of some friendly spat between them. With no rancor
toward Enid she envied the girl, that she was allowed to receive such
easy, innocent affection from him publicly. More than any other
upset of the past half hour, that moment made her want to weep.
Even if Brychan brought a reprieve, even if he miraculously announced that there was no one in Gwynedd for Noble to propose
to, she would never be allowed that casual embrace with Gwirion in
the courtyard.

Around her, behind her, before her, the people waited, their attention torn between the hall entrance and the chapel. Their peerless
monarch was victorious against the Mortimers; his queen had
proven herself his worthy consort; together they had foiled even
Llewelyn's craftiness. They were the stuff of bardic ballads. Why,
went the unspoken but universal cry, should they be deprived of such
magnificence?

THE king pulled closed the chapel door behind him. It was
warmer here than out of doors, but not by much; the utter
stillness of the air felt icier than wind. "Brychan," he said softly. The
bard was kneeling before the altar, eyes half closed, his lips moving a
little as he wandered through internal corridors of sacred memoriza-
tion. Noble watched him for a moment, troubled.

The divorce itself did not disturb him; it was plain to all that the
marriage had accomplished, and would accomplish, nothing. Isabel

had turned out to be an interesting woman, but that was not the value or purpose of a royal match. Her removal would not be a significant loss, and in some important ways would be a boon. What he did resent was having to contemplate mutual reliance on Llewelyn to ensure his own kingdom's independence. Turning to the man he knew hoped to rob him of his sovereignty, as a means to *keep* his sovereignty—it was the sort of thing that Gwirion, in an exercise of witty nonsense, might try ironically to justify. But he could not continue without allies, and allies these days did not come easily. At least a tie of marriage was not as onerous as an outright pledge of subjugation. It was, in the larger picture, the closest thing he could imagine to a panacea.

Brychan opened his eyes. Noble took a deep breath, found that he had clenched his fists.

"Tell me my future," he said quietly. Brychan opened his mouth to speak and Noble held up a warning hand. "Quickly and simply," he ordered. "I do not need a litany of the house of Gwynedd, I want only to know if there are potential brides within two degrees of Llewelyn himself."

Brychan nervously shook his head. "Not within even four degrees, Your Majesty," he said apologetically.

"*Damn it!*" Noble hissed, and struck out furiously at the wall he stood beside. The wall shuddered and a small wooden statue of St. Cynllo tumbled off a shelf nearby. He forced himself to calm with a long, slow exhale. "You did not see that," he informed the bard. Cowed, Brychan nodded.

Noble stared across the room at nothing for a long moment, an unreadable expression on his face.

When he turned back to the bard, he was entirely transformed: smiling, poised. "This is excellent news," he announced in his convincing, reassuring baritone, as if to an awaiting throng. "Now we are entirely free to pursue what has clearly been our intention all along, to rely entirely on our own particular strengths in ruling our own particular people." Brychan regarded him wide-eyed, and with an indulgent smile Noble continued, polishing his act with this captive audience, "You are wondering, perhaps, what those strengths are?"

"I would never question—" Brychan stammered, but Noble silenced him with a grand flourish of his hand.

"Come and see for yourself."

He threw open the door and left the chapel, as the bard scrambled to his feet to follow him out into the courtyard. Scores of onlookers, shivering and stamping the slush from their boots, had gathered round the steps, and withdrew slightly at His Majesty's apparently ebullient appearance. The yard felt silent, uncertain how to decipher the unexpected flush of triumph on his face. Every single pair of feet shifted an inch or two closer to the steps where Isabel stood. Gwirion, with Enid beside him, risked a glance up at Isabel. Her strained expression made his heart hurt.

Without a word, Noble walked briskly down the steps and across the courtyard, the crowd parting all around him, giving him beseeching looks that he ignored. He headed toward his wife in the hall doorway, her red wool mantle wrapped around her, proud and pale, not certain where to put her eyes as the king approached her. She felt Gwirion looking at her but she did not dare look back.

When her husband reached her, he pivoted to face out over the yard, and without looking at her he took the cup of spiced metheglin from her hands. He raised the cup high and finally spoke. "A toast to your eternal queen!" he called out, as if he were proclaiming the start of a festival.

The courtyard burst into explosive cheers and Isabel nearly fainted with relief. Feeling her falter, Noble handed the cup to Angharad, and wrapped both arms around his wife, then pulled her toward him and kissed her hard and long on the mouth. The cheering grew louder.

As he pulled away from her, he kept his mouth near the side of her head. "An hour ago we were a people in crisis," he whispered, "and now we're joyfully celebrating our blessings."

"Was this just a charade, then?" Isabel asked, not believing it.

"You know it wasn't," Noble said warningly, his voice still low. He kissed her forehead, softening. "You are content with this?"

She averted her eyes. "Beyond content, sire. Grateful and obediently yours."

He looked pleased with the description. Still he asked, whispering, as the courtyard began to quiet down, "You don't regret the freedom you might have known had I divorced you?"

"I hardly consider the status of a divorced woman very free," she answered, forcing a smile.

"But, madam, then you would be free to take a lover," he said in a meaningful voice, "without it impinging on your precious popularity."

Appearing not to notice how she started at this, he laughed and nudged her affectionately with his shoulder, then took the cup from Angharad's waiting grasp to publicly salute his wife again.

16

BY PROXY

Late Winter, 1199

 SABEL SPENT a panicked week believing both that Noble knew about them, and that he didn't care. Or if he did care, he needed her too much now. He had made her the darling of Cymaron, which made Cymaron that much dearer to the kingdom at large. With Mortimer to one side and Llewelyn to the other, it was largely force of personality that was keeping Maelgwyn ap Cadwallon on his throne, and she was part of that mystique now, amplifying it. She played her role beautifully for her husband through the grey, end-of-winter doldrums that had settled on the castle. She rode uncomplainingly for hours with him through hellish weather for brief "social" sojourns to remind Maelienydd's aristocracy in person how fortunate they were to have such a powerful and charismatic first couple attending to their interests. They made many of these visits to the south, near to Anarawd's estates and friends. She would return from these trips—two days out and back at most—exhausted and yet strangely

sleepless, and only the harp could soothe her nerves. Her women, growing accustomed to the noise, came to sleep so soundly through it that there were nights when they would have sworn the harpist, although summoned, did not play at all.

Mortimer was still stalling on providing the promised resources for the earth defenses, complaining that no work could be done in winter anyway, and the barons whom Noble had assigned to be his watchdogs, all of them fearful of Mortimer's wrath, were too half-hearted to demand results. And Llewelyn's rising popularity to the north, outside Maelienydd's borders, seemed unstoppable—to Noble's great annoyance, for he understood the source of it: Lord Rhys of Deheubarth had been a boon to all of Wales, lending support to almost any skirmish against the Normans. But Rhys was dead now, his kingdom in shambles; men wanted a new font of manpower and Llewelyn seemed to have it. Noble himself had shown his own army that by taking Llewelyn with him to the front. Owain reported duly that the king's northwest barons, learning Mortimer was not abiding by the terms of treaty, could not understand why Noble would not pledge himself to Llewelyn. The prince of Gwynedd was not a conqueror, he was a unifier, and asked only appropriate respect from those whose lands he would protect. In their minds, Maelgwyn ap Cadwallon's demotion from sovereign to petty prince would be a small price to pay.

As relief from these and other plagues, Noble craved distraction, but Gwirion had not been up to form and he was beginning to resent it.

But perhaps something was afoot now. The king was pleased when he saw his friend revert to old familiar habits of scuttling around dark corners of the castle, speaking hurriedly in whispers to people who later denied seeing him, and disappearing for hours at a time into dank basements. Surely he was staging an event of some sort, and he was staging it for Noble. This was all that mattered to the king. The less he could afford time for such distractions, the more he needed them.

THE morning of the March new moon, the castle awoke under a damp snowfall that melted underfoot, leaving the courtyard a mess of slush made slushier by the predawn brigade of Gwirion's bribed assistants. When the muffle of fog and darkness eased enough for light to enter the courtyard, the guards on the keep tower briefly started: There were strangers in the bailey, standing in formation as if awaiting orders. Their stillness in the face of the guard's warning calls suggested an intimidating martial discipline, and Gwirion appeared at the watch's elbows just as they realized the things weren't alive. He crossed the soldiers' palms with what was needed for them to respond as he wished and at once the trumpet sounded the five-note siege alarm. The castle population assembled, half-dressed, groggy, and shivering in the hall, already suspecting this had to do with Gwirion, because no one would be insane enough to attack in this weather. The queen had been summoned to her husband's bed in the middle of the night, and came with him now straight from his room to the hall, one of his shorter robes wrapped over her shift for warmth, without stopping to collect her jewelry, her rosary, or even her wimple from her own room. People stared at the thick tumble of her hair in the lamplight, unused to it.

The grey daylight grew, and features on the figures became discernable. That created the first buzz: All of them were dressed as women. They were effigies, enormous poppets, life-size and sometimes bigger, held upright by stakes shoved into muddy cracks between the courtyard paving stones. The mock siege alarm was called off and everybody in Cymaron, following the king and queen in their bedrobes, grabbed wraps and wandered outside into the wet, grey morning to see what strange immobile army had invaded them.

The creatures themselves were simply made, limbs of rags wrapped around branches and heads made of leather with facial features drawn or glued onto them, but all of them wore actual clothing stolen from women in the castle. In fact—

"This is Marged!" Noble cried out with a delighted chuckle, reaching an especially short, round one near the kitchen. He took a closer look. "That's her nose!" He glanced around at the rest of the figures. "Did he make everyone?"

The sewing bevy had just discovered their unflattering statuary: three beings identically dressed and decorated with feathers. "Yes, sire," Generys said in a clipped voice, her nose running in the cold. "At least the women."

"Let me see my wife," Noble called out to the courtyard as a whole. "If someone finds the queen—"

"Here she is," Gwilym announced, his lips squirming as he tried to squelch a smile. He gestured to a small figure with an enormous metal crown hanging cockeyed over a long wimple that was one of the queen's own. There was a black-and-white belt around its waist and from it hung a remarkably good imitation of her rosary, complete with the cross housing the relic of St. Milburga. The royal couple admired it from across the courtyard, laughing.

For nearly half an hour, all activity was suspended as the entire population wandered about marveling and chortling over the likenesses. The more Noble smiled, the easier Isabel felt. For several nights now, Gwirion had not come to her, explaining only that he was at work on an enormous secret project designed to please the king. She regretted that their trysting had to be eclipsed for this to manifest, but it was necessary insurance. Her husband was still affectionate to her in court and amorous in bed, but she had become more anxious than Gwirion about his possible suspicions, and anything to alleviate them met with her instant approval. If Noble knew and felt trapped into looking away, she was grateful that Gwirion at least gave him something else to look at.

Gwirion watched them all from the highest point of the wall walk, hidden from view in the tower that housed the bridge to the keep, wearing his entire wardrobe for warmth: four tunics, two britches, and two pair of hose, all of it too large. For the first time in his life, inventing mischief had felt like labor to him, harder not only to dream up but to find the energy to realize. He had rallied himself to do it as a patriotic duty: His king required it of him.

When he sensed the hubbub dying down, he crossed along the wall walk and descended the stairs closest to the king's tower. "Attention, people!" he cried out from the last step, affecting a dreadful French accent. He was bulky in all his layers and he'd slicked his dark hair back on his head with water and spit, although a curl from the cowlick lay obstinately askew. "My dear students! And faithful assistants! I am glad to see you here at the convocation of my school!"

Noble grinned. He was impressed with the effigies, but he'd have been disappointed if that was as far as the effort went. "What school?" he prompted.

"My dear king! You do not know about this great school I have created? Just for your men? Just for the men of this castle? You have so many beautiful virgins and so many beautiful prudes and it is so frustrating for your men. So I have invented the school of proximal fornication! Behold!" He grabbed the skirt of the nearest figure—the butler's wife—and flung it up over her head. The actual wife, standing near it, shrieked when she saw it exposed, and everyone else in immediate view had such an enormous reaction that the rest of the yard squelched through the slush to see: The effigy was crudely anatomical. The butler himself thought it was amusing, and after a moment his wife started laughing even as she blushed.

"Here we are!" Gwirion cried out happily. "In full working order—every one! I have tested each myself, only this morning, so you may have to clean up a little." The beaming teulu at once dispersed to hoist the skirts of all the figures, and found with hilarity that every one was similarly outfitted. Noble leaned against the wooden staircase to his room in the cold morning air, clouds of laughter bursting from him, and the women present were wrestling with different levels of amusement, shock, embarrassment, and fury; amusement generally won out. It was an egalitarian offense, at least, with every servant and every lady equally obscene.

The one effigy whose skirt was not upended was the little wimpled one.

"Is my wife not worthy of your lechery?" Noble called out to Efan and his band. He embraced Isabel from behind and rested his chin on her still unwimpled mane.

Efan looked extremely clumsy for a moment. "Nobody would presume to gape at the queen's private parts, sire."

"Don't be absurd—Gwirion *made* the queen's private parts." Noble laughed. Gwirion suddenly felt the need to focus all of his attention on adjusting the sewing bevy's veils, and Isabel willed herself not to tense in her husband's arms. "Go on, then, have at her."

The teulu exchanged glances, but all hesitated to take the first step.

"You silly children," Gwirion said with forced casualness, in his own voice, and ran to the queen's figure to flip up the skirt. "It's just another cunny, lads." He instantly busied himself again in the sewing bevy's veils.

Noble kissed Isabel's head quickly and went to study her double. She knew going with him would seem most natural and lighthearted, but she could not bring herself to do it. Everybody chuckled with anticipation as Noble knelt down to view the artificial copy of his wife's loins. Screwing up his face with exaggerated scrutiny, the king poked and pried, examining the artifact with such vulgar fascination that even Isabel herself, blushing, had to laugh. Gwirion was apparently having a devil of a time getting the veils to sit right on the sewing bevy, and missed the king's performance. Noble finally stood again, shaking his head. "You didn't quite capture it, Gwirion. You must study your subject in more depth next time."

The queen's blush vanished and she looked ill, but nobody noticed her reaction because Gwirion shrugged theatrically and answered, "I made them all alike, sire. Just like women really are." This brought roils of indignant amusement from both sexes and gave him an excuse to resume his French persona and push on with the prank. "Come along, students, we will be getting started for the first lesson now. Let us begin! I need a volunteer boy and a volunteer girl. If there is no volunteer girl, I will substitute myself. I choose..." He looked around the courtyard. Madrun, the queen's youngest woman, was standing clutched and giggling beside the hall serving girl whose breasts Gwirion, with his new wonderment about the female form, often found himself staring at.

"And I will choose the fair Madrun over here..." As she squealed, he stomped through the slush to her and dragged her over to her effigy. Her face was pink from both the cold and the thrilled embarrassment. "And for the man I find..." Nobody said it but everyone knew whom he was looking for. Madrun and the marshal's son Ednyfed had been besotted with each other for months, but Ednyfed's mother Elen would not allow him to court a woman from the south; she considered that stock infected with the blood of Flemish settlers and therefore beneath him. "Aha, here is the young man I am searching..." He found the boy, blushing but hearty, and dragged him briskly toward the effigy as well. "Now this is the game we play, yes? He wants to relieve his burning desire with her. But he cannot relieve his burning desire with her. So—he has use of the proximal fornication. Pull your drawers down, lad, and make yourself at home." Gwirion flipped the skirt up and casually threw it over the effigy's face. The assembly laughed. He knew that nobody would actually strip in such weather—although he wondered briefly if there would be any takers had he tried this in summertime. "And you, fair Madrun, you will be providing the sounds! You will stand behind and mo-o-o-o-an and gro-o-o-an for all of us to hear, to make it seem more real, yes?" She covered her face with one hand, laughing and blushing, and tried to swat him away with the other hand. "No, no such gestures, only sounds. Very well. Are we ready to begin?"

For the next several hours, Gwirion teased and goaded random couples to bond over the figures. Almost everybody, including all of Noble's teulu, who came over from the keep or up from the village, took the dare at some point, although no man went so far as to drop his drawers. At one point Noble pretended he was about to engage with the effigy of Marged the cook, with Gwirion offering to provide the sound and even giving a spirited demonstration. For over two hours, nobody touched each other, removed any article of clothing, or even made much eye contact, but Gwirion had roused as much flirtatious mirth as was usually reserved for the Spring Rites of May Day. It was an antidote to the weather, the winter, and the threat of war. *Give us this every day and I can endure anything,* Noble thought gratefully.

The hilarity might well have lasted into the afternoon if Noble had not decided to try coaxing his wife into participating with him. There was no problem with her enthusiasm—she agreed to it, and the crowd cheered and applauded her as she crossed, blushing slightly, over to her small effigy. The moment she was beside it, however, her face changed from pink to purple and she was instantly enraged. She grabbed at the fake rosary hanging from the figure's belt and snatched it away so hard the belt broke.

It wasn't fake.

"Gwirion!" she nearly screamed. *"This is my rosary!"*

Gwirion, who had almost succeeded in getting the buxom hall servant to have a go with the falconer, glanced over his shoulder and called back pleasantly, "Of course it is, that's why I put it on you."

"You had no right to take this!" she shouted. People in the path between them stepped away—this was not hysteria or whining, it was righteous wrath. She held up the chain and shook it in her fist. "You *know* what this means to me. And *this.*" She held up the cross, her hands shaking, and spoke very slowly and clearly. *"This is the relic of a saint.* You know that."

The courtyard was instantly silent and all eyes turned to Gwirion. With a quick nod he excused himself from the black-haired girl and walked to the royal couple. Even Noble looked slightly cowed by her announcement.

Her eyes blazing, she pushed the cross out toward Gwirion, daring him to further insult it. He took the rosary from her politely and examined the crucifix. "But you see, it's just an *English* saint," he declared dismissively, and handed it back to her.

Nobody laughed. People stood silent, ruddy cheeked, suddenly noticing that their boots were leaking in the slush. Gwirion looked to

Noble for support; the king shook his head slightly. "What does this mean, then?" Gwirion said, raising his voice to address the crowd. "I'm allowed to mock the men who persecute us, but not the church that justifies their doing it? What hypocrisy!" There was an uneasy shifting of legs and exchange of glances, but still nobody spoke. "Oh, for the love of ale!" Gwirion said, laughing. "It's a strand of hair! It was probably cut off some leprosed peasant who died on the side of the road near the shrine. If half the relics out there are real, the saints were all eight feet tall with sixteen legs and triple rows of teeth." The silence grew even more absolute. He had never in his life so utterly misjudged his audience. He tried to think of some way to bow out gracefully and decided that it had to be at her expense. "Surely you can afford to buy another one, if that one's been desanctified," he suggested sarcastically, and addressed the crowd again: "You do understand that's why she has it, don't you? It was a purse that earned her that little tidbit, not merit. Just a purse, and probably Mortimer's at that. But go ahead, please, be incensed on Uncle Roger's account."

It didn't get the response he'd hoped for, but there were finally mutterings that sounded more questioning than damning. She looked like she truly would have killed him if she could. "You stole something of mine," she said, quickly shifting the emphasis away from her family.

"No, I stole several somethings," Gwirion corrected with forced cheeriness, and lifting up the makeshift crown, he pulled the wimple off the effigy. "Here, you can have this back too. Would you like me to strip her for you? Or shall we ask the king to do it, he has *much* more experience than I do. In fact maybe he should strip them all!" Finally there was a very slight ripple of chuckling around the yard.

She was unappeased, and all the angrier for not being able to chastise him with the bluntness this deserved. "Adèle made that rosary for me. It's the most cherished object I possess."

"I didn't damage it, milady," Gwirion said, trying to avoid being cornered into defensiveness or worse yet, apology. "I didn't even disrespect it. I had it hanging from your belt like it ought to be—

believe me, there's a dozen other more creative places I could have set it! Shall I list them for you?" She stared at him, saying nothing, and nervousness began to dictate his behavior. "And there's a dozen other *things* I could have done with it," he babbled. "For example, I could demonstrate its essential Englishness and my essential Welshness by flogging myself with it, like this!" And he reached out to take it from her grasp. She snatched her hand away but not before his finger had caught a loop of the chain, and the length of the rosary was stretched taut between them. He didn't want to be accused of stealing it again and she did not want the chain to break under tension; they both re-leased it at the same moment and the rosary plummeted. The clear glass crystal that encased the relic in the center of the cross struck the stone paving of the courtyard first, and struck it hard.

Isabel said nothing, which was the harshest possible condemna-tion. She knelt at once without looking at him and picked up the cru-cifix, wiping the slush and dirt away on the yellow woolen robe, almost too horrified to speak. Reflexively, Gwirion got to his knees to help her, but she pushed him away, so abruptly and angrily he toppled into the slush. "Leave me alone," she said in an icy voice. "Go away. You've done enough damage." She clasped the rosary and crucifix against her chest and stood, then walked out of the courtyard without another word or glance at anyone. Everyone watched her go in silence.

The king found her in her solar, fuming, the rosary and crucifix drying near the hearth. The crystal hadn't shattered, but it was scratched. "Do not even try to defend him," she blurted out in lieu of greeting. "Even without the relic, even if there was only the fact that Adèle made it for me and he knows that—"

"I agree," Noble said quietly. "I'm making no excuses." She shut her mouth, disarmed. "I came up here to see how you were faring, nothing more." He gave her an affectionate look. In the warm light of the fire, his broad face looked paternal. "We all forgot breakfast entirely this morning, but dinner will be ready soon."

"I don't want to see him," she said.

Noble pursed his lips. "I assume you are not asking to eat in your chamber."

Instead of answering she peered through a rip in the sealed parchment covering the window, tried to make out the different hilltops an inch at a time. "Very well," Noble said. "I'll tell him to take dinner in the kitchen."

"And supper," she added at once, her eyes still on the abbreviated landscape.

"This will *not* be a return to the hostilities of last year," he announced firmly. "I don't have time to relive such nonsense now. I require the two of you to be civil to each other."

"Tell *him* that," she snapped, forcing herself to be fascinated by the little she could see out of the window.

She did not call for Gwirion that night and relished, for the first time, the power she had in their affair: He could not come to her unbidden.

GWIRION tried the next morning, after mass, to apologize. She requested him to do so formally, in front of the king and court as they broke fast, and he agreed even to this humiliation, even knowing that for the first time, perhaps ever, he was not the congregation's secret darling. He stood before the high table where the royal couple sat, feeling rows of diners' eyes on the back of his head, self-consciously penitent in stance. "What exactly are you apologizing for?" she asked sharply, when his two-word declaration—"I apologize"—was over.

"Whatever you want me to regret," he said after a moment. It was an honest response; he had no other answer.

"What *do* you regret?" she demanded severely from her chair. He reviewed the whole event mentally as king and queen waited, watching him expectantly, and finally he answered, "I regret that I released the rosary. Then it wouldn't have fallen and gotten scratched. That's the only real harm that was done—and we're equally responsible for it," he pointed out reasonably, adding in an exaggeratedly indulgent

tone, "but if you'll apologize for your part in the mishap, I'll certainly apologize for mine." This got no reaction from the hall. But
Noble was making a steeple with his fingers before his lips, his signature of suppressed laughter, and Gwirion knew he was amusing the
only one who mattered. He relaxed a little, reassured. There was no
harm done, then—in fact, a public falling out like this, suggesting
things were somehow as they'd always been between them, was strategically savvy, although he was glad it was over now and things could
go back to normal. After only one night apart, he missed the feel of
her hair between his fingers.

She gave him a disgusted look. "I accept your apology," she said
coldly. "And when you figure out what you should really be apologizing for, I'll accept that as well. Until then, please refrain from placing yourself unduly in my presence."

FOR three days she ignored him. He did not dare approach her,
even given a chance to. But he ached with missing the smooth
warmth of her skin, would have been content even catching a hint of
her scent at the hearthside. And yet the young hall maid seemed more
attractive every hour. He found his own fickleness oddly reassuring,
proof that it was only flesh he missed, and flesh could come from
other sources. Hall maids, for example.

Isabel was glad he'd reminded her of just how callow he was, for
she'd been teetering on the edge of real attachment, and this had
helped her to collect herself. She was grateful for the affair, it had
brought her pleasure and a sense of power, but Noble seemed
wholeheartedly devoted to promoting her adoration and contentment now, and deserved the whole of her in kind. Gwirion would be
her lover only on the physical level, and as physical levels went, what
Noble offered was easily superior in both form and technique. So
there was no profit to an intimate reconciliation. It was not guilt or
even loyalty that prompted her decision; it was simply pragmatism.

Let Gwirion find himself a woman better suited to him, she thought, and when each was confident that the other was independently content, perhaps a treasonless friendship could mature between them. It would be a graceful and sensible resolution to an otherwise impossible scenario.

WHEN his wife had first become seized by insomnia and insisted on retiring to her own bed each night, he realized he missed feeling a feminine body asleep beside him. He had seldom kept a woman in his bed after lovemaking prior to his marriage, and was surprised to find that he had developed an attachment to it; he was not surprised to find, however, that he had no attachment whatsoever to the feminine body actually belonging to his wife.

There was a young woman who had caught his eye weeks earlier. She was black-haired, with the curves and generally wild look that he liked so much, but a sweet, almost childlike face. He asked Gwirion about her and learned that she was new to Cymaron, that she was orphaned but well past the age of consent, with a younger sister who like her worked in the hall. One night shortly after Gwirion's wan apology to Isabel, Noble saw the girl standing with a group of others, mostly Marged's assistants, listening to Gwirion play. When he had finished the tune, the king called him over. The rest of the clique broke up to return to their chores, but the black-haired girl, curious, followed Gwirion's path of travel with her eyes. Servant and queen both watched the two men in whispered conversation. Noble's gesture, and Gwirion's eyes following after, left no doubt who the subject of the conversation was. The girl, her face wide-eyed but unreadable, darted out of sight into the kitchen. Isabel felt a stab of jealous anger in her gut as she realized Noble was openly setting up a tryst; it mocked her assumption that they were working toward at least the appearance of adoring monogamy. *Perhaps I misunderstood*, she decided with a dismissive mental shrug. *Perhaps the girl is simply meant for Gwirion.*

Suddenly she couldn't breathe.

AFTER supper Isabel excused herself to the chapel and sat for a long time in the light of a single votive, the rosary on her lap and her eyes fixed above the altar, staggered by the unwelcome enlightenment about the state of her own heart.

Back in the hall, she found Gwirion in his usual loitering spot by the kitchen screens, cleaning his teeth with a hazel twig. He made to walk away at her approach, but she signaled him to stay. Being close to him again made her palms clammy. It took her a moment to corral her thoughts into words.

"That Christian spirit you find so contemptible is coming to your aid," she finally whispered. "The moon is far from full tonight, so people will be sleeping soundly. Except perhaps for me."

He was surprised. "You don't think I'm beyond redemption?"

"Oh, you might be," she answered, still whispering. "But that's not for me to judge." She crossed her arms awkwardly. It made her look, as certain gestures did, like a little girl playing at adulthood. "I know you felt you had to do that, and I forgive you, Gwirion, but you must understand something. I don't think you realize just what an insult you committed that morning." He decided it would be best not to comment on this. "What you mocked was the very part of me that is choosing to forgive the mockery. You may find devotion absurd, but if I were not devout, I would not be speaking to you now—or ever."

"I don't believe that," Gwirion said quickly. "I'm not devout but I'd forgive you nearly anything." And then he was quiet, looking almost embarrassed.

"Then you're a better Christian than you realize." A pause, as he graciously refrained from mocking her for saying this. "I know that nothing is safe from your derision, least of all me. I don't care, give him what he wants. But I do ask that you *hesitate*, at least, before you mock my piety again."

He grimaced for a moment, chewing on the hazel twig. "I'll do that for you, not for your piety. Good evening, sire," he went on brightly in a louder voice, his eyes widening, and she jumped as Noble's hands squeezed her shoulders from above. She whirled around to find him grinning at her.

"I see there's some progress being made here. Excellent. Life is much easier for the entire castle, frankly, when the two of you are not at odds. Is the battle over?" Both nodded, slightly sheepishly. "Who took the honors?"

They exchanged glances. "She did," Gwirion conceded.

"That's fine," her husband hummed. "As long as you don't rub off on him." The king nudged her toward the door. "I'll be up in a few moments, go and warm the bed for us."

She nodded, said good night to Gwirion politely, and left the hall. Noble turned his hypnotic gaze on his friend. "Thank you," he whispered, squeezed Gwirion's shoulder, and exited after his wife.

A N hour later, as the castle was settling in to sleep, Gwirion received two summonses at once—to play the harp for the queen, and to play the pander for the king. Grudgingly he took up his old vocation of royal procurer, a job he had once approached with a certain amusement and, if nothing else, vicarious pleasure. Now it felt seedy, even shameful—and annoying at the same time, for it was the young woman he had very nearly asked the king to give him as a mistress. He found her lying on a pile of rushes and meadowsweet not far from the hall fire. When asked, she said her name was Nest, and she seemed not only prepared to follow him upstairs, but, in fact, quite pleased about it. As they traveled through the night-fogged courtyard, he was close enough to her to catch her scent, the kind of sweet muskiness that would have excited any man; Noble's taste was impeccable. He led her up the outside stairs to the king's chamber, pausing at the door with a nod to the bored and smirking Gethin. "Here we are," Gwirion said, and she laughed with nervous pleasure. He gently nudged her through the door and closed it behind her.

In his bedchamber, Noble lounged propped up on one elbow near the fire, throwing a few sticks into the hearth to keep the new flames hot. He heard brief, excited laughter outside, and smiled. Then the door opened and he saw the girl enter. Somebody pulled the door shut and after a moment, realizing she'd been left here, she turned and faced the king. Her eyes went very round as she saw who her companion was. She looked confused for a moment, then nervously dropped into a curtsy.

"You don't need to do that in here," Noble said expansively. "Come sit by me."

Her jaw went slack and she gave him a stupid, stunned look. "Your . . . Your Majesty has called me?"

"That surprises you? You came willingly along, didn't you?"

"Yes, sire. I didn't realize this was your room, sire, I've never been upstairs before."

"Whose room did you think it was, then?"

She swallowed uncomfortably, radiating embarrassment. "I thought the room was unoccupied, sire."

For a moment he was confused by this answer, then understanding, he lay back on the floor and shook with laughter. "That's brilliant!" he crowed. "You, my dear, are a *godsend*."

HER women were asleep by the time Gwirion arrived and he did not even bother with the pretense of playing the harp. They were impatient to touch after days of separation; he had just undressed and they were running their hands along each other's bodies with breathless awe as if it were for the first time. A moment later and he might have been too absorbed in her warmth, but he was still alert enough to realize that it was the king who was whistling "Rhiannon's Tears" as he descended from the wall walk. In barely a second Gwirion had blown out the candle, scrambled out of her bed and into the shadows near his harp. She barely had time to register what he was doing before he leapt back, pulled the bed curtains closer together and disappeared again into the shadow to frantically pull his tunic on.

"Noble!" Isabel managed to sound normal as her husband abruptly flung open the door and entered.

"I have extraordinary news," the king announced cheerfully, throwing open the bed curtains and placing his candle lantern on the side chest. His cheeks were flushed from the cold and he slid his chilly hands under the covers, pressed them against her warm abdomen.

She shrank away from his hands and gestured at the tapestry that shielded the sewing bevy. "Be quiet, you'll wake them," she shushed.

"I don't mind if they overhear," he said as Gwirion emerged, miraculously dressed. "I thought you'd both enjoy hearing that my evening's assignation failed utterly."

"What a pity," the queen said sardonically, although at this moment she hardly cared. "Why?"

"Because the girl thinks she's in love with Gwirion." Noble laughed.

Gwirion was astounded. "But she seemed eager to go to your room—"

"She didn't know it was my room. She thought it was some special bower you were taking her to for your own devious purposes. She was so adorably earnest that I decided to reward her for it. So she's waiting in your room downstairs—I promised her you'd be right down."

The two of them started violently in the darkness, and Gwirion felt a weight lift from his chest. This was the perfect solution for him, the perfect out, and he knew she knew that because when he risked a glance at her, he saw on her face exactly the look he had wanted never to see there: fear. Anything else he could have managed—derision, amusement, sulking, even jealousy or anger. But the vulnerable look that begged him not to wasn't something he was equal to. The alternative he wanted—the safe, relatively moral, and very delectable alternative to the worst kind of adultery—was dangling within reach and the only thing keeping him from grabbing it was that look on her face. As if reading his mind, she caught herself and turned her head away, forcing her expression into a neutral mask.

"Thank you, sire," Gwirion finally managed to stammer. "Did you mean . . . now?"

"Of course now," Noble said, laughing at him. "Now and later too. I think it's an excellent long-term proposition. Go on, then. She's practically edible."

"Thank you, sire," Gwirion said again stupidly, but his legs were unwilling to move. Inexplicably he felt compelled to take her emotions into account—an alien, confusing impulse. He resented her for it but the resentment did nothing to dull his disorienting sense of duty to her.

She read his mind and forced the hardest sentence of her life out of her mouth. "Go on, then, Gwirion," she said, managing to sound like a teasing older sister. "The night's not getting any younger."

Noble chortled. He nudged her, grinning, incredibly pleased with himself. "He's stunned by his good luck." He turned back to Gwirion. "Go *on.*" He wafted his hand in a grand wave of mock imperiousness. "You are dismissed," he intoned, sitting on the edge of Isabel's bed and loosening the tongue of his drawers belt. "My wife and I will celebrate your good fortune on our own."

With a terse good night to both of them, Gwirion collected the harp and left the room awkwardly. He was angry, and mostly he was angry with her. What she'd said to cover herself didn't count. He'd seen her expression, her one unguarded moment. Earlier in the evening she had been with the king, and he was being sent away so that they could be together again and she'd dared to give him *that look?*

He left the harp in the hall, and paused outside the opening to his own little room. There was a slight rustle within and his heart al-

most stopped. "Sir?" Nest's voice whispered from beyond the opening, and suddenly he remembered how good she'd smelled. He closed
his eyes in the darkened kitchen, and rested his head against the stone
wall a moment. Finally, with a heavy sigh, he knelt down and crawled
into the space.

"Good evening, Nest," he said quietly, and reached for her hand.

T HE next morning in chapel, Isabel prayed in vain to be released from the torment that had kept her awake, a fever of
emotions she knew she was not the least entitled to. He was being
paired off with a mistress who would be free to show him tender affection every day, in ways both casual and intimate. In front of other
people. That would be seductive. Over time, Nest would win him
away from her by offering him what the queen was not allowed to.
Her envy of Enid paled by comparison.

At board, her angst was only worsened by a sharp slap of guilt
when she saw her husband's face, as he was brooding over messengered dispatches he'd asked to read before breakfast. While she was
nearly falling apart over the petty luxury of personal emotions, he
was struggling to keep the state intact. Absurdly, she envied him the
burden. He gave her a weak smile when she sat beside him and gestured to the scrolls he'd been perusing. "As usual. Llewelyn is doing
things he said he wouldn't and Mortimer is not doing things he said
he would," he said, sounding tired. "While Anarawd is querying his
neighbors on the royal bed's fecundity." Then his eyes flickered to
something behind her and his face brightened a little. "And speaking
of fecundity, here is Cymaron's newest stud!" Gwirion had approached the table, and without a word or look of greeting, settled
quietly upon his stool. Noble gave him a lecherous wink. "Entertain
us with tales of your nocturnal exploits, then, you little satyr. I'm
taking my wife back to bed immediately after breakfast, so you may
be quite explicit."

Gwirion's face went very red and he looked into his lap. "I ... don't think that would be gentlemanly of me, sire."

"When have you ever been gentlemanly?" Noble snorted, and his eyes were once against drawn to something behind his wife's head. Nest had just entered the hall, as unreadable as Gwirion, skimming the sides of the room cleaning up after the servants and guards who had slept here. "Never mind," Noble announced smugly. "I'll go straight to the source." He rose and ambled over to the girl. Isabel and Gwirion avoided looking at each other. While the chaplain intoned his usual Latinate thanksgiving, she watched the king approach Nest and speak to her for a moment. He patted the girl's arm with a parental joviality.

But after he'd left her and returned to the table, he paused and looked appraisingly at Gwirion. Gwirion tried to ignore the gaze and then realized it was going to continue indefinitely if he didn't acknowledge it, so he finally looked up. Their eyes locked and they maintained the silence for another moment.

"You really are a fool," Noble said. He was annoyed. Gwirion simply shrugged. Out of the corner of his eye, he saw Isabel relax and close her eyes in gratitude for a moment. She who willingly spread her knees to another man every evening was tormented by the thought of his being with another lover even once. He almost wished he had taken the girl after all, just to give Her Royal Majesty a taste of what he went through each evening.

THAT night when she called him, Gwirion almost sent back the message that he was busy with his stud duties by order of the king. But he couldn't bring himself to refuse her. He retrieved his harp from its chest in the hall, his gaze lingering briefly on Nest's sleeping form curled near the hearth.

He stopped. Even if Noble did not suspect them, even if he never came to suspect them, what had happened last night would be only the first of interminable irritations.

He turned to Llwyd and whispered, "Please apologize to Her Majesty, but I'm unable to attend to her, I've other commitments."

Her doorkeeper was confused by the obvious lie, but nodded and headed back for the stairs as Gwirion, trying to breathe calmly, watched him. There. That simply, it was over. He started back to his stone warren, imagining her as she imagined him taking Nest. For one dazzling moment this gave him extraordinary, vengeful satisfaction and then he was disgusted with himself.

And he had not, after all, actually fantasized about taking Nest this time—only about Isabel fearing it. He cursed softly to himself, understanding what the difference meant.

Clutching his harp under his arm, he turned back toward the stairs. Nest, as he passed her, slept peacefully. He intercepted Llwyd just before he reached the balcony and mumbled an excuse to go in.

He sat himself near her bed and began to play without greeting her, and played for nearly half an hour in the sad Irish tuning that he knew she liked. Then he silenced the strings and rested the harp on the dried meadowsweet that fragranced and padded the floor.

He waited for her to tug the bed drapes apart and gesture for him, as she always did, but there was no movement from within. After a long moment, he tentatively opened the curtains himself, unused to taking the initiative.

She was sitting up on the far side of the bed in her shift. She made no movement toward him as he crawled in; he left the curtain open behind him for the candlelight to come in. She looked anxious.

"Why didn't you?" she whispered.

"Isn't it enough that I didn't?" he whispered back.

She shook her head. "If I didn't care *why* you didn't, I probably wouldn't care if you did it at all. I want to know . . ." She hesitated. "I need to know how I figured into your decision." She shrugged self-deprecatingly. "If I figured into your decision."

He looked at her unspeaking for a long moment in the obstructed candlelight. "You *are* my decision," he finally said.

Her breath caught. She had so hoped for that answer and so doubted it would come. She held her palm out toward him and he met it with his own. His large eyes in the muted candlelight made him look almost childlike.

"I thought it was a trap," he said, sheepish.

"So did I."

"But then I realized it couldn't be."

"How can you say that? Wasn't it strange, when he came in here last night? As if he was being deliberately naive."

Gwirion shook his head. "He knew you were sleepless, so he expected that I'd be up here, there's nothing odd in that. And you covered beautifully when you told me to go downstairs."

"The whole thing just felt...too pat, somehow. Like a well-planned game."

He shook his head again, this time sympathetically. "Noble's always playing games, it's second nature to him. You'd drive yourself to distraction trying to track every one he plays."

"What if he suspects, and he's setting us up to get caught?"

"He could have caught us last night. If I hadn't heard him whistling—"

"Exactly!" she hissed, hating that they had to whisper. "He was whistling!"

"Which he would not have been doing if he was trying to catch us at something," Gwirion said reassuringly, interlacing his fingers with hers. "I'm far more attuned to him than you are, why are you so nervous?"

She sighed. "He says things sometimes, gives me funny looks, that make me think he knows."

"He would have done something already."

"No, he wouldn't, he needs me now."

"Noble doesn't need *anyone*," Gwirion said, almost dismissively. "If he wants something, he always finds alternatives. He would never subject himself to wearing horns because you'd somehow become indispensable to him—nobody is ever indispensable to him."

"We have to be more careful," she said with vague stubbornness.

He grimaced. "Should I come to you less often?"

"No!" She crawled over to him and leaned against him. This was the longest conversation they'd had by far since their first tryst in this room, and its timbre bothered her. She cuddled into his arms, pressed against the body that she feared she now knew better than the person. "It isn't fair," she sighed. "It's so *simple* for *him* to tryst."

He hesitated. "This is much more dangerous than his liaisons. You know that."

"But I'm *damaged*," she said bitterly. "Even if he suspects my fidelity, he knows I can't conceive a bastard."

"That isn't what I meant," Gwirion said. After a self-conscious pause he added, "I meant he doesn't fall in love."

That night they lay together for hours, holding each other.

·17·

DRUNKARD'S TUNING

Approaching Spring Equinox, 1199

FTER COUNCIL the next day, the king summoned his wife to meet with him alone in the receiving room, a strangely formal request. When she entered, he was so drawn and somber he was almost grey. For one fleeting, irrational moment she was afraid this was about Gwirion's refusal to take a mistress.

"Are you indeed the Lady of Maelienydd?" he asked quietly, not looking at her, staring into the flames of the fire.

"Please don't start that again," she said.

"I have my reasons."

"Tell me what you suspect me of, Noble, I haven't the energy for games."

He looked deeply troubled. "I understand the world, but I resist it," he whispered bitterly. "Is it possible, do you think, to betray a loyalty that is deeper than blood, and not burn in hell for it?"

She swallowed, trying to breathe calmly. "What loyalty is that, sire?"

"Sire?" he snapped, and looked up at her, enraged. She took a step away from him, paling, and almost fell onto the settle. "I call you in here as my wife, my consort, my confidante, and you treat me with obsequiousness? Is that how you show me I can put my faith in you?" He turned back to the fire, disgusted.

"Noble, please, speak plainly," she begged. "I don't know what you're talking about."

He sighed, then looked back up at her, more civil this time but still dour. His mouth had the grim, firm set to it that she had only ever seen in sleep before. "This is about Llewelyn."

She relaxed a little. "How can your loyalty to Llewelyn be deeper than blood?" she asked.

He shook his head slowly. "I don't care about Llewelyn. I care about my kingdom. *My. Kingdom.*" He whispered both words as if they were a foreign phrase he was trying to recall. "I need you to support me if I sin against my fathers in order that my sons might prosper."

Still not understanding him, she rested her hand tentatively on his arm. "You need my support as the Lady of Maelienydd?" she asked.

Even his blue eyes had lost their spark. "I need your support as a Mortimer," he whispered at last. Then he told her what he meant to do, and would not be talked out of it.

THAT evening, Gwilym the steward and Hafaidd the usher requested Gwirion to perform for them privately in their shared chamber when he was finished playing for the king. He was fond of them both, and indebted to them for enduring decades of his rascal wit, so he cheerfully agreed. He finished his ale, offered Noble a parting good-night witticism concerning leeks and bodily orifices, wrapped a wool mantle around himself, and headed toward the door of the great hall, his harp in its sheath tucked under his arm. The queen had been crossing the hall not quite toward him through the

smoky amber light. She paused to speak with Elen, the marshal's
wife. As Gwirion passed nearby, she excused herself, smoothly intercepted him and murmured, "Go up the stairs, not down, when
you've finished," then returned her attention to the other woman.

He could barely focus as he played for them, at once hoping and
dreading that she had arranged a tryst where they might have the luxury of real privacy. The two older men murmured unhappily together, in phrases rife with "Roger" and "Llewelyn," and sometimes
"Anarawd." Gwirion's gaze drifted to the planked ceiling of their
room, wondering whether she was even now waiting in the chamber
above, and he was so flushed throughout his performance that they
offered to damp the fire if he was too warm. Gwirion refused, with
many awkward thanks, and declined to share a horn of ale before departing. The harp he left with them, on the flimsy excuse of not
wanting to expose it to the cold.

Outside, the black night was thickly smudged with clouds. The
mantle wrapped around him, he hesitated on the stairs before taking
a step up. But the commitment of that one step seemed magically to
catapult him to the floor above. He stopped at the door of the guest
chamber and carefully pushed it open.

The room was sealed with wax parchments at the window, frigid,
and completely black. It was too silent for her to have been here, but
then he heard her voice calling quietly from what he guessed was near
the fireplace, "Come here."

"They're not asleep downstairs yet," he warned, everything in his
body quickening at once. He dropped his wrap by the doorway.
"They'll get suspicious if they hear noise up here."

"It can't possibly be as bad as it is in my room," she replied. "It's
safe to make a little noise—Madrun trysts with her lover here, I've
heard her tell the other girls. I said come here. It's straight across, I
moved everything that was in the way."

When he was beside her, he sank down onto a soft nest of blankets she had laid out that afternoon before the sun went down.
"How did you know I'd be in their room?" he asked.

"I suggested it." She laughed a little, pleased with herself. "My women think I'm with Noble for the night, and Noble thinks I'm tucked into my own bed with a sour stomach. I could get quite good at this."

He smiled despite his nervousness, and let her undress him. Naked, jaw clenched from the cold, he loosed the side ties of her kirtle and ran his chilly hands under it, along her body, and she shivered. He helped her wriggle out of the kirtle, and after she laid it carefully aside, he grabbed her gently by the hips and pulled her toward him, drawing the blankets over them into a cocoon. His mouth found her breasts and his hands lost themselves in the satin hair he so adored.

They were quiet, but quiet felt raucous compared to the silence they'd been constrained to in her room for weeks. Hearing each other's voices as they touched and pressed themselves together drove them nearly into seizures of affection and they found themselves almost laughing—quietly—at the intensity of their desire. She marveled as always at the difference in the two men. Noble treated their coupling, both in his satisfaction and hers, as further evidence of his sovereignty—it was another thing she was pleasantly useful for, both to his senses and to his pride. To Gwirion, physical pleasure seemed to be eternally miraculous, and she was credited for all of it. That had been strange to her at first; it lacked the manly arrogance that was part of Noble's sexual charisma, but now she cherished it.

But what she cherished most of all was that in the aftermath of conquering each other, it was finally safe for them to speak. They lay with arms and legs entwined and bodies pressed together, her hand draped over him, brushing against the scar on his back.

"Say my name," she whispered, but he shook his head. "Please." He wouldn't. "Then call me some pet name. I want to hear an endearment from your lips."

"There is no endearment that suffices," he whispered. "Words pale." He sounded almost bashful.

"You *always* have a word at your disposal."

"Not for you. You defeat me."

"Aha! The Normans win a round!" She grinned.

"You're Welsh to me," he said, with a simple sincerity that touched her until he added snidely, "Except for that ridiculous accent."

She began murmuring incomprehensible things with her lips brushing his. He smiled, but shook his head. "I have no idea what you're saying."

"It's shockingly filthy," she promised. "Worse than pagan. Something that would leave even that heathen August war god of yours speechless."

He gave her a condescending smile. "Do you mean Llew? He's not a war god, first of all, and he's Welsh, which means that *nothing* leaves him speechless."

"Of course he's a war god, all Welsh heroes are war gods."

"And I really can't imagine why we should feel the need for that," Gwirion muttered dryly, then went on to correct her, as if it were something any child would know. "But Llew is the god of harvest and the sun. I pity your people having a history that's limited to human mortals, how very dull for you. No wonder you were such a witless prune when you arrived." He quickly kissed her to stave off her protestations and kept his tongue pressed against hers until her muffled indignant growl had given way to giggles.

"Is he the one who—" She tried to remember what he'd been blathering about in the courtyard last summer. "The one who puts . . . a divine spark, isn't it, into every oat stalk?"

"He puts a divine spark into everything," Gwirion said, running his hand across her nude belly. "Except the English. He tried, but they're allergic to divine sparks."

"You!" Laughing, she tried to hit him but he used it as an excuse to grab her hands above her head and rolled on top of her again.

"Tell me what the shockingly filthy French meant," he ordered, the tip of his nose resting gently on the tip of hers.

"Would you like me to demonstrate?" she offered.

They came together again, but for most of the night they simply talked, teasing and laughing softly, saturating themselves with the intimacy they'd reached in their imprisonment under Cynan. Something within Isabel quivered nervously on behalf of her eternal soul, but she could not abide the thought that something so joyful could be wrong. Anyhow, it was a joy she could not bear to live without now. Such genuine, immediate companionship was more seductive to her than an eternity of angels.

Before it was light enough to see, they folded the blankets up and she slipped them into chests whose locations she had memorized by feel the day before. They helped each other to dress. This took a long time, as it required stroking and tickling and hands slipping into places where they did not really belong, but eventually they were both presentable, in ragged linen and fine silk, respectively. The slightest grey glow had begun to illuminate the far horizon, but not yet the air, as they stepped together out of the room, she in her purple mantle and he in the dull grey woolen one, his arm still fastened around her waist, not wanting to relinquish her back to reality. They should have disciplined themselves, he thought, they should not have lingered until nearly dawn. By day they belonged to Noble, not to each other. And the days were growing longer.

"One more kiss," he begged, and a smile lit her face: He never asked for kisses, never bothered with parting terms of endearment. They pressed their lips together for a long moment that wasn't nearly long enough, then he squeezed her once more tight against him, whispering, "I hope you have insomnia tonight." She laughed softly, and they began to separate, she to the left and Gwirion to the right.

Gwirion turned smack into the teulu's stiffened leather breastplate, hurting his nose and jumping back in protest. She heard the noise and spun fully around, then froze. There was an awkward, horrible moment of silence as the guard stared at the two of them, eyes narrowed in his young pockmarked face, trying to imagine some acceptable explanation for what he was seeing. Gwirion recognized him with a silent groan: It was Caradoc, the catalyst for his misadventures last summer on the road with Enid.

"What's going on here?" he demanded angrily, sparing no niceties for the queen. She opened her mouth to speak but nothing came out. Caradoc took a menacing step toward them and began to draw his sword. "Answer me!" he growled.

Before the sword was out of its sheath, Gwirion darted back and snatched the queen's eating knife from her belt, threw his arm around her and held the knife to her throat. "What's going on is I've taken the queen hostage," he said fiercely. "Back off or I'll make mincemeat of her." She stiffened but said nothing as Caradoc gave him an incredulous grunt. "Endear yourself to the king," Gwirion urged. "Tell him to come out here and negotiate with me for her release. Go on—" He poked the eating knife against her neck and she had the sense to cry out in a terrified voice. "I'm a bit mad you know, you don't want to fool with me. Go on, Caradoc!" The young soldier, confused and disturbed by this bizarre turn, started down the steps as other teulu and guards around the bailey, hearing her cry and sensing the commotion in the predawn darkness, headed toward them. "Quick," Gwirion whispered urgently. "Up to the top of the tower, but make it look like I'm dragging you."

The two of them scrambled up the dark tower stairwell, Gwirion cursing quietly when he stumbled on his blanket. They burst out under the leaden sky, onto the pitched-round roof of the tower as shouts and calls began to echo around the walls of the bailey and from the lookout of the keep. Gwirion, eyes wild, sat her down on the conical crown of the roof and desperately tried to figure out what to do next.

"Is this a prank or the end of our lives?" she asked, pulling the mantle tighter around her and trying to stay calm as voices of angry, anxious protest came closer from below.

"I don't know yet," Gwirion said shortly. The tower rose a floor above the wall walk, and the only way to reach this roof directly was by the one stairway, a weakness in the design that he was acutely grateful for. There was a wooden cover for the stairwell hatch to keep the rain out. It lay on the sloped roof, and he struggled to move it into place. She slithered down the incline to help him.

"Don't," he grunted between labored breaths. "You're my captive, remember? They're watching from the keep, the light's rising and they mustn't see you help me." The cover was in place now but wouldn't keep anyone out long—it could easily be pushed up from below. He had to secure it. To start with he picked up Isabel herself and placed her on top of it to give it a little bit of extra weight. There was nothing else up here. "That will have to do for now," he said. "Don't move, don't get off that. If they see you on it they'll be reluctant to muck with it much for fear of hurting you."

"What now?" she asked, alert but unafraid, and distractedly fingered an abandoned bird's nest wattled into a gap in the stone.

"I don't know," he snapped, almost annoyed with her for not being more distressed. He thought of sending her down on her own and barricading himself up here on some pranklike pretext, which would no doubt sound as feeble as what he'd pulled with Caradoc. That would at least separate them and possibly remove suspicion from her. But if they had, indeed, just irreversibly revealed themselves, sending her down to Noble might literally be fatal.

He sat beside her, and the scent of her softened his edge at once. "I want to take your hand right now," he whispered. "I don't dare because of the men in the keep. I think there's enough light now that they can see right down here."

She shrugged her mantle off one shoulder so that it covered both their hands, and ran her fingers over his. He took a quick breath, startled. "What else do you want to do to me?" she asked in a playful voice.

"It's not the time for levity," he insisted. "I don't know how to save you from this, Isabel."

He'd said her name without thinking and it startled both of them.

"The crazy fool is scolding the rigid Saxoness for levity?" She seemed delighted, and he decided it must be a peculiar kind of nervous attack.

"I am truly sorry about this," he said. "I wish to God there was some way I could shoulder all responsibility."

"Taking me captive is effective," she said. "Should I struggle? Do you want me to bite you?" She leaned in toward him. "I'd love to bite you."

He laughed. Then he stopped himself and shook his head to clear it. "I'm floating right now," he said, perplexed. "I've been caught in treasonous adultery, and we're probably both about to be killed, and I'm . . . I think this is joy." She squeezed his hand under the mantle, smiling so prettily it made his eyes smart. "You don't know how desperately I want to kiss you right now," he whispered.

"Yes I do," she whispered back. "But tell me what else you would do to me if you could. If it were ever safe."

"I . . ." He winced. "I'd make an ass of myself."

"Really?" She looked gleeful at the declaration. "How?"

He blushed. "I'd make up dreadful poems about you, about your hair and your nipples and your kneecaps. I'd stare at you in silence for hours wondering what I did to deserve all the good and bad of this, and being grateful for all of both." He plucked a denuded oat stalk from the abandoned bird's nest and said softly, "I'd ask the great god Llew to fill this humble stalk with the divine spark of all my good regard for you. He would endow each straw in all of Wales with the power to bestow my love upon you."

"Good heavens," she said in a choked voice. "Is there a bad poet hidden under all of that?"

"And then of course," he went on in his normal voice, tossing the oat straw away, "I would summon the spirit of King Arthur to wrench your wretched Norman throat while I ravished your horse."

She grinned, nodding. "That's more like it," she said heartily. "That's the charming lad I lost my heart to." They laughed together. Nervously. Terrified, in fact.

HEARING from Caradoc only that the queen had been taken hostage by "the villain," who had possibly already forced himself on her, Noble had leapt out of bed and frantically thrown a woolen robe over his tunic and drawers before running down the steps and into the still-slushy yard.

Around the wall walk and the towers, fifty teulu archers stood ready with arrows on the string, waiting for the king's word.

Hafaidd and Gwilym were standing with a small crowd of servants staring up at the northwest tower. "Where are they?" Noble demanded anxiously.

Gwilym looked uncomfortable. "Up there, sire." The steward gestured with a nod of his head.

"And he'll parley?"

Gwilym and Hafaidd exchanged bemused glances: Apparently the king did not realize who the villain was. The steward cleared his throat. "Only with you, sire."

"Get his attention, then."

Gwilym nodded to the herald, who put his horn to his lips and blasted a long, steady note that silenced the yard. Immediately, a head crowned by a mop of dark hair popped up over the edge of the parapet and gazed down at them.

"Good morning!" Gwirion called out.

Noble relaxed. "For the love of the saints!" he scolded. "What are you doing? Where is my wife?"

At a gesture from Gwirion, Isabel rose and showed herself. "I'm safe, Noble," she called down reassuringly. "It was one of his less-inspired pranks. He told me you were up here waiting to show me something."

"I thought Your Majesties might like to view the sunrise with me," Gwirion overlapped, loudly, and scowled. "I was on my way to fetch Your Majesty when that idiot soldier ran into me and went quite mad—does that amuse you?" he interrupted himself, when he saw the expression on Noble's face.

The king was looking up at them with a knowing smile, his hands clasped behind him. "I was merely appreciating your most extraordinary gift for timing." As he said these words, he gestured to the door of the great hall as Thomas, Walter, and Ralf emerged from it out into the yard, in expensive but ill-insulating mantles. They followed everyone's upturned gazes to the top of the tower.

"What the *devil* are you doing to her this time?" Ralf demanded, instantly enraged.

G WIRION accepted a hand slap—a real one, in the presence of the uncles—when he had brought the queen back down into the yard. He sat quietly through Ralf's berating him in the council chamber, in front of Noble, while Isabel watched mutely; Gwirion had insisted she play the innocent. When the old man was finally out of breath, Gwirion gave him a pleading look. "Does this mean you won't be wanting me to play for you at supper? I had something special planned." But the glow Isabel had seen in his eyes when they were alone on the tower roof was gone. Just when she knew he was truly with her, he disappeared again.

This time it was for her sake, not his own. When they came downstairs into the courtyard, she had been glowing with the particular light of a woman rapturously in love, and to Gwirion's cautious eyes Noble seemed attentive, and curious about it. Their night-long tryst had been too easy and seductive; they were both dangerously close to tripping into a fantasia of something that could never be, and he would blame himself if she slammed into reality too hard too late. He could not let her fall; he would remind her, with her family's unwitting assistance, of their very narrow limits. If he had to he would make himself despicable.

G ENERYS was fastening the underpinnings of the queen's wine-red wimple as Gwallter rearranged the drape of Noble's mantle over his red silk tunic. It was evening. The visitors had been sequestered all day, nursing a severe chill born of unexpected troubles on their travels. "Still they arrived a day sooner than I expected, which is excellent, it means I can begin the spring circuit earlier," Noble said.

"What happened to them? It's a day's ride from Wigmore, why did they arrive here in the morning?"

He tipped his head to the side as Gwallter fastened the draping with a brooch. "They lost their way and got in very late last night. I don't know how your entire race has managed to avoid self-destruction. The moon is not half full and it was clouded over completely, but they just kept *going*. They were halfway to the Severn when some scouts found them and brought them back south. Thank God they had my writ of safe conduct or they might have had their throats slit."

She pulled away from Generys and sat down hard on the bed, alarmed but not about that. "Last night?" She tried to sound casual. "Where did they sleep?"

Noble bent over a little so Gwallter could place the circlet on his head. "I had Gwilym put them in my audience chamber." He straightened, nodded toward the door, and waited for Gwallter to open it. "I was going to put them in the guest chamber above Gwilym's room but thought better of it. Illicit couples use it sometimes to rendezvous and I didn't want your uncles embarrassing anyone. I'll see you at supper." He left.

She reached out to grab the bedpost as the room wobbled.

"Milady?" Generys said tentatively, and reached toward the queen's half-assembled headdress. Isabel held up her hand to stop her. She desperately needed an hour alone to think; there were too many complications begging for resolution. "No wimple this evening," she said at last, pulling the barbet off. "Tonight I wear a Welsh veil."

THE family would be dining privately in Noble's receiving chamber, with a proper table set up and chairs brought in especially for all of them. This was an uncommon way to entertain visitors, but the visitors noticed nothing uncommon about it. To them one's exclusion from the populace, not one's adoration by it, defined rulership.

The queen went down from Noble's room to the hall, where the rest of the castle population was assembling for their supper. The first servants who saw her murmured little sounds of surprise at the white veil, and their murmurs caught the attention of the entire room. As she crossed toward the receiving chamber, she basked in the fascinated attention of many dozen pairs of eyes. When she was near the door, she finally looked up and acknowledged the glances. There was silence for a moment, and a strangely intimate sensation between the people and their queen. Then one pair of hands in the back of the hall began to clap, and almost instantly the entire hall burst into applause. She flushed with pleasure and nodded acknowledgment with a humble smile. She knew where the applause had begun.

When she entered the audience room, her kinsmen eyed the veil, looking confused. Noble himself blinked once in surprise, then flashed her a private smile of appreciation, and her pulse, still racing from his parting comment in the bedroom, calmed a little.

They held conference as they supped. It was Noble's only chance to speak to the visitors entirely in private without rousing the worry and suspicion of his council, which he was beginning to suspect of housing secret Llewelyn sympathizers. Since Gwirion's presence would have been inflammatory, Angharad had been called in to play softly for them by the hearth; she was the quietest and most circumspect of the sewing bevy and above all did not know French.

Thomas seemed much older, only in part for the trauma of the past few months. He was taller by an inch or more since last autumn and he looked gaunt; he had outgrown the doughy, pallid look that made it impossible to take him seriously. And he had sprouted a real beard at last. He was still young, but he was a Norman gentleman now. The uncles seemed slightly lost, as if they had no identity or reason for being without overseeing his interests.

Of Mortimer, they had little news but many rumors. They'd heard he was negotiating with William deBraose, whose lands bordered the southeastern expanse of Maelienydd, and that the two of them were corresponding with King Richard's brother John, now the likeliest contender for the throne. They were leery of delivering what they assumed to be unwelcome news, but Noble seemed untroubled. "John coming to the throne will be a boon for Wales," he insisted. "He understands the barons better than Richard does. He wouldn't see Mortimer overrunning us as a victory for England, he'd see it as a victory for Mortimer, and it would make Roger more powerful than John wants any one baron to be. He'll control Roger. I thank you for the news, but actually I want to discuss another matter." He paused, looking pained for a moment, and glanced again at his wife's Welsh veil. She knew what he was about to ask, knew how hard it was for him and why. She herself had tried to talk him out of it the day before, but having failed, had resigned herself to playing her role of consort and supporting him without comment. "I need your help," he said at last. "Against a fellow Welshman."

"Family problems?" Walter asked wryly. The Welsh propensity for fighting one's own was well-known to the Normans, who had exploited it for decades.

Noble shook his head. "A would-be empire builder. A man I would embrace as my brother if I didn't think him capable of fratricide."

"Llewelyn," Thomas said stiffly, and the king nodded. "I don't see how he's a threat to me."

"He's a threat to your sister," Noble said meaningfully.

Thomas flushed. "My sister? We thought . . . you . . ." He glanced at his uncles, who looked equally awkward. "We thought you wanted a divorce. We thought you were summoning us here to . . ." He hesitated. "To take Isabel back to England."

The royal couple stared at him, stunned. "What?" Noble demanded. "How could you presume—"

"We heard a rumor and it sounded plausible," Ralf interrupted bluntly. "This marriage affords you nothing, especially as your cousin Anarawd inherits if Isabel does not conceive. It makes sense that you would try to wed into Llewelyn's family."

Noble gave a short, harsh laugh of exasperation. "Where did you hear that?" he demanded. "It was never more than an idea and as an *idea* its life span was perhaps an hour!" They said nothing and he looked accusingly at his wife, but saw that she was as shocked as he was. "The rumor is unfounded," he said flatly, and rested his hand on the queen's. "I'm cleaving to your sister and she is cleaving to me. She is in fact part of the bedrock of my sovereignty now. Will you help her?"

Thomas was not prepared for this. "I don't have an army."

"Your uncle does."

Thomas blinked. "You want me . . . to negotiate on your behalf with Roger Mortimer . . . for him to fight with you against another Welshman?"

"The boy matures," Noble said with approving bitterness.

"Why would he—"

"Because it will endear him to John."

Thomas shook his head. "You've lost me."

"John will be king soon."

"Why do you say that? Richard is invincible—"

"So was my father," Noble said. "It only takes one arrow. John will be king soon. I predict within a year, two at most. Richard is about force, John will be about politics—I'm sure we're all aware of that. He won't want anyone in his realm having too much power, or in any way challenging the crown's absolute authority. Roger already has a strike against him there—he disregarded King Henry's writ of safe passage when he attacked us and killed my father twenty years ago. He'll need to endear himself to John. Llewelyn has it in him to become far more powerful than John will be comfortable with. Someone needs to stop Llewelyn before he gets too powerful, and that person will endear himself to John."

The uncles exchanged glances but Thomas's gaze never left the king's face. "That is the tortuous thinking of a man who is running out of options," he announced.

"Thomas!" his sister gasped, but Noble put a hand on her arm to quiet her.

"Yes," he said simply. "It is. I congratulate you on the exquisite education these last few months have clearly visited upon you. It may be tortuous but it's accurate. The question remains: Will you help your sister?"

"I need to consider the situation," Thomas said evenly. "I'll write you when I feel ready." King and queen exchanged glances. She still did not like this scheme, but she knew better now than to speak out against him.

"That's fine," Noble said. He was thrown, but pleased, by Thomas's transformation. If nothing else, it rendered Ralf and Walter obsolete. The king smiled politely. "Then the discussion is closed and we may enjoy the rest of our meal."

G WIRION, after spending the day penned up under guard in his closet, alternating between dozing and chastising himself for adolescent daydreams, performed that night in hall for the other diners. The visiting servants spoke no Welsh, which meant he was performing solely for the castle, and this crowd was so lenient that impropriety was never an issue. He improvised some debauched songs making fun of the king and the queen—as people, as partners, as rulers, and as would-be parents. It was a safe and harmless way to let out some of his own frustration. And he decided on a brazen experiment to determine if anyone suspected the affair: After one particularly bawdy verse concerning the many positions the king used to try to get the queen with child, he went on to sing,

"At long, long last His Majesty
Saw what had to be seen
He said, Gwirion, you mocker,
Exercise your cocker
And dick the devil out of the queen."

He felt a thrill of fear as he actually sang the words, but the response reassured him: It was such a ludicrous proposition to all of them that they roared with mirth. He could see no looks exchanged or elbows nudged; there was only tremendous, good-natured guffawing and Gwirion decided to end the song with this. Young Ednyfed the marshal's son offered him a cup of mead, and he was reaching out to take it when a hand gloved in fine leather grabbed the cup and doused the contents roughly in his eyes. The room uttered a brief collective gasp and fell silent, and Gwirion, blinking in surprise through stinging drops of alcohol, found himself looking at Ralf's enraged face.

"Oh, damn," he said loudly, without thinking, and Ralf slapped him with the back of his hand. Gwirion had been slapped too often—usually much harder than that—to flinch. He wiped the mead away with a bored, annoyed look.

"What are you doing?" the queen's voice cried out. All eyes turned to see the entire dining party crowded in the doorway to the audience chamber.

"This *animal* has been—"

"That animal saved my life," she said with some heat. She switched to French. "It's disgraceful enough he wasn't welcome to sup with us at table—"

"Sup with us!" Walter snorted from the doorway, beside her. "Independent of the fact that he took you *hostage* this morning—"

"That was a prank," Noble said mildly, "although I do think, my dear, there should be limits to how you reward him for his nobility." He did not look at either of them, but a shiver so intense rattled Isabel's spine that she had to grab her brother for balance. He misread the gesture as a request for support.

"I have no objection to his joining us," Thomas said.

"You did not hear what I just heard," Ralf seethed from across the hall.

"Why don't you tell us, then?" Noble called out, smiling. The crowd stared at them, unused to hearing Noble speak what was, to most of them, simply the queen's native gibberish.

"It does not bear repeating," Ralf said, looking sickened. "Come, return to the room." He headed back toward his family.

"Gwirion," the queen said in her strongest voice, and went back to Welsh. "We would be honored to set a place at table for you."

This was exactly what he'd feared—that one of them would start to lose perspective of what was rational behavior. He made a sneering face. "No, Your Majesty, I don't belong there."

"I say that you do."

"Then Your Majesty has a mistaken notion of my place in the world. I would offend your venerable uncles with my manners. Like *this*," he explained, and belched into a sound hole in the harp, which made it echo resonantly. "Or *this*," he added ferociously, rising briefly to fart. The crowd in the hall cheered him on as the pleasure drained from Isabel's face. "That is my personal method for responding to English windbags. In the presence of ladies I do try to mend my ways, but this tends to be the result." He belched into the harp's sound box again, this time somehow in falsetto, which set the room to laughter again. The queen, her face stony, turned without a word and retreated into the audience room, as Walter harrumphed, "I told you he was a villain." Only Thomas appeared serenely indifferent to the insult.

When he knew his guests were safely back in the audience chamber and could not see him, Noble grinned and saluted Gwirion, who made himself grin and salute back, and the room again erupted with merriment.

LATER that evening, after the chandler had lit the way to the guest quarters for the righteously indignant visitors and the queen had retired in silence to her own chamber, Noble called Gwirion to his room. He dismissed Gwallter after the chamberlain had neatly laid out piles of traveling clothes for him; he announced that he would condescend to sort through them on his own, but while doing so he wanted only entertainment and distraction.

For a month he would tour the kingdom on circuit, spending most of his time in the northwest, a night or two at the larger castles and fortresses, watching the muster of troops, stopping by the smaller landowners along the way, and checking the border in certain key defensive areas, especially the area closest to Llewelyn. He had a three-pronged challenge facing him: first to convince barons who were weary of fighting and already well-disposed toward Llewelyn to consider a military stand against the prince of Gwynedd if he moved closer to Maelienydd; second and much harder, to consider doing it in concert with, of all people, Roger Mortimer. Finally, should this idea be utterly rejected, he had to at least press them to agree to resist Llewelyn's crusade.

He was leaving at dawn, avoiding the company of Thomas and the uncles on their homeward trip by setting off at once northward. For logistical reasons, he was not taking the usual full-circuit retinue, which included all his officers. So far he had mentioned bringing neither Gwirion nor Isabel and they had both been hoping with nervous delight that they might have the whole month together.

When Gwirion was alone with Noble, he felt so comfortable and normal that he could almost believe there was no secret, no betrayal, nothing outside this room. It always startled him when the queen interrupted them, a rude reminder that the rest of their shared life was getting very complicated.

Tonight, her presence more than startled. It provoked.

There was a knock on the door and Gwirion paused in his playing as Noble called out, "Come." She entered, still dressed formally from the family dinner, including the stony expression that she'd worn for the last hour. Her husband looked up from the pile of clothes on the bed. "Good evening, my lovely veiled companion. This is a surprise. You didn't seem in the spirit of visiting. Come to warm my bed, are you?"

"Actually, sire," she said stiffly, "I'm here to speak with Gwirion."

"Certainly. Come in."

She hesitated. After Noble's loaded comment earlier about the guest room, she was sure that asking to be alone with Gwirion would equal a confession. So she entered the room and closed the door behind her.

"Did you lose your wimple, milady?" Gwirion asked.

She ignored his comment and perched on the end of the bed so that she could face Gwirion with her husband behind her. "Gwirion, I would like to know why you behaved that way tonight."

"I'd like to know why it matters to you, milady."

"So would I, for that matter," Noble said, looking curiously at the back of her head.

"I don't care that you insulted them," she lied. "Apparently that's why Noble feeds and clothes you. But you might have used a little wit to do it. I would like to think our friendship at least entitles me to have my family mocked with a sophistication worthy of our amity."

"I think, Your Majesty, not." Gwirion laughed. "You have a rather romanticized notion of this amity we've reached. It doesn't raise me to your level any more than it degrades you to mine. It doesn't mean that in a few years I may travel with you and your husband to visit your family and sit among you as a peer. If the king's regard for me doesn't earn me a place at table, your regard won't either." She gave him a hurt expression and he pressed on, feeling desperate. "We are irreconcilably disparate spirits and we've only become friends for the convenience of the king, not the exaltation of his fool."

"You're a better man than you used to be. I'd simply like them to see that."

Her sad, affectionate look pierced too acutely for him to continue a campaign of estrangement. The urge to comfort her was overwhelming. He chuckled nervously and insisted, "I'm no better than some old oat straw in an abandoned bird's nest, milady," as Noble, laughing behind her, said over him, "A *better* man? I beg to differ, madam! I was just telling him before you came in how annoyed I was with him for having grown so dull. Until that magnificent exhibition in the courtyard with the effigies, I was convinced we were all lost— don't you know that the fate and fortune of the country rises and falls on Gwirion's wit?"

"That's not the point I was making to Her Majesty," Gwirion said firmly. "I'm nothing, I'm just Noble's parasite to them, and they have no interest in a parasite. Why should they?"

"*We're* interested in you," she protested. "*We* see there's more than a parasite—why mightn't they?"

"Listen to that—*we.*" Noble smiled, shaking his head. "How far she has come! To appreciate Gwirion is the measure of a mind. Your family simply isn't subtle enough to understand him."

"That also wasn't the point I was trying to make, sire," Gwirion said blandly. "I was speaking not of *their* limitations, but of my own." He hesitated, knowing he shouldn't continue to offer up the image, but unable to stop himself: "I say again, I'm no worthier than an oat stalk."

She blinked quickly as the meaning of the image became clear to her. Then, her back to her husband, she gave Gwirion a grudging smile. "Yes, in some old bird's nest," she said with affectionate sarcasm. Gwirion's stomach flopped over; he looked away quickly, defeated by the inability to estrange himself from her.

Noble laughed dismissively. "If we are through with the vegetative metaphors, my dear, you'd best go pack."

She grimaced, grateful her back was to him. "Pack, sire?"

"I'm bringing you with me, didn't I mention it?" Noble glanced with some disdain over the collection on his bed.

"You didn't, actually," she responded, and stood up to face him, inured by now to frustration. Gwirion plunged into a new tune. "My ladies will not be pleased to have such short notice."

"It doesn't matter, they won't be coming with us, they ride too slowly. Except Generys. You may bring Generys."

"And who else will be coming with us?" She tried to make it sound very offhand, and pointing to a side-slitted tunic on the bed she added in the same voice, "That one sits better on you when you're on horseback."

Noble picked up the tunic and tossed it onto a nearby chest where two others already lay. "Thank you. Goronwy has been asked to consult on a case near Llanidloes, so he'll be coming, but we need to cover a lot of area in a little time so we're taking the smallest possible entourage. And we'll be going to Huw's so Gwirion, for one, is definitely staying here. Huw still wants him dead—with better reason than your charming uncle Ralf ever gave." He grinned at Gwirion, who was pointedly giving all of his attention to the harp. "I'm sorry about that, Gwirion—I do still owe you a night with Lady Branwyn."

"I forfeit," Gwirion said evenly without looking up.

Noble frowned. "If you continue to pass up these delectable morsels I shall begin to suspect you of being a secret Cistercian. Or worse." Then he smiled. "I suppose I'll just proxy the night with Branwyn for you. But I'll tell you all about it if you like." He continued to sift through the tunics and missed his wife's shocked indignation, as Gwirion suddenly started playing louder and wilder, hiding behind a shower of notes.

"*Must* you flaunt that in front of me?" she demanded. "Could you not practice a little discretion in how you speak when I'm present?"

With a cascade of smothered plunking, the harp music stopped and Gwirion stood up. "This is private," he said. "I'll leave."

"Oh, sit down, Gwirion," Noble said, impatient but informal, and Gwirion, not sure if it was a request or an order, hesitated. "A sense of propriety in you is ludicrous. There are no secrets here, thank God. Keep playing." He turned to his wife and said politely, "And you were saying?"

To her, it felt like a dare. She no longer really cared what he did with Branwyn or anyone else, but admitting that now would give him more fuel for suspicion. She waited until Gwirion had reluctantly taken his seat and picked up the instrument again, then said in a low voice, "I take no issue with your life before you were committed to me. But now——"

"Now I'm married to a woman who obviously cannot conceive, and it's in the interest of my kingdom to sow my seed more widely and in more fertile fields."

"That's a feeble excuse," she retorted. "Branwyn's free to be with you because her husband knows she can't conceive."

"That's true," Noble admitted. "In that case, I'll make sure to have a go with her attendants as well. They all looked fairly fecund." He smiled pleasantly at her and continued to pick through his clothes, tossing the desired ones onto the chest to be packed by the chamberlain later.

"Could you at least practice enough discretion so as not to insult me?"

He raised one eyebrow. "You are the most privileged woman in the kingdom. Considering the concessions I grant you, you might be the most privileged woman in Wales, perhaps all Britain. If one minor insult is pushed in your direction, I should hope you have the fortitude to survive it with grace."

"I'm an intruder here," Gwirion insisted desperately, standing again and fidgeting with the harp's lion-head finial.

"Why? We're only discussing unorthodox sexual relations, it's your favorite topic," Noble said. He threw a hearty grin at his friend. "In fact, you being an expert in the field, give us your judgment—is it unreasonable for the queen to oppose my intentions toward Branwyn?"

"Your intentions toward Branwyn had better not require taking any children along for her husband," Gwirion replied, his voice rising.

Noble returned his attention to his wardrobe. "If you insist. Huw's tastes are dictated by aesthetics, not anatomy. Anything petite appeals to him. I'll just offer him my wife."

"You will not!" she snapped. Gwirion stayed quiet, which annoyed her.

"The boy or the queen," the king mused. "A difficult choice." He turned to her as if she were not the woman being discussed. "Let's leave it to Gwirion," he suggested cheerfully. "Gwirion, whom do you think I should offer?"

"Offer him your own damn buttocks," Gwirion snarled.

"You weren't paying attention, Gwirion—the choices are the boy or the queen." When Gwirion made no move to answer, Noble added with a sigh, his attention on the display of tunics, "It's not like you to refuse to play a game with me. Tell me what has put you out of humor. Or would you rather that I guess?"

"Of course not, sire, I'm your devoted player," Gwirion said quickly, fighting not to clench his jaw. Isabel tensed.

Noble gave him an approving smile. "I'm glad to hear that. In that case, whom do you propose I offer up to Huw?"

"It's detestable to dole out sexual favors as a means of ruling a kingdom," said the queen in a faint voice, already knowing she would not be listened to.

"Is it?" challenged Noble, archly. "Loyalties are forged by kinship. Huw is not kin to me, Llewelyn seduced him ideologically and although he returned to the fold I need some enterprising way to keep him there, as he is dangerously close to straying once again. So I must offer him power. But what power can I offer him?" He shrugged. "Land? It's too small a kingdom. Gold? It's a poor country, I have to keep a tight hand on the coffers. Security against the English? Llewelyn has a better offer. The only other forces that have universal power are sex and death. I can't free him from death or—for now—kill him, so sex seems the obvious choice. And now Gwirion will tell us precisely how I'll do that."

For a moment the two men stared at each other in a way that reminded her, unpleasantly, that they already shared more memories than she could ever have with either of them.

"Obviously," Gwirion said suddenly, in a strained attempt to sound rascally, "if the purpose is political expediency, you must give him what is of the greater value. I assume that would be your queen and not your stable boy."

"Gwirion!" Isabel cried out. When both men looked at her curiously, she stammered, "The man who is . . . who is an *oat stalk* has no right to say such things about his queen!"

"While the man who is the king's fool has an *obligation* to," Gwirion said, fumbling with his tuning key.

Noble looked satisfied. "Well, that's settled, then," he said in a chummy tone. "I'll just trundle Isabel off to Huw's bedchamber when we get there."

"No you won't! There must be statutes against prostituting one's own wife!" said Isabel furiously.

The king laughed, lips pulled back coldly at the corners—and when Gwirion realized Noble's eyes were boring into him, he forced himself to fake a laugh as well. "No statutes that apply to me. But this was just a little pastime—I don't intend to act on it, Isabel, don't get hysterical," Noble said. "However, I must say I'm very glad to see that Gwirion stands ready to play with me."

"It is the very reason I exist," Gwirion said wearily, in a voice unctuous with sarcasm.

Noble smiled at him with a paternal warmth. "Yes," he informed him affectionately. "In fact, it is."

18

SNARE

Early Spring, 1199

OR WEEKS the royal couple, a few immediate attendants, and the teulu were out of the castle. As usually happened when Noble was away, Gwirion became lackadaisical, doing always what was asked of him and absolutely nothing more. Gwilym often asked him to play for the household after supper but quickly despaired of any other satisfaction from him—as always, his wit went into hibernation in the king's absence.

But unlike other periods of ennui, he had a new preoccupation. In a castle not much given to higher learning, he had found a book. It had been at the bottom of a chest in the storage room beneath the great hall, where he with his uncanny memory recalled its being tossed fifteen years earlier. He spent every free moment wrapped in a velvet mantle he'd inherited from Noble, his nose to the brittle pages of the codex, muttering to himself, but he was possessive and secretive about it. Nobody ever managed to get a clear look at it, and from what Marged's workers could glean from a quick glance at the cover, the letters were put together in odd, insensible ways. The rumor quickly spread among the servants that he was studying sorcery. Because it was Gwirion, this did not bother them much—if anything, they were looking forward to seeing how he would supplement his pranks with a bit of magic. Each night after their dull Lenten supper of salted trout, oat bread, and ale, the castle workers would beg him to practice spells for them. He would intone strange-sounding words and phrases with intricate arm gestures, and then inform them all that somewhere in Scotland a pig had spontaneously combusted, or that he had prevented a boat from capsizing off the Isle of Mon. Nobody was sure whether he was serious or mocking, but they would always ooh and ahh respectfully. He would swap wry glances with Gwilym or the other officers, barely keeping a straight face as he resumed his seat and returned his attention to the book, which had been written for Prince Maelgwyn when he was eight years old. It was a primer of the French language.

A week into the circuit, after damp but gleeful spring equinox rituals that he could barely rouse himself to join, Gwirion was summoned to play for the royal party at Owain's manor. It was to celebrate the king's birthday—which, Gwirion's own birth date being a mystery, was always celebrated as his own as well. He was not in a celebratory mood and a trip away from Cymaron generally made his stomach sour with tension. It was a long day's journey, a dreary exodus on a muddy road between clouds so low they seemed within reach, and treeless hilltops carpeted red with last year's dead bracken. The air was wet and chilling and they had nothing to eat along the way but salted trout. Everyone was sick of trout.

Owain's manor was a hillside, wood-framed compound in an inhospitable part of the kingdom. The soil was poor, but the manor was ingeniously built so that a small tributary of the extreme upper Wye River, almost at the Severn, meandered through the courtyard,

and there was a plentiful supply of trout. Gwirion and his escort of
teulu arrived during supper and took their meal, mostly trout, in the
kitchen.

Noble and Efan were dining in private conference with their host
to discuss the ruins of a Roman hill fort on Owain's land. This fort
overlooked a difficult pass into Maelienydd from the northwest. The
king and his chief soldier wanted it refurbished and garrisoned with
his own men—but at Owain's expense, on the grounds that Owain
would be the first to be affected by a "visit" from Llewelyn. Gwirion
pressed his ear to the door in time to hear Owain's polite rebuttal,
which brought nothing but derisive rebuke from his sovereign. The
hill fort was centuries abandoned because the pass was extremely challenging to cross, Owain explained, but more important, the land was
simply too impoverished to support a garrison without imposing beyond reason upon his shepherds and farmers.

"I don't want to challenge my sovereign," Owain ventured, "but it
really should at least be my own teulu up there, they're my kin and all
sons of the local freemen. At least there would be ties of blood and
affection to mitigate the burden." This was met with equal contempt.
Gwirion grimaced and walked away. He did not hear the rest of
Owain's quiet reasoning: "If Your Majesty forces troops onto my
lands, just to scare off someone who may not even be an enemy, Huw
and all the others in the area will be up in arms—they'll call you a
tyrant, and they'll use it as an excuse to go over to Llewelyn."

Coming from anyone else, it would have been a threat; from Owain
it was merely a regrettable description. But Noble's expression darkened
and stayed that way through supper. By the time he rose from the table
he knew, annoyed, that he would have to force the issue.

WHEN Gwirion arrived, Isabel was closed up with Owain's
mother and sister, who wanted to practice their atrocious
French. He wanted desperately to catch a glimpse of her but didn't dare

try too hard for fear of seeming suspicious, especially when he heard that Noble had himself left his supper conference in search of her. Gwirion retreated and spent a little time peering about the homey wooden manor house, imagining the life he would be having here if he had taken Owain's offer at the December war council. He could not, even now, make himself regret his choice, although the young man had not exaggerated: He could easily live out his years anonymously in this godforsaken corner of the kingdom. It was the first time in twenty years the royal circuit had even bothered stopping here.

Owain's hall was stuffy and Gwirion, seeking fresh air, eventually slipped out into the central yard. The moon was a night short of full, and with the slight cloud cover the sky had a silver-midnight haze bright enough to cast vague, unnatural shadows across the wet grass. To Gwirion's surprise, Owain had come out here too, leaning heavily on the railing of a bridge that crossed the stream, fidgeting with a small, dense fishnet that he'd pulled up out of the water to repair.

"Good evening," Gwirion said.

Owain spun around. "Oh, it's you," he said, relaxing. "I thought it was His Majesty come to torment me some more."

"Is he still on you for what happened during the war council?" It was unlike Noble to waste effort on a grudge.

"No, he's after the hill fort," Owain said in a tired voice. "He doesn't understand his own people. They can barely survive the winter but they're peaceable, they help each other out. They haven't the time or the inclination for any sort of skirmish. What I'll have to ask of them to maintain a garrison will push them beyond the edge— they'll end up desperate and resentful and they'll be a bigger problem than the supposed enemy the soldiers are being sent here to watch for in the first place."

" 'Supposed'?" Gwirion frowned. "Llewelyn's not the enemy?"

The two dark-haired, slender figures considered each other for a moment in the half-light, and then Owain looked away. "That depends on who you are," he said uncomfortably.

"If you're the king, Llewelyn is the enemy," Gwirion said, and added bluntly, "which means if you're the king's subject, Llewelyn must also be the enemy."

Owain made an evasive gesture and tried to smile. "Come inside with me. I have a flagon of brandy wine, if you care to share it. Then we'll get the harp out for you. It was my father's, it hasn't been played since his funeral, six months ago."

They crossed the damp lawn toward the cellar where Owain kept his butlery, but as they passed a side gate that opened into the stable yard, they saw and heard something that brought them to an instant freeze.

The sound that made them turn was Isabel's voice, and the scene that brought them to a stop made Gwirion shudder and Owain gape. Noble had brought his wife outside into the night and had her pinned between a barrel and the side of the stable. Beneath his red woolen cloak he wore only his tunic; beneath her lighter linen one she was naked, and he was possessing her. Her face was unreadable in the muted moonlight, but every movement he made against her stood out in sharp relief, lit by the flames of a freestanding stable-yard brazier.

In unison, the two men automatically turned away and then immediately looked back again. Owain made an embarrassed sound and dropped the fishnet without noticing. Gwirion thought for a moment that his knees would give out, and instinctively he grabbed at Owain's sleeve.

"Yes, I see it," Owain whispered, misunderstanding the tug on his arm. He blinked and shook his head slightly, as if he could not make himself believe what he was seeing. "Why——"

"I don't know, but look away," Gwirion said in his ear. "We're just playing into his hands if we stand here."

Owain nodded and walked away. Gwirion started to follow, but his eyes, against his will, strayed back to the stable.

Noble had pulled her away from the wall and laid her on her back across the barrel, her mantle in a heap on the ground by her head. As he began to climb on top of her, he murmured something too quietly for Gwirion to hear, and she made a feeble cry of protest in response. Gwirion stiffened. *You have to go away,* he told himself furiously. *Leave. There is nothing you can do.* He managed to lower his eyes from the scene, and saw the little fishnet Owain had dropped. He felt himself bend over to pick it up. *Don't,* he ordered silently. *You're not going to do it.* But then on the other side of the gate, she cried out again, louder this time, and Gwirion saw red.

H IS wife cried out as he had told her to, as if she were in pain, and then a second time, but the bait was obviously not luring. Seeing her shivering and tensed against the late March air, Noble was about to offer her a hand up and his own mantle for warmth. He ran a finger down her trembling abdomen—when he heard her gasp in surprise and then the world went black.

Somebody shoved him hard from the side and threw a foul-smelling rag over his head, twisting it tight around his neck and knocking him off her. He stumbled away from the barrel, reaching for his throat as his assailant shoved him again, knocking him to his knees. He leapt up at once and tore off the sack—it was actually a net—but the attacker was already fleeing. Following Isabel's astonished face and the sounds of speeding footsteps toward the inner yard, he rushed to the gate and saw the slender dark-haired figure as it disappeared into the great hall. He uttered an oath of infuriated triumph, then turned back to the queen as she scrambled to wrap her mantle around her. Confused and traumatized by the charade, she braced herself, afraid he might strike her, but he followed Gwirion. She sank to the ground, too exhausted to be frightened, almost relieved that the end had come.

Y OUR Majesty?" Owain cried incredulously, confused. He had been brought under guard before Noble at the hall hearth, and he stared stupidly at the net. "Yes, that's from my stream, and I had it out there with me, I was about to repair it, but I didn't . . . I would never assault—"

"Did you see me with my wife?" Noble demanded, his eyes an intense unnatural blue. He was standing near his captive in only his tunic, his hair in wild disarray. The queen was seated behind him, looking down. She had retreated long enough to don a long wool kirtle and surcoat. Her braids were disheveled and she was shivering from cold; at Noble's order Generys was fetching her mulled cider.

"Yes, sire, I saw you. I . . . went inside afterward." He cleared his throat awkwardly.

"Do you have any witnesses?"

"I was with Gwirion. He can back me up. I invited him in for a drink."

Noble made a dismissive face, but he signaled one of the teulu to summon Gwirion. His wife remained exactly as she was, her face grim but otherwise unreadable, her posture stiff. She did not glance up as Gwirion walked past her to stand before the king, and he made no attempt to communicate with her.

Noble stared at Gwirion. He stared back, his face the epitome of innocent curiosity. "Sire?" he asked. "I was just searching for the moon, they seem to have misplaced it. Is it time for the birthday celebrations?"

"I was assaulted," Noble said. "Tonight. I was by the stables—"

"I know where you were, I saw you," Gwirion said in a quick, tight voice, so cold Isabel thought Noble must realize at once who his attacker really was. Gwirion nodded with his head toward the shackled young man. "And you think Owain did it?"

"We are already aware of his extreme partiality toward my wife. And I was nearly strangled by that," Noble said, pointing to the netting on the floor. "He admits he had it out there. And I saw him flee."

After a flicker of hesitation, Gwirion said calmly, "No, you didn't. You saw me."

"You?" Noble smiled as though this was the beginning of some new game.

"What's amusing about that? You don't think I'm capable of assaulting you?"

"Of course not," Noble said with maddening affection. "But I'll indulge you. How did you get the netting?"

"He dropped it," Gwirion said promptly. "Ogling you. He left it behind when he went into the house."

Noble glanced at Owain. "How much did you bribe him to cover for you?"

Owain looked affronted. "I didn't, sire," he protested. "I don't know if Gwirion attacked you, but I swear it wasn't me."

"Well, it certainly wasn't Gwirion, so if it wasn't you, who else could it have been?" Noble demanded. He gestured, elegantly and vaguely, around the hall. "Who else in your household has your general build and coloring?"

"I would have to think about that, sire."

"Yes, do that. You'll think more clearly if you're not distracted, so to keep you from distractions you'll be put in prison overnight. You have one here, I presume?"

Owain's face contorted with disbelief. "Sire?"

"Your Majesty, may I speak with you alone?" Gwirion said through clenched teeth, taking a step closer to him.

Noble signaled Efan to bind Owain's hands. "Find out where the cellar is and take him down. Goronwy and I will decide on his punishment in the morning."

"*Sire,*" Gwirion growled urgently.

"In a moment, Gwirion. Efan, see to the watch yourself. Bring the prisoner to us after breakfast."

"What are you going to do to him?" the queen's voice said suddenly in the dark hall. She had risen stiffly to her feet but was still staring at the floor.

"I'm not a tyrant, Isabel, I do observe the rule of law. He'll have a fair trial in the morning, with the judge presiding." Noble glanced around at the random manor servants, guards, and teulu who had collected nearby to watch the drama unfold. "You are all dismissed.

Our birthday observations are canceled." Efan, towering over Owain, began to lead him from the hall. "Gwirion, we will not be using you tonight after all. I regret you troubled yourself with the journey for nothing." He turned to leave.

"Sire," Gwirion said again, barely getting his voice above a whisper. "I require an audience in private."

"Of course you do," the king sighed. "Come along, then." He gestured for his wife to follow them out into the misty yard. She stayed as far from Gwirion as she could without it seeming obvious, and resolutely avoided looking at him. He obeyed the unspoken edict.

Noble nodded toward the door to their room. "Go in, my dear, I'll be right along." Still without a word or look for Gwirion, she turned awkwardly away and went inside. The king glanced at him. "Yes?"

He hated that his breath was visible in the diffused moonlight, it would reveal his anxiety. "I did it and I know you know I did it," he said, his eyes feeling glued open. "I don't know why you're doing this but please don't bring that boy into it, he's innocent."

"Nobody is innocent," Noble said with a soft, bitter laugh.

"He didn't do it, Noble, I did."

"What you must understand, my perennial crusader against sexual predation, is that I don't need you to have done it. I need Owain to have done it. Therefore, Owain did it. You will not confess to it. Do you understand me?" Gwirion stared at him, shocked. The king frowned as if he was hurt by the look. "I'm not a monster, Gwirion, I am a monarch. I think you afford yourself the luxury of forgetting that sometimes." He patted his friend on the arm. "Get some sleep now. I think they've made a bed for you in hall." He walked through the dewy grass after his wife.

G WIRION found his ability to meddle suddenly stymied. He wrapped a brychan around himself and squatted in the moon-illuminated yard outside the king and queen's ground-floor sleeping chambers, as close to their small shuttered window as he dared, to eavesdrop. He heard Isabel insist Owain was innocent, but she would not name another culprit in his place, and anyway, the king seemed entirely uninterested in her protestations. Then Gwirion, slipping inside and down a staircase, tried to speak alone with Owain in the cellar—a room far larger, drier, and more habitable than the cell at Cymaron—but Efan the penteulu refused to cede them any privacy.

Gwirion tried, quietly, to share his wisdom with the imprisoned young baron despite this: He did not know what Noble's plan was, but he was certain that the way to foil it was for Owain to do the one thing Noble would never expect him to do: make a false confession. "Say it was a mistake, that you thought it was a vagrant harassing one of your servants, and when you realized whom you'd attacked, you panicked and fled. That makes it an accident, not treason."

"That's a stupid risk," Owain whispered, nervously, through the iron bars.

"He knows it wasn't really you," Gwirion whispered back. "His scheme, I think, depends upon your claiming it wasn't you. So if you *admit* it was you, somehow you will undermine his scheme."

"If I admit it was me, I will be *hanged*," Owain insisted. "If I claim innocence, there will be a trial and I'll be acquitted."

"That might be true if you weren't dealing with a tyrant," Gwirion muttered despairingly. Efan heard him use the word "tyrant," and with glowering eyes chased Gwirion from the cellar.

THE following morning after breakfast, Noble ordered one of the trestle tables left up, and he sat behind it, with porcine Goronwy to one side and Owain's own chaplain holding a quill to the other. Across from them stood the prisoner, hands bound, unshaven, unwashed, and generally the worse for his night in the cellar. Gwirion perched near Owain's household workers and the rest of the retinue. The queen was placed directly behind Noble, so that she and Owain could not see each other. She folded her hands in her lap and kept her head bowed, barely hiding how furious she was.

The simple questioning of the evening before was repeated for Goronwy. Owain quietly maintained his innocence, and Gwirion testified that he'd seen the baron leave the yard without touching the king. The warning look Noble shot him kept him from making an actual confession again. But then, it hardly seemed necessary: Within ten minutes the judge had acquitted Owain, who smiled with relief. "Now, Gwirion," Goronwy continued, "as you're our only witness—"

"Just a moment," Noble said, stretching and yawning in his chair with a deliberate informality. "We're not quite done with Owain."

"He's been acquitted, sire," Goronwy said.

"As the plaintiff, I'm questioning your judgment," Noble announced. "And so in keeping with the custom and the rule of law, it shall be decided on appeal." He swung his smiling face directly front toward Owain. "By your king."

Owain gaped at him in disbelief.

"That's outrageous," the judge announced, slamming the table with one stubby hand before he could stop himself.

"I'm certainly outraged," Noble said agreeably. "People shouldn't wander about attacking their sovereigns with fishnets. Owain, on appeal, based on the information available to us, I find—"

"I did it!" Gwirion said desperately. "Stop it, Noble!"

Noble gave him a sardonic look. "Don't interrupt, Gwirion, it's rude. Owain, I find you, on appeal, guilty of treason. Assault per se is only punishable by fine, but treason, as I suspect you know, is a capital offense. According to the law I would, ordinarily, have no choice but to hang you. But this being my birthday, I am inclined to indulgence, so I have decided to spare your life."

"Thank you, sire," Owain said in a voice choked with relief.

Gwirion, although confused, relaxed a little. But Isabel pursed her lips, waiting for the next twist, a twist she suddenly realized she should have seen from the beginning.

"However," the king continued, sounding very pleased with himself, "there is still the fact that you are capable of performing an act of violence against my royal person, and I must be protected against that. So your life is spared, thanks to my graciousness, but you are hereby banished from Maelienydd." Owain looked up sharply, horrified, and half the room cried out in shock: Banishment was almost worse than death.

Isabel, hardly knowing she was doing it, leapt to her feet and opened her mouth to protest. Noble glanced over his shoulder at her. "Yes, madam?" he asked in a lazy voice. "Is there something you would like to tell us regarding this travesty?"

She stared back at him, trying to calm herself. *Don't do this,* she wanted to beg him. *You will turn every baron against you.* But she realized with a sick feeling that she was too compromised to say anything at all. She shook her head once, hurriedly, and sat again.

The king nodded with approval and returned his cool smile in Owain's direction. "As you will be in Ireland—a kinder sentence, you must agree, than sending you to England—there is the matter of your property. As you have no immediate heir, since I doubt you've ever had an emission in your life, it will of course come to the crown, and the crown in turn is awarding it to the brotherhood of Abbey Cwm-hir. Seeing as that will make it church land, our friend Llewelyn is less likely to come trooping through it than he would if it were yours. However, against the unfortunate chance that he might stoop to such a sacrilege, we will write at once to the head of the brotherhood in Bordeaux and ask for a church-financed company to refurbish and garrison the old hill fort we spoke of earlier. They at least will certainly not be seduced by Llewelyn's siren call. Do you have any final words before you go to pack, Owain?"

Owain looked as if he would be permanently speechless. Goronwy was furious but silent; the king had done nothing outside his lawful warrant. Gwirion shuddered and sat down as steadily as he could.

Owain muttered something under his breath.

"What?" Noble asked. "Speak up, man."

"I said I didn't recognize you in the torchlight," Owain said, still mumbling. "I didn't recognize either of you. I thought you were some vagrants using my stables for unsavory activities. I . . . I attacked you and then I recognized the queen's face, and realized I had made a mistake, and I was frightened and confused, so I fled. I apologize for attacking Your Majesty, especially at a . . . moment of intimacy. I'm prepared to accept whatever punishment you see fit, but I hope you will bear in mind that it was an honest mistake. It was ignorance, not treason."

Noble rose in annoyance, and above the muttering that whirled round the periphery of the room, Goronwy quickly announced, "There will be a retrial with this new testimony." He sat up straighter and asked Owain, "Have you been coerced into making this confession?"

The young baron answered with a pained smile, "Only by experience, Your Honor."

"I hope that is the same experience that has suddenly convinced you to invite a garrison of my men to your hill fort," Noble growled.

Owain hesitated and glanced at Gwirion, looking torn. Gwirion felt the king's eyes on him too and his impulse was to turn and leave; the last thing he wanted was to become anybody's strategist, especially against the king. He knew no details, only that it was Noble's will against another's, and his was a conditioned response: He looked at the king for a moment, then glanced back to Owain and nodded.

There was the briefest pause and then: "The garrison will be welcome, sire, whenever they appear." Owain spoke in a voice of depressed capitulation. "I'll make sure my fellow barons know that your men are there by my own invitation."

"Yes, you will, and you will counsel your fellow barons against supporting Llewelyn."

Owain appeared to physically grow smaller. "Of course, sire."

"Thank you," Noble answered, instantly serene again. He resumed his seat. "That is a generous birthday gift. This has been a remarkably productive twelve hours. I'm only sorry," he added in a quiet aside, over his shoulder to his wife, "that Gwirion came all the way out here for nothing."

He gave her a knowing smile that froze her blood.

19

Tyrant Spring

April, 1199

GWIRION WAS SENT back to Cymaron, and the rest of the circuit was a blur to Isabel, a rushing bustle of public audiences in strange manor houses interspersed with private moments with her husband. Each time they were alone together she was certain he would finally confront her. He never did—but he adopted, at least in her imagination, an air of constant private amusement and she was certain he was gloating over her unease. He remained affectionate in bed, which confused her more than reassured her, although at Huw and Branwyn's he flauntingly spent each night in their hostess's bedchamber. His wife, too frightened to object, remained demurely silent. *He needs me*, she reminded herself with growing anxiety, *he needs me to secure English aid against Llewelyn*. In this corner of the kingdom, it seemed unlikely that anyone but the English would assist him to deflect the prince of Gwynedd: Huw was not the only baron to insinuate that it was solely Noble's pride hindering the bounty of Llewelyn's generosity. Noble needed his Mortimer wife. That was her security.

Gwirion, returning home directly from Owain's, retreated at once to his French primer with a sense of furious impotence. Without Noble's presence demanding his humor or Isabel's inspiring it, he was, he knew, a disappointment to the villagers. The days extended and the Easter feast passed without the usual antics of Cymaron's favorite comedian. The whole of the village and castle climbed up the high slope to the east of the castle, to breathlessly salute the sun with spiced bragawd cider at dawn on Easter Monday. Except for Gwirion. This was more than his usual mental hibernation; it was spiritual retreat.

When the royal party's return was trumpeted through the bailey, when the usual hustle began to fly the flag and strew the roads with daffodils, Gwirion simply disappeared.

He had not been discovered by the time the royal party made its celebratory entrance through the barbican. The castle and all the village turned out to cheer home their handsome king and his beloved bride. Noble was on his grey charger and Isabel behind him on a bulkier but smaller dun palfrey, her face veiled up to the eyes behind a linen travel kerchief. Even with the cold dust of the road on it, the king's garnet-studded circlet, the crown he wore for all but the most important state occasions, gleamed. His famous blue eyes blazed with a fatherly affection for his audience, barely masking ragged exhaustion. After their retinue had ridden entirely into the bailey and children had thrown flowers at the palfrey's feet, and finally the cheers had subsided, Noble relaxed in his saddle and asked for Gwirion. "I don't know where he is, sire," Gwilym said. "We summoned him an hour ago and I've had Marged's Dafydd looking for him."

As if on cue, the boy popped out of the stables, darting comfortably between the tired horses that stood waiting to be freed of their riders. He bowed hastily to the king and turned to Gwilym. "I can't find him, sir, but the pony he rides is missing as well, and all her gear."

The crowd murmured as Noble's eyes, and the queen's behind him, widened. Looking automatically back to the gatehouse, he saw the herald up on the wall walk start slightly at something just outside the bailey, something apparently on the road up to the barbican. The king reined his grey charger around to face the gate, and the crowd shifted with him. The trumpeter, after gaping at whatever had startled him, slowly brought the instrument to his lips again and sounded a few hesitating notes of fanfare.

Through the gateway, up into the courtyard, and straight to Noble's charger trotted Gwirion's little mount, with her rider standing upright on the saddle, bobbing with her gait and gripping the leather with his callused unshod toes, his arms held out to the crowd in mimicry of Noble's public greeting. This alone would have been a mild but risible gesture of mockery. But Gwirion had done something that changed the timbre of it dramatically: He had spirited himself into the king's coffers and was wearing the heavy crown that Noble saved for solemn ceremonial events. He'd also donned one of the king's red silk outfits, identical to the riding costume the king himself now wore. He looked absurd, the clothing too big and fine for him and far too regal for anyone to wear while standing on a pony.

"Thank you, my loyal subjects!" he crowed. "How kind of you to lay down your useful labor to spend an hour feeding my pride. You'll each receive a chicken for Christmas." There was a nervous titter from the crowd. Noble was thrown for a moment, then decided he liked the cheekiness of it.

"You do know that impersonating the king is a treasonous offense, don't you?" he said.

"Then you'd do well to stop it before I decide to have your head!" Gwirion said in a menacing voice. Although the charger was hands higher than the pony, Gwirion standing up found his head above the king's.

Noble gave him a droll look. "You're the real king, are you?"

"Of course I am," Gwirion announced loftily. "I have the bigger crown. And my head is higher."

"Your head will be a *lot* higher if you don't watch yourself," said Noble, straight-faced. He pointed beyond the curtain wall to the exalted keep tower. "Up there. On a pike."

"But may I keep my crown?" Gwirion said with sudden childlike eagerness. He took it off to admire it. "I would sooner have my head on a pike than give up my crown."

Worried anger flashed across the royal face and Gwirion realized his mistake: To the king's wary ears, it had sounded like veiled criticism, a suggestion that his insistence on retaining his kingship would make his kingdom suffer. Even Gwirion understood that was not for joking, and tried to change the tenor of the comment. "And why must it be my head?" he asked, loudly. "Impale me through the arse, milord, that would at least give your people something prettier to look at."

"What an excellent idea," the king said. Relaxing, he finally granted his friend a small grin. For Gwirion, the impromptu jest was over. He was about to dismount when Noble's grin mutated into a grimace. "Is that *all*?" he demanded. "Gwirion, you're hardly up to form. Spin it out a little longer, won't you? Perhaps do something with the queen."

"Pardon?" Gwirion said lightly.

"If you've stolen my crown you may as well abduct my wife," Noble said in a reasonable tone of voice. And smiled again.

The crowd guffawed in its unsuspecting, collective personality as a huge unseen hand squeezed Gwirion's guts and he blanched. He reached down to the pony's neck for balance and slid into the saddle, willing himself not to look at Isabel.

"I . . ." He brightened, relieved by the rare chance to be honest. "I already have! The day before you left! You had to bring her family all the way from England to rescue her, remember? Please don't press me to do it again, it truly was a *chore*."

Noble laughed. "Very well, never mind, then. Cadwgan!" He dismounted and turned his attention easily to other matters, and the invisible hand relaxed its grip on Gwirion's guts.

THE queen was somehow spirited through the hall and into her room before he even caught an indoor glance of her. Desperate for contact, he brought wine up to her solar. The door was closed as he approached carrying the small clay flagon, and the phlegmatic Llwyd stood to bar his way.

"Her Majesty has not asked to see you," he intoned.

"I haven't asked to see her either," Gwirion retorted. "I'm only here as wine bearer, under orders from the kitchen." That wasn't entirely a lie. He had been standing in the kitchen when he gave himself the order.

"Wait a moment, then," the man growled, and opened the door slightly. There was an indistinct exchange of voices and Gwirion blushed just hearing the muffled intonation of her accent. Finally Llwyd pulled his head back out and gestured lethargically for Gwirion to enter.

Gwirion stepped into the room, pulling the door closed behind him. Isabel had her back to him and was looking out the window over the russet hills, her hands clasped around her rosary. Gwirion, after a nervous pause, set down the flagon near her bed and went to her. She turned at his approach but did not move toward him; she looked startled, almost frightened, like a cornered deer. Gwirion pulled from his belt the silly, meager gift he'd made: a braid of oat stalks. Sheepishly, he took her left hand and placed the little token in it.

"The great god Llew and I have missed you very much," he said. In French.

She smiled hearing it, especially the way he mangled all the vowels. Then she burst into tears.

They were frightened tears and he hugged his arms around her to steady her and calm the sudden shuddering of his own heart. Her anxiety surely wasn't for their safety: Not even Noble could have affected such levity in the courtyard if he knew about them. He kissed her ear, brushed the side of his thumb across her lips, wished a primer for a prepubescent boy might have included even a single word of romantic endearment.

When she had calmed enough to speak, she nestled herself deeper into his embrace and said in a fatalistic voice, "He knows."

"No," he said reflexively. "I'd be able to tell."

"You haven't been near him for over a fortnight."

"Exactly, so there's been nothing to reveal us."

She looked up at him. "He knows you were the one who attacked him, Gwirion, he'd have to be an idiot not to know why."

He enveloped her in his arms again, gave her a reassuring squeeze, and smiled. "No, no, thwarting rape is in my bag of tricks. He doesn't question why I did that. In fact he was *relying* on my doing it."

"Yes, because he knows about us!" she insisted impatiently.

"No, because he knows about *me*. I hardly knew that stable boy, but I went to his defense, remember?" He tilted her head up to look straight at him, and said with quiet confidence, "I was just a pawn in his game against Owain. So were you. Please trust me. Every time his behavior makes you think he knows, I promise you, there's something else at play. Owain's was a perfect example. You don't appreciate his subtlety, you think he's playing one very simple game with us, when there are half a dozen games he's playing all at once with the world at large. Like marrying into Llewelyn's family—"

"That was a bluff to test us," she said firmly.

He shook his head. "No it wasn't, there was much more going on. And in the end, he cemented your popularity—he wouldn't have done that if he wanted to get rid of you."

She shook her head. "He did that for a reason and the reason isn't working. Even his most faithful are intrigued by Llewelyn now."

"You're still an asset and he won't squander that. Doesn't he need you for that repulsive scheme of his, to fight in league with the devil—I mean your uncle?" He gave her a tentative peck on the tip of her nose, wishing he could will away the little crease between her brows.

"I'm scared of him, Gwirion."

"Everyone's scared of him, he's the king."

"He's not acting like a king, he's acting like a tyrant. Roger Mortimer looks benign in comparison. I shudder to think of what he's become capable of."

With every atom of his being resisting it, he offered, "I'll stop coming to you if it would—"

She clamped her hand over his mouth, looking miserable. "I

know I should say yes, but I hate that you can even make that offer." She removed her hand and kissed him impulsively, slipped her arms around him, almost clinging to him. He was heady with the rareness of this, the simple act of standing up together fully clothed in daylight hours, embracing. Noble was an idiot, he thought bitterly, an utter imbecile, for estranging the woman whom he had a right to enjoy this way.

There was one loud rap on the door and they leapt away from each other, Gwirion frantically trying to remember his excuse for being here. He scuttled for the flagon just as the door opened and the king entered the room.

"Sire," they both said at once, sounding hollow. Gwirion stood upright, holding the vessel before him to make sure Noble understood the reason for his presence. Noble nodded to his wife, then crossed his arms and gazed at Gwirion with his head tilted to one side. "That was witty, what you did in the courtyard earlier," he began. "And you know that I would never curb your wit. But, Gwirion." He hesitated. "These are difficult days. It's fine for you to mock my office as long as everybody else understands that they mustn't. This is not the time for that."

"You're censoring me?" Gwirion asked, incredulous.

Noble looked very annoyed. "I've just told you I'm having trouble holding on to my kingdom and that is your response?"

He was instantly contrite. "I'm sorry, sire, but I don't see you having trouble. What you did at Owain's—"

"What I did at Owain's would never have been necessary if I were secure," Noble interrupted. "You have a wide array of targets, Gwirion, I'm requesting you choose one other than me for now. Content yourself with something safe, like fornication." He left the room.

The queen shot Gwirion a troubled look, but he waved his hand dismissively. "That was just a passing comment. Is *that* the sort of thing you take as evidence he knows? That's so . . ." He risked an impish grin. "So *French*. The preoccupation with romantic distress and all that. Think like the Welsh, milady. We're ferocious and verbose, but we're always very practical."

By day Noble became more and more insistent on the company of each of them, and they were both diligent in attending him. But the hours they gave themselves alone were what they lived for now, and for a week they were together every night. Isabel was still cautious and often troubled; she grew daily more convinced that Noble was aware of them, daily more adept at reading double meanings into his expressions—and yet daily more needful of her time with Gwirion to calm her. It was frightening, ironic, that she felt safe only in the arms of the one person whose proximity was dangerous. Their silent lovemaking was as intense as ever, but her craving for his nearness was almost independent of that—there was something soothing in his presence. When close to Gwirion, she felt more *known* than even God could know her.

She tried to believe his insistence that the king's behavior toward her had not changed. Certainly in bed Noble was as affectionate as ever, a detail she did not share with her lover. And during the day, he continued to encourage her popularity at court, among the local population, and at the abbey. Perhaps Gwirion's argument was sensible; perhaps her worries were all a trick of a guilty imagination. Perhaps, she fretted, but likely not.

Gwirion himself felt almost reborn, impervious and undyingly grateful to the God he'd never before taken heed of. That there could be no future, no development, in what they had together meant nothing; they had it now and now was all. They learned that they could speak in silence by mouthing words against the other's ear. One night they didn't even make love but simply lay together looking at each other in the candlelight, bashfully seeking expressions of regard. They knew better than to arrange another tryst out of her room, and reestablished their many silent ways of making love.

At least, they hoped their ways were silent.

T HEN one rainy evening, Angharad was relieving Gwirion at
       the harp; the queen reclined alone on a pelt rug before the fire,
pretending to do needlework and waiting for Noble to join her for
the evening entertainment.

Madrun very awkwardly approached her. "Your Majesty," she
stammered, "we have a request and are uncertain whom to petition."

"A request for what?"

Madrun gave her a sheepish smile. As the only member of the
sewing bevy with a lover, she had been deemed the most apt to discuss these things, but she was also the youngest and most easily flustered. "We would like to hang a second set of tapestries around our
beds."

"Is it too cold? Shall I have the chandler build a larger fire?" she
asked, giving up on the embroidery.

"No, milady it's for . . ." She lowered her voice and blushed. "It's
for the noise."

The queen started. "The harp?" she said hopefully.

Madrun shook her head. "After the harp, milady. When . . ." The
girl lowered her voice. "When His Majesty comes to you at night."

She could breathe again. That had been close but safely avoided.
And it was to her own advantage to grant the request, as long as she
didn't have to explain it to Noble—whom she suddenly realized was
standing right over them.

Seeing them in huddled, conspiratorial conversation, he instantly
dropped down to his knees to join in. "Good evening," he said, and
grinned at Madrun's blush. "I was coming over to talk politics with
my wife, but apparently I've interrupted something far more interesting." He examined the girl's embarrassed face with avuncular amusement. "Is this the talk of women? Is the fair Madrun suffering an
ill-mannered love?"

"No," the young woman said, smiling shyly. "Just an ill-insulated
sleeping chamber."

"I'm seeing to it, Noble," Isabel said firmly, holding her hand out. He gave her a funny look.

"This is a secret? How very intriguing."

"It's not a discussion for mixed company," Isabel insisted, desperately adopting the air of being Madrun's protector.

But Noble only smiled more broadly. "Then I *insist* upon hearing it." He grabbed a nearby wooden stool and perched on it, so that his head hovered very close above theirs.

"Madrun, you're excused," the queen said with a look at her husband. "I will explain the situation."

The girl bowed her head and began to rise, but Noble grabbed her arm and held her in place. "Oh, no, no, no." He grinned. "Half the fun is in watching her squirm. She's adorable." He looked beyond their heads at the figure who had been eyeing them from a careful distance, and beckoned. "Gwirion, you bore, come here and enjoy this with me."

The queen's hand moved instinctively to her rosary, and she had to fight the impulse to pray aloud as Gwirion joined them with a forced smile of anticipation. "Yes, sire?" he said, settling onto the rug across from Noble, a woman to either side. He nodded politely to the queen. As he lowered his eyes he noticed her hand fidgeting nervously with the rosary beads and he looked up quickly, examined all three faces. "What's going on?"

Madrun was by now that particular shade of scarlet achieved only by redheads. "Have you ever seen anything like that?" Noble asked, delighted, as if she were an exotic animal. "She knows a secret and my wife doesn't want her to tell us what it is. Go on, Madrun."

Gwirion hesitated for a moment, trying to grasp at once all the possible calamities that could arise from this encounter, to determine if his presence or his absence would be preferable. His hesitation cost him the choice, as Madrun began to speak, haltingly, cheeks flaming with embarrassment.

"We only wondered if you might like more privacy when you come to the queen's bed late at night, sire."

Noble started violently.

Then by turn he looked alarmed, enraged—and terrifyingly controlled. "Ah," he said shortly. "I see. We're making too much noise, are we?" He looked sharply at the queen. The queen looked down at the rosary in her lap.

Gwirion had to choose between fainting and scheming and almost made the wrong choice. But he pulled himself together enough to utter one short sentence. "What exactly do you hear, Madrun?" He had no idea if he sounded panicked, amused, or merely curious. The fact that he could speak at all was a miracle.

"Those . . . those sounds. Hard breathing. The bed moving." She was bright red again.

"Oh, *that*," Gwirion said with what he hoped sounded like a dismissive laugh. He brushed his hand in the air to show how blasé they should really be about the issue. "And maybe sometimes stifled groans with it, no doubt." She nodded, wide-eyed. "That happens all the time when I play for her. First she can't sleep and then when she does she has nightmares." He turned to Noble. "That's all it is. No offense, milady, but it's rather unbecoming, to be honest. I'd wake you but that would be presumptuous of me." He laughed nervously. "Perhaps the problem is my playing."

Noble looked narrowly first at Gwirion and then at Isabel. "You've never had a nightmare in my bed," he said.

She forced herself to meet his eye, and then harder yet made herself say, "That's true, sire. I wonder if you might allow me the pleasure of staying the entire night with you from now on."

Good girl, Gwirion thought, even as it wrenched him. Noble, still looking hard at her, nodded very slowly. His face relaxed gradually, shifting from anger to calm to something strangely vulnerable. He looked touched by her request and reached out to grasp the hand that had been fingering the rosary. With a small smile, he brought her fingers to his lips and brushed them with a kiss.

"I would like that," he said softly. "My apologies for thinking—" But she graciously waved it away.

"Well, thank the saints," Gwirion said after a brief pause, in a voice that managed to sound lively. "Maybe now I'll catch up on my sleep and capacitate my wit again."

"I hope a little sleep is all it takes," Noble said dryly. "Or I'll have to put you out to pasture."

"I always did like sheep," Gwirion said agreeably, feeling himself die inside.

"Is it sheep now? I thought you had a predilection for your pony—what is her name?"

"Jenny," Gwirion echoed, sounding wistful. "I once had a mare named Jenny, she was worth a pretty penny. But *then*, I met a ewe named Annie, and she had *quite* a darling fanny."

Madrun giggled, turned bright red again, and covered her face. Noble chuckled. "I hope you appreciate how quick his wit is, madam, however lame," he said pleasantly to his wife, and then back to Gwirion, "Keep going."

"I don't actually have a close acquaintance with much livestock, sire," Gwirion fumbled. He could see how shaken Isabel was by the king's comment, how clearly it seemed to have a double meaning to her. But he knew those looks: Now the king was in a purely impish mode. He wished that he could reassure her.

"What about girls, then? I can think of many girls you've known." Noble smiled. "Let's see—I think there was a Breila—"

"I once knew a girl named Breila . . . it was great fun to defile her."

"That was rotten," Noble said, making a face. "Yes, you do need sleep."

Madrun's face lit up: Young Ednyfed her lover, the marshal's son, had entered the hall. She rose tentatively. "Sire, do you require my presence any longer?"

Noble followed her gaze, saw what fueled her glow, and smiled approvingly. "No, run along. But, Madrun"—he held her back with his voice, and gestured for her to lean in so that he could speak softly to her—"you will not mention your mistress's nightmares to a *soul*, do you understand me? I don't want her embarrassed for it. Tell Angharad and Generys, and then do not discuss it even among yourselves again." His expression was unnervingly serious. Finally she realized she was expected to nod, so she did so, earnestly, and departed. He turned back to Gwirion and Isabel. The queen was the color of plaster.

"Gwladys," Noble said in a conversational tone.

"I once knew a girl named Gwladys," Gwirion tried shakily, "Whose . . . buttocks were loved by all the laddies."

"That's dreadful," Noble declared. "Go along to bed, then. I expect a full recovery by morning." He kissed his wife on her ashen cheek. "From both of you."

Gwirion was standing first. "Good night, then, Your Majesties," he said. He bowed and left as quickly as he could without actually fleeing.

"Isabel, are you ill? You're pale as fog." She stared at him, her fear too raw to hide or even control. She wanted to confess, it would be less terrifying than his toying with her like this. With a silent prayer for deliverance, she opened her mouth, and found she could not speak. "Isabel? For the love of God, what's wrong? Shall I call Madrun back?" She was about to faint. He took both of her hands in his, looking very concerned. "Let me take you up to the room. Can you walk?" She nodded, spastically, but had to lean against him to keep from falling over.

IN his room, Noble finally stopped asking about her health. Ignoring her peculiar fevered stare, he gently helped her out of her kirtle, which was already wet just from crossing through the rain-drenched courtyard. He slipped in beside her under the blankets. For actual sleep he usually wore shirt and breeches, like any Welsh warrior trained to be forever at the ready, but tonight he stripped entirely and wrapped himself around her gently as she lay facing him, without pressing further intimacy. The gesture was physically soothing, almost mothering, and finally, as he seemed about to fall asleep himself, she began to relax.

Isabel draped an arm over his torso as they lay facing each other, and her fingertips rested against the sleekness of his back. "Your skin is smooth," she murmured, grateful to have something natural to say. He had to know, it was too obvious for him not to know. But for some reason he was electing to be gentle with her now, and even if he was setting her up for a harder fall later, at this moment his behavior was genuinely comforting and she was in need of comfort. He made a purring sound of contentment and pulled her closer to him, tucking her head under his chin. The skin of his neck had the warm scent that had nearly drugged her with lust the first few weeks of marriage. That attraction had never truly diminished, it had just become dwarfed by all of the other things between them. She pulled back to look at him. In the candlelight she ran her eyes across the wide span of his shoulders, his beautiful broad lion's face, the well-muscled chest. He was a magnificent creature in a way that Gwirion wasn't, but Gwirion's touch incited something in her Noble's never had, something more personal than lust.

"Do you know," he muttered sleepily, as if they had been in the middle of a conversation, "how Gwirion saved my life?" He went on in a rambling tone as if he were talking in his sleep. "He distracted your uncle. Long enough for me to hide safely in the bracken. Then Mortimer tried to draw me out . . ." He paused so long she thought he had fallen asleep. She was about to pull away to roll over to her other side when he took a breath and went on, ". . . by hurting Gwirion quite a lot."

She stiffened. "Are you accusing Roger of torture?"

"Judging by the wounds," he continued, eyes still closed, voice still muffled and rambling, "they used everything they happened to have with them—he had been cut, and lashed, and burned, and beaten. And other things." The recitation was so casual he might have been discussing crop rotations. "He still has scars from it, old now, faded. But there's one spot that was lacerated badly, the skin was torn away, it was such a mess they couldn't sew it up quite right, and there's still scar tissue dense enough to feel. It's in the spot you're touching," he finished placidly. "You would feel it if you brushed your fingers over his back exactly as you're doing now to mine."

She stopped breathing and her hand despite itself pulled away from his skin. He said nothing, and she forced herself to return the hand, forced herself to draw a gentle breath, and waited for the next move in the game, to see in what droll manner he would finally confront her. She wished Gwirion were here for the unmasking, then was glad he wasn't. But she wished that she could warn him.

She turned her attention back to her husband in anticipation of the worst, and found that he had fallen asleep.

GWIRION feared that the king and queen actually sleeping together would bond them in a way that would make him redundant—not to the king, as he had feared nearly a year earlier, but to the queen. Since her return from circuit, the hours with her had been thrilling and sweet, and he relished recent memories all through that first night of many that he would no longer be called to her room. It was the innocent moments that nagged at his attention, not what made them lovers but what made them fond: the tilt of her head in the candlelight, the rosewater scent of her hair, her nervous amusement when he tried to stifle a sneeze, all the foolish little things he used to mock lovers for. He ached for them, but there could be no nighttime trysts now, and privacy in daylight hours was impossible.

The next morning, awake but still curled up in his blankets, he steeled himself for what would be the hardest thing now: that although he could not touch her he would be forced to be around her all the time because Noble wanted them both near him almost constantly. Gwirion cringed. It would be torture. He pondered morbidly on the new state of things. If they would never make love, never spend time alone together, never show affection or share intimacy in any way, then by definition, it would seem, they were no longer lovers. He felt unexpectedly disoriented by this revelation; he couldn't rest with it.

The king and queen were crossing to the high table to break bread after mass, casually acknowledging the morning bows of servants, when Isabel saw Gwirion from the corner of her eye and almost started crying on her husband's arm. The only sane thing for him to do was to dismiss her; she promised herself not to blame him for whatever coldness he had to show her. She gave Noble and their congregation a vague smile as the royal couple neared their chairs.

Noble released her arm, moving around the table to his seat, and Isabel blinked, stared at her own seat, then sat beside him carefully. She leaned back against the object that had caught her attention, hiding it from view: a single oat stalk, no bigger than a straw, had been placed neatly on her cushion. Gwirion did not otherwise acknowledge her, but she glowed with a private smile all through breakfast, and later wound the stalk gently around her rosary.

But as days wore on, the little crease between her brows became etched into her skin. He thought and hoped it lessened each time he was in her company. Still he worried for her; she grew paler and more withdrawn each day, bedeviled in a way that the king either did not notice or did not mind.

Noble had his own bedevilments to contend with. There was no word from Thomas yet, and rumors reached them that Mortimer, in defiance of the newly crowned King John, was gathering troops again within striking distance of the border with Maelienydd. The chaos of Powys and Deheubarth moved daily closer, and although Noble's barons had men to reckon with it, it was a constant tax to the collective manpower of the kingdom. Anarawd wrote several times, asking after the queen's health.

And then there was Llewelyn. The great Llewelyn, already both rebel folk hero and entitled aristocrat, Llewelyn who promised the Welsh a unified land again, entirely free of the English. All Noble need do to protect his people was to offer up his sovereignty. Gwirion wrestled no such demons; knowing that the king genuinely needed him, he unstintingly forced himself to perform his prancing wit, even when Noble listened with his wife upon his lap caressing him.

ONE chill sunset well into April, while the trestle tables were being set up for supper, Gwirion sat down at his tripod stool by the fire to play. Out of habit, he ran his fingers across the harp to remind himself what tuning it was in, but he arrested the movement as he neared the higher strings. One of them had some thin filaments wrapped and tangled around it. With a cluck of annoyance he began to unwind it—then realized he was holding several strands of Isabel's hair. He rested his head against the shoulder of the harp, tucked toward the fire and away from the hall so nobody could see him blink back tears.

During supper that night, a courier from England was admitted to the hall bearing a scroll with Thomas's seal. It was addressed, very formally, to Maelgwyn ap Cadwallon of Maelienydd. Noble eagerly received it in his chair by the fire as Isabel and the councilors hovered near.

He scanned it quickly and naked shock washed across his face. He read over it at least three times, the alarm in his eyes rising, then stood, flung it furiously to the floor, and stormed toward his audience room. At the door, he turned back into the hall, irritated. "*Gwirion,*" he said impatiently, as if Gwirion should have known to follow. The harpist leapt up with the harp and rushed after him. When the door slammed closed, the queen picked up the scroll, read her brother's message, and nearly panicked.

In the audience chamber, Gwirion curled up near the hearth on his usual cushion and began to play the descending arpeggios that were normally so effective at calming the king's wrath. Noble hardly seemed to hear them. Gwirion had never seen him so enraged—he stormed across the room, kicking aside the pelt rugs that lay in his path, and as he passed the settle he grabbed it and violently upended it, sending it smashing against the wall. He kicked the ornamented chest, growling, and threw himself with aggravation into his leather chair. But he couldn't sit; in a moment he was up again, knocking the chair angrily across the room as well. "That *whoreson!*" he shouted, "That weasly bastard *puppet!*"

"What's wrong?" Gwirion asked nervously, almost afraid to hear the answer. "Did Mortimer refuse to help against Llewelyn?"

"*No,*" the king spat. "He couldn't refuse because Thomas never *asked* him. Thomas went straight to John."

"And?" Gwirion prompted, not seeing the problem; surely having England's royal army on their side against Llewelyn would be helpful.

"He proved himself a loyal and useful subject by offering his services to John, to act on John's behalf—*diplomatically*—with Llewelyn, should the need arise. He explained that he was the best man for the post because he not only spoke Welsh, but he had firsthand knowledge of Welsh culture, as his sister was married to"—he was so angry he almost laughed—"his sister was married to a minor Welsh chieftain."

"Oh Christ." Gwirion winced. He had stopped playing, but Noble didn't notice.

"There's more," Noble went on, righting his chair and trying to sit, but still too agitated. He began pacing again. "He did, *generously,* tell John that the minor Welsh chieftain had offered to participate in limiting Llewelyn's progress, but," and here he impotently oozed derision, "they discussed it further and decided it was not in *England's interest* to accept the offer. They don't feel it would be appropriate to interfere internally, they want history to take its course. In other words they want to wait until one of us has subdued all the others, then ride in and demand that the victor submit to England. Thomas has just joined the growing ranks of those who *want* to see Llewelyn overwhelm me. The next time he sets foot in Wales it will be not as my ally, or her brother, or even Roger's nephew, but as King John's lackey." He sighed heavily and finally came to a stop. "She's absolutely useless now."

"What?" Gwirion asked, trying not to sound alarmed.

Noble shrugged with resignation. "I've done everything I can to keep her politically relevant, to squeeze some semblance of utility from the marriage. She's lost any believable value as the potential mother of my heir, but I thought she'd have some pull getting Thomas to work with me on Mortimer." He shook his head and settled into his chair. "That opportunity is gone—Thomas sold us to John's vagaries and he sold his sister with us. She's worthless."

"Your people love her. You made her beloved."

"That was probably a mistake," Noble said wearily, rubbing one temple. "I wanted to secure popular sentiment for the throne, and I did that, but I've also taught them that an outsider deserves their good regard. If they could come to love a Norman woman, they could surely come to love another Welsh prince." He leaned his elbow on his knee and rested his head in his hand, looking exhausted.

"They could love a Norman woman because she proved herself lovable," Gwirion said carefully. "Llewelyn has done nothing but enrage your subjects."

"That's only true here at Cymaron," the king corrected miserably.

There was a gentle rapping at the door and at Noble's weak nod, Gwirion admitted the queen. She looked fragile. This was the closest he had been to her in days; he could smell her scent and had to take a step away to keep himself from touching her.

This situation was, she knew, as dangerous to her safety as adultery was. Seeking something to say, she finally managed to stammer, "I'll estrange myself from Thomas—" but she stopped at an enervated gesture from her husband.

"That's useless, it does nothing but chastise him. He's not a boy anymore, Isabel, he doesn't care about chastisement." There was a long silence. "If I don't get a child soon, Llewelyn is becoming an option by default," he said at last, grimly.

She hurried nervously across the room and knelt on Gwirion's cushion, near the king. "What option is that?" she challenged. "You give up your sovereignty to him so that your people are absorbed into his united front, which will be broken up by John as soon as it's too powerful?"

"What is my alternative?" he demanded with quiet harshness.

"But Llewelyn isn't actually conquering by force," said Gwirion with a small grunt—needing something to do with his hands, he had begun trying to right the settle. "He's using personal persuasion. Make it clear to him you're not one to be persuaded and send him home. It's not as if he's planning an armed assault, it's not as if he poses the sort of danger Mortimer would."

Noble looked up at Gwirion in amazement. "Your grasp of politics makes *Enid* sound well educated," he announced irritably.

"What's wrong with what I said?"

"He won't have to use force against me because he'll find a way to win my people to him."

"Your people love you, they won't break with you," Gwirion declared, as if that ended the discussion, and dragged the bench back into the middle of the room.

Noble gave him the slow, hypnotic stare. "Won't they?" he asked. "You would be amazed, my friend, by what seduction can achieve."

Gwirion, afraid that Isabel would hear this as some sort of threat, hurriedly changed the subject. "Independent of my understanding politics only as well as Enid—"

"Not quite as well as Enid," Noble corrected tonelessly. In a dry attempt at levity, he added, "But then sometimes I think women have a deeper understanding of what it means to be overtaken."

"Noble," Isabel interrupted from the cushion. She took his hand, looked up at him. "Let me be useful. Tell me what to do."

He considered her for a moment, gave her a sad, paternal smile and planted a kiss on the crown of her veil, resting his chin on the top of her head. "End the treachery," he said quietly.

Gwirion sat down very hard on the settle, certain the queen would faint. Isabel tensed and barely kept herself from leaping away from Noble. She held his large rough hands between her own petite ones and said, with frightened resignation, "Tell me how to do it and I will."

"Oh, for pity's sake, Isabel," he said breezily, as if she were naive. "I was being ironic. Gwirion seems to have misplaced his own ironic powers, so we are trading roles a little, he and I."

That night it terrified her to even undress before him, but he was very natural with her, caressing her as always and holding her against him. He was the same considerate lover who had taken her virginity, who had gotten her with child, who had taught her everything about making love except what love was. His physical presence was so unthreatening that each night her internal siege alarms were calmed. If he knew, her body whispered to her mind, he would be too hurt and angry—nobody that angry could have been so gentle to vulnerable flesh.

THAT Llewelyn would finally send an emissary surprised no one. That the message would be a request for a sworn "alliance" was assumed, however odd it might be to ask it of an established ally. That it would be worded to present Llewelyn as de facto overlord was equally expected. What nobody foresaw was that the bearer of the message would be Cynan.

He arrived on a sunny morning a few days shy of May Eve, without his full teulu, only an honor guard of four swarthy mountain men. Gwilym was summoned by the porter; the steward came to the gate and discovered, to his disgust, that the baron from Gwynedd was entirely unchanged from his January infestation. He inhabited the bailey, large and jolly and this time well dressed, in an elegant blue silk tunic, red hose, and expensive leather knee boots. Those who recognized him either fled or skulked after his party in outraged disbelief. The castle children armed themselves with hoof picks, skewers, and flinty rocks, spying on him from a safe distance and earnestly believing themselves ready to spring on him to save their queen.

Poor diplomatic Gwilym envied the children the liberty to be enraged. His face an inexpressive mask, he grudgingly led Cynan into the great hall. By the hearth sat the king and queen in their high-backed, carved oak chairs, listening to Hafaidd's and Marged's plans for the May Day supper feast. Steward and baron made a peculiar duo as they crossed the hall: Both men were tall, but Gwilym moved with a sleek efficiency of movement in a direct line toward the hearth while Cynan, twice as large in girth, meandered energetically behind him, of a speed with Gwilym but covering far more lateral ground along the way. Hafaidd and Marged, recognizing him, took several steps back from the throne almost in unison; hall servants froze in shock.

"Milady!" he cried joyfully when they approached, before Gwilym could intercept with introductions. "You are a vision of beauty in your sweet Welsh veil!"

The queen turned an unpleasant color and her jaw dropped open. Noble, who had never seen the visitor before, glanced curiously from one to the other. Isabel closed her mouth and pointedly looked away, but she clenched her fists so tightly that her arms shook. Then Gwilym formally presented the grinning visitor and Noble closed his eyes for a moment, calculating how to handle this, enraged. He could imagine the prince of Gwynedd chuckling as he thought of it, and he wished he'd slit Llewelyn's throat when he'd had the chance. He opened his eyes again to study Cynan—Cynan who was waiting, knowing exactly what Noble was debating and determined not to let the moment ruin his pathologically chipper mood.

"It's an honor to finally meet you, Your Highness." He beamed.

Isabel caught the nuance of his comment and corrected him at once. "My husband is a king, Cynan, not a prince," she said stiffly. "You will address him as Your Majesty."

"Of course I will." Cynan smiled, and finally bowed. "Your Majesty." Noble looked at him unblinking. Cynan met the gaze comfortably, unimpressed.

"You must excuse the chill reception you're receiving," Noble said at last. He reached out and took one of his wife's fists from her lap, rubbed it between his palms to try making her relax it. "We have long memories in Maelienydd and your last visit left a sour taste in everybody's mouth for introducing us to the concept of betrayal."

Isabel shuddered. She was almost getting used to these comments, these potential threats, but she wished Gwirion had heard that one so he would understand that she wasn't hallucinating the danger.

"If you're worried about loyalty, Your Majesty, you might want to mind your northwest border," Cynan suggested offhandedly. "Did you know your young Owain ap Ithel is in league with my lord Llewelyn?"

"What?" Noble demanded, stiffening, his own grip tightening around Isabel's clenched hand.

Cynan grimaced cheerfully, reeking with mock regret. "It seems Owain was quite panicked, having some difficulty feeding troops—yours, apparently—who for some peculiar reason have been visiting a hill fort on his property. His concerned neighbor Huw ap Maredudd mentioned it in passing to my prince, and Llewelyn was pleased to lend Owain some provisions—in fact, I delivered them myself on the way here. Lovely lad, Owain. Not well stocked above the ears, if you'll excuse me, but your soldiers are very grateful to have their bellies full again." He smiled at the king, who had gone pale. Cynan raised his voice a little. "You see we're prospering in Gwynedd under my lord Llewelyn, we've grown used to hearty meals when our bellies growl. Even after I paid the fine you levied against me for our silly little misunderstanding, my pantries and cellars were full to bursting through the winter." He looked around the hall and boomed to all the hovering servants, "Do you like the sound of that?"

"You will not address my people," Noble snapped from his throne. He released Isabel's hand, almost throwing it away from himself, and leapt to his feet, barely in control of his mood. "You must excuse our rudeness, we have neglected to offer you proper hospitality. Hafaidd," he said tightly, and the usher stepped toward them again. "Find someone to wash the baron's feet. If you will excuse me, Cynan, I need a moment with my councilors."

"Oh, certainly, Your Highness—"

"*Majesty,*" the queen corrected, glaring.

"Certainly, Your Majesty, but you haven't even heard my message yet."

"Yes I have," the king said evenly, and gestured with his eyes to Gwilym.

For an hour the senior council met behind the heavy door of Noble's private audience chamber. Cynan, eternally amused by circumstances, wandered comfortably about the hall affecting interest in the well-being of certain female servants he remembered. Quiet, child-faced Nest had the misfortune of being assigned to wash his feet. Watching her, Isabel was overwhelmed by an uncomfortable combination of guilt and protectiveness, and when Nest had finished her task the queen excused her, and every other female, from the hall. Cynan at once turned his effusiveness entirely on Isabel.

She had never been fond of Efan, but she wished he were out here and not locked away in the audience chamber with Noble. The penteulu was the only man at Cymaron big enough to overpower Cynan; although Cynan had never lifted a hand to her in violence, she felt terrified of him. His breezy chatting distressed her as much as any threat would have, and by the time the audience-room door opened, she was severely dyspeptic.

They filed out somberly: king, steward, penteulu, judge, chaplain. "No bard?" Cynan queried from the middle of the room, and added helpfully, "We have an excess of bards as well in Gwynedd, if you need a good one."

Ignoring him, Noble crossed to his chair. He gave his wife's hand a reassuring squeeze, then sat straight-backed and silent, looking abstractedly into thin air. Cynan sauntered through the hall again toward him to resume his friendly conversation, but Gwilym stepped in front of him to stop him. The steward managed to present an officious-looking smile, hardly his natural demeanor. "You will speak to me, sir, not to His Majesty," he informed Cynan.

"Pardon?" Cynan said, surprised, but made no effort to push past him.

"His Majesty has many appointments to attend to. I will hear your petition in the receiving room and bring it to His Majesty's attention. Should I find it worth his while."

Cynan leaned back on one heel and crossed his arms with an appraising grin at Gwilym. "But my message is for the king," he said.

"If your prince needs to discuss matters directly with my king, he will be welcome to Cymaron at any time. If the matter is trivial enough to send a deputy, my king appoints a deputy as well. I have the honor of that office." The steward, without shedding his dignity, still looked uncomfortable. This was easily the longest speech he had given to an outsider in his life. "As a messenger of Llewelyn's, you are of course a welcome guest. Castell Cymaron certainly has the resources and the spirit to embrace you—and then to send you safely back to your very distant home."

Cynan laughed and asked over Gwilym's shoulder, "Did you compose this for him, sire?"

Without acknowledging the question, Noble kissed his wife's hand rather ostentatiously, rose from his chair, and walked through the hall toward the yard, Efan trailing him. "His Majesty does not have time to receive you just now," Gwilym explained politely. "He is organizing a supply train to his baron Owain's, now that you have been good enough to bring the message that there is need of it, for which we thank you. Will you speak with me, or would you prefer to tell your prince that my king is pleased to receive him in person?" His voice was uninflected and yet almost timorous.

"I would prefer to tell my master that your master refused to receive me." Cynan was pleased to hear the king's footsteps stop abruptly on the threshold at this declaration.

"I am receiving you on His Majesty's behalf."

"I wasn't sent to speak to you."

"Your posturing is childish," Isabel said sharply from her chair. From the doorway, Noble gave her a warning look and she pursed her lips angrily but said no more.

Cynan, to nobody's surprise, would not agree to waste his breath on one he deemed to be subordinate. Nonetheless, before beginning his journey home, he convivially invited himself to dinner, an invitation Noble graciously seconded. Isabel choked back her indignation, understanding her husband's choice and yet resenting it. The tension of the moment was making her begin to feel genuinely ill. She took Noble aside by the kitchen screens to ask to be excused from the meal for fear of being sick in public. He would not allow it.

"We want to slight him, don't we?" she argued. "My absence at table surely does that."

"We want to *invalidate* him," Noble corrected her. "Acknowledging that he has the slightest effect on any of us works against us now. You are the Lady of Maelienydd and you will not be cowed, enraged, or in any other way affected by a baron of Llewelyn's." He put his hand firmly on her arm and led her to the table.

Dinner was almost unbearable. She couldn't count, let alone name, the blur of emotions Cynan's presence provoked in her. Noble placed him with the lower officers at table, a subtle insult Cynan blithely refused to acknowledge. He was boisterously social with the room at large, and Noble in turn was unfailingly civil and charming to him throughout the meal. Isabel, although too shaky to mirror the king's suavity, forced herself to participate in chitchat. This was at first more to show up her husband than the baron, but Noble's obvious approval and appreciation calmed her spirit, if not her stomach. By the end of the meal, although she still would have preferred to be almost anywhere else, she sensed that she had carried some of her husband's burden for him. Even given the warped circumstances, it was reassuring to know that they could work together.

When the ordeal of the repast was behind them the royal couple accompanied their unwelcome, indulged guest outside to the bailey. The silent communal alarm over Cynan's presence was still in full force and people clustered around the courtyard, waiting for him to appear. Somebody tried to start a rumor that he would shrivel and die in direct daylight.

It was a spring day, still cool but windless and unusually dry and sunny; Isabel wished she had the presence of mind to appreciate it. The king had dismayed her by inviting Cynan to stay through the afternoon and overnight, suggesting that he might like to hear their marvelous harpist play. Cynan said, smilingly, that he was aware of the harpist's many talents, but he was eager to return to his beautiful, fair Gwynedd and his beloved prince. That was the first moment Isabel realized Gwirion had been absent since Cynan's arrival. She wondered if he'd heard they had a visitor.

His appearance, moments later, made it clear he hadn't.

The circumstances of their meeting were so perfect for catastrophe that half the castle workers in the yard were openly choking back hilarity: Just as Noble and Isabel were escorting Cynan down the wide wooden stairs into the bailey, Gwirion, doing the huntsman a favor, was exiting the kitchen carrying a large wooden pail of bloody meat scraps for the dogs. He stopped short when he saw Cynan and even took a small step backward, gaping. Everyone watched him, fascinated to see what he would do. He did nothing. He stared at the visitor without expression but unblinking, saying nothing, doing nothing. Cynan grinned and waved. Gwirion did not respond.

"We have a visitor," Noble called out unnecessarily. "An old friend of yours, to whom you owe your recent popularity. Why don't you come to greet him."

Gwirion, with difficulty, collected himself. He took a step toward them and Noble added, dryly, "Without the bucket, Gwirion."

Gwirion's eyes glanced from Noble to Cynan and back again. He began to lower the pail of meat slops. Then he looked between them at the queen and stopped lowering it. "Her Majesty is not well," he said with genuine concern, barely hiding how distressed he really was by her appearance.

"Her Majesty is absolutely fine," Noble said in a voice of deliberate offhandedness. "As are we all." His expression explained the entire situation to Gwirion as plainly as spoken words would have—especially the fact that Gwirion was not, under any circumstances, to misbehave.

"Christ, sire," Gwirion urged. "Let her go. She looks as if she might vomit on him."

"You're mistaken, Gwirion," the king said serenely. He turned to the baron. "We have so enjoyed your appearance, however brief. Do accompany your prince when he has the leisure for a visit. Are your horses ready? Put the bucket down, Gwirion."

Gwirion glanced briefly at the bucket as if he hadn't realized he was holding it. "Sire, are you implying I'd dump this gore all over him, simply because he's deserving of abuse? What do you take me for, a fool?"

"There is no license for fools today, Gwirion," the king said in a slightly strained voice.

Gwirion mused thoughtfully. "What about avenging angels?"

What happened next seemed physically impossible, but Gwirion did it. Still holding the bucket, he continued walking toward them, then tripped so elaborately that he either flipped or turned a handless cartwheel—nobody was ever certain which—and landed on his feet much closer to the three of them, the gory contents of the pail miraculously in place. There had been a collective gasp when the trick began, and then nervous laughter when he seemed to right himself. And then, in another move nobody ever quite deciphered, Gwirion himself was suddenly, spectacularly, wearing the contents of the bucket. Fat trimmings, gristle, stringy bits of rabbit flesh, and bloody juice covered his hair, his face, his tunic, his legs, and splattered onto the paving stones around him. It was somehow not so much gruesome as farcically outrageous, and Isabel almost started laughing from sheer nervousness. Instinctively she backed away from the three men.

"Oh, dear," Gwirion said quietly, blinking in the sunlight he'd just cartwheeled into and using a gory hand to wipe at his gory face. "I've made a mess of it."

He avoided Noble's outraged, killing glare and began, apparently, to seek something with which to wipe his face clean. The king immediately stepped in front of Cynan, but Gwirion nimbly veered around him and went straight for the long side-split skirt of Cynan's riding tunic. Grimacing, the baron pulled away, but Gwirion held tight and kneaded the smooth blue silk with his bloodied hands, then lowered his face to wipe it clean on the skirt panel. He had not actually gotten that much gore on it, so he blew his nose into it as well. Cynan tried in startled disgust to shunt him off, but Gwirion calmly grabbed the loose hem of his sleeve and coughed into it fluidly, leaving gobs of sputum, while everybody stood watching in stunned silence. "I suppose I ought to change before this dries on me," Gwirion said matter-of-factly, and trotted back into the kitchen dripping meat juice.

The king, using every jot of self-discipline to control his own fury, turned to Cynan with a forced smile. "You must forgive Gwirion, he's terribly clumsy, he's forever bumping into things."

Cynan's gaiety was replaced by a sour sneer. "I see." He nodded. "That would explain why the queen's gown was so askew after we'd shut them up alone together."

Noble's knife was at Cynan's throat almost before he'd finished speaking. The king threw an arm around the larger man, a violent, mocking gesture of camaraderie, although his face was a mask of calm. "Rephrase that statement."

Cynan glanced down at the knife, his humor instantly restored, delighted that he'd unnerved his host.

"If you don't rephrase that statement, I will give my good friend Gwirion the pleasure of opening your well-fed midriff," Noble informed him sternly. "You slander him and you slander the woman he risked his own welfare to protect." Cynan said nothing, just kept grinning down at the gleaming blade. "Gwirion!" Noble called out, and several of the servants near the kitchen excitedly went in to search for him.

Cynan sighed. "The light was dim," he said in a voice of concession. "Perhaps her gown was not askew."

"That's not enough," Noble said, and pressed the knife into his flesh.

Cynan gave a grunt of pain. "Her gown was definitely not askew. Her gown has *never* been askew."

Noble pulled the knife away and avoided looking at his wife, who had first blushed and then turned very pale. He shoved the blade back through his belt and slipped one arm around her shoulders with a private grimace, pulling her away from Cynan. He looked at their guest with a smile that was little more than a lifting of his upper lip. "I'm so glad we cleared up that misunderstanding," he said in a voice lifeless with civility.

He kept his arm around her even when she was revived, offering Cynan the picture of marital and state stability. Finally, after more supercilious ceremony than Noble engaged in when he really was sorry to see a guest depart, the baron was gone.

In silence, the king led the queen back into the hall, where Gwirion, cleansed and changed into one of his other cast-off tunics, was seated calmly by the fire tuning his harp. His hair was wet, and he had managed to steal some of the queen's rosewater so he smelled unusually floral; otherwise there was no evidence he had done anything this morning but rise from bed, get dressed, and settle into his usual routine.

The royal couple took their seats, which had been moved near the hearth across from Gwirion. There was a tension to the quiet: the deceptive, heavy calm before a storm breaks.

Gwirion nonchalantly sounded one string against its neighbor. "Is Her Majesty feeling any better?" he queried innocently.

She opened her mouth to answer him but Noble cut her off. "Yes, thank you, she's much improved. We established the source of her unease and she is now recovering from it."

"And what was that?" asked Gwirion, smirking into his harp. "An ugly visitor? A rude visitor? A villainous visitor?"

"Oh, no," Noble said pleasantly. "It was much more domestic. Her gown has been askew."

20

USES OF SOVEREIGNTY

May Eve, 1199

T THE DEADEST hour of the night before the dawn of May Day, Gwirion was summoned to the king.

Since Cynan's departure two days earlier, nothing had felt right. Noble hardly spoke to either of them, had not called Gwirion to play for him or make him laugh, never once expressed affection in public, or private, toward his wife. There was an oppressive, airless cloud around the king. Gwirion had been trying not to panic, trying to convince himself that this was the passing mood of a beleaguered monarch.

Marged's grandson, almost sleepwalking, stuck his head through the hole in the wall to wake Gwirion on behalf of the king, who sat writing by the hearth in the great hall.

"Sire?" Gwirion whispered as he stumbled out, cautious and befuddled. "What's wrong?"

Noble was reclining in his cushioned, high-backed wooden chair, across his lap a broad oak board that he was leaning on to write. "Nothing's wrong," he said. He carefully underlined something he'd just written. He was already dressed for May Day, elegant in the long green-and-gold tunic he'd worn a year ago to celebrate his wedding. He'd thrown a light green cloak around his shoulders for warmth, and as if color had a spiritual dimension, the brightness seemed to have affected him: He looked more relaxed than he had for days, perhaps for weeks.

"Shall I do that for you, sire?" Gwirion asked. Noble hated writing.

"No," Noble said offhandedly.

"Sire, I don't mean to pry but it's the dark of the morning and you rarely write your own correspondence and when you do, you do it in decent light in your audience chamber. What's wrong? Is this about Llewelyn?"

Noble looked up and smiled at him casually. "No. Nothing's wrong," he said. "These are just instructions for Gwilym about some minor changes in the May Day celebrations. Christ in heaven, I'm looking forward to an occasion free of politics." He returned his attention to his work. "Play for me while I finish, won't you?"

Some two dozen servants were trying to sleep, either beside them or in curtained cubicles, exhausted from the wild romps of May Eve around bonfires enormous enough to blaze despite the intermittent spring showers. Gwirion chose quiet melodies. He tried to convince himself that this was like any of the ten thousand evenings he had passed with Noble; the king seemed utterly oblivious of the tension of the past few days. A small part of Gwirion hovered upstairs, wondering which room the queen was in and wishing there were a way to escape Noble's attention just to be alone with her for a moment.

The queen's doorkeeper Llwyd descended into the hall, the man who for months had escorted him to her side believing that he was merely fetching her a lullaby. When he saw that Gwirion was already engaged, he crossed to them and bowed. "Excuse me, sire," he said woodenly, "but the queen has requested the harp. Perhaps when you are finished with him, he might go to her chamber?"

"I'm never finished with him," the king said. "But if I feel like sharing she'll be the first to know."

"Her Majesty is not in your room?" Gwirion asked, hoping he sounded disinterested. "I thought she wanted to stay with you because of her nightmares."

"She hasn't had them for some time now and she wanted to see how she might sleep alone." He elaborately added his signature to the letter, laid the quill aside, and blew on the ink to dry it.

Gwirion picked up his tuning key and slipped it over one of the pegs, hoping he did not look too blatantly delighted with the news. He sounded the string very lightly as he lowered it half a tone, and dissembled, saying, "I'm concerned about Her Majesty. If the nightmares prove to continue, I'm honored to be of service to her but I believe she'll need more than I provide."

Noble smiled a lazy, leering smile. "I think you're right about that." He folded the note over without sealing it. "To start with, tonight she needs a final good rutting to tire her out. So come along," he said, rising from his chair and gesturing to Gwirion to follow him.

"Sire?" the harpist croaked, staring, his stomach in his throat.

"Between the two of us, let's see if we might help her sleep."

"Sire?"

Noble gave him a puzzled expression as if he couldn't imagine what Gwirion was protesting. Then he grinned. "You filthy-minded little swine," he said approvingly. "I meant you be her bard, I'll be her lover."

"At the same time?" Gwirion asked feebly.

"Of course, like the old days."

"Those women were different. I don't think the queen would welcome—"

"Really, Gwirion, you must give her a little credit!" Noble laughed. He signaled toward the lower hall, and Gwirion was surprised to see tall, quiet Gwilym, who never showed himself in hall before mass in the morning. He too was already dressed in his bright May Day outfit, but he was hardly in the spirit of revels; in fact, he seemed quite wretched about the early hour. When he approached them, Noble handed him the note. "As we discussed," the king said lightly. "Ignore it otherwise." Gwilym took the note, wordlessly, and bowed. He did not acknowledge Gwirion; Gwirion thought he was too tired to even see him.

Noble nodded toward the stairs. "Come along," he said to Gwirion with a smile of anticipation. He hoisted a rush light out of a wall brace near the bottom of the stairs and began to ascend. Gwirion followed miserably, willing himself to faint if not expire. For nearly a month, he'd dreaded what was about to happen.

But then the king paused. He mused on something for a moment, and finally handed the torch down to Gwirion. "Go up without me, there are some more logistics I must see to here. Send her women down to Gwilym, would you? I'll be up in an hour or so."

Gwirion shook his head, confused. "You want her women down here? Now? It's hours until dawn, sire, why must they rise so early?"

"And when did you become the guardian of their best interests?" Noble retorted. "The steward has years of organizing May Day rituals. You do not. Please send them down, and tell my wife to be awake for me when I come up in an hour."

WHEN the grumpy, sleep-fogged sewing bevy had been dismissed to hall, Gwirion and Isabel looked at each other in silent amazement, thrilled and yet afraid to act on the opportunity. Finally she held out a hand, smiling in the torchlight, and he nearly threw himself on her. He straddled her, bent over her, covered her face with kisses, and nuzzled his nose into her hair as she squeezed him to her. Nothing in his life had ever felt so good to him. "An hour alone in a room with you and a bed," he whispered ecstatically into her ear. "I'm the most blessed man alive."

"Why just an hour? It's ages until dawn."

He tugged at her shift while she wriggled under his weight; she grinned and ran her hands through his hair, trying vainly to tame the cowlick. "He's coming up here in an hour," he murmured, and kissed her earlobe.

She froze, then with genuine terror pushed him up and away from her. "What?" she demanded.

"I was just downstairs with him, he said he'd be up in an hour."

"Are you daft?" she cried, pushing him away with something approaching sudden hysteria. "It's a trap! Get off the bed—get out of here, leave the room! It's a trap! You *idiot*—get off the bed!"

Gwirion stared at her, confused. She pushed her shift back down around her legs and sat up in the bed, straightening the blankets, trembling. "It's not a trap," he said at last. "Noble's traps are subtle. That would be too obvious."

"He's counting on us to think that," she insisted, slapping frantically at his legs to make him back away. "He sent me to my own bed tonight. He sent you up here alone, and he called my women away. And he let you know we'd have an hour. It won't be an hour, it will be any moment now, as soon as he hears incriminating noises."

"If he knows," Gwirion insisted, "he wouldn't bother staging something like this."

"Of course he would, it's more distressing for us that way. *Leave,* Gwirion, that's an order."

Instead of leaving he took a step closer to her and she tried to draw away, but he snatched her hands in his and sat on the bed beside her. "I gave you the wrong impression," he said in a soothing voice. "He was coming up here with me—he stayed downstairs at the last moment."

"That was staged," she said firmly.

He gazed at her pale face in the candlelight and sighed. "If his goal is to distress you, he's succeeding. And if his goal is to distress you by keeping you eternally on edge, do you think he'd ever actually confront you?" She rolled her eyes in agitation, but when he reached out to brush his thumb against her lips, she let him. He kissed her cheek. "We haven't been alone together for a month and you're still terrified every day, I see it in your face. I swear to you I would never do anything to give you more cause for that fear." She looked down and shrugged, a little reassured by his calm, trying to control her breathing. Tentatively, he perched on the edge of the bed and put an arm around her, rocking her against him. Her little body was warm and familiar in his arms, and he felt too glad to speak. She closed her eyes and let herself collapse against him.

He smiled down at her. After a moment, he reached under the blankets with his free hand and began to lift the hem of her shift, his pulse and breathing quickening. She stiffened and pushed the hand away, but he threw his arm around her, trapping her in his embrace, and rolled over until she was beneath him. Her face flashed fear again.

"Get off of me! You fool, it's a *trap*."

"We just had this conversation," Gwirion whispered, and kissed her on the lips. Isabel uttered a smothered sound of despair and yielded. His kiss, after weeks of missing it, erased the world. She reached for his bed tunic and he at once tore it off, while she fumbled with the string to his breeches belt and pushed the blankets away. They made love silently but frantically, an almost violent act unlike any coupling of theirs had ever been, his slender body driving against her bare legs and silk shift.

Afterward, at her insistence, Gwirion immediately drew away to dress, but safely clothed again he returned to her side and held her, rocking her. For a very long time, they sat in silence.

Then abruptly, whether it was nerves or gladness, Isabel began to giggle and Gwirion, because it soothed his soul to hear it, joined her.

They settled back into a comfortable silence.

He nuzzled her cheek with his nose and whispered affectionate obscenities in an exaggeration of her accent. She tried to teach him the French erotic phrases Adèle had never wanted her to know. He invented elaborate stories about all the livestock he claimed to have seduced since they'd last been together, and she laughed again. She rubbed her head against his chest and reached up to stroke his hair. "You should take a lover," she said. "I feel childish for resisting the idea of Nest."

"It's too late. You've spoiled me, I can't settle for anything less now."

"I'm serious, Gwirion. You need more than this, and it will throw him off the scent."

"Oh, yes? And he's ardently *on* the scent now, is he?" Gwirion asked.

"I'm telling you, this is intended to be a trap."

"How original," Gwirion mused archly. "To make us think we'd have an hour, and then giving us nearly two. That cunning lad. Whatever is he up to, do you think?"

"It hasn't been two hours."

"It's been at least an hour and a half. If the plan was to surprise us before we were expecting him, he's slightly tardy. And that, madam," he added, imitating Noble's affectionately condescending tone for the epithet, "is not the sort of error he would ever make."

Isabel sat up a little straighter. "I was wrong?" she breathed, relieved but incredulous.

A few moments later, they heard Noble's voice outside the door cheerfully bidding an early good morning to her doorkeeper. In one move, Gwirion slipped to the floor grabbing for his harp while Isabel pulled the blankets back over herself. They were a picture of innocence when Noble entered, carrying a second torch and smiling.

"Did you keep her awake for me?" he asked, closing the door. He rested the torch in a sconce near a window. "What a nuisance all these ritual details are. I couldn't wait to be up here at last."

Gwirion braced himself as Noble tossed down his cloak and moved to the bed. But he remained fully clothed as he slid casually under the blankets to lie beside his wife. "Ah," he sighed contentedly, warming his hands against her upper arms. She shuddered from the cold touch. "That's much better. Play us something, Gwirion. Play 'Below the Ford.' "

"Below the Ford" was the tune Gwirion had always used after supper to signal to Isabel that he would be available if she called him.

"I'm in the wrong tuning for that," he said quickly.

"We'll wait."

As Gwirion retightened the string he had lowered downstairs, Noble reached under the sheets and then up under Isabel's silk shift to stroke her hip, moving his fingers toward her groin. She stiffened and he stopped, looking mildly disappointed. But he wrapped an arm around her outside the sheet, spooning her to him in a half-reclining position, and she nestled in against him, reached down to kiss his hand. When "Below the Ford" was over, Noble called for "Rhiannon's Tears" and then two other tunes. Gwirion, to avoid looking at them caressing, played with his face bent so close to the harp that his hair nearly brushed the upper strings. Noble nuzzled his wife's ear. There was such a sweetness to the moment: the mildness of the damp spring night, the warm flickering of the torchlight, the dancing cadence of the harp, the silent presence of his dearest friend, and the soft, yielding, milk-smooth body of his wife beside him. And best of all, Llewelyn, Mortimer, and the rest of his concerns locked outside the door.

There was a comfortable silence when Gwirion finished the final song.

Then Noble ruined the mood.

"Gwirion," he announced genially, "I've decided you'll lead the Spring Rites this year."

His wife had no idea what this meant, but after a glance at Gwirion she knew it wasn't good. He had said it in an affectionate, indulgent tone, so she guessed it was something disgusting and perverse that Gwirion would once have leapt at.

"Why?" he asked, when he could finally find his voice.

"What are the Spring Rites?" she asked, looking back and forth between them. She had heard the term several times before, especially recently, and surmised it was some spring folk festival, probably involving large-scale, drunken debauchery, but the speakers—even Gwirion—always seemed sheepishly determined to avoid details.

"Don't be dim, Gwirion. Because of your derring-do with Cynan in January. You've earned it."

Gwirion looked completely at a loss. He moved his harp from one spot to another on the floor, fidgeting with it, trying to balance it upright and taking particular interest in the grain of the wood where it rested on the floor. "I don't think I deserve that honor, sire," he finally said with a nervous, self-effacing laugh.

"I make that decision, Gwirion, not you. You can't be telling me you don't *want* it."

"What are the Spring Rites?" she asked again.

"It just seems unfair to the girl," Gwirion stammered. "After all—who am I? She's expecting the king."

Isabel sat bolt upright, the blankets almost falling away from her. "One of you tell me what you're talking about," she demanded.

"Gwirion, you explain," Noble said, easing her back down against him.

Gwirion used his finger in a futile pretense of dusting out the lion's tiny ears at the top of the harp's forepillar. "We have a . . . tradition of sorts here."

"Don't tell me there's a ritual deflowering of a virgin," Isabel said.

"No, no," Gwirion said hastily—then hesitated. He continued swabbing the lion, trying to sound casual. He really did not want her to associate him with this story. "Well, that is, it doesn't *have* to be. What's important is that she seems . . . appropriately . . . fulsome. Fecund. For her night. With the king."

"What?" she said sharply, and pulled the sheet up to her neck, breaking out of Noble's embrace.

"Perhaps that sounds worse than it is," Gwirion said. He couldn't bring himself to look at her. "The girl is always willing—in fact, everyone makes a big fuss over her. She's *chosen*. No one's ever *forced* to it. It's just . . . something that's always been done."

"They say it guarantees a better harvest," Noble said, conspiratorially playful.

"That is the most superstitious, backward barbarism I've ever heard of!" Isabel declared. "That's absolutely *cretinous!*"

"What do you think *you* were?" Gwirion said impatiently, trying not to snap from the tension.

She gave him a look. "I was the king's *bride.*"

Noble laughed. "What was the date of our wedding, madam?"

Her eyes widened and she turned to stare over her shoulder at him.

"Not a coincidence." He smiled.

She was disgusted. "But it's not the same at all!"

"Oh, of course not," Noble said lazily. "You came here willingly to partake in an ancient ritual that would culminate in our bedding together for the good of the kingdom, but it's not at all the same."

For a moment she couldn't even speak.

"It's considered a huge honor for the girl," Gwirion said, trying to be helpful.

"Oh, yes, I'm sure it is!" she sneered, and elbowed her husband away as he tried to nestle up closer to her.

"Tell her the rest, Gwirion," he ordered, smiling.

"There's more?" she said, appalled.

Gwirion desperately wanted this conversation to be over. He was actually blushing. After an awkward pause, he explained, "Um. Yes. Afterward. There's a bit of a free-for-all."

"Oh, is that all?" she said with sarcastic offhandedness. "I had pretty much expected *that*." But she sobered. "And you participate?" she asked Gwirion, then added hurriedly, to cover, "All of you, I mean—everybody?"

Noble laughed beside her in a tone that made both of them wince. "There have been years at a time when May Day has provided Gwirion his only stab, so to speak, at female flesh."

She looked away. There was nothing she could say in front of Noble, but Gwirion read her silence and it made him heartsick. He rested his head on the shoulder of the harp as if it were a person who might comfort him.

"However, this year," Noble continued grandly, "he takes the honors." He leaned down over her and murmured in her ear, "King's prerogative, to appoint a proxy for the main event, when there's a deserving champion."

Gwirion immediately protested, "Sire, I told you that I don't want—"

"I visited the girl tonight," Noble went on, as if Gwirion hadn't spoken. "She's staying with Cadwgan's family. She's very pretty, a little like that hall servant who took a fancy to you, but more flirtatious. I'll—"

"Thank you, sire, but I am respectfully declining the honor,"

Gwirion said, and lifted his tuning peg from his belt again to fiddle with the harp pegs.

"No you're not," Noble informed him, his cheeriness abating slightly. "This isn't a dinner invitation, it's a sacred tradition."

"It's not *sacred*," Gwirion said. "It's actually *profane*."

"That makes you the perfect acolyte," Noble retorted. "You're profane."

"I'm working on that," Gwirion muttered under his breath, fidgeting with the peg of the lowest string.

"Yes, I've noticed, and I wish you wouldn't, it makes you a dreadful bore," Noble said. "But you see, *I* mustn't do it anymore." He looked down at Isabel with a sly expression. "My wife resents it when I stray."

"I would make an exception if you strayed for the proper reasons," she said with forced levity.

Noble pushed her shoulder down, twisting her supine onto the bed. He hovered over her with an intrigued expression. "Would you?" he said, imitating her tone. "And what would you consider a proper reason to stray from the royal marriage bed?"

She blanched and stammered up at him, "Whatever is in service to the throne, sire. We know I'm damaged and you need a son. Don't let my harping on monogamy come between you and our people's expectations." He looked impressed by the response, and she continued, a little more confidently, "If you really consider it imperative that Gwirion stand in for you, I've no objection and I can't fathom why he would, but I would think the need to get a royal heir comes before offering Gwirion an hour of pleasure he seems too squeamish to accept."

He gave her a searching look, seeking something beyond her words. Finally he released her and smiled, patiently. "Well spoken. Gwirion, you will simply participate as you always have in the bacchanalia."

The chance to be alone with her again—while the entire castle was distracted—was too tempting. "I don't want to do that either, sire," he said cautiously. Noble started.

"No, Gwirion, that is going too far! It would hardly be worth it without you there." Almost out of the side of his mouth he told his wife confidingly, "Gwirion at such a gathering is a thing of wonder."

"I'm sure I'd like to see that, sire," she said with a wan attempt at humor.

Gwirion hesitated. "You must excuse me, sire, I've no desire to participate at all."

The king stared at him. "Yes you do," he said sternly.

"No, I don't." He tried to meet Noble's eyes as they bored into his but he couldn't, and turned his attention again to fidgeting with the harp pegs. Somehow, he had to pass this off as his usual contrariness.

Noble suddenly sat up and threw the sheets off himself with such vehemence that he almost uncovered his wife as well. She scrambled to reclaim a blanket, passably pretending to be shy of Gwirion's eyes upon her. Noble leapt up from the bed, and with quick, controlled steps swung down around the foot of it to stand over Gwirion. "Listen to me," he said in a threatening voice. "You will attend tomorrow. Of your own volition. You will enjoy it."

"Is that an order?" Gwirion asked with an edgy laugh, still pretending to tune.

"It shouldn't have to be—don't make me order you," Noble said. "You ass. Do you know what thin ice you stand on right now?"

"No, but I'll retreat at once to solid ground," Gwirion offered with nervous pleasantness. "And pen myself up in the kitchen tomorrow night."

"Why are you being so contrary, Gwirion?" Isabel asked in the most offhand tone she could affect. She risked a pleading glance at him but he didn't see it.

Noble's expression darkened, but she saw a flash of desperation behind the anger; then it was brushed away. "Aren't you man enough to handle it?" he taunted.

"Aren't you man enough to handle it without me?" Gwirion taunted back as if they were playing at bickering. "Why are you so desperate for my presence?" He fluttered his lashes at the king. "I'm hardly equipped to receive your particular attentions for the evening."

"That is not the point!" Noble thundered. He snatched the tuning key from Gwirion's fingers and hurled it furiously across the room. "You don't know what you're meddling with! For the love of the saints, behave yourself!"

"Is that an order too?" Gwirion prayed for any graceful way out of this standoff. He hoped his frantic pulse was not actually audible.

The king stared at him for a moment, looking troubled. Then: "I am leaving now," he announced with deliberation, his voice trembling with tension. "You will remain here and play for Her Majesty. Later today, you will attend the Spring Rites with me."

"And if I don't?" Gwirion asked, desperately clinging to the pretense of banter.

Seeing Noble's eyes widen with annoyance and frustration, Isabel immediately announced, "You will attend, Gwirion," but the king turned on her, outraged.

"*Be quiet!*" he ordered. "Ignore her, Gwirion! You will not choose to go because *she* told you to. Do you understand? You are not to do her bidding. This is your own free decision and your own free decision is to attend."

Despite the strain, Gwirion laughed nervously at the absurdity of this. The laughter snapped some final string holding Noble's fury in check; he lunged at the harpist and snatched the harp from his hands. He clutched it high over his head and for a moment seemed about to smash it down on Gwirion. Gwirion stopped laughing at once and cowered.

Noble turned and in three long, sure strides had crossed to the window—and hurled the harp out into the grey dawn air.

Gwirion leapt to his feet in disbelief and cringed as the sound of splintering wood and snapping strings echoed faintly up to them from the bottom of the castle mound. He raced toward the window but Noble stepped in his way and caught him, an outstretched hand grasping each arm. "Now," the king said, devoid of all expression. "I am leaving. You will remain here and play for the queen and later today you will attend the Spring Rites with me. *Do you understand?*"

Isabel did, and shuddered, drawing the sheet up around her as if it could somehow give protection, but Gwirion just looked confused. "How can I play?" he cried plaintively. "You just destroyed my harp!"

"My harp," Noble corrected at once, and pushed him back toward the bed, shoving him down so that he nearly fell on Isabel.

Gwirion sprang back scowling. "Bastard!" he spat. "That was your father's harp, Noble! *Bastard.*"

"Come with me to the Rites and I'll give you a new harp."

Again Isabel thought she saw desperation behind the firm expression in her husband's eyes. "That sounds like a fair exchange," she said in a cajoling tone to Gwirion.

"That harp was irreplaceable!" he protested furiously.

"Dammit, you idiot!" Noble shouted, and grabbed him by the high collar of his tunic, shaking him. He jerked the fool toward him so their faces were very close; they could feel each other's breath. "I don't care if you sit in a corner and sulk the whole time, you must attend!"

Gwirion twisted away from him, shrugging and shuddering as if his touch were repellant. "*Why?*" he demanded.

Noble abruptly slammed the back of his hand against Gwirion's mouth. Isabel cried out as Gwirion collapsed to the floor, both hands cupped around his jaw. Noble grabbed him like a shepherd would a wayward sheep and hauled him impatiently onto the bed. "Because," the king hissed through clenched teeth, inches from his face, "you are *expected*. If you do not attend, people will talk. If you do not attend because you are in this room, people will do more than talk—people will *know*, and, Gwirion, I am trying very hard to keep people from knowing. Do not further rob me of incentive." Then, very softly, almost a whisper: "And *damn you*, Gwirion, for bringing me to this."

They both stared at him in horrified silence, Gwirion dumbfounded, Isabel resigned and pale. Noble sighed, looking both exhausted and annoyed. He released his captive and took a heavy step away from the bed.

Gwirion cradled the side of his face, his tongue feeling thick in his mouth. He swallowed and made the mistake of playing innocent. "What do you mean, sire?" he asked timorously.

Instantly ignited again, Noble whirled around, grabbed the front of Gwirion's tunic and hoisted him up until he teetered on his toes for balance. "You have one opportunity to cease insulting me."

"But how am I insulting you?" Gwirion babbled, tasting blood behind his teeth. Isabel closed her eyes in defeat.

The king's jaw clenched. "You have now wasted the opportunity," Noble informed him. "You stupid wretch." He shoved Gwirion hard onto the bed, glaring at him, then pulled his dagger from his belt and smacked it against Gwirion's chest, pressed the point hard against his heart. Gwirion stared down at it, stunned, not quite believing this moment had arrived. Noble looked at him furiously— but far more than that, with sorrow, and for a moment Isabel, watching them, thought she was looking at the face of amnesty. Then, too fast for her to see it happen, the blade flashed up and cut into the skin of Gwirion's temple, exactly where the childhood scar was, the scar she'd noticed the first time she'd watched his sleeping face. As badly shocked as pained, Gwirion clamped one hand to the wound, cursing. He stared in disgusted terror at the king.

"Is that not both poetic and economical of me?" Noble demanded with satisfaction. "The first wound you survived and the last wound you'll survive, on the same small patch of flesh? You will *not* survive another wound from me."

Isabel tore at her shift, ripped away a piece of silk from the skirt and pressed it hard against Gwirion's bleeding forehead. Noble slapped her harshly and she recoiled. Gwirion, dazed, tried to move between them to protect her, but the king pushed him aside. "*You* are a very foolish child," he told his wife angrily. He settled on the foot of the bed, facing them, and sheathed the dagger. His taut face transformed immediately, unnervingly, into a personable, almost chatty aspect. "Shall we begin negotiations for surrender? There's so much to consider and dawn will be here soon." Only his breathing, shallow and quick, betrayed his real mood now.

For a long moment there was silence. She gave Gwirion the piece of silk to press against the wound himself. "Move away from him," Noble suggested in a conversational voice, which under the circumstances was more distressing than an outright threat. She retreated several feet, still under the blankets.

"How long have you known?" she asked at last.

Gwirion could not speak. His distress, Noble noted with grateful satisfaction, was much more complicated than hers was. He, at least, still loved the man they'd wronged.

"A long time," Noble answered. "But you knew that, of course, I made it very clear to you." He gave her a chill smile. "And then, sometimes, I didn't."

"What gave it away?"

"I suppose Gwirion *telling* me the moment I returned from the front raised my suspicions—"

"You didn't believe me," he objected in a reedy voice.

"True," Noble said. "It took at least three minutes of watching you both gawk stupidly at me to wonder if there might be something to it." He saw the expression on his wife's face, outraged castigation aimed at Gwirion. Noble smiled at her. "But, my dear," he went on, "the honors for giving it away go all to you. I offered you a cure for an insomnia you'd never had—and suddenly you had it nearly every night."

She pursed her lips. "Why did you do that?"

He shrugged. "I was curious to see what would happen—you cannot deny the inherent fascination of the situation for me. I was sure the whole thing would explode in your faces, and once it was safely behind us I could tease you about it. But it didn't explode. And then I realized it was more than merely lust. Which is when it all became so interesting. You're each in your way the two most honest people I know—Gwirion to the point of cruelty and you to the point of boredom. Two honest people being dishonest is a fascinating thing to watch. Most of the time, I was impressed, and I was almost always entertained. I had some brilliant moments along the way myself, driving you to distraction."

"And what did it serve to do that to me?" she demanded.

He gave her a smile of private meaning. "It was a *whim*."

"You said you never indulge whims."

"Usually I wouldn't. Usually I wouldn't indulge cuckoldry either. Obviously I made exceptions. I did what I required to keep myself sane—I've had a kingdom to tend, you know, we haven't all had the luxury of making this adultery the center of our lives. But generally, I've been having a grand time with it. I could have kept it going for years, maybe forever."

"Then why this now?" she asked.

"To begin with, you're both becoming sloppy, and I can't risk that any further. You might at least have practiced enough discretion so as not to insult my office—if I may paraphrase you, my dear. But far more urgent, to be honest, is how you're ruining him. I can't condone that any longer. The Spring Rites were suddenly upon us and I realized that would be the touchstone, so I had to act." He made a gesture that was at once self-deprecating and self-satisfied. "I believe His Majesty has been a paragon of thoughtfulness. I deliberately gave you a final hour alone together tonight—I do hope you took advantage of my generosity. And I never once succumbed to the obvious temptation of making him watch us, I never once summoned him to serenade our mating—although believe me, I have considered it almost every evening." He turned his complacency on Gwirion. "This is hardly a significant detail, but my male pride compels me to inform you that nothing matches the ardor of an unfaithful woman trying to distract her husband from her unfaithfulness. I've been very satisfied by her this month and I have satisfied her greatly in return." He smiled at Gwirion and concluded, "While you have not."

"What are you going to do with us?" Isabel asked before he could prolong the taunting.

"With *us*?" he echoed, amused. "Are you under the delusion that the two of you are a unit? I shall do something with you and something with him, but there is no more *us* between you as of this moment. Is that understood?" He took Gwirion's face in one hand and lifted it toward him. "You understand that, don't you?" Gwirion stared at him, still too distressed to speak. After a moment, satisfied, Noble nodded.

With a small flourish, he again unsheathed the dagger and displayed it to them like a child revealing a personal treasure. "This small piece of metal," he informed them, "goes by many names: dagger, stiletto, dirk, dudgeon. It's intended to rend flesh. Human flesh. It is not a hunting knife, nor is it used to slaughter livestock."

"We know what it's used for," Isabel said impatiently. She pressed the torn bit of silk more firmly to Gwirion's bleeding forehead; he had forgotten it entirely.

"This particular dagger," Noble went on, gazing at it fondly and ignoring her, "was given to me by my father a week before he was cut down by your despicable uncle. I held it sitting in the bushes nearly twenty years ago wishing I could slit Roger's throat. It was forged by the grandfather of our current smith, and despite its simplicity there is a genuine grace and elegance—"

"For the love of God!" she snapped. "If you're going to kill us with it, just—"

"Not *us* again," Noble said with a chastising smile. "I told you, no more us. You may say, 'If you're going to kill *me* with it—'"

"If you're going to kill me with it, just get on with it," she said between clenched teeth. Angrily, she slipped her shift off, pushed the sheets away, and kneeled upright beside him, nude, her arms at her sides, her hair cascading heavily behind her and her head held back slightly. "Here's my heart and here's my throat. I'm sick of your Celtic verbosity."

Noble laughed with genuine affection and glanced at Gwirion, who was still staring at them both slack jawed. "She's quite marvelous, isn't she?" He looked back at her. "Since you offered, you may assist my presentation. If I were to use it this morning, I would have a variety of options. Sit."

He pulled her down so that they all faced each other in a triangle, but he kept his free hand cupped hard around her arm. "The uses of a dagger," he intoned didactically, regarding with dreamy reverence the one he held. "First, of course, there is the resource of the cutting blade. This would most commonly take the form of slitting the throat." He whipped the dagger up toward her bare white neck and Gwirion impulsively grabbed at it. Noble pushed him away without effort, elbowing him in the stomach so that he staggered back against the edge of the bed trying to breathe. "It's just a demonstration," Noble said. "Don't become hysterical." He turned back to her and lightly drew the blade across her throat where a lethal slice would be made. She took a sudden breath when she felt the metal cold against her, but did not flinch. "There is also the tip, which offers us a number of options. First, the straightforward piercing of the heart, which might have a certain poetic appropriateness here." He rested the tip of the blade against the meat of her left breast and pressed it just enough to dimple the flesh. Gwirion sat staring, worried that any gesture at all from him would push the king too far. Isabel didn't move. She did not look at the blade, just gazed at Noble with a look that was both calm and vulnerable.

"Of course," Noble went on, removing the dagger and turning her to sit with her profile to them, "an approach with greater resonance would be the stab in the back." He pointed the blade just to the left of her spine, and pushed a little harder this time so that blood rushed to the skin. She winced slightly, which made Gwirion sit up in alarm. Noble lowered the dagger. "You handled that very well," he announced as she turned back to face them. "I was quite tempted to go ahead with it."

"I know," she replied. "But since you didn't, would you please tell me what you are going to do instead?"

"But you are hard!" he said with feigned dismay. "When did you come to be so hard?" She waited, unspeaking, and he nudged her. "Tell me your preference." She said nothing. "Let me guess, then. You with your dreary English artlessness—you would just want a straightforward direct hit, wouldn't you? Obvious and efficient."

"I doubt you're capable of straightforwardness," she replied. "I am still waiting for an answer."

"Answer?" Noble frowned. "Ah, yes—what am I going to do

with you? Let me ask you the same question: What were you planning to do with yourselves if I hadn't interfered?" Neither of them spoke, and after a moment he sighed with apparent satisfaction. "Well, at least there was no full-scale conspiracy going on. That puts you on a *slightly* higher plane than those whose betrayals are merely political. I must admit that's reassuring." Without relinquishing his flip exterior, he sobered a little. "I, on the other hand, am somewhat organized. We must consider the situation in a larger context, beginning with an enumeration of each sinner's sins. Not that you are devout, Gwirion, but the commandments are not to be broken lightly. Thou shalt not covet thy neighbor's wife. Have you heard that one? Thou shalt not bear false witness?"

"Thou shalt have no other gods before me," Isabel interrupted. "Which is really the only sin he can commit against you."

"Tut, my darling, you verge on sacrilege," Noble said mildly. "But certainly, an examination of your sins gives us more cud to chew. You've taken a lover out of wedlock. You've compromised the sanctity of the womb that is supposed to conceive my heir. You've stolen the affection of my closest friend. But really, at the end of it all," he concluded, a little smile creating the passing deception that he might forgive her, "your worst offense, madam, has been your womanly effect on him. I warned you last September not to become the agent through which I could ever lose him. As I said, I might have been willing to endure the infidelity if you hadn't ruined him in the process."

"I haven't ruined him," she argued. "He's a man, Noble. He used to be your puerile little shadow and now he is his own man."

"What good is that?" Noble demanded. "My court is full of men, why couldn't you have taken one of them? Did you ever consider that I might *need* him as a puerile little shadow? Why did you have to *mature* him?"

"I matured myself," Gwirion protested, finally finding his voice.

"Ha!" Noble said with amused disbelief. "The maturity of dumping meat slops on oneself to defend the honor of one's mistress." He turned his full attention, his glittering blue eyes, back to Isabel. "So, madam, those are your sins. As I still have some regard for you, I would prefer to find a way to absolve you of them, and with that in mind, it seems to me that it is in your best interests—and mine too, perhaps—for me to free you of the bonds of matrimony."

She gaped at him, and even Gwirion drew in a breath. "Free me?" she asked.

"If you were not my wife, then most of those offenses would fall away."

"But can you . . . do that?" she asked. "The church won't grant a divorce."

"Welsh law would. What a pity you insisted we be married under canon law." He shrugged. "We must try a different course."

"Annulment?" she ventured, trying to understand his meaning.

"Do you desire that?" he responded.

"Annulment?" she repeated. What had once terrified her was suddenly a panacea. "How? Will the church agree?"

"If you and I both desire it, as royal citizens of a true state of Britain, there are steps we may take together to enact our own annulment, so that the church will have to acknowledge our uncoupling. But I need your full willingness."

"We would be annulled?" she said, as if she could not get the idea to stay in her mind. "You would agree to it?"

"I certainly agree to take steps toward it," he answered. "We began this in good faith, but it seems to have brought nothing but trouble for everyone." He smiled gently at her and brushed the back of his hand against her cheek. The gesture was so uncharacteristic, so intimate, so simple and sincere, that Gwirion looked awkwardly away, feeling like an intruder. "And I'll make sure you're taken care of. You will never go hungry or homeless, you have my word."

"What are the conditions?" she asked, as a year of seasoning prodded her to be skeptical.

Noble shook his head. "No conditions. I want Gwirion to stay with me, not go with you, but that is his choice too."

Gwirion was stunned. "If I chose—" he began, but hesitated. Noble nodded, grimly.

"I have little experience in granting you freedom, but I want to redress the failing. So it will be your choice."

Gwirion blinked in amazement, but Isabel warily pressed on. "And how do we go about initiating this annulment?" she demanded. She tried not to sound too eager. It could not possibly be this simple.

"We don't petition the church," Noble answered. "We go directly to the source." She frowned at him, uncomprehending, until he said: "God loves beauty, and I doubt He can resist a pretty face. So you are going to petition him directly." He smiled at her with a sudden intensity that unnerved her. "And you are going to do it now."

"No!" Gwirion screamed, understanding, but she frowned in confusion even as Noble rushed her with the dagger and sank it through her breastbone. As she realized what was happening, it was shock more than pain that washed over her face. The king made a strange sound between a cry and a laugh and kissed her hard on the lips.

Gwirion, after a moment of horrified inertness, leapt at Noble to pull him away. Like an enraptured acolyte in some arcane religious ritual, Noble pushed the sagging body against Gwirion's chest and intertwined their arms, propping her up as Gwirion frantically embraced her. He pulled the dagger out of her and hurled it away; as the wound began to spurt he tried, uselessly, to stop it with his hands. Sobbing, screaming, he kissed her, then pulled away again to see her face, trying desperately to make eye contact, trying to pull her away from death with his look. She couldn't focus on him but she knew he was there, and a sad smile tickled her lips as her head lolled forward onto his shoulder and she was still.

"Apparently God said yes," Noble said, wrestling with hysterical, triumphal laughter. "Would you rather join her or stay here with me?"

Gwirion thought he screamed and threw himself at Noble in a blind rage—but when he came to himself he realized he had not moved. He was holding her body. Her head was still resting on his shoulder, tucked against his neck. The blood had seeped from her and soaked the sheets; it was all over him, he was lying in it, slipping farther into it. With a cry he leapt away and fell off the bed and onto the wood floor, his tunic heavy with her blood.

Noble had calmed completely, retrieved his dagger, and crossed to the window, staring out over the hills. Gwirion's commotion in ripping his blood-sodden tunic and drawers off, wiping the blood from his naked limbs in a frenzy with the bed curtains, made the king look over toward the bed, serene and expressionless.

"Please dress yourself properly," he said. "I am not through with you." He looked back out the window.

"Sire," Gwirion said in a small, horrified voice. "Noble. Look what you've done."

Noble, without looking, nodded, facing out. "It's very final, isn't it?" he said pensively. "In the field, you have so many opponents, you have more than one chance to get it just right. In politics, the dance can last for years as you refine it. This is different." His eyes still gazing in abstraction out the window, he held his hand up and away from him to reenact the movement. "One jerk of the wrist and it's over."

Gwirion stared at him aghast. "Is that all this means to you? You've just *murdered your wife*." And as if speaking it finally made it real to him, he caught back a cry and scrambled around the bed to cradle her body from the far side. He avoided her open, sightless eyes, but he touched her skin, still soft and pliant but unnaturally still, and his breath caught raggedly.

"If you must continue to paw her, at least put on some decent clothes," the king insisted. Gwirion looked about unsurely, and Noble pointed across the room. "If I'm not mistaken, you'll find some just inside the door." Gwirion took a hesitant step toward the threshold. Lying there neatly folded was the black silk outfit Noble had worn the day before. Beside it was a large basin of lukewarm water and a pile of washrags.

"The note to Gwilym," Gwirion said quietly, understanding, feeling his body turn to lead.

Noble nodded.

With one traumatized eye on the king, Gwirion sponged the blood off himself and then began to dress. He realized as he pulled on the long-sleeved tunic that somebody had taken the seams in; it fit him almost perfectly. Just like the last time he had faced his execution. The king had seen to every detail of this production.

"When you've finished dressing, open the door," Noble said calmly. "We shall continue this in a slightly less intimate setting."

"May I have a moment with her?"

Noble shrugged. "Very well."

"Alone?"

"No," the king said immediately, and settled into the tapestried cushions of the window seat. He looked untroubled, exquisitely regal, in the sunrise.

Gwirion put on the rest of the clothes, pressed the bandage from her torn shift to his wound again, and returned to the side of the bed. She was paler and already cold. The blood had long stopped. With a knot in his throat, he reached out and gently pressed her eyelids down so that they covered her unseeing tawny eyes. He stroked her cheek and the seductive silky hair, said her name, and sobbed.

Noble waited, basking in the early light at the window, marking time patiently by the shifting shadows of a cloudless morning. He was willing to go slowly now. Despite the game with the dagger, his fury had barely found relief in her quick dispatch, but he was weary and there was still so much he would have to wring from Gwirion to be satisfied. He could wait.

After what felt to Gwirion like weeks, his tears dried and he settled from a rage of grief to the exhausted numbness of resignation and mourning. "Now," Noble said gently. "Open the door."

One hand still pressing the fabric to his temple, Gwirion nodded dully and obeyed.

He was shocked to find a small crowd clustered on the landing, waiting for the door to open. Beside the usual morning doorkeeper there was the sewing bevy, the physician, the queen's priest, and Efan, shadowed by another soldier from the teulu. The women's eyes were red from crying; the men were somber and would not look Gwirion in the face.

He stumbled back in surprise and spun around to Noble. "What is this?" he demanded. "This isn't anybody else's business!"

"This is everybody's business, Gwirion," said the king, rising from the window seat and nonchalantly retrieving his cloak. "These good people are here to take care of her. It's time for you and me to quit her."

"No!" Gwirion yelled automatically.

Noble raised the dagger. "Yes," he countered placidly. "Downstairs. We'll conclude this where I'm almost certain it began."

Efan stepped into the room, avoiding Gwirion's gaze. He had the doleful awkwardness of one who had intended to gloat over a fallen adversary but found he couldn't. The same was true of his fellow soldier, who—on Noble's orders—happened to be Caradoc.

Gwirion, staring at Caradoc, muttered to the king, "Your sense of spectacle is relentlessly perverse."

"I consider it poetic," Noble said with serenity. The guards each clapped a hand on one of Gwirion's shoulders. They pushed him gently out of the room, onto the darkened balcony and toward the stairs.

As they descended to the hall, Gwirion grew more and more astonished: Most of the castle had gathered near for the shameful promenade. Everyone looked stunned—and yet no one looked surprised. *They all know*, he realized, feeling sick, and once again he remembered the note to Gwilym. Even plump, protective Marged, standing discreetly near the kitchen screens, obviously knew now. He gave her a distressed stare across the hall and her response was to shake her grey head helplessly and shrug. She had not known for long enough to warn him.

He looked down, but some of the eyes upon him were so intense he felt their attention as physical slaps. He never knew their actual expressions, only that they stared. Marged's grandson Dafydd. Madrun's beloved Ednyfed, his mother Elen, his father Cadwgan the marshal. The butcher and his son. Nest, and all the other hall servants, all the kitchen workers, all the teulu. Einion the porter. Father Idnerth. Gwilym. Hafaidd the usher. Goronwy the judge. All the other officers. The stable boy whom Gwirion had saved from Huw. And there were dozens more.

The silence, in such a crowd, was unbearable. As Gwirion reached the bottom step and pivoted toward the round white audience chamber, he glanced at the collection of faces and announced, loudly, "Thank you all for your petitions, but we've already selected our chief fool."

It wasn't witty but it broke the awkward silence, and they released their collective breath. Nobody—except Gwirion, who wasn't looking—could fail to see the king's affectionate expression. Surely, the castle denizens thought as one, surely the king would punish him but then forgive him. She had come to them as an outsider, and however worthy she had grown in their eyes, she'd lived among them only a year—but Gwirion was nearly the only constant in the king's life since infancy. He could not be so rudely dispatched.

WHEN they were inside and the door had been shut and locked from without, Noble tossed down his cloak against the wall and casually settled, lolling, into his comfortable leather chair. All the sconces were blazing brightly; the room looked far too cheery. "May Day is not off to a promising start," said the king.

"She didn't wrong you," Gwirion said mournfully. "I did."

"I know you wronged me," he answered calmly. "But so did she."

"I wish you had punished me for both our sins," Gwirion said.

Noble looked up near the ceiling, an unreadable expression on his face. "The irony here is that your only sin is saying that."

"I don't understand you."

"Gwirion. Anything I have is yours. If you wanted her, you had only to ask me for her. I would have found that rather titillating, in fact."

"You're disgusting. That's not what I wanted."

"Yes, it took me a bit to realize that. I threw far more tempting morsels in your direction and encouraged you to nibble, and you never did. That was the real problem."

"The sin wasn't sleeping with your wife, it was falling in love with her?"

"It was falling in love with *anyone!*" Noble shouted. He leapt at Gwirion and grabbed him round the neck, hurling him to the ground and bashing his head against the wood floor. "How could you do that? Traitor!"

Gwirion grabbed at the king's fists trying to get them off his windpipe, hearing his own breath rattle in his ears. He forced himself against instinct to let go of his clutch on Noble's hand to swipe at the king's face. Noble pulled away for a moment with a curse, taking one hand from Gwirion's throat, but before Gwirion could twist away Noble was clutching him again, now really clutching, hard, and shouting. Gwirion's legs flailed the air, trying to find something to kick, striking nothing. He saw blood snap across his vision every time Noble struck his head to the floor, and imagined that the gurgles of his constricted breathing were bubbles of blood seeping into his throat to drown him. He couldn't hear what Noble was saying anymore, couldn't even see the frenzied face and contorted mouth. A metallic taste in the back of his mouth calmed him, and although he knew it was the first taste of death, he relaxed with it, grateful to escape.

Almost too late, Noble realized what he was doing and released him. There was a horrible silence and the body lay inert. Then Gwirion convulsed and began gasping for air.

When he came to, he found himself lying on the settle, the king regarding him intensely from his chair.

Gwirion took a moment to regain his senses, and struggled slowly to his feet. He stood, dazed, trying to remember where they had come from, why they were here, where the queen was—and then he had to face it all over again. "What have you *done?*" he shrieked, and hurled himself at Noble.

Noble was ready for him with quicker reflexes than Gwirion's, and they were snarled up together tearing at each other—for a few seconds only, until Noble pulled the dagger from his boot and had it at Gwirion's throat. Gwirion stopped, tried to leap back, and smacked into the chest. Noble moved forward just enough to keep the blade at his throat.

For a long moment they stared at each other, breathing hard, the knife hanging between them. "Why don't you just *do* it," Gwirion spat.

"I've always believed in delaying satisfaction."

"That's not what your wife told me."

Noble smacked him hard across the face even as he burst out laughing. "That's the lad I miss!"

"You won't get him back by slitting my throat."

"I know," said Noble. "That's why you're alive right now. You have a chance to save yourself, if you choose to take it."

Gwirion's laugh was brittle and sarcastic. "I won't like it, will I?"

"No, it's simple," Noble assured him with vicious cheerfulness. "Just give me what I want."

Gwirion fluttered his lashes at the king and lisped, "But, Noble, you know I'm not a loose woman."

Again, the king smashed him across the face and laughed.

"Please hit the other side next time," Gwirion said, forcing his voice to stay calm. "I want to keep the bruises symmetrical."

"Remember what it was like before we ever knew her," Noble whispered earnestly. "That's all I want."

Gwirion looked from Noble to the blade. He felt the blood trickling again from the cut at his temple. He knew he couldn't win a physical fight, and he wasn't even sure he could win a mental one now. He didn't trust himself to outsmart the king's fury, and he was too tired in his bones to win back his life with laughter. He thought of the dead woman upstairs and wondered what she would do in his place. She was so direct, so artless. He had never tried artless.

"Would you let me live freely?"

Noble hesitated. "I would let you raise hell. I would let you shock and insult me and everybody around me. I'd let you put my reign in peril with your pranks. I would sooner lose my kingship to your scheming than to Roger's or Llewelyn's."

"That's not what I asked. I want to know if you'd let me live freely—for myself, and not just for you."

Noble shook his head. "That's what you did when you fell in love with her and nothing good came of it for any of us. I'm offering you your life so things can be as they were between us."

"Then, sire, the answer is no," Gwirion said softly, meeting Noble's eyes comfortably for the first time in months.

Noble blinked in disbelief. "What do you mean, no? This is a dagger, Gwirion." He spoke with slightly exaggerated diction. "I'm holding it at your throat and I'm going to kill you with it unless you say yes. Under the circumstances, one says yes."

"I am saying no," Gwirion replied calmly.

"Don't test me, you whoreson."

"I'm not. I expect you'll kill me." And he slipped under the blade as Noble, with a roar of fury, stabbed at him.

They were wrapped about each other again, Gwirion trying to hold Noble's right arm back and leaping away as the dagger slashed toward him. Gwirion bit at the knife hand, but Noble shoved him off and tossed him across the room, then threw himself after him. Gwirion scampered from under the assault and was up and around, throwing himself on Noble before Noble realized where he had gone to. Gwirion's teeth sank into the flesh of the king's hand, until he felt something grainy give way under his teeth and he tasted blood. Noble cursed and dropped the dagger, pushing Gwirion away from it as it fell to the floor. But Gwirion, smaller and more agile, twisted away from the king and lunged for it. Picking it up, he made an awkward stab at Noble. Noble ducked and tripped on his long tunic, and Gwirion threw himself on top of him, landing astride his chest with the dagger against Noble's throat.

Noble looked up at him and laughed sarcastically. Gwirion was white and his hands were shaking.

"You're going to let me live as I want to," he rasped.

"No I'm not," Noble taunted. "You'll have to kill me if that's what you want."

"Don't be stupid," Gwirion ordered in an unsteady voice. "I have only myself to think about, you have the entire kingdom. You have to save yourself for them, they need you. You *must* agree with me."

Noble shook his head. "As much as I resent it there are others who might rule the kingdom, Gwirion. There are no others who might be my fool. Or my friend. If you want the life you spoke of, kill me."

"Don't make me do that," Gwirion begged, losing any pretense of bravado.

"You can do it," Noble prodded in a seductive whisper. "It's easy. Just reach under my chin and slit my throat. I'll go quickly. It will hardly hurt. Llewelyn will be good to my people. And you'll be free."

"I can't do that!" Gwirion screamed, sobbing, trying to hold the point of the knife against the king's throat.

"I know," Noble whispered, gently now. "So take the dagger away from my throat and put it in my hand."

Gwirion closed his eyes with a sob of resignation as he lowered the dagger, slackening his grip.

THE king had told them not to open the door under any circumstances, but the inhuman shriek alarmed even the teulu and brought people running from all over the castle. The sound dissolved into a wailing moan, the voice of a fatally wounded animal abandoned by its pack. As if there were no need to draw breath, the moan went on and on, a furious lamentation from a bellowing set of lungs unused to grief. Like a caterwaul, it grew worse and more frantic rather than dying down, and finally Marged demanded that the door be opened.

Efan threw it ajar and Caradoc thrust a torch into the room, but it wasn't needed—all the sconces were lit and the whitewashed walls had an almost gaudy brightness to them.

Piled together against the far wall were the king and Gwirion. One of them was screaming. Blood was splattered in a bright, sparkling arc just above them, dripping down on them. Madrun, who had come down to ask about funeral proceedings, fainted at once. Elen gasped and ran out of the room. But the others stayed where they were, staring at the tangled mess of limbs and clothing. Gwilym covered his face with one broad palm.

Oblivious to the intruders, the mourner keened on. He was so animated when he gasped for breath that both bodies seemed to heave for air, and at first they thought and hoped both men were still alive. Finally, he quieted, lay limp for a moment in his friend's rigid arms, and then began to disentangle himself.

It took a few moments to get free; he was gentle and respectful, moving the royal limbs until Noble sat still and peaceful against the wall. As a final gesture, Gwirion took the king's green cloak, kissed it in homage, and draped it high across Noble's shoulders to hide the gaping neck wound. With the wound hidden, the king looked as if he were sleeping. Gwirion pulled himself up to his feet and the onlookers, finally registering what had happened, grasped each other in horrified shock. They stared at Gwirion and Gwirion stared back at them, blinking the last of his tears away, rubbing the blood from his forehead.

"Are you going to kill me?" he asked the steward, in a tired voice.

Gwilym shook his head. He folded and unfolded the letter Noble had written hours earlier. "He said that if he allowed you to survive, we were to do the same."

"I see," Gwirion sighed. Hesitantly, he walked toward the door.

"But I must ask for the weapon," Gwilym said uncomfortably, stepping in his way.

Gwirion looked up at him. "Apparently I am the weapon," he said quietly. "But the knife is with the king."

They all turned to see. Noble's hand clutched the knife in a death grip. Nobody spoke.

Gwirion turned toward the door again and walked out of the room.

HE stumbled through the great hall, where dozens of eyes peeked at him in fear from the corners. He pushed the great double doors open and walked out into the yard. The bells were ringing. The early-morning sky was bluer than he had ever seen it, bluer than the best of their days out riding. He took the few steps to the unattended barbican, walked through the gate and down the castle mound into the village.

People were huddled in small clusters in the open air, staring toward the chapel tower where the bell was ringing, wondering what disaster was unfolding and when the news would reach them, debating if the villain of the hour would be Mortimer, Llewelyn, Anarawd, or Thomas. Many turned to him, expecting him to fill his frequent role of herald, but he walked past them as if he didn't see them.

When he came to the village gates he paused. He had never passed this spot alone before. The guards, sensing it would not do to question him, moved aside and he walked out, the sun warming his back and the road lying before him, offering him everything and nothing.

AUTHOR'S NOTE

aelgwyn ap Cadwallon, ruler of Maelienydd, really existed. But this story is a work of fiction, and takes creative license with some well-established historical facts for the sake of crafting a tale. To honor what really was, I would like to acknowledge the more obvious and egregious ways I have played with history. Almost without exception, every change I have made has been in the interest of simplifying an extraordinarily complicated political scenario, and I've done this by removing certain real-life figures, consolidating kingdoms, and telescoping the time line.

The land I call Maelienydd was known in earlier times as both "the land between the Severn and the Wye" and Cynllibiuc. In the 1190s, the region was made up of a few smaller kingdoms; the largest of these was Maelienydd, and I have consolidated them all into one kingdom with one ruler. Maelgwyn ap Cadwallon actually died in 1197. At the time of this story (1198–99), Roger Mortimer had control of Castell Cymaron and Maelienydd; he had taken Cymaron in 1195 and Maelgwyn spent the last two years of his life fighting, with the help of Lord Rhys of Deheubarth, to try to win it back. I have fictionalized nothing about the intensity of the Mortimer feud with the native ruling family, and the assassination of Cadwallon (the prologue) is factual. Isabel and Thomas, however, are both my creations, and by extension so are all political and military activities predicated on their existence.

The historical figure most clearly warped by my alterations is Llewelyn ap Iorwerth of Gwynedd, later known as Llewelyn the Great. His trajectory of power did indeed go from a small part of Gwynedd to an enormous swath of Wales. He did not, however, accomplish this in a year, as I have him doing—it took many years and the consistent mandate of the people; by the time he was a real force to be reckoned with in Maelienydd, Maelgwyn was long gone. Accelerating his rise to power as severely as I have risks presenting him as Machiavellian (particularly considering some of his actions in the story)—but he wasn't. Gwywynwyn of Powys does not appear by name in my story at all, but was a formidable figure of the time. Maelgwyn had brothers and cousins, some of whom ruled small sections of the area I call Maelienydd. I have either ignored them or diminished their significance, for simplicity's sake. Maelgwyn actually had sons (and daughters), although none of them ever had the chance to rule. There are many other simplifications. In general, in the era of this story, the land between the Severn and the Wye was not as cohesive, safe, or stable as I've depicted it.

Although most Welsh rulers of the time were, in written records, known merely as lords or princes, Cadwallon was referred to as "king" by at least one English chronicler, and I have taken the liberty to pass that honor on to his son—who may have been called "king" by his subjects, regardless of what the English called him. Abbey Cwm-hir really existed, including its enormous church; it was founded by Cadwallon. Gerald of Wales (chapter 4) was real, as was the book of his to which Isabel refers—and so was the encounter Maelgwyn had with him.

Depictions of the court, council, laws, and customs are based upon real medieval Welsh law (with very occasional creative license); obviously, both Isabel and Gwirion constantly fly in the face of established convention and get away with it. All folk rituals and formal ceremonies, with the exception of the Spring Rites, are true to life. What we today call "Celtic Christianity" had died out by 1198, but certain core beliefs and values predating Christianity were still deeply imbedded in the popular mind-set. People would have seen nothing heretical about blending native beliefs and myths with Christian dogma into one fairly seamless belief system, which they would have considered fully Christian.

Gwirion is not only fictional, but historically improbable, as the Welsh court had no known position corresponding to the concept of a European fool or jester. The word "gwirion" means both "innocent" and "foolish," but beyond that is based on the root word for "truth."

HOW TO NOT WRITE
HISTORICAL NOVELS

he first decade I tinkered with this novel, I never thought of it as historical fiction. I thought of it as a story about three specific people. Such a story could easily be set today, but it's easier for me to write about things when I have a little distance from them, and I decided that about eight hundred years was a nice comfortable distance. After culling possibilities, I chose the Welsh/English border near the end of the twelfth century.

But my research soon disheartened me: there were three kingdoms in Wales at the time, and on close examination, none of them fit the bill. I decided, feeling sheepish, that I'd have to invent a fourth kingdom. (It's not like this was historical fiction, after all; it was just a story about three people.) I made up various things about this kingdom, including a feud between my rulers and the Mortimers of England. Then, wracked with guilt for faking it, I began frantically researching the period in greater detail so I could include something authentic.

That's when I learned, to my surprise, that there actually was a seldom-mentioned fourth kingdom, exactly where I had set "my" kingdom . . . and its ruling family had suffered a long-running feud with the Mortimers. Several other details I'd invented also turned out to be true to life. (You can read more about this on my Web site, www.nicolegalland.com.) Fascinated by the coincidences, I shifted my focus to research what had actually happened in that part of Wales in the 1290s. Serendipity, incredible coincidences, and a few generously insightful individuals provided me enough information for a lifetime of writing historical fiction. It truly felt as if the universe was conspiring to make it possible for me to write the ultimate historical novel about medieval Maelienydd.

But what I wrote, in the end, was really a story about three people. And despite the cornucopia of historical detail I was able to put into the book, these three people are not inherently Welsh, nor inherently medieval—mostly because neither am I. Of course, they're not modern Americans, but all I can say about them with any certainty is that they are *mine*. Virtually every historical novel I've read has revealed things about the period in which it's set, but has equally revealed its author's perceptions of humanity; I am no exception. We think we're merely writing plots but we're often writing personal metaphors of some sort or another. The use of historical detail simply makes a great *trompe l'oeil*.

This insight occurred to me again in a different way while writing my second novel, which will be published in 2006, and which, as of this writing, is still untitled. (Titles can be tricky!) It's set in the court of the Holy Roman Emperor, and I did exhaustive research on the era. But it's not *about* the Holy Roman Emperor. It's about things that are hidden (information, objects, actions, birthmarks, lovers), and all the repercussions of concealment. As with *The Fool's Tale*, the story could easily be set today, but it's still easier for me to write about things when I have a little distance from them, and eight hundred years is *still* a nice comfortable distance.